THE TALENT

Praise for *The Talent Sinistral*:

"To say I enjoyed this book would be an understatement. It is a compelling and powerful tale that will delight fantasy fans everywhere."
— David Gemmell (2003)

"L.F. Patten takes readers on a rousing adventure with two delightful heroes in this thoroughly enjoyable tale. A vivid and colorful ride."
— Carol Berg, author of *The Collegia Magica Series*

"Masterful storytelling. *The Talent Sinistral* is a splendid fantasy, brimming with adventure and wit, yet informed by moving portrayals of serious themes. Patten's world is evocative and completely real, tinged with Celtic elements and subtle magic. *The Talent Sinistral* gives readers that rare experience: a book that satisfies but leaves you wanting more. Patten is a writer to note."
— Mackay Wood, author of *Wolf's Cub* and *Gryphon King*

"L.F. Patten has created a bright, wide and boisterous world filled with adventure and character. A solid read!"
— Patrick LoBrutto

"L. F. Patten weaves a web of adventure and intrigue which beguiles and delights, while always keeping the reader guessing. Richly panoramic when describing its war-torn setting, yet always believable in the depiction of its large cast of interesting characters, *The Talent Sinistral* breathes new life into a tired genre."
— M.S. Harris, for *Renaissance Magazine*

In memory of David Gemmell: Bard, Visionary, and Eternal Hero,
who did indeed possess *the talent sinistral.*

Huge thanks to all who helped bring this story to life. To the exceptionally talented Markus Harris for his expertise in combat and all things Medieval. To my amazing writers' circle: Susan, Carol, Curt, Brian, Catherine, Courtney, and the late Glenn Gillette, for coaching, coercing and keeping me on track. To to my first "mentor," Dr. Morris McGee, for setting me on the path. And most of all, to Bob, for his unyileding love, patience, support and encouragement, even through the insane times. I love you all!

This is a work of fiction. All characters, places and incidents portrayed in this book are products of the author's imagination. Any resemblance to real persons, living or dead, is purely coincidental.

Published by **Crystal Sword**, an imprint of **Stone Dagger Publications**
P.O. Box 260423,
Lakewood, Colorado 80226
www.stonedagger.com

Cover graphics by M. S. Harris
Maps by Curtis Craddock

ISBN 978-0-9668701-4-5

The Talent Sinistral
by
L. F. Patten

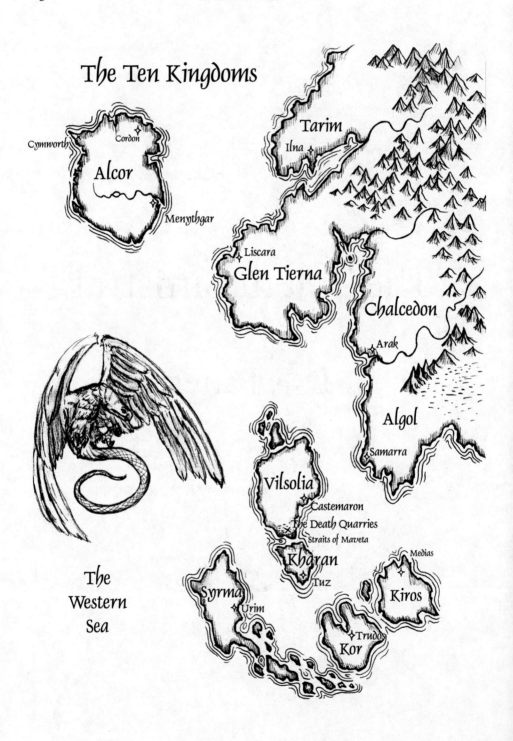

The Ten Kingdoms

Alcor
Cymworth
Cordon
Menythgar

Tarim
Ilna

Liscara
Glen Tierna

Chalcedon
Arak

Algol
Samarra

Vilsolia
Castemaron
The Death Quarries
Straits of Maveta

Kharan
Tuz

Medias
Kiros

Syrma
Urim

Kor
Trudos

The
Western
Sea

The Island of Alcor

Ruins
of
Nwtyrra

Carreg
Cymworth
(ruin)

Cymworth

Castle
Correth
(ruin)

Carrow
Moor

Midlam
High
Moor

Malton
Moor

Cordon Castle

Evorick

East Downs

West Downs

The
Wilderwood

R. Elas

Glenneth

Dorcalon

Chirt Castle

Derwenth

Millferry
Bridge

Averford

R. Averin

Berwyn Forest

Loch
Alainn

Caerllyn

Menythgar

Spire of Galglenneth

Galwyn

Caer
Morthund

Caerdewi

Anlawth

West
Ruthland

Ceorl's Ford

The
Southerwood

Castle
Garth

Ruthland
Castle

East
Ruthland

R. Bron

Hlanneth

Dandryth

Castle Kennet

Part I: The Brassy and the Jackal

Chapter One

"You shall encounter, this night, one who will forever change the course of your life."

Master Gwythion's words. Their unsettling message continued to gnaw at Kier. He dared not doubt the truth of the old monk's prophecy, for the Fithlon Brotherhood probed the mysteries of *Infinite Mind,* and Gwythion wore the sash of the Twelfth and highest Tier. His *seeings* were always dependable. Apprehension pricked Kier's belly like an irksome saddle burr, refusing to be dislodged. He'd labored years to create this life for himself, melding and shaping it to fit his own particular needs. He did not want it *changed.*

High above, a midnight wind rattled the treetops, driving sooty cloud rags across the Ladymoon's alabaster face. The pitted copper crescent of her consort perched atop the western hills, looking for all the world like a half-round of ripe, Llynshire cheese—or so Kier's empty belly told him. Maybe it was hunger and not just foreboding that bedeviled his gut. He'd eaten nothing since dawn, while still on shipboard, and Gwythion had offered naught but talk, which was all the sustenance the aging monk seemed to require.

"... forever change the course of your life." Kier gave his head an impatient shake to drive out the nagging presage. Two hours of plodding this rutted cart track back to the city had left him testy and bone weary— in no mood for puzzles. It was hardly how he'd imagined his first night back in Castémaron. If not for Gwythion's urgent mind-summons, that found him before he'd even disembarked, he'd have spent a peaceful evening, tankard in hand, recuperating from a exhausting three-month mission and an especially rough crossing of the Inner Sea—always chancy during storm season. Instead, he'd had to sit for hours, struggling to remain awake, while the Fithlon Master intoned passages from one ancient text

after another—moldy histories of fallen kingdoms and dire foretellings—as if their relevance should be self-evident. It wasn't. Yet try as he might, Kier could coax no explanation for the urgency that had compelled him to the Fithlon's musty cloister, leagues beyond the city walls, with scarcely time for a wash and a change of clothes. But being cryptic was the Fithlon way. Kier still felt a certain loyalty to his former mentor and was willing to humor the old monk at need. But he sorely hated feeling manipulated.

Off east, above the harbor, a horde of roiling black storm clouds devoured the stars. Kier chided himself. None but a fool, or a madman, would be abroad on Castémaron's unpatrolled approaches at this ungodly hour. Right now, he accounted himself both. When he'd first set out for Fithlon monastery, the weather had been balmy, and stretching his legs after days at sea had seemed a welcome respite. Had he realized his mentor would keep him so long past nightfall, he'd have rented a mount from the inn's stable.

"... *encounter, this night, one who will forever change...*" The dread portent refused to be dislodged. Kier tossed back a corner of his cloak to leave his sword arm unencumbered; his weapon visible. No sense tempting trouble; it seemed to find him readily enough without invitation. Yet, like enough, Gwythion's presaged life-changer awaited him, not on the midnight roads, but back at the inn—some envoy from Alcor, bearing his new orders. That could certainly alter his life. Kier considered quickening his pace, just to get the dreaded encounter over with, but chose otherwise. The inn was yet a half-league off, nestled against the harbor wall on the city's far side. The mysterious messenger would just have to wait.

Another gust ruffled Kier's hair and flapped his cloak behind him like demon wings. The dank air felt clammy against his face, laden with the threat of rain—and worse: the noisome pall of refuse and decay so common to Castémaron. The city infested the marshy plain like a fungus blight, its building stones infused with crystalline *magien* sands, causing the ancient walls to glow faint amber in the clouded moonlight. He'd come to hate this foreign port, however eloquently bards might praise Vilsolia's luminous capital as *Empress of the Civilized World*. She was far too crowded for his taste; too decrepit; too blasted big.

A yawning sentry at the West Gate waved him into the city with barely a glance at the brass medallion that identified Kier as an imperial ally. Kier touched two fingers to his brow in cursory salute. These past five years, his duties as Alcor's military liaison had taken him the length and breadth of the Deg Tirith—the Ten Kingdoms of the known world—to exotic realms most only dreamt of. Kier savored the independence his constant travel afforded. Now, at last, he was master of his fate—an impossible prospect back in hate-ravaged Alcor, where his very looks proclaimed him traitor to both of his homeland's warring races. There was no disguising it: the thick black hair and sharp features of the conquering Tiernai, set against a rock-solid build and a complexion that was Dynian fair. And most damning of all, his eyes: neither Dynian blue nor Tiernai umber, but dark amethyst flecked with gray—the eyes of a despised halfblood. Here in the outer kingdoms, his mixed race bore no stigma. Kier curled the fingers of his left hand into a fist. Would that the same could be said of ...

An icy prickle at his lower spine wrenched Kier's attention back to the city's midnight streets. He slowed; cocked his head. The rising wind swirled dust and dead leaves among the sagging stalls of the deserted market square. It carried on its wings the echo of music and laughter from a nearby tavern and, in the distance, the measured clang of a harbor buoy. Nothing obviously amiss. Yet his Fithlon-trained senses tingled. Someone lurked nearby. Hostile? Uncertain. With a last, swift glance around the moonlit square, Kier turned and quickened his pace toward the inn.

The feeling of threat intensified as he wended his way through the tangle of feculent streets and alleys of the city's harbor district. Above the plaintive cries of seabirds, Kier could now make out the faint rhythm of footfalls behind him, slowing and quickening in response to his own. His mind raced. Who might be stalking him here? He'd made no enemies in Castémaron—at least, so far as he knew. Kier's baser instincts exhorted him to run. Yet years of Legion discipline won out: *Keep your head. Never be made a victim. Engage the enemy on your own terms.* Not far ahead, he recalled a small plaza where several narrow byways intersected at an ancient shrine. Room to maneuver, and multiple paths of escape. As strategic a site as he was likely to find in this urban cess pit.

A tremulous flash gilded the harbor clouds, followed by a low, predatory rumble. Kier reached the plaza and ducked into the first alcove he found—the mouth of a refuse-choked alley. Here, he could wait out his pursuer; get a look at him as he passed and, if need be, subdue him from behind. There was light enough, barely. The pearly sheen of Denia's moon, diffused by low clouds, lent the cobbles a faint luminescence. But that wouldn't last with a storm moving in.

Tiny hairs pricked Kier's neck. He doffed his cloak and silently drew his sword, then felt for the reassuring firmness of the small dagger strapped inside his left sleeve. The certainty of danger pulsed like venom in his veins, steadily closing in on him from behind ...

No. That was wrong. This sensation came from *within* the alley.

Kier wheeled an about-face, recognizing the trap. Too late. Something hurtled toward him through the darkness. Kier jerked aside, barely in time. The missile glanced off his brow and shattered on the slimy cobbles.

Kier's skull erupted in pain. Swinging blindly at his attacker, he staggered back into the plaza.

Footsteps scrambled up behind him. The pursuer! Before Kier could spin to confront him, a solid weight smashed down between his shoulderblades.

Stunned, Kier fought to maintain his stance. A swirl of colors did a mocking pirouette before his eyes. In helpless horror, he felt his legs begin to buckle beneath him. The sword slipped from his nerveless fingers as, with a groan, he crumpled to his knees.

The surrounding tenements swam in a crimson blur. Kier struggled to regain his feet, but someone pounced on him from behind, holding him down. A gravelly whine bored through his throbbing consciousness like the bray of an ill-played sack-pipe.

"Are ye sure 'e's the one ol' scarface at the tav'rn were talkin' of?"

A blot of shadow bobbed before Kier's eyes. "Aye, he's a cap'ain awright. See 'is brass? Here, grab 'is arms." Kier felt his elbows yanked behind him and pinned. The thief in front slashed Kier's jerkin and shirt, and began to paw through them. His breath stank of rotted teeth. Practiced fingers found Kier's leather purse. "P'taw," he spat, rattling its contents. "Not much 'ere, e'en fer a brassy." He tucked the pouch into his belt.

"But does 'e 'ave that am'let, like the man said?" came the other's grating voice.

His partner snapped a chain from Kier's throat and squinted hard at the charms on it, then deftly stashed that away as well. Kier felt the cold pressure of a knife blade against his naked ribs. "Where d'ye hide the amulet, cap'ain?"

He could make no sense of the query. Yet, deep down, Kier knew his attackers would not wait long for an answer. Far easier to despoil the dead. He had but seconds.

Willing down panic, Kier directed his taut muscles to relax. As he'd hoped, the thief behind let the grip on his arms slacken. A subtle wrist flick and Kier felt the hidden dagger drop dependably into his palm. Its solidness gave him confidence. Mustering strength, he stabbed the small weapon into his captor's thigh.

The man yowled and jolted backward. The abrupt motion wrenched the precious dagger from Kier's fist. It clattered to the cobbles as he threw himself clear and staggered to his feet.

The thief in front scrabbled after him. Kier felt a seam of fire where the man's blade had skittered across his ribs. He barely managed to grab up his fallen sword before his attacker caught up, long knife glinting in the lightning flash.

Kier backed toward the nearest wall, shaking his head to clear it. Blood from his forehead blurred his left eye and his responses felt sluggish. Breathless, he fought the torpor in his limbs.

The wiry thief watched with the glowing eyes of a predator. Where his left hand should be, Kier made out only a tarred stump, but the disability did not seem to hamper him. His shabby knife darted for Kier's thigh. Kier caught the flash of steel and instinctively parried. There was a grating clash as his blade slid his attacker's weapon aside.

Where had the man's accomplice gotten to? If he should creep up from behind... Kier groped back for the protection of the wall, but felt only emptiness. The alley mouth?

The thief's blade streaked in from Kier's blinded left. Kier parried across his body, but the motion taxed his balance and he stumbled. His boot lit on something that crushed beneath his weight. The stench of rotting flesh assailed his nostrils—human flesh. Bile seared Kier's throat. With fevered desperation, he battled to free himself.

The sword hilt slimed in his sweaty palm as he slashed at his enemy's darting shadow. Left, right, his longer blade drove the man back into the plaza.

The sky overhead crackled white, revealing his attacker about to strike. Kier seized the opportunity and drove in hard—a killing stroke.

It whistled through empty air. A swift kick, and the thief's ragged boot sent Kier's sword clanging to the cobblestones.

Kier sought about him for some last defense. He spied movement beside the plaza's central font. The accomplice? His hopes sank. He was weaponless; outnumbered.

Grinning wolfishly, his captor leveled his blade at Kier's heart, herding him back toward the gruesome alley. Kier raged at himself as cold reality set in. Death in battle he could face, but this? To die a victim, like a beggar in a gutter, because he'd failed to win a simple street fight?

Failure. The word recalled blistering taunts from his boyhood. How long before he was even missed? Days? Weeks? Stripped clean by roving scavengers, his body could lie ignored and unidentified till it rotted to carrion, like the luckless creature he'd trodden upon. Resolve girded Kier's belly. He'd not give in to that. Better to die fighting. One well-timed lunge and he might seize his captor's knife. It was the slimmest of chances, but...

Rain began to pelt the cobbles. Thunder rumbled. As Kier steadied himself for a last, desperate leap, a dark form slipped up behind his attacker. There was a sudden jerk; a strangled scream of anger—or astonishment—and the thief sagged, dead, at Kier's feet.

Kier stared, baffled, as a tall shadow-figure ambled to where his sword had fallen, picked it up, and formally presented it back to him, hilt first. Then, as the stranger stood illuminated by the heaven's-rent, he halted Kier's questions with an impudent chuckle.

"Well met, brassy," the lanky fellow drawled, touching his brow in mock deference. "And now, as you owe me your life, perhaps you'd care to buy me a drink?"

Chapter Two

The Dragon Sword boasted as seamy a reputation as any alehouse in the
Ten Kingdoms—a reputation more than subtly suggested by the tavern's
weathered signboard. Its main face simply pictured an elaborate sword hilt
in the form of a coiled dragon, above the establishment's name. But the
panel facing the rough Harbor District had been redesigned—the work
of some anonymous prankster, years before—and never repaired, due to
the increased popularity the tavern had enjoyed since that date. Depicted
there, in vibrant reds and greens, was the graphic image of a leering dragon
in formidable rut, beneath the bold caption: *The Dragon's Sword*.

The sign groaned back and forth on rusted hinges as Kier's mysterious
rescuer led the way up the worn stone steps. Kier held back. He'd never
had occasion to visit the *Sword*, yet he'd overheard soldiers from the nearby
garrison boast of lusty exploits there. After his mortifying ordeal in the
alley, Kier's own desires went no farther than the peace and solitude of
his fireside, back at the inn. But he owed this stranger a blood debt. And
he'd be fool indeed to return to the streets in this condition. He needed a
chance to settle himself; regroup.

The dissonant clamor of music and rowdiness that assailed him as
his companion threw open the tavern door almost changed his mind. A
glare of amber light spilled onto the rain-slicked cobbles accompanied
by a draught of air so laden with the pungent reek of ale, sweat, and the
intoxicating blue-green smoke of jirash pipes, Kier felt nauseated.

The din inside was absolute. On a platform across the commonroom,
a dark Syrmian dancing girl whirled and preened to the skirling music of
pipes and drum. Nearer at hand, a scuffle erupted between two drunken
seamen. Fists flew and furniture crashed, while the brawlers' shipmates
stomped and cheered raucous encouragement. Few others paid more
attention than to duck as need required. Kier's rescuer shouted something

that went unheard above the noise and pointed to the bar. Steeling his resolve, Kier followed.

They'd just signaled the tapster for food and drink when a shapely Kirosian cocotte with eyes of deep topaz sidled toward them through the crowd. She flung willowy arms around the neck of Kier's companion. "JonMarc, my fair one," she cooed, her voice a breathy alto. "When will you come upstairs and let me make you... *comfortable*?" Skillfully, she executed a lewd hip-rotation against the young man's thigh.

JonMarc grinned broadly and curled his arm about the courtesan's waist. "Ah, Shanya," he said, pressing his open lips to hers. Kier discreetly turned away. It was some time before the two came up for air. "Later," JonMarc promised, running his hands longingly over the courtesan's ample curves as though loath to abandon them. "There's someone I want you to meet. This is... "

Kier stepped up and cleared his throat. "Captain Kier Fitzmorwen, Alcorean Royal Legion."

A spark kindled Shanya's golden eyes. "A foreign brassy, eh?" Her lips narrowed in a pretty pout. "Oh, but look JonMarc, he's wounded!" She reached up to caress Kier's swollen brow. Kier drew back. Mischief danced in Shanya's splendid eyes. With the grace of a pampered malkin, she cornered him against the bar and playfully walked her fingertips up his exposed chest. Then, sliding one hand behind his head, she drew his mouth to hers while her hips pulsed a slow, insistent rhythm against his loins.

Kier's every muscle tensed. A shadowy specter from his past thrust its way to the fore: a pair of vixenous brown eyes; the stab of mocking laughter. Kier stuffed the humiliating memory back into the deep, dank pit from which it had arisen. Feeling supremely self-conscious, he disengaged himself from Shanya's determined embrace. "Perhaps... another time," he managed awkwardly, then turned and beat a tactical retreat toward a newly vacated table in the corner.

His companion did not follow. When Kier looked back, he saw the pair again passionately intertwined. But then, to his surprise, JonMarc left Shanya to ply her wiles on other prospective clients and forged a path across the smoky commonroom to the platform where the dusky slavegirl danced. He dug inside his tunic and held aloft a silver coin.

An anticipatory "Ahhh" rose from the press of onlookers as the girl sank to her knees, allowing JonMarc to place his offering in the valley between her bare breasts. Skillfully, she set the coin somersaulting like a darting fish over the rippling waves of her belly muscles, then slid it into the hip band of her tawdry pantaloons. She rewarded the donor's generosity with a sultry wink.

Grinning like a satyr, JonMarc started back across the crowded hall. His route carried him past a long table where a boisterous party of garrison troops sat drinking and dicing. Abruptly, JonMarc's feet tangled. He pitched sideways, right into the arm of a crop-haired legionary who was about to cast. His throw ruined, the beefy veteran spun with a snort while his companions hooted and jeered. "Blundering *spoil-hand!*" he bellowed, hurling a furious fist that JonMarc deftly evaded. That made the veteran even angrier. "Ghedrev flay your miserable hide. Go carry yer cursed-luck elsewhere!"

JonMarc retreated a prudent distance, then darted a contemptuous glare at his assailant, who had already returned to his gaming. Content that no one else paid heed, JonMarc calmly made his way toward Kier's table in the corner. Kier motioned him to a seat.

JonMarc searched the bottoms of several abandoned tankards until he found one yet unemptied. Cradling it in his palm, he planted himself in the chair opposite.

The gesture roused Kier's curiosity. Why would someone flush enough to offer silver to a common dancing girl need to scrounge discarded tankards for ale? It was one of several contradictions that intrigued him about this JonMarc. The lanky fellow seemed entirely at ease in these seamy surroundings, yet he was better attired than most, and his fair features clearly proclaimed him an outlander. Kier aimed a questioning nod toward the soldiers' table. "What was that about?"

JonMarc simply shrugged. "I slipped."

Hardly. Kier had glimpsed the wayward leg that caught JonMarc up, and its owner's malicious grin as he withdrew it. The incident was no accident and JonMarc knew it. So despite his attire and apparent wealth, JonMarc enjoyed little, if any, status among the tavern's raucous patrons. One reason for that was made clear from the surly veteran's gibe. The flickering lamplight revealed the back of JonMarc's left hand. There, indelibly seared into the flesh, was a mark Kier found all-too-familiar—the iron-red serpent spiral that branded JonMarc a spoil-hand. *Sinistral*. That was cause enough for abuse among this superstitious lot. Did JonMarc also possess the arcane mind talents that sometimes accompanied spoil-handedness? Kier hadn't sensed any at work.

JonMarc slid the incriminating hand into his lap and his tone turned acerbic. "You want me to go sit elsewhere so I don't ruin your luck as well?"

Kier shrugged. "Sit wherever you like. But you saved my life tonight, and I'm grateful. I've no quarrel if you stay."

The truculence drained from JonMarc's face like liquid from a punctured wineskin and he sat back to savor his scavenged ale. Spoil-handedness aside, the fellow stood out among the slight, dark-featured natives of Vilsolia like a milk-flower in a weed patch. He was unusually tall—at least three fingers taller than Kier—and he wore his shaggy, flax-colored hair tied back with a leather thong. His eyes, cornflower blue, angled downward at the edges, lending them a somewhat lazy cast. Only one race in all the Deg Tirith possessed such fair features: the Dynian of Kier's native Alcor. JonMarc had the look of a pureblood.

Yet the embattled Dynian seldom left their island homeland. What would JonMarc be doing here in far-off Castémaron? Gathering support for the Branwyn insurgents back home? That was a disquieting thought. Despite the Tiernai blockade, weapons smuggling to the rebel forces on Alcor remained rife. Yet if JonMarc aided the Dynian rebellion, surely he'd view Kier with suspicion, as an officer of his Tiernai enemy. Thusfar, JonMarc had betrayed no sign of distrust.

"What brought you here to Castémaron?" Kier asked, not in the common speech, but using the ancient Dynian language he'd spoken as a child. If JonMarc were a Branwyn agent, his reaction would surely betray some clue.

JonMarc's fair brows knitted in puzzlement that appeared genuine. Either he did not comprehend his own native tongue—a prospect difficult to credit—or he was well accomplished at deception. Kier tried a more direct approach. "Do you live here in the city?" he asked, this time in the common speech.

JonMarc took an unhurried swig from his tankard and nodded. "Western heights."

The affluent quarter. That accounted for the attire. "What do you do here?"

JonMarc's expression broadened to a rakish grin. "Whatever I can get away with."

Kier shook his head impatiently. "I don't mean in this place. What's your employ in Castémaron?"

Another leisurely swallow. "Oh, this and that. I manage to keep busy."

Evasion. So JonMarc *did* have something to hide. Kier tried to glean more by touching his companion's thoughts. But whether due to the crowdedness of the room or the fact that his head still pounded like a stonemason's maul, Kier's Fithlon-trained talents picked up nothing, except...

Anger. A fiery swell of it suddenly flooded his senses. But it did not come from JonMarc. Kier's eyes flew up in alarm, seeking its source.

A harried-looking tapgirl, hefting an armload of food and two brimming tankards, stalked up beside JonMarc. With no fanfare, she plunked her load onto the tabletop, snatched the unfinished tankard from JonMarc's hand and hurled its contents in his face.

JonMarc sputtered like a landed carp, obviously caught off guard. If he possessed any sinistral sensing talents, they must be minimal at best. He seized the girl's wrist. "Valerey, what in the...?"

The tapgirl yanked her arm back, brown eyes ablaze. "Aren't you the generous one!" she snapped. "Tossin' silver coin about like you're some kinda toff. What 'bout *me*? When I came back with nar a sull for my services, Eliém basted me royal! What was I to tell him? That you'd pitched me so you could go alley-romp with your hoodlum mates?"

The comment pricked Kier's curiosity. He found himself secretly enjoying his companion's discomfiture. Clearly, JonMarc was working more angles than he could handle.

JonMarc tried to snake his arm around the tapgirl's waist, but she was having none of it. "Come on, Val," he chided, "you know I wouldn't do that to you. When we overheard that scuffle, I sent you off so you wouldn't get hurt. Then I went back to save this brassy's arse."

Kier's amusement died. So— JonMarc had taken the tavern girl out for a midnight tumble, but abandoned her in order to come to his aid? It was unsettling to think he might owe his life to his companion's penchant for lechery.

Valerey eyed Kier up and down as if noticing him for the first time. Kier straightened. He'd given little thought to his appearance. Now his gaze dropped, with hers, to the slashed jerkin; the bloodstained remnants of what, until tonight, had been his best shirt. He brushed a lock of blood-crusted hair from his brow and winced. The knot on his scalp felt the size of a calabash.

The tapgirl nibbled her lip, considering. JonMarc flashed her the most disarming smile Kier had ever seen, and Valerey's anger melted like frost at orb-rise. "Well..." she began."

JonMarc fished inside his tunic and deposited a small stack of coins onto the tabletop—far more than the cost of the food and ale. With a self-satisfied smirk, Valerey scooped up the generous sum before its donor could reconsider. Then, bussing JonMarc lightly on the forehead, she scampered off to answer a hail from another table.

Kier looked on in wonder. Female behavior mystified him at the best of times. Ignoring JonMarc's sly wink, he tugged his cloak about him to hide his ravaged attire.

"You needn't fret your looks," his companion quipped. "You're little worse off than the rest of the scum who frequent this fair establishment—and you, at least, have an excuse."

"Thanks," Kier muttered. He was ready to concede that his rescuer was probably no rebel agent. The cocky Dynian was far too reckless for undercover work. But then, what was he doing here, so far from his homeland? JonMarc presented a web of contradictions Kier was determined to unravel. He took a sip from his tankard, then winced and nudged it aside. The tavern's sludgy brew was more than his empty stomach could handle just now. And he needed to keep his wits about him. He reached instead for a chunk of the black bread and sharp, rindy cheese Valerey had left, while a few scraps still remained. His tablemate was well on his way toward devouring the lion's share. "I'm sorry to stick you for the cost of all this," he said. "I haven't forgotten I owe you that drink…"

JonMarc waved it off. "No worries. Must be tough, losing your purse. Was there much in it?"

Something in the way he said it triggered Kier's caution. This was no time to let on that, in fact, he was not so destitute as he pretended. When on assignment, liked to keep his more valuable coin tucked safely in a pouch at the front of his breeches where, he reasoned, no self-respecting street cull was likely to go groping for it. The stolen purse had merely held pocket change. He shook his head. "Maybe a few coppers."

"Twelve."

Kier raised his eyes.

"Twelve coppers, eight bronze tanirs, and an Algolian silver dalmar." JonMarc reached into his tunic and deposited the purse and several other items on the tabletop: a broken neck chain, two silver charms, and a slim throwing dagger with a gold-filigreed hilt.

Kier's suspicions plowed into each other. It must have shown on his face, for JonMarc's eyes twinkled cunningly through the blue-green jirash haze. "C'mon, brassy, you don't think I'd take on a pair of croakers in an alley if I didn't mean to profit by it?"

So— JonMarc might be as much a scoundrel as the two who'd assaulted him. The tapgirl had spoken of his "hoodlum mates." What if...? A warning chill. This JonMarc might be the second thief. He never got a good look at that man, and lost track of him once the fight began.

But no, the voice was all wrong. Kier couldn't forget that strident whine. And his dagger had raked that attacker's thigh. JonMarc showed no sign of injury.

JonMarc flashed an impudent grin and nudged the stolen items toward him. "Look, I recovered your belongings. The least you can do is show some gratitude."

Kier wasn't sure what to make of the gesture. If his companion was so willing to return the stolen items, how indeed had he profited? "I *am* grateful," he said. "I hated the though of losing these. But how did you get them? I searched the thief's body and found nothing. You hardly even came near him—except to knife him in the back." Kier's tone implied that, while he thoroughly approved the action, he was less than enthusiastic about the method. Still, he'd been in no position to argue. He gathered up the charms and their broken chain and tucked them into the recovered purse, now almost empty of coin. Kier dangled it quizzically.

"Ah," said JonMarc. "Well, if it makes you feel any better, you actually did pay for the drinks."

"What about the silver dalmar?"

JonMarc flicked his glance toward the dancing girl's vacated platform.

Kier sucked in his cheeks. He'd presumed as much. Still, it was scant enough compensation for the debt he owed. "How did you know these items belonged to me and not the thief himself?"

"Charms of the Tiernai stag and the Dynian dragon?" JonMarc shrugged. "Who but an Alcorean halfblood would wear both? And as for this pretty rat-sticker—" He bounced the dagger in his left hand, then hurled it unerringly into a wood beam, scarcely an inch from Kier's scalp. "It's a noble's weapon. And for all your brassy ways, you're noble-born or I'm a dung hauler."

The reckless gesture startled Kier. Irritated, he yanked the dagger free and slid it back into the sheath at his wrist. "All right," he snapped, "if you're so blasted astute, what else do you think you know about me?"

JonMarc was quick to snatch up the verbal gauntlet. "Well, I imagine mixed-race marriages are rare on Alcor, what with the civil war and all, so I'm guessing you were stable-get. And you wear a crest ring, so your sire's a Tiernai noble. That means your mam must've been some compromised Dynian wench—a servant, maybe; or a peasant. The other way 'round and you'd not have managed a Legion captaincy by age— what, twenty-five?"

"Twenty-*one*," Kier said. "Five years ago." He regretted issuing the challenge. JonMarc's cavalier tone rankled him—all the more because he had shot uncomfortably near the mark. Clearly, the Dynian knew something of Alcor's politics, even if he did not speak its tongue.

JonMarc beamed, looking smug. "So wealthy papa bought his bastard a captaincy. Who is he?"

"A duke," Kier replied testily. "And he didn't buy my commission. I *earned* it."

A shrug. "Have it your way. All that experience didn't help you much tonight."

Kier glowered. He didn't need to be reminded.

JonMarc tossed down the last of his ale and gestured toward Kier's scarcely-touched tankard. "If you're not gonna finish that…" Without waiting for a reply, JonMarc emptied its contents into his own mug and took another long draught. He wiped his mouth on his sleeve.

Kier could scarcely believe the Dynian's audacity. Was JonMarc deliberately trying to unsettle him, or was he truly as oblivious as he seemed?

"There's one thing bothers me," said JonMarc, lacing fingers behind his shaggy head. "Why would a couple of street culls jump a brassy officer? Garrison rats don't usually carry much worth stealing. Everyone knows that. And brassies avenge their own. Why take the risk?"

Kier shrugged. "From their talk, I got the impression they'd been sent after a specific captain."

"Sent? By who?"

"They didn't bother to *tell* me that. One of them pressed me about… some kind of talisman, I think. But I don't carry anything like that."

"Maybe he meant your neck charms."

"These? There's nothing exceptional about them. I've worn them since I was a boy—a gift from my father." Kier shook his head. "I expect those two mistook me for someone else."

"A lot of Alcorean captains roaming Castémaron these days, are there?"

Kier ignored the sarcasm.

"Well, if I were you, friend," JonMarc went on, "I'd have a care where I strolled alone, so late at night. Next time, I may not be around to save your brassy cods."

"I'll try to remember that," Kier growled. "And while we're at it, *friend*, why don't you tell me how you come to know so much about 'street culls?'" He thought he sensed slight uneasiness in JonMarc's reaction. Good. It was high time he took the offensive.

But JonMarc masked it well. "Hang around this piss bucket long enough, you'll be surprised what you learn." He flashed that cocksure smirk. "Tell you what: Let's see you work out my past as well as I have yours. I'd like to see the skills that *earned* you that captaincy."

JonMarc's amiable sarcasm was growing ever more annoying. It troubled Kier that he could glean almost nothing from his companion's thoughts. He disliked relying on his Fithlon training, preferring to hone his skills at deduction, yet this JonMarc was an enigma. Though he lacked obvious sinistral talents, his mind defenses must be potent indeed, to deflect a probe.

"All right," he said. "You appear to be pureblood Dynian, yet you speak like a Castémaron native. Either you've a keen ear for accents, or you've lived here a while. I'll guess the latter." He sought JonMarc's reaction, but his tablemate's expression never altered. Kier stroked his chin. "A pureblood would likely come from Alcor's western provinces. That was a fair target for Syrmian corsairs till some eighteen years ago, when the Tiernai started patrolling the coast. Let's say you were taken in such a raid. That would have made you—seven or eight?"

JonMarc's brows rose. "Hey, you're better at this than I'd thought." Kier's satisfaction proved short-lived. "But the truth is, I've no memory from before I was captured. I had to piece a lot together to come up with what you've just worked out—and I can't be sure it's true."

"You mean you don't remember *anything*? Your family; your home?"

JonMarc shook his head. "I might as well have been new-born when I awoke on that galley." He smiled wistfully. "I don't even know my right name. The Syrmians called me *Jaha'an Maurek*. It means *the white jackal*," he added proudly. "I shortened it myself."

Kier nodded to himself. No wonder he could detect no recent contact with Alcor in the Dynian's thoughts. There was none. It also explained why JonMarc failed to understand his native tongue. "What became of you after you were taken?"

JonMarc settled back in his chair, long legs stretched out before him. "Well, I spent close to a year with the Syrmian pirates. When we were sunk off the Kharan coast, I got rescued by a merchant vessel. They brought me here to Castémaron, where I lived on the streets for a while."

"Alone?" Kier reminded himself that nothing about this JonMarc should surprise him.

"Nah, this city's a breeding pit for street brats. You learn to live by your wits and watch your back. I did all right." A glint of pride. "Better 'n most. Then, after a few months, I was recruited by a *jackman*. He gave me food, a place to sleep, and some protection, in return for whatever trinkets I could acquire for him."

"You mean he taught you to steal."

JonMarc's expression fairly dripped condescension. "Hell, I already knew how to steal. You think anyone can live out there just by begging? No, he wanted someone experienced; someone small and agile enough to creep into wealthy homes through rat-hole crevices older thieves couldn't use. It gave him an edge on the competition—and me, a reputation I was sorry to outgrow."

Kier could not fathom JonMarc's willingness to reveal so much about his obviously shady past, especially to a military officer. The Dynian seemed to feel a need to impress, or at least shock him. "Do you still thieve?" he asked, hoping the directness of the question might shake JonMarc composure.

His companion simply shrugged. "Don't need to anymore."

Kier suspected otherwise. "I imagine your spoil-handedness proved advantageous to you on the streets. I've heard that among pick-purses it's considered a valued trait."

JonMarc grinned. "Well, I admit it sometimes comes in handy for..."

"*Comes?*" Kier locked his gaze.

A look like curdled cream spread over JonMarc's face. "Blast it, Kier, that's not what I meant." He darted an anxious glance at the party from the garrison, now dealing a noisy hand of jack's-bluff. At the table's far end, a swarthy sergeant took little interest in the card game. His eyes, like black lodestones, fixed on JonMarc as if he'd overheard the exchange—unlikely, above the din. When he saw Kier watching, he sullenly turned away.

"For an honest man, you haven't much use for soldiers," Kier noted.

Genuine bitterness weighted JonMarc's response. "Even less than they have for me. They're as worthless a pack of lying scum as any culls you'll find thieving on the streets."

"Then why did you risk your life to aid me tonight?"

Pinned down, JonMarc seemed at a loss—either uncertain of the reason himself, or hesitant to divulge it. He passed it off with a casual shrug. "Bored, I guess." His words were slightly slurred—the ale starting to work on him. "You think I don't know your type, brassy? The fine, brave officer, noble-born and full of his own morality—with no more street sense than a yokel from the provinces. It's no wonder you blundered into trouble and had to be rescued."

Kier's anger flashed. "You know *nothing* of me! At least I've proved myself in combat. What have you done? I see no honor in stabbing a man in the back."

"*Honor*? Is that what you think it's about? The man I stabbed was about to gut you like a capon. Where's the honor in being a corpse?"

Kier shook his head. "That's not what I meant. I'm grateful for the rescue. Truly. But to murder a man by stealth, without even bothering to confront him—it just isn't..."

"*Honorable.*" JonMarc spat the word. "Then tell me, how would you have done it, Captain?"

"I'd have tapped his shoulder and taken him as he turned."

A caustic laugh. "He'd have plugged his blade hilt-deep in your gut before you even touched his shoulder. Take my advice, brassy. If you mean to explore Castémaron's back alleys after dark, learn to respect those who make their living out there, preying off such as you. Leave your highborn niceties behind. It's no place for honor or conscience. You learn to survive, or you die."

JonMarc's patronizing tone infuriated Kier. He'd traversed slums every bit as deadly as Castémaron's with his principles intact. Until tonight, he'd never been victimized. "That's a load of tripe. Without those so-called 'niceties,' we'd all live like wild beasts, preying off one another. What kind of survival's worth that?"

"*Mine* is."

"Are you trying to tell me you have no conscience?"

JonMarc swallowed down the last of his ale. "Why would I want such responsibility?"

Kier studied his companion again: the belligerent chin, the stubborn, if lazy, blue eyes. Odd he hadn't noticed it before: a deep, white scar at the corner of JonMarc's right eye. Sometime in his youth, JonMarc had been dealt a blow that came within a fraction of blinding that eye. A consequence of living on the streets? Probably. Still, Kier doubted JonMarc was ever as ruthless as he tried to pretend.

He let it pass. The argument was irrelevant, anyway. The attack tonight had nothing to do with honor or conscience. He'd been vigilant and offered no advantage. If anything, it came down to skills; hard won skills that, though it galled him to admit it, failed him tonight. It was an unnerving thought, for experience had taught him that only through training and discipline could he hope to overcome the impediments capricious *Fortunea* pleased to set in his path.

What had gone wrong? He remembered the battle through a frantic blur. Never had he felt so powerless; so bereft of control. He'd even lost his sword—a squire's error. True, the blows to his head accounted for his disorientation. Yet it was as if the battle had followed its own course—as though, despite anything he did, the outcome was pre-ordained...

Pre-ordained? The revelation smacked Kier like a gauntlet. Gwythion's prophecy. How in blazes had he forgotten it? He stole a glance at JonMarc. Was this Dynian the one the Fithlon Master predicted would change his life? In effect, he already had, just by saving it. If that outcome was foreseen, then perhaps the battle had simply been un-winable. That possibility made Kier uneasy. It suggested he was no more than a string puppet, with no control at all over his destiny. He absolutely refused to concede that. Yet if the incident indeed fulfilled Gwythion's prophecy, the outcome had turned out better than he'd dared hope. A change that brought no lasting change. His life could continue on its course, unaltered. Kier felt a weight lift from his heart.

JonMarc was tracing his left forefinger through the ale rings on the tabletop. Every now and then he cast furtive eyes toward the tavern's corner stair. With each glance, he seemed to grow more edgy. "I suppose you'll be wanting to get on your way," he said, as if prompting Kier to do so. "Before you go, brassy, there's something you need to know: I didn't kill that second thief tonight—the one whose leg you bloodied." JonMarc sighed. "I dunno, maybe I do have some honor in me." It sounded like a self-indictment. "The bastard put up no fight, so I just pommeled him cold. If you really were his target, he'll be back. You can bet your rank on it."

"I'll be watchful," Kier assured him, though he doubted the need. Now that the presaged event was over, such an eventuality seemed unlikely. He cast his gaze about the smoky commonroom. After the slave girl's final dance, the place had emptied quickly. Aside from a handful of soldiers still intent on their gambling, no more than a dozen customers remained, in varying degrees of alertness. JonMarc was right. It was time he started back for the inn. But first—

"Look, JonMarc, I won't be in Castémaron long. I need to know how to repay this blood debt I owe you." In truth, he could ill afford not to. If his association with JonMarc were truly linked to prophecy, it implied a certain measure of obligation. The only way to rid himself of it was to formally pay off the debt, either in money or compensatory service. The sooner he did that, the sooner he could put this unfortunate debacle behind him

For the first time all evening, JonMarc looked truly disconcerted. "*Repay?*"

"All I can only offer you now is what little's left in my purse. But if you meet me tomorrow at the Gull's Nest Inn, I'll make it worth your while."

The Dynian looked as if he'd swallowed wormwood. "You'd actually *do* that? I mean... a brassy? I never thought... " He stopped himself. Kier sensed some internal battle raging within him, but could not begin to divine its cause. Straining to read the Dynian's thoughts took too much of a toll on his aching head.

From atop the upper landing there came a peal of drunken laughter. A portly gentleman of middle years started down the stair, clinging fast to the arm of a buxom courtesan. His stubby legs wobbled beneath him like rotted pier pilings. "JonMarc!" he bellowed as he reached the lower steps, bleary eyes scanning the commonroom. "Where's the blasted slave got to?"

Slave?

JonMarc cringed, his air of craft bursting like a soap bubble. "Here, master," he cried, scrambling from his seat.

So *that* was it—the reason for all the tales; the evasion. JonMarc wasn't embarrassed about his past. He was ashamed of his present.

The gentleman had barely taken two unaided steps into the commonroom when his unsteady legs gave way. He toppled sideways, right into the path of a laden serving wench. The girl tried to in vain to avoid the collision. Her armload of tankards went flying, spattering them both in ale and shattered crockery.

Kier hurried over to help JonMarc hoist his master out of the wreckage. The gentleman seemed completely unfazed by the mishap. He leaned complacently against the stair rail, humming softly to himself while

JonMarc toweled him off.

For Kier, the revelation of his companion's unfortunate status changed nothing. Slave or no, JonMarc had saved his life and Kier felt duty-bound to repay him. That in mind, he slipped off his cloak and directed JonMarc to drape it about his master's ale-soaked shoulders. "Tell him I expect you to return it to me tomorrow, at the Gull's Nest," he murmured in the Dynian's ear.

JonMarc looked supremely uncomfortable. "Kier, I…" It was all he could manage.

His master drew himself upright, centering Kier in his unfocused gaze. "Do I know you, sir?" he declaimed, in a mellifluous baritone.

"I'm… an acquaintance of JonMarc's."

"Ah, well." The merchant cocked his head toward his slave. "He is something of a rogue, you know." He spoke behind his hand in a resonant aside. "He has *taking* ways."

JonMarc turned a deeper shade of green. If looks could throttle, Kier suspected the portly merchant would be choking on his words. The reaction seemed excessive. Surely JonMarc couldn't think the revelation came as a surprise.

With scarcely a parting nod, JonMarc turned and bustled his master out the door. Kier was about to follow when the tavern's churlish owner accosted him, demanding compensation for five broken tankards. Kier settled the debt with the last of the coins from his recovered purse.

By the time he finally exited the tavern, the rain had ended. The pre-dawn streets were silent, but for the amorous laughter of a staggering couple disappearing around a corner. Kier turned the opposite way, lured by a tantalizing image of hearth and pillow.

He'd not gone twenty paces when a woman's startled scream sliced the thick air behind him. Such sounds were not uncommon to Castémaron's streets, and Kier was sorely tempted to ignore it; he wanted no more trouble this night. Yet he owed his own life to a stranger's intervention. Against all better judgment, he turned and dashed after it.

A block beyond *The Dragon Sword*, he overtook the couple he'd seen. The woman, apparently unscathed, was being steered away by her shaken companion. Sprawled across the moonlit cobbles, Kier made out two prostrate forms. His stomach lurched when he recognized the one struggling to his knees.

JonMarc's face was blood-spattered and a spreading stain darkened his left sleeve. Kier dropped to one knee and seized the Dynian's shoulders. "What happened?" he demanded.

"Someone... attacked us!" JonMarc's brow crinkled as though he scarcely believed such an outrage could have been directed at him. "I drove him off, but..." His distraught gaze fell to his master's body, sprawled face down in the gutter.

A clutch of soldiers departing the tavern had evidently heard the woman's cry. The light of their torches cast spidery shadows on the surrounding tenements as they hastened up, weapons drawn. One yanked JonMarc to his feet while their sergeant, the swarthy fellow Kier had noted earlier, crouched to examine the body.

Kier suspected what conclusion must be racing through the sergeant's mind. "Which way did your assailant go?" he asked JonMarc, hoping to forestall the inevitable interrogation.

JonMarc pointed to a nearby alley. At a gesture from their sergeant, two soldiers ran to investigate. They returned but a moment later. "Nothing," said one. "It's a dead end. No one could escape that way."

The sergeant stood, rubbing beefy hands together, his expression gleeful. "So the harlot *Fortunea's* caught you up at last, JonMarc, you thieving son of a maggot." He snatched a knife from JonMarc's belt and thrust it into his own. "Yer cursed spoil-hand skills won't get you out of this one."

JonMarc's pale eyes widened as the implications of his plight began to creep in on him. "Devoreth's blood, Elrin, you can't think that... *I* killed him?"

"Don't be playin' the innocent with me. 'Tis plain you attacked Lord Sethrin and he fought back. Who'd have better cause to murder a man than his slave?"

"But I didn't *do* it!"

"Sergeant," Kier broke in, "I see no such evidence. I was with them when they left the tavern. This Lord Sethrin was in no condition to fight anyone. Surely you saw him. He could barely stand up, much less inflict a wound like this."

"Keep out o' this, captain. You've no authority in Castémaron. You know, of course, that this slave has murdered afore."

No surprise there. Kier recalled JonMarc's lack of compunction at stabbing a man in the back only this evening. "Then why is he not imprisoned?"

Elrin spat. "Because he's one of demon Ghedrev's own. Should'a had that 'cursed spoil hand of his severed years ago. But that'll soon be remedied." Grinning smugly, Elrin directed two of his men to take up the body while a third bound JonMarc's wrists before him. "We've a cozy lock up for you, slave. Enjoy it while you can. Tomorrow, you'll be slogging it to the Death Quarries."

JonMarc's face blanched whiter than the moon-washed stucco. His pinioned hands grappled for at Kier's forearm. "For the love of Devoreth, Kier, you're an officer. *Do* something!"

Kier loosed a grim exhale. "Sergeant, *wait.*" His tone of command jerked Elrin to a halt. "I want a word with him." At the sergeant's angry nod, JonMarc's guards backed off. Kier led the slave a short way aside. "JonMarc, tell me straight. *Did you kill your master?*"

"No, Kier, I swear it. Sethrin was good to me. I had no cause to murder him."

Kier recalled the scathing look JonMarc had offered his master not ten minutes earlier. "Then what did your attacker look like? Where might he have gone?"

"He took us from behind. I never saw his face. But he hasn't left that alley; I'm sure of it. And Elrin's men are right; there's no other exit. He's still in there."

"But the soldiers searched!"

"Blazes, you think they *want* to find him? He's skulking in the darkness, waiting for the commotion to die. It's a common enough trick. Once things quiet down, he'll make his move." Desperate fingers clawed Kier's sleeve. "Wait for him, Kier. It may take a while before he feels safe. But if he escapes into the streets, you'll never track him." JonMarc's voice shook with genuine fear. "Kier, I'm *begging* you. You owe me your life!"

Elrin, who had managed to eavesdrop, issued a contemptuous snort. "The slave has you gulled. There was no attacker. He killed his master himself. The knife was in his fist when we found him." A scornful laugh. "You're a fool, captain."

"And you're a liar, *sergeant.* I saw you lift that weapon from JonMarc's belt. He didn't even have time to draw it. Do you say he stabbed his master with a sheathed blade? And himself as well?" Kier displayed JonMarc's bloody forearm. "Where's the weapon that did this?"

"Say what you like, this spoil hand's got a record long as your arm. I've waited years to pack him off to the quarries, and I'll not lose him now on account of you." Elrin jostled his captive's shoulder. "Move along, maggot."

The rude shove dislodged something concealed in JonMarc's belt. It jingled to the ground at the slave's feet. Elrin snatched it up and laughed aloud. "Well, what've we here? Lord Sethrin's purse. And a goodly sum, by the weight of it. What more proof do we need?"

Blood drained from Kier's face as he recognized his hide-out purse. How in blazes had JonMarc managed to lift it? He'd been careful to keep the table between them all evening. The answer came to him: the courtesan, Shanya. Only she had come near enough. The two must be in league.

JonMarc would not look at him. Kier swallowed his indignation. "The purse was mine," he said. "You can see it bears an Alcorean crest. I offered it to JonMarc as reward for saving my life."

Elrin's gape of astonishment was exceeded only by JonMarc's. "Well, he won't be needin' it where he's going. I'll take it as evidence."

Kier clapped a firm hand on the sergeant's forearm. "I think not."

Elrin hesitated. Then, furious, he flung the purse in the mud at Kier's feet. To save face before his men, he cuffed his prisoner so hard JonMarc nearly sprawled headlong. "Move along, you thieving son of a whore," he barked, and prodded JonMarc off toward the garrison prison.

Chapter Three

The troop escorting JonMarc and his master's corpse disappeared around the corner. Alone on the empty street, Kier rubbed his arms against the pre-dawn chill while his eyes darted swift reconnaissance of his dismal surroundings. Wisps of spectral mist rose from the scummy cobbles that still gave off the faintest luminescence. No sounds broke the stillness but the snarl of a prowling malkin and the chitter of rats wriggling in an open sewer. Victims and predators. That about summed up all of Castémaron.

Cautiously, Kier approached the alley where JonMarc swore his attacker had fled. The corridor was still as a death vault. Hard to imagine anyone still hid there. Kier sensed no presence within, though with so many restless souls asleep in the surrounding tenements, it would be all but impossible to isolate a single, unfamiliar mind. Still, he owed it to JonMarc to make sure. Though the theft of his purse rankled Kier, simply forgiving the crime was not enough to balance a blood debt. Only saving JonMarc from a murder charge would accomplish that. And that meant bringing in the real culprit. Kier chose a spot directly beside the alley mouth and settled against the crumbling brickwork to wait.

The brisk air, welcomed after the stifling warmth of the tavern, now felt frigid as the long minutes trudged by. Kier wished he'd thought to retrieve his cloak from the merchant's corpse. He felt a fool standing here in the cold when he might be warm asleep at the Gull's Nest. And the prospect of encountering another cutthroat in the dark was not exactly heartening.

Of course, that presumed there *was* an attacker. What if Sergeant Elrin was right and JonMarc had indeed committed the deed himself? He had motive enough. It was clear he chafed at his captivity. But why do it now, so near the tavern, with a troop of soldiers within call? To finish the job and make an escape before Kier discovered the theft of his purse and reported it? Kier had to admit it was a possibility.

He shifted uncomfortably, his toes numb from standing in cold muck that reeked of slops and rotted fish. He longed to depart, yet to do so would condemn JonMarc to certain death. Kier recalled his single visit to the infamous hell pit known as the *Death Quarries*. Gruesome images of heat-seared rock and plodding, hollow-eyed slaves still plagued his dreams. No prisoner survived the stone pits of Maveta. Whatever crimes JonMarc might have committed, he surely didn't deserve that fate. Kier silently damned the slave, and Gwythion's prophecy, for getting him into this. At first light, he'd inspect the alley. If it proved empty, there was little more he could do. Guilty or not, JonMarc would pay with his life. And Kier himself would face whatever penance the gods should devise for one who abandoned a blood debt.

Beyond the harbor, the eastern sky began to brighten. Drowsiness enticed Kier like a warming blanket. To combat it, he set about his training drill, flexing and releasing his muscles, one by one, to keep them limber. The familiar routine revived him, though it did little to break the tedium. A few minutes more and he'd be quit of this obligation, for good or ill.

An all-too-familiar warning skittered up Kier's backbone. He straightened, weariness forgotten. Had something stirred within the alley? He sensed movement—footsteps, drawing nearer. So JonMarc was right.

Kier held his breath, muscles poised. An inky blot distorted the alley mouth, taking the form of a man as it broke from the darkness. Kier sprang. Before the lurker could react, Kier grabbed his outstretched arm and hurled him into the adjacent wall. The man's forehead met the brickwork with an audible crunch that left him stunned. Kier slipped off his own belt to bind his captive's bony wrists. But as he worked to secure them, the creature snapped to. With the wiry strength of a slime adder, he squirmed his way free. Kier made a grab for his ragged cloak, but the scrawny fellow shrugged it off like an out-grown skin and bolted away down the narrow street.

Kier flung the filthy garment aside and took off after him. He could make out the rasp of phlegmy breath as the man skidded around the corner ahead. Kier followed. In the dim pre-dawn, he saw his quarry some dozen paces ahead, about to disappear into the shadows between two ramshackle tenements. Kier yanked his dagger from its wrist sheath and hurled it.

There was a startled yelp and his victim's momentum faltered. Kier raced up behind and snagged his arm. Again, the creature shook loose, lurching backward into the gloom. He did not see the wall behind him until he slammed into it. The impact drove Kier's blade deep into his back. With a strangled gasp, he sagged to the ground.

Kier grasped his victim's wrist and dragged him into the growing light. Ragged breath bubbled in the man's chest. The blade had punctured a lung. Kier's conscience harangued him for the means he'd used to take the fellow down. He'd intended his small blade to slow him, not to kill. JonMarc, he knew, would view the outcome with smug satisfaction. Kier only prayed he could find some proof that this unfortunate had indeed murdered the slave's master. He tugged his dagger free and rolled the man onto his back.

His victim gasped and coughed, spattering blood on Kier's sleeve. His upper lip was split—some birth deformity—exposing well-rotted teeth. A bloodstained rag bound his left thigh. As Kier retrieved a shabby dirk from his victim's belt, the man's glazed eyes fluttered open. Abruptly, they widened in puzzled recognition. "But... I left 'e dead!" he gasped, in a gravelly whine that obliterated Kier's last doubts. Hoisting the dying thief over his shoulder, he turned for the garrison prisons.

The city was coming alive with the promise of a new day. A street-crier loudly intoned the hour while fishmongers maneuvered heaping barrows toward the market square. Few raised eyes to Kier, laboring beneath his unwieldy burden. Those who did quickly looked away. Kier could only imagine how he must appear, his clothes ripped and bloody, his face sprouting a day's growth of dark stubble. He only hoped his own stench did not match that of his luckless victim.

The black-walled fortress loomed beside the harbor, a stark bastion of order dominating the city's cluttered chaos. Kier knew the place well. As an officer of an allied land, he was usually accorded a measure of deference there. Today, his intimidating looks afforded him even more. A young sentry waived him through the iron portcullis with little question. Kier adjusted the thief's weight on his shoulder. It was some time since he'd heard breath whistling through the hole in the man's back, so he presumed he must be dead. He lugged the body through the dark barbican tunnel and across the yard toward the prefect's office.

A cluster of bedraggled prisoners stood shackled in the outer ward, waiting to be led off to the Death Quarries. Most were barefoot; one or two coughed convulsively. Few would survive the grueling five-day trek through the parched southern wastes. Kier breathed relief that JonMarc was not among them. But the very fact that they were being assembled renewed his urgency.

The door to the prefect's anteroom stood ajar. Kier shoved his way in and paused before an immaculately tidy desk. The pudgy adjutant behind it scarcely raised an eye.

"I request an audience with the prefect," Kier said.

The adjutant continued to make entries in his ledger, tracing each figure with meticulous care. Kier's patience ebbed. Abruptly, the young aide wrinkled his nose. Only then did he deign to look up, and his eyes narrowed. "Imbecile! Take that disgusting thing out to the yard. Does this look like a morgue?"

Kier's free hand curled in a fist. The body on his shoulder evidently concealed his medallion of rank. At this point, he didn't care. He found the adjutant's supercilious attitude infuriating. "I told you," he said, laboring to keep an even tone, "I need to see the prefect, *now*."

The adjutant fluttered a dismissive wave. "The prefect sees no one without an appointment." He turned back to his ledger.

Kier's temper snapped. "Here's my appointment!" He heaved the ragged body onto the desk with a dusty thud, sending ink and parchments flying.

The astonished adjutant leaped back and started to protest. Then he took in Kier's harrowing looks, the now-visible medallion, and the retort melted on his lips. He stumbled backward toward the office door. "I... I'll see if the prefect can be disturbed."

"You do that," Kier said. Gingerly, he worked his shoulders, relieved to be quit of his bulky load, and tried to make himself look remotely presentable—a wasted effort, he decided.

A moment later, the adjutant returned, his manner contrite. "The prefect will see you now." His eyes dropped to the filthy corpse sprawled across his desk. "But Captain, what shall I do with...?"

"Take it to the yard," Kier grunted, stalking past him. "Does this look like a morgue?"

As he entered the austere chamber, he spotted Sergeant Elrin, standing in the light from a small oriel window. The sergeant looked none too pleased to see him. Kier suspected he'd just submitted his report.

The prefect rose slightly from his chair, his nod cordial but chill. "Captain Fitzmorwen."

Kier returned a salute. He'd dealt with Castémaron's prefect on previous visits, and had worked hard to earn the man's respect. Coming before him in this condition undoubtedly lost him ground. Though the prefect did not comment, his furrowed brow suggested disapproval.

Kier went right to the point. "There's your murderer, Elrin." He jerked his head toward the anteroom door. "He was skulking in that alley, just as JonMarc said. I took this from his belt. You'll find recent blood on it." He laid the dirk on the prefect's desk.

Disbelief hardened Elrin's blocky features. He bowled past Kier into the outer chamber and rolled the body over, ignoring the flustered adjutant. "It's Urd, the ferret-lip," he said. "He an' his brother Kortha are hired knives. But they work as a team. Kortha's the brains of the pair."

"Kortha is dead." Kier addressed his comments to the prefect. "Killed last evening when the two attacked me on the street. The slave JonMarc risked his life to aid me." Kier judged it best not to name JonMarc the thief's killer. The last thing the slave needed was another murder charge on his head. "This Urd escaped with my knife-wound in his thigh. Apparently, he awaited us outside *The Dragon Sword* and mistook JonMarc's master for me, as I'd loaned the man my cloak. He indicated before he died that he thought *I* was the one he'd killed."

The prefect folded his arms. "And why were these villains targeting you, captain?"

"I don't know, sir," Kier admitted. In fact, he could think of no one in Vilsolia who might pay to have him killed. It was tempting to dismiss the incident as mistaken identity, but like JonMarc, he found that explanation hard to accept.

Elrin returned, more bellicose than ever. "So you found a cowering thief. What's 'at prove?"

"It proves JonMarc did not murder his master. I'll testify to that at his trial."

"Trial? For a slave?" A scornful laugh. "He'll go straight to the quarries." Elrin glanced up at the window and his dark eyes betrayed a knowing glint. "Prob'ly already on his way."

Kier recalled the line of shackled prisoners in the ward. "Just pray he's not, sergeant."

The prefect sat patiently observing their exchange. Once or twice he stroked his graying goatee. "What is your interest in this slave, captain? That he's from Alcor? I understand the races are still at war in your homeland. Why would a Tiernai officer—a nobleman's son, if I remember aright—trouble himself over the fate of condemned Dynian slave?"

"The fact that he's of Dynian race has naught to do with it. The slave's committed no crime."

"Hasn't he?" said Elrin. "Lemme tell you about your spoil-hand friend. He's a smart-mouthed street whelp who flouts the law and turns 'is thumb at authority. Whenever we lock him up, he *conjures* his way out again. He once gulled the garrison swordmaster into buyin' his release, then did the same with Lord Sethrin." Elrin eyed Kier with scorn. "An' now it's plain he's bespelled you, captain."

Kier bristled. He was under no spell. JonMarc might be a skilled conniver, but any sinistral mind skills he possessed fell far short of the talent to bend wills. "I don't give a cleft copper for his past. You know as well as I that JonMarc did not commit *this* crime, and right now it's all you can hold him for." Kier looked to the prefect, hoping he would concur. The little he could read behind the officer's impassive facade told him that at least he wasn't hostile.

"Captain Fitzmorwen is right, sergeant. Unless you can show me better evidence of the slave's guilt, I'll be forced to free him."

Elrin looked as if his fury might choke him. "But *why*? He's naught but a spoil-hand pick-purse. What point savin' his miserable hide? So he can thieve again? He's *worthless*."

"Aye," said Kier, "brand him worthless and you can pack him off to his death with a clear conscience. Who made you the judge of anyone's worth?" Elrin turned away, seething.

The prefect rose, indicating he considered the matter closed. "You are dismissed, Sergeant. Have the slave released to Captain Fitzmorwen's custody."

Kier's heart skipped. "*My* custody?"

"Is that not what you intended, Captain? The slave's master is dead. Someone must be accountable for him. You can hardly expect me to release him on his own recognizance."

Kier hadn't considered that. The last thing he wanted was to be answerable for JonMarc. "But I'll be leaving Castémaron within the week."

"By that time, Lord Sethrin's estate will doubtless be settled and the slave's new owner will take possession." The prefect noted Kier's reluctance. "It's that or the quarries, captain."

Kier sighed. At least he had one consolation. The blood debt was repaid. Another day, maybe two, and he'd be quit of JonMarc for good.

The prefect dismissed him with a brusque nod. Kier followed Elrin out. The line of ragged prisoners still loitered in the ward, shuffling in their heavy leg-irons. "They're ready, sergeant," said the prison warden. "We only awaited your word on the last—"

"Release him to the captain here." Elrin nearly choked on the words.

"*Release*? But he's your prize catch! I thought—" Elrin glared and the burly warden swallowed the rest. "Aye, sergeant." He turned for the keep.

"This ain't the end of it, Captain," Elrin warned. "The slave'll slip up again. Don't think you're any better 'n the other fools he's gulled. Such as him don't risk their life for no one, 'less they got somethin' to gain by it." Elrin chuckled malevolently. "You best watch yer back, Captain."

Kier bit back a retort. There was no point bandying insults with a lout like Elrin.

The warden returned with his prisoner. Squinting against the bright orblight, JonMarc spied the wretched line of prisoners ready to be marched away and tried to wrestle free. The warden cuffed him in the head. "I'll take him," said Kier, before the man could strike again.

JonMarc raised his eyes at the familiar voice. His anxious gaze darted to the ragtag procession, now lumbering toward the gates, then back to Kier, regarding him as if he were an apparition he feared might evaporate.

The moment the iron gate clanged shut behind them, he seized Kier by the shoulders and swung him around. "Kier, you did it!" he cried, laughing. "I never thought... How'd you convince the prefect to free me?"

Kier quickly extricated himself from JonMarc's embrace. The slave looked little worse for his few hours' imprisonment. His face and clothes were grimed, and dried blood matted his hair and torn sleeve, yet he seemed animated, even exuberant, as they started across the plaza.

"Elrin had no evidence against you. When I brought in the real culprit—" Kier briefly summarized the morning's events.

JonMarc shook his head, incredulous. "And the prefect took your word over Elrin's? Ghedrev's cods, Kier, you've more clout than I'd guessed."

The comment tweaked Kier's suspicions. He did not doubt JonMarc's propensity to take advantage where he could.

The streets near the Harbor Gate were a-bustle with foot traffic. Out on the quay, a brisk sea wind rocked ships at their berths, while the angled rays of Devoreth's Orb ignited the dark harbor waters into a field of shimmering crystal. Kier turned for the shadowed lane that led to the Gull's Nest's rear entrance.

JonMarc hastened along beside him, combing fingers through his tangled hair. Abruptly, he slowed. "Kier, about your purse. Y'see, I never expected..."

"To be caught?"

JonMarc winced. "No! I never expected you'd offer to repay the debt. And, well... no one's ever lied to *save* my life before. Why'd you do it?"

"I didn't lie. I *had* offered you the money. I saw no reason to make my task of defending you any more complicated." Kier gave a grim chuckle. "Let's just call it a matter of *honor.* "

JonMarc's downcast eyes could have scorched the pavement. "Then—I guess the debt's repaid."

"I'd say so. Just do me one favor, JonMarc. Stay out of trouble, at least until you've left my charge. I haven't time to keep track of you every moment, but that Elrin will be watching you like a bloodhawk. If you slip up, don't expect me to run to your rescue again."

Kier rubbed his cramped neck muscles, eager for a wash and some sleep. They had reached the inn's rear door. JonMarc stood silent, looking as pathetic as a chastened spaniel. "Where will you go now?" Kier asked.

JonMarc shrugged. "My master's villa, I guess—to learn what's to become of me, now that he's dead."

Kier conceded a touch of sympathy for the slave. "Well, you'd best get that arm wound seen to first." He gestured toward the door. "C'mon, I'll buy you breakfast."

The Gull's Nest was a flurry of activity. Kier managed to snag a house boy and ordered their meals and hot water for bathing. Then he led JonMarc up to his room by a back stair, to avoid attention.

He was just toweling his hair dry when there came a loud knock on the door. Kier threw on his last clean shirt and hastened to answer, hoping to find the boy with their breakfasts. But the apple-dumpling figure that fretted in the hall belonged to the innkeeper's wife.

"Sorry t' trouble you, Cap'ain," she said, nodding steel-grey curls at him. "I'll but keep you a moment." Kier sucked in his cheeks, knowing better.

The woman craned her neck to see inside the room. Kier reasoned why, and the recognition both amused and annoyed him: he'd asked for *two* breakfasts. She'd come to see what doxie he was harboring in his garret chamber. Her gaze instantly fell on JonMarc, seated on the edge of the sleeping pallet, his shirt unlaced, and her expression fairly sizzled with righteous indignation. "I keep a respectable 'ouse 'ere, Cap'ain. I'll not 'ave such going's on!"

Kier halted her nascent rant with an upraised hand. "What did you have to tell me, Mistress?"

The landlady huffed, drawing herself up to full height—still more than a head shorter than he. Frowning, she withdrew from her ample bodice a letter sealed with wax. "This came for you yestereve. The lad what fetched it here came off a vessel just put in from Alcor. He waited a good while for you to return. When you didn't, 'e told me 'twas to be delivered to no 'ands but yours." The lady raised her head proudly. "I've kept it safe beneath me pillow all night."

Kier imagined the letter must have burned a sizeable hole in the landlady's pillow. "Thank you," he said reaching for it.

She wafted it out of reach. "Said 'twas urgent, 'e did, sir."

"Well then, *give* it to me."

The landlady bristled as if Kier had charged her with thievery. Grudgingly, she handed the letter over. "*Urgent*," she reminded, as he eased her out the door.

JonMarc chuckled under his breath.

Kier paid no heed. So there *had* been a messenger from Alcor waiting for him last night. Did it have aught to do with Gwythion's foretelling? Perhaps he'd been wrong to think the prophecy fulfilled. Kier turned the letter over. It showed signs of much handling. Yet the seal remained intact, despite what must have been a valiant effort by the landlady to discover its secrets. It was dated a month since. "It's not my orders," he said, as much to himself as JonMarc. He recognized the seal and the graceful script, and his heart leapt. "It's from my cousin Cariwyn!" Eagerly, he broke the seal and read in silence.

His elation plummeted. Kier sensed JonMarc staring at him and turned away to hide the sudden grief now weaving icy tendrils about his heart.

"It's my father," he said. "Cari says—he's dying."

Chapter Four

Kier re-read his cousin's letter yet a third time, struggling to grasp the full import of its content. His father the duke was only fifty, hale and strong five years ago, when Kier had left Alcor. How could he be dying? Kier set the message down and cradled his head in his hands, the foundations of his carefully constructed world crumbling beneath him like a desert sinkhole. "I have to get back to Alcor," he muttered.

JonMarc's voice intruded on his grief. "Let me go with you."

Kier raised his eyes. He'd all but forgotten the slave was there. JonMarc sat cross-legged on the bare wood floor, filching scraps of bread and bacon from Kier's untouched breakfast plate, seemingly unconcerned with his companion's troubles. Kier refused to meet that hopeful gaze. "Why would I take you to Alcor? You've lied to me from the start."

"I never *lied*. I just—didn't tell you everything."

Kier dismissed it. He didn't want this argument. Not now. His whole being rebelled at the thought of re-visiting his war-ravaged homeland, and his emotions around his father's impending death were yet too turbulent to dwell upon.

"Look, it's the perfect chance. Until my master's estate's settled, I don't really belong to anyone. If I disappear, no one'll even miss me."

Kier wrenched his mind from the grim prospects ahead. "The authorities won't see it that way. Surely your master has an heir; a wife or something."

"He's got a wife. Ruthira. But she won't inherit. She's in the same fix as me. Both our futures rest on who takes over the estate. But that won't be decided for some days, and I'm not waiting around to learn the outcome. I've been through this before."

"So you plan to escape anyway." Kier shrugged it off. "Well, I won't stop you. I've enough to deal with right now. But if that Elrin gets wind of it..."

"He won't. Not if you help."

"*Help*? Blazes, JonMarc, I'm *accountable* for you. I said I'd look the other way. That's all I'm willing to do. Don't ask me to break Vilsolian law."

"Why not? You serve Alcor, not Vilsolia." A cunning look wormed across JonMarc's face. "Besides, what better way to account for me than to take with you?"

It didn't even merit a response. Kier felt no further obligation to JonMarc. He'd done his part, and more. This journey would be grim enough without a self-absorbed miscreant hounding his steps. Carefully, he folded his cousin's letter and slipped it into his pack, then stood to gather his belongings, hoping JonMarc would take it as a sign the discussion was ended. He didn't.

"What good's it do me to escape the city if I can't get off this blasted island? Just let me board the ship as your slave. Then I'll go my own way. No one'll ever know."

"An Alcorean officer with a slave? Who's going to believe that? Slavery's outlawed on Alcor."

JonMarc brightened. "All the more reason to take me there." He scrambled to his feet. "Look, I was brought to Vilsolia against my will. As an Alcorean officer, it's your *duty* to rescue captives like me. Just think of it as... as confiscating stolen property."

"Don't tell me my duty. I've already saved your hide from the quarries. Just because I let my guard slip last night, don't think I'm another fool you can gull."

JonMarc was not to be put off. In fact, he seemed hardly to be listening. "If you're worried about the extra passage money, I can come up with that."

"How? By thieving? I don't need that kind of help."

"Then I'll pledge to serve you till the debt's repaid."

"And I don't need a servant." Kier heaved an exasperated sigh. "Look, JonMarc, it's not the money. I'm Alcor's military liaison. To break Vilsolian law would completely destroy my credibility." He slumped back into his chair. "Why in blazes would you want to go to Alcor, anyway?"

"Kier, I'll go *anywhere*, as long as it's away from here. But you said it yourself: slavery's illegal there."

"Believe me, JonMarc, there are worse things than slavery."

JonMarc favored him a look that seemed to question his very sanity. "*Name* one."

"Race war. Since the Tiernai conquered Alcor, they've ruled with an iron gauntlet. The Dynian are hounded; persecuted at the slightest provocation. You could be maimed, even killed, by any Tiernai who decided to make sport of you, and no one would dare interfere."

JonMarc's chin rose defiantly. "I'll chance that. I know how to take care of myself. Besides," he added, "you're part Dynian. If Alcor's so terrible, how'd *you* manage to survive?"

"By getting the blazes out of there. And trust me, I'd rather face a whole fleet of Tarimian war galleys than return."

JonMarc plopped down on the edge of Kier's sleeping pallet, propping elbows on his knees. "Well, anything's better than being trapped here; having to leap at everyone's call. *Keep out of trouble, JonMarc. Tend my bath, JonMarc. Kiss my gold-plated backside, JonMarc.*" Intensity lit the slave's pale eyes. "I want my own life, Kier! This might be my only chance to get it."

Kier massaged his aching temples. He sympathized with JonMarc's plight. But simply turning his head while a slave in his custody escaped was enough to challenge his standing with the Vilsolian High Council. He dared not chance more, even if he wanted JonMarc's company—which he didn't. And though the slave might chafe at his captivity, he did not appear ill-used. In that sense, he was better off than most of his Dynian brethren back on Alcor. Yet, perhaps there was another course. "Who's likely to inherit your master's estate?"

Wariness edged JonMarc's response. "Probably his brother, Lord Correlin. Why?"

"It might be week's end before I find a ship heading for Alcor. If the estate's awarded before then, maybe I can use what influence I have to try and negotiate your release."

That hardly mollified JonMarc. "And if you fail? By then, I'll have no chance to get away."

Probably true. But it was the most Kier was willing to concede. He feared to make any gesture that might raise JonMarc's hopes. The Dynian had an annoying habit of twisting words like lanyard cord. "At least I can try. If that doesn't work, then..."

As he'd feared, JonMarc seized on his nebulous "*then*" like a drowning man to a spar. "Kier, I swear you won't regret it."

Kier shook his head ruefully. He already regretted it.

They parted company outside the inn. JonMarc's towering blond head quickly disappeared amid the bustle of foot traffic headed for Castémaron's central plaza. Weary in body and spirit, Kier turned the opposite way— toward the harbor and a ship that would carry him back to Alcor.

Most mornings, Kier enjoyed the salty bustle of the wharves: the shouts of dockhands hoisting cargo onto sun-browned shoulders; the sing-song chant of fishmongers peddling their night's catch. Yet today, the sights and sounds brought no comfort. Rather, they triggered a surge of bitter memories of Alcor and the home he'd left, all too willingly, five years before.

The harsh cry of sea birds melded with a torrent of unbidden images: kerlews, wheeling and swooping above jagged chalk cliffs, accompanied by the endless thunder of the surf; a bitter wind rippling across Alcor's craggy moorlands; the stark gray walls and towering keep of Cordon Castle, overlooking the wide sea. Kier recalled his first glimpse of that castle, standing lonely and proud atop its high motte. He'd been a lad of twelve, also lonely, and a bit frightened, yet stubbornly proud as he rode behind the raven-haired stranger he knew to be his father.

The man had come alone in the night to the tiny hamlet, nestled in Alcor's western mountains. Kier remembered listening from his pallet in the stable loft as the stranger haggled with Kier's aunt in the moonlit yard below. Despite her protests, Kier knew the sharp-tongued widow would gladly be rid of him—for a price. He'd endured her tirades against the fate that burdened her with this *child of abomination* after his mother's untimely death. Never did she let him forget the risk her family took by harboring him. "*Fruit e'er falls near the tree,*" she'd said, and though Kier displayed no outward sign, he knew that, like his condemned mother, he too possessed despised *sinistral* talents.

The stranger had entered the stable then, mounted the rickety ladder and knelt in the straw beside him. "Prepare for a journey," he'd said. For six agonizing years Kier had awaited that moment. Now, he could scarcely believe it had arrived. His father, come to deliver him at last from the loveless hovel where taunts and blows were the daily routine.

The duke had studied him in the flickering lantern light, his dark, Tiernai eyes probing deeply into Kier's own, which, the duke said, were so like his mother's. On their long journey across the breadth of Alcor, he had spoken much of Kier's mother, as though his son's haunted face resurrected her memory from the shadowed past. He'd told Kier of the cold day, years before, when she had come upon a young noble, thrown from his injured mount, and nursed him until he was fit to rejoin his hunting comrades. Kier had heard the tale before—recounted lovingly by his mother, and the cruder version forced upon him by his aunt—and he knew why the villagers despised him; why, when they spoke to him at all, it was but to remind him he was a worthless halfblood. The Tiernai were the enemy. They had taken Alcor by force; murdered its High King; brought years of degradation upon the native Dynian. And Kier's father was Tiernai. Worse, he was of the hated nobility, a class accustomed to taking Dynian women at whim and discarding them once noble lust was sated. No wonder that when the tall man searched his son's eyes, he found there only guarded distrust and shadowed pain.

Then, at last: Kier's first glimpse of the mighty castle that was to be his new home. His heart had leapt with awe and excitement at the thought of dwelling in a place so grand. Perhaps here, amongst his father's folk, he might at last gain acceptance. Yet as the duke led him into the gaily tapestried hall, Kier again found himself confronted by hostile glares and whispered jibes. From that moment, he realized that life at Castle Cordon, though more opulent, would be little different from what he'd known since his mother's death. He would ever be an outcast.

Plodding wearily along the bustling quay, Kier still carried that burden—a deep wound that five years abroad had barely begun to heal. His father had recognized his anguish. When Kier came of age, at sixteen, the duke suggested he journey to Menythgar, Alcor's capital, to train as a squire in the royal court. Kier had gone eagerly, for at court he need no longer endure the stinging hatred of his step-mother, the Duchess Yssolt, or his half-brother's blistering taunts. Malcolm, three years Kier's junior, had at first been elated to find a comrade to ease the tedium of life at Cordon, and their father heartily encouraged their friendship. Yet when the duke was away, as he so often was, presiding over Alcor's Royal Council, the Lady Yssolt used her greater influence over her son to instill a festering resentment of his father's bastard.

So Kier escaped to Menythgar, and learned much there in service to the old king. It was at court that he'd met the inscrutable Master Gwythion, who recognized the sinistral talents Kier had so long kept hidden, and singled him out for training in the arcane ways of the Fithlon. Yet the taunting continued, now from his peers, sons of other Tiernai lords, who delighted in tormenting the halfblood upstart who could never be one of them. Kier staunchly stood his ground, though oft enough it left him bloodied and humiliated. As years passed, he found he could thwart the ridicule by driving himself to excel at all he attempted. His mastery of weapons and horsemanship earned him the respect of Alcor's iron-willed Legion Commander, though it elicited scant notice from the one man Kier most yearned to please: the duke, his father.

At last, seeing no future on Alcor, Kier requested a military posting abroad, and blissfully left that hate-ravaged island, free for the first time in his life from the constraints of his mixed birth.

He had never been back. With Master Gwythion now retired to a Fithlon cloister outside Castémaron, there were only two persons in all Alcor that Kier truly cared about. One was his father, though there had been times, when the indignities seemed beyond endurance, that he'd cursed the duke for ever giving him life. The other was his gentle cousin Cariwyn, who always accepted him without condition. Had Tiernai law not prohibited marriage between a daughter of nobility and a bastard, he'd have asked for Cari years ago. But that could never be.

And so, he stayed away, forging a life for himself among the far flung realms of the Deg Tirith. Now Cari's urgent message compelled him to return. Kier almost wished no ship would ever again embark for Alcor, and so relieve him of his torment.

§

As Kier made his weary way along the crowded wharf, a gaunt figure, cloaked and hooded in common gray, peered from behind a stack of wool bales to observe his passage, shading his eyes from the morning orblight with one pale hand.

So, Fitzmorwen still lived. The fools he'd hired to dispose of him had clearly botched their task. He'd suspected as much when they failed to report. Perhaps they'd perished in the attempt or run off in fear. No matter. He'd see they met death soon enough. Incompetence merited no clemency. Yet their cursed negligence now faced him with an unsavory task—reporting to his Master that the prophesied talisman had not been recovered. The news would be ill received.

The young captain had nearly passed by when his confident stride slowed. He darted a glance about him as if sensing something amiss. The watcher retreated into shadow, clearing all thoughts of vengeance from his mind. He must remember to be more cautious. His Master had warned him Fitzmorwen was Fithlon trained.

The halfblood officer resumed his progress along the wharf, stopping at times to make inquiries. A gnarled seaman pointed him to a barque several berths beyond. The watcher followed at a prudent pace.

As he emerged from the cover of a weathered tack shed, a rude jolt from behind hurled him off balance. "Ahay there, graybeard," bellowed a surly dockhand, his soiled jumper reeking of sweat and stale beer. "Move yer sorry bones out o' the way!"

The watcher spun with a snarl. The impact had skewed his woolen hood, exposing the features he took great pains to hide.

At the sight of the disfigured face before him, the dockhand's eyes saucered. "D...*demon spawn!*" he hissed, bulbous fingers fumbling the protective sign of Devoreth's Eye.

The slur ignited the watcher's fury. With strength that belied his gangly build, he seized the burly oaf by the throat and shoved him back into the shadows.

The dockhand gasped for breath. His lips mouthed incoherent syllables as sinewy fingers ripped away his cap and buried themselves in his unwashed curls. The other hand clamped around his stubbled jaw, jagged nails raking flesh. The dockhand's face went pale as rancid suet as terror froze his limbs.

The watcher's thoughts turned oddly wistful as he savored a moment that was always too fleeting. Then, with a thrill that tingled the blood, he jerked the dockhand's head at an angle it was not designed to go. There was a satisfyingly squishy pop of dislocated bone, and his victim sagged to the weathered planks, limp as a gutted mackerel.

Heedlessly, the watcher tipped the man off the pier's edge, taking silent satisfaction as the mass of helpless flab sank beneath the waves. The grimy woolen cap floated out on the tide.

Demon spawn. Aye, they called him that—the *perfect* ones, whose unmarred flesh bore no vengeful god's curse. The watcher drew up his hood to once more hide his features from a hostile world and fingered the scalded seam across his left cheekbone. Fitzmorwen was no longer in sight. He'd probably boarded the barque. The watcher's lips compressed. The dockhand's terror had renewed his spirits. What matter that Fitzmorwen survived the first attempt? Soon he would be bound for Alcor. Time enough to finish the job there.

Chapter Five

JonMarc ambled up the tree-lined avenue to his master's villa on Castémaron's prestigious western heights. Though situated somewhat lower on the slope than its more affluent neighbors, the villa imposed itself upon the hillside like a painted courtesan, its effusive ornamentation hinting at its owner's very recent rise to social acceptance.

JonMarc slowed as he neared the gates. The bright pink stucco was now draped in the somber brown of mourning. That triggered a pang of regret. Despite Lord Sethrin's eccentricities—perhaps because of them—he had genuinely liked his late master.

That feeling was quickly replaced by a chill of concern for his own future. A litter stood out front. JonMarc recognized it as belonging to Correlin, Sethrin's brother. That did not bode well. He circled to the rear.

"JonMarc!" The old cook's exclamation greeted him as he ducked in through the kitchen. The room was dim and homey, warmed with the smell of baking bread. "Devoreth be praised you're safe, lad. When we heard about poor master Sethrin, we feared—"

JonMarc bussed the stout woman affectionately on the cheek. "Ah, sweet Belindra. Always concerned for me."

Belindra waved him off with impatience. "But Nan overheard the soldiers tellin' mistress Ruthira that you'd been arrested for the master's murder."

JonMarc pulled up a chair and straddled it backwards as a handful of kitchen maids clustered about him, eager for news. "Well, they were wrong." he said, savoring his new status as a celebrity. He snatched a joint of cold fowl from one of the funeral trays. No one stopped him. "They held me a while, but when they caught the real culprit, they let me go." Belindra eyed him dubiously, starting to question further. JonMarc cut her off. "How'd Ruthira take the news?"

"Which news?" asked one kitchen wench, with a knowing smirk. "That the master was dead, or that you were in prison?" Belindra glared at her. The girl tossed it off with a shake of her stringy curls.

"Go see for yourself," said Belindra, cocking her head toward the stairs. "Wasn't that Correlin's litter out front?"

"Aye, 'twas. He was here with the mistress when the soldiers came."

"And for several hours before that," chirped the serving wench.

No surprise there. Ruthira was not one to sit still for her husband's infidelities. She preferred to take them lying down—with whoever happened to be at hand. The mistress' escapades provided endless fodder for gossip among the household staff—gossip that frequently included JonMarc.

As he stood to leave, JonMarc grabbed up several freshly baked tarts from a nearby platter. "Now you let those be," Belindra scolded. "They're for the funeral feast tomorrow."

JonMarc evaded her grasp and scrambled for the stairs. He made his way around the balcony that overlooked the courtyard fountain. The Lady Ruthira maintained a suite of rooms as far as possible from those of her late husband. JonMarc was no stranger to them. The mistress of the house preferred to be attended by males. Her personal slave was a eunuch—an imperious fellow named Imille. JonMarc had never trusted him.

He halted outside Ruthira's door. There were voices within, drawing nearer. The latch moved. JonMarc swiftly ducked into a niche beside a plaster sculpture of two simpering water nymphs. A moment later Correlin emerged, impeccably attired, as always.

JonMarc had seen his master's brother many times, always when Sethrin was away from home. The siblings made no secret of their mutual enmity. JonMarc suspected the rift had to do with Correlin's blatant attentions toward Ruthira. Correlin was an influential man with a reputation for getting what he wanted. What he desired now was his late brother's wife and property. And he would have them; he declared as much as he embraced Ruthira at her chamber door.

Ruthira appeared less enthusiastic. "But dearest, don't you think this a bit hasty? The neighbors are bound to talk..."

"Let them," Correlin snapped. "I didn't become First Expositor to the Emperor by sitting on my hands. I'll approach the Council this afternoon. By morning I will be your new lord." He moved to leave, then touched a finger to his brow and did an abrupt turnaround. "Here." He thrust into

Ruthira's hand a small satin pouch. "Wear this for me from now on." It was not a request.

Ruthira studied the pouch but did not open it until the echo of Correlin's confident stride faded beyond the courtyard gates. JonMarc slipped up silently behind her. The gift turned out to be a portrait pendant, such as were currently in vogue. Ruthira stared at the haughty image in the frame—the narrowed brows; the thin, almost cruel, mouth. She sighed. It was a faithful likeness.

"You might at least have waited till my master was in the ground," JonMarc growled.

Ruthira spun, clutching Correlin's portrait to her breast. "JonMarc! Where did you come from? I thought you were imprisoned."

He backed her into the doorway. "Aye, and by now I'd be packed off to the quarries, if you and your new lord had your way."

"*I* never wanted it. Correlin said you must pay the penalty for Sethrin's murder."

"Blazes, Ruthira, you know I didn't murder him. I owed him my life. It was just some common street cull." JonMarc's eyes sparked as he stepped nearer, trapping her against the door frame. "Did you even bother to wonder what might become of me?"

Ruthira flushed. "Of course. But what could I do? I cannot argue with him; not until all this is settled and..."

"And your position is secure. I know."

Ruthira fumbled behind her for the latch. The door swung inward. She laid bejeweled fingers on JonMarc's arm and drew him into the chamber. Her slave, Imille, hovered just inside. Ruthira dismissed him with a nod and he discreetly shut the door behind him as he left.

Ruthira paused to admire herself in a copper mirror as she passed. Though several years his senior, JonMarc had to admit his mistress was a handsome woman, full figured, with the jet black hair and smooth, olive skin common to natives of Vilsolia. A vixenish gleam lit her almond eyes as she turned to him and ran a tinted fingernail down his cheek.

"My poor JonMarc. You know I'd have done everything in my power to save you. Why, I planned to go to the prisons this very afternoon to implore them to set you free."

It was a lie. JonMarc knew it. Yet how could he fault her for putting her own needs first? He'd have done the same. Right now, Ruthira's position was nearly as tenuous as his own. There was a time, long past, when he'd taken her overtures seriously. But he'd quickly learned that Ruthira's affections were a sham, intended only to fulfill her own love-longings. She toyed with men, letting no one penetrate the shell she'd built around her heart. Following her expert example, JonMarc had taught himself to be equally manipulative—or thought he had.

He'd already mapped out his strategy. He needed money, and time to get away. Those, Ruthira would never grant if he told her he intended escape. His mistress would not stand for—as she would see it—being abandoned. JonMarc might be sold or sent away, but never could the departure be his own idea. No, to accomplish his aims he must appeal to her vanity; play whatever game Ruthira indicated, and remain in control long enough to satisfy her. If experience were any guide, she would then favor him with whatever he asked for—within reason. The only challenge lay in divining what would please the lady today.

The cue was quick to come. Ruthira's gaze dropped to his bandaged arm and her dark eyes lit with concern. "Oh, but you're hurt! My poor angel, did they torture you?" Taking his hands in hers, she led him to her sumptuous bed, still disheveled from Correlin's sojourn, and made him lie down.

JonMarc chuckled to himself. So the game was to be maternal sympathy. Fine. He'd let Ruthira think he was in desperate need of her ministering. He only regretted that he'd cleaned up so thoroughly back at the inn. In this mood, Ruthira would undoubtedly prefer him bloody and disheveled. Of course, once she removed his clothes she'd see he hadn't been tortured. Still, JonMarc was confident his mistress's ripe imagination would fill in any missing details.

Ruthira gently pulled off his boots, then sat and began to unlace his tunic. JonMarc let her bathe him and linger over his flesh with hennaed fingers while he pretended to be too weak to respond. Ruthira loved to think she alone had the power to rouse him. In fact, the longer he resisted, the more enthusiastic the lady became. JonMarc secretly watched as she leaned over to kiss him. She'd thrown off her chamber robe and allowed her gown of pale green silk to slip from her fleshy shoulders. Lightly, she slid the garment across his loins. "My sweet love," she purred in his ear. "Do your wounds pain you?" She placed JonMarc's branded left hand between her soft breasts and buried her face in the crook of his neck. Practiced fingers sought him elsewhere.

JonMarc groaned. It was no use; he could no longer maintain the charade of indifference. Time to let Ruthira think she'd won. He groped for her.

Gently but firmly, Ruthira moved his hand away.

JonMarc's eyes popped open. That wasn't part of the game.

Ruthira's brown eyes filled with mocking concern. "Rest, my sweet. You mustn't exert yourself. In fact, I think it would be best if we continue this another day."

What...? Had he responded too quickly? JonMarc raised himself onto his elbow.

Ruthira pushed him back down. She draped her robe about her shoulders, smiling as her eyes tracked boldly over his torso. "You said I should wait till poor Sethrin is buried before I dally with another man, and of course you were right. We must postpone our pleasure."

"Postpone? But I thought ... I mean...don't you...?" Was she *serious*?

Ruthira's voice fairly dripped. "Ah, but your pain must be unbearable. How can I think only of myself?"

"No, it's all right. I'm not that badly hurt..." JonMarc's jaw trembled, his physical response anything but feigned. "Blast it, Ruthira—I *need* you!"

The victorious gleam in Ruthira's eyes told him exactly who had won this bout. "I know you do," she said, her tone venom-sweet, yet hard as flint. "I just wanted to hear you *admit* it."

By the time JonMarc awoke, Devoreth's Orb cast angular shadows across the lavish chamber. Ruthira lay curled in the crook of his arm, looking smugly satisfied, her plump legs entangled with his own. The pale blue covers lay twisted and scattered. They'd coupled three times—no, four—and after the second, the pleasure had all been Ruthira's. JonMarc's calves and buttocks ached as if he'd run ten leagues. He wondered if the body were intended to endure such rigors, all in the name of pleasure. With care, he disengaged from Ruthira's possessive embrace.

"Oh, JonMarc," she murmured, regarding him with languorous eyes, "that was wonderful! I'm so glad you were not sent to the quarries."

"Me too," he grunted, hunting for his clothes among the tangle of silken sheets. "But I soon will be, if Correlin returns to find me here."

That seemed to rouse her. "But you're innocent of Sethrin's death. Why should Correlin condemn you?"

"Do you imagine he'd let me stay here to be your lover? Once he learns I'm out of prison, he'll waste no time packing me off to the slave block, or the galleys—or worse."

Ruthira pouted. "But that means I shall never see you again."

"It does, unless we can think up a plan."

"What kind of plan?"

"Well, *you* could send me away—someplace I'd be safe."

"No," Ruthira said flatly, "I could not bear to part with you."

JonMarc's lip took a bitter twist the lady did not see. Ruthira cared
for him no more than she cared for the other young men—from soldiers
to craftsmen's apprentices—who passed through these apartments with
amazing regularity. To Ruthira, it was all part of the same self-gratifying
game.

"You think I like it any better? But we've no choice. At least I can hide
until Correlin develops a routine and forgets about me. Surely he'll leave
the city at times. I can come to you then."

Ruthira donned her robe and paced back and forth beside the bed.
"Let me think," she said, pressing a knuckle to her upper lip. "I know! We'll
make a place for you in the cellar."

"Someone's bound to find me there."

"Well then—you could hide at my friend Lenina's. Surely she'd keep you
for a time."

"Lenina? Is she the attractive one with the red hair?"

Ruthira frowned. "No, I don't trust her that far." For a moment she was
silent. Then she snapped her fingers. "I have it. There's a place Correlin
knows nothing of. Remember that cottage on the beach near Penyon's
Point, where we spent that glorious week while Sethrin was away in
Duhira? You could live there."

Perfect. He could be gone for days before Ruthira thought to check on
him. JonMarc disguised his enthusiasm. "I'll need a pass to leave the city,
and money to buy food."

Ruthira unlocked her jewel chest. "I can only give you a little now. I'll
send Imille with more as soon as I can. In the meantime, take some of
these. You may be able to sell them."

JonMarc lined his purse with the cheap trinkets Ruthira offered—and
some of the better ones, once her back was turned. The pendant with
Correlin's portrait lay beside the chest. JonMarc eyed it with pretended
disgust. "I don't like leaving you here to be wife to that lecherous boar."

Ruthira's face brightened. "Why, JonMarc, you're jealous."

"Can you blame me? He'll be here with you every night, while I'll be stuck alone in some drafty hovel by the sea."

Unexpected spite crept into Ruthira's voice. "And what of all those nights I lay here while you and Sethrin dallied at that dreadful tavern?"

"That wasn't *my* choice."

"No? Are you saying you don't have a doxie there who keeps you company? More than one, I shouldn't wonder."

JonMarc cautioned himself to tread warily; this was dangerous ground. "Ruthira, going to *The Dragon Sword* was Sethrin's idea. I was only his bodyguard."

Ruthira favored him a dark look. Then suddenly she smiled and ran playful fingers through his hair. "Ah, my poor JonMarc. To be forced to sit there, hour after hour, while my loving husband practiced his *swordplay* upstairs. And all that time you might have been here with me."

"Correlin was always here with you," JonMarc grumbled.

"Ah, but I was ever *thinking* of you."

JonMarc grinned to himself. "And I of you, lady."

He took his leave of Ruthira just as Correlin's litter, borne by four tall Kirosian slaves, approached the front gates. JonMarc exited through the rear. He tossed the small bundle that contained the sum of his belongings over the garden wall, then followed it.

Ruthira watched from her chamber window. She beckoned Imille. "Follow him," she said. "If my young gamecock has a rendezvous with one of his chippies at *The Dragon Sword*, I'll see he pays a high price for it."

Early twilight dimmed Castémaron's narrow streets as JonMarc approached *The Dragon Sword*. It felt odd coming here alone; odder still the realization that if his plans succeeded—and especially if they did not—he might never see the place again. That thought raised mixed emotions. At times, he'd hated the tavern; the tedious hours spent waiting for his master to come down. Yet those very hours had made the place a home, as familiar as any he'd ever known. Surely there'd be no harm in treating himself to a last, farewell tankard.

A party of soldiers ambled up from the direction of the garrison. They were rowdy; already drunk. JonMarc recognized two from last night. Best not to take chances. He waited until they had stumbled inside the tavern, then slipped around to the rear.

The innyard was a strew of dilapidated structures and moldering trash heaps that stank of offal. JonMarc managed to snare the eye of a scullery wench who had stepped out to discard kitchen slops. Her work-weary face brightened. "JonMarc, you're safe! The soldiers said—"

JonMarc pressed a coin to her palm to halt her flurry of questions. "Look, Bett, do me a favor and tell Ma'ardhi I'm here."

Bett cast an eye toward the tavern door. Strains of music echoed from within. "She's in the middle of her dance, JonMarc."

"I'll wait." JonMarc grabbed her arm as she turned to leave. "Don't let Eliém find out."

JonMarc slogged across the innyard, a sea of muck after last night's rain, and crept into the empty stable. The evening squalls were blowing in early. The sagging walls trembled and creaked with every gust. JonMarc leaned against the doorframe, loose hair feathering his cheek.

Despite its battered condition, the stable had a comforting feel. He'd spent many an hour here—not with courtesans, like Shanya, whose services he could rarely afford—but with any number of serving wenches. He'd been here with Ma'ardhi only once, but that night meant more to him than all the rest. JonMarc loosed a sigh. If only there were an easier way.

A thumping on the stair caught his ear and he turned expectantly, but it was only a patron en route to the privy. The man staggered halfway across the muddy yard, then gave up and relieved himself against a sagging post. As he headed back, JonMarc followed with his eyes, longing to join the warmth and revelry within.

After what seemed an eternity, the music ended. Moments later, Ma'ardhi's cloaked form appeared on the landing. She hesitated, squinting into the gloom. JonMarc softly called her name, hoping she would hear above the wind's restless moan. She came running and threw dusky arms about his neck, kissing his mouth and throat. JonMarc lifted her off her feet and buried his face in her thick raven hair that smelled of tavern smoke. He carried her into the stable.

"My sweet Jaha'an," Ma'ardhi murmured. "I feared that I am never again to see you!" Her voice against his ear sounded innocent, almost childlike. The lilt of her Syrmian accent speaking his boyhood name almost melted him. "You are safe? The soldiers have not hurted you?"

JonMarc set her down and shook his head. "No, I'm not hurt. But..." Now came the hard part. Better just to say it. "Ma'ardhi, I can't stay in Castémaron. I have to leave before I'm sold."

She'd wrapped her slender arms around his middle. "I know this." JonMarc fancied he heard tears in her voice. "I am only grateful you came to say me goodbye."

JonMarc shut his eyes, clutching her to him. Why did it have to be like this? He did his best to make light of it. "You'll find someone else and forget all about me soon enough."

Ma'ardhi drew back to look at him. He saw reproach in her shimmering eyes. She smiled through the tears. "Who will have me?" she chided, "now that I am..." She patted her belly.

Guilt stabbed JonMarc. Ma'ardhi had never known any man before him. Her very innocence allowed him to experience his manhood in a way no pampered harlot like Ruthira ever could. "Ghedrev's blood, if only I could take you with me."

"You cannot. I would be too quickly missed." She stroked his cheek. "I am sorry, my Jaha'an, for making it more trouble for you to say goodbye. You must not think of me."

"Have you told Eliém yet, about...?"

Ma'ardhi shook her head. Her black hair rippled like wind-tossed silk. "I will—soon. But first you must be far away." She touched her finger to his lips when he tried to argue. "Do not worry, my Jaha'an. I will be well. The other girls are much caring of me."

JonMarc managed a smile. "They'd better be, or I'll be back to find out why." He heard the clomp of boots on the stair—another customer looking for the bog. Heavy drops of rain began to fall. JonMarc drew Ma'ardhi deeper into the shelter and held her in silence until the man left.

"Where will you go?" the girl asked, when they were again alone.

JonMarc hesitated. He wanted to tell her his plans, uncertain though they were, but caution warned him otherwise. She could not be forced to divulge what she didn't know. "As far from this cess pit of a city as I can get. I've found someone who'll help me escape."

"The one you drank with last night? But he is a brassy. You are sure you can be trusting him?"

"I don't trust anyone. I'll only use him to get me out of Vilsolia."

Ma'ardhi lowered her eyes. "You are too much using of people, Jaha'an. It will bring you hurt one day."

"Blast it, I've been used all my life. What's the harm in taking a little of my own back?" He placed his finger beneath Ma'ardhi's chin. "Trust me, I know what I'm doing."

The dancing girl turned to wander down the aisle between the empty stalls. Her slippered feet made swishing sounds as they swept aside the scattered straw. JonMarc followed.

"Valerey said she was with you when you found this brassy in trouble." Ma'ardhi cocked her head. "But you never take a girl into streets. Why did you go there? Had you another *seeing*?"

JonMarc stiffened. Sometimes Ma'ardhi's insight made her seem far older than her sixteen years. "Aye," he reluctantly admitted, "just before it happened. I used Val as..." He stopped; rephrased. "I needed an excuse to go out there—to see if it was true."

"Did you tell the brassy this?"

JonMarc laughed bitterly. "What, that I had some kind of *vision* that he was in trouble? Blazes, Ma'ardhi, he already knows I'm a thief; you want him to think I'm mad as well?" He shut his eyes and brushed his cheek against her hair. "You're the only one I've told."

Ma'ardhi wrapped her delicate brown hands around his bandaged arm. "You are feared of these seeings. Do not be. When I was a temple novice, in Syrma, the holy mothers told us of such things." She patted his left wrist. "Your seeings are caused of this."

"What? The knife wound?"

"No." Ma'ardhi held his branded left hand. "This. *Sham ia'ad*."

JonMarc delved into his fading memory of the Syrmian tongue. "You mean because I'm spoil-handed. I've had that thrown up to me all my life."

Ma'ardhi shook her head. "Not *spoil*-handed. *Sihe'er* ia'ad."

"Sihe'er?" JonMarc chewed his lip. "Magic? *Spell*-handed?"

"Aye. Spell-handed. Among my people it is said the Sham ia'ad possess sihe'er. Magic."

"I've heard that, but it's nonsense. I don't have any magic."

"You have seeings."

"But they only started a few weeks ago; right after I met you."

"No matter. You are Sihe'er ia'ad. Spell-handed. My people fear such magic. Sihe'er ia'ad are hunted; cast out. Long ago, many were killed. But then followed—" Ma'ardhi struck her palm to her forehead. "*Kha'atar*."

"Kha'atar? Bad luck?"

"Aye. Bad luck. Storms and fire mountains. Now my people no longer kill Sihe'er ia'ad. They still fear, but also—respect."

JonMarc scratched his head. "I guess that's why the Syrmian pirates who captured me didn't slit my throat when they found I was a spoil-hand, though they were none too pleased."

"Of course. They feared that to kill you would bring even badder luck.

They guessed you had magic, for they named you *Jaha'an*. Jackal. In our legends, Jaha'an is trickster—always in trouble, but with strong magic."

JonMarc chuckled. "Well, the first part fits. I wish I had some of the magic; it might make this escape a lot easier."

Another gust rocked the stable, spitting rain through cracks in the rotting timbers. JonMarc pulled Ma'ardhi against him. Her head came only to his chest.

"I must go, my Jaha'an. Eliém will be missing me." She drew back. "Do you carry still the charmstone I gave to you?"

"Aye." JonMarc dug inside his tunic and drew out a small crystal on a braided silk cord. He held it out to her. "I wanted to give it back before I left."

Ma'ardhi halted his gesture with an upraised palm. "Keep it. It will guard your life."

"But you said it was sacred..."

"Please, Jaha'an. It will protect you from spells and bring you *kha'asir—good* luck." Ma'ardhi pressed the charmstone into his palm and wrapped her small hands around his. "Promise me you will wear it until, in your new land, you find someone you would give your life for—as I would for you."

"But I can look after myself. I've done it all my life. You'll need the charm more than I—"

Ma'ardhi refused to take it. Reluctantly, JonMarc draped the silken cord over his head, hiding the crystal pendant inside his shirt. "Ma'ardhi, I..." The words wouldn't come. JonMarc wiped a hand across his cheek.

Ma'ardhi turned for the door. Abruptly, she spun back. "I am almost forgetting. There was, early this day, a man here asking about your brassy captain. He said he is a friend to him, but if that is the look of his friends, I think you should not be trusting him so much."

"Why? What did he look like?"

Ma'ardhi drew her dark brows together. "Perhaps so high." She measured her hand to the level of JonMarc's eyes. "Under his hood was long hair, white, like goat milk." She wrinkled her nose in distaste.

"An old man," JonMarc acknowledged.

"No, not old. Only white-haired. His eyes, too, were white—and very strange. There was a scar on his face—brown, like henna." Ma'ardhi grimaced. "I did not like him."

"You say he asked about Kier—the brassy? What did he want to know?"

"What hour he left. Where he stayed."

"What did you tell him?"

"Only Eliém spoke to him, and he could not tell much—only to try at the fortress for news. All talk this day was of you, and your master's murder. No one cared about the brassy captain." Ma'ardhi frowned. "There is another thing. I did not hear it, for my talk is not so good, but Valerey said the man spoke like an out-lander. Maybe from Alcor?"

"That's Kier's home. So it might be a friend of his, or a messenger. I'll pass the word on."

Ma'ardhi started to reply but was cut short by a salvo of curses coming from the tavern. An angry voice bellowed her name. Ma'ardhi froze. "That is Eliém! Again it is my time to dance. I must go. He is in a black mood. If he finds you here..."

"He won't. Look—" JonMarc rummaged in his pouch for some of the better trinkets he'd lifted from Ruthira's jewel chest. "Take these; hide them. When the child's born, you'll need..."

Another roar from the tavern drowned his words. Eliém came stomping down the stair.

"I am coming!" cried Ma'ardhi. "Oh, my sweet Jaha'an. You will be careful of yourself?" She grasped his hands. JonMarc wrapped her once more in his arms.

Eliém was slogging through the mud, cursing as he came. Reluctantly, JonMarc let the girl go. She hurried out to waylay the lumbering innkeeper. He shoved her aside. "Who's in there with you? If it's that thieving Dynian spoil-hand, I'll have his cods for a wall hanging!"

"There is no one." Ma'ardhi insisted. "I only had—a woman's sickness."

Eliém snorted disbelief and barged into the stable. But he'd brought no lantern. With an angry snarl he seized Ma'ardhi by the wrist and dragged her back to the tavern.

JonMarc pictured slitting the fat innkeeper's throat. He waited until he judged them safely inside, then dropped from the stable loft. A moment later he clambered over the innyard wall and disappeared into the night.

Chapter Six

A chill wind hummed and moaned around the Gull's Nest's ancient gables. It started the shutter outside Kier's window clacking. The noise broke his concentration from Cari's letter, which he'd re-read a dozen times in the sputtering tallow light. Blurred specters of his cousin's graceful script danced before his eyes even as he rose to fix the shutter.

The rain-slicked street below was dark and deserted. A block away, the great bell in the Harbor Gate tower chimed four times: four hours past orbset. Kier secured the latch and stumbled back to the table. He leaned his head on his fist.

Having purchased supplies and passage for the voyage to Alcor, he'd returned to the inn and collapsed across his lumpy pallet like a dead man—his body's attempt to heal his aching mind and spirit. Yet upon waking, the pain descended again, accompanied by a deep sense of foreboding. At dusk, he'd ventured downstairs for a bite to eat, but the inn's crowded commonroom proved too noisy. He'd quickly retreated to the solitude of his garret chamber, carrying with him three small jugs of the landlord's best Kirosian wine. He now stared into the dregs of the second.

From the littered tabletop, Cari's framed image reproached him. It was a portrait the size of his palm, a treasure he carried with him wherever he went, though seldom did he muster the will to remove it from his pack. Cari's knowing brown eyes seemed to follow his every move, and Kier found it hard to convince himself it was simply a trick of the artist's brush. At fifteen, his cousin's gentle image looked exactly as he remembered—the slim, delicate features; the lustrous brown hair. That was five years ago. She'd be a woman now, of marriageable age. The thought of some other man possessing her was more than Kier could bear. He shoved the portrait aside and uncorked the last wine jug.

The tart liquor succeeded in numbing his senses, but did little to banish his fears. Beside Cari's letter lay another, delivered today—a message from Legion Commander Donal. It provided grim detail of his father's condition and urged Kier's immediate return to Alcor. The duke, Sir Donal reported, had collapsed in Council. The problem was thought to be his heart, and— the words weighed like lead upon Kier's soul—he was not expected to live beyond the Feast of Renewal. That festival was less than a fortnight hence. Even with fair winds and gentle seas, the voyage to Alcor would take ten days. It left precious little time.

Kier had to admit that he and the duke had never been close, perhaps because they were so much alike. Both shied from overt displays of emotion. Yet Kier had always wished it otherwise. When he was training for the Legion, the duke had sent him costly gifts: a fine cloak, boots of supple Algolian leather; his sword, dagger and crest ring. But such gestures, however generous, could not take the place of what Kier wanted most: his father's affection. Duke Morwen was clearly ashamed of his bastard son, for no success Kier ever achieved could rouse from him more than cursory acknowledgment. Even so, Kier held deep, if conflicted, feelings for his father that he now feared he might never have a chance to reconcile.

He shut his eyes, cradling his head in his hands. For a long while he let his thoughts drift. Perhaps he even dozed. He only knew that a voice suddenly burst into his mind—and it was not his own.

"You are leaving. We must meet again ere you depart."

Kier winced—not at the message, but its intensity. He straightened, rubbing his eyes with his palms. The Fithlon Master's timing was lamentable. Normally he could shield his thoughts from his mentor's probes. Tonight, Gwythion had caught him completely off guard. Kier hastened to rebuild his mind defenses. "I haven't much time," he responded silently, a bit irked that Gwythion would even make such a demand, for if his mentor knew of his intended departure, he must also recognize his need for haste. "My ship sails tomorrow, at eventide."

"Come to me in the morning. We have urgent matters to discuss."

"*What* matters?" His mentor had cited such urgency yesterday, when summoning him from shipboard. Kier prayed this did not involve another prophecy.

"That, you will learn when you come." As usual, Gwythion was both brusque and infuriatingly cryptic. Yet, for an instant, Kier thought he detected something darker beneath the monk's message—something distinctly out of character for the Fithlon Master. Fear.

"*You have encountered him—the one I foresaw.*" It was a statement of fact. Gwythion knew his prediction was accurate. "*Tell me of him.*"

Kier shrugged as if they sat face to face. "He's a Dynian slave, and branded *sinistral*. He rescued me from attack on the street..."

"*Sinistral, you say? Does he possess talents?*"

"None that I detected. He's just a slave and a pick-purse. I doubt he can even write his name."

"*Bring him.*"

The demand caught Kier by surprise. "Why?"

"*Because I ask it.*"

Kier bristled. He found Gwythion's penchant for secrecy infuriating. "He's gone. He may not return."

"*Then find him. I shall expect you both at second hour.*"

There was nothing more. Gwythion's presence vanished as swiftly as it had come. Kier snorted annoyance and lurched to his feet—too fast. The chamber wheeled. He braced his hands on the table.

How in blazes was he supposed to find JonMarc at this hour? He had no idea where his owner's villa lay. For all he knew, the slave might already have escaped. Someone at *The Dragon Sword* might know. Kier had no wish to return there, but Gwythion left him little option. He belted on his sword and threw his cloak about his shoulders.

Outside the small window, rain pelted harder than ever—a miserable night to be abroad. Kier tensed. Beneath the overhang of a chandlery across the street, a lone figure stood hunched and sullen. Kier drew back, but not before the lurker spotted him. Tossing back his hood, the lanky figure waved both arms and pointed toward the inn's side entrance.

Kier breathed profound relief. Grabbing the lamp, he hurried downstairs to unlock the door before JonMarc's knock could awaken the household.

"How long have you been standing out there?" Kier asked, as the slave stepped inside.

"An hour, maybe." JonMarc followed him up the stair and dropped his small bundle onto the floor. "Hope you don't mind my coming. I'd no place else to go." He flung his sodden cloak across Kier's chair, shaking his wet hair like a terrier. Kier leaped back to avoid being spattered.

"Actually, I'm—glad you're here." It was only true in that JonMarc's arrival saved him an uncomfortable search. Kier had no wish to relinquish his solitude—especially to an opportunist like JonMarc. He snatched the blanket from his bed and offered it, along with his last jug of wine.

JonMarc gratefully accepted both. He shrugged out of his sopping clothes and draped the blanket about him

Kier took a seat on the pallet's edge. "I thought you might've left the city by now."

JonMarc lowered himself onto the mat before the fire, extending bare hands and feet toward its welcome warmth. "I had—business—to finish at the *Sword*. Then I just walked a while, to work out my plans." He cast a quizzical glance at Kier's discarded cloak. "Were you going out?"

Kier rested his elbows on his knees. "Actually, I was about to go looking for you. I have to visit my old mentor in the morning. He's invited you to come along."

JonMarc cocked his head. "How does your mentor know about me?"

"I told him you'd saved my life. He's eager to meet you."

"So—you were ready to brave the streets in this downpour just 'cause some old grizzlebeard wants to meet me?"

Kier groped for an answer. How could he explain his mentor's motives when he didn't understand them himself? "Gwythion can be rather— insistent."

A calculating glint crept into JonMarc's eyes. "Blazes, I'm sorry Kier. But my master's wife gave me a pass to leave the city. It's only good for tonight."

"But you said you had no place else…"

JonMarc ignored him. "Of course, if you were to help me leave Castémaron by *sea*, I'd have more time. A ship would be out of Vilsolian waters as soon as it left the harbor. In that case, I could probably stick around to meet this mentor of yours."

There was nothing slow about the slave's wits. Kier had expected an escape scheme to reveal itself, but not so soon. He was tempted to call JonMarc's bluff: if the slave indeed had a gate pass, surely he'd be long gone by now. Yet, the prospect of showing up at Gwythion's without him was not one Kier wished to contemplate. Given the sorry choice of alternatives— his mentor's wrath or that of the Vilsolian High Council—Kier preferred to risk the latter.

JonMarc was watching him, wary, expectant. "All right," Kier grumbled, "I'll help you get to Alcor—on one condition: there'll be no thieving while you're in my charge. Is that understood?"

JonMarc soberly traced an X of oath-taking across his right palm. Kier sensed his exuberance ready to burst forth like ale from a shaken keg, but JonMarc held it in check. Hands nested behind his head, he stretched out before the fire, a self-satisfied grin splayed across his face. Kier doubted he'd look so smug once he discovered the *old grizzlebeard's* affiliation.

After a moment, JonMarc raised up onto his elbows. "You got anything to eat around here? I'm starving."

Kier nodded toward a sack of provisions he'd purchased for the voyage. JonMarc got up and helped himself—so generously Kier was about to take exception. He'd bought enough for a ten-day voyage. If they should be delayed… Yet he hesitated. The frayed blanket had slipped from JonMarc's shoulders, revealing a deep criss-cross of scars patterning the slave's bare back. Kier's protest died on his lips. He could buy more food.

JonMarc dropped a double handful of jerky and biscuits onto the table, sweeping Kier's letters aside with his forearm. He spied Cari's portrait and picked it up. "She yours?"

"My cousin."

JonMarc gave the image closer scrutiny. A rakish gleam lit his blue eyes. "Not bad!"

The moment he set the portrait down, Kier whisked it away to the safety of his pack. "Have you learned who's to inherit your master's estate?" he asked, to change the subject.

"His brother Correlin, like I said."

"Is he the type to pursue an escaped slave?"

JonMarc took a moment to answer, having crammed an entire biscuit into his mouth. "He hardly knows I exist," he mumbled, spewing crumbs. "As long as I don't draw attention…"

"In that case, I'm surprised you returned to *The Dragon Sword*. That Sergeant Elrin's sure to be watching for you."

JonMarc shook his head, swallowing hard. "I didn't go in. Ma'ardhi met me out back. We had something to… settle."

"Ma'ardhi?"

"The dancing girl." JonMarc gulped the last of the wine and wiped his dripping chin on the blanket. "Guess you may as well know; everyone else will soon enough. Ma'ardhi carries my child. I couldn't leave without at least saying goodbye."

Something inside Kier went taut. "Why are you leaving at all?"

JonMarc shrugged. "I told you, I want a life. And anyway, I haven't much choice. Ma'ardhi's not like Eliém's other girls. Her dancing's so valuable he won't let her keep company with men.'"

"But you just said—"

"Look, I never meant for it to happen, all right? But I'd had a few ales, and she was—well, you know. One thing led to another and..."

Aye, Kier knew. His own father had done much the same with a Dynian peasant lass, then rode off to re-join his comrades, leaving her to raise their bastard in poverty and disgrace. Inwardly seething, he said, "What will happen when Eliém finds out?"

JonMarc gave a dark chuckle. "I don't even want to think about it. He's a bellowing ox at the best of times. You can see why I have to get out of here."

His blatant indifference was more than Kier could stomach. "What about the *girl*? She's not leaving. What will Eliém do to her?"

JonMarc appeared startled by his reaction. "Nothing. She's too valuable. In a few months she'll dance again, and Eliém will have a new slave—without cost." A smug grin. "A damned attractive one too, I'll wager. That'll more than make up for his losses."

Kier could hardly believe what he was hearing. JonMarc had to be the most self-involved scoundrel he'd ever met. He felt like he'd been sucked into a crime by helping the rogue escape. "How can you just abandon her—the mother of your child? Don't you feel any responsibility at all?" He sensed emotion swelling behind JonMarc's passive exterior. At least the slave was capable of feeling.

"What do you expect me to do? I can't take her with me. Even if I stayed, Eliém'd never let me set foot in the *Sword* again. What could I do for her here except make things worse?"

"Seems you've already done that," Kier muttered. "Why don't you just marry her?"

JonMarc regarded him as if he'd sprouted antlers. "Slaves don't marry, Kier. They're mated sometimes, if their owners choose, but it's never permanent. I thought you knew that."

Kier did not know. He'd had few dealings with slaves. He suddenly realized just how little he understood of JonMarc's plight.

JonMarc sat back in his chair, clasping the moth-eaten blanket around him. "Anyway, I'll bet you're a fine one to talk. I've seen how brassies operate. How many little bye-blows have *you* got running around?"

Kier reddened. His response was barely audible. "None."

"Oh, right. You expect me to believe..."

Kier's gaze held daggers. "*I* was someone's *bye-blow*. You think I'd inflict that on another?"

The statement fell like a brick between them. As if eager to ease the tension, JonMarc began making ready for bed. He curled up before the hearth, Kier's blanket wrapped snugly about him.

Kier was willing to let the matter drop. He, too, felt sleep coming on and embraced it like a welcome comrade. He sank back on the straw mattress, drawing his cloak up to his chin.

His overwrought mind had just surrendered to blissful numbness when JonMarc's voice wrenched him back.

"I almost forgot. Ma'ardhi said a man came looking for you at the *Sword* this morning—an odd sort with milky hair and a scar on his face. He claimed to be a friend of yours."

Kier rolled onto his side. "I don't know anyone who looks like that. What did he want?"

JonMarc related what the dancing girl had told him.

Kier scowled. "Why would someone seek me at *The Dragon Sword*? I'd never been there before last night. All my messages come through the garrison."

"That's where Eliém sent him."

"So—he could've found me by now, if he'd wanted to." Kier tried to make sense of the disquieting news. Who in all the Deg Tirith would be seeking him here? A man from Alcor; white hair; a scar. A shiver lanced through him. "JonMarc, one of my attackers last night spoke of a man with a scar..."

The slave was already snoring peacefully, the tattered blanket bundled about him like a woolen cocoon. Kier envied him that deep, untroubled sleep. He was wide awake again. And the more he replayed the attack, the more certain he became that it was no case of mistaken identity. Someone in Castémaron wanted him dead.

Chapter Seven

A sharp nudge on the shoulder roused JonMarc from sleep. He groaned, and squinted at the small window where the first slanted rays of Devoreth's Orb peeked around the shutter. Kier stood above him, already dressed. JonMarc sat up with a yawn and knuckled his eyelids. He was accustomed to early morning, but only as the culmination of a long night's carousing. Beginning his day with it seemed a quaint and not altogether agreeable concept. He threw on his clothes and ran a wooden comb through his hair, then followed Kier down the back stair.

Two horses stood saddled in the stableyard. "It's nearly three leagues to Dolwythion," Kier said. "We'll be less pressed for time if we ride." He stroked the muzzle of a thick-limbed roan that had seen better days, then swung easily into the saddle. "You've sat a mount before, haven't you?"

JonMarc responded with a dismissive wave. Now that he'd finally begun to gain ground with this brassy, he wasn't about to let on that, in twenty years of living in crowded Castémaron, he'd had neither the need nor opportunity to actually stride a horse. Brashly, he strode up to the dappled mare and seized the reins. The beast shied away. JonMarc reached out again, this time for the saddle, but the mare whinnied and sidled off.

"You might find it easier to mount from the left," Kier suggested. Amusement sparked his amethyst eyes. Reddening, JonMarc stalked to the other side and hoisted himself across the beast's back, then swung his right leg over. He gripped the reins tightly as they made for the open gate.

The mare proved docile enough, content to follow her companion's lead through the winding streets. JonMarc sniffed the humid air and gazed about, enjoying this new, lofty perspective on the surroundings he'd known since boyhood. He tried to fix their image in his mind. After today, he'd likely never see Castémaron again, and the memory of some home, even a wretched one, seemed preferable to none at all.

Ahead, Kier looked entirely at ease in the saddle. JonMarc hadn't yet made up his mind about this brassy. Two nights ago, he'd thought he had him pegged: the pampered son of a foreign lord, crippled by an outmoded sense of honor, and hopelessly naïve on the streets. But twice now, Kier had surprised him: first, in refusing to fix blame for his stolen purse; then, by going out of his way to repay a blood debt common wisdom said need not be repaid to a slave. What had the brassy to gain? Only a fool put himself out for another if it earned him nothing.

On the other hand, Kier had proved incredibly easy to gull. JonMarc still exulted over his coup last night, when the prize he'd come to wheedle for had simply dropped into his lap. He murmured thanks to hunchbacked Ghedrev, the patron god of rogues and cast-outs, for giving Kier such a demanding mentor. JonMarc wasn't exactly sure what a mentor was, or why Kier should have one, nor did he understand why that mysterious personage wanted to meet him. To reward him for saving the brassy's life? That must be it. JonMarc chuckled. His circumstances were definitely looking up.

They found the winding streets around the market square hemmed in with carts and barrows of tradesmen jostling for advantageous spots to set out their wares, while early risers wandered amongst the stalls, haggling for bargains. JonMarc wistfully inhaled the aromas around a sausage vendor's brazier. Kier's eagerness to be on the road had allowed no time for breakfast.

Overwhelmed by the flood of incoming carts, the Westgate's harried sentry waived them out the gate with scant acknowledgment. JonMarc breathed relief. Traveling with a brassy had its advantages. He relished the opportunity to spend the day outside the walls. If Correlin should perchance discover his absence, the haughty lord would doubtless search within the city first. Though he'd concealed it from Kier, JonMarc could not shake his nagging concerns about his dead master's heir. Last night, in restless dream, he'd seen himself and Correlin locked in a mortal struggle, while the floorboards pitched and heaved beneath them. JonMarc forced the unsettling image aside. As long as Ruthira believed he waited at their seaside hideaway, she'd cover his absence with a convincing lie. That might give him several days. He needed only one.

The air grew freer as they left the city crowds behind. The cobbled road quickly deteriorated to a muddy track flanked by open fields and the occasional cluster of peasant cottages. JonMarc had never traveled this far beyond the city's western gate. Feeling more confident of his riding skill, he urged the mare up beside Kier. "How much farther?" he asked.

"Not much," Kier murmured, his first words since they'd left the gates.

JonMarc shifted his seat. Thusfar, he'd viewed this trip as something of a lark. Now, the bucolic landscape was starting to make him uneasy. He recalled marketplace tales of dangers that lurked beyond the city walls, like demons at edges of old sea charts—rumors of a black fortress-cloister, home to a mysterious brotherhood of monks whose arcane powers inspired fear in all who encountered them. JonMarc upbraided himself. Why hadn't he thought to find out more about Kier's mentor before making his bargain?

Not half a league beyond, they came upon a high boundary wall crowned with gleaming razor shards of obsidian. Behind it, atop a long hill, towered a stark black edifice, its many jagged turrets pricking the clouded sky like impalers' pikes. Within its lofty walls there rose a massive spire, capped with a dome of dull silver—a giant's finger, probing the heavens. JonMarc slowed to gape at the daunting sight, torn between fascination and a fervent desire to bolt.

Kier cantered on, following the boundary wall, and for a moment JonMarc thought they might pass the intimidating edifice by. Then the brassy reined to a halt before a gate flanked by two stout pillars. Cautiously, JonMarc drew up behind. He studied the intricate ironwork with the eye of an experienced cracksman, wondering if, and how, Kier meant to enter. He saw no bell or knocker.

As if in answer to his thought, the heavy gate gave a sudden jolt and slowly began to grind open on its own. As it swung inward, the angled shafts of Devoreth's Orb blazed upon its worn, bronze center panel, cast in deep relief with a sigil JonMarc recognized from tale and rumor: the eight-pointed *Nwtyrran* star.

"Holy chancres of Ghedrev," he muttered under his breath. "Blazes, Kier, you never told me your mentor was *Fithlon*!"

"You never asked." Kier calmly dismounted and walked the roan through the open gate. He turned back. "You coming?"

JonMarc's palms sweated. An anchor-stone weighted his belly. Every chilling tale he'd ever heard of the Fithlon assailed him. Kier stood waiting, hands on hips. JonMarc rallied his courage. He tried to focus on the reward Kier's mentor would likely offer him. He slid off the mare's back and cautiously led her inside. "You might at least have warned me," he grumbled.

There was a groan of hinges, and the gate shut behind them with a clang that nearly stopped his heart. He risked a glance over his shoulder. A stout, grey-cowled monk stepped away from the latch. So—the gate did not move by magic. JonMarc felt a bit foolish.

"If I'd warned you, you might not have come," Kier replied simply.

True. No right-minded soul sought out the Fithlon. JonMarc recalled how clever he'd thought himself last night, when he made his pact with Kier. Who had actually gulled whom?

The gatekeeper stepped up to take the horses. At Kier's nudge, JonMarc handed over the mare's reins, being especially careful not to touch the monk's fingers. He stuck close to Kier as they turned up a long tree-lined path.

They passed several more monks, silently working the grounds. All wore grey robes, belted with cords of various hues, their faces hidden beneath deep hoods. JonMarc gave them wide berth.

"You needn't squirm like a frightened squirrat," Kier said wryly. "They won't eat you."

"But—they're sorcerers, aren't they? I mean, I've heard..." JonMarc toyed with the dirk at his belt. "The Covenanters say that if a Fithlon looks you in the eye, your brain will melt to jelly; that they can force a man to strangle himself, or plunge hot pokers through his own eyes!"

Kier laughed softly. "Aye, I expect most Fithlon have power enough for that."

Blood drained from JonMarc's face. He couldn't tell if Kier was jesting or not.

"But Fithlon don't go around melting people's brains for amusement. Their doctrine forbids them using their powers to cause harm. Nowadays, most choose to be left alone."

In that case, JonMarc saw no need to disturb them. Wouldn't it be more courteous just to leave? Gravel popped and crunched beneath his reluctant footsteps. "How'd you get involved with them?"

Kier never raised his eyes from the ground. "Master Gwythion and my father are old friends. I suppose that's why he chose me to be his pupil. That was ten years ago, back in Alcor. I'm afraid I've been rather a disappointment to him, since I abandoned my studies when I accepted my commission."

JonMarc regarded the brassy with new respect, and a measure of concern. "Do *you* have Fithlon powers?"

"Some. Gwythion's trained me to the First Tier. That's all any Fithlon's allowed to teach an outsider. He knows I've no interest in joining the Brotherhood."

"Why not?"

"Because I've no mind to shut myself up in a cloister the rest of my life."

JonMarc detected some reticence in Kier's reply and wondered how much he'd left unsaid.

They were nearing the end of the path. Through the trees, JonMarc spied the black fortress he'd seen from the road, towering before them like a bastion of death. If anything, it looked even more menacing up close.

"Welcome to Dolwythion," Kier said.

JonMarc wanted to run. No reward was worth this. The notion of following Kier into that place made his insides squirm. Yet he didn't wish to appear a coward; not when this brassy held his very future in his hands.

The massive, iron-bound doors opened silently at their approach, and another faceless monk ushered them inside. He seemed to know their business without asking. Kier returned a sober nod, as if in response to some unspoken query, then led the way down a dim, vaulted corridor.

Despite his trepidation, JonMarc gawked about him like a yokel at a city faire. The polished floor dazzled with a million grain-sized magien crystals. Frescos and tapestries adorned the walls, their colors muted with age. One panel, in particular, caught his eye: a massive slab of gleaming black calstone, embedded with nine colored jewels that formed the well-known constellation of the *Life Tree*. At the center of the familiar double trident, where the lower cross-piece met the stem, the sacred *Life Star* blazed forth, a faceted yellow crystal the size of his fist. JonMarc breathed a low whistle, imagining the price such a treasure would bring on the streets.

The cavernous hallway seemed to pulse with an eerie watchfulness, accentuated by the distant drone of chanting and the hollow echo of their footsteps. As they mounted a tall, turret stairway, an odd smell began to weight the air—deep and musty, like an ancient storeroom. Its source became apparent as Kier led him through an arched doorway at the top.

Books. They filled the chamber, stacked onto ceiling-high shelves and spilling over onto chairs, tables, and haphazard piles along the floorboards. None but the wealthy could afford to own books. Here were more than JonMarc ever imagined could exist. They shared the circular chamber with scores of dusty artifacts of every shape and description: intricate carvings of birds and beasts, blown glass spheres dangling from the ceiling, clusters of multi-hued crystals that sparkled in the firelight, and, in a curtained alcove, a finely-crafted brass cylinder balanced atop a tall stand.

In the center of the room, a pair of stout candles flickered on a ponderous desk that, too, was littered with volumes, some open, others weighing down the edges of charts and scrolls. Behind it, dwarfed by a massive stack of parchments, sat an elderly monk, poring over a yellowed manuscript, his features largely shaded by a dark grey cowl.

"Ah, you are here," he said, without looking up. "Come. Sit."

Every chair was piled high with books. JonMarc followed Kier's lead and began to stack the ancient volumes onto the floor, one by one.

"Take care with those," the Fithlon Master snapped, still engrossed in his studies. "They're worth more than the entire Vilsolian treasury."

JonMarc hesitated. The treasury? In his hands? He flicked a glance at Kier. The brassy was preoccupied with his task. Almost without thinking, JonMarc snatched up a small volume, bound in red leather, and slipped it inside his jerkin. With so many books, the Fithlon Master would never miss just one. He took the seat beside Kier.

A moment later, Master Gwythion set aside the pair of clear, wire-rimmed discs he wore perched atop his nose and scrutinized his visitor in a way that made JonMarc's innards crawl.

"So *you're* the one." The statement sounded like an accusation. "Dynian, eh? Of what lineage?"

"I... don't know," JonMarc stammered, taken aback. "I was..."

Gwythion's keen eyes snared his and held them a moment. "Ah."

JonMarc blinked hard and shook his head. It had happened so fast. He had an uncanny feeling the Fithlon Master knew what he'd been about to say, and more. How much more? Could the Fithlon probe deeper than his immediate thoughts? JonMarc's belly writhed. What if the Fithlon Master had learned about the stolen book?

He was left to agonize as the aged monk turned his attention to Kier.

§

Kier leaned back in his chair, arms folded across his chest. If he didn't know the Fithlon ate and slept like other men, he might have thought his mentor hadn't stirred a whit since their last meeting. Nothing seemed to have changed—except that the care lines in Gwythion's face were perhaps a little deeper. Kier wondered why.

"*Well, I've brought him,*" he said silently. "*I hope he's all you expected, because, thanks to you, I'm now saddled with him till I reach Alcor.*"

"*We shall see,*" came Gwythion's reply in his mind. "*There is more to this Dynian than you guess—more even than he himself suspects.*" The Fithlon Master raised one bushy brow. "Now, tell me what is really troubling you, Kier," he said aloud.

The query caught Kier up short. He was never quite sure just how much his mentor gleaned from his unprotected thoughts, though if Gwythion were truly reading his mind, the monk would already know the answer. "Why didn't you tell me my father is dying?" he said. "You must've had word of it before you contacted me. Else, how did you know I was preparing to leave Castémaron?"

Gwythion soberly shook his head. "In truth, Kier, I did not know. I learned of your departure, and Duke Morwen's illness, only when I touched your mind yester-night, and the news troubles me deeply. Still, I have long known *something* would necessitate your return to Alcor."

"Known? How?" Kier tried to probe behind his mentor's thoughts, to no avail. "Something's happened since my last visit, hasn't it? When will you finally tell me..?"

A muffled crash cut him short.

§

JonMarc's hands trembled. How long before Kier's mentor discovered the theft of the book and turned his brain to fish guts? What in Ghedrev's name had possessed him to steal from a Fithlon Master? Now he had to find a way to return the book to the stack before Gwythion realized what he'd done and told Kier. The brassy would certainly hold him to his promise not to thieve, and refuse to take him to Alcor—assuming he even survived this audience.

On the edge of the Fithlon's desk lay a bowl of honey-dates. Perhaps if he pretended to reach for those, he could discreetly slip the book back onto its pile without being noticed. Kier and his mentor were busy conversing. It might work. Cautiously, JonMarc reached out.

With a heart-stopping clatter, the pile toppled. JonMarc recoiled. He hadn't even touched it. He saw Kier's frown and hastily stooped to rebuild the stack, managing to slip the small volume onto the top without being detected. Then he slunk back to his seat and desperately groped inside his tunic for the charmstone Ma'ardhi had given him, their first night together.

He only prayed it had power enough to shield him from the Fithlon's wrath.

Master Gwythion remained silent so long JonMarc began to wonder what melting brain tissue would smell like. A rivulet of sweat trickled down his nose.

At last the Fithlon spoke. "My apologies, JonMarc. I should have realized: one who has known starvation takes his mealtimes very seriously." He nudged the bowl of dates. "Pray help yourself."

JonMarc slowly raised his eyes, hesitated, then snatched a date from the bowl. He didn't even think to put it in his mouth; he was too busy pondering his narrow escape. So Kier's mentor hadn't divined his thoughts after all. JonMarc congratulated himself. He'd actually managed to deceive a Fithlon Master. Yet... if Master Gwythion hadn't read his mind, how did the monk know he'd starved? JonMarc's elation wilted. What in Ghedrev's name had he gotten himself into? He sensed Master Gwythion studying him and gripped the charmstone through his shirt.

"*May I see it*?" the monk asked.

JonMarc gave a start, both at the request, and the realization that he'd heard the Fithlon's voice, not aloud, but from inside his own head. Was that how the Fithlon communicated? He feared to comply. What if this were simply a trick to make him relinquish his only protection?

"*Trust me*," said Master Gwythion, in his mind.

Such trust did not come readily. Still, there was something irresistible about the Fithlon's request. If Master Gwythion meant to punish him, wouldn't he have done so by now? And what might the monk do to him if he refused? Reluctantly, JonMarc slipped the pendant over his head.

Gwythion studied the clear, thumb-sized crystal intently, and for a moment his stern features softened, as though his mind wandered the mists of the past. "Do you know what this is?" he asked, aloud this time.

"Ah— it's a charmstone. They're supposed to—"

"Protect against Fithlon spells. Yes, yes, I know." Master Gwythion clearly found that explanation tedious. "It is a *dathana* crystal. You see here? It has a heart of fire. Such stones are rare—and powerful. Where did you get it?" JonMarc started to answer. "Ah," the Fithlon master said. "And she who gave it to you—did she know its powers?"

The speed at which Master Gwythion read his thoughts unnerved JonMarc. He felt uncomfortably transparent. "I ... I don't think so," he stammered. Gwythion's expression said he suspected otherwise. JonMarc's curiosity overwhelmed his remaining fears. "What *are* its powers?"

"You may come to know that, when you are ready." Gwythion held the crystal to his brow. "This stone is very ancient. It came from Nwtyrra, before its fall."

At the mention of that legendary realm, JonMarc caught his breath. Even Kier glanced up.

"It has many stories to tell. Perhaps one day you will find the skill to hear them. It has traveled countless leagues; passed through many hands to get here. And you, JonMarc, are but another courier. Keep it safe until the time comes to pass it on—as your dancing girl did."

Gwythion wrapped the silken cord around the charmstone and pretended to toss it back to him. JonMarc jumped, instinctively reaching out with his left hand. The monk gently placed the small crystal in his palm. JonMarc began to suspect the Fithlon was toying with him. Or—the insight came in a flash—*testing* him?

There was a power about this Fithlon Master that seemed to make the very air tingle, and an agelessness in his dark eyes that belied the deep creases surrounding them. Master Gwythion had thrown back his hood, revealing a freckled scalp, haloed by slate-grey hair that hung to his shoulders. His bearded face was long and gaunt, with high cheekbones flanking a sharp, somewhat crooked nose. Yet it was his eyes that fascinated JonMarc—eyes as deep and black as a bottomless lake, and as compelling; eyes that darted with the quickness of a sparrowhawk, seeming to take in all they saw, and more that lay beyond normal sight. Behind Kier's eyes, JonMarc knew, there lay a fortress, solid and impregnable. But Master Gwythion's eyes encompassed the vastness of the universe—easier to penetrate, yet impossible to fathom.

JonMarc cocked his head. "Why did you ask me here, Master?" He knew now it had nothing to do with a reward.

"Aye, I'd like to know that myself," said Kier, betraying some impatience. "Why the urgency? Couldn't you have told me what you needed to when I was here the other night?"

Master Gwythion eyed him sternly. "I needed *both* of you to hear what I have to tell. In a few weeks an event will occur, of such magnitude its outcome will determine the future of the Deg Tirith; indeed, of all Éclatan. In it, I am now convinced that you, Kier—and perhaps JonMarc as well— are destined to play roles."

The statement stunned JonMarc. An event that could change the world?

And involve him? The revelation was so far from anything he'd expected he could scarcely muster speech.

It was Kier who gave his questions voice. "What kind of event could possibly affect the entire world?" The brassy sounded unmistakably skeptical. "And what makes you think either of us might be involved? Did you foresee it?"

"Not I," Gwythion replied. "Yet it *was* foreseen, nine centuries ago, by Dyveth Aneryn, Nwtyrra's exiled king."

JonMarc was now so thoroughly captivated the Fithlon Master might melt his brain to syrup and he'd scarcely notice. "You spoke of Nwtyrra before. Yet I thought... I mean, isn't the Fallen Realm just a fable?"

Master Gwythion's candescent gaze seemed to probe JonMarc's very soul. "It is not! Tell me, JonMarc, how much of that *fable* are you familiar with?"

JonMarc flushed. He'd stuck his foot in it again. Not that he'd meant to. He'd always loved such tales, and would sit for hours in the marketplace, listening to any itinerant bard or Covenant priest willing to tell them. Often enough he paid for his idleness with floggings, but that never deterred him. Still, the thought of relating such stories to a Fithlon Master...

"Only snatches," he returned weakly, hoping Master Gwythion would relent. The old monk prompted him on. JonMarc decided that if he must recount the tale, he'd best do it precisely as he'd memorized it in the market, complete with every pious intonation. He pressed his palms together as he'd seen Covenanters do.

"Nwtyrra was a kingdom in the midst of the Western Sea, where dwelt a race of false gods, cast from the heavens." JonMarc tentatively glanced up. Gwythion's gaze never left his face. Swallowing hard, he continued. "In that land, they discovered a source of vast power, and used it to build for themselves an empire which they filled with vile mechanisms and unholy devices. But the great god Devoreth saw their iniquities and cursed them, causing them to battle amongst themselves. At last, the Nwtyrrans and all their evil magic were consumed in flame and swallowed by the sea."

JonMarc lifted his eyes hopefully, only to see Master Gwythion scowling. His spirits fell.

"Evil magic? Devoreth's curse? You obviously heard that account from a Covenant priest." The Fithlon's irate snort suggested he ranked the god Devoreth's self-proclaimed ministers somewhat lower on the rungs of creation than garden slugs. "The power the Nwtyrrans discovered was not evil. It was evilly *used*. No power is tainted of itself. Still, I suppose it is a hopeful sign that Nwtyrra is still remembered in some fashion, if only by those committed to its vilification."

Gwythion stared into his steepled fingertips. "Be assured, JonMarc, Nwtyrra did indeed exist, but not as the Covenanters relate. She was once a glorious realm, proud and fair. Never before or since has our world of Éclatan seen such a civilization. Yet in her pride, she grew reckless. Within her fair breast she allowed a pestilence to grow: the disease of fear; the scourge of intolerance. For you see, JonMarc, the Nwtyrrans were not gods, false or otherwise, but men like ourselves—men whose knowledge and control of nature far surpassed our own. Yet when they imagined themselves threatened, they took their new-found power—sprung from the element *miril*, which occurs nowhere else in Éclatan—and directed it against their brethren. That power proved greater than the Nwtyrrans' wisdom to control it. It dragged them to a ruin so complete their own minds could not comprehend it, even as their wondrous civilization crumbled about them."

JonMarc reverently fingered the dathana crystal in his palm. It made him feel somehow linked to Master Gwythion's tale. "But if the Nwtyrrans were destroyed, how did my charmstone get here? And how could you know their history?"

"A worthy question," said Gwythion. "There were survivors. One man, at least, saw the darkness coming: the Nwtyrran king, Dyveth Aneryn. Blessed with the gift of foresight, he prophesied that the Nwtyrrans' fears would ultimately drive them to ruin. Yet few listened; fewer still believed. Obsessed with jealousy over Aneryn's arcane talents, the king's enemies overwhelmed him and seized the throne, declaring Aneryn, and all others who possessed such talents, traitors. So Aneryn gathered about him a small band of followers: thirteen in all. They dubbed themselves the *Lidialis*, the 'visionaries,' and renounced all use of miril, which enhanced their powers. With the enemy upon them, they commandeered a vessel, bade tearful farewell to their beloved land, and set sail to the east.

"They had no notion whence their journey might lead, for they retained little knowledge of the lands beyond their shores. When they were but three days out, the skies behind grew dark, and all Éclatan convulsed in smoke and flame. A monstrous cloud arose, accompanied by a rain of ash that lasted twenty days, until the fugitives sickened and longed for the light of Devoreth's Orb.

"Throughout that ordeal, Aneryn refused to look back. He had foreseen Nwtyrra's fall in his vision and could not bear to witness it again. As their tiny craft tossed directionless on blackened seas, a vast wave overtook them and bore them many leagues, to deposit them at last on a rugged strip of coast along Alcor's western shore—a land known as Cymworth."

JonMarc listened in awe. Never before had he heard Nwtyrra's story recounted in such detail, nor with such passion. Beside him, Kier rested one elbow on the arm of his chair, veiling his expression behind a calloused hand. He'd plainly heard all this before.

"I related that," said Gwythion, "because it has tremendous bearing on what I am about to tell you." He turned to JonMarc. "Can you read?"

The query took JonMarc aback. "Uh... a little. I had a master once who taught me..."

"Ah." Gwythion cut him off. JonMarc still found the monk's brusqueness unsettling. "There is a book in the stack beside you—small, with red binding. Find it."

JonMarc blenched. He knew exactly where the book lay—right atop the pile where he'd returned it. Hesitantly, he picked it up and offered it to the Fithlon. Gwythion shook his head.

"Keep it. Read it thoroughly. You must become familiar with its contents."

JonMarc's jaw dropped. "You're... *giving* me this?"

"I trust you will treat it with the reverence it deserves." Master Gwythion regarded him from beneath furrowed brows. "Only bear in mind, JonMarc: when I speak of the book's value, I refer to the knowledge it contains. You might find its street price highly disappointing."

JonMarc flushed with embarrassment. So Gwythion knew of the theft all along—and did not mean to punish him. He turned the volume over and leafed cautiously through the handwritten pages. His attention focused on the title, embossed in gold, and he carefully traced his finger across the shiny words. "What is *The... Book... of... Ygair*?"

"It is the Fithlon sacred text, compiled over centuries from the chronicles of the Nwtyrran refugees, though it also contains a good deal of Fithlon commentary."

"But how do the Fithlon fit in? They're not from Nwtyrra, are they?"

"No, the Fithlon Brotherhood is native to the Deg Tirith. Yet they owe their existence to the Nwtyrran exiles. You see, when Aneryn and his folk arrived in Alcor, they did not realize how difficult life would be without the power of miril to aid them. They were forced to enlist the aid of local villagers just to survive their first winter. In return, they taught the village elders about Nwtyrra—her laws, arts, philosophies—so memory of those things would not be lost. They also introduced tools and innovations to make the villagers' lives easier. Those elders selected for training became known as the Fithlon, or *faithful*. They studied the Nwtyrran tongue and, when the last of the exiles died, compiled their writings into *The Book of Ygair*.

"Yet as years passed, the Nwtyrran teachings became obscured. The generations of Fithlon that followed began to interpret the wonders they read of as sorcery. Much of *Ygair* now reflects that confusion." Gwythion glanced at Kier, who sat silent, staring at the floor. "Kier will help you sort out those parts. He studied *Ygair* years ago—and it would not hurt him to do so again."

Kier raised his head. "Why? You still haven't said what any of this has to do with me."

"It has *everything* to do with you. The demesne of Cymworth, where Aneryn and his followers made landfall, is to be your inheritance."

Kier's brows narrowed. "That can't be. Alcorean law forbids a bastard to inherit."

"Nonetheless, Cymworth is to be yours. Your father agreed to it years ago."

"But why would he challenge Alcor's laws just to grant me Cymworth, of all places?"

"Because I persuaded him. It is vital that anything found at Cymworth be legally yours."

Kier's frown deepened. "What could you possibly expect to find at Cymworth? I scouted there once, for Commander Donal. The peninsula's desolate—just chalk cliffs and the crumbling ruin of a fortress. Even the Dynian don't go there, and it borders their lands. Surely, if there were anything of value at Cymworth, the Tiernai would have plundered it years ago."

"The ruined fortress you saw is all that remains of Carreg Cymworth, built by the Nwtyrrans during their first year in exile. Because the tomb of King Aneryn is said to lie somewhere near those ruins, the Fithlon have long forbidden travel to that sacred spot. And though Alcor's Tiernai conquerors may scoff at such a proscription, the native Dynian respect it. Their lore runs deep. To them, Cymworth is a site of reverence, its legend shrouded in the mists of the past."

Kier still looked skeptical. "So, you want me to inherit a Fithlon holy place. Why? Am I supposed to build a shrine there or something?"

"Nothing so trivial," said Gwythion. "There is another reason the Fithlon forbid travel to Cymworth. It has long been rumored that some dread secret lies hidden amongst the ruins. Some believe a remnant of the power that destroyed Nwtyrra might have been carried to Alcor. For centuries, Fithlon scholars sifted through the Nwtyrran texts, seeking some clue to the mystery. Yet naught could be been found, save a cryptic passage in an obscure manuscript that never found its way into *Ygair*. It was written in Nwtyrran script, and declares:

> *May proud Nwtyrra's Doom smite All who dare*
> *To seek her lost Power without True Purpose;*
> *To subdue it without Compassion;*
> *To wield it without Restraint.*

"To some, this seemed to confirm the rumor, for if a remnant of Nwtyrra's power did indeed escape destruction, where would it likely be hidden but at Cymworth? Yet the nature of that power, and how it might have reached the Deg Tirith, remained a mystery. With the oppressions of the Covenant Priesthood increasing, the Fithlon Synod forbade further investigation of the matter, lest their sworn enemies learn of it."

"So what happened?" JonMarc asked. "Was the search abandoned?"

"It was—for a time." Gwythion rose and began to pace, knobby hands clasped behind his back. "Then, after many years, I, and a learned Master of the Tenth Tier named Maelguin, again took up the matter. We feared that, should such a power exist and fall into the wrong hands, it might wreak upon the Deg Tirith the same ruin that befell Nwtyrra. Scrupulously, we retraced the steps of each of the Nwtyrran refugees, combing their journals for any reference that might illuminate the mystery. Yet we found nothing. At last, convinced there was no other way, we defied the Fithlon Synod and journeyed to Cymworth to search its forbidden ruins—not for the power itself, which we had neither the wisdom nor experience to control, but for a clue to its nature and purpose.

"After many grueling days, we discovered what we sought, hidden deep in a crypt where it had lain undisturbed for nine centuries: an iron-bound chest containing manuscripts that could only have been left there by Dyveth Aneryn himself."

Gwythion halted, his dark gaze scrutinizing each of them, in turn. "Those writings confirmed our deepest fears. They indicated that a power had indeed escaped Nwtyrra's ruin—a *cábretaur*, or unrefined crystal of miril, borne in secret to the Deg Tirith by Dyveth Aneryn, unknown even to those faithful few who accompanied him here."

A tingle skittered up JonMarc's backbone. The room suddenly felt stifling.

Beside him, Kier ran a nervous palm across his cheek. "But why would Aneryn bring such an accursed thing here, knowing its destructive powers?"

"Ah," said Gwythion, "long have I pondered that. I now believe I understand his motive. You see, when Aneryn realized the imminence of Nwtyrra's fall, he was faced with a terrible decision. He knew the cataclysm he had foreseen would destroy all of Nwtyrra—her magnificent achievements as well as the power that had wrought them. For understand: *there is no substance powerful enough to destroy miril, save miril itself.* Therein lay Aneryn's dilemma, for while Nwtyrra's destruction would be caused by the misuse of miril's power, the crystals themselves were blameless. They had been formed at the world's beginning, and existed, harmless and unknown, on that single island, until the Nwtyrrans came and learned to use them. Their power had potential for great good. Was it right to deny that to others, who might one day learn to use it wisely?

"The dread decision lay solely in his hands: to allow *all* miril to be destroyed with Nwtyrra, and so remove forever its dangers—and potential benefits—from the world; or to preserve the single cábretaur he possessed and bequeath it to future generations, allowing them to take responsibility for their own destiny."

Gwythion rested against the edge of his desk. "In the end, Aneryn chose the latter course, his rationale: that any civilization which loses the wisdom to keep from destroying itself has perhaps outlived whatever justification it had for existence in the first place."

"In other words, he left us on our own," Kier grumbled.

"In a sense. Yet our well-being concerned Aneryn deeply. By explaining all he could of Nwtyrra's fall and the circumstances that preceded it—of which I have related only a small part—he hoped to provide us a tool with which we might learn from his people's mistakes and avoid repeating them. Through this, he hoped to lend some meaning to Nwtyrra's tragedy."

All this was well beyond JonMarc's scope; hardly a part of the mundane world he knew. Rather, it felt as if he'd stepped inside a fable—a feat he'd often wished he could accomplish. He fingered the charmstone at his throat. "So what became of the Cábretaur?"

"Aye," Kier echoed. "If it's remained hidden for nine hundred years, isn't it best left undisturbed?"

Gwythion shook his head. "It would be, if that were possible. The peoples of the Deg Tirith are not ready to face such challenge as the Cábretaur represents. They may never be. Unfortunately, Aneryn's design worked out differently.

"You see, while Nwtyrra thrived, her rulers chose to keep their civilization isolated. When Aneryn escaped here to the Deg Tirith, he was dismayed to find its people living at what, to him, seemed a primitive level—tribal, warlike, certainly unprepared to receive the treasure he'd borne so far in secret. As the Cábretaur could no longer be destroyed, he chose to hide it until the inhabitants progressed enough to understand its potential. He made certain observations—predictions, if you will—concerning the time he foresaw when the Cábretaur would again come to light, though he could in no way *control* when that would be. Then, without divulging his true purpose, he sent his followers amongst the populations to speed their progress toward that day.

"In part, the Nwtyrrans achieved his goal. Our calendar is one example; the Tyrric Laws, another. They form the basis for nearly every legal system in the Deg Tirith. Both were introduced by the Nwtyrrans, nine centuries ago."

Gwythion circled back to his tall chair and leaned his palms on the edge of his desk. "As the exiles died, one by one, they entrusted responsibility for carrying on their work to their Fithlon disciples. Yet as centuries passed, the common folk began to renounce the Fithlon, their fears ignited by the Covenant Priesthood, whose function has ever been to keep the peoples of the Deg Tirith trapped in the ignorance of the past." Gwythion's dark eyes smoldered. "The Covenanters fanned those fears into hysteria. Thousands were slaughtered, not only Fithlon, but anyone suspected of possessing powers the Covenanters deemed *ungodly*. Sadly, the heaviest Fithlon losses were incurred by those who lived and worked amongst the people, advancing Aneryn's cause. When the purges ended, the few Fithlon who escaped locked themselves away in cloister-fortresses like this one, turning their focus inward. Most now devote their lives to mysticism and the powers of mind, caring little for the ways of the world.

And Aneryn's purpose is forgotten."

Gwythion brushed clutter from the unrolled parchment on his desk and beckoned them nearer. JonMarc pressed in eagerly. Kier looked on from his seat.

"Yet despite this setback, the appointed hour approaches. Maelguin and I discovered Aneryn's predictions in the manuscripts we found at Cymworth. They detail the time when the Cábretaur will reappear: *The Second Conjunction of the Life Tree*. My calculations indicate that conjunction is less than a month hence. Last night I observed, through my glass, the approach of the wandering star the Nwtyrrans called the *Death Seer*. Its last appearance, nine centuries ago, heralded Nwtyrra's fall. That is why I summoned you, Kier. Soon the *Death Seer* will be visible to the naked eye. And when it conjoins with the *Life Star*"—Gwythion tapped a spot on the chart, circled in red—"the fate of our world will be decided."

JonMarc darted an uneasy glance at Kier, whose fingers clutched the carved arms of his chair as if straining to keep some deeper emotion at bay. "I don't understand," Kier said. "How is this Cábretaur to reappear? Will it just pop out of the ground for anyone to find?"

"Of course not. It must be sought. Aneryn described the circumstances in his predictions."

Kier's expression turned wary. "And who is to attempt that task? Aneryn didn't happen to mention any names, did he?"

"No. But he did describe characteristics that would set this individual apart. These I have studied for many years. I am now convinced that only one man in all Éclatan fulfills Aneryn's conditions." Gwythion looked directly into Kier's amethyst eyes. "That man is *you*."

Chapter Eight

Kier's belly churned like boiling pitch. Ever since Gwythion first chose him as a pupil, he'd suspected some hidden agenda behind the Fithlon's tutelage. He knew now he'd been right. The revelation brought no comfort. He felt trapped.

Resentments hammered him like siege missiles. That his mentor would try to foist so outrageous a burden on him, especially now, with his life already veering out of control: his father's impending death; the dreaded return to Alcor; his career, perhaps his very life, in jeopardy. To heap upon that some bizarre responsibility for the world's fate?

Kier clamped his jaw to stop it trembling. He wanted to smash something; to hurl Gwythion's parchments to the floor. He willed the impulse down. He'd not give vent to his frustrations—not in his mentor's presence, and certainly not in front of JonMarc.

He sensed Gwythion awaiting his reaction. What could he say? That he didn't believe a substance so powerful as his mentor described could even exist? Gwythion was a revered master—the only Fithlon ever to attain the Twelfth Tier. Kier had never known him to be wrong about anything. He might have accepted the tale on faith alone, were it not for its devastating implications. For if, as Gwythion maintained, his actions were ordained by prophecy, it meant he had no control whatever over the course of his life. Kier utterly refused to concede that.

"No," he declared flatly, "I will not be anyone's pawn. Find someone else." His own temerity astounded him. Seldom had he dared defy his mentor's wishes, and when he did, his pride paid a hefty price.

He heard a hiss of intaken breath: JonMarc, clearly astonished by his refusal. The slave had been hanging on Gwythion's words like an expectant puppy, totally engrossed in the tale. Blazes, if he was so keen to be Fortunea's trinket, let *him* go seek this accursed Nwtyrran gemstone.

Gwythion sat, unmoving, behind his great desk, an immense presence trammeled within a wizened frame. At any moment, the Fithlon's fury would burst forth. Kier braced for the eruption.

Yet his mentor surprised him. "Finding another is not an option, Kier," he said simply. "*You* are the one foreseen and *you* will find the Cábretaur. There is no way around it."

"There is if I refuse to search."

"Even so, you *will* find it. You will be drawn to it, by what means I cannot say. If Aneryn's vision was true—and I cannot believe otherwise—it will come to pass, whatever course you may chart for yourself."

The statement only heightened Kier's exasperation. "I cannot accept that. I won't have my actions *controlled*—certainly not by some fugitive king who died nine centuries ago!" He saw embers spark behind his mentor's eyes—the Fithlon's temper, finally beginning to slip. Right now, he didn't care.

"Your actions are your own, Kier. No one else controls them. I say only that some of what you have done—will do—has been *foreseen*. It is not the same thing. Because I foresee a horse will lose a shoe today does not mean I cause its loss. And because Aneryn saw, nine centuries ago, that you would one day seek his hidden Cábretaur does not mean he is *compelling* you to do so. He merely witnessed the event before it happened. That means that, somehow, it *must* happen."

The nuance of interpretation hardly mollified Kier. He glowered at the floorboards.

"Why tell him, then?" JonMarc asked. "If it's all to happen anyway, why not just let it?"

"Because there is much Aneryn did *not* foresee. Kier's finding of the Cábretaur is but a single event, viewed out of context. What will occur before and after remains unknown. It is my task to prepare him for any eventuality."

"But—if that event is fixed, then all the rest must be as well, even though Aneryn didn't foresee it. How can anything you tell Kier change what's destined to be?"

Kier cocked a glance at the slave. He'd hardly expected such astuteness from him.

"Ah," said Gwythion, "you have hit upon an age-old question, JonMarc; one the Fithlon have debated for centuries. Is man's destiny fixed? If we could step out of time and look back, we might find it so. But seen from within, how can one tell if he follows a prescribed path or one of infinite alternatives? To worry over whether you can change your fate is to assume the path you may be destined to tread is not the one you would choose. How do you know they are not the same? How would you recognize a change if it occurred? In this case, my very act of telling Kier of Aneryn's vision may be what sets this cycle of events in motion. Or it may simply be part of a predetermined continuum. There is no way of knowing."

JonMarc's brows narrowed as he ruminated on that. Kier allowed himself a mirthless chuckle. His companion was in for a brain-full if he chose to argue philosophy with a Fithlon Master. Kier had more pressing questions. "What *exactly* did Aneryn say to make you so certain I'm the one he foresaw?"

Gwythion had clearly anticipated the challenge. "Aneryn made three major predictions. Of those, only the second pertains to you. The first simply states:

> *The Miril Cábretaur will shine again for Aneryn*
> *In the Second Conjunction of the Life Tree.*

That conjunction I have already discussed. The second reads:

> *Born of Love and of Hatred;*
> *Skilled of the Stag and of the Serpent;*
> *Heir to the Hand of Lidialis:*
> *He who bears the Amulet bears the Crystal's Key."*

"So the first lines are supposed to refer to my mixed parentage?" Kier gave a dismissive snort. "That proves nothing. There are halfbloods aplenty on Alcor. What does the next one mean? I've never heard of the *Hand of Lidialis.*"

"It is another part of your inheritance," said Gwythion, "a token your father entrusted me to give you when the time was right." The Fithlon drew an intricate key from about his neck and, with it, unlocked an age-worn trunk beside his desk. JonMarc eagerly pressed in to glimpse the chest's contents as Gwythion rooted through it, and Kier had to acknowledge his own curiosity. His mentor's vast collection of artifacts and oddities had always intrigued him, though he could identify little amid the jumble: only the carved head of what appeared to be a broken walking staff, and the graceful curve of a small, unstrung harp. At times Kier wondered just how old Gwythion must be, to have accumulated so much. Never had he found the audacity to ask.

The Fithlon removed from the trunk a polished wooden box slightly larger than his fist. It was unadorned, save for an etched gold panel on the lid. With a solemn nod, he presented it to Kier. "Open it," he said.

Kier did, and caught his breath. Inside lay a silver charm nearly the length of his forefinger, cunningly cast in the form of a pointing hand. As he drew it out, the colored gems set in gold around the wrist winked in the candlelight like tiny fireflies.

"The left hand pointing to the future," said Gwythion. "The symbol of the *Lidialis*, Aneryn's Nwtyrran followers. It, too, is a relic brought here by the exiles."

JonMarc drew close. His eyes betrayed a calculating glint. "Ghedrev's cods, that thing must be worth..."

"It is beyond price," Gwythion snapped. "Your father discovered it, Kier, some eighteen years ago, while surveying his lands at Cymworth. When he showed it to me, I realized it must be the *Hand of Lidialis*, which Aneryn's writings indicated would be found in the years directly preceding Conjunction. At first I thought the duke must be the seeker Aneryn predicted. Yet he did not fulfill the prophecy's conditions, nor did your half-brother Malcolm, the only *heir* to the Hand I was aware of. So I pressed the duke: was there not another heir?

"At first he denied it, for he feared the consequences should your existence become known. Yet, in the end, he told me of your birth; that he had beheld you only once, as an infant. After your mother's tragic death, guilt kept him from returning to your village."

Gwythion's words stirred emotions Kier would sooner have left entombed. He, too, bore the guilt of that death.

"I related to Duke Morwen the history of the Cábretaur and my belief that you must be the one foretold to find it. I encouraged him to fetch you from your village and acknowledge you, for only thus could your safety be assured. Fortunately, he took my advice. And when you came of age, he sent you to be my pupil, so that I might prepare you for the task ahead."

"You mean, rescuing me from the village wasn't the duke's idea at all? That without your intervention..."

Gwythion sensed his turmoil. "Be assured, Kier, in time, your father would have sought you out without my urging. He delayed only because he feared your step-mother's wrath."

It was scant consolation. While Kier was all too familiar with the duchess Yssolt's fiery temper, it hardly seemed reason enough for Alcor's *Iron Duke* to abandon his son.

He felt JonMarc nudge his elbow. The Dynian pointed to the silver hand. Against his better judgment, Kier passed it to him. JonMarc studied the talisman keenly.

"Master," he began, "you said that *I* might have a role to play in all this as well. What role? What does Aneryn say about me?"

"Nothing specifically," Gwythion admitted, "though his writings suggest that Kier will not undertake this task alone. I myself have foreseen as much, though I cannot be certain the companion I beheld was you."

Wonderful. Kier frowned into his laced fingers. Wasn't it bad enough to be trapped in this quagmire of moldering prophecy without having his every step dogged by a self-serving opportunist only looking for a chance to take advantage?

"*Do not so readily discount him,*" came Gwythion's thought, in his mind. "*Have I not said there is more to this Dynian than meets the eye?*"

Oblivious to their exchange, JonMarc continued to scrutinize the silver hand, his expression puzzled. "Why would Aneryn and his followers chose a *spoil* hand for their symbol?" he asked. "Wouldn't they consider that—well, you know..."

"Demeaning?" Gwythion regarded him from beneath darkened brows. "Quite the contrary. Nearly all the Nwtyrran refugees who escaped to the Deg Tirith were *spell-handed*. It is the reason they were driven from their land."

That pricked JonMarc's interest. "Were they branded?"

"Certainly not. It was the Covenant Priests of the Deg Tirith who devised that atrocity." Gwythion's words smoldered. "In Nwtyrra's early days, few even noticed which hand a person favored. Yet as years passed, a small portion of their population began to exhibit extra-ordinary talents: heightened sensing, the power to read others' thoughts; in rare cases, even foresight. It appeared that, in a select few, prolonged exposure to miril crystals enhanced the minds' innate abilities. Yet it was impossible to predict which individuals would be thus affected. The only outward trait those few had in common was that the majority favored the use of their left hand.

"As you might guess, such a discovery did not set well with the rest of Nwtyrra's populace. Suspicions grew, rooted in the fear that those who possessed so-called *sinistral* talents might use their advantage to dominate all who did not. The revelation that Nwtyrra's own ruler possessed such skills seemed to lend credence to those fears. Aneryn's enemies made it their excuse to seize power, condemning the ousted king—and all *spell-handed*, whether they possessed sinistral talents or not—as traitors, while secretly devising miril-powered weapons to annihilate them."

Gwythion sighed. "You know the rest. In response to that imagined threat, Aneryn's enemies unleashed a power so unmanageable it devastated the very civilization they sought to protect. Only the king and his meager following managed to escape. To them, the pointing left hand came to symbolize their brothers' sacrifice."

JonMarc fingered the spiral-serpent image seared into the back of his left hand. "So exposure to miril enhances sinistral talents. But you said there isn't any miril here in the Deg Tirith—except the one crystal Aneryn brought with him. Why do people still fear spoil... ah, *spell*-handers, if they have no powers?"

"Fear is not rational, JonMarc, especially when spurred by religious fervor. Long before Nwtyrra even existed, the Covenant Priesthood of the Deg Tirith sought to eliminate anyone with abilities they deemed *unnatural*. And make no mistake, many spell-handed, even here, possess at least *some* measure of sinistral talent. Exposure to any kind of crystal, even the common magien sands that make the ground glow, enhances it to some degree."

JonMarc's eyes brightened. "Then, is Fithlon magic simply enhanced sinistral power?"

The Fithlon Master nodded.

"So... all Fithlon must be spell-handed."

"Most," said Gwythion, "not all. Some are equally adept with either hand. And it is possible for even a *skill*-handed individual to possess a high degree of sinistral power. *Abominari*, the Covenanters call them, and fear them above any spell-hand, for they defy outward identification."

Kier remained silent. Though his mentor did not press the point, he had noted the reference in Aneryn's second prophecy. While not spell-handed, he possessed the *sinistral* talents symbolized by the serpent, as well as the right, or *skill*-hand, abilities dignified on Alcor by the Tiernai stag. *Abominari*. It was the dread secret that set him apart from normal society—even from other sinistrae. Kier found Aneryn's reference to it the most compelling evidence that his mentor's tale might indeed be true.

"So what is the purpose of this *Hand of Lidialis*?" he asked. "Is it simply a memento, or does it serve some function?"

"According to Aneryn's prophecy," said Gwythion, "it is *the Crystal's Key*." Note that the forefinger is of a different mineral than the rest of the hand. It possesses powers of attraction not unlike a ship's stone. As a key, I presume its function is to release a lock of opposite attraction. It seems clear that anyone who wishes to acquire the Cábretaur must first possess this amulet."

Amulet? Kier belly knotted. "Gwythion, who else knows about the hand amulet?"

"You mean who else knows it exists? Only those few Fithlon who have read the parchments Maelguin and I discovered at Cymworth. But none but ourselves and your father know it has actually been retrieved. Why...?"

"Because the two ruffians who attacked me the other night said they'd been sent to find an *Amulet*."

Gwythion stiffened visibly. "Are you certain that is the word they used?"

Kier nodded. "I'd forgotten it till you spoke. They demanded to know where I kept it hidden. But how could a pair of common street culls know about something that's supposedly so secret?"

Gwythion's face was granite. "They were clearly under orders from someone who did."

JonMarc stirred at that. "Kier, that scar-faced man Ma'ardhi said was looking for you at *The Dragon Sword*. Do you think...?"

"If he's the one that hired them, he must've assumed I'd received the silver hand that night." Kier cocked his head, puzzling. "But who would even know I'd been here, or that you had it to give to me?"

"Aye, who indeed?" Gwythion rose from his chair and began to pace, a bulbous knuckle pressed to his upper lip. "Whoever he is, he'd not be seeking the Amulet for its own value, but because of its connection to the Cábretaur. And if he knows of that, he must have some connection with the Fithlon."

"Or with the Covenant Priests," JonMarc suggested.

A sibilant exhale escaped Gwythion's bearded lips. "I truly hope *that* is not the case. It would be disastrous. As far as I can determine, the Covenanters know nothing of the hidden writings, or of the Cábretaur. Even the Fithlon Synod officially denies the Cábretaur exists. When Maelguin and I presented them proof, they denounced us for seeking it against their dictates and refused all discussion of the matter. They know the truth, but fear to acknowledge it openly."

"Could it be someone here at Dolwythion?" Kier asked, "or that Maelguin you spoke of? What if he now seeks the Cábretaur for himself?"

"I know the pursuits of all who dwell here. And Maelguin has been dead nearly thirty years. When the Fithlon Synod rejected our findings, he took it as a personal affront. He shut himself away in his fortress of Caer Morthund, on Alcor's southwest coast, and never emerged again. In his later years, it was rumored that he took an apprentice, but that association ended with the master's death. His pupil was later burned by the Covenanters." Gwythion leaned against the desk, restless fingers toying with a large onyx ring on his left forefinger. "Since Maelguin's demise, no other Fithlon has shared my preoccupation with the Cábretaur. As we remain constantly aware of each other through the *Infinite Mind*, it would be nigh impossible for one member of the Order to pursue such a course unbeknownst to the rest."

Gwythion dropped back into his chair and focused his gaze on one of the stout candles on his desk. Its amber light cavorted against his pupils like a Midsummer's bonfire. Kier knew the old monk's thoughts were ranging outward, through secret realms Kier could scarcely imagine. It was some time before his mentor wrenched his eyes away.

"I find nothing."

"What were you looking for?" JonMarc asked.

"A feeling. A sense of hostile purpose. But all is as it should be, unless..." Gwythion's brow furrowed. "There may be, at one point in the field, an *absence* of thought."

Kier tilted his head. "I don't understand."

"I'm not sure I do, either. I seemed to detect a silent place—a void that should not be. I cannot explain it."

"What might cause such a void?"

"Nothing I have ever encountered." Gwythion massaged his brow. "This is very strange. I shall have to probe it further."

The knot in Kier's belly cinched tighter. "What exactly are the Cábretaur's powers?" he asked. "I mean, besides enhancing sinistral talents. You've said it can destroy, but surely the Nwtyrrans prized it for more than that."

"Indeed," said Gwythion, "yet no one truly knows the answer. Though Aneryn's writings speak much of the element *miril*, and the greatness that was wrought with it, never does he discuss the scope of its powers or how they might be tapped. I suspect that omission was intentional, so none could wield the Cábretaur without first studying it." He loosed a troubled sigh. "The truth is, no living man even knows what *miril* looks like."

The statement only fueled Kier's exasperation. "Then how in blazes are we supposed to find the damned thing?"

"The Cábretaur is enclosed in a protective casket. Aneryn provided clues to its location in his writings: three additional verses that describe the stone's resting place and the means by which to acquire it. I transcribed them myself into JonMarc's copy of *Ygair*. Study them well."

"And if we do chance to retrieve it," said Kier, "what then? The people of the Deg Tirith still aren't prepared to deal with so deadly a responsibility. What's to be done with it?"

"As I have said, Aneryn did not know the populace would be unready. His only provision for the Cábretaur lies in his third prophecy:

> *He shall rightfully claim the Cábretaur who owns*
> *The Patience to probe its Nature,*
> *The Knowledge to train its Power,*
> *And the Wisdom to see its Peril.*
> *Beloved Son and Adept of the Faithful, He shall receive his Legacy*
> *At the Hand of the King."*

"What does he mean, *At the Hand of the King*?" JonMarc asked.

"It is too early to say. Perhaps, as Maelguin believed, Dyveth Aneryn himself will return from the Death Realm and present his legacy to its rightful heir. Yet, you need not concern yourselves with that. To find the Cábretaur: that is your task. And to keep others from laying hold of it. As is the way with prophecy, once that part is accomplished, the rest will likely come clear."

Kier took no pains to hide his skepticism. "And what then? Are we supposed to bring it here to you?"

"That will not be necessary. I shall meet you on Alcor when the time is right. Until then, tell *no one* of your purpose, especially no Fithlon or Covenant Priest. Until we know who else seeks the Amulet, we must be doubly wary. I have trained you, Kier, to recognize and block most Fithlon mind probes. You must teach JonMarc to do the same, for he will certainly need that skill. I think you will find him an apt pupil."

Excitement radiated from JonMarc's blue eyes. He actually looked forward to this accursed hare's-chase. Kier wished he'd never met the slave—or Gwythion.

"One more thing will I warn you of," his mentor said. "Once you secure the Cábretaur, do not, under *any* circumstances, attempt to use it. You may be hard beset before this is ended. Do not probe the gem or test its authenticity by trying its power. Do not even look at it, if you can avoid doing so. Above all, you must *never* remove it from its protective casket. Aneryn warns most urgently of that. Unshielded, the Cábretaur's powers are beyond anyone's strength to wield."

Somewhere beyond the firelit chamber, a deep-toned bell chimed a single, clear note: one hour past mid-day. Kier shot a look at JonMarc. It was later than he'd thought. "We need to get back," he said. "It's a long ride to the city and we've a tide to catch." As they stood to go, Kier hesitated. "Gwythion, you know more about this than anyone. Why don't you come with us?"

The candlelight deepened the creases on Gwythion's face. He looked older, more weary than Kier had ever seen him. "I cannot. Not yet. There is much still to do here. I need my instruments to calculate the precise moment of Conjunction. And I must strive to learn the identity of your rival." Gwythion tapped a finger to his brow as though fixing a thought in his mind. "I must seek audience with the Fithlon Synod, though I fear they will be loath to grant it. But you, Kier, can afford no delay. Your father's condition will not wait. I will contact you when I have news."

"But the duke is your friend. Surely you'd wish to see him once more, before..."

"Duke Morwen and I shall meet again," Gwythion assured him, "though perhaps not in this realm." He laid a reassuring hand on Kier's forearm. "As to the task ahead, Kier, do not let concern over Aneryn's prophecies constrain you. For good or ill, they will work themselves out. It is not prophecy that determines a man's destiny, but the choices he makes along his path."

Kier turned away. Fine words. Yet how could a man's destiny truly be his own when some other hand had already chalked out its course?

Chapter Nine

"*Ayeee-aah!*" JonMarc's exuberant yell sliced the afternoon stillness. It reminded Kier of a Dynian war cry. Head thrown back, the slave galloped past him, pale hair flying wild in the tepid breeze. Atop the next rise, he tugged the mare up short and waited for Kier to catch up.

The speed with which JonMarc had taken to the saddle supported Kier's suspicion that, at some time in his forgotten past, his companion must have been a credible horseman. No surprise there. JonMarc was Dynian born. Whether he knew it or not, horses were in his blood. Right now, he acted as if he hadn't a care in the world. Kier wished he could share that naïve contentment. He felt only apprehension for the journey ahead, and a growing pang of urgency.

Here in daylight, Gwythion's tale of the portentous Nwtyrran crystal seemed curiously unreal. Kier prayed his mentor was wrong about the matter, though he knew such hope was futile. Master Gwythion was never wrong. Still, he'd insisted the circumstances would unfold on their own, and Kier was determined to let them. He would not alter his plans to search for a prize he scarcely believed existed. Of greater concern was the identity of their mysterious rival. The bruises on his neck and scalp painfully attested to *that* one's existence.

Yet even that paled beside his need to see his father. Gwythion's revelation had shaken him to the core. That the man he admired above all others, whose praise he'd striven to earn all his adult life, had required prodding to rescue and acknowledge his own son? Why? Gwythion said it was fear of his lady wife's anger, but Kier could scarcely credit that. Duke Morwen never feared anything. Yet that left only the bitter alternative: his father had deemed him unworthy. Kier could think of but one reason for that. The duke blamed him for his mother's death.

Devastating or not, he had to learn the truth. And, anchored in the harbor, the small barque *The Albatross* was his only hope. She sailed with the evening tide, and her captain, a swarthy Syrmian named Pa'alaf, had warned he would not wait for stragglers. Kier measured the height of Devoreth's Orb above the western horizon, then factored in the time it would take to reach the wharves through streets a-throng with market-goers. He frowned and nudged the roan to a canter.

Up ahead, JonMarc grinned to see his pace quicken. The moment Kier reached the crest, the Dynian gave another ecstatic whoop and charged the mare on. Kier's gelding labored to catch up.

Halfway up the next rise, Kier felt the beast's gait go short and his stomach sank. He reined to a halt and dropped quickly from the saddle to inspect the left forehoof.

JonMarc came trotting back. "What's wrong?"

"Blasted shoe's hanging by a nail. No wonder he's off." With his dagger, Kier pried the mud-caked iron free, then wiped the shoe in the grass and stood to examine it. The edges were worn thin as parchment. Muttering a curse, he spat on the iron for luck, then hurled it into the adjacent field.

JonMarc shaded his eyes to follow the horseshoe's flight. It landed with a plop amid the scrub at the field's far edge. He whistled low, impressed.

Kier had already gone to check the other forehoof. That shoe looked in little better shape, but at least it felt secure. With a resigned sigh he gathered up the gelding's reins and trudged off on foot.

JonMarc reined in beside him. "You're not going to ride?"

Kier shook his head. "He's already favoring that leg. My weight would only make it worse."

"What difference does that make? The beast isn't yours."

Kier bit back a caustic retort. JonMarc's unwillingness to accept, or even comprehend, responsibility reminded him why he preferred the company of horses to that of his fellow men.

Once he determined no response was forthcoming, JonMarc, too, dismounted and hastened up beside Kier. "But what if we're late for the ship?"

Kier hunched his shoulders, unwilling to dwell on that possibility. With no further delays, they'd still make their deadline, though with less time to spare than he'd counted on. He grasped the gelding's bridle to urge him along faster. "Guess I should've expected this," he muttered, after a time. He caught JonMarc's quizzical look. "Gwythion predicted it. Didn't you hear? He said that just because he foresaw a horse would lose a shoe today didn't make him the cause of it. I thought he was only making a point."

The Dynian chuckled. "Maybe he was."

Kier allowed a grim smile. JonMarc had a lot to learn about Fithlon inscrutability. Kier had no doubt at all that his mentor had foreseen this setback—and how much more?

They reached the city gates without further incident. So focused was JonMarc on the promise of adventure ahead, he paid little heed when the gate sentry halted them. But Kier's belly knotted as the soldier scrutinized his medallion, and the fair-haired slave at his side, with what seemed more than passing interest. Yet he read no hostility in the sentry's mind, and as the man made no move to detain them, Kier kept his misgivings to himself.

They found the city predictably crowded as the market day neared its close. Dray mules lined the square, flicking dunflies with their tails. JonMarc remounted to forge a channel through the sweltering press while Kier led the roan along behind, grateful for the protection the beast afforded his flank. He could not dismiss the knowledge that someone in this city was ready to kill him for the silver amulet hidden inside his shirt.

They had left the busy square and were wending their way down an empty side street when Kier overheard a sound he'd come to dread: the swift patter of footsteps approaching from behind. His fingers closed around his sword hilt as he glanced back over his shoulder.

A slight figure swathed in a faded shawl was hastening to overtake them. A woman. Kier slowed, but the pursuer passed him by as if he'd gone invisible. "JonMarc!" she cried, breathless, as she scrambled up and tugged on the Dynian's sleeve.

JonMarc turned with a start. "Valerey! What are you doing he...?"

The tavern girl's silencing gesture cut him off. Urgently, she beckoned him into a narrow passageway between two ramshackle dwellings. JonMarc slid from his saddle and followed.

Kier took up the mare's reins and positioned himself beside the passage entrance, where he could listen and observe discreetly. He only hoped their business would be swift.

Valerey appeared on the brink of tears as she drew back her shawl. "Thank the gods I've found you, JonMarc. Soldiers came searching the *Sword* this morning. Your new master knows you mean to run."

Kier's breath escaped in a low hiss. That would explain the gate sentry's interest.

"Ruthira," JonMarc growled. "Plague take the bitch. What did Eliém tell them?"

"All he could, which wasn't much. He didn't know where you were. But he did describe your brassy friend." She acknowledged Kier with a wary nod.

Kier cursed their ill luck. The patrols must be seeking him now, as well. Yet if they were sought by the authorities, why hadn't the sentry detained them? An Alcorean officer with a tall, fair-haired slave would be difficult to mistake. The mystery troubled him as much as the news.

"I'm grateful for the warning," JonMarc said. "How'd you even find me?"

"I've been wandering the streets for hours, JonMarc! I was so afraid they'd find you and send you back to..." Valerey's strained voice finally broke. She flung work-reddened arms around JonMarc's middle and clung tight, sobbing.

JonMarc gently stroked the tapgirl's mousy hair, his expression detached. "I'll be all right," he assured her. "Correlin won't stop me."

Valerey wiped her eyes on her tattered shawl. "There's more. Eliém knows about you and Ma'ardhi—about the child. He's like a wild man. If he finds out I warned you..."

Kier winced. From what he'd seen of the churlish tavern owner, Valerey was taking an immense risk. He secretly wondered if JonMarc was worth it.

"But how did he find out?" JonMarc pressed. "Ma'ardhi swore she'd say nothing until..."

"Someone saw you together last night. When Eliém heard about it, he dragged her to the yard and beat her till she confessed."

An anguished moan escaped JonMarc. "I've got to go to her!" He tried to shove past the girl.

Valerey stood her ground. "No, JonMarc, you *can't*. Eliém will kill you." Her voice dropped. "She'll be all right. Shanya's looking after her." She touched JonMarc's sweaty cheek. "She won't lose the child."

JonMarc allowed himself to be dissuaded—a mite too easily, Kier thought. Valerey laid her forehead against his chest. "Ma'ardhi said that, if I found you, I was to bring her a lock of your hair. She wants to weave it with her own into a spell-token for the child." The tapgirl smiled a little through her tears. "So he'll grow up to be like his father."

A dim spark ignited JonMarc's pale eyes. "She thinks it will be a boy, then?"

Valerey wiped her smudged cheek with the heel of her hand. "Late last night, I took her in secret to an Osha'ana woman from Syrma. Ma'ardhi had her cast your fate in the Tsa'arat crystals. The witch saw much danger before you, yet she foretold that you would one day return to Castémaron—and find your son by the token he wears."

JonMarc appeared strangely awed. He drew the dirk from his belt and sliced off a lock of flaxen hair. Valerey clutched it to her breast as if it were a holy relic.

"Val, tell Ma'ardhi I...."

"I will." The girl raised reddened eyes to his and kissed his cheek. "Take care of yourself, JonMarc. The Lady's blessings go with you." As she drew up her shawl to leave, she turned a last, suspicious glance at Kier, who stood in shadow, rubbing the gelding's muzzle. She obviously judged him as likely as any to turn JonMarc in.

JonMarc watched the girl scurry away down the narrow street. He wiped his eyes with the heel of his hand. Kier found himself regretting his earlier doubts. Perhaps he'd judged the slave too harshly. JonMarc's feelings for the dancing girl appeared genuine enough.

"You all right?" he asked.

JonMarc nodded in silence. But when he looked up, his blue eyes sparked as bright and eager as ever. "So, what now?" he asked, as if the entire episode had never happened.

The reversal took Kier aback. Was JonMarc simply putting up a brave facade to hide his distress? If so, the act was convincing. Again, he wondered if the slave was capable of genuine concern for anyone but himself.

He set doubt aside and glanced up at the westering orblight. Little could be seen beyond the overhanging rooftops, yet he needed no shadow angle to tell him the afternoon was wearing quickly. With patrols seeking them, they'd have to proceed with caution. It scarcely mattered that they hadn't yet broken any laws. They dared not risk capture. "How much can your new master have learned of your plans?" he asked.

JonMarc shrugged. "Nothing."

"You're *sure*?"

A skewed smile. "Kier, until last night, *I* didn't know my plans."

"Well, we have get the horses back to the inn and retrieve our supplies. If the patrols are looking for *two* of us, it might be safer to split up and head to the harbor by different routes."

The alarm on JonMarc's face said that was no option. "I'll get us past any patrols," he said, exhibiting more confidence than Kier was wont to share, and instantly set off in the direction of a particularly noxious-looking side street. Kier swallowed his misgivings and followed along with the horses. He prayed JonMarc knew what he was doing. They had no time for blunders.

For the next half-hour, JonMarc led them on a circuitous route through some of the city's most derelict neighborhoods, areas that, even armed, Kier had never dared traverse. JonMarc's ease in such surroundings lent credence to his tales of his unsavory life on the streets.

"How much do you know about this Correlin?" Kier asked, as soon as their route widened enough for them to walk abreast. "You said he's wealthy. What's his occupation?"

Shoulders hunched, JonMarc pressed ahead. Kier was about to repeat the query when his companion's response wafted back on the putrid air. "I've heard he's some kind of merchant."

A merchant? What simple merchant had authority enough to call on garrison troops to track an escaped slave? "Is that all?"

Only the squelch of JonMarc's boots in the muddy ground answered him. Kier huffed. Getting the slave to divulge information was like prying nails from a tarred post.

At last there came a reluctant reply: "I think he may be—some sort of official."

Kier didn't like the sound of that. "You mean a local consul or something?"

Silence again. Then: "I heard him tell Ruthira he's—First Expositor to the Emperor."

"*First Expositor…*" Blood drained from Kier's face. They were eluding the Emperor's chief advisor? Deep in his gut, Kier felt a familiar knot cinch tight. It was barely two days since Gwythion predicted JonMarc would change his life. Could even the Fithlon Master have foreseen how much?

Whether due to luck, or JonMarc's skill at evasion, they reached the Gull's Nest without encountering any sign of pursuit. While the slave waited in shadow, Kier led the horses to the stableyard. Moments later he returned, laboring beneath two heavy bundles.

"The hostler said a small troop came by this morning, asking questions, but they never returned. They can't have learned much. I'd told no one my plans." He cast anxious eyes skyward. "Let's get to the ship."

They were relieved to find no soldiers loitering near the Harbor Gate. Yet from beneath the overhang of a wharfside tavern, they could see a sentry stationed beneath the high gate arch, meticulously checking the passes of all who exited. Kier's hopes dwindled.

"This is your last chance to back out, JonMarc," he said. "Till now, you've only accompanied me outside the city. As you were placed in my charge, that can be explained. But once you step onto the wharf, your intention to escape is clear." As was his own complicity. Should Correlin charge him with abetting, there was little Kier could argue in his own defense. His career would be ruined, and with it, any chance of seeing his father alive. But there was no backing out now. Even if Gwythion hadn't obligated him to take JonMarc to Alcor, his own promise had.

"I'm going with you." The determination in JonMarc's eyes said he was ready to face the risk.

"Then you'll need a cap or something to hide that Dynian hair."

JonMarc flashed a grin. "No problem." He dug a small coin from his belt pouch and bounded up the tavern steps.

"No, wait..!" Kier began, as JonMarc burst inside.

He emerged an instant later, flourishing a grimy fisherman's cap which he tugged over his head, unmindful of the outraged shout that followed him through the door. "I paid for it," he said.

The cap was little more than a woolen sack, so faded its true color could scarcely be guessed. JonMarc tucked the last flaxen strands underneath, then hoisted their bundles over his shoulders. Kier took the lead, maintaining a confident stride, though his entrails writhed like vipers.

As at the Westgate, the harbor sentry took peculiar interest in Kier's medallion and the tall slave standing behind him, blue eyes carefully averted. Kier held himself rock still. He'd taken pains to concoct a tale that, if needed, could explain their departure, but he doubted the sentry would believe him. Anyone assigned this post must have heard all the tricks.

The stocky sentry leafed through his small sheaf of parchments a second time, then scratched his balding scalp. "Everything appears to be in order," he said, though his puzzled expression spoke otherwise. "Safe passage to you, Captain. Devoreth's breath be at your back."

Kier returned a half-hearted salute, struggling to hide his astonishment.

"He gave up!" JonMarc whispered behind him as they hurried down the wharf. "Correlin called off the search. I *knew* Gwythion's magic would get us through."

The comment jolted Kier from his perplexity. "Fithlon powers can't manipulate events…"

JonMarc would not listen. He frolicked along, swinging their bags in a circle, while passersby eyed him as if he were moon-crazed. Kier tried to temper that exuberance until he could sight down the quay. The handful of ships making their way out of the harbor told him the tide had turned. If *The Albatross* was among them it might be days, even weeks, before another vessel put out for Alcor. By then, his father would be dead.

He hastened on, dodging heaps of tangled nets that stank of seaweed, and shaded his eyes. Near the end of the wharf, a small barque bobbed at her berth, yellow sails still furled. She rode low in the water, fully loaded and ready to depart, her prow brightly painted with the protective eyes of the goddess Denia. "They waited!" he mouthed, hardly daring to speak their luck aloud. JonMarc favored him with an *I told you so* look.

The dockside air hung heavy with the pungent aroma of Kharan hemp. JonMarc halted at the gangplank's base, allowing Kier to mount first. The slave mercifully wiped the idiot's-grin off his face before ascending. "Wait here," Kier said. "I'll tell the captain we've arrived."

JonMarc shook his head. "My job." He started toward the stern.

An eruption of fiery argument halted him. It rose from below deck, growing so loud even the scurrying crewmen paused to exchange uneasy glances.

"Obey orders or you're off my ship!" The strident voice bore a thick Syrmian accent. A door slammed and a wiry seaman with sun-bronzed skin, his graying hair tied back in a short queue, stomped across the deck, cursing under his breath. Kier allowed time for the heat of the altercation to dissipate, then gave JonMarc a nod. The slave disappeared down the stair.

He returned a short time later to join Kier at the rail. "Captain Pa'alaf's invited you to dine with him," he said, looking unusually somber.

"What's wrong?"

JonMarc's sigh was lost on the breeze. "Nothing, I guess. It's just… the way the captain looked at me—like I was a prize capon. It reminded me of…"

He broke off abruptly at the clomp of heavy boots ascending the stair. A swarthy seaman appeared, broad-shouldered, with a paunch like a bloated jellyfish protruding over his frayed rope belt. His curling black hair gleamed from oil and lack of washing. His gaze instantly fixed on Kier and he swaggered to the rail. "Name's Balik," he said, extending his beefy hand in an amiable way. "First Mate of *The Albatross*."

Kier nodded and returned the gesture. "Captain Kier Fitzmorwen, Alcorean Royal Legion."

Balik grinned, displaying teeth stained deep ocher from years of chewing ko'oqwa nuts. His fleshy fist tightened around Kier's fingers like winch cable.

Fire shot through Kier's hand and his lips hardened. It seemed he was forever encountering churls like Balik, who viewed anyone of rank as a potential rival over whom they must prove their authority. Kier focused his will on his straining hand.

Balik's grin abruptly faded. Sweat beads popped across his brow. With a snort, he pulled his hand away, darting an embarrassed glance about him. Satisfied that none of the crew had witnessed his discomfiture, he drew up his chin and squinted hard into Kier's amethyst eyes.

"Ne'er seen glims o' that hue afore," he scorned, cuffing Kier sharply on the shoulder. "Who's yer sire—some barbarian Skelding?" He threw his head back, roaring amusement at his own joke.

Kier pictured landing a withering blow beneath the big seaman's stubbled chin. But this wasn't the time. "My father is a duke," he replied pleasantly, but with an edge of tempered steel. "Who, pray, is yours?"

Balik hesitated to answer, unsure whether he'd been insulted or not. He drew himself up and spat a viscous glob of ko'oqwa that landed a hair's breadth from Kier's boot. He then turned and swaggered off, shouting orders to the crew to cast off.

JonMarc melted up beside Kier, blue eyes agleam. "Nicely played. Served the fat oaf right."

Kier leaned against the rail, basking in appreciation that was worth a few aching fingers.

The Albatross's saffron sails bellied with the wind, and the dusk-shadowed city receded. Above the western hills, Devoreth's Orb floated low, casting silver daggers across the waves. Sentries, now no more than tiny specks, marched in silence along the garrison walls, no longer a threat. Despite his worries, their escape had gone flawlessly. Kier was almost tempted to accept JonMarc's assertion of Fithlon magic. He knew he should feel elated, yet his apprehensions remained.

JonMarc had hauled their baggage to an out-of-the-way corner of the deck and returned to offer a promptive nudge. "The captain's expecting you."

Kier wrenched his mind from his concerns. "On my way," he sighed, and headed below.

Chapter Ten

Kier mounted the short stair from the captain's cabin and paused, clinging to the rail until his flaccid legs adjusted to the rocking deck. Behind him, the heavy door thudded shut, followed by a bolt's sharp clack. Formalities ended, Captain Pa'alaf wanted privacy. So did he.

A brisk wind snapped the canvas above his head and hummed a dissonant elegy through *The Albatross's* high rigging. Kier forced his legs up the last steps and squinted into the gloom. "JonMarc?" he called. The wind blew the name back in his face.

He made out JonMarc's lanky form hastening toward him. "Here, master."

Kier frowned. Now that they'd left Vilsolian soil, he saw no reason to continue the charade of forced servitude. While JonMarc had agreed to attend him until the passage money was repaid, never again would he be a slave.

JonMarc draped Kier's cloak about his shoulders and ushered him to their appropriated corner of the deck. Kier settled himself beside a tack chest while JonMarc sat cross-legged beside him.

"How was your dinner with the captain?"

"Cordial," said Kier. "That Pa'alaf's a cagey one. The evening felt like one long verbal joust." Kier rubbed the back of his neck. "He sets a good table, though. His Kirosian wine's the best I've tasted in years." Indeed, either Kier had drunk more of it than he'd intended, or the wine had been especially potent. He leaned a shoulder against the rail to steady himself as the ship rolled with the waves. "Anything happen while I was gone?"

"Naught to speak of. The helmsman, Jarl, invited me to share mess with the crew, and we got to swapping tales. Seems Pa'alaf and Balik have quite a reputation around the docksides for underhanded dealings—smuggling and the like."

"I'm not surprised. He pretends gentility, but he struck me as a pirate at heart. Still, he captains a good ship. Honest or no, he must be doing well for himself."

JonMarc drew close. "Jarl says Pa'alaf's only captained *The Albatross* a few months. The crew's already fed up. They've been jumping ship at every port. Even Jarl plans to leave, once we reach Alcor. He was first mate till Pa'alaf took over and brought Balik aboard."

Kier watched whitecaps dance across the sea's moon-shimmered surface. "I don't much care who commands, so long as he gets us safely to Alcor." He sniffed the air. "Weather's moving in. I wonder if they'll anchor for the night. There are sheltered coves all along this coast." Kier waved his hand vaguely to port, though no lights showed to indicate the shoreline.

JonMarc was busy hauling Kier's bedroll and his own threadbare blanket from their packs and did not see. "I can barter you hammock space below, if you like," he said. "The stench down there could nobble an ox, but if you want to be out of the weather..."

Kier shook his head. Whenever possible, he preferred to spend his shipboard time on deck, breathing clean air. He'd never been much of a sailor, but as most of the Deg Tirith was only accessible by water, sea travel became a necessity. At times he even enjoyed it—once he got past his initial queasiness. Right now, any smell rank enough to earn comment from JonMarc was certainly more than his tentative stomach could handle. Clutching his cloak about him, he shoved the worn bedroll into the corner and sat on it to pad the numbing deck planks. Beside him, JonMarc curled up contentedly in his blanket cocoon. A moment later he was snoring.

Kier sighed, envious. Between the meal and the choppy seas, he anticipated little rest tonight. To take his mind off his discomfort, he leaned back and let his eyes wander the heavens, idly seeking familiar patterns among the scatter of cold sparks.

Overhead, the *Life Star's* white brilliance winked down at him. She was by far the brightest object in the night sky save the two moons, now muted by cloud. Gwythion once told him the star had brightened over the years; that when worshiped by the ancient Nwtyrrans, she was merely a speck, visible only on the darkest nights. To Kier's memory, she had always been the same: the all-seeing eye of the goddess Denia, whose clear glow on the horizon heralded the season of Renewal. Tonight her presence seemed cold—almost alien—associated as it was with the Cábretaur and Aneryn's prophesied conjunction.

Uneasiness tugged at Kier's mind and he scowled at the stars, now giving them his full attention. Either his reckoning was completely wine-befuddled, or the *Life Tree* constellation's double trident was pointing the wrong way. He raised up on one elbow and scanned the skies for the *Eagle's Eye,* the pole star, that should hang above the prow if they followed the route Pa'alaf had traced for him. He finally found it, winking between the clouds above the port stern. So the ship wasn't heading north at all, but south.

But why round the island's southern point? It took them leagues out of their way. And the waters of the rocky Maveta Straits were especially treacherous in choppy seas. Only one sizeable port lay along this route, and it was known mostly for...

Kier's blood iced. He prodded his companion's shoulder. "JonMarc!"

The Dynian sat up, rubbing his eyes.

"Have we been sailing south all evening?"

JonMarc just stared at him, struggling to throw off the fuzzy mantle of dream. "Ah... I guess so. Hadn't thought about it. Why?"

Kier cursed under his breath. "Because Pa'alaf told me we'd be rounding the *northern* point."

It took a moment for his words to sink in. "He changed the course? But, why?" Kier watched comprehension slowly work across JonMarc's moon-washed face. "This route will take us past..."

Kier returned a sober nod. "The Death Quarries."

JonMarc looked stricken. "Then Correlin *didn't* give up. He must've bribed Pa'alaf to deliver me to the quarries." His fists clenched. "And I fell for it like a prize chub. Blazes, I'm *nothing* to Correlin. He's scarcely noticed me. Why would he go to such trouble to have me recaptured?"

Kier suspected Correlin noticed far more than JonMarc gave him credit for. Gruesome images assailed him. "We've got to turn this ship. I visited those quarries once, years ago. You can't imagine what it's like, JonMarc. Chains and blood; starved corpses heaped like firewood, to rot in the sun. The stench! I've seen my share of death in battle, but—" The memory proved too much for Kier's queasy stomach. Choking back bile, he clawed for the rail.

"I'm sorry," he gasped, once the spasms subsided. He wiped his clammy face on a rag JonMarc provided, feeling drained; mortified. "Must've been... all that wine."

JonMarc nodded, allowing him that excuse. "I've no need to *imagine* the quarries, Kier," he said, his voice barely audible. "I lost three years of my life there."

Kier raised his eyes, recalling Elrin's words the night JonMarc's master was killed. "Because you murdered a man?"

JonMarc chuckled bitterly. "You don't miss much, brassy." He shut his eyes a moment, as if struggling with his own memories. "I was to be freed," he said. "My master wrote it in his will. He was the garrison swordmaster when I was locked up for thievery. I was fourteen. By some bizarre chance, he took pity on me; paid my bondage fee; welcomed me into his home. For five years he was like a father to me, Kier—the only man I ever knew who cared about my fate.

"But when he died, a noble's son—" JonMarc spat the words. "A swaggering piss-whelp the same age as me—he claimed my master owed him money; some gambling debt. To settle it, he seized all my master's belongings, including the papers that would have freed me. When I panicked and tried to run, he flogged me like a hound." JonMarc sighed, gingerly fingering the white scar beside his eye. "This was the last blow he ever struck."

Kier regarded his companion with new insight. "How did you kill him?"

A chill breeze feathered JonMarc's hair. He flexed his fingers. "They say I strangled him. I don't remember it—only his dead eyes staring at me as they carried him away."

"So they condemned you to the quarries. But how did you survive there—for *three years*?"

JonMarc eyed him dubiously, as though appraising his condition. He shook his head. "You don't want to know that. You wouldn't understand. No one would, unless they'd been there."

"I have. I told you…"

"You were never *enslaved* there." JonMarc's pale eyes took on a hollow cast. "The moment you arrive they set you to work, hauling rock from the cliffs—from orb-rise till it's too dark to see, day upon day without rest. And all the while, the guards stand by with whips and clubs to make sure you don't falter. At night, you sleep where you drop. And if you're sick or injured, they throw you on the dead heap—alive—for the carrion eaters to rip apart. Life's worthless there. More wretches are always arriving to fill the needs."

JonMarc cradled his head on his forearm. A quaver edged his words.

"After a while, you forget you're a man. You become some mindless, plodding creature with no thoughts, no hopes. Death is everywhere, Kier. You train yourself not to see it—not to smell or taste it, in the water; the food. Gods, the food. I don't know what they fed us. When you're starving, you don't ask."

JonMarc turned to the open sea. His voice carried back on the wind. "They say hardship brings out the humanity in men." A caustic laugh. "It's a lie. I've seen men bludgeoned to death for a moldy crust. The dead become *things*. The dead heap is where you find rags to cover your heat-blistered back—if you can get there quick enough—and shelter from the winter gales, because rotting flesh is warm." He jerked his eyes back to Kier. "Does that disgust you?"

Kier evaded his gaze. "I— I only wonder that men can learn to live like that."

JonMarc gave a vacant shrug. "A lot can't. Most die within weeks. But if we were reduced to beasts, the guards—they're something worse. You get to know who they are, the ones who enjoy their work. You try to stay clear of them. Once I learned the routine, I saw there was only one way to survive. I sold myself to the guards—as often as I could—for food, for clothing; just to stay alive another day." JonMarc chuckled softly to himself. It had an eerie sound.

Kier felt a chill and shifted uneasily, wondering what other dread secrets lurked beneath JonMarc's impudent guise. "So what happened?" he prompted, after a lengthy silence. "How did you escape?"

JonMarc looked back with a start, as if he'd forgotten Kier was there. "I didn't. I was released. I'd been servicing a guard who'd taken a liking to me—an ignorant lout, but not as bad as some. To keep me around longer, he had me assigned to do facing work, dressing the stone for shipment. Prisoners there are better used. They work in an area that's usually shown to stone merchants and visitors like yourself—those who don't want to see any more than they have to."

Kier ignored the swipe.

"One day, part of the cliff face gave way. While scrambling to save my own hide, I shoved a visiting merchant out of its path. In gratitude, he bought me to be his body slave. And these last few years I served him faithfully—till he was mistaken for you, the other night, and murdered."

Bitter intensity charged JonMarc's words. "I won't go back there, Kier. This time they'll have to kill me." He turned and strode to the opposite rail.

Kier scrambled after him.

JonMarc shielded his eyes from the salt spray. The glow of the coastal cliffs shone faintly through the deepening mist. "We can't be more than a league from shore. I can swim that far."

Kier shook his head. "I've sailed these waters. The currents will drag you under, if the man-eaters don't get you first. Even if you make it to shore, how long can you hide out in Vilsolia before you're recognized? You don't exactly blend in, you know."

"I'll chance it. I won't give Correlin the satisfaction of knowing he's won." JonMarc clapped Kier on the shoulder and his voice softened. "But thanks. For everything. More than I deserved. Tell Master Gwythion..." JonMarc sighed. With a deep breath to work up his courage, he swung his leg over the rail.

"No, wait!" Much as Kier wanted JonMarc out of his life, this wasn't how he wished it to end. "How much coin do you have?"

"Not enough to bribe Pa'alaf, if that's what you're thinking."

"How much?"

JonMarc hesitated. Having committed himself to action, he seemed reluctant to let it go. Finally, he clambered back and reached into his belt pouch. He drew out the last of Ruthira's baubles. "They're mostly paste. My lady mistress has the taste of a three-sull whore."

Kier added the contents of his own purse and weighed the result. "It might work."

JonMarc rolled his eyes. "Come on, Kier. Pa'alaf's no fool. He knows Correlin's the one with the money. At best, he'll accept our bribe, then deliver me to the quarries anyway."

"Maybe so. But we've got to try something."

"*Why*?" Suspicion swelled in JonMarc's voice. "I can't fathom you, Kier. Why risk so much to help me? The blood debt's repaid. Blazes, I had to gull you into taking me along." JonMarc threw up his hands, genuinely bewildered. "Is it because of Master Gwythion? Or have you found some advantage to keeping me in your debt?"

Kier tried to formulate an answer, but none would satisfy someone like JonMarc, who weighed every act on the balance of self-interest. "Believe what you like." He turned for Pa'alaf's cabin.

JonMarc seized his arm. "Wait! Don't throw your money away. Maybe we can come up with a better plan."

The scheme they concocted was iffy, at best. Still, it was a course of action, and right now, any action seemed preferable to the alternative. "Simply stopping Pa'alaf won't be enough," Kier pointed out. "If we're to take control of the ship, we've got to constrain Balik as well."

JonMarc rubbed his palms together against the wind's deepening chill. "Then I need to let Jarl in on our scheme. He's the only other one who can captain her."

Kier frowned. "Can you trust him? We're talking mutiny, here—punishable by hanging."

"Not if the plan works. So long as Jarl leaves matters to us, no one'll get hurt. We'll just keep Pa'alaf and Balik locked up till we reach Alcor. As far as they'll know, we forced Jarl to follow our orders as the price of keeping them alive. That's hardly mutiny."

"You think he'll go for it?"

JonMarc shrugged. "I can ask. If he says no—well, there's still the rail."

Kier liked the wiry helmsman instantly. Jarl was of middle years, tough and sinewy, with a face as creased and weathered as a parched canvas sail. Kier recognized him as the man who'd stalked from the captain's cabin when they first came aboard.

Jarl seethed when told of Pa'alaf's treachery. "Aye," he growled, "there was a course change ordered just as you two were sighted on the quay. Pa'alaf spoke of off-loading goods at the quarries. I told him 'tis madness to ply the Maveta straits in squall season, but he'd not listen. With these winds, we'll reach the first pillars in less than an hour. I daren't take her about 'til I know the captain an' Balik are—restrained."

Kier eyed the lowering clouds. "Then we'd best be quick. Will the crew cause trouble?"

Jarl scratched his stubbled chin. "There's some as'd follow me into a maelstrom if I led 'em. But a few came on later; I canna answer for 'em. An' there's been talk—fears at havin' a spoil-hand aboard." He bobbed his head toward JonMarc. "Still, you may count on my help."

JonMarc clapped the helmsman's muscled arm. "Thanks. And don't forget: send Balik to us in half an hour. No sooner." Jarl nodded and hurried off to take his shift at the wheel.

"Are you sure you can do this, JonMarc?" Kier asked. "You're not a street brat anymore."

JonMarc flashed him a feral grin. His spirits had risen considerably, now that they had a plan of action. "I can do it. I used to earn fair kit crawling in through the chimney-holes of the highborn, and those openings were narrower than Pa'alaf's porthole." He stripped to a breechclout and slung a coil of rope over his shoulder. "Just keep Pa'alaf's attention. Do whatever you have to; just don't let him turn around." He clamped his worn dirk in his teeth and headed for the stern.

Kier swiftly descended to Pa'alaf's cabin. He took a breath to calm himself, then set his fist to the door. "Captain! Captain Pa'alaf." He pounded louder. "Open up, I have to speak with you."

"Go away," came a muffled voice. "Don't you know the hour? I'll talk in the morning."

"You'll talk *now*. I know we're headed for the Death Quarries. I want this ship turned back." Kier jingled the purse. "I can make it advantageous to both of us."

"Pah. You've nothing I want."

"What harm to look?" Silence. Kier held his breath, his heart thudding like a dirge drum. At last he heard footsteps; the snick of a bolt. The timber door squealed open a crack and Pa'alaf's tawny face peered out. Shrewd black eyes drilled into him. Kier jingled the purse to show its weight. The greedy face retreated and the door opened to admit him.

Pa'alaf was fully dressed and his bunk looked undisturbed. On a table near the center of the small cabin, a lantern gave off a feeble orange glow. The musty air smelled of smoke and fish oil. Pa'alaf nodded him to a seat. Kier purposely chose one that faced the small porthole in the stern. It placed his back to the door, a position that made him feel uncomfortably vulnerable.

The stubby sea captain slipped into the chair opposite, twirling his finger through ringlets of oiled black hair. "You are observant, Captain," he said. "I did not expect you to discover my little ruse till orbrise found us in Maveta harbor." The Syrmian tossed his hand. "No matter. Show me what you bargain with. But first, lay your sword on the table." He shrugged in a friendly way. "To show good faith."

Kier's innards writhed. He hated giving Pa'alaf the advantage, but he had to keep up the charade. Reluctantly, he drew his sword and laid it between them. Pa'alaf shoved it out of reach.

"Now, empty the purse." Pa'alaf inspected its contents and his fleshy lips curled in scorn. "You expect to bribe me with *this*? This wouldn't satisfy a camel driver." He tossed a string of gaudy beads onto the table, scattering the coins. "Go back to your slave. Tell him he will spend the last of his short life in the stone pits." Pa'alaf pushed back from the table.

"Wait!" Kier hastened. "I've another item." He'd hoped it wouldn't come to this, but at all costs he must hold Pa'alaf's attention. "It is a treasure such as you've never beheld—a rare prize from the hoard of an ancient kingdom." Kier reached inside his jerkin for the Amulet.

Pa'alaf's entire demeanor changed. He snatched up the silver hand and held it to the lamplight, leering hungrily at the gem-encrusted gold around the wrist. "It is indeed from a king's hoard," he agreed, fondling the trinket in a way Kier found obscene.

"Do you want it? It's yours, if you turn the ship about and take us to Alcor."

"I want it. But Lord Correlin offers more—a pouch of silver and ownership of this vessel."

"Ownership?" Kier paled. "You mean...*he* owns it?"

Pa'alaf grinned slyly. "Ironic, yes? You buy passage on a ship belonging to the very man you try to steal from." With a quick move, Pa'alaf snatched a jeweled dagger from his belt and motioned Kier to his feet. "Lord Correlin will have his slave. And the sale of your trinket will make me a wealthy man."

Pa'alaf slid around the table's edge, forcing Kier against the wall. Kier submitted to the indignity, but it galled him.

The ship creaked with the rising waves. A waft of fresh, sea air fluttered the lantern. Pa'alaf was too preoccupied to notice. He braced his free hand on a chair back and raised his blade to Kier's throat. "You, Captain, will simply vanish into the sea. No one will ever—"

"*I wouldn't count on that.*" Bare feet plopped down on the plank floor behind him.

Pa'alaf's dark eyes narrowed and he started to turn. There was a quiet *thwop*, and JonMarc's dirk pinned his sleeve to the chair. "That could as easily have been your back," the Dynian snarled.

Kier seized his chance. He rammed his boot heel into the captain's kneecap. Pa'alaf yelped in pain and stumbled backward, taking the chair with him. Kier grabbed his flailing knife arm and cracked his wrist against the table's edge. Squealing like a lanced boar, Pa'alaf let the blade drop. Kier curled fingers through the pudgy man's collar and shoved him into JonMarc's waiting arms.

The Dynian flung his captive into a chair like a sack of beans. Fielding the dirk Kier slid to him across the table, he wrenched its edge against the throbbing vein at the dazed sea captain's neck. "Nice work," he said, grinning.

"It was all I could do to keep from watching you back there." Kier fingered his nicked throat. "You certainly took your time about it." He strode to the open porthole and sliced off a portion of the rope JonMarc had used to lower himself over the rail. He tossed it to JonMarc, who set about binding Pa'alaf's limbs. "You know, I saw it the whole thing and I still can't believe you squeezed yourself through there."

"Talent," JonMarc murmured, the dirk in his teeth.

Pa'alaf wriggled against his bonds and tried to cry out. JonMarc struck him a savage backhand. "One whimper," he seethed, "and I'll slice you into shreds so small even the man-eaters won't find them." He ripped the sleeve from Pa'alaf's linen shirt and wadded it into the Syrmian's mouth. Pa'alaf's beady eyes goggled.

Kier scooped his belongings off the table and reverently tucked the silver Amulet back inside his shirt, praying Gwythion would never learn of the risk he'd taken.

He heard the clomp of heavy boots on the outer stair. "That'll be Balik," he said, "right on schedule." He motioned JonMarc to the shadows. "I'll take this one."

The Albatross's first mate hammered on the door, grumbling resentment at his captain's late-night summons. Pa'alaf flashed a sidelong glance at JonMarc and tried to cry a warning. His voice carried no volume through the linen wadding. Kier reached out and shot the bolt.

The ox-like Balik thrust the door wide. His jaw dropped at the sight of his captain, bound securely to a chair in the center of the room. He ducked inside and took two lumbering steps before his sluggish mind reasoned that someone else must have let him in. He wheeled about.

His fleshy jowl met with a right cross that carried all Kier's resentment behind it.

Balik stood firm, blinking owl-like several times. Then his eyes glazed over and he toppled to the floor like a felled oak. Kier cradled his aching knuckles.

"Enjoyed that, did you?" said JonMarc, already busy binding Balik's wrists.

Kier nodded. "Look, I'll finish here. You go above and tell Jarl to take the ship about."

By the time Kier came on deck, the drizzle had dwindled to a thick mist. He spotted Jarl and JonMarc conversing at the helm, above a halo of lantern light. JonMarc nodded soberly.

"Jarl thinks we should stay put," he said, as Kier climbed up to them.

"Aye," said Jarl. "We've already entered the Maveta passage. Y'can see the beacons ahead. But the fog's closin' fast. If we try t'sail round the point, or e'en come about, we'll risk runnin' up on the rocks afore we see 'em. I say we lay anchor mid-harbor and wait till the fog lifts."

Kier wiped damp hair from his brow. "You're captain now, Jarl. We'll rely on your judgment. I don't relish entering Maveta Harbor for *any* reason, but if you feel it's our safest course, I'll go along. What do you say, JonMarc?"

JonMarc gave a tense nod and quickly turned away.

By mid-morning the rain had ended, though the harbor remained blanketed in billowing gray. JonMarc stood on deck, oblivious to the chill, gazing bleakly at the fog-bound coast. Kier watched him from across the deck. JonMarc had stood there, silent and staring, since before dawn. Whenever a light breeze veered from the west, he would wince and turn his face from the stench of death and decay. Kier sensed his anguish. He, too, was eager to be quit of the place.

It was nearly noon when the clouds began to lift. JonMarc looked up hopefully as Jarl came on deck to assess conditions. Even as he searched the horizon, a seaman stationed on the mainmast gave a yell. "Vessel a'starboard."

Kier followed the sailor's arm. The shrouded hull of a small galley broke from the fog, turning to come abreast of them. Still at anchor, her sails furled, there was no way *The Albatross* could elude their visitor. Troubled, Kier went to join JonMarc.

The Dynian never took his eyes off the craft as it swiftly closed the distance between them. His fingers suddenly whitened around the rail. "What's wrong?" Kier asked.

JonMarc stared a moment longer, a dead look in his eyes. "It's Correlin."

"What, *here*?" Kier studied the boat's nine occupants. The rowers were likely soldiers, for they seemed uncomfortable managing a sea craft. Kier picked the portly man in the center for Correlin. A brawnier figure sat behind him. Kier stiffened. "He's brought Sergeant Elrin."

JonMarc barely acknowledged.

"So, he planned to rendezvous with Pa'alaf himself." Kier blew a tense exhale. "I see no choice but to let him board, JonMarc. He's the Emperor's chief advisor. We can't drive him off without a fight, and that'll put Jarl and the crew at risk, should they ever return to Vilsolia. We've landed them in enough peril already."

JonMarc said nothing.

"At least we control the ship. That gives us some leverage." That control, Kier knew, ultimately depended on where the crew chose to place its loyalties. With the popular Jarl in command, he'd seen no need to establish his own authority. But who would they support now that Correlin had shown up? Kier saw trepidation in JonMarc's eyes and laid a reassuring hand on his shoulder. "We'll get out of this. Remember, Aneryn foresaw us on Alcor."

"He saw *you*," JonMarc replied.

The galley scraped *The Albatross's* tarred hull as it drew alongside. A crewman threw down a boarding ladder. Jarl looked to Kier, his dark eyes troubled. He knew the gentleman in the vessel below was the owner of the ship he'd mutinied to take.

Elrin easily mounted the rope ladder, followed by six of his men. The wily sergeant's lip curled in triumph when he spotted JonMarc, but he did not speak.

Correlin emerged last. He clambered on deck, pale and wheezing, but quickly recovered his lordly demeanor. Despite the weather, and what must have been a hellish ride the twenty-odd leagues from Castémaron, he was fastidiously attired in a surcoat of wine-colored brocade, as if en route to an Imperial ball. He brushed himself off with an air of authority, thin lips compressed in a gloating smile. He completely ignored JonMarc.

"Where is Captain Pa'alaf?" he demanded, dabbing his brow with a silken cloth. "Why did he not dock, as arranged? I nearly froze to death in that leaky tub."

Kier whispered to a seaman, one of Jarl's trusted men, and sent him running. Then he stepped forward, hands resting casually on his hips. "Captain Pa'alaf has met with some unexpected entanglements. I'm afraid you'll have to deal with me."

Correlin's brows narrowed. "Who...?" Elrin murmured in his ear. "Ah, of course, the brave Alcorean officer of whom I learned so much at the garrison. My congratulations, Captain. It seems I underestimated your intelligence." Correlin looked up as Pa'alaf and Balik were half-led, half-carried onto the deck, still bound and gagged. His countenance darkened. "Clearly, I over-estimated theirs." He halted the soldier Elrin had dispatched to untie the pair. "Leave them so. Let them stew awhile in their incompetence."

Pa'alaf glared and struggled. Correlin turned back to Kier and, for the first time, deigned to acknowledge JonMarc, standing rigid behind him. "So, you two now control my ship. And myself too, you are thinking." Correlin's voice bore a note of secret delight.

"I don't want you or your ship, Correlin," JonMarc said hoarsely. "I only wish to return to my homeland in peace."

"Is that all?" The merchant sneered. "Have you forgotten that you belong to me?"

"I belong to *no one*. We're no longer on Vilsolian soil. You've no claim to me."

"Have I not? Your memory is short, JonMarc. Let me refresh it. You are responsible for my brother's murder. You were his bodyguard and failed to protect him. For that alone, your life is forfeit. And now, by attempting escape, you try to steal from me a valuable piece of property."

"Valuable? You've already spent more than I'm worth just to recapture me!"

"Quite right. By sparing no expense in your pursuit, I discourage others with similar intent." Correlin waved a be-ringed hand. "As for my ship, those who aided you in this mutiny will join you in the quarries." He signaled Elrin. "Shackle him."

Kier drew his sword. "I don't think you quite understand your position, Correlin. *I* control this ship, and I alone am responsible for your so-called mutiny." A steely glance warned Jarl's protest to silence. "I suggest you depart with your men before anyone gets hurt. You have my word that the vessel and all its cargo will be returned to you, once we reach Alcor."

Correlin's face twisted in contempt. "Your *word*? What is that worth? The slave JonMarc was released to your charge, yet you stole him from me. *He* is the cargo I am after."

A shiver lanced through Kier. For an instant he sensed something in Correlin: raw; terrifying—the barest glimpse into a raging cauldron of emotion.

Correlin strode past him. "Let us see what control you really have." He addressed the gathered crew. "By Vilsolian law, each of you is guilty of mutiny, whether you took part in the deed or not. I am prepared to carry out the death sentence immediately." He gestured for a rope. "To follow this officer is to admit your guilt. Who will be first to hang for him?"

There was some uneasy shuffling as the crewmen grumbled amongst themselves.

"'Tis all the fault of that 'cursed spoil-hand," muttered one, to general agreement. "I'll not take the drop for one of 'is kind."

"Nor will I," chimed another. The rest muttered grudging concurrence.

"As I thought." Correlin sneered. "You see, captain? These men owe you no allegiance. You control *nothing*."

Kier's eyes hardened on the ragged line of seamen. He'd gambled that their loyalty to Jarl would color their allegiance. Yet in the face of certain death, how could he fault them for placing their own safety first? This was never their fight.

Elrin flicked his hand and four soldiers quickly encircled Kier, weapons drawn. "Disarm him," Correlin ordered. "Kill him if he resists."

Kier glanced about. He might yet battle free, but it would cost him. There was no escape, and his death would hardly help JonMarc. He felt the pressure of a blade at the small of his back. Better to wait; see what transpired. With a snort, he let his sword drop. One of Elrin's men kicked it aside.

"Be assured, Captain," said Correlin, "I have the Emperor's ear. When his allies on the Alcorean Council are informed of your actions, your future will be ruined." He flapped his arms to warm himself as a rising wind keened among the halyards. *The Albatross's* weathered timbers groaned. "Let us finish this accursed business and get back to shore." He pointed to Jarl. "That one is a ringleader; he comes with us. And now, JonMarc..."

JonMarc had drawn his dirk and was backing along the rail, desperation in his eyes.

"Don't be a fool," Correlin snarled. "You cannot escape."

"Then I'll die in the sea." JonMarc swung his leg over the rail.

"And what of your little dancing girl?"

The slave froze. "What do you mean?"

"I understand congratulations are in order, JonMarc. You are to be a father."

Horror crept across JonMarc's face. "What will you do? Buy her?"

"Buy?" Correlin scoffed. "That ale-bellied oaf of an innkeeper will *give* her to me." A gloating smile. "She'll make me a fine concubine, don't you think? Is she lusty in bed, JonMarc? Does she make a slave feel like a man?"

JonMarc groaned like a gored bull.

"And when I tire of her, I shall donate her services to the garrison, where you know they will be well appreciated. The child, of course, will be destroyed."

JonMarc gave a strangled cry. Kier struggled to reach him, but his captors held him fast.

"And if I come with you, Correlin—what then?"

"Then I will leave the girl at *The Dragon Sword*, unharmed."

JonMarc breathed hard and licked his lips as he balanced on the rail. Kier could see he was battling with himself. "What of the others: Jarl, and the crew? You'll let them go?"

"Of course. It is you I want, not them."

JonMarc seemed to be weighing his alternatives. Kier spotted movement. Elrin had circled around the row of crewmen and now crept up on the slave from behind.

"JonMarc, look ou—!" Kier cried. One of his captors jabbed him with a sword pommel.

Elrin sprang. Before JonMarc could leap one way or the other, the sergeant dragged him from his perch and hurled him to the deck. JonMarc tried to grapple to his feet. Elrin kicked him in the ribs—again, and yet again. JonMarc writhed and hugged his side, yet each time he tried to rise, a savage thrust of Elrin's boot flattened him to his face.

Kier's fists clenched with rage. Beside him, some of the crew began to fidget uneasily.

"Enough," Correlin said at last, casually slipping off his leather gloves. "Get him up."

Elrin seized JonMarc's collar and hauled him upright. The Dynian no longer resisted. His expression was utterly desolate.

Correlin rubbed his milk white hands together, relishing his victory. He had Elrin drag JonMarc to the center of the deck. "Strip him," he ordered. "Let everyone see him for the miserable vermin he is."

"Blast it, Correlin," Kier seethed, "you don't have to humiliate him as well."

Elrin and a second soldier tore away JonMarc's clothes. They shackled him hand and foot, and turned him, naked, to display his scarred back to the crew. The Dynian stood, battered and bleeding, hugging his right side. The charmstone on its tattered cord dangled against his chest. Elrin yanked it free and hurled it across the deck.

Kier overheard a crewman mutter angrily under his breath, and his hopes rose. Correlin's attempts at intimidation seemed instead to be eliciting sympathy for JonMarc.

A strange gleam appeared in Correlin's eye, and Kier sensed again the primal emotion he'd detected earlier—a hatred so intense it made his flesh crawl.

"*That* was for the years you forced your filthy attentions on the Lady Ruthira."

JonMarc's brows narrowed in confusion. "Forced?"

Correlin smacked his glove across JonMarc's face. "Do not talk back to me, slave. You think she hasn't told me what's been going on? For years, you've used your accursed spoil-hand powers to compel the lady to your will, and my fool of a brother did naught to stop you. But *I* have. You'll never debauch her again. She belongs to *me!*"

JonMarc seemed scarcely to comprehend Correlin's words. But Kier saw the wild look distorting the merchant's face and recognized it for the madness it was. With a subtle flick of his wrist, he let his hidden dagger slide into his palm.

"Get him to the boat," Correlin snapped. "The helmsman too. And pick four crewmen to accompany them. Let their fates stand as a lesson to the rest."

JonMarc's head flew up. "But you promised they'd go free!"

Correlin laughed, a curdling sound. "What promise? These mutineers will die in the stone pits, like yourself."

JonMarc's body trembled. "What... about Ma'ardhi?"

Spital whitened the corners of Correlin's mouth. "Your little whore? She will join you in the quarries. Such a pretty creature will be well received, don't you think?"

Something inside JonMarc snapped—like a stout tree limb that endured the weight of one snowflake too many. Rage kindled his eyes. With an anguished shriek, he shoved Sergeant Elrin off balance and lunged for the grinning merchant. He locked his hands around Correlin's throat.

Elrin recovered and raised his sword. Kier saw his chance. He stabbed free of his astonished guards and charged, bowling the sergeant belly-first into the rail. He hammered Elrin's fist against the stout oak until the sword dropped into the sea. Then he lifted the brawny sergeant by his belt and the scruff of his neck and heaved him after it.

He was vaguely aware of shouting and howls of glee as Jarl and the crew turned on their captors. Soldiers hit the waves, some discovering too late that they could not swim. Kier shoved the dagger in his belt and clamped his hands around JonMarc's wrists, trying to tear them from Correlin's pasty throat. "JonMarc," he cried, "you're not a murderer. Let him go!"

The frenzied grip would not loosen.

Correlin's arms flailed behind him like a stuffed doll's. Tiny gurgling sounds issued from his throat. His suet face was already going blue. JonMarc burrowed his thumbs deeper into the merchant's windpipe.

Kier thrust himself between the pair. "I'm sorry, JonMarc," he whispered, and rammed his knee into the slave's groin. With a groan, JonMarc broke his hold.

Correlin gasped and wheezed. "I'll have...that slave's cods..."

He never completed the thought. With a whoop of victory, Captain Pa'alaf snapped his bonds. He hurled his own secret dagger right at JonMarc's exposed back.

It found a different mark as JonMarc doubled over.

Correlin gave a garbled scream and sank to his knees, his pierced throat spurting hot crimson onto the rain-slicked deck and down the front of his elegant surcoat. Bulging eyes staring disbelief, he toppled face-first into the darkening pool.

PART II: THE HEIR OF EVORICK

Chapter Eleven

Level shafts of dawn the color of freshly spilt blood broke through a cleft in the distant hills and skittered across a coppered sea. Kier yawned and shaded his eyes. Beneath fair skies, last evening, they'd traversed the rocky Maveta passage and by sundown, rounded Vilsolia's southern point. Now, foam churning at her prow, *The Albatross* fleeted northward, soon to turn for open sea.

A keen wind flapped Kier's cloak. Salt spray stung his nostrils. He breathed it in to help him stay awake as he reflected on the events of the past three days. For someone prophesied to change his life, JonMarc had certainly made a good start.

Someone touched his arm. Kier spun, fingers instinctively flying to his sword hilt. The pock-scarred cabin boy shrank back. Kier smiled by way of apology and nodded for him to speak.

"Your servant's awake and asking for you, sir."

Kier clapped the lad's shoulder and hurried below.

He found JonMarc lounging in the captain's bunk—nearly a foot too short for him. One sinewy leg was crooked against the footboard, the other sprawled over the edge, a frayed blanket strategically draped between, like a garland on a painted nymph. The lantern had gone out, but the open port hole channeled a shaft of morning orblight into the cabin, and a fresh breeze to clear out the sour stench of sweat. Kier dragged up a chair and straddled it backwards, rubbing a palm across his stubbled cheek. "How do you feel?" he asked.

"Alive. Guess that's a start." JonMarc cocked his head. "What happened up there?"

"You don't remember?"

"Not the end. The cabin boy told me Correlin's dead. He said *Pa'alaf* killed him."

"It's true. I don't know which of you he was aiming at. Maybe he didn't either. They took him ashore, charged with murder. Balik went too. No one's sorry to see them go." Kier worked the sore muscles at the back of his neck. "It took some *persuasion*, but you're in the clear—for now. The Emperor may see it differently. I suggest you stay well away from Vilsolia for a while. I split Pa'alaf's silver among Jarl and the crew, to compensate for what we put them through."

"What happened to Elrin?"

"No one saw him surface." Kier's eyes drooped. He never enjoyed causing a man's death.

JonMarc clearly felt no such remorse. His fingers crept to the charmstone Kier had re-strung about his neck while he slept. "Maybe Ma'ardhi was right and this thing really does protect my life."

Kier chuckled. "Maybe so." It seemed JonMarc's murderous fury had left no obvious after-effects. Its internal toll was another issue. Kier had sat beside him most of the night, often struggling to shield his own mind from the fiery horror of the Dynian's nightmares.

JonMarc shifted position on the cramped bunk and winced. Kier reddened. "Look, I'm sorry about... I saw no other way to stop you killing him."

The Dynian's features hardened. "You should have let me finish it."

"That would only have made things worse."

"*Worse*? How? At least I'd have bought myself a quick death. If not for Pa'alaf's lucky blunder, I'd be lying bloodied in some cess pit out there while Correlin gloated over his victory."

Kier drew an uneasy breath. "Believe me, JonMarc, I wouldn't have let him take you."

A mirthless laugh. "What, did you think you could talk him out of it? You saw him, Kier. He was crazy as a..." The words died on his lips. He stared into Kier's face. "Ghedrev's blood," he murmured, "you'd have killed him yourself!"

Kier turned away. Was it truly what he'd meant? A day ago he'd have scoffed at the very notion. Yet the rage, the loathing he'd felt for Correlin in those final moments had cut a trough to the black chasm beneath his soul; a heinous place he dared not delve too deeply. Kier rubbed his brow, unwilling to try the matter further. Some things were best left unexplored.

Thankfully, JonMarc let the issue pass. "You look completely frayed out," he said. "Where are my clothes? I'm going topside for some food. Why don't you stay here; get some sleep." He winked. "I promise to wake you once we reach Alcor."

The rest of the journey passed without incident. The weather held, a blissful procession of sun-caressed days and cool, starry nights, lulled ever by the rhythmic swell of the waves.

JonMarc spent most of his time curled in a corner of the deck, practicing the mind exercises Gwythion had charged Kier to teach him, or laboring line by line through the Fithlon sacred text. Kier often stood nearby, leaning thoughtfully against the rail. Now that his stomach had settled, he felt he could sail forever these foaming seas, eyes ever to a clear horizon. He dreaded the day that knife-edged boundary of sea and sky would be broken by the dark hills of his homeland.

There was a change in the air as they entered northern waters: a cool dampness that carried the brisk scent of snows, abiding still in Alcor's western ranges. On their tenth day out, as rainy mists again began to close, a lookout atop the mast eagerly shouted the sighting of land.

JonMarc scrambled to the rail to peer at the dark smudge of coastline ahead. Kier moved up beside him as *The Albatross* broke through a fog bank and entered the dark harbor waters. A shudder passed through him, and it was not from cold. "Welcome home," said JonMarc.

Kier said nothing, but his face was stone.

The darkening sky threatened rain as they took their leave of Jarl and the crew. Kier's first duty was to report to the Legion commander, an obligation he was eager to discharge. After ten days at sea, he was desperate for news of his father.

As they left the quayside, a pair of pale eyes observed their movements. A hooded form crept from its bale-strewn lair and, flitting from shadow to shadow, it followed them.

§

JonMarc surveyed his new surroundings with interest as he struggled to match Kier's determined stride up the steep Serpentine Way that led, with many the twist and turn its name implied, to the upper city. He found his first glimpse of Alcor's capital disappointing. Compared to the worldly bustle of Castémaron, Menythgar seemed no more than an overgrown fishing port, shabby and grey, with rows of slate-roofed houses stair-stepping down to the harbor. Even on this, the start of the three-day Renewal festival, the limply-garlanded streets looked less than festive. There was more mist in the air than merriment. A small troupe of tumblers, resplendent in soggy motley and drooping feathers, hurried by, muttering to themselves. Most revelers had carried their merrymaking indoors, to one of the city's many taverns. JonMarc was eager to join them—it seemed months since he'd visited an alehouse—but Kier's dogged pace never faltered.

Up ahead, a jagged black wall ringed the city's heights. To JonMarc, it looked out of place, like an iron crown gracing the head of a fishmonger. "The Citadel," Kier explained. "The Tiernai built it fifty years ago, once they'd conquered the city and killed Alcor's High King. The Dynian were never fortress-builders. The invaders caught them completely unprepared."

JonMarc noted many passersby with fair features like his own shaded beneath drab woolen hoods. They hurried past, eyes averted, stepping into the gutter to grant the narrow walkway to Kier, with his dark Tiernai hair and officer's stride. JonMarc, they regarded with wariness, returning his cheery greetings with tense nods, if they responded at all. "Then why do Dynian still live here?" he asked. "I thought the races were at war."

"They are. But a lot of Dynian make their living in Menythgar, and so, must submit to Tiernai rule. The real opposition lies to the west, where the Branwyns—the Dynian warrior clan—have their base. I'm told there've been skirmishes, but no actual battles since Ceorl's Ford, five years ago. Both sides lost leaders there: the Tiernai Crown Prince, Eduard, and the Dynian war chieftain, Jerrod Branwyn. Since then, relations have been quiet, but strained."

They were nearing the hillcrest. JonMarc dug out a small treasure he'd picked up on *The Albatross's* deck: Correlin's leather gloves. He'd cut off the fingers to leave his own unencumbered. The rest would hide his serpent brand. Throughout the Deg Tirith, it was illegal to disguise such a mark, and discovery might cost him dear. But the chance to start his new life free of the constraints that marred his past seemed well worth the risk.

Passing beneath an imposing victory arch, they entered the wide, walled plaza before the Citadel gates. "Wait for me here," Kier said. "This shouldn't take long." He flashed his medallion at the Tiernai sentry within. The dark-eyed soldier opened the gate for him, but warned JonMarc off with a daunting glare.

An hour later, JonMarc still sat waiting. He'd removed from Kier's pack his companion's warmest cloak, black leather lined with the white fur of snow hare—too elegant a garment for a soldier, but not for the son of a lord. Snug beneath its folds, JonMarc drew up his feet on the stone bench and hugged the thick bulge inside his tunic where the precious Fithlon book lay wrapped in oilskin. He dared not expose it to the damp, though in truth, he'd never found reading a pleasurable pastime. It seemed the harder he concentrated, the more the letters on a page gamboled before his eyes, whirling and switching partners like dancers at a wintertide masque. Instead, he chose to occupy himself by observing the plaza's intermittent passersby.

The square had clearly been the focus of earlier festivities. The paving stones lay strewn with food scraps and trodden spring blossoms. The remaining vendors were packing up their wares, content to try their luck on the morrow. All but one.

Across the plaza stood a young girl—at least, JonMarc presumed it was a girl. Her face and figure were hidden beneath a hooded cloak that exposed only waif-like eyes and the hem of a tattered skirt. She displayed upon a pole an array of ribbon garlands for sale, though no one was in the market for such frivolity on this murky afternoon. Now and again, she would steal a glance in JonMarc's direction, and he flattered himself to think she might be watching him. Yet whenever he tried to snare her eye, she quickly returned to the pointless rearranging of her wares.

JonMarc set his attention to other things, but his eyes always found their way back, only to see hers swiftly turn away. This interplay went on for some time before JonMarc hit upon a plan. True, Kier's instruction during the voyage had aimed at blocking thoughts, not sending them, but what if the skill worked in reverse? JonMarc shut his eyes and concentrated on touching the girl's mind.

He lost all track of time, but when he opened them again, a figure stood at his elbow and a soft, slightly husky voice spoke beside his ear. "Art thou ill, m'lord?"

JonMarc's head shot up. He found himself gazing into a pair of huge, sea-green eyes. "No," he replied, a little rattled, "I'm—fine." Ghedrev's cods, it had worked!

"I greatly wonder why a Dynian lord takes his ease outside the Tiernai Citadel?"

The girl appeared no more than eighteen, fair complexioned, with a wealth of reddish curls that peeked out from beneath her shabby hood.

"I'm no lord," JonMarc assured her. It must be the costly cloak that gave that impression. "I'm just waiting for my friend."

"A Dynian has been admitted to the Citadel?" The girl sounded incredulous.

"He's only half-Dynian—and a Legion officer."

"Ahh," she said, apparently satisfied with his response.

"And what of you? Why do you stand here in the cold, peddling garlands that no one buys?"

The girl shrugged and shyly took the seat JonMarc offered beside him. She regarded him curiously. "Your accent is strange. Are you not of Alcor?"

"I'm from Castémaron. I just arrived today."

"Then—will you now make your home here in Menythgar?"

JonMarc smiled. She sounded hopeful. "No, I'm afraid we'll be riding out tomorrow." And pity it was, too, if this were a sample of what the city had to offer. He sidled closer and slipped his arm around the girl's waist.

"If you wish, I could show you the sights of Menythgar," she said. "When do you and your friend ride north...?" She caught herself. To cover her blunder, she boldly laid her hand on JonMarc's thigh. As a result, when his muscles tensed, they did so for several reasons at once.

"I never said we were riding *north*. How did you...?"

The strident blare of a hunting horn cut him short. From beyond the plaza came a loud baying of hounds and the clatter of horses cantering up the Serpentine toward the Citadel.

The girl's eyes widened in panic. She tried to pull away but JonMarc seized her wrist. The object of her terror conveyed nothing to him, and his question wanted answering.

"Tell me, girl! How did you know we were riding north?"

"It was—just a guess," she cried unconvincingly, and battered him with her fists. "Please, let me go. 'Tis the Connails' horn call. If they..."

A dozen hunting hounds sped into the square, racing before their masters. They broke like a flood tide as they dashed for the gates, yammering in expectation of their warm kennel. Their leader veered off when he scented JonMarc and the girl. Hackles bristling, he charged the stone bench. The rest of the pack followed.

The girl screamed when she saw them turn. JonMarc leaped to his feet on the bench, hauling her up beside him. In seconds they were surrounded by a roiling sea of fur and snarling fangs.

Three of the hounds tore at the girl's cloak, dragging her off balance.

She shrieked and groped for the wall. JonMarc seized her arm and shoved her behind him. His dirk sheared through the taut fabric. Two hounds plummeted backward. JonMarc's blade plunged through the skull of the third. With an awful howl, it fell back amid its companions.

JonMarc wiped the bloody dirk on his thigh. The weapon wasn't enough. He seized the garland pole and cracked it across his knee, strewing sprays of color over the seething mass. Before he could position his makeshift spear, another hound leaped high, raking his arm with its fangs. The staff lit hard across its muzzle and sent it yelping back. JonMarc skewered another through the neck. Once more, blood spurted over slavering tongues and bright, crimson eyes.

The fur-lined cloak was rent and bloodied. JonMarc's right arm throbbed where yellowed teeth had sunk into his flesh. He stole a swift glance toward the center of the plaza where three horseman sat watching—Tiernai horsemen. Each wore a silver falcon emblazoned on his surcoat. One of them held a hunting horn, but did not blow. Their laughter told why: they were enjoying the spectacle. JonMarc growled and booted another beast that tried to clamp its jaws about his ankle. Some of the milling hounds had discovered the blood of their wounded packmates and seemed uncertain what to do. JonMarc knew their indecision wouldn't last.

Suddenly, above the yammering, a male voice called out—not loud, but cold as frosted steel. "Liam, call off the hounds." A horn blast brought the pack to heel. The surviving hounds gathered about their keeper and obediently followed him through the gates. "And you—" The speaker addressed his remaining henchmen— "Put those creatures out of their misery." He glanced first at JonMarc and the girl, huddled on their narrow perch, then at the wounded beasts yelping on the pavement before them. His men set their crossbows and shot. The yelping ceased.

"Now." The speaker's measured tones built to a crescendo of rage. "Tell me how this quarry of yours warrants the lives of five—*five*—of the finest hunting hounds in all of Alcor."

The three henchmen exchanged uneasy glances. "He's a Branwyn spy, m'lord," said one. "Obviously, he awaits a chance to pass unnoticed through the gates..."

"I am no spy." JonMarc leaped from the bench, eyes ablaze.

There were five horsemen in all: the three retainers, and the two newly arrived in the plaza. It was the taller of the newcomers who had spoken. He appeared about JonMarc's age, with a neatly trimmed beard, and black hair that hung to his velveted shoulders; a strikingly handsome young man—or would have been, had a broken nose not marred his sharp Tiernai features. There was an air of hauteur in the way he sat his spirited ebony stallion. The other was a youth of about fourteen, slight of build and downy-cheeked, whose dark eyes mirrored his companion's arrogance.

"Your dogs' attack was unprovoked." JonMarc cried. The girl tugged his arm, urging him to leave while he could. He gestured for her to go, too furious to take the prudent course himself.

The henchmen glared. "M'lord Aric," one said, "what matter if he be spy or no? Surely you'd not deny us a little sport? After all, what's one Dynian the less?"

"Your *sport*, Gart, has cost me five of my best hounds. No Dynian is worth that, be he accursed Ross o' Branwyn himself."

"But how could we know he was armed?" said the largest of the three, a burly man with a thick black mane and beard. "It's unlawful for his race to bear weapons. An' your hounds are trained to attack Dynian. We did not think..."

"Aye, that is your trouble, Modron; you do not *think*. Do you imagine you're still in the wildwood, tracking witless peasants?" He turned his restless mount. "But enough. Let us see what game my hounds have procured for us. The wench appeared passing fair, don't you agree, cousin?" His young companion nodded eagerly. "Bring them here."

Two henchmen dismounted to intercept JonMarc, who was already striding toward them. The other cantered off after the girl. Her cry startled JonMarc, for he had hoped her safely away. Yet he found himself cut off from aiding her. The henchman deposited her on the ground, none too gently, just as the others closed on JonMarc. He required no escort. He stalked up to the one called Aric with murder in his eyes.

"So," said Aric, "this is the Dynian who thinks naught of destroying a prize hunting pack."

"Had your creatures not attacked, they would still live," JonMarc replied evenly. "I hold my life above that of a hound."

Aric looked down his broken nose at him. "Well, *I* do not. Tell me, churl, have you not learned the imprudence of talking back to your betters?"

Contempt spread across JonMarc's blood-spattered face. "I'll tell you when I meet one."

Aric Connail went livid. "This Dynian whoreson needs a lesson in manners. Disarm him."

Hands clamped like iron around JonMarc's upper arms, and his dirk was wrested from his belt. JonMarc lodged a powerful elbow thrust into the belly of the one called Gart and the henchman doubled over with a grunt. He halted Modron's answering blow with a sharp, side-handed chop. The huge man leaped back, seizing his wrist.

"Fools!" Aric bellowed. "Hold him."

JonMarc crouched, ready. Yet he froze when he heard the girl scream. Her captor held a dagger to her breast. "Yield, or the wench dies."

JonMarc's spirits fell. Grudgingly, he dropped his arms and allowed himself to be taken.

Aric's face broke into a triumphant sneer. "Excellent. Now, perhaps you can show this traitor-spawn what happens to the Dynian worm who dares think himself equal to the Tiernai stag."

The liegemen's eyes lit with enthusiasm at this chance to redeem themselves. Gart pinned JonMarc's elbows behind him while the surly Modron grinned and kneaded his knuckles.

JonMarc planted his feet. A ham-sized fist plunged into his belly. He managed to stifle a groan, thankful for once that he hadn't eaten since early morn. Gart jerked him upright by the collar as Modron's follow-up smashed into his cheek. JonMarc turned his head with the blow, to ease the impact. The pain that surged was accompanied by a frantic cry he knew could not be his own. He raised his eyes with effort, tasting blood.

The girl had struggled free of her captor. She fell to her knees before Aric. "Please, m'lord Connail. He is new to the city and does not know who you are. I beg you, let him go."

"If he does not know, he must be taught." Aric's tone sounded gentler than before, yet his smile remained cold. "Come, stand before me, wench. What do they call you?"

"Rowenna, m'lord," she replied.

"Remove your cloak. I would see you better." With trembling fingers, Rowenna unfastened the brooch at her throat and let the ragged garment drop. Aric nudged his young companion. "Aye now, Tuán, is that not a prize for any man's bed?"

"For many men's beds, lord," said Gart. "She's a trollop from the Dynian tavern, *The Jackal and Hounds*."

The statement surprised JonMarc. Most of the women he'd ever known were whores—admitted or not. This girl possessed an innocence that didn't fit the mold.

Aric's face hardened. "So, wench, you would give yourself to Dynian and Tiernai alike?" Rowenna flushed and lowered her eyes. "What shall we do with her, Tuán? She's as handsome a creature as I've seen in this accursed city; and she has spirit. Yet I doubt my lady wife would care to lie three in a bed tonight. Will you have her?"

Tuán's brown eyes nearly popped from their sockets. He leaned forward eagerly. "I would know better what I'm getting." He stole an uncertain look at his cousin, who shrugged as if to say "go ahead."

The henchmen exchanged ravenous glances. JonMarc rolled his eyes, foreseeing the inevitable. He began to formulate a plan.

"Come here, wench," Tuán commanded. His voice broke and one of the henchmen snickered. The youth glared at him.

At a nod from Aric, Rowenna's captor slid his knife through her bodice laces and tore the garments from her shoulders. She stood straight, biting her lip, her body flushed despite the cold. Tuán leered at her bare breasts. A pendant glittered between them. He pointed. "What is that?"

The henchman reached for it, managing a grope as he snapped the chain. "A harp emblem—sigil of the Dynian traitor, Gerit Mawr." He tossed the locket on the ground and stomped it with his heel. Rowenna cried out and tried to go after it. Her captor held her wrist. "So, you're one of his rabble, are you, little one?" he laughed, and kicked the pendant out of reach.

"Well, cousin?" said Aric. "What say you now?"

Tuán's jaw trembled. "I—I would see the rest of her."

Rowenna moaned as the manservant again went for her gown. He moved slowly, prolonging the moment.

JonMarc seized his chance. While all eyes were riveted on the girl, he wrenched free of Gart's slackened grasp and charged into Modron, bowling the giant onto his back. The liegeman's shaggy head hit the cobbles with a thud. Gart lunged at him. JonMarc executed a well-planned somersault and landed in a crouch beside Rowenna's fallen cloak. Eyes trained on the company, his nimble fingers found what they sought and he tossed the ragged garment aside.

No one moved. None of Aric's men could guess JonMarc's intent. Aric was having trouble calming his skittish stallion. Beside him, Tuán seethed at the interruption.

JonMarc straightened. He made a feint toward the girl—the gesture he knew they would expect. The swarthy liegeman behind her raised his weapon. JonMarc leaped in the opposite direction and stabbed the brooch pin into the rump of Tuán's mount.

The horse reared, catching its rider by surprise. JonMarc dragged the youth from his saddle and yanked him to his feet. Wrenching Tuán's arm tightly up behind, JonMarc pulled a knife from his own shirtsleeve and pressed it to the youth's lower vertebrae. "Now we can talk," he said, his smoldering eyes fixed on Aric. Young Tuán trembled and stained his breeches.

"Imbeciles!" cried Aric. "I ordered him disarmed."

"But, my lord, he *was*," Gart protested.

"Aye, lord. I have his blade right..." Modron reached to his belt and found it empty.

"Here." JonMarc jerked the weapon so that Tuán screeched in terror. Modron's thick fingers fumbled the sign against evil.

JonMarc disarmed the youth, sliding Tuán's jeweled poniard into his own belt. "You." He addressed the third manservant. "Stand clear of the girl. The rest of you, move away."

The liegemen hesitated. "Do it!" Tuán shrieked. Aric nodded sullenly, and the three retreated. Rowenna instantly caught up her gown and held it about her.

"Go, quickly," JonMarc ordered.

Rowenna started to depart, but halted, frantically searching the ground for her lost pendant.

"Leave it!"

The girl flashed him a desperate look, then turned and ran from the plaza.

"You'll not get away with this, Dynian," said Aric. "Harm the lad, and you die—in agony."

"I'll take that chance. How will you bargain for his life?"

"Aric!" the youth whimpered.

"Oh, have done," said Aric with disgust. "I gave you credit for manhood. By the gods, Tuán, even *she* had greater courage." He turned to JonMarc. "All right, Dynian, we will bargain. I'll send my men within as soon as you release the lad. We'll then each go our own way. But I warn you, look to your life should e'er we meet again. What say you?"

JonMarc didn't like the odds—not at all. But he could expect none better. He couldn't stand here holding Tuán until reinforcements from the

Citadel overwhelmed him. "What promise will you make that I can trust?"

"I swear to you on my honor as a lord, heir to the Earldom of Ruthland."

JonMarc laughed bitterly. "I'd sooner take your word as a bully and coward, for I *know* you're that." He chewed his lip. He'd known few Tiernai but Kier and Jarl, and they both honored their word. It was little to go on, but his position was shaky at best. "All right," he said. "Take him." He shoved Tuán toward his waiting horse.

The youth slipped on the slick cobbles and foundered headlong. Gart rushed to help him up. Tuán elbowed him aside and limped on, crestfallen, swiping miserably at a bloodied nose.

JonMarc fingered his dirk and backed quickly across the darkening square toward the entry arch.

Aric waited until his cousin was within reach of the Citadel gates. Then he gathered his men about him. With eyes of searing vengeance, he cocked his head toward JonMarc and quietly issued a command:

"*Kill him.*"

Chapter Twelve

JonMarc was halfway to the plaza arch when he saw Aric's men
fan out in pursuit. His fingers tightened around the dirk and he cursed
bitterly, though the Connail lord's betrayal surprised him far less than the
realization that he could still trust enough to feel betrayed. One of the
henchmen jumped onto his horse and dug in his spurs. An icicle of fear
lanced up JonMarc's spine. He scrambled backward a few more paces, then
turned and ran.

Freezing drizzle had started again. JonMarc heard hoofbeats clattering
up behind him and leaped aside. He caught a potent whiff of horseflesh
and wet leather as the beast charged past. JonMarc skidded to a halt and
doubled back. Aric's henchman reined the horse around—too fast. With a
grunt, the animal lost its footing on the slick cobbles and went down. The
rider's skull hit the pavement with an audible crack. The horse clumsily
heaved to its feet, leaving its rider on the ground, unmoving. JonMarc
didn't stay to watch; he turned and raced for the plaza's single exit.

Aric reached it first. The Tiernai lord pranced his stallion before the
arch, a self-satisfied smirk creasing his distorted face. No escape that way.
JonMarc halted several yards away and swiped icy droplets from his cheek.
"So this is the worth of your sworn word, Connail?"

Aric regarded him with consummate contempt. "Dynian scum. Did
you truly think I'd bargain with one of your accursed race? This land would
be well rid of the lot of you—and soon *shall* be. Think on that as you die,
Branwyn swine."

JonMarc spared a quick glance about him. Gart and Modron were
advancing swiftly. The rest of the plaza was deserted. If anyone watched,
it was from the safety of the Citadel walls. JonMarc sucked in his cheeks.
Early dusk was falling fast.

The henchmen separated as they approached. He'd have to engage them singly or be butchered where he stood. He drew Tuán's poniard from his belt. Grasping his dirk in the other hand, he edged toward Gart, the stockier of the pair. "Hop it up, lard arse," he yelled, hoping to rile the man to independent action. "You think I've got all night?"

With an outraged shout, the liegeman charged. JonMarc ducked his flailing knife and drove his dirk into the man's side. The point pierced Gart's jerkin. It halted at a rib. Gart turned, snorting like an angry boar. He seized the front of JonMarc's tunic and tried to disembowel him with his hunting knife. JonMarc parried low, deflecting the stroke. He thrust his boot into the liegeman's shin. Gart plummeted backward, ripping JonMarc's tunic as he fell. The charmstone on its frayed cord batted JonMarc in the nose as he, too, slipped on the slushy cobbles and landed on his rump.

Gart lunged, long knife streaking for JonMarc's chest. Panicked, JonMarc scuttled sideways. He managed to raise the dirk just as Gart pounced. The point pierced the liegeman's thick riding breeches and sank deep in his groin. With a shriek, Gart tore himself free, ripping the blood-slimed dirk from JonMarc's left hand. He staggered drunkenly, then collapsed.

JonMarc had barely regained his feet when Modron rammed him from behind, hurling him against the wall. The impact took his breath. Modron seized JonMarc's right hand and wrenched it up behind him, nearly popping his shoulder from its socket. Pain screamed through his arm and the poniard dropped. JonMarc flung his head backward, catching the liegeman square in the nose. With an astonished grunt, Modron loosened his hold. JonMarc jerked free and spun around.

Modron was not so easily undone. The giant slammed his weight against JonMarc's chest, flattening him against the wall like a squashed spider. JonMarc tried to move, but the liegeman's greasy head pressed his face so hard he could scarcely breathe. He felt the point of Modron's dagger against his ribs. It punctured his leather tunic; the woolen shirt underneath. JonMarc gasped and strained to shove the huge man off. It was like fighting a crushing boulder. The steel point burrowed deeper, piercing the sacred Fithlon book. It wormed through the ancient pages and pricked JonMarc's skin above his heart. JonMarc shut his eyes, bracing for the pain.

From out of nowhere, a flash of brilliant white seared his eyelids while a raucous screech nearly burst his ears. Modron's weight vanished. JonMarc's eyes flew open. Through a shimmering glare he saw Modron, now backed well away, clawing at a crystal stud in his earlobe. The liegeman stared at him wild-eyed. "Conjuror!" he cried, fumbling the protective sign of Devoreth's Eye. Ears still ringing, JonMarc could only goggle.

The piercing light faded, and with a start JonMarc realized it centered at his chest. The charmstone. But how...? No time to ponder. JonMarc bowled past the stunned Modron and scrambled into the square.

Aric Connail blocked his path. JonMarc doubted the Tiernai lord would stoop to fight him, but that wouldn't stop Aric from preventing his escape. JonMarc's legs wobbled like jelly. His chest heaved—raw, aching. He saw Modron stalking toward him, hatred submerging fear in the liegeman's eyes. JonMarc clenched his fists. He had no weapons; no retreat. But blast it, they wouldn't kill him easily. He'd take that half-wit liegeman with him. He braced for the final assault.

"*Connail.*"

JonMarc's heart leaped. Never had he been so relieved to hear a familiar voice.

Kier dashed toward them, eyes ablaze. He slowed to a determined stride as he neared. "Call your man to heel."

Modron slowed his advance, uncertain. For a moment his smoldering gaze locked on JonMarc's. At last, Aric waved the liegeman off.

"Well met, Fitzmorwen," the Connail lord said. His face betrayed purest loathing. "I'd not heard you'd returned. Be not perturbed. Our quarry is a Dynian firebrand, but we have quenched his flame."

Kier spied JonMarc's exhausted form and purpled. "Get you gone, Connail, or by the gods, I'll see you in irons."

Aric spat. "Dynian lover. You've always sided with your own traitorous breed. This Branwyn broke the law. 'Tis death for his race to bear weapons."

"I see no weapon," Kier said.

Aric's stallion pranced nervously. "I own the right of revenge. The Dynian whoreson downed two of my liegemen."

"Only two?" said Kier. "Then be thankful you brought no more."

Seething, Aric went for his sword. Kier drew his own—quicker. His unyielding gaze skewered Aric like a javelin. "Are you sure you want to fight me, Connail? You may recall the last time…"

Aric's free hand rose as if to touch his marred face. Instead, it balled into a fist. With a snarl, he rammed the weapon back in its sheath. "Not here," he said. "Not now. But payment *will* come, Fitzmorwen. You'll feel my blade soon enough." He reined his stallion for the Citadel gates.

Suddenly, Modron's knife flashed. JonMarc caught the movement through the corner of one eye and instinctively dodged the crucial inches. The blade scored his left shoulder. Choking back a cry, JonMarc dropped to his knees, tears of frustration stinging his eyes.

He was dimly aware of Modron's retreating laughter. Then Kier knelt beside him. Cautious fingers probed the wound. "You'll live," the brassy said. "The blade bit bone, and thank the gods, your bones are as thick as your Dynian head." The levity was forced. JonMarc heard strain in his companion's voice.

Kier ripped the sleeve of JonMarc's mangled shirt to stanch the bleeding. His lips compressed. "I warned you how dangerous it is here for Dynian. And it'll only get worse as we head north."

JonMarc tossed it off. Despite the altercation, he had no regrets about coming to Alcor. "That's... two I owe you," he said. "I never guessed you had such authority over lords."

Kier loosed a snort. "Aric's no lord. His father and uncle rule the provinces of Ruthland, but Aric holds no fief. His only power lies in his sword and his treacherous tongue."

"How'd you know he wouldn't fight you?"

"Aric only fights when he's confident he holds all the advantages." Kier finished tying the makeshift bandage and wiped his palms on his thighs.

JonMarc flexed his fingers. "So, what took you so long?"

"Sir Donal's aide kept me waiting nearly two hours, then bade me return tomorrow." Kier got to his feet. "At least I learned my father's still alive. You wait here while I fetch our packs. There's a decent inn nearby where we can have that wound seen to. Then you can fill me in on what happened with the Connails. It's plain this wasn't the first stroke to find you tonight."

By evening, JonMarc sat in relative comfort on the floor of the cramped chamber they would share with six other lodgers. Due to the festival, accommodations were scarce throughout the city. The Tiernai innkeeper, noting Kier's rank, at first offered his last private room. Then he spotted Kier's amethyst eyes, his Dynian companion, and remembered the room was already promised. They settled instead for two bedrolls' worth of space in the garret. JonMarc didn't mind. He had plans for his one night in Menythgar, and no mere shoulder scratch was going to stop him. But for the tightness of the bandage, he felt very much himself. Still, it took some wheedling before Kier finally agreed to accompany him to the place the Connail minion had mentioned: a tavern called *The Jackal and Hounds*. In light of the day's events, JonMarc found the name oddly apropos.

Kier accepted the lamentable condition of his best cloak with scarcely a comment. For that, JonMarc was grateful. Kier paid the landlord's young daughter to patch the more conspicuous rents, then presented it to JonMarc as a gift, granting him what he jestingly termed *squatter's rights*. It made no difference to JonMarc that the cloak would never again look new. It was still the finest garment he'd ever owned.

The chill evening air felt exhilarating after the inn's stuffy attic. They had just rounded the first bend of the Serpentine when the stillness was broken by the measured tread of marching boots. JonMarc stiffened and drew up his hood to hide his pale hair, fearful Aric might have used his influence to dispatch soldiers after them. Kier seemed to share his concern, for his hand crept to his sword as he motioned JonMarc to the shadows.

The troop of six came abreast of them and halted. The leader seized a torch from one of his men. "I seek Captain Fitzmorwen," he said, thrusting the light close.

"You've found him." Kier's tension melted. "Gaelin! What are you doing here in Menythgar?"

Gaelin removed his helmet, freeing a tousle of dark curls. JonMarc studied him warily. He looked scarcely out of his teens, a slender youth with the dark eyes and typically angular features of the Tiernai. "I just rode in two days ago," the young officer said, aiming a curious gaze at JonMarc. Kier indicated it was safe to continue. Gaelin lowered his voice. "With the threat of renewed war, Sir Donal's called all auxiliary forces back to duty."

Kier acknowledged grimly. "So you think it will actually come to that?"

"I do fear it, Captain. Tension's already rife. And with Duke Morwen's death imminent..." Gaelin flinched. "I'm sorry, Kier, I didn't mean..." Kier nodded him on. "Well, with the duke gone, and your brother in his council seat, the Connails will have the support they need to beseige the Branwyn base at Dorcalon." Gaelin's voice dropped to a near-whisper. "Aric's here in the city, lording it over the Dynian, as is his wont."

"Aye, we've met him," said Kier.

"His uncle, Covenant Penitarch Tor, is with him, and his cousins Niall and Tuán. I'm told they spend considerable time with young Prince Rhynion, though that's no surprise. Rumor says the prince is soon to be named Regent."

"How is Rhynion?" Kier asked. "I've not seen him since his father was killed."

Gaelin shook his head. "Not well. I've heard he had a fever last week and spent five days abed. He's better now, but when I saw him at Renewal rites this noon, he looked frail. And the old king is shut away in his chamber. They say his wits have left him. He never recovered from his son, Prince Eduard's, death. Being nigh eighty, none expect he'll last much longer."

"And that will leave a power void."

"Aye, with the Connails intent on filling it. They only await the Council vote, in three weeks. And your half-brother Malcolm has joined their ranks."

JonMarc did his best to keep track of all the new names, filing them away for future reference. The more he remembered, the better he'd likely fare in this alien land.

"What of the Branwyn rebels?" Kier asked. "Do they too seek war?"

"In all fairness, the Branwyns have striven to maintain the peace, though they've been sorely provoked. Last year, the Connails pushed the *Black Laws* through Council, forbidding Dynian to bear arms or even speak their own tongue. That's prompted huge unrest. And lately, the Connails have renewed their raids on the borders—burning villages; murdering Dynian at whim. Penitarch Tor and his Covenanters treat it as a holy crusade."

Kier's eyes smoldered. "They would."

"The new Branwyn war-chieftain, Ross, is said to be a canny leader. He won't endure such provocation for long."

"Aye," said Kier, "I met him as a boy. We competed at tournament. Even then, he had the makings of a stalwart captain." Kier's eyes dropped to the brass medallion on Gaelin's chest and he smiled. "And what of you? You've made centuriant, I see."

Pride shone in Gaelin's dark eyes. "Aye, thanks to you. I don't know what you wrote Sir Donal about me, but after three years as your aide, he decided I was ready for command."

Kier clapped him fondly on the shoulder. "You are. Now tell me, why were you seeking me? We're on our way to *The Jackal and Hounds* for a pint. Will you join us?"

"*The Jackal...?* But—that's a Dynian tavern."

"Aye." Kier nodded toward JonMarc. "My companion is Dynian."

Gaelin eyed JonMarc up and down. "So it's true. I heard you kept a Dynian servant." The young officer looked troubled. "If I may counsel you, Captain, be careful. You've been long away. Feelings run especially strong in the city these days. As for the pint, I regret I cannot join you, though I doubt I'd be welcome at *The Jackal and Hounds*. I'm sent to escort you to the Citadel."

"But I just left there an hour past. Sir Donal's adjutant told me to return in the morning."

"Aye, and for that he'll be mucking the Legion stables for a week. Sir Donal's been awaiting your return. He wants to see you *now*."

Kier sighed. "JonMarc, I'm afraid we'll have to postpone that pint. Maybe you'd best wait for me back at the inn. After what happened this afternoon..."

JonMarc dismissed his concern. He wasn't about to waste his only night in Menythgar moldering in a stuffy garret. He had a nose for finding taverns, and what he hoped to accomplish there might actually go better without Kier's company. "Don't worry," he said. "I'll be fine."

Kier looked uncertain. "Don't forget, we leave the city at dawn tomorrow..."

JonMarc waved assurance and ambled off into the gloom.

Muggy night had settled on the city. The diffuse glow of Devoreth's red moon lent the fog a coppery sheen and made the wet cobbles glisten like ripples in a molten stream. JonMarc jaunted down the slope toward the lower city. The streets were all but deserted, most gallivants having found their way to some snug haven, out of the weather. JonMarc passed one such oasis, a boisterous alehouse called *The Silver Stag*. It bore an air of disrepute not unlike *The Dragon Sword*, an allure JonMarc found almost irresistible. The tavern's signboard pictured a proud, victory-crowned stag treading on the throat of a writhing dragon. Even one new to Alcor could not mistake its racial implication. JonMarc prudently passed it by.

Gradually, the wide, ordered avenues of the upper city gave way to winding confusion as JonMarc descended to what Kier had said was Menythgar's Dynian quarter. Sagging frame-and-stucco dwellings huddled against each other like fearful fugitives, their protruding upper stories shadowing the narrow street. Though poor, the place had a different feel than Castémaron's perilous slums—shabby, but not squalid or even especially threatening. JonMarc was sure the tavern must lie somewhere nearby. He rounded a corner, and halted.

Directly ahead of him, the street split. The main route sloped down toward the fogbound harbor. The other curved off in more or less the direction he wanted, yet it looked little more than an alley, scarcely wide enough for three to walk abreast. JonMarc rubbed his brow.

His instincts suddenly warned him he wasn't alone. He cast a cautious glance about him. No one. Unless... At the fulcrum of the intersection sat what he'd first taken for a heap of refuse stacked against a wall. Closer attention showed it to be a man, though JonMarc could hardly imagine a more wretched creature. He wore a collection of rags, no single piece of which could rightly be called a garment. A tattered hood pushed back from his brow revealed him to be hollow-eyed in the truest sense: empty sockets gaped specter-like into the moonlit mist.

JonMarc regarded the luckless creature with suspicion. Back in Castémaron, thieves sometimes posted a beggar—usually feigning blindness behind a loose-woven bandage—at the entrance to their lair to signal the approach of any ill-guarded passerby. This held such an aura of treachery, but for one thing. Unless the man's powers of sight sprang from some unprecedented source, this beggar was unquestionably blind. And of what use to an ambush was a lookout who could not see?

JonMarc drew closer. Almost imperceptibly, the old man cocked his head. "Good even', Father," JonMarc said. Even in Castémaron's back alleys, where beggars were as plentiful as street rats, a graybeard of this one's years would be accorded respect simply for having the pluck to survive so long. "I seek a tavern called *The Jackal and Hounds*."

The beggar remained silent. JonMarc considered repeating the question louder, in case the man's hearing had gone the way of his sight. But at last the mound of rags stirred. A bony finger pointed toward the narrow lane. JonMarc frowned. He'd expected as much. He'd simply have to be on his guard; that, or return to the inn and forget about the tavern—and the girl. After ten long nights at sea, the latter seemed no option at all.

JonMarc drew a copper from his pouch and pressed it to the beggar's palm. With unexpected strength, the creature seized his arm. JonMarc shuddered as claw-like fingers perused his face. "*Angwaled ébared colléstra,*" the man whispered, his voice harsh and dry as an old raven's.

JonMarc did not recognize the syllables. Disconcerted, he jerked free and backed away.

He'd scarcely entered the lane when, from behind, he heard the harsh

cry of a night-wing. Yet this call came from no bird. It was clearly a signal
to some lurker that here was fair game for their enterprise. JonMarc
hesitated. The eeriness of his encounter with the beggar had unsettled him.
He shook the feeling off and chuckled. He was in his element now. Let
someone try to jump him. He knew tricks no street-cull in this backwater
port would ever dream of.

The lane proved, not the ominous alley he'd expected, but a tidy row
of tradesmen's shops; probably quite a merry place in daylight. He'd gone
some twenty paces when his ready eyes spotted a flicker of movement
ahead. JonMarc pursed his lips. Amateurs. Palming his dirk, he crept to the
recess where he'd seen the figure retreat and flattened himself against the
wall.

Ten heartbeats. Twelve. The lurker must be growing impatient for his
victim to pass so he could jump him from behind. JonMarc's limbs tingled.
He heard the rasp of anxious breath. Twenty. Twenty-five. Cautious fingers
crept around the corner. A hand appeared.

JonMarc seized it. The lurker gave a startled yelp as JonMarc yanked
him from his lair and shoved him, kicking and squirming, into the wall.
Only a boy, JonMarc realized as he struggled to control two small fists
and a pair of flailing legs. The lad fought with a fiery determination that
reminded him of his own youth on the streets. A sharp kick sent pain
shooting through his knee.

"Hold still, boy!" he grunted. "I won't hurt you—"

A blade pricked the side of his neck. "Loose him."

JonMarc cursed himself for an ass. Of course the lad had an
accomplice. He'd willingly have done as the voice demanded, were his
captive's limbs not taut as bowstrings. To release him…

The blade at his neck jerked. "Now."

Reluctantly, JonMarc loosed his hold. Like a sprung catapult, a knotted
fist flew up, catching him squarely in the nose. JonMarc gave a sharp hiss,
blinking back tears. The lad scrambled free.

"Who are you?" demanded the one behind him. "What is your business
here?"

"What's it to you?" JonMarc replied, rubbing his nose. "If you want my
purse, take it."

"I've no need of your purse." The voice sounded youthful, and not
especially menacing. "I ask again, why are you here?"

JonMarc puzzled at the response. This was the oddest band of thieves he'd ever encountered: a youth, a boy, and an old blindman. They hadn't even bothered to take his weapon. JonMarc suspected he was missing something. "I seek a tavern called *The Jackal and Hounds*."

He heard his captor's thoughtful exhale. An unhooded lantern flashed its mottled gleam on the wall before him. The pressure of the blade at his neck eased. "Turn 'round."

This was the perfect chance. A thrust of his dirk and he could escape before his captor even knew what killed him. JonMarc did not take it. He couldn't have said why, except that he was now as curious about his attackers as they were about him. He turned slowly to face a youth he could tell at a glance was no street cull.

The lad stood half a head shorter than himself, a sturdy fellow of about sixteen, with ginger curls and a wide, trusting face. The weapon poised at JonMarc's throat looked ancient—the re-sharpened hilt shard of some broken sword. "You are Dynian," the youth said, as though the fact relieved a number of problems, "yet you speak like an outlander."

"I'm from Castémaron."

The youth eyed him with curiosity and a glint of distrust. "What is your errand at *The Jackal*?"

JonMarc shrugged. "I come to return a token to a lady."

"Show me."

JonMarc reached into his tunic and handed the youth the trampled silver locket with the sigil of the harp, that he'd retrieved from the Citadel Square. His captor studied it intently, then passed it to his young companion. "'Tis Rowenna's!" the boy exclaimed.

"Aye," said the other, warily. "She told us of the losing of it. She said 'twas the Connails' doing. 'Tis why we stand guard tonight—to give warning should they try to do her further harm. But *you* are not of their number. How came you by it?"

"If she spoke of the attack, surely she mentioned she didn't face the Connails alone. I retrieved her trinket once the fight ended."

The youth nodded, apparently satisfied, and handed the locket back. "'Tis well. Old Ewan signaled he thought you a friend. But when you seized my brother..." He slid the sword shard into a battered scabbard at his hip. "Why did you not answer Ewan's challenge?"

Challenge? The beggar's words? "I speak no Dynian," JonMarc replied.

The youth studied him with wonder. "Rowenna said you were a strange one; that you dared face Aric Connail alone." His face fairly glowed with admiration. "Pass, outlander. Our sister will be relieved to know you still live."

The atmosphere of *The Jackal and Hounds* was somber—in fact, it was downright grim. JonMarc felt every eye trained upon him with distrust as he shut the heavy door and made his way to the bar. Tankard in hand, he found a small table in the corner and quickly buried himself in the depths of his brew.

This was hardly a proper tavern. Where was the merriment, the cheerful rowdiness? JonMarc eyed his drab surroundings: the age-cracked walls, the sagging beams, all dreary gray. No sign of Rowenna, yet she must be here. Her brother said as much.

A debate was brewing at the bar. JonMarc resisted the distraction. Chin propped on his fist, he tried to lose himself in the fantasy of frothy images that formed on the surface of his ale. The bobbing breast of a Kirosian veil-dancer slowly stretched until the jeweled nipple broke free and dissipated into amber oblivion. A pair of shapely thighs took shape and parted alluringly to reveal their foamy secrets... The jab of JonMarc's finger dissolved them into a sizzling mist.

What in blazes was all the arguing about? Couldn't a man even dream in peace? JonMarc tossed down his ale and signaled the barkeeper for a refill. The gesture went unnoticed.

"Now, don't ye be saying such things of the lad," the barman admonished a ruddy-faced patron. "He cannot help his parentage. He came here oft enough when he lived in the city, and were ever fair-spoken, what little he spoke at all."

"Aye," replied the ruddy one, a surly man whose voice rasped like a spade through wet gravel. "And all the while he were spying out our secrets, I'll wager."

The barkeeper set down a tankard he'd been wiping with a frayed rag and placed pudgy hands on the bar. "An' what secrets had we then, Iain?"

Iain ignored the question. "Why'd he bother t' return? We've Tiernai enough on Alcor without another halfblood to..."

"He obviously has a care for his dying father."

"His *Tiernai* father. All the more cause to distrust him. Here, Dickon, fill 'er up."

Dickon topped off the proffered tankard along with those of several more patrons who had gathered close to listen. JonMarc suddenly realized who they must be discussing. It surprised him that Kier was regarded as a person of note here in his homeland. Yet how could these folk know he'd returned? JonMarc abandoned his table for a seat near the bar where he could better hear the conversation.

"What harm's the old duke done you, Iain?" Dickon asked. "Of all the council lords, he has e'er dealt fairly with our race. 'Tis said he truly loved the lad's mother."

"Aye," Iain cackled, "so do they all love our women—long enough to bed 'em. Is that not so, Rowenna?" He aimed his loud remark at a door behind the bar. JonMarc stirred at hearing the girl's name. He silently cursed Iain for his boorishness.

Dickon angrily wiped his hands on his soiled apron. "Leave the child alone. Has she not been through enough today?"

"Who d'ya think the lad'll side with if the war renews?" asked a portly man with a soft, round face like a soup dumpling. "His father's race, or his mam's?"

Iain rolled his eyes. "He's a Tiernai captain. What side d'ya think he'll take?"

"Now, now," said Dickon, "we cannot be sure o' that. The lad's been gone a long while. Alcor has changed. Now, Gerit Mawr believes—"

"Gerit Mawr? Denia's blood, I don't know what's worse—t' trust a halfblood bastard who knows not where his loyalties lie, or a turncoat coward like Gerit Mawr."

"Speak no ill o' Gerit Mawr, Iain. He, at least, stands for peace."

"Aye, an' 'tis a good fat piece of Alcor he's after, I'll wager, with himself t' wear Ross Branwyn's rightful crown."

"Nonsense," the barkeeper retorted. "Can you not see that peace is our only hope?"

"How can you talk of peace, Dickon, after what the Connail swine did t' your daughter today?" The speaker was a stubbled graybeard in a frayed doryman's cap. "I say, if the Tiernai want war, let's give it to 'em. It may be our chance to drive 'em forever from our shores."

"But we've not the strength for it, Huw," said the dumpling-faced man. "The Tiernai grow e'er stronger, while our own folk dwindle. E'en fifty years ago we were no match for 'em. The Tiernai live for war while, until their coming, the Dynian knew only peace."

The one named Huw eagerly leaned across the bar. "Ah, but we nearly won at Ceorl's Ford. Jerrod Branwyn, rest his valiant soul, had the Tiernai bastards on the run—till he was foully cut down. The ranks of the Branwyn rebels are growing, an' their men are well trained. 'Tis said young Ross is a doughty captain."

"Aye, and so were Jerrod, and Glyn, and their father Gareth before them," said Dickon. "Yet they were all destroyed."

"Well, as to Glyn, who can say? Though he vanished five years past, there's many believe an heir to Dynian kings will one day return and bring us victory." Huw spoke behind his hand. "From what I hear, Glyn Branwyn travels abroad, gathering arms and support for our cause. The Branwyns still hope—"

Dickon flourished his ragged towel. "Aye, they *hope*. They hide safe in the mountains at Dorcalon and put their trust in prophecy. What hope have *we*? If war comes, 'tis we in the city'll first feel its bite. Will the Branwyns gallop to our aid?" He huffed. "Not bloody likely."

"That's traitor talk," snapped Iain.

"You think so? Look at us—old men, eking out a living amongst our enemies, in a city that once was ours alone, while our leaders skulk up in the hills. How many of our young men'll die if this war of yours is fought? Our only hope is peace."

"*Or a glorious death.*" The words came from across the room. All eyes turned toward the speaker, a hooded man who sat alone at a table near the door. JonMarc hadn't seen him enter. His pale eyes gleamed as if a furnace blazed behind them. Fanatic's eyes. A brown scar, like a deep, muddied river, traced the line of his left cheekbone.

"I say we give up this cowards' talk. We must fight the invader to the last man. I've been abroad. Do you know what those of other lands say of us? *Craven*, they call us. Cowards. How else could we stand by while our race is trampled into the very mud our fathers died to defend—stripped of our arms; of even our own tongue?"

There was a sullen murmur of agreement from those around the bar. The fiery man stood, thrusting his chair aside. "My brothers, must we *surrender*? Must we grovel at Tiernai whim? Must we sue for peace when our enemy arms for war?" He pounded his fist on the tabletop. "I say no. I say we fight this war, that is so long overdue—aye, and mayhap we shall lose. But is it not better to die valiantly than to live as sniveling bondsmen? If we live, we must live as *men*. If we die, we shall die with honor! *Angwaled ébared colléstra.* For the blood of brothers lost."

As one, the roused patrons leaped to their feet, answering the familiar challenge: "*Éremyn áreth Alcor*. For the liberation of Alcor!"

JonMarc was astounded at the energy that so quickly infused the room. The fervor would die soon enough, yet the hooded man had talent. He did not strike JonMarc as a leader—more a manipulator of emotions for his own purposes—whatever those might be.

"The key to the whole speech was *death*," muttered the dumpling-faced man to Dickon. JonMarc voiced agreement and suddenly found himself intimate to their conversation.

"Makes me surer than ever that Gerit Mawr is right," said Dickon. "If the Tiernai cannot be driven out, our only choices are death—as this riot-monger promotes—or to learn to live with them in peace. I, for one, believe that can be done. 'Tis better than seein' my family, my people, destroyed for the sake of what this one would call *honor*."

"Aye," said the other. "Yet mayhap there was a worthy purpose to all this—air passing, for look, it has coaxed your sweet daughter from her brooding. Come, Rowenna. Sit by me, lass. Sing to us of a time when the Dynian were proud, and not cat's-paw to some charlatan's whim."

JonMarc hastened to his feet when he saw the girl enter. Rowenna's eyes lit with recognition as she took the proffered stool. "I am pleased to see thee well, milord," she said, her voice as provocative and warm as his memories had made it. "You are—unscathed?"

JonMarc smiled. "Nearly. And I'm still no lord. My name's JonMarc. Can we talk, Rowenna?"

His request was nearly drowned out by the swell of voices that rose in growing insistence for a song. The tavern's patrons were once again united, if only in their desire to be entertained. Someone brought the girl a small harp, intricately carved and clearly very old. She flashed JonMarc a helpless smile and made her way to the center of the room.

"I would first dedicate a song to the stranger who so valiantly came to my rescue this afternoon," she said, with a nod to JonMarc.

Her grateful father hastened to fill JonMarc's tankard, and roused the company to drink to his health and that of all his descendants, before allowing the song to proceed.

It turned out to be a bawdy number entitled: *The Lay of the Traveler*, that told of a rogue who wedded and bedded a lass, swearing ever to be true, only to find that she had a husband in every town in which he had a wife. By the time the tune ended, it was clear that the passions of a moment before had been skillfully redirected, and Rowenna was taking measures to keep it so.

JonMarc maintained a secret eye on the hooded man near the door. He seemed oddly unconcerned that his efforts had come to naught. He sat, scrawling a message on a scrap of cloth. Perhaps he was a spy for the Branwyns. If so, the spectacle of his lately roused recruits singing and stamping time to a bawdy ballad paid sorry tribute to his energies. Whatever his motives, JonMarc did not trust him.

He set his musings aside and lent his voice to the enthusiasm that greeted Rowenna's latest roundelay. From the shouted requests she selected a madrigal and began again to spin her magic over the crowd. The melody was sad and beautiful—painfully so—its passion wrenched from a people's ancient soul. The lyrics told of change and defeat, of innocence lost and beauty defiled, of senseless waste and the passing of young life. JonMarc found himself drawn into it, sensing for the first time the unifying spirit of this ancient folk to whom his birth had tied him.

He did not know how long he sat under the enchantment of the girl's playing—whether through one song or a dozen. His tankard seemed always to be full, however many times he seemed to remember emptying it. He had reached the familiar state in which he became acutely aware of his thought processes, indicating they had been reduced to an observable speed, when his hazy mind informed him that the tune had again changed.

Rowenna sang this new melody in what JonMarc presumed must be the outlawed Dynian tongue. The strange words floated into his mind on wings of cloud as delicate as lace and fragile as flower petals, and seemed to paint pictures on his thoughts. He felt something oddly familiar about this tune, though he couldn't imagine where he might have heard it. As its final notes hung on the smoky air, the last words to touch JonMarc's mind remained there. He repeated them to himself again and again until a thunder of applause broke his trance.

"Did you like it?" Rowenna asked, slipping into the seat beside him.

JonMarc nodded enthusiastically. "That last song left a few moist eyes."

"Aye, it always does. 'Twas a lament for Giordon Telynor, the last Dynian High King, who was murdered by the Tiernai invaders upon his eighteenth nativity. The last verse declares: *There is no glory in senseless death*. 'Twill keep them thinking."

JonMarc softly repeated the syllables he'd heard. Rowenna's sea-green eyes narrowed.

"I'm sorry," he said. "The words of your song keep running through my head."

Rowenna regarded him quizzically. "Those words were not in my song, JonMarc."

JonMarc struggled to make sense of that. "But—they *had* to be. They came into my mind just as you finished. What do they mean?"

"'*Angoran neth tedynian, Fimabri*'? They say: 'Forget not thy people, my son.'"

JonMarc frowned. "That's impossible."

"'Tis what the words say."

"No, you don't understand, Rowenna. I speak no Dynian. None at all. Either I heard those words in your song—or my mind's playing some pretty strange tricks on me."

Rowenna glanced disdainfully at JonMarc's half-empty tankard. She pushed it away. "Come," she said, "tell me why you are here. When I left the Citadel Square I ne'er thought to see you alive again."

JonMarc retrieved his tankard, not so much because he wanted it as in stubborn defiance of Rowenna's conviction that he should not have it. He quickly summarized his encounter with the Connails.

Rowenna's eyes flashed. "So you came to learn if the lies they spoke of me were true."

JonMarc felt suddenly sheepish. Her words did hit very near the mark. He reached inside his tunic. "I came to return your locket."

Rowenna accepted the pendant with a glow of relief and dropped it into the straining confines of her bodice. JonMarc's eyes followed it longingly. Yet in the midst of an unspoken plea, something abruptly usurped his attention.

A man entered the tavern and slipped into a seat across from the hooded fanatic. Neither spoke, but the cloth missive changed hands. The hooded one then rose and departed. The newcomer glanced at the missive, then stuffed it into his belt and made his way to the bar.

JonMarc's curiosity was roused. "Who is that?" he asked Rowenna.

"His name is Enic. He comes in now and again. Why?"

"What about the man who just left? The one in the hood?"

"Oh, him." Rowenna crinkled her nose. "I know neither his name nor his business. He oft disappears for weeks, only to turn up again unheralded. Tonight was the first I've heard him speak, and I wish he had not. These men—" her gaze encompassed the tavern's ragged patrons— "they mean well, but they are so confused. They do not want war. They've no wish to lose all they've labored for. Yet they have pride. They were shamed today by what happened to me at the Citadel. It forced them to remember what humiliations their women suffer at Tiernai hands. But they have no redress. If they press suit against the Connails, 'tis their lives they'd lose, and still the assaults would continue. I did not wish to remind them of that, so I kept hidden. Yet when a man such as that one rouses them, who knows what mischief it might spawn? So I sang to them, hoping that, like gentle Killian of legend, my melodies might soothe the torment within. It worked, this time, for he is gone and they are of their own minds again. But I cannot sing away a war, JonMarc."

As Rowenna spoke, JonMarc kept his eyes on the small man at the bar. He wanted a look at that message. Swallowing down the last of his ale, he rose and sauntered off for a refill.

The task was child's play. His mark had no suspicions at all when the lanky stranger stumbled into him. JonMarc slipped the cloth scrap into his shirt. His drunken act was evidently convincing—and not entirely feigned. He returned to his seat and shoved the brimming tankard aside, sloshing half its contents on his sleeve. Rowenna frowned.

Before JonMarc could explain, the tavern door burst open. The youth from the alley stumbled in, carrying the limp body of his young brother. Rowenna cried out and ran to them as others helped ease the boy onto a tabletop. "No time!" the youth shouted, breathless. "The Connails are right behind. I fear they killed old Ewan. Someone take Robyn to the back. An arrow found his side. Hurry!" Dickon and Rowenna carried the boy away.

The remaining patrons—some dozen in all, mostly elderly men—eyed one another nervously. Swiftly, they gathered up anything they could use as weapons—pewter mugs, fire irons. A few drew shabby knives they dared carry despite the Tiernai ban. Grim-visaged, they lined up facing the entrance, gleaning strength and resolve from one another.

JonMarc positioned himself at their left flank, to defend the door to the back rooms where Rowenna had gone. "How many?" he asked the girl's brother.

The youth recognized him. "Four," he said, "armed and drunk. If they dare touch my sister..." A murderous gleam lit his eyes. "'Tis death to kill a Tiernai, but I'll risk it." He fingered his refurbished sword.

From the stair outside came a peal of harsh laughter. An instant later, the tavern door burst wide and four hulking men crowded in. JonMarc recognized Modron in the fore. The rest were strangers, though all wore the silver falcon of the Connails.

Lamplight kindled Modron's eyes as he canvassed the room. His bearded lip curled with scorn at the ragged line of Dynian arrayed against him. He missed JonMarc, hidden in shadow at the end of the bar. With a contemptuous laugh, he strode forward, his comrades right behind.

The Dynian defenders did not waver. With a thrust of one mighty arm, Modron sent the scrawny Huw and another man careening into the furniture. The rest moved aside to let the Tiernai pass, but tightened their ranks behind. A few darted anxious glances at Rowenna's brother. The youth signaled patience.

Modron slammed down his giant fist. "Barman."

Dickon stepped out of the kitchen, his apron soiled with blood.

"Four mugs o' yer best ale. We been huntin' Dynian traitors all day, and it's thirsty work." Modron nudged his nearest comrade and grinned. "Looks like we come on a whole bloody nest of 'em, don' it?" He spotted the ferret-like Enic, edging his way toward the exit. "Hoy. You, there." He lunged for the small man's wrist. "Where be you off to, wormlet?"

Enic cringed. "I don't belong here. I am no traitor. I serve..."

A fierce backhand silenced him. "I'm not interested in your excuses. You were about to buy our drinks, ay?" Enic trembled like a snared rabbit. He reached for his purse. Modron clamped a fist around his hand and squeezed. Enic shrieked and fell to his knees. His purse jingled to the floor. Laughing, Modron scooped it up. "Barman," he said, "hurry it with that ale. The wormlet here's offered to pay."

"Be done with your bullying, Connail," said Dickon. "Ye'll get no drink here. You've had too much already. Now *get out!*"

Modron seized Dickon by the collar and hauled him across the bar until their foreheads nearly met, then shoved him back against the wall. Dickon's head hit with a thud and he slid to the floor. Modron's eyes gleamed. "You'll do as I say, Dynian." He seized a torch from his comrade and held it perilously near the frayed curtains. "Where's the whore we seen at the Citadel? She'll bed with me tonight or I'll burn this vermin-hole to cinders—with as many o' you as try to stop me."

"We may burn," choked Dickon, "but you'll burn with us. 'Tis a fate you've long deserved."

JonMarc had seen enough. Modron still hadn't noticed him. Time to change that. With a gesture to halt Rowenna's brother, who looked ready to attack, JonMarc strode into the light.

Modron's face hardened when he saw him. "So you still live, you conjuring spawn of a harlot." Modron swaggered toward him. "That's easily fixed. Thought to have the wench yerself, did you? Well, let's see what she thinks when I've done with you." He thrust the torch in JonMarc's face.

The sudden move caught JonMarc off guard. He stumbled backward, clumsily fending off the blow with his injured arm. If only he weren't so infernally drunk.

Modron thrust again. JonMarc dodged and nearly stumbled. He heard Rowenna scream a warning from behind the bar. Somewhere in his fuzzy mind he wondered why she'd left the safety of the kitchen. He lurched aside as a hulking form behind him fell to the floor, brained by a well-aimed tankard. A shout went up from the Dynian defenders. Encouraged by this minor victory, they attacked the Connails, wielding stools and tankards against their enemies' steel. JonMarc was forced to rely on their enthusiasm, and Rowenna's attentive warnings, to cover his back.

Modron swung the flaming brand like a sword. Another blow grazed JonMarc's ear. He smelled singed hair as he scrambled aside, stabbing his dirk at the big man's forearm. Modron yelped. JonMarc seized the torch and managed to wrest it free.

Cursing, Modron jerked out his knife. JonMarc shifted the torch to his injured left hand and concentrated on hefting the dirk with his right. Modron slashed. JonMarc ducked the blow and swung to counter. With lightning speed, Modron seized JonMarc's dirk hand and pinioned it against the bar, useless. The giant raised his weapon for the kill.

JonMarc's instincts took over. As Modron's dagger streaked for his heart, he plunged the sizzling brand straight into the burly liegeman's face. The action ripped wide his injured shoulder. Pain seared through him like a hot poker, followed by a bloodcurdling shriek that all but dwarfed his own hoarse cry.

Modron's bearded face was wreathed in flame, blackened lips curled back from his teeth in a bellow of hate. The stench of seared flesh filled the air. JonMarc gagged at the hideousness of it, and of a deeper, inexplicable horror welling up from the unfathomed dungeons of his memory.

His senses whirled. With a strangled moan, he lurched toward the bar. The wooden rail floated up to meet him. It smashed his forehead with a shower of silent sparks, and his mind went dark.

Chapter Thirteen

JonMarc woke with a start, his pulse racing from ghastly dreams of fire and death. Every heartbeat was like a quarry hammer, amplifying the dull ache in his forehead. He forced himself to one elbow, shivering as the furry coverlet fell from his sweat-drenched shoulders. Pain lanced his left arm and he collapsed back with a groan.

Gradually he began to piece together events, but they were indistinct, as though viewed through a smoky pall: the assault on the tavern; dodging Modron's deadly blows; his enemy's bearded face consumed in flame. Then—nothing. And now he was here. But where was *here*?

He lay on his side on a pallet of thick furs, in the corner of a small, smoky chamber. Silhouetted against the embers in the hearth opposite, he made out a heap of clothing strewn haphazardly across a low bench. His? He ran an exploratory finger down his side, encountering only the smoothness of his own bare flesh. No wonder he itched like a penitent. Panic seized him and he groped for his charmstone. He found it dangling against his armpit. Its touch gave him comfort. Perhaps it again deserved credit for preserving his life.

But where was he? At the inn with Kier? He didn't recall returning there. And this room had a different smell—not the pungence of road-weary travelers, but the sweet aroma of strewn herbs, and a muskiness his lower brain recognized as the comforting scent of woman flesh.

Something stirred behind him, and a graceful hand, kitten soft, slid around his waist, then drifted languorously across the hard plane of his belly. Where the fingers brushed the hairline, JonMarc's muscles fluttered. He was instantly aware of the rest of her—the full, firm mounds that pressed against his back, rising and falling with the gentle rhythm of her breathing. She gave a long, satisfied purr and moved closer, sweeping silken toes against the wire hair of his calves, and cupping his rump into the warm cradle of her naked thighs.

JonMarc struggled to recall their lovemaking. His mind remained blank. Could he have been that drunk? "Rowenna?"

"Hmmm?" the dreamy response. She drew herself up, cushioning his left arm between her breasts, her cheek resting lightly on his bandaged shoulder. Her fingers twirled playful circles in the hairs below his navel. A chill skittered up JonMarc's spine and back down to his toenails.

"Rowenna, what happened tonight? The Connails..."

"Defeated."

JonMarc shifted onto his back to look at her. "What about us? Did we...?"

Rowenna's lush curls fell feather light across his chest. The gleam of the embers reflected in the dewy sheen of her eyes. "Do you not remember?"

"No, nothing since the fight. I—passed out, I think."

"Aye, and I brought you here to tend your wounds."

"Then—we didn't..." He thought her lips parted in a playful smile, but couldn't be sure.

"If you cannot recall, m'lord, scarce does it matter what we might have done."

JonMarc retrieved her hand that was inching southward. Right now he wanted answers.

Rowenna sighed and again nestled her head against his arm. "You have slept like a restless babe—all night."

JonMarc breathed relief. At least his memory was intact. He hated to think he could forget such an encounter. "You stayed with me?"

"Of course. 'Tis my bed." She snuggled closer. "I chose you."

Warning bells sounded in JonMarc's mind. "What do you mean, *chose* me?"

"Among the Dynian, 'tis a woman's right to choose what man she will lie with. But surely you know that."

"I'm—not familiar with Dynian ways, Rowenna. I've never lived among them. Tell me..."

Rowenna touched a silencing finger to his lips. It smelled of lavender. "My lord," she whispered, nibbling lightly on his earlobe, "surely there are more pleasurable matters to think on." Her hand again slipped beneath the covers. It slid across his belly and kept going. This time JonMarc did not stop her. She wouldn't be disappointed. As Rowenna's fingers lightly touched him, he felt the muscles of his loins tremor, then spasm hungrily.

With a primal moan, he rolled over to cover her open mouth with his.

A chill, lead-grey dawn was seeping through the edges of the roughhewn shutters when JonMarc again opened his eyes. He slid noiselessly from beneath the covers, careful not to disturb Rowenna, whose gentle breathing whispered in a soft, unbroken rhythm. Squatting awkwardly before the hearth, he fumbled to resurrect a flame, while snatches of frosty breeze played an exasperating game of hoodman blind with his exposed flesh.

He was halfway into his breeches when a rustling from the pallet him told him Rowenna was awake. JonMarc glanced back. The girl lounged amid the furry throws, ivory arms tucked behind her head, seemingly untroubled by the cold. Sea-green eyes watched him with curiosity—and a hint of smugness.

She'd be eyeing the lash marks on his back, of course. Women always did. They seemed somehow drawn to them with a perverse fascination JonMarc often wondered at, but never understood. Some claimed to find the scars appalling. The courtesan, Shanya, desired only to smother him in a well of maternal sympathy. He'd even known a few, like Ruthira, who found his marred back to be a source of arousal. Whatever a woman's perceptions, JonMarc had never known one who failed to be intrigued.

"So you're leaving." Rowenna's voice betrayed no emotion. JonMarc eased his injured arm into his shirtsleeve and nodded. "A pity you cannot stay longer, JonMarc—a week. A day."

He smiled. "I'd like that. But there are things I have to do."

"I know," she sighed. "You accompany your friend Fitzmorwen to Castle Cordon. Nay, do not look so surprised. 'Tis known throughout the city that he is returned, and I, at least, know you are his companion. I watched you leave your ship together."

JonMarc frowned. "And then felt the need to spread the word?"

"Fitzmorwen needs not my small voice to herald his arrival. He has been much looked-for of late. Many would know his stand on the coming war. The half-Dynian son of a Tiernai duke may have influence in Council, should he choose to use it." Her eyes narrowed. "Will he?"

"I don't know," JonMarc replied honestly. "We've never discussed it. I doubt Kier realizes anyone cares. From what he's told me, neither race ever exactly welcomed him."

"Aye, he always saw it so. Yet there were some—" Rowenna broke off.

JonMarc wondered what she'd left unsaid. "You knew Kier when he lived in Menythgar?"

Rowenna sighed. "I think no one truly *knew* him. When he trained at the Citadel, he sometimes came to my father's tavern. That was long ago. I was but a girl—and love struck, I admit. He was so tall and strong—and noble, despite his mixed birth: a youth to turn any maid's heart." Rowenna smiled wistfully. "Of course, he saw me as naught but a gangly girl who was forever splashing ale upon his sleeve. He paid me no heed."

JonMarc could just imagine. Kier's raven hair, and eyes the color of Ruthira's amethystine ear jewels, allowed him his pick of women. JonMarc had seen their attention kindle whenever his companion passed. Yet Kier remained stubbornly oblivious, and swiftly changed the subject whenever JonMarc brought it up. JonMarc suspected his lack of interest had to do with the pretty dark-eyed girl whose portrait Kier carried in his pack—and guarded fiercely. From his own brief glimpse, he could understand his companion's preoccupation. "So the questions you asked me at the Citadel—what you really wanted was news of Kier."

Rowenna lowered her eyes. "In part. After so many years, men change—as do women's perceptions of them. I needed to be sure the man I had seen was truly Fitzmorwen. We hardly expected him to be companioned by a Dynian. 'Tis a hopeful sign."

"Don't read too much into it. I saved Kier's life in Castémaron and he took me into his service. That's all."

"Yet 'tis you I came to know, JonMarc—the man who twice delivered me from the Connails, at the risk of your own life. Because of that, 'twas you I chose to share my bed."

JonMarc's uneasiness crept back. "I don't understand this *choosing* of a man, Rowenna. If you expect me to pledge—"

"I expect nothing. You may be Dynian born, JonMarc, but 'tis obvious you did not come to manhood among us. You think like the Tiernai: that it is man's place to choose and woman's to humbly submit. You will not find it so among the Dynian. Blessed Denia's law declares that those who bear responsibility for continuing the race shall decide what men may contribute their seed. 'Tis an honor to be so chosen. Yet it does not mean I wish to wed you."

JonMarc stroked his chin. He had much to learn about his own race. It was flattering to think that, after only one night on Alcor, he might already have contributed to its future. He snatched up his tunic. "What became of the Connail minions last night? You said they were routed?"

Rowenna's eyes glowed. "Aye, they lost their taste for blood quick enough when you destroyed their leader."

Fiery images flashed across JonMarc's mind. He winced. So Modron was dead. "What of the others?"

"They live, though they'll doubtless be in some discomfort for a time. Only Modron was killed—and poor Ewan. But that was not unlooked for. The old man longed for death. Twenty years ago, the Connails burned his home, raped and murdered his wife and children, then put out his eyes and left him to live with the horrible memory of it. 'Twas fitting he should now die so—in defense of his people. At last he shall know peace."

"But the Connails! You can't mean you let them go? If they tell Aric what happened, you'll all be in danger."

"Aric will learn naught of it. Our men are sworn to silence. And the big one's body will ne'er be found—though scarce could it be recognized if it were. The minds of the rest have been cleansed and all memory of the incident erased. My father summoned a monk of the Faithful, who worked with them all night. Before dawn, they were carried to the seaside, there to wake and wonder at their ill fortune."

JonMarc looked up with a start. "The Faithful? You mean, your father called in a *Fithlon*?"

"Aye, Master Demias is Dynian born, and well known to us. 'Tis his talent to turn thoughts, and other like mysteries. But you must know more of these things than I; you, a spell-hand with a conjuring stone, who carries the Fithlon sacred book. Are you of their order, JonMarc?"

"I... no. I've only had a little training. I never realized the Fithlon could erase thoughts. Can the spell be broken?"

Rowenna shrugged. "Mayhap by another Fithlon. But the Connails despise the brethren. And such a thing would doubtless take time. For now, I think we are safe from Aric's revenge."

JonMarc picked up the precious Fithlon book and smoothed its punctured pages. He slipped it safely inside his tunic. "I've got to go, Rowenna. I told Kier I'd be back by dawn and it's past that now." As he tugged his boots on, his eyes lit on a crumpled scrap of cloth, fallen to the floor—the message he'd filched at the bar last night. He snatched it up. "In all the excitement, I forgot about this. Let's see what Enic and his fire-eyed comrade were so privy about."

He'd barely struggled through the first line when his stomach sank.

Rowenna sensed his alarm. "JonMarc, what is it?"

JonMarc sat on the edge of the pallet and let her read aloud over his shoulder.

"*Fit-M is returned. Proceed with plan. Three watch the Tower Inn and await your signal to move. Others hold the M-bridge.* He must mean the Millferry Bridge," Rowenna interjected. "It lies on your road to Cordon. *Come alone to me with the token. I go to Lord M tonight.* Signed— *R.* Then: *It must appear the work of Branwyn. Pedigc a methenu. Em Areth endylian.*"

"What's that last part?" JonMarc asked.

"It says: *Fail not, our Master is watching.*" Rowenna frowned. "I don't understand..."

JonMarc lurched to his feet. "I do. They're still after him. Ma'ardhi warned me of a man with a scar. What if he followed us from Castémaron? Blazes, I was looking right at him and never made the connection."

"But what do these men want with Fitzmorwen?"

JonMarc hurled her a panicked look. "They want him *dead.*"

"But *why*?"

"So they can steal—" JonMarc caught himself. "Listen, Rowenna, the Fithlon you spoke of—that Master Demias—what's his connection with the scarfaced man?"

Rowenna shrugged. "None. I've known Master Demias all my life. He would never wish Fitzmorwen harmed."

JonMarc wasn't convinced. "But they're both Dynian, and so's Enic. So this must be a Dynian plot."

"No, JonMarc. That cannot be. Why would Dynian wish to blame such a deed on the Branwyns—their own people?"

"I don't know. None of this makes any sense." JonMarc raked fingers through his hair. "In Castémaron, the scarfaced man tried to have Kier killed. This time he might succeed. I've got to stop him." He hurried for the door.

"Wait!" Rowenna wrapped a blanket around her slender frame and hastened after him. "The note says the men will only be watching; that they require a signal from Enic to act."

JonMarc took a deep breath to calm himself. "You're right. What became of Enic last night, after Modron broke his hand? Did he get out before the fight?"

"When last I saw, he lay upon the floor in a swoon. My father threw a blanket over him."

"Then maybe he's still there. If not..." JonMarc didn't want to think about it. He grabbed his cloak, kissed Rowenna brusquely on the forehead, then rattled down the narrow stair.

The commonroom was a ruin of overturned furniture and shattered crockery. The stench of burning hung thick on the chilly air and murky puddles glinted like steel in the rising dawn. A blanket lay crumpled on the floor. Enic was gone. With a quick glance into the adjoining rooms, JonMarc unlatched the tavern door and hurried out into the morning.

Chapter Fourteen

JonMarc reached the Serpentine and leaned against a shop corner to catch his breath. Sweat soaked his back and trickled freely down his face. His knees felt close to buckling from the long race uphill. He wiped a sooty sleeve across his brow and sighted up the winding street. Another few blocks to the inn. He thought of Kier and exhorted his legs to run.

A growing throng of Menythgar's Tiernai citizens, all gaily attired, were headed down to the Renewal festivities near the city gates. Some glared at JonMarc as he dashed past, or shouted obscenities as he shouldered them aside, but no one moved to stop him. At the next curve, he left the avenue to pick his way through back alleys with the second sense of one who had spent his life on city streets. He soon found himself facing the stout brick wall that encompassed the inn's rear stableyard. He clambered over.

The innyard was astir as a small company of travelers loaded their mounts amid the flap and cackle of geese and the general flurry of kitchen maids preparing for market. JonMarc hurried around to the front. Here, the street was largely deserted. JonMarc saw no sign of Enic's watchers, though they were hardly likely to make themselves obvious. He offered up a silent prayer to crook-backed Ghedrev that the stolen message was false, his fears groundless. His gut knew better. He thrust open the inn door and hammered up the stair.

A human barnyard of gruntings and snorings assailed him as he entered the stagnant chamber where, but for the grace of Rowenna, he'd have spent the past night. His spirits fell. Kier's corner was empty, their packs gone. But surely the brassy wouldn't have abandoned him just because he'd failed to return by dawn.

Down in the commonroom, the harried innkeeper made it clear he neither knew nor cared where the halfblood officer had got to. His dark-eyed daughter proved of greater help. The captain, she said, had gone to the horse markets. He would return by first hour. JonMarc was instructed to wait. "Strange," she added, whisking a stray lock of auburn from her brow. "Another man came asking for him not half an hour since; a nervous sort— one of your own race."

JonMarc tensed. "What did you tell him?"

"Same as I've told you." She shrugged. "I thought it no secret."

JonMarc's stomach sank. He slipped the girl a copper for her trouble and walked out into the broadening daylight.

Enic had beaten him here. The treacherous creature now knew as much about Kier's movements as he did. How would Enic use that knowledge? A dreadful image flashed across JonMarc's mind: Kier, his only guide in this alien land, overpowered on the streets. He might already be dead. JonMarc banished that thought. He tried to consider rationally. The scarfaced man clearly intended Kier be taken as he departed the inn, but Enic had arrived too late. Would he risk missing his quarry on the crowded streets when he knew Kier would soon return? Here, position and surprise could be his. JonMarc's spirits rose. There was still a chance.

But from which direction would Kier approach? JonMarc had no idea where the horse market was held. A block to his right, the steep Serpentine hair-pinned out of sight as it climbed toward the black-walled Citadel. Downward, it clove a wedge between two rows of shopfronts, then curved back again on its sinuous path to the harbor. JonMarc scanned the muddy cobbles. No sign that hay wains or unusual numbers of horses had recently passed. So the market must lie nearer the city gates. If he headed downhill, he might catch Kier returning.

As he stepped into the street, a flutter of movement snared his eye. Some distance down from him, on a rooftop overlooking the Serpentine's lower slope, a slight figure waved a signal to someone on the ground. From a recess nearby, another man answered. He, in turn, motioned in JonMarc's direction. JonMarc drew back into shadow as a third figure, not twenty paces from him, leaned from a passageway to acknowledge. JonMarc glimpsed a full quiver slung across his back. Icy dread froze JonMarc's belly. The lookout on the roof was almost certainly Enic. He must have spotted Kier. Cocking his ear, JonMarc could make out the steady clip-clop of horses approaching up the Serpentine. A moment later, they appeared around the corner. Kier sat astride a thick-limbed gray, leading a smaller chestnut by the reins.

To JonMarc's street-trained eye, the stratagem became clear. The attackers would let Kier pass between them, then strike him down from both directions at once. He was already within the first bowman's range, his mounted form an easy target.

Blazes, Kier, you're riding into a trap! JonMarc barely bit back the shout. A warning cry would simply provoke the enemy to shoot. JonMarc racked his brain. How could he alert Kier to the danger without speeding the attack? Perhaps… a diversion? Without further thought, JonMarc launched himself into the street. "Gwythion!" he shouted, hastening toward Kier, his arms wide. "Good to see you, friend. Are you here for the festival?"

Kier reacted instantly. He ducked low over the saddle and slid to his feet between the horses.

The nearest bowman pulled his shot as his target dropped from view, and drew back into hiding. JonMarc breathed relief. He'd gambled that the attackers had been told their quarry's identity; that their split second of indecision would stymie Enic's plan. It seemed he'd been right. He caught up with Kier and, with the horses as cover, escorted him up to the inn.

"Get inside," he hissed, as they reached the front stair. "I'll take the beasts around back."

Kier stole a swift glance over his shoulder, then nodded and slipped through the door.

"What was that about?" he demanded, as JonMarc entered through the kitchen. "I sensed danger; that I was *riding into a trap?*"

So—Kier had read his warning thought. JonMarc thrust the purloined message into the brassy's hand.

Kier's face darkened as he read it. "Where'd you get this?"

"Lifted it from a man at the tavern last night. I'll explain later." He glanced toward the yard. "Might be safer if we wait till they're gone."

"You think they'll give up so easily?" Kier shook his head. "We caught them by surprise. Now we've got to roust them before they can regroup." He tucked the note in his jerkin and strode for the door.

JonMarc stayed him with an upraised hand while he leaned out to scan the stableyard. "Looks clear," he said, and hastened down the short stair. Kier followed.

There was a soft *zzzip*, like the hiss of a stinging serpent. Before JonMarc could place the sound, Kier gave a startled cry and stumbled on the worn steps, a grey-fletched arrow jutting from his thigh.

JonMarc cast about him for the shooter. An agile figure, bow in hand, was cautiously picking his way across the stable's angled roof. He dropped to the ground and scrambled away toward the arched passage that led to the street. JonMarc shoved past two astonished kitchen wenches and took off after him.

He nearly had the bowman in reach when his left boot slid in a pungent equine mound. JonMarc careened headlong across the muddy flagstones. His quarry vanished around the corner.

Grunting a curse, JonMarc struggled to his feet and hurried back to the stair where Kier was unsteadily trying to stand. The two maids clucked and fussed over him, but drew aside at JonMarc's approach.

"Lost him." JonMarc whistled low when he saw the snapped arrow shaft lying on the step and the bloody stain where the point still lodged in Kier's thigh. Kier had bound the wound with a maid's kerchief. "It should be seen to…"

"Later." Kier took a pained breath. "Just… give me a leg up."

JonMarc knew better than to argue. He laced his muddy fingers and helped his companion mount, then swung onto the chestnut mare. Kier swayed a moment in the saddle, but steadied himself. At his nod, they turned for the arched passage.

They paused as they neared the street. "There," said JonMarc, pointing. Some twenty yards below, four men stood arguing. Two had thrown back their hoods, revealing pale hair bound with leather brow bands. A small balding fellow in their midst harangued at them unmercifully. "Enic," JonMarc murmured, and glanced at Kier. "We can get past them—"

Kier shook his head, his eyes glacial. "I want answers." He surged the gray forward.

With a shout, JonMarc kicked the chestnut to follow.

The conspirators panicked when they saw them bearing down and backed out of the street, fumbling for weapons. JonMarc charged one, who gave a terrified shriek and bailed for cover. JonMarc trampled his fallen bow and turned after Enic. He was the one with the answers.

Fear flashed in Enic's pale eyes when he found himself singled out. He turned and raced down the cobbled slope. As he skidded around the first curve, he cast a breathless glance over his shoulder and choked a cry. JonMarc reined the mare to across his path. Reaching for the small man's shoulders, he launched himself from the saddle and grappled him to the ground.

JonMarc was first to his feet. Pain seared his wounded shoulder as he dragged Enic up by the collar. "Who sent you to kill Fitzmorwen?" he demanded, in no mood for clemency.

Enic's ferret eyes darted side to side. Bandaged fingers edged toward his belt. JonMarc saw, and clamped his hand around his captive's wrist. A sharp jerk, and Enic's dagger dropped. JonMarc wrenched the limb up behind the small man's back. "Try that again and I'll break your arm. Now tell me, who is the man you plotted with last night at the tavern?"

Enic's glare was venomous. "I don't know what you're talking abou..."

JonMarc jerked the arm tighter. "The man with the scar. His name, and who he serves."

Enic squealed. "He... he calls himself Roderig. I know nothing more."

The sound of commotion drifted down the slope—shouts of soldiers breaking up the scuffle. JonMarc made out Kier's commanding voice above the din and breathed relief.

"You've failed, little man. Fitzmorwen lives. You'll get no mercy from Tiernai troops. Answer my questions and I'll free you before they come. Who is this Roderig's master?"

Enic's struggles abruptly ceased. His round face went deathly pale. "*Master?*" He winced, cowering as if the very air had ears. "I have failed... my Master. He will know. He sees all; hears every thought. He won't forgive..."

"Who?" JonMarc demanded. "*Who* won't forgive?"

Enic's whole demeanor changed. With the snarl of a trapped sewer rat, he rammed his foot into JonMarc's shin. JonMarc gave a startled yelp and his grip momentarily slackened. Enic wriggled free, scrambling for his fallen dagger. JonMarc sprang after him. He seized the smaller man by the scruff of his neck and hauled him to his feet.

He heard a sharp hiss of intaken breath, and Enic slumped over his arm like a bean-sack doll. JonMarc felt wetness on his hand. Alarmed, he let his captive sag to the ground.

Enic's pasty hands were wrapped around the dagger hilt, it's point sunk deep in his midsection.

JonMarc berated himself. His clumsiness must have forced Enic onto the blade. Somehow, that explanation didn't sit well.

Blood was leaking from Enic's mouth. JonMarc shook him, hoping to dislodge the last, stubborn answers, but Enic's eyes had glazed. Aching and frustrated, JonMarc rounded up the chestnut and hoisted Enic's limp body over her saddle, then plodded back up the hill.

§

"The attack was unprovoked. I sought no quarrel with them." Kier carefully adjusted his cloak to hide the dark stain that spread like spilled ink across his thigh. Two of his attackers had fled the moment the soldiers arrived. The third lay twisted and staring, his yellow hair matted with blood. A few curious bystanders had gathered to gawk. Kier turned away in disgust.

The Tiernai centuriant beside him patted the gray's neck. "He wears the badge of the Branwyns. Those heathen need no provocation. By the gods, they grow bolder by the day. To attack a Legion officer here in the city, within bowshot of the Citadel? You!" he shouted to one of his men. "Bring that one to me. The Branwyn cur will be well interrogated, before he's hanged."

As JonMarc mounted the slope, he suddenly found himself ringed by a hedge of Tiernai pikes. Two hefty guardsmen seized his arms. He aimed an indignant look at Kier.

"Not that one, Centuriant," Kier said. "He's with me."

"Captain?" the officer rejoined, incredulous.

JonMarc shook off his escort like so many irksome flies. "Question *him*," he said, tipping Enic's body off the chestnut's back. It fell to the cobbles in a bloody heap.

"Let's get out of here," Kier growled, and turned his gray for the lower slope.

The crowd of Renewal celebrants milling about the city gates slowed their departure to a crawl. By the time they reached open road, Kier was feeling chilled and clammy. He did his best to attend JonMarc's account of the fight at the tavern, but the fire in his thigh bedeviled him. Gwythion had taught him Fithlon methods for suppressing pain and blood loss, but they required a level of concentration difficult to achieve on this rutted road. Kier said nothing of his discomfort. He only prayed that when it came time to dismount, he could do so without falling on his face.

A half-league beyond the gates, they found a quiet grove beside the road, where they could rest in privacy. To Kier's relief, he managed to keep his feet under him as he slid from the gray's back. He was aware of JonMarc watching as he hobbled to a low outcrop studded with gorse and maidenthorne, and eased himself to the ground.

The Dynian handed him a full wineskin. Kier appreciated the gesture, but did not drink; it would only lessen his ability to concentrate.

JonMarc set about gathering brush and tinder, and soon had a small pot of water simmering. Kier drew out his dagger and had JonMarc place its blade, and a silver coin, into the boil. Then, dropping his bloodstained breeches, he allowed his companion to probe the wound.

JonMarc clicked his tongue. "Here's the shaft fragment. But the dart's come loose. I'll have to dig it out." He took up the dagger. "Go ahead and yell if you want to. There's no one to hear."

Kier set his jaw. He had no intention of yelling. He shut his eyes and turned his mind inward, focusing ever deeper on another place and time: his uncle's fair castle at Hlanneth. There, a youth, he rode the lush grounds with his cousin Cari at his side, hearing the sounds and smelling the smells of a scene as far removed as possible from his present discomfort.

For a time, the stratagem worked. Then JonMarc began muttering to himself. The sound tugged at Kier's consciousness. The blade became a searing adder, burrowing into his thigh. Kier fought to remain detached, but sweat beaded his brow and burned his eyes. His carefully constructed world unraveled like a beggar woman's shawl, and the pain surged in.

"Got it."

Kier choked down his rising gorge and opened his eyes. JonMarc squatted before him, triumphantly displaying the bloody iron point between thumb and forefinger. It was nearly a thumb's breadth across. "You want it for a souvenir?"

Kier emphatically shook his head. This was not an episode he wished to remember.

JonMarc wiped his bloody hands in the grass. "The wound's too deep to cauterize. It might fester while we're on the road."

"Poultice it," Kier said, holding pressure on the wound with a scrap of rag. He was already feeling less light-headed. "There's a pouch of medicinals in my pack. Bring it and I'll show you what to use."

JonMarc sorted through the assortment of folded parchment packets. As Kier directed, he mixed the dried herbals with wine and water to make a paste: "Ladymoss and woundwort to halt the bleeding; goldenroot for healing. And bind the coin in with it," Kier added. "My mam was a Dynian healer. She always used clean silver to prevent wounds from festering."

JonMarc bandaged his handiwork with strips of cloth from one of Kier's discarded shirts, saved for such a purpose. When he'd finished, Kier hoisted himself to his feet and took a few tentative steps. With luck, the injury wouldn't cause him too much trouble. Then he settled back against the outcrop and tried not to watch as JonMarc ravenously assaulted the provender. To take his mind off his queasiness, he dug out the stolen message and studied it more closely.

"Do you really think this Roderig you saw at *The Jackal and Hounds* could be the same man we were warned of in Castémaron?"

JonMarc gulped down a mouthful of barley cake. "He fits the description: pale hair and eyes."

"That can be said of most Dynian."

"But he has a scar on his face, just like Ma'ardhi described. I figure he could easily have arrived here ahead of us, since we took the long way around Vilsolia. And the message speaks of a *token*. That's got to mean he's still after the Amulet." He squatted beside Kier. "Lucky I learned of the plot in time to warn you."

Kier voiced his gratitude, though it occurred to him that if JonMarc had returned to the inn before dawn, as promised, they could have left together, purchased the horses and been well out of the city before Enic even reached the inn.

"We need to find out who this Roderig serves," he said. "You couldn't get Enic to talk?"

"Oh, he talked quite a bit, but none of it made sense. He kept ranting of how his master could see everything and hear his thoughts." JonMarc rubbed the back of his neck. "I might've coaxed more out of him, if he hadn't fallen on his knife."

Kier doubted that. He found Enic's words unsettling.

"What about the *Lord M* Roderig speaks of?" JonMarc asked. "Any idea who that might be?"

Kier had an idea, but it pained him to consider it. JonMarc took his reticence for uncertainty. "Well, there must be *some* lord on Alcor with the initial *M*."

"I can only think of two," said Kier. "One is my father."

"And the other?"

Kier wished there were some way to avoid the issue. "My half-brother, Malcolm. But he wouldn't be part of a plot to *kill* me—especially a plot hatched by the Dynian."

"Rowenna didn't think it was a Dynian plot."

"Well, Enic and his men certainly weren't Tiernai."

JonMarc shrugged. "Even so, she says you're a great hope to her people."

Hope? The revelation baffled Kier. What kind of hope could he be to the Dynian? As a youth, they'd shown him no more regard than had the Tiernai.

JonMarc sucked in his cheeks, clearly hesitant to voice what Kier knew was on his mind. "Kier, what if your brother Malcolm is Roderig's Master?"

Kier shook his head. "He can't be."

"What makes you so sure?"

"Because Gwythion said that whoever seeks the Amulet must have a Fithlon connection. If Roderig's not Fithlon, then his Master must be. Enic revealed as much: *Sees everything; hears thoughts.* Those are Fithlon skills. My brother has no such training. He hates the Fithlon." Kier snapped a dry seed head and crumbled it in his hand. "Almost as much as he hates the Dynian. Anyway, the message only says Roderig will *go* to Lord M, not that he's actually involved."

JonMarc looked dubious. "What about that Master Demias Rowenna mentioned? He might be the one. He's both Fithlon *and* Dynian."

"I've never heard of him. But if he's Roderig's Master, and he was in the capital last night, why would the note tell Enic to deliver the Amulet elsewhere?" Kier rubbed his brow. "I wish we'd hear from Gwythion. It's been more than ten days. He should've made contact by now. I've held my mind open every night. It's not like him to be silent for so long."

JonMarc doused the fire and began re-packing their saddlebags. "We're not out of this yet. Roderig said his men would be holding the bridge. Is there any way around them?"

"None I can think of. We've got to cross the river somewhere, and the only fording place is leagues up-stream. Just getting there and back would add another day to our trip. I can't risk more delay if I'm to reach my father in time." Kier limped to his horse. "We'll just have to chance it."

§

A long, low cloud hung over the valley of the river Averin. Like steam rising from a deep fissure, it hugged the river's course, winding through the rich bottom acres of the King's Hold, finally to dissipate in the amber haze that veiled the rocky heights of the capital, now leagues behind. JonMarc followed it with his eyes.

They crouched on a low hillock. Directly below, the Millferry Bridge loomed out of the mist, its either end flanked by trees still scant of leaf.

JonMarc wondered how long Kier would take to decide their course of action. The brassy hadn't spoken for some time. He hunched, unmoving, beside a scrubby hawthorn, eyes fixed on the bridge below, head cocked attentively to the breeze.

`   JonMarc heard only the raucous cries of cairn-jays swooping overhead. "Can't see a thing through that accursed river mist," he grumbled.

"Be glad of it. Whoever's down there can't see us any better. We've little cover up here."

JonMarc turned, grateful to be conversing again. "Where d'you think they're hiding?"

Kier rubbed his chin. "If they're bowmen, like the last lot, they may be in the trees at either end of the bridge, waiting to shower us once there's no retreat. It's a common Dynian tactic." He struggled to his feet. "Truth is, I don't sense *anything* down there, threatening or not."

JonMarc accepted that his companion possessed certain Fithlon skills, though Kier seemed loath to discuss them. If they were as potent as Gwythion suggested, he wondered why Kier didn't rely on them more often. "Is this sensing of yours ever wrong?" he asked.

Kier shrugged. "Sometimes. But not usually at such close range."

"So what do we do?"

Kier gingerly hoisted himself into the saddle. "Rush it. Just keep low and don't slow down till we reach the other end. Even the finest bowman would be hard pressed to hit a moving target in that porridge."

Kier held them to the quiet of the greensward until they could follow it no farther. Then he urged his mount to a gallop. Tall gateposts loomed out of the fog like stony sentries; the only sound: the churning river below and the hollow drumming of their horses' hooves on the bridge's weathered planks. JonMarc braced for the stab of an arrow piercing his back. But as abruptly as it began, the drumming ceased. Devoreth's Orb grew warm again and the sky turned blue as they mounted to the top of the rise and looked back.

The swollen river roared invisibly below, the fog undisturbed by their passing.

"Seems they've abandoned their post," said Kier. "Or their orders miscarried. Still, if they're not here, where are they? I'm going to have a look around."

"You're *what*? Kier, why don't we just leave?"

The brassy was already off his horse and limping down the bank. JonMarc heaved a martyred sigh and followed.

"There are tracks here," Kier called over his shoulder. He half-crouched in the mud at the bridge's base, wincing at the strain on his wound. Beside him, turbid waters swirled and churned, swelling their banks. "They were made since the rain last night—or during it. It's too jumbled to be sure, but I think there were four or five horses here, and two at least were unshod. That means their riders were likely Branwyn rebels, though the Branwyn base lies leagues west of here. I don't like to think what they might be doing so far east."

"Maybe it's just meant to *look* like the Branwyns, like the note said."

"Maybe," said Kier. "But I'm with your friend Rowenna; I can't fathom why a Dynian like Roderig would go to such lengths to defame his own people."

As they climbed back, Kier stopped to tug something from a tree. "A crossbow bolt. That's a Tiernai weapon. And shot from the bridge, by the angle of it."

"Dynian horses and Tiernai weapons." JonMarc shook his head, bewildered. "Are both sides in league against us, or did they attack each other?"

"The latter, most likely. The tracks lead north. If Roderig's men were somehow driven from the bridge, they may be awaiting us on the road ahead."

For a while, there seemed little chance of that. North of the bridge, the road was no more than a muddy path through open fields, with few banks or thickets where attackers could lie hidden. After several hours, the tracks they'd been following played out and Kier at last conceded that the evidence at the bridge might have had nothing to do with them at all.

Devoreth's Orb hung low in the west when they finally reached the skirts of the Wilderwood, a dense patch of forest that straddled the border between Derwenth and the rocky, northern province of Evorick. As only a narrow finger of forest touched the road, Kier determined to reach the villages on the other side before halting for the night.

JonMarc's rump and thighs already ached from unaccustomed hours in the saddle. Yet he knew his companion was anxious to make up the time they'd lost this morning. Though Kier insisted on regular stops to rest and water the horses, he paced and chafed at every delay.

"Kier," JonMarc began, to take his mind off his discomfort, "you speak Dynian, don't you?"

Kier barely glanced up. "I was born to it. Why?"

JonMarc hesitated. He wasn't eager to relate his unsettling experience during Rowenna's song, when words unknown to him suddenly popped into his mind—not, at least, until he'd had time to make sense of it. *Forget not thy people, my son.* Words from his past. A father's entreaty? Or a mother's? Try as he might, he remembered neither. And, indeed, he had forgotten whatever he might have known about the Dynian. "Will you teach me?" he asked.

Kier chuckled. "Whenever you like. Have you decided to make Alcor your home, then?"

"Maybe. But I'd like to learn more about Dynian ways. Maybe that'll help me find what I'm looking for."

"And what's that?" Kier still sounded amused.

"Don't know yet. Back in Castémaron, I never thought much beyond the next night's ale and tumble. What point making plans, when your life can change at a master's whim?" JonMarc eyed Kier sidelong. "How about you? What are *you* looking for?"

The turnabout clearly caught Kier off guard. He darted his glance away. Getting the brassy to talk about himself was like begging coin off a miser. Yet gradually a wistful expression eroded the staunch bulwark behind Kier's eyes. "I guess I've always imagined buying some land—maybe in Chalcedon, or the Tarimian highlands—and settling down to raise horses."

"Just horses?" JonMarc found it odd Kier did not mention the pretty dark-eyed girl in the portrait he carried.

"Horses accept you for what you are. They make no impossible demands. I've seen enough of men's intolerance to last a lifetime, JonMarc. The farther I can get from lands where people are preyed upon just for being different, the happier I'll..."

Kier broke off abruptly and shot his gaze to the surrounding forest. "*Ride!*" he yelled, and kicked the gray in the flanks.

A feathered shaft split the air across their path. With a *whizz* and *thwop* it lodged, trembling, in the bole of a tree, mere inches from the gray's muzzle. JonMarc reined in hard as another arrow stung the bark of a sapling, just behind his shoulder. Kier's gelding reared as a dozen brown-clad men dropped from the trees to surround them in a bramble of steel-tipped arrows.

JonMarc's belly churned. Beside him, Kier quieted the gray and cursed his own inattention.

From the rear of the dour company, a dark man emerged. He was thick-limbed and heavy-bearded, and so wide of girth he overflowed his saddle like a sack of grain on a dray mule.

"Kier Fitzmorwen?" he said, his voice deep and gruff as any garrison commander's.

Kier drew himself up lance straight. "Aye."

"You and your companion are requested to hand over your weapons and come with us."

Chapter Fifteen

"Requested!" JonMarc spat. "As if we had a *choice*."

They sat back-to-back on a floor of tamped earth, arms encircling their knees and bound, wrists to ankles. JonMarc squirmed and shifted his rump on the unrelenting ground. They'd been sitting there nearly two hours.

Kier made no reply. His wound bedeviled him, but the delay frustrated him more. How much longer might his father cling to life?

Outside their tent, darkness had fallen. Campfires sprang up like will o' the wisps. Their flickering light glimmered through the rents and patches in the sagging walls. The smell of woodsmoke mingled with the succulent aroma of spitted meat. JonMarc's belly rumbled.

"Will they feed us, do you think?"

"I expect so," said Kier. "If they plan to kill us, they'll doubtless choose a swifter means than starvation." As if to emphasize his words, a ragged shriek sliced the evening's stillness. Kier felt JonMarc go rigid behind him and realized his own nerves were none too steady.

"What do you think they'll do to us?" A quaver edged JonMarc's voice.

"Depends on what they're after."

JonMarc's volume dropped to a harsh whisper. "But these are Roderig's men, aren't they? Surely they're after the Amulet."

"I'm not convinced. They only searched us for weapons. And there are too many to be hirelings. Even blindfolded, I sensed this is a good-sized camp. If it's Roderig's base, why have men waylay us at the bridge? Besides, some of our captors were Tiernai. So far Roderig's preferred to recruit Dynian for his dirty work."

"But they expected you. Who but Roderig knew you were headed this way?"

Kier pursed his lips. "Your friend Rowenna, for one. And any number of those at the Citadel. It's no secret I returned to Alcor to see my father."

"Well, if it's not Roderig, then who?"

Kier was about to voice his suspicions when they heard low murmuring outside. The tent flap flew back and two men in ragged foresters' garb entered. Without a word, one squatted to untie their ankles, then gestured toward the door. Kier and JonMarc struggled to their feet and ducked out into the chill evening where four more men, similarly clad, closed around them.

They were escorted along a forest path, legs still tingling from their long confinement. Kier counted the cookfires glimmering through the trees and made some mental calculations. This camp must house hundreds.

They came at last upon a clearing where a cabin of rough-hewn logs stood nestled among the trees. Firelight peeked past the edges of the hide door and voices rumbled within. A heavyset man awaited them. Kier recognized the leader of the war band that had captured them.

"I am Druric," the man said, his voice a resonant baritone, "lieutenant of this camp. Our captain is now returned and invites you to share meat with him." Druric's black brows narrowed at Kier's dubious expression. "'Tis a most singular honor!" he insisted. Clearly it was an *honor* they had no option of refusing.

Druric dismissed their escort. He drew a huge knife from his belt and sliced their wrist bonds. "Attempt nothing foolish," he said, holding back the hide curtain. "Our weapons will be trained on you at all times, though you may not see them."

A long, crowded table dominated the smoky hall, laden with jugs and platters of food. On one wall, a fire crackled merrily in a stone hearth. Kier counted eighteen seated men, some fair, others dark. A few possessed the amethyst eyes of a halfblood. Silence fell as they entered and all eyes fixed on them, expressions ranging from keen curiosity to outright suspicion.

At the table's far end, there sat a massive bear of a man, russet hair drawn back in a thick braid. His flowing beard glinted in the firelight like molten bronze. He leaned casually upon one elbow, legs like treetrunks thrust to the side, and trained ice-blue eyes on Kier.

Kier homed in on that gaze. "Gerit Mawr," he said, nodding satisfaction at having his suspicions confirmed. "When last we met, you were raiding Tiernai supply wagons."

The captain's shaggy brows narrowed. "An' you were but a fledgling aide, tagging along in Sir Donal's shadow." He rose, grinning, and stretched out a brawny hand.

JonMarc's jaw dropped. Gerit Mawr's bronze pate nearly brushed the roof beams. He accepted the proffered bear paw with obvious trepidation as Kier introduced him, and Gerit Mawr pumped his arm mightily. "So, 'tis true you ride with a Dynian, Fitzmorwen. A healthy sign. Come join us." Gerit Mawr indicated two empty chairs to his left. "Tonight, we feast in your honor."

This was too much for Kier. "My *honor*? You waylay us on the road like common brigands, force us to your camp bound and disarmed, then have the gall to name it honor?"

Gerit Mawr's face fell. "Ah, I do apologize for the misunderstanding. I was gone from camp, and my men were not sure of you. There have been strange happenings of late. Druric felt it best to take precautions, even if they be proved unnecessary. Yet I know you to be a man of honor, Fitzmorwen, and as such, you shall not sit weaponless in this company."

At Gerit Mawr's gesture, a guard hastened forward, bearing their confiscated arms. Kier quickly sheathed his sword and wrist dagger, masking his relief at their return. He did not trouble to mask his impatience. "I'm grateful for your trust, Gerit. Yet my father is near death. I've wasted too many hours here already."

"Aye, I do lament the duke's illness," said Gerit Mawr. "Though Tiernai, Duke Morwen has e'er dealt fairly with the Dynian. Still, you cannot ride all night. Why not rest among friends? For we *are* friends, Fitzmorwen—or should be, as our cause is the same: the well-being of Alcor. Stay. I promise you will learn enough to make the detour worth your while." Gerit Mawr signaled one of his men. "Food and drink for our guests."

Their host was clearly as bullish of mind as he was of build. Kier gave in, determined, as a Legion officer, to glean whatever information he could from the outlaw captain.

They were served thick slabs of venison and a porridge of lentils and onions. What the meal lacked in variety it made up for in quantity. JonMarc attacked his food ravenously. By his third cup of mead he was inclined to forgive his captors for his sore limbs and numbed buttocks.

Gerit Mawr lounged back in his chair, toying with a pewter goblet—a child's cup in his enormous hand. "I understand you've become quite a traveler, Fitzmorwen," he said. "You must find that life agreeable, to have stayed away from Alcor so long."

Kier shrugged. "I go where the Council orders me."

Their host clearly desired more substance. He re-directed his questions to JonMarc. "How does a son of Denia come to travel with a Tiernai officer? 'Tis a bond seldom seen in this sorry land."

JonMarc felt Kier's warning nudge. "I serve Fitzmorwen in repayment of a blood debt," he said carefully. "I was raised in Castémaron, not Alcor, and know little of the Dynian or their land." Kier dipped his head in approval and JonMarc relaxed. "But tell me of yourself, Gerit Mawr. I heard your name spoken in Menythgar, and I've seen a locket stamped with the same image of a harp as on the ring you wear. What does it signify?"

The room went suddenly still. A gangly youth seated at the captain's right leaned forward intently. His violet eyes bored into JonMarc like augers.

"*The Kreuth of Killian*," said Gerit Mawr, caressing the sigil on his forefinger. "It recalls the Dynian legend of old." He sought recognition. "Ah, but you are not of Alcor. The legend tells of a youth, one of the five Dynian heroes, who wandered our hills at the dawning of our age. In those years, the Dynian were not a single folk, but many tribes, constantly at war. None knew from whence the youth came, for unlike the Dynian, he was dark of countenance, and slender as a willow. He carried with him a silver *kreuth* that he would at times play, and the people named him Killian, for his gentle song recalled the bird of that name. 'Twas said that all who heard it would lay down their weapons and be at peace—and so were the tribes united."

"But why choose such a symbol?" said JonMarc. "Your folk are armed, and not all are Dynian." His gaze flicked to the halfblood youth at their host's right.

"But they are all fugitives, and weary of this war as a slave is weary of his bonds. You have but glimpsed our camp, JonMarc. 'Tis ragged as any pauper's hovel, yet we house entire families—wives and children of the men seated here, and countless others, fleeing the ruin that has cost them their homes and many their dear ones."

JonMarc could appreciate the analogy. "But why do they fly to you? What can you offer them here, except poverty?"

A doleful smile edged across Gerit Mawr's craggy face. "That, I do *not* provide. Most bring it with them. For my part, I offer protection, and a haven where they can live in peace, not as islands in a warring tide. For as you say, JonMarc, there are Dynian *and* Tiernai among us, and many of mixed race who can find refuge nowhere else. All are wearied of war and would see it end, for whatever their blood, they are native to Alcor. This conflict is of their fathers' making, not theirs."

JonMarc sat back thoughtfully. If Gerit Mawr spoke truth, his numbers could only increase. In time, his motley rabble might prove a force to be reckoned with. Kier's tight-lipped expression indicated he must be thinking the same. "You don't look like peacemaker, Gerit," JonMarc observed slyly. "Would you not fight your enemies, Dynian or Tiernai, if they came against you?"

Gerit Mawr stroked his burnished beard. "Aye, we would fight—if our lives depended on it. But we do not seek battle. 'Tis but a tri-month since Earl Ruark of Galwyn drove us from the Southerwood—and in midwinter. Yet we departed peaceably, for so long as there are other havens to fly to, 'tis not worth the shedding of blood. But 'twas a sore trial, for you judge aright. I am not by nature a man of peace. At times my fingers ache to wield a battleaxe.

"Years ago, I led men against the Tiernai, and was accounted a formidable foe, as Fitzmorwen will tell you. I had lost my wife and four sons when the Tiernai o'erran our village in Galwyn, and I was filled with hate. Yet as years passed, I found that doling similar hardship on my Tiernai foes could not return those I'd lost; indeed, it only increased my torment. I resolved then to seek an end to this conflict that has sundered more lives than e'er I could with ten thousand at my back. So I took another wife and made more sons, of which Manogan here is eldest." Gerit threw an affectionate arm around the violet-eyed youth seated beside him.

"Your son?" said JonMarc. The slender Manogan bore little resemblance to his ursine father. He was not a comely youth by any stretch, his face ruddy and pitted from some childhood disease. Dark hair hung limp to his shoulders. "Then... your wife is Tiernai?" The outlaw captain nodded. So, in making his peace, Gerit Mawr had traversed the forbidden boundary and wedded his enemy.

Manogan's thin lips curled. "The stranger asks questions that do not concern him. What matter whether my mother be Dynian or Tiernai? At least I know what man *sired* me." His eyes nailed JonMarc's in brazen challenge.

"Manogan!" Gerit Mawr snapped. "You'll not speak so to our guests."

"Fitzmorwen is our guest. The other is but his lackey. I would know where he has seen this locket he speaks of that bears your sigil."

JonMarc did not pretend to understand how he'd won the youth's animosity. "I told you, I saw it in Menythgar. It was worn by a maid."

"What maid? What had you to do with her?"

"That, I think, is none of *your* concern."

"It *is* my concern." Manogan reached inside his stained leather jerkin and drew out a pendant identical to Rowenna's. "There are but two of such make. The locket you saw, worn by the daughter of Dickon Terengar of *The Jackal and Hounds*, is mate to this, just as Rowenna is *mine*."

JonMarc tensed. His mate? Why hadn't Rowenna told him? He masked his discomfort with a casual shrug. "What's that to me? I saved the lady from Connail villainy. In the struggle, her locket was lost. I simply returned it to her."

"She cannot have *lost* it. She keeps it well concealed. The truth! How came you to see it?"

"I told you—"

Manogan leaped up. "*Liar*. A poor excuse to dally with another man's betrothed. I challenge you, Outlander, in defense of Rowenna's honor. Declare yourself, if you be not craven."

JonMarc was more than ready to give this surly pup a comeuppance. Kier stayed him.

"*Manogan!*" Gerit Mawr's bellow shook the hut. "Apologize to our guests and leave this hall."

With a defiant snort, Manogan backed to the doorway, his forefinger leveled at JonMarc. "We shall see, Outlander. We shall see which of us she chooses." He stomped out.

Gerit Mawr signaled one of his men to follow. "I beg you, pardon my son," he said. "He has been enamored of Rowenna since they were children, and the maid has not been unsympathetic. This summer, 'twas arranged that they should wed. Yet by Dynian law, 'tis the woman makes final choice, and Rowenna has not yet agreed to the match. Until she does, Manogan will be consumed with jealousy for any man who ventures near her." He eyed JonMarc, not unkindly. "I hope there was little of substance between you, though I do not ask. You appear to be fullblood Dynian, and Rowenna would find that appealing, for she is a maid wholly committed to her people's plight."

JonMarc recalled Rowenna's talk of choices. For all their sakes, he hoped Manogan would never learn what had passed between them.

"'Tis I myself bear blame for this," Gerit Mawr admitted, "for 'twas through me you chanced to meet the girl. You see, Dickon's folk, and Rowenna in particular, are my eyes in the capital.

"We have long anticipated Fitzmorwen's return." Kier glanced up warily at that. "'Twas Rowenna's task to watch for him and send word when he made port. That word we received only this noon. I regret I was not here. We would have offered a warmer reception."

"It was warm enough," Kier grumbled. He knew their host's history. Gerit Mawr's reputation as a Tiernai foe was second only to that of the legendary war-chieftain, Gareth Branwyn. Despite his apparent change of heart, Kier was not ready to trust him. "Come, Gerit, you've made worthy account of yourself, yet the evening passes. Why did you bring us here?"

Gerit Mawr folded brawny arms across his chest. "To be plain, Fitzmorwen, I would know your loyalties."

"My *loyalties*?"

"In two weeks time, the Tiernai Council will gather in Menythgar to decide whether or not to renew their war against the Dynian. You are the son of a duke; a respected leader of men. How do you stand on this issue?"

Kier's brows narrowed. "What does my stand have to do with it? I'm a Legion officer. I serve the king, and when he dies, I shall serve Prince Rhynion. If the Council votes for war, and King Brendan supports it, then war it will be. I've no power to change that."

"But if you could influence that decision?"

"How could I do that? I've no voice in Council."

"But if you *had*, Fitzmorwen, how would you vote?"

Kier could not make out what their host was getting at. He was hesitant to share his private convictions with anyone, especially a one-time enemy. Still, what harm could it do? "I'd vote for peace," he said. "I've no wish to see the war renewed. But why talk of *ifs*?"

Gerit Mawr folded his big hands on the tabletop. "Much has happened in your absence, Fitzmorwen, that you may not know of. The Connails strive with evil purpose to control young Rhynion. They cleave to him like leeches, sapping his strength, filling his mind with venomous counsel. More than half his subjects are Dynian, yet the Connails would turn the prince against them, convincing him of threat where there is none. To that end, they seek to rule the Council. Earl Hannon is already in their sway, as is your brother Malcolm."

Kier nodded, impatient. "I've heard all this."

"Have you also heard that the Connails scheme to reestablish the renegade line of Anlawth?"

"Anlawth? But—that family was attainted for high treason decades ago.

I didn't know any still lived." Kier cocked his head. "How do you know this? Rowenna cannot have told you. Even Sir Donal said nothing of it to me, and he bears no love for the Connails."

"No, Rowenna knows naught of it. I said she is my eyes in the capital, not my ears. I have other sources. There are not a few, Fitzmorwen, who are loyal to Alcor, yet oppose the Connails.

"As for Anlawth, you remember aright. Fifty years ago, Benyck of Anlawth headed the Dynian High Cyngor. Yet he sold out his people to the Tiernai invaders and instigated the murder of Alcor's High King. As reward, the Tiernai conqueror, Melchor, made Anlawth an earldom and gave Benyck his royal sister to wed. Yet soon Benyck's black heart changed. He turned against the new king as he had his former master, and plotted his death. The plan was discovered and Benyck executed, his entire family declared traitors—including King Melchor's own sister, who had recently borne Benyck a son. 'Tis he that still lives. His name is Táranos. I know little more of him than that—except that the Connails strive to reinstate him to his father's old Council seat."

"But why would the Connails support him?" Kier asked. "He's half Dynian, a race they're sworn to destroy."

"Because, in return, he has pledged to vote for war. The Connails are a devious lot, Kier. They shrink at nothing to achieve their ends. To provoke the Branwyns, they've begun raiding the Dynian villages that lie on Connail borders. The last incident was less than a fortnight ago: the hamlet of Caerdewi, razed to cinders. Only a handful managed to escape, making their way through the mountains to take refuge with the Branwyns, at Dorcalon."

Kier felt blood drain from his face. "Caerdewi, you say?"

"Aye. You know the place?"

"I was born there." Kier's anger swelled. He'd seen his mother murdered by of one of Penitarch Tor Connail's Covenant priests. Now the rest of her family—his aunt and cousins—were likely dead as well, at Connail hands. Though they'd never wasted any love on him, they were simple, decent folk who, despite the risks, had taken him in when he'd had no other home. "They've no right," he seethed. "The war's not yet declared."

"But it soon shall be. When Malcolm succeeds your father as Duke of Evorick, he'll throw his support behind the Connails. Duke Morwen was e'er a man of principle. Malcolm is but a pawn."

Kier struggled to calm himself. "My half-brother is what he is, Gerit, for good or ill. Our wishing will not change him."

"So should I say also, were things well at Cordon. But there have been troubling rumors. 'Tis said Malcolm behaves strangely if late—that he forbids any to see or speak with the duke save those of his choosing. Even the Duchess Yssolt and your cousin, the Lady Cariwyn, are barred."

Kier's distress at the news collided headlong with a rush of excitement. Cari—at Cordon? Then he would soon see her! He thrust elation aside. "You say these are *rumors*?"

Gerit shook his head. "My sources are reliable. Though the duke still lives, Malcolm has proclaimed himself ruler of Evorick. And there is more. Some say your brother is possessed."

Kier clicked his tongue. "Surely a leader like yourself cannot heed such nonsense."

He heard rumblings from around the table. Gerit Mawr's officers evidently took the charge seriously. Gerit himself remained unperturbed. "When first I heard the tale, I reacted much as you. Yet the man who reported this is no fool—and he has suffered mightily for his experience. You know him. He served your father these thirty years. His name is Stethan."

"Cordon's steward, aye. Yet he is Tiernai. How does he come to report his tales to you?"

"For lack of anyone else to listen. Stethan and I have an understanding. Years ago, he secretly took to wife a Dynian maid, who bore him twin sons. Sadly, she died in the birthing and, as Stethan could hardly raise his halfblood brood at Cordon, he left them in my care."

"So in return, he acts as your spy." Kier found it hard to condone such betrayal by his father's most trusted servant

"Let us say, he shares with me his growing concerns. Yet this week past, I received word that Stethan was dead—attacked in the night by Dynian brigands. Much did I lament the news, though I could scarce credit the cause. There are no Dynian brigands within leagues of Castle Cordon. Still, I mourned the passing of a good man.

"Then, two nights past, a peasant lad arrived, summoning me in secret to a cottage on the Evorick moors. There I found Stethan, beaten and broken, but very much alive. He told me he had indeed been set upon, but not by Dynian. 'Twas lord Malcolm's own henchmen who lured him beyond the castle walls, beat him senseless and left him for dead. Why? Because he chanced to witness something he did not understand."

"And what was that?" Kier asked, his uneasiness growing.

"According to Stethan, at supper last week, Malcolm complained of head pains, and Stethan thought to check on him before retiring. Concerned at receiving no answer to his knock, he entered the chamber, only to find Malcolm writhing on the floor, clutching his head and crying out to some unseen demon. Stethan tried to run for help, but Malcolm discovered him. Enraged, he demanded to know all the steward had overheard. Eventually, he calmed and let Stethan go, on threat of death should he reveal what he'd witnessed. Yet it seems Malcolm reconsidered and sent henchmen to silence the old man for good. Only by fortunate accident was Stethan found and borne to safety."

Gerit Mawr's keen eyes probed for Kier's reaction. Kier struggled to keep his face impassive. He had an idea what the aging steward had blundered into. Yet how could his Fithlon-hating brother have experienced such an encounter? "Could Stethan repeat anything he overheard?"

"He said he seemed to witness but one side of a bitter discourse that he could scarcely fathom. One thing he did recall: Malcolm was much concerned with finding some token amongst your father's effects."

Kier felt JonMarc's nudge and shook his head. The exchange was not lost on Gerit Mawr.

"So, you *do* have some idea what this means."

"No clear one," said Kier, "and I do not care to speculate. I'll see for myself how things fare at Cordon before I judge."

"What is there to judge? Your brother will soon hold Alcor's future in his hands. If war is renewed, thousands will perish. Yet Malcolm is possessed." Kier shot him a sharp look. "All right, his actions are suspect. You must at least concede that."

Kier frowned. "I'll talk with him, Gerit; try to urge him from the Connails' sway. As we've been apart so long, he may be willing to listen— though I doubt it."

Gerit shook his shaggy head. "'Tis past time to talk."

Kier's frustrations peaked. "Then what is it you want of me?"

The chamber went silent but for the crackle of hearth flames. Gerit Mawr stared into his steepled fingers as though carefully selecting his words. Then he locked his ice blue gaze on Kier.

"Unseat your brother. You are Morwen's eldest and may rightfully claim the dukedom. With my forces behind you, Malcolm cannot oppose you long."

Kier's astonishment quickly flared to indignation. He took a breath to calm himself. "I'll forget you suggested that, Gerit," he said, rising to his feet. "JonMarc, we're leaving." Several of Gerit Mawr's followers lurched from their seats to block his path. Kier glared back at their host. "Am I still your prisoner, Gerit?"

Gerit Mawr hesitated, then jerked his hand, ordering his men off. "We must talk of this, Fitzmorwen! Devoreth curse your stubbornness. 'Tis the future of your people we speak of."

"My *people*? Who are my people, Gerit? The Dynian? The Tiernai? How can I be champion to one and not traitor to the other?"

"Your people are those of Alcor. Will you burden them with another war? Claim the dukedom and use your voice to turn the Council to peace. We are already pledged to support you. And our numbers are greater than you guess."

"*How* great?"

Wariness. "Are you with us or against us?"

Kier willed his clenched fingers to relax. "I've no wish to be your enemy, Gerit. But I'll not dispute my brother's birthright. Even if Malcolm relinquished the dukedom willingly, it would not pass to me, for Tiernai law forbids a bastard to inherit—as you well know. Though I disapprove his actions, Malcolm is my father's true heir. My duty demands I oppose any who challenge that."

"Does your duty also demand that Alcor founder in innocent blood?"

"The matter is not so simple. To prevent a war, you ask me to *start* one. It's a reckless plan and I'll have no part of it."

Gerit Mawr's shrewd eyes sparked. "What if you had proof Malcolm seeks your death?"

Kier went rigid. He felt JonMarc's hand on his arm. "Kier, if that's true, then Roderig—"

Kier cut him off. His gut felt as if he'd swallowed rocks. Reluctantly, he took his seat. "I'm listening, Gerit."

"As I've said, we learned of your return to Alcor only this noon. Rowenna dispatched two riders with the news yestereve. They'd have arrived sooner, had they not been waylaid."

Icy dread engulfed Kier's heart. He hung on Gerit's words, suspecting what was to come. A part of him wanted to stop his ears before he could hear it.

"As they crossed the Millferry Bridge at midnight, they were attacked by three they took to be Tiernai highwaymen. After a bloody struggle, our men prevailed. Two attackers were killed."

"And the third?"

Gerit Mawr deferred to Druric. "Our prisoner," the stout lieutenant said. "We questioned him most of the day, but he revealed little—only that *you* were their intended target. In searching his dead comrades, we found this." He handed Kier a folded missive.

Kier opened it and read in silence. JonMarc nudged his arm. Kier struggled to keep his voice steady. "It seems my brother does not wish me to reach Cordon."

"What say you now, Fitzmorwen?" said Gerit Mawr. "How can you defend a brother who openly plots your death?"

Kier evaded the question; he needed time to think. "Did you say the attackers at the bridge were Tiernai?"

"Aye. But what else would Malcolm's men be?"

"Aye, what else? If they were truly Malcolm's. Yet this is neither my brother's hand nor his seal. I've seen its like before. We were attacked in Menythgar this morning by men whose orders bore this same hand—that of one named Roderig. And those assailants were Dynian."

"Dynian?" Gerit Mawr's rugged face betrayed astonishment. "Since when does the heir of Evorick hire Dynian henchmen?"

"Never, to my knowledge. The deed was meant to appear the work of Branwyn, no doubt staged for the benefit of those in the Citadel, to cast the Branwyns in even greater disrepute. Yet I cannot believe Malcolm would concoct such a plan. He lacks the subtlety."

"Mayhap the subtlety belongs to this traitor, Roderig. I've heard naught of him from my spies at Cordon. Perhaps Malcolm employed him to dispatch you in such a way as to keep any blame from falling upon his lordship."

"Or perhaps someone is slandering my brother." Kier rubbed a palm across his stubbled cheek. The smoke-filled chamber felt stifling. "This man you captured—may I speak with him?"

Druric looked uncomfortable, but ordered a guard to fetch the prisoner. "I doubt he'll tell you more than he told us."

Gerit Mawr sat back, arms folded across his broad chest. "So, Fitzmorwen, will you ally with us? Forget Tiernai law and claim your brother's Council seat. Your father's blood runs truer in you than e'er it did in Malcolm. For years Duke Morwen has labored to unite this land in peace. Yet now, as he nears death, Malcolm threatens to destroy all he has achieved. Is it not a greater issue than birthright?" Gerit Mawr clapped a beefy hand on Kier's forearm. "You alone can complete your father's work. Seize the dukedom and, with your vote, turn Alcor again toward peace."

"*Peace?*" said Kier, throwing off the captain's grip. "Do you know what you ask, Gerit? If I steal my brother's birthright, it will not bring peace. Surely you cannot not believe his friends the Connails would simply sit by and allow it. Their cries of *treason* will unite all the Dynian-hating rabble who now but lack impetus to fight. Oh, we'd give them that. And with them would march the king's own legions, as well as all loyal Alcoreans who only want the proper order restored. Those few in Council who stand against war would be swept aside, compelled by their very allegiance to Alcor to take up arms against us.

"And once the momentum began, who would have the might to stop it? Once we were defeated—and do not delude yourself, Gerit, we *would* be—they'd turn against the Dynian with renewed hatred, inspired by my own Dynian blood, and yours. Would the Branwyns have the strength to withstand them? I doubt it. Either way, there would be a bloodbath to make the battle of Ceorl's Ford look like a springtide festival. Is that what you ask me to support, Gerit?"

The cabin went eerily still. Then, as if released by a floodgate, every voice surged forth at once. Gerit Mawr pounded his fist for quiet. "It need not be so! There are some in Council—Duke Morwen's brother, Edmund of Hlanneth, for one—who regard you above your brother and would doubtless take your side, especially when it is revealed that Malcolm is possessed."

"And how do you mean to prove that? No, Gerit, I desire peace as much as any, but this is no way to achieve it. I don't want the dukedom or anything that goes with it. I've no intent to remain in Alcor any longer than my present business requires. This land holds only torment for me."

Gerit Mawr's retort was cut short as the hide curtain flew aside. "Captain," cried the breathless guard. "The prisoner is dead."

Druric leaped to his feet. "How?"

"I entered his cell thinking him asleep. When I reached out to rouse him, he seized my knife."

"You had to kill him?"

"He killed himself. Plunged the blade into his belly before I could stop him."

Kier felt JonMarc stir beside him. "Did he say anything before he died?" Kier asked.

The halfblood guard shook his head. "Naught of consequence. He must have been a servant or a bondsman, for he ranted of his master's wrath."

"'Tis unfortunate," said Druric. "We might have coaxed more from him."

"It seems he chose an easier death. I can't say I blame him." Kier stood. "Gerit, I thank you for your news. We will retire now, for we've a long journey tomorrow."

Gerit Mawr sat sullen, tapping his beefy forefinger on the table. "I did not expect you would be easily swayed. You share your father's stubbornness. Yet consider what we've said, Fitzmorwen. And be watchful at Cordon. Your stay there may well change your mind."

They were escorted back to their tent. By the time the guards departed, JonMarc appeared ready to burst from the need to share his thoughts.

"Kier, Druric's prisoner didn't kill himself because he feared torture—at least, no torture Gerit's men could devise. It's just like Enic. I tried to convince myself he fell on his knife because I couldn't make sense of it otherwise. But it's plain he took his own life, the same as Druric's prisoner—all the while raving of his master's wrath."

Kier looked up from re-dressing his wound. He'd reached the same conclusion, and the implications worried him. "The Fithlon Synod forbids any Fithlon from using his powers to dominate others. Yet it seems someone isn't deterred..." Kier halted abruptly and held up a hand.

Outside their tent, a shadow stirred against the glow of a nearby campfire. Kier hastened to fasten up his breeches while JonMarc dropped to all-fours and silently crawled to the rear of the tent. He slipped out beneath the hide wall.

There were sounds of a scuffle. Kier raised the tent flap in time to see his companion sail over the intruder's shoulder, to land with a grunt in a patch of scrub. Kier lunged out of the tent before the skulker could run off, his dagger poised for throwing. The hooded figure raised empty hands and made no attempt to escape.

"You all right?" Kier called to JonMarc, unwilling to take his eyes off his captive.

JonMarc groaned, struggling out of the thornbush. "Aye," he muttered, sucking a scratched hand. He limped up beside Kier.

"Fetch a light," said Kier. JonMarc ducked into the tent and returned with the lantern. Its amber gleam flickered off the bronze medallion on the robed intruder's breast: a circled, eight-pointed star.

"Kier, he's Fithlon!" JonMarc yanked out his dirk.

"Why were you spying on us?" said Kier.

"I was not spying," the monk replied simply. "I needed to speak with you, Fitzmorwen, and but awaited an opportunity." He shook back his cowl. Shaggy, silver-grey hair glinted in the lamplight. "Will you not invite me in?"

Intrigued by the monk's audacity, Kier drew aside the tent flap and ushered him inside. The spry fellow promptly took a seat on JonMarc's open bedroll. Kier and JonMarc exchanged wary glances. "Who are you?" Kier demanded.

The monk calmly placed his palms together. The back of his left hand was branded with the serpent scar of the sinistrae. "My name is Demias."

JonMarc started. "Demias? Rowenna spoke of a Master Demias. You were in Menythgar just last night." He eyed the monk with suspicion. "What sorcery brought you here so swiftly?"

Demias arched his pale brows. "My horse."

Unabashed, JonMarc squatted before him. "Rowenna said you probed the minds of the Connail minions and erased their memories of the tavern brawl." The round-faced monk nodded placidly. "Did you probe mine as well?"

A shrug. "I tried. But you wear a dathana crystal; my vows forbid me to remove it."

JonMarc fingered the charmstone through his shirt. "You mean, a Fithlon can't probe my thoughts while I wear this?"

Demias smiled indulgently. "We can if you willingly open your mind. Otherwise, such a task requires considerable power. I was weary after my work with the Connails and in truth, my son, I did not consider your thoughts to be worth the effort."

JonMarc looked almost offended. "Master Gwythion didn't have any trouble," he grumbled.

"Master Gwythion is an adept of the Twelfth Tier. I am only tested to the Sixth."

Kier still stood near the tent flap, fingers tapping impatiently on his swordhilt. "You said you wanted to speak to me. Well, here I am. What have you to say?"

Demias looked up, his expression grave. "Beware your brother, Fitzmorwen. Gerit Mawr is right. Young Malcolm is indeed possessed."

"So you heard that." Kier could scarcely repress a snort. "The main thing that possesses Malcolm is his own ambition."

"There is that," Demias conceded. "Yet I speak of something more dire."

Kier turned away. "I know. The encounter Stethan described sounded like a Fithlon mind-touch."

Demias shook his head. "Worse. He who bends his will toward your brother has the skills of the Fithlon, yet is *not* Fithlon."

Kier stared at him. "How can that be? The Fithlon are forbidden to teach their secrets beyond the First Tier to any but those sworn into the Brotherhood."

"True. Yet he possesses those skills—and has demonstrated he does not fear to use them."

Kier regarded the monk sidelong. "How do you know this?"

"Master Gwythion approached the Synod with his suspicions nine days ago."

Right after they'd left Castémaron. "How well do you know Gwythion?"

"I was his pupil. He told me of your quest; that you seek the Cábretaur of Aneryn."

Kier eased himself to the ground. Gwythion warned them not to speak of their mission to anyone—especially any Fithlon. Yet Master Demias already knew of it. Kier sensed no deception in the monk's mind, though an adept of the Sixth Tier might well detect Kier's feeble probe and conceal his true thoughts. One thing was certain: something troubled the silver-haired monk.

"Who is this false Fithlon," he asked, "and what is the extent of his powers?"

"So far, the Synod has discovered little. He has somehow managed to keep his existence hidden from them by shielding his thoughts from the *Infinite Mind*. The *how* of that is of great concern to us, yet it is not so distressing as the *why*."

JonMarc drew forward. "If he was so easily overlooked, how great can his powers be?"

"Great enough, I fear. Think on it: one who possesses Fithlon skills, yet does not bow to the Synod's restrictions on their use. Merely to hide his thoughts from the *Infinite* requires more skill than any true Fithlon—even Master Gwythion—has achieved. And it seems he has maintained the deception a very long while. If such a one should acquire the Cábretaur's power..."

"He would be invincible," Kier muttered. The revelation troubled him more deeply than he cared to let on. "I thought the Fithlon Synod refused to acknowledge that the Cábretaur exists."

"Officially, yes. But they cannot ignore the possibility, especially in view of this apostate's accomplishments."

"Well, if they expect us to risk our lives to retrieve their damnable crystal, they'd better learn this false Fithlon's identity soon. We're not likely to evade him long, especially if my brother is in his sway. What do they know so far?"

Demias stared into his delicate hands. "Only what I have said. Master Gwythion took that investigation upon himself."

"So why haven't we heard from him?" JonMarc whispered, echoing Kier's thoughts.

"Has he discovered nothing in all this time?" said Kier, impatient for a solid answer. "Surely you must have some idea."

"Master Gwythion suffers no one to share his thoughts—not even those he claims to account his friends."

Demias's disgruntled tone convinced Kier that the monk had tried to dissuade Gwythion from his present course, whatever that might be. Tried, and failed. He didn't like the sound of it. "What is Gwythion doing?"

Demias avoided his gaze. "I know only that his life essence in the *Infinite Mind* has vanished. I can think of but one way that might occur. Master Gwythion has crossed the forbidden portal and entered the *Death Realm*."

Fear laced icy fingers around Kier's heart.

"I don't understand," said JonMarc. "What does that mean—the Death Realm?"

"It is the shadowland to which the life force flies after death, to be purged of its worldly identity and reunite with the *Infinite*."

"Then—are you saying Gwythion is *dead*?"

Demias's face was somber. "Whether his body still lives, I do not know, but his mind—his essence—no longer inhabits this realm."

"But why?" JonMarc sounded unnerved. "Surely one with powers as great as Gwythion's wouldn't just—*die*. There must be some reason he's chosen to do this."

"I do not pretend to know Master Gwythion's mind," Demias admitted, "nor do I understand the mysteries of the Twelfth Tier. Yet this I do know: none may cross the forbidden portal except in death. Should Gwythion survive, I fear he will lack the strength to return."

Kier stared into the flickering lamplight, fingers knotted at his sides. He'd never known his mentor to shrink from risk or do anything without good reason. "He'll return," he said. "He's promised to meet us on Alcor. Gwythion has never abandoned a trust."

His voice was firm, yet he doubted. What if this time Gwythion had indeed pressed himself too far? His mentor possessed extraordinary skills, beyond those achieved by any other Fithlon. Yet even the greatest skill had its limits. Kier tried to convince himself that Gwythion knew what he was doing and all would turn out well. Yet his gut churned a more ominous warning—and in stronger terms.

Chapter Sixteen

Kier raised a heavy hand to wipe crust from the corners of his eyes. It was a gesture more of habit than need, for he hadn't slept—or at least, if sleep had come, it had so melded with his wakeful musings as to make the two inseparable. He certainly did not feel rested.

Ahead, JonMarc gave a hollow yawn and squirmed in his saddle. Kier nodded silent empathy, remembering well the discomforts of a long journey to one unaccustomed to sitting a mount.

They rode single file through the pre-dawn wood, following the youth Gerit Mawr had sent to guide them back to the road. There had been no farewells, and no further sign of the mysterious Fithlon. For the latter, Kier was grateful. His mind swirled like a rip current over the monk's disturbing news.

Gwythion had descended into darkness, risking his life, perhaps his very soul, to learn the identity of their renegade Fithlon rival—an identity it now seemed his half-brother might already know. Kier couldn't imagine how Malcolm had become involved with someone even remotely connected to an order he patently despised. Surely his ally, Covenant Penitarch Tor Connail, would object. The Covenanters and the Fithlon had ever been mortal foes.

And Malcolm knew about the Amulet. Kier felt for the silver hand, now strung on a chain about his neck. At their next halt, he'd find it a better hiding place, out of reach of the brother who apparently sought his death. Kier still could scarcely countenance that. As a boy, Malcolm had idolized him, imitating his walk, his speech, his every endeavor. Kier prayed there was still a part of his half-brother he could reach. He hated the thought of riding blind into an enemy stronghold. Yet he could only go on. Since dawn, his heart had warned him he must reach Cordon tonight or never again see his father alive.

By the time they reached the road and their laconic escort left them, Devoreth's Orb perched upon the horizon, a yellow globe veiling the countryside in a web of spun gold. From atop a rise, they looked out over the broad plain of Derwenth, a patchwork of meadows and dotted forest. Leagues to the north, the broad river Elass glinted, a thread of silver beneath the distant hills.

They made good speed across the flatlands and, by mid-day, crossed into the great northern province of Evorick. Here the countryside changed. Evorick was a land of crags and rugged uplands, culminating in the high, barren beauty of the moors. Kier's spirits rose as the land took on familiar contour. As a youth, he'd loved galloping among these windswept hills— his one escape from the ordeal of life at Cordon.

JonMarc proved an inexhaustible font of curiosity. Kier did his best to address his companion's seemingly endless queries about Castle Cordon and his boyhood there. He'd have preferred to spend the time in private reflection. Yet, despite the chatter, JonMarc's company was proving far less burdensome than he'd feared, back in Castémaron. He'd had no traveling companion since Gaelin left his service, two years past, and Kier began to wonder if his discontent of recent years might, in part, have been due to loneliness. It was a startling recognition for one who had spent most of his life solitary.

It was near midnight when they left the road to cover the last league overland. The night was cold and crisp, the sky pricked with a billion stars, shimmering like jewels in the moonless dark. Kier picked his way with surety among the tumbled rocks whose edges still glowed with a faint magien sheen. Half an hour later, they passed through the sleeping village of Cordon. Every cottage was shut tight. Somewhere in the fog-fingered valley, a dog yipped. All else was silent, save the chill wind rippling through the broom, and the hollow thump of their horses' hooves on the bridge's ancient planks.

They were both bone weary as they ascended the last slope. Before them, Castle Cordon's mighty keep shone dim amber against the starry backdrop. Torches gleamed from sconces beside the gates, but upon the castle walls they saw no movement.

Kier pounded the iron ring until the drawbridge planks trembled beneath them.

A light appeared in the gatehouse above. "Get ye gone!" came a sullen voice. "No one enters Cordon after nightfall. Come back tomorrow."

Kier's temper flared. He hadn't journeyed leagues only to be turned away like a beggar at the gate of his own home. He unbuckled his waterskin and hurled it through the open window.

There was a loud splat, followed by bellowed rage and a distinctly feminine squeal.

"You're on duty, soldier," Kier shouted. "Get your indolent face out here or, by Devoreth, I'll see you flogged."

They overheard some choice obscenities. Finally, a tousle-haired sentry appeared on the wall above the gate, fastening up his breeches. "State your business," he snarled.

"I've come to see the Duke of Evorick."

The sentry swaggered. "Have you now? Lord Malcolm sees *no one* after retiring. You can cool your stinking heels till the gates be opened, at dawn." He turned to go.

Malcolm—the *duke*? Panic overrode Kier's anger. But had his father died, surely the castle would be draped in mourning. "I speak not of Malcolm," Kier snapped. "It is Duke Morwen I've come to see. I am his son, Kier Fitzmorwen, Captain of the King's Legion."

The sentry's eyes widened and his whole demeanor changed. "*You*? But I was told— Wait one moment while I fetch..." His final words were lost as he scurried out of sight.

Kier aimed JonMarc a troubled look. "If my father were still in control, the knave would pay dearly for his arrogance. I fear my brother has no head for command."

The sentry soon returned with another man. At first, Kier thought it might be Malcolm, but he quickly realized otherwise.

"You claim to be the son of his Grace, Duke Morwen?" the newcomer challenged.

Kier struggled to mask his irritation. "If you don't believe me, bring out someone who—"

The newcomer raised a placating hand. "No, no, I accept your word. You have the duke's voice and bearing. I am Halistan, Captain of the castle guard." He paused as if awaiting acknowledgment. Kier gave him none. "In truth, we did not expect you, Fitzmorwen. I was told one might arrive bearing tidings of you, but that you yourself had been... delayed."

"Wishful thinking," JonMarc murmured. "He's stalling, Kier."

Kier agreed. "How long am I to be kept waiting, Captain? I'm an officer of the king. You cannot deny me entrance."

"I know it well," Halistan replied amiably. "It is your companion concerns us. Lord Malcolm permits no Dynian to enter Cordon."

"I'm Fitzmorwen's squire," JonMarc shouted, before Kier could open his mouth.

Halistan chuckled. "An impudent squire, to speak before his master. Yet my orders are clear. I cannot allow him to enter without authority. He may, after all, be a Branwyn spy. There have been Dynian brigands abroad of late."

"You have *my* authority," Kier said. "I will personally vouch for this man before the duke, my father. Will that satisfy your orders?"

Halistan stroked his short beard, pondering. Finally, he nodded at someone unseen and the portcullis groaned open. Kier and JonMarc dismounted and led their weary mounts inside.

No sooner had they entered the torch-lit courtyard than they found themselves surrounded by an armed detachment. "Well met, brother," came an unctuous voice from the shadows.

Kier spun, automatically reaching for his sword.

"Disarm them," Malcolm barked, stepping into the light. He looked older than Kier remembered; more careworn, his slender frame wrapped in furs against the night's chill. Yet the years had only deepened the contempt in his shadowed brown eyes.

"Malcolm, there's no need of this. You know why I've come."

"You did well to summon me, Halistan. My father's bastard looks weary, does he not? He has traveled far this day—praise Devoreth for his *safe* arrival." Malcolm turned a vicious eye on a hooded figure lurking beside him.

JonMarc touched Kier's arm. "Roderig," he whispered. A soldier prodded him to silence.

Kier's innards churned. Surely Malcolm would not dare to murder him—an officer of the King's Legion. Not in front of so many witnesses. The brother he'd been raised with would shrink from such a prospect. But under a renegade Fithlon's influence...?

"Malcolm, I must see our father. There's little time. You know it is the only reason I returned."

Malcolm motioned to Halistan. "See that Fitzmorwen and this... *creature* of his are housed for the night. Tomorrow we may find occasion to grant him audience."

"Malcolm, please!" Kier cried, as two stocky guardsmen clamped hands around his biceps. "Let me go to him. Tomorrow may be too late."

Malcolm's aura of composure shattered. "Too late for what? To grovel for a share of *my* inheritance? You think I don't know why you suddenly return now, after five years absence?"

Kier's jaw trembled. "I don't care a cleft copper for your inheritance. Our father's *dying*. I only want to see him once more." His eyes darted, taking stock of his position; the stony-faced guards. There was no escape. "Blazes, Malcolm, I'm your brother. I've never done you harm."

Malcolm regained his control. His thin lips curled. "*Brother*? I share no blood with you, serpent-spawn." He turned and walked off, tossing a thoughtless wave over his shoulder. "Take them away."

A warning chill wormed up Kier's backbone. *Serpent-spawn*? No Tiernai but the duke and Gwythion knew his mother had borne a serpent brand. Even the Covenant priest responsible for her death made no connection between the sinistral potioner he killed and Duke Morwen's bastard son. How did Malcolm know of it? And what did that portend? The scion of a *sinistra* was always suspect. And though Kier did not inherit his mother's spell-handedness, he still possessed sinistral talents—enough to threaten his career, even his life, should they become known.

They were escorted to a chamber in the castle's south tower. With every step, Kier fought the urge to wrestle free. The sullen pair flanking him, and the two brutes behind, jostling JonMarc, weighed against his chances of success. Indeed, such an attempt might provide Malcolm whatever excuse he needed to have them both killed.

The guards unlocked the chamber's heavy door and shoved him inside. Kier expected JonMarc to follow, but their captors had resentments to vent. At the spongy thud of fists on flesh, he scrambled back to the open door. In the torch flicker, he saw JonMarc double over as three of Malcolm's men took turns pummeling him. "Dynian scum," one snarled, planting an indignant fist in JonMarc's belly. "Ye can die wi' the rest of your beggared breed."

JonMarc let out an agonized wail that might have waked the castle dead. Kier tried to claw past the door guards. "Blast it, he's just a servant. If you want to fight someone, fight *me*!" Gods, he was aching for it. The butt of a quarterstaff found his midsection and he reeled back, gasping.

JonMarc's groans quickly weakened to pathetic whimpers. As they did, his tormentors seemed to lose interest. "Bloody craven," one snarled, as they flung him into the chamber. JonMarc sprawled across the slate floor and lay still as death. Kier staggered to him, fighting nausea.

The moment the door bolt clacked, JonMarc raised his head, eyes bright as ever in the glow of a candle stump. He waved aside Kier's offer of aid and crawled to the edge of the pallet, the chamber's single piece of furniture, feeling for broken ribs.

"I should never have let you accompany me here," Kier muttered.

JonMarc worked his tongue around his mouth and spat out a chip of tooth. Despite the blood on his lip, he managed to flash his unquenchable grin. "You think I'd miss all this?"

"JonMarc, they might've killed you."

The Dynian chuckled. "Nah, I gave them what they wanted."

Kier stared at him. JonMarc's piteous moans had sounded so genuine it was hard to believe they'd simply been for show.

His relief was swiftly overshadowed by the looming reality of their plight. He had to find a way out of here. Malcolm's jealousies would not keep him from his father.

He glanced around their dreary prison. He was familiar with the room; it had been his bedchamber during the years he'd lived at Cordon. Since then, it appeared to have gone unused, for dust lay thick on the hearthstones, and the floor was littered with debris blown in from the unshuttered window. Kier tested the door. The bolt held fast. Voices in the stairwell told him at least two of Malcolm's guard remained outside. He crossed to the window and gazed down at the star-shot waters of the moat, three stories below.

There was a way. He'd used it as a boy, whenever his stepmother locked him in for some perceived transgression. If he could climb to the roof, he could re-enter the keep by the watchtower stair. It wasn't far above. He only needed rope, and something long and rigid enough to catch behind the merlons. Years ago he'd used a fire iron, but there was none to be had. Kier unbuckled his sword belt and tested the bronze-banded scabbard for strength. It might briefly bear his weight. He sat and began to shred the bedclothes.

The aged fabric ripped with ease. Kier bound the ends together and tugged the knot to test its strength. The cloth began to fray. He'd have to braid the strips.

JonMarc stood near the door. He frowned at Kier's determined efforts. "What in Ghedrev's name are you fussing at?" he hissed.

"I'm going to climb out of here. It's the only way."

"Way to kill yourself."

Kier ignored him and went on with his task. His fingers worked nimbly. Soon, he had a line he judged long enough to toss up to the roof. He knotted one end around his scabbard.

JonMarc knelt with his ear to the door. "Kier, *wait.*"

Kier gathered the braided linen and headed for the window. He didn't need JonMarc to tell him the risk he took. He knew. But he had no choice. He hadn't journeyed all this way just to have his father die while he remained imprisoned at Malcolm's whim.

He heard a sharp snap and turned with a start.

JonMarc dropped a tool into the leather pouch at his belt and cautiously pressured the door. It opened with a muted squeal. "The guards have gone," he said. "Let's go find your father."

"You might at least have warned me." Kier's disgruntled whisper echoed through the empty hall like a host of hovering spirits.

"I tried to. You wouldn't listen."

They'd descended to the keep's main level and now tip-toed along a circular hallway. With only a hooded candle, they could scarcely see more than a few feet ahead. Kier ran a hand along the wall, trying to recall which chamber was used by his cousin Cari. He'd need her help to locate the duke. *This one*, he motioned at last. He raised his fist to knock.

JonMarc laid a cautionary hand on his forearm and shook his head. Selecting a tool from his pouch, he knelt before the lock.

Kier shifted uneasily. Using such tactics to escape a prison was one thing. To break into a lady's bedchamber..? Yet they dared not raise an alarm. He jerked a grudging nod and stood back, feeling uncomfortably like a felon.

The bolt released with a soft snap. "I'll go first," he whispered, and slowly eased the door open. The amber gleam from JonMarc's candle splayed his shadow across the rush-strewn floor as he slipped noiselessly inside.

He sensed movement. Something flew at him through the darkness. Instinctively, Kier dodged. The projectile whisked past his brow and smashed to tinkling shards on the stone floor.

Kier threw himself at his attacker, pinning slender wrists against the wall. "Let me go!" the girl cried, pummeling his shins with her bare feet. "How *dare* you enter my chamber, Halistan? The duke shall know of it and have you banished!"

"*Cari!* Cari, it's me. It's Kier."

He felt the tension in her limbs lessen as his words sank in. "Kier?" Her dark eyes trapped the candlelight as JonMarc brought it nearer. Then they softened, and she flung herself into his arms.

Kier had never known such ecstasy. Within his heart, a pang began to ease—an abiding ache he'd scarcely realized was there until he felt it leave him. He buried his face in Cari's hair, drinking in the sweet scent of her. She felt small and fragile in his arms, and he held her close, protecting her from the phantoms of her fears.

Eventually Cari raised her head and noticed the stranger in the room. She struggled to disengage herself. Kier let her go unwillingly. "This is— JonMarc," he stammered. "We traveled together from Castémaron."

Cari nodded cordially and blushed as JonMarc's gaze lingered on her torso. Annoyed, Kier snatched a blanket from the bed and wrapped it about his cousin's slender frame, acutely aware of her supple curves beneath the chemise. Since he'd last seen her, Cari had indeed become a woman.

Cari smiled up at him. Her fingers stroked his unshaven cheek. "My darling Kier. You come in answer to my prayers. When did you arrive?"

"An hour ago. Malcolm saw fit to detain us in the tower, but JonMarc has a—*talent* for escape."

Cari eyed the tall Dynian curiously, even as he studied her. "You'll have to tell me about it," she said, "and how you managed to enter my chamber without a key. But not now. Now, you must go to the duke. He was terribly weak when I left him this evening."

"Then you *do* have access to him? I was told otherwise."

Cari took up a gown and waited for them to turn their backs. JonMarc required prodding. They sat on the edge of the bed.

"Only these past few days has Malcolm allowed me to sit with him unaccompanied, and that because the physicians assure him your father is beyond speech. Yet each day, when they leave, the duke entreats me for news of you."

Kier rested elbows on his knees and stared dismally at the floor. "I should've come sooner."

"Aye, he'd have liked that. But at least you are here now. We can go to him as soon as—" Cari huffed. "Ah, these dreadful laces. Will you help me, Kier? I've not yet got the way of them."

Kier nearly stumbled over himself hastening to her aid. "Why are you unattended?"

Cari gave a bitter laugh. "Malcolm does not want me here. Two days ago, he ordered my ladies back to Hlanneth, hoping I too would go. But I cannot leave the duke; he's like a second father. And he is ill used by Malcolm's folk. So I manage on my own. Generally I do quite well."

"Aye, I noticed," Kier replied, a warped eye to the crockery shards littering the floor.

"Oh, Kier, I am sorry. I took you for your brother's swaggering guard captain. He's paid me much attention of late, all of it uncourted. A stroke upon the helm would do the rascal good. He's far too enamored of his own importance. But you—and with the chamber pot!" Cari suppressed a snicker. "Can you ever forgive me?"

Kier let it pass. "Where is the duke? I overheard a guard say Malcolm has taken the main apartments for himself."

"They have him in the east tower, where they say he'll not be disturbed by the comings and goings of so many."

Kier frowned. "Whose decision was that?"

"Malcolm's, of course. He insists the air is more wholesome up there, and the view more pleasant—both true. Albeit, at times the wind from the sea can chill to the marrow, and with the shutters closed against it, the duke cannot see the view. It is Malcolm alone derives the benefit, for the tower has but one access—the easier to keep out those not yet in his service. We must find a way past his guard."

The task proved simple enough. The glimpse of a Dynian head poking around the corner quickly lured Malcolm's sentry from his post. He stalked it as far as the stairwell before Kier's sledgehammer fist crumpled him. Kier hauled him to a storeroom for safekeeping while JonMarc donned the man's sword and helmet.

Cari slipped into the chamber to check on the duke. When she emerged, her face was grave, and Kier recoiled at the message there. Since Castémaron, his driving fear had been that if he reached the duke's bedside too late, his questions might go forever unanswered. But—what if the answers proved even more damning? Dread constricted Kier's throat. He suddenly wanted to flee. He willed the impulse down and entered alone.

The room stank of illness—of sour bedclothes and bodily waste— scents he'd never associated with his father. They lent the fire-lit chamber a surreal quality, while making the truth of the duke's condition unavoidable. Until this moment, Kier had pictured his father as he'd always known him: strong, commanding, ruggedly handsome. How could this hollow-eyed specter propped against pillows be Alcor's *Iron Duke* Morwen? He set his candle on the night table and drew up a chair beside the bed.

The rumpled covers stirred. "So, you've come at last." The voice was barely recognizable, Duke Morwen's rich baritone now broken and grating, like a hinge on an old cellar door.

Yet even that was welcome to Kier. He bowed his head. "Your grace, forgive me. I came as soon as I learned you were ill."

"So *that's* what it took." The duke worked to clear congestion from his throat. In the feeble light, he looked far older than his fifty years. His scraggly hair, once raven black, had faded to the dull gray of hearth ash; his seamed and stubbled face clung to the bones of his skull like a death mask. "Five years. In that time... you could not manage to return... even once?"

Kier started to protest. He'd have come back eagerly, had his father but requested it. Still, there was no point casting blame. "I'm sorry, your grace. My duties..."

"*Duties.*" The duke's temper quickly lost its edge. He sighed. "I'm not blind, Kier. I know you never felt welcome here. And—not without cause. I, too, found reasons to stay away."

The candid admission took Kier aback. He recalled that, during his boyhood, his father spent little time at Cordon, always citing his responsibilities in the capital. His frequent absence was ever a trigger for the Lady Yssolt's furious tirades.

The duke struggled to raise himself amongst the cushions. "Does Malcolm... know you're here with me?"

Kier shook his head. "My lord brother had me locked up the moment I arrived."

"Aye, that sounds like Malcolm. But you outmaneuvered him." The duke's eyes crinkled with perverse glee—and admiration. Kier soaked it in like a desert rain. "There is so much... I want to say to you, Kier. So many years... to make up for. We've scarcely..." Phlegm tangled his throat and he broke into a paroxysm of coughing.

Kier hastily poured a glass of brandywine from a carafe beside the bed and helped his father drink. "Please, my lord, don't exert yourself."

"No, let me speak. Your coming is all I've awaited." Duke Morwen dropped back against the cushions, his complexion wan even in the dim candlelight. Yet his voice, while hoarse, grew steadier as he spoke, as if he'd long been mustering strength for this encounter.

"I do not fear death, Kier. I've looked him in the face so oft his countenance has become familiar to me as my own. You, a soldier, will understand that."

Kier dipped his head. He'd steeled himself against that visage often enough, though he could not yet claim to have lost his fear of it.

"Malcolm does not. He has been too much coddled by his mother. The blame is mine. I abandoned him to her years ago."

"And while I was gone, she taught him to despise me."

"No," Morwen said, "she only taught him fear. Yssolt ever feared the past; my feelings for your mother." His face clouded. "I know I've scarcely been a father to you, Kier, though some say even the little I gave was too much. Bring the candle nearer. I want to look at you."

Kier did, and the duke appraised him up and down, his gaze keen and penetrating as ever. "You've become a fine man. Sir Donal's reports make me proud." A ragged sigh. "You look much as I did at your age, do you know that? Except the eyes. Those are your mother's."

Kier recalled the duke saying much the same thing years before, on their first journey together. Then, Kier had been too young, too intimidated to question. "My mother was no halfblood," he noted quietly. "Her eyes were *blue*."

"I speak not of color, but what lurks behind: the pain; the longing."

The duke's insight made Kier feel naked as a newborn.

A look of enduring sadness washed across Morwen's haggard face. "I only pray my sweet Allyn has forgiven me."

Like tar from a noisome pit, Kier's harbored resentments bubbled up inside him. "My mother never blamed you."

The duke's narrowed gaze skewered him like a lance. "But *you* do."

Kier looked away. He'd never voiced his feelings to his father. Indeed, in all the years since he'd come to Cordon, they'd seldom conversed— and never as man to man. Kier steeled himself. This was the hour he'd readied for. "Why did you abandon her?" he asked, unwilling to disguise the accusation in his voice. "Why did you leave her in the village, to be humiliated; disgraced?"

The duke's grimace was more of pain than anger. "I never meant to hurt her, Kier." His voice was as coarse as dried grit-weed. "You must believe that. I *loved* your mother. The hours I spent in her arms were the sweetest of my life. I begged her to come away with me. In Menythgar, I'd have found her lodgings with others of her race. We could have been together, at least some of the time." The duke shook his head dolefully. "But she refused. Your mother was a determined woman, Kier. She would not leave the villagers without a healer. Even then, I think she knew there would be a child, and she refused to raise a halfblood among strangers."

Kier scarcely saw how that would have made any difference. While the village folk relied on his mother's healing skills, they made no secret of their contempt at her decision to keep her bastard son. Kier could not recall her ever mentioning that the duke had offered to take her away with him. His tone softened. "Then why did you never come back?"

"I did! When I learned of your birth, I stole into the village by night. I saw you in your cradle: a sturdy boy, the first child of my loins." Morwen's lips softened in a wistful smile. "You gripped my finger with such strength.—as if to keep me from departing. Yet I dared not tarry, for the war still raged. Had the villagers discovered I was a duke's son, and not some lesser knight, as your mother gave out, they'd have delivered me to the Branwyns.

"After that..." Morwen's shoulders slumped. "I don't know, Kier. I was young—younger even than you are now. In youth, there is ever tomorrow. I always meant to return, to watch you grow. But the war; my duties..." He winced, as if suddenly deeming his own excuse as inadequate as he'd earlier judged Kier's.

"Then word came to me... of her death; the rumor of a sinistral potioner put to the ordeal by a Tiernai Covenant Priest." Morwen's eyes shimmered. "For days I was frantic to learn the truth. I sent a trusted spy— Sir Donal—to discover the circumstances of her death and whether you, at least, survived. To my relief, he brought word that you were safe; taken in by your mother's kin. I sent them coin to care for you."

Coin? Kier had never heard that. His aunt and her brood always treated him like the lowliest drudge, as if he were beholden to them for every morsel. Yet—why hadn't the duke come himself? There could only be one reason. "You blame me for her death."

"Blame *you*? Why would I?"

Kier felt suddenly flustered. "Because... if it weren't for me… the way the villagers tormented her... I tried to use my sinistral skills to... " Guilt stopped his tongue. If he were to reveal that his own actions might have prompted the Covenant priest's attack, his father would surely despise him.

"I couldn't save her!" he ended lamely.

"You were but six, Kier. What use could a child's untrained skills be against a Covenant Priest? Thank Devoreth the villain did not discover you possessed *talents* or he'd have destroyed you as well." Morwen's head drooped. "No, Kier, the blame was mine. I should have known the dangers she faced, dwelling on the Connail border; disdained by her own kin because of me. I should have protected her." The duke shut his eyes. Moisture glistened on his sunken cheeks. "Ah, my sweet Allyn, had I but *taken* you from that pit of hate, you might have lived." He sank back against the pillows, his breath rattling like a parched husk.

Again, Kier offered the wine cup and held it while his father sipped. "Shall I leave you to rest, my lord?" he asked.

"No, stay with me, Kier. I need you here."

The answer unsettled Kier. He'd never heard Duke Morwen admit to needing anyone. He leaned back in the chair and closed his eyes, suddenly aware of his own weariness. The chamber felt peaceful, with no sounds but the duke's labored breathing and the muted echo of the surf, thundering against the rocks, far below. Yet it was an eerie peace—one that brought back with painful clarity the memory of Kier's first grief. The elements were the same: the fire-lit chamber, the stale bedclothes.

His mother cradled his small hand in her own as he sat by her bed, and whispered soft words to allay his fears. His father was a nobleman, valiant and honorable. One day, very soon, he would ride to the village on his fine stallion and bear Kier away, to raise him in a palace, as was his due. The glorious creature his mother described could only be one of the great heroes of legend, and it thrilled Kier to think such a man was his sire. But then... murmured voices outside the door—the Elders and the Covenant priest, come to drag his mother away.

A strangled cry escaped Kier's throat. He lurched upright. The motion shattered his dream.

His father was watching him. "You are weary, my son. You've ridden hard, this day."

"I'm all right," Kier said, embarrassed. He hadn't meant to doze off.

Morwen smiled sadly. "I'll not keep you long." His voice dropped to a whisper, as though he feared the very walls might overhear. "Has Gwythion told you—of your inheritance?"

Kier judged it best not to tell the duke of Gwythion's mysterious disappearance. "He spoke of Cymworth."

"Good. But be aware, Malcolm will oppose you— "

"I know. He thinks I only returned to steal what is rightly his."

The duke's face hardened. "He is grown so distrustful, that one. It seems the more he gains, the more he covets." He paused to catch his breath. "Did Gwythion give you... aught—?"

"The silver hand? Aye, I have it with me. He said you found it."

Something like a sigh rasped in the duke's throat. "It seems an aeon ago. I was loath to surrender it to him, for I suspect its worth is more than any dare imagine. I'd thought its existence known only to Gwythion and myself, yet somehow Malcolm has got wind of it. He's questioned me about it several times since I fell ill—the last, only this morning." The duke chuckled slyly. "I feigned weakness and told him naught. It was meant to be yours, Kier. Of that I am certain."

The duke coughed again, his weakness anything but feigned. But he seemed determined to continue. "Gwythion told me of the Nwtyrran prophecy—that you are the one appointed to fulfill it. I cannot say I believe in it. Long ago, I rejected such tales as fodder for weak minds. Yet, to lie alone with Death makes a man see things anew. There is a great paradox here. The Amulet is real; solid and whole, yet it is not of our time, our world." The duke fought for breath. "Gwythion says such treasures are not given to mortals, but only lent, in fulfillment of some greater purpose. Perhaps that is true. I'm only an old soldier. Such puzzles of the mind never concerned me. Yet I do know that... when a task needs doing, it is folly to entrust it… to one whose only motive is ambition. Though Malcolm is heir to my title, my lands, you, Kier, are the child of my heart. I know Gwythion's faith in you... is not misplaced."

The duke dropped back, his chest heaving. Kier struggled with himself. Should he tax his father with one last question? Perhaps there would be another chance to ask. No, not if Malcolm had his way. He had to know. "Gwythion said it was only because of the Amulet that you agreed to acknowledge me as your son. Why did you wait *four years?* Were you ashamed of me?"

The duke's silence seemed to last an eternity. With each second, Kier's misgivings grew. He shouldn't have asked. Some secrets were better left un-probed.

"Not ashamed, Kier," Morwen said at last. "*Never* ashamed. I was... afraid. Afraid you would reject me; that, like your mother's kin, you would despise me as your Tiernai enemy; that you blamed me for her death. By then I had inherited a dukedom; wedded a woman I foolishly hoped might ease the longing in my heart. I had fathered an heir. I feared the upheaval, should I bring you to Cordon, and convinced myself you were better off among your mother's folk." He shook his head. "The longer I put it off, the more daunting the prospect became. I tried to banish you from my mind. When, at last, Gwythion pressed me to acknowledge you, I lashed out at him; bade him keep to his own affairs. But he was right—as he always is—and I knew it.

"So I went to fetch you. That journey, Kier, was the most difficult of my life. I, who had faced Branwyn swords without compunction, was terrified of how my own son would receive me. And when I found you, and saw the damage they had done... You had already turned inward. You scarcely spoke. To this day, I feared that you resented me."

"I… I only wanted your approval," Kier said, his voice nearly as husky as his father's.

"You've *always* had that, though I did not know how to tell you. I feared to show you favor over Malcolm." The duke touched Kier's knee—a tentative gesture of affection. Kier tensed involuntarily and his father drew back, shaking his head sadly. "I know your life has not been easy. There are many you have cause to hate: the Covenanters, for stealing your mother's life. The villagers who abused you. All who have caused you torment over the years. Malcolm. Yssolt. And myself, most of all."

"I don't hate..." Kier began.

"Good. Hatred is but a mask for fear. It blinds a man and keeps him from seeing what truly is. Remember that, Kier, for whatever path lies before you, you will need clear sight."

Shouting suddenly erupted in the hallway outside. Someone pounded the door. Kier jerked to his feet, flashing his father an urgent look.

Duke Morwen met his eyes calmly. He grasped Kier's hand with both of his own. "You have ever been... my true son, Kier. Do not tell Malcolm we spoke."

Kier hesitated, loath to leave the duke's side. Having at last found the father he'd longed for, he was unwilling now to let him go. There was so much more he wanted to say. He'd rehearsed the words over and over in his mind on the long road north. Yet now, they would not pass his lips. "Father, I—"

The duke squeezed his hand. "Go my son. I am weary and must rest."

"We'll speak again," Kier promised. "I'll find a way past Malcolm's guard..."

From beyond the door came the strident clang of swordplay; a cry of pain. Someone shouted his name. Kier had never felt so ripped apart. At last, desperate, he pulled loose of his father's slackened grasp and ran for the door.

Chapter Seventeen

JonMarc had fought Malcolm's men to a standstill. Two chain-mailed guards had him cornered in the door alcove, but still he managed to hold them off, flailing his sword with both hands, like a club. A third knelt groaning in the corner, bleeding from the shoulder.

Cari had given herself up immediately, for Malcolm dared not harm her. But a Dynian life wasn't worth a random thought among Malcolm's private guard. Despite Captain Halistan's promise of clemency, JonMarc refused to surrender his weapon. The word of a Tiernai he would not trust. That lesson had been painful in the learning, and JonMarc was not about to repeat the mistake.

"Hand over the key, fool," Halistan urged from Malcolm's side. "My sergeant will soon return with another, and these futile efforts will cost you your life."

JonMarc did not answer. He had no key; Kier had taken it with him and bolted the door from within. But he was willing to let them think he did, to allow Kier more time with his father.

It was not long, though, before Halistan's sergeant trotted up the last steps and handed his captain a full ring of keys. At the same moment, a bolt snapped and the door behind JonMarc edged open. Kier peered out. His face darkened as he assessed the situation. Warily, he stepped into the hall.

The two remaining guardsmen moved to intercept him. JonMarc slipped the sword into Kier's ready hand and stepped aside. Kier held the weapon low, point raised—to defend, not provoke. The guards halted.

Malcolm instantly dispatched his waiting physician to check on the duke. Kier stood by to let the black-robed creature pass. The fellow emerged a moment later, capped head bowed in studied solemnity. "M'lord," he intoned, "Duke Morwen is dead."

Cari gave a sob and covered her face. Kier looked as if he'd been gut-punched. "*Dead*?" he managed. "But—he was alive when I left him." He tried to shove his way back into the chamber. Malcolm's men moved to prevent it.

"Treachery!" Malcolm cried. "All knew the duke was too weak to receive visitors. Yet you, insolent as always, disobeyed my direct command. *You*, brother, are to blame for his death."

"Your Grace," the physician began, "I think the visit had little to do with..."

"*Silence*, fool."

The old man cowered.

Malcolm gestured his sergeant to seize Kier's sword. Head bowed, Kier did not resist. His defiance seemed to have perished along with the duke.

Only when Kier was disarmed did Malcolm dare advance. He thrust his sharp nose in his half-brother's face. "Tell me what passed between you."

Kier turned away, eyes shut.

"I will know what was said!"

"Oh, *have done*, Malcolm," Kier replied, exasperated. "Our father is dead. Is that not enough for you? I'm going to my chamber to mourn him in peace." He elbowed past Malcolm and the uncertain guards as if they were no more than shadows and strode off toward the torch-lit stairwell. Momentarily forgotten, JonMarc scurried along behind.

Malcolm stared after them, his mouth agape. "My lord," Halistan said in his ear, "your physicians assured you his Grace was too ill to speak. I doubt any conspiracies were hatched this night. I daresay no more passed between them than a few expiring glances."

"I hope you're right," Malcolm grumbled, "for I like it not."

Alone in the dark of their tower chamber, Kier recounted to JonMarc a little of what had passed between him and the duke. Most, he kept to himself. Just knowing his father never blamed him for his mother's death was a relief. More than that. It was a blessing. Yet the miraculous prize he'd discovered had as quickly been stolen away. Kier mourned Duke Morwen's passing. Even more, he lamented the father-son camaraderie that now could never be.

"Why couldn't I tell him... that I loved him?" he murmured, as he and JonMarc settled down to sleep. "When the moment came, the words stuck in my throat."

JonMarc did not answer. Kier assumed the Dynian had grown bored and dozed off. But then, from out of the darkness: "Have you ever said that to *anyone*, Kier?"

The words stabbed Kier's heart like a dagger thrust. Aye, he'd said it—long ago, before he learned that affection meant loss. First, his mother had abandoned him among villagers who despised him; now the duke, the father he'd barely re-discovered, was gone as well. The only remaining person Kier loved was Cari—and he dared not tell her, lest she, too, depart.

Outside in the bailey, an exuberant cock crowed a chanson to the dawn. It gave no thought to love or death, but only the all-encompassing moment. Swallowing back tears, Kier rolled over and buried his face in his blanket as grief and exhaustion overtook him.

It was late afternoon when a servant rapped on the door of their chamber to summon them to supper. Kier acknowledged groggily. As he turned from the door, it occurred to him that his half-brother hadn't bothered to lock them in again. With the duke dead, Malcolm clearly felt no need to constrain him. Kier had been too exhausted to even notice.

By the time they dressed and made their way to the great hall, the family was already at meat. Cari's face brightened when she saw them. Malcolm's expression could have curdled new milk, and his mother, the Duchess Yssolt, refused to look at them at all.

Kier took the seat beside his cousin while JonMarc, acting his part as squire, dutifully stood beside his chair. Before setting fork to plate, Kier turned to his stepmother. "Madam," he said stiffly, "my condolences on the loss of your husband."

Yssolt raised one eye and offered an almost imperceptible nod, as though she had not expected such civility from him. Cari touched his thigh in reassurance. Kier covered her small hand with his own, squeezing it gently, as if it were a thing of porcelain he feared might break.

They passed the meal in strained silence. Yssolt stared into her lap, having ceased to eat. She pointedly ignored JonMarc, who showed no sign he noticed. He'd managed to snare the eye of a rosy-cheeked serving lass and gazed after her intently as she retreated to the kitchens.

At last Yssolt had had enough. "This is intolerable!" she snapped. "I cannot abide this—*heathen* standing over me. It's bad enough the land swarms with them. Must I now endure one in my own dining hall?"

At a nod from Kier, JonMarc happily skipped off after the serving wench. Cari watched him disappear around the corner. When the sound of flirtatious laughter echoed from the pantry, she murmured some excuse Kier could not fathom and left the hall in the opposite direction. A piece of Kier's heart went with her.

Malcolm, too, growled something under his breath and abruptly departed. Throughout the meal he had seemed withdrawn, hunched over his plate, his slender, almost feminine hands shading his face. Kier welcomed his absence. He glanced at Yssolt, expecting her to follow her son, but the lady sat, cold as calstone, avoiding his eyes.

Kier had to admit the years had been kind to his stepmother. Her face and doll-like figure reflected the dusky, delicate beauty of the Tiernai. Her long hair, now bound beneath a silken veil, remained lustrous and black as jet. Kier recalled rumors, even as a boy, that Yssolt used some concoction of oil and soot to keep it so.

"You had no right to bring that creature into my home." Yssolt said at last.

Kier set down his knife and pushed his plate away. Hungry though he was, the tension in his belly made it impossible to eat. "I remind you, madam, that it is my home as well. We're both here by the will of the same lord."

Yssolt straightened, dark eyes afire. "Not for long. When my son is proclaimed duke, you will no longer be welcome at Cordon."

Kier bit back a retort. He'd *never* been welcome at Cordon. He rose, eager to depart. The last thing he wanted was a confrontation with his father's widow. To his astonishment, Yssolt motioned him to stay. The lady appeared on the brink of tears. "I wish you had never returned," she whispered vehemently.

"I would there had been no need of it, madam." What did she want of him?

Yssolt's raised her eyes, red-rimmed and glistening. "You were ever Morwen's favorite. Only *you* held his love. My son knew it not. And now you return to flaunt his adulteries in my very face."

Kier's temper slipped. "Hardly adultery! You were not yet my father's wife when he lay with my mother."

"His *wife*? Was I ever truly his wife? Even in my own bed, his thoughts were ever of her. How many nights did he waken me from sleep, crying her name? You and your Dynian mother stole Morwen's love before I could even lay claim to it. I shall always despise you for that!"

Kier was unsure how to respond. The lady Yssolt had never before opened her heart to him. Why choose to do so now? Despite the years they'd lived under the same roof, they remained less than strangers. "I've learned to bear your hatred, madam," he said. "I've no doubt the duke, my father, tried to love you, in his own fashion. Had you not been so consumed with jealousy, you might have recognized that what you so long desired was ever yours for the asking. My mother was never your enemy. Until her death, she loved a man she *knew* she could not claim."

Yssolt's eyes welled. "I wish she had *lived*. Oh, Kier, you cannot know how oft I wished that. For if she had, you would now be a warrior of the Dynian, and Morwen would have judged you an enemy. And she might have found another to wed her, and so betrayed his love. In time, he would have forgotten her. Dead, she is too powerful. I cannot fight her memory." Yssolt covered her face in her hands.

Kier felt both awkward and confused. He'd never seen his stepmother so vulnerable. The pain of the duke's passing forged a bond between them that almost transcended the many years of hostility. Kier hesitantly laid his hand upon Yssolt's sleeve. "You no longer need to, madam," he said, with less gentleness than he felt.

Yssolt stiffened at his touch. "I'm sorry," she said, recovering her composure. "I did not mean to trouble you with that."

Kier was certain of that. For years, he'd doubted the Lady Yssolt felt any affection at all for her husband. Clearly, he'd been wrong. "How may I serve you, lady?" he asked.

Almost against her will, Yssolt raised tortured brown eyes to his. "I think... there is little you can do. Between us there can never be more than tolerance. It is too late to alter that. Yet my own son is so—*changed*. These past months he has grown cold to me, almost a stranger, and I do not know the cause. It is as if there is no longer any love left in him. It frightens me, Kier, for Malcolm has ever been my life. Without him I have no one to turn to. *No one*."

Yssolt's anguish won out. She choked back a sob. Before Kier could reply, she rose and swiftly fled the hall.

§

Eyes wild, Malcolm paced the floor of his chamber in the keep's high tower. The blood-red crystal that allowed his Master to find him showed fire at its edges. It would be soon.

He dreaded this encounter. The throbbing in his head would last hours afterward—probably longer tonight, for the news he had to impart would surely evoke the Master's wrath.

It was a heavy price to pay, yet worth it to see his greatest ambitions fulfilled. Only three months ago, he had experienced the first of these visitations. Then, he had welcomed it. Like his allies, the Connails, this outcast noble who pleased himself to be called *Master* recognized his potential. Duke Morwen's heir had greatness in him. They all said so. With their help, he'd prove it to the world.

It was gratifying to have powerful friends, despite the humiliation it sometimes caused. This Master was arrogant. Though he boasted Fithlon skills, he did not know his place. And lately, his demands had become increasingly tiresome. Yet there would come a reckoning. Once Malcolm's wishes were fulfilled and he no longer had need of accursed Fithlon magic, he'd remind this presumptuous renegade who ruled. Until then, this *Master* needn't know he was being used.

A rush of wind tore through the open window, plunging the room into darkness. Malcolm reeled into his chair, grasping his head.

"*What have you to report?*" demanded a voice that seemed to force its way into his skull. An image took shape in his mind. He had never beheld that countenance in life, yet he recognized it as if they stood face to face.

"Duke Morwen is dead," he responded, managing to sound triumphant despite his agony. "I am at last Duke of Evorick."

"*As I promised. And that is but the start. Our enterprise fares well. Yet time is short. Did the duke speak of the Amulet before he died?*"

"Not to me." Malcolm braced for what he knew was to come. "But to my half-brother, he may have…"

The voice exploded in his brain. "*Fitzmorwen lives?*"

"He arrived last night with a Dynian servant and stole into the duke's chamber before my guards could stop him. But—" Malcolm hesitated. "You assured me he was not to be killed, only disabled. The gods frown upon a brother's murder. I warn you, I'll take no part in that."

"*Warn me?*" The voice sounded bitterly amused. "*You still think to tell me what you will and will not do? Have I not shown you what happens to those who cross me?*"

Malcolm shuddered. He hated debasing himself before this creature. "I do not cross you. I say only that if you desire my brother's death, I want no part of it."

"*Ungrateful wretch. I suppose you still wish to be king.*" Malcolm did not answer, but the menacing voice in his mind knew his thoughts. "*So I suspected. You know that I alone can bring it about. In return, I expect you to keep your bargain: to do my bidding without question. Do you understand that, Malcolm Morwensen?*"

"I understand." Infuriating, to humble himself before a halfblood outcast. Yet as long as this Master took the risks while he need only reap the rewards, the agreement was worth maintaining.

The voice in his head chuckled maliciously, sending an icy blade up Malcolm's spine. "*You say a Dynian accompanied Fitzmorwen?*"

"Aye, an insolent rogue. My brother claims he is his squire."

"*And you believe him? Fool. It is as I've said. Your brother plots with the Branwyns. Using Cymworth as his base, he will try to wrest from you the whole of Evorick. You must prevent him acquiring that land, for it is rightfully yours. Above all, he must not journey there to spy out its defenses.*"

Malcolm hunched his shoulders. "You've spoken of this threat before. Yet without proof, how can I imprison him?—especially with so many due to attend the duke's funeral. My brother has friends among those in power."

"*As have you. Yet you needn't concern yourself with imprisonment. Fitzmorwen will not leave Cordon before the old duke is entombed. Set a watch upon him to note his movements. We shall deal with him later. Now, where is Roderig? I must have words with him and I do not sense him in the castle. Did he not arrive?*"

"He came yestermorn. But after Fitzmorwen arrived, he set off to bear that news, and word of the duke's death, to Earl Connail." Malcolm could not resist a small gloat. "It seems your creature has again failed you."

Pain, like a fiery spike, lanced behind his eyes. "*That is none of your concern. Why did he not await my instructions?*"

"He—he feared that, since we'd had no word from you in some days, you might be in difficulty. He sought Earl Aran to try to learn your mind."

Silence. Then: "*I admit I was—delayed. A minor inconvenience. One of the simpering Fithlon dared challenge me. But he'll no longer trouble us. I've dealt with the meddler, as I shall with all who oppose me or fail in my demands. Do you understand that, Malcolm Morwensen?*"

Malcolm cowered, arms thrown up to shield his mind from searing waves of thought that were not his own. "I have never failed you, Master!" he stammered as the pain grew. "I've performed all you've asked of me."

"*You have failed to locate the Amulet.*"

"I will!"

"*Perhaps. But the true test of loyalty lies ahead. Serve me well and your reward shall exceed your greatest imaginings. Fail, and be assured I will know of it.*"

The pain in Malcolm's skull crescendoed. With an agonized shriek he slid to his knees, rocking his head between his hands. When the torment finally subsided, it was like cool liquid seeping into his brain, draining his will and washing away any notion of duplicity or revenge.

"*Now*," the voice said, this time low and soothing so that the very sound of it was a balm to his writhing mind. "*I know you are my faithful ally, Malcolm. When the time is right, you shall be ready to assume your place as ruler of this land. Until then—*"

"I shall obey your commands," Malcolm whispered.

"*Good. When is the duke to be buried?*"

"Five days hence."

"*Ah, that suits our purpose. Prepare to receive a royal visitor. Prince Rhynion shall attend.*"

"The prince? But he is unwell. Surely Sir Donal won't allow him to leave the Citadel."

"*Does the Legion Commander's will override that of the prince? I shall see that Rhynion is persuaded to attend. His presence is vital to my—to our plans.*"

Malcolm nodded somnolently. "What would you have me do?"

The voice in his mind gave a malignant laugh. "*Return your brother's weapons. Perhaps it is as well he did not die. I've a better use for Fitzmorwen. How ironic that he should aid us in our enterprise, yet earn for his trouble only the bloody name of traitor.*"

Chapter Eighteen

Kier dashed across the torch-lit courtyard and clambered up the ladder to the stable loft. His breath hung like smoke on the frosty air. Yet the scullery who'd directed him there had earned her copper. He could already make out the rhythmic rumble that said JonMarc slept contented.

They lay nestled in the hay, JonMarc's right arm curled about the chambermaid's bare shoulder, the other propped behind his head. Despite the night's chill, his fur-lined cloak draped them only from the ribs down. All around, the hay was strewn with clothing, hastily discarded.

Kier hesitated, feeling supremely awkward. He made it a point not to delve into JonMarc's personal life. Urgency spurred him. Cautiously, he reached across the tangled petticoats, the round hillocks of the girl's pale breasts, and prodded JonMarc's shoulder.

The girl woke instantly. With a squeal, she yanked the cloak up to her chin.

JonMarc barely opened one eye. He stretched in a lazy way and nuzzled his face in the wealth of raven curls at the crook of his playmate's neck. "What is it, Kier?" he drawled.

So much for the pretense of servitude. "Get dressed and come with me. We've been summoned."

"By who? Your brother hasn't spoken to you these past two days..." JonMarc's eyes popped wide and he sat up. "Master Gwythion?"

Kier winced, wishing he'd been quick enough to prevent that slip. In a hostile environment like Cordon, some names were best left unspoken.

JonMarc thrust his legs into his breeches and hastily gathered up the rest of his clothes. He hurried down the ladder after Kier, leaving the girl to wonder at his abrupt departure from beneath the furry warmth of his cloak.

"What did he say?" JonMarc panted, struggling into his boots as he labored to catch up.

Kier spared a glance over his shoulder but did not slow. Since the ominous news of Gwythion's disappearance, he'd been desperate for this contact, fearing it might never come. Now that it had, he rued any further delay. "Only that he required us *both*."

"But, when...?"

"Half an hour ago, while I was at vigil in the chapel. It's taken me that long to find you."

JonMarc threw his hay-flecked woolen shirt on over his head, scrambling to keep pace with Kier's determined stride. "Then Master Demias must've been wrong."

"I don't know. The contact was weak; I could barely make out Gwythion's thoughts." Kier refused to divulge more until they reached the privacy of their tower chamber.

JonMarc lit a taper from the torch outside. As its feeble light dispersed the gloom, his mouth fell open. "Ghedrev's bloody shiv!" he gasped, eyeing the shambles before him. "What happened here?"

Kier righted a toppled candle stand and heaved his slashed straw mattress back onto its frame. Disgusted, he wiped his hands on his thighs. "I found it like this when I came looking for you. Malcolm's been hunting for the Amulet."

"He didn't..."

"Only its case, and he flung that across the room. I doubt he realized what it was." Kier took a seat on the ruined mattress and settled back against the wall, anxious to renew the contact.

JonMarc continued picking though the scattered wreckage. He found his haversack torn apart and began gathering up his strewn belongings, the number of which had increased suspiciously in recent days. Kier made no comment. He had more important worries than JonMarc's penchant for acquisition. He shut his eyes and focused attention on the dark void behind his eyelids.

"So, where'd you hide it, then?" JonMarc asked. "You said an icon of a pointing hand was too awkward to wear around your neck. Where'd you put it?"

Kier evaded the question. In the years he lived at Cordon, he'd carved himself several secret crannies behind the stones of this chamber. And secret they would remain, especially from JonMarc. "It's in a safe place," he said, working to maintain his concentration. Gwythion's thoughts must still be bent toward Cordon. He need only snare them.

An explosive snort. "No wonder the serving wenches have been so hot after you lately. And here I thought it was *my* influence."

Focus disrupted, Kier struggled to make sense of the statement. Abruptly, he tumbled: the secret pocket at the front of his breeches where, back in Castémaron, he'd stowed his hide-out purse. Of course JonMarc's mind would go to that. Even in the direst circumstances, it seemed his companion could not get past his preoccupation with sex. "Don't flatter yourself," Kier grunted. "I've told you, the servants here are Malcolm's spies—including that pretty thing you bedded tonight. They've no interest in either of us; only in the information we might let slip."

JonMarc's smugness sagged like a wilted stamen. "Oh come on, little Dierdre? She's no spy." He fidgeted, uncertain. "Even if she were, what information could she hope to get from me?"

"At the very least, that we're in contact with a Fithlon Master. You even blurted his name. Gwythion's no stranger at Cordon. By morning, Malcolm will know all about it."

Soberly, JonMarc took a seat on the floor. Kier hoped the lesson had finally sunk in.

"So what do we do now? Will Gwythion contact you again?"

"I hope so, if I can just concentrate long enough to signal him we're ready." Again, Kier shut his eyes and sought out the level of his mentor's thoughts.

JonMarc's fingers drummed a nervous rhythm on the floorboards. He squirmed and cleared his throat. Kier threw up a mental barrier and drove his focus deeper. Still, he failed to detect any sense of the Fithlon's presence. Had he completely lost the contact? It was only Gwythion's insistence that JonMarc be present that had caused him to break off in the first place. Neither had expected the search for him to take so long. What if the Fithlon Master had given up?

"Maybe he's too far off," JonMarc whispered, trying to be unobtrusive.

Frustrated, Kier set the task aside a moment. "Distance is no object when communicating through *Infinite Mind*. The problem is isolating a specific individual among so many others. Usually, a Fithlon will give his pupil a beacon crystal attuned to the master's thoughts, to make him easier to locate. Gwythion's skills are so precise, he's never needed to…"

Kier raised a hand to hold off JonMarc's nascent response. A presence hovered at the edges of his mind. He tried to snare it, but it remained elusive. He vaguely sensed JonMarc's thoughts seeking out his own. Good, the Dynian had finally settled down and was trying to apply the lessons Kier had taught him on shipboard. Kier projected his own thoughts into the void: "*Why can I barely hear you? Yes, he's here now. Can you not detect his presence?*"

JonMarc nudged his knee. "Kier, what if my charmstone's blocking him? I can put it..."

"No!" Kier hastened. A fragile message filtered through—uncomfortably tenuous. "Gwythion wants to tap its power to enhance his thought-sending." Kier's uneasiness grew. Why would a Twelfth Tier adept require such rudimentary aid? Something was very wrong.

"What should I do?"

"Open your mind. Gwythion will manage the rest."

"But how? I'm concentrating as hard as I can."

"*Don't* concentrate," said Kier. "Your natural defenses are too strong. Drop them." He sensed JonMarc trying to comply.

All at once, Gwythion's thought burst through, impatient and predictably testy.

" *... a near thing! Had I lost the contact... with my powers depleted... might have been hours, even days, before I could attempt it again.*" The Fithlon Master couched his message in words, a more cumbersome process than mere thought-sending. Whether he did so because it was easier for JonMarc to understand, or because he wished to prevent them from detecting anything deeper, Kier could not tell, but the little his mentor said confirmed his fears.

"What's happened? We met a Master Demias who said you'd entered the *Death Realm.*"

Gwythion's irritation crackled like summer lightning. "*Demias talks too much.*" A tense silence. "*Is the Amulet safe?*"

"Yes, though Malcolm's done his best to locate it. I fear he's in league with—"

"*There is little time, Kier. Let me read from your memory all that's passed since we parted.*"

Kier froze. He hated having anyone, even his trusted mentor, rummage through his thoughts as if they were cheap peddler's goods. The events of the last few days had dredged up emotions he had no wish to share.

"*Open your mind,*" Gwythion insisted. "*I've no wish to force you.*"

"Can't you read my memory instead?" JonMarc suggested. Privacy was something he'd seldom experienced and never particularly valued, while the prospect of delving into the Fithlon's mind was too exciting to pass up. He sensed Kier's gratitude and cached it for future leverage.

Clearly, Gwythion had not considered the possibility. "*Do you understand what I ask?*"

"I think so. But what of my charmstone? Master Demias said the Fithlon can't probe my mind while I wear it."

"*It is no obstacle if you open your thoughts willingly. A dathana crystal is but a tool for channeling energy. It strengthens whatever you wish to do—allow a thought in, or keep one out.*"

"Or send one?" JonMarc ventured.

"*That too—when you are ready. But this is no time for lessons. I am weary and there is much to relate.*"

JonMarc shut his eyes and allowed the Fithlon Master to search his memory of the events since they'd left Castémaron. He found hosting Gwythion's mind rather like reaching through a crack into the most massive treasure vault ever conceived, yet barely being able to touch the coins in the nearest pile. The enticing experience ended all too quickly.

"*Thank you, JonMarc. You have a most—singular way of viewing things.*"

JonMarc chuckled, wondering which of his memories Master Gwythion found most *singular*. His liaison with Deirdre, perhaps? He'd never thought to wonder whether, like Covenant Priests, the Fithlon were sworn celibate.

"*Kier,*" Gwythion said, "*I am most grieved to learn of the duke's passing. Our situation is more urgent than I'd feared, for I did not realize how deeply your brother Malcolm is involved.*"

"I cannot believe Malcolm is responsible for..."

JonMarc stirred. "Not responsible? Blazes, Kier, Malcolm's made it clear he wants you dead. What will it take to convince you—a dagger in your sleep?"

Kier bristled. "If Malcolm truly wanted me killed, he could have ordered it at any time. He may be selfish and ambitious, but I can't believe he's evil. Someone is using him."

"*True,*" said Gwythion. "*Yet so long as his will is not his own, you dare not trust him.*"

"I never said I *trusted* him," Kier muttered. "Have you learned who manipulates him? Master Demias said it's one who possesses Fithlon skills but isn't of the Brethren. How can that be?"

"He was Fithlon—years ago, when Maelguin lived. I told you of Maelguin, the master who helped me search for Aneryn's writings. Years later, he took an apprentice; a true prodigy, it seemed. Then Maelguin died and his pupil vanished. Rumor said he was captured and burned by the Covenanters. Yet this, I have learned, is only partly true. He was taken, but escaped. At the time, none thought to pursue the matter further, for Maelguin's research was controversial and the Fithlon Synod wanted it ended."

"What did he study?" Kier asked.

"The use of crystals in expanding the mind. Maelguin became obsessed with it. He was ever sending his thoughts outward, seeking deeper, more obscure levels of perception. That search became an opiate to him, and finally it destroyed him.

"Through it all, his pupil watched and learned, yet received little guidance. When his Master died, he continued to study in secret, turning his attention to areas of greater allure: the power of crystals to increase his already formidable sinistral talents so that he might compel others to his will. And to prevent the Fithlon from discovering his pursuit, he taught himself to shield his mind, taking refuge in the one place he knew they dared not follow—beyond the Forbidden Portal."

"The Death Realm," said Kier. "And you pursued him there?"

"I saw no other way to learn of him."

"But how can the living enter such a place and remain alive?" JonMarc asked.

"Through no simple means. The Death Realm is not a physical place, but a level of perception. With sufficient powers of mind, one may learn to enter. The difficulty is in finding one's way out again, as Maelguin discovered, to his peril. His body wasted away while he tarried there, and his spirit dwells there still.

"Yet his pupil is of cannier stuff. Through years of searching, he discovered a weakness in the fabric of the Portal through which he can enter and depart at will. Could, rather, for I challenged him, to lure him out, and occupied him while those within repaired the rift. That route is barred to him now. He must find another, should he wish to take refuge there again.

"Yet while that confrontation weakened me, it hurt him little. His time of secrecy is ended. I think it pleased him to reveal his power at last, knowing the Fithlon can do naught to stop him."

Kier shifted uneasily. "You talk as if his power is greater than theirs."

"It is."

"Not greater than yours, surely. How can he be a match for a master of the Twelfth Tier?"

"*He is* more *than a match. He nearly destroyed me! For three days I lay helpless in my chamber, too weak to contact you. Even now, I am barely recovered. Why else would I be forced to rely, like a novice, on a dathana crystal, just to be heard?*"

"But how could he have learned so much with no master to train him?" JonMarc asked.

"*It happened* because *he studied alone. Fithlon doctrine is based upon balance, JonMarc. At each level, a Fithlon's abilities are tempered with discipline. As his powers increase, so does his wisdom in their use. It is an arduous process, and every Fithlon recognizes that the study of Mind is but a tool for reaching the ultimate goal: communion with the Infinite. But balance is the key: power and discipline, always hand in hand. No Fithlon may teach one without the other. Yet after Maelguin's death, his pupil ignored the Synod's dictates and became his own teacher. Like most novices, he cared naught for discipline. The lust for power consumed him. Using his Master's research, he progressed rapidly through the training, for he studied only half of it.*"

"Then what tier is he?" Kier asked.

"*He is of no tier. He has never been tested. Yet his mind skills are staggering. I sensed his rashness. He does not fear to unleash powers any true Fithlon would quail to use. If he should acquire the Cábretaur—the last remnant of the energy source that destroyed Nwtyrra—and learn to tap its power, he will be invincible. All the Fithlon together could not vanquish him, for their powers are not cumulative.*"

It was a chilling revelation. "Were you able to learn this renegade's identity?" Kier asked, feeling the press of time. Despite the added power of JonMarc's charmstone, Gwythion's mind-touch was swiftly weakening. They dared not lose the contact—not with so much still to learn.

"*I was. He calls himself* Táranos."

"Táranos? But—that's the attainted heir of Anlawth! The Connails and my brother strive to restore him to the Alcorean Council. But why play at petty politics on Alcor when he has the might to challenge the Fithlon Synod? What does he hope to gain?"

"*Revenge. Táranos is obsessed with it. The halfblood son of a double-traitor, despised by Dynian and Tiernai alike, and nearly burned alive for his sinistral skills—he seeks the ruin of Alcor, and will laugh aloud as the races* destroy each other at his command. And that is but the start. He desires no less than the domination of all Éclatan. He must be stopped."

"How?" Such a task seemed impossible. "How can JonMarc and I even hope to vanquish one so powerful even the Fithlon Synod cannot stop him?"

"You need not vanquish him. Only evade... Keep him from acquiring the Cábretaur. Táranos does not understand foresight; does not possess it. Thinks if he steals ... Amulet, ... he can recover the Cábretaur himself. He is wrong. Aneryn foresaw you."

Gwythion's tenuous connection to their minds was dissipating like fog in the wind. "Then what do you want us to do?" Kier asked.

"Get to Cymworth... as swiftly as you can. Locate the Cábretaur. Be ready to seize it ... at Conjunction. I calculate... fifteen days. I will join you there..."

"Where's Táranos now?" JonMarc interrupted. "Won't he be waiting for us?"

Gwythion's strength seemed all but spent. "Still at his fortress in Anlawth. Our battle weakened him ... but not enough. ...He will depart soon. You must reach Cymworth first."

One last question haunted Kier. He'd harbored it since they'd first been told of the task. Now, he almost feared to ask it. "Gwythion, has your foresight shown you that we will succeed in this?"

When Gwythion responded, his thought was like a cobweb fluttering on a breeze. "Conflict with Táranos ... cost me my foresight. I approach this ...as blind as you."

Chapter Nineteen

The morning of the duke's funeral dawned gray and dreary, and ragged clouds, like sheep shearings, hung low and thick in the valleys. By mid-day, the fog had turned to drizzle.

On a slope below the castle, a vault had been carved into the low cliff. Within that lightless cavern, Morwen Devon, the third Duke of Evorick, would be laid to rest beside the bones of his ancestors.

As the funeral procession wended its solemn way down the muddy slope, the wind picked up, chill from the sea. By the time the ceremony ended, everyone looked forward to the wine that would flow freely at the funeral feast to come.

"At least 'twas short enough, an' there's a mercy. Old Morwen could ne'er abide a long-winded priest."

Kier hung back in the shadow of the wind-fluttered canopy until the speaker passed. He recognized the crusty voice and thick Tiernai brogue of Antony Ruark, the Earl of Galwyn—his father's trusted ally. Ruark walked with his neighbor and inseparable companion, Earl Jeremy Lochlainn of Derwenth. Kier admired both men, especially the stocky Ruark, who made no effort to mask his rough edges—the legacy of a lifetime of campaigning. But right now he was in no mood for conversation.

Most of the guests already moved, like a sluggish tide, back toward the castle. Nearby, the Lady Yssolt was helped to her litter by her brother, Norris Hannon, the Earl of Dandryth. She had held herself tall and straight throughout the ceremony, and if she wept at all, she'd hidden it well. Only Cari had broken down when the rocky tomb rumbled shut. She walked now, head bowed, behind the prince's litter, leaning on her father's arm. Kier had thought to return to the castle with them, but these last few days his cousin seemed to be avoiding him. Kier hoped his inattention had not offended her.

JonMarc slipped up beside him and tugged his sleeve. "You all right?" He peered into Kier's face with the look of a worried aunt. Kier returned a grim sigh and nodded. "Why didn't you sit up front with the family? Duke Edmund was looking for you."

"I needed to be alone."

Workmen began to dismantle the canopy. One aimed JonMarc an indignant lour and muttered an ethnic slur. Kier led his companion into the drizzle. Together they trudged back to the castle.

"It was more than that," said JonMarc, kicking a stone into the lank weeds beside the path. "Even standing in back with the servants, I could see what happened. Your brother invited that Covenant priest, Tor Connail, to sit with the family, and left no place for you. Why didn't you press your rights, Kier? He might as well have slapped you in the face."

Kier stared down at the trodden mud. "I won't play Malcolm's game. He was hoping I'd make a scene before the prince and all the nobles. I'd never insult my father's memory that way. Besides," he added, trying to sound more cheerful, "we leave for Cymworth tomorrow. I never mean to return to Castle Cordon. It's here I learned how it feels to be a fortress under siege."

They found the great hall a seething mass of peasantry, all clambering for a bountiful helping of their new duke's generosity. Along the tapestried walls, torches guttered and smoked, giving off a feeble orange glow that did little to dispel the gloom. The atmosphere was already stale.

Kier paused beneath the entry arch and surveyed the crowd, commoners and nobility alike, with disgust he made no attempt to conceal. He was in no mood for festivities. The overpowering stench of boar grease sizzling on the open spit all but nauseated him. He seemed to be the only one in this oppressive hall who displayed any grief at Duke Morwen's passing.

JonMarc spied a familiar figure in the crowd and, with Kier's nodded permission, dashed after her like a hound to the chase. Kier marveled after him. His own experience with the gentler sex—admittedly limited— indicated that Tiernai women regarded with contempt any man who bore even a vestige of Dynian blood. Yet for some reason that did not deter JonMarc, perhaps because it hadn't occurred to him it might be a problem.

Kier elbowed his way toward the dais, where a handful of nobles clustered about young Prince Rhynion like crows around carrion. Lady

Cariwyn sat alone at the far end of the table, staring out at the sea of faces with eyes that seemed to envision another world. Kier circled behind and gently bent to kiss her forehead.

She leaned against him and smiled, her dark eyes sad. "How quickly they set aside their mourning mien," she sighed. "They seem to forget 'tis but an hour since they laid to rest the most fair and loving lord in all of Alcor."

Her words helped ease the painful chasm in Kier's heart. Cari had ever been his soulmate. She alone saw through the cloak of reticence he wrapped about himself to keep the world at bay. "Yet a full nine-year of mourning would not bring him back," he replied. "Is it not fitting they now celebrate the investiture of their new duke, my lord brother, who provides so *generously* for their entertainment?"

Cari regarded him sidelong and her expression softened. "Your eyes betray you, Kier—as they ever did. You do not think as you speak."

"No," he admitted quietly, taking the seat beside her.

Cari squeezed his hand and gazed out over the crowd. JonMarc's flaxen mane stood out like a beacon in a churning sea. He was clearly in his element, surrounded by a bevy of eager peasant lasses who giggled and squealed as he treated himself to whatever liberties he could get away with. "Your companion is popular with the serving maids," Cari noted, with a lightness that somehow seemed forced. "Tell me about him. Is he truly an escaped slave, as rumors say?"

"Well, he *was* a slave, but now he's as free as you or I."

"Ah," Cari murmured, "I think he must be freer. He and I conversed a little, outside the duke's chamber. He seems a fascinating man, and with such tales to tell! I scarcely know whether to believe them or not."

Kier flashed a rare smile. "With JonMarc it's hard to be sure."

"You two seem so well suited. I'm glad you've found such a friend. And you know, he does not speak at all like the Dynian peasants I've met. He almost seems—a golden princeling of the elder days, so tall and fair."

Kier chuckled. "He'd like that."

"Oh, Kier, you mustn't tell him I said it."

Kier shook his head, still smiling. "Never fear, sweet one." He lifted her delicate fingertips to his lips. Just having her near was a balm to his spirit. "I see you're still a fantasy weaver, as when we were young, always concocting tales to entertain us."

"And you always teased me for it because I made them end happily. You said the real world was not like that. Do you still believe that, Kier?"

He shrugged. "I've seen nothing to change my mind."

Cari sighed ruefully and rested her head on his shoulder. "Oh, my darling Kier, what is to become of us now?"

"What do you mean?" he asked, a bit surprised by her change of mood.

Cari hesitated. "My father has not spoken to you?"

"About what?" Kier raised her chin and looked deeply into her trusting brown eyes. "What troubles you, sweet one? Tell me."

Cari grasped his other hand. "Kier, I am—betrothed."

His fingers beneath her chin trembled slightly, despite his desperate effort to control them. He looked away. "We both knew it would happen, someday."

"Aye," she said, "yet, I'd always hoped..."

"A fool's hope." Kier fought back a surge of bitterness, and failed miserably. "I'm a duke's bastard. A halfblood. By Tiernai law, there could be no marriage between us. We faced that long ago—or should have." He aimed the accusation at himself, for as long as Cari remained unwed, he'd never quite abandoned a remnant of hope. Now that door had slammed shut forever.

"So," he said, recovering, "who is the lucky lord? I suppose I must congratulate him."

"Caulder Hannon, the heir to Dandryth."

Kier choked down bile. If he stayed another moment, he knew he'd say something he'd regret. "I hope you'll both be—very happy," he managed, and stood to leave.

Cari laid her small hand on his sleeve. "I know you do not like him. I remember how, at court, Caulder always played the sycophant to Aric Connail, and together they tormented you cruelly. But don't you see, Kier? I have a chance to change that. Dandryth is not fully in the Connail sway. This marriage may help ally Earl Hannon with my father's party and prevent a war. If I can influence Caulder..."

"Caulder's a weakling. He sides with whoever shouts loudest. You pit your small voice against Aric Connail's, and he's far more adept at this game than you are."

"Perhaps," Cari admitted. "But still, I must try. That, or resign this wretched land to a future of bloodshed and misery."

Kier did not answer. How could he fault Cari for choosing to sacrifice herself for her principles? It was a noble gesture, just what he'd expect of his cousin. But why such a futile one?

"I'm nearly twenty-one," Cari went on, forcing lightness into her tone. "I cannot remain a maid forever." She gently squeezed Kier's arm. "Perhaps you too should consider taking a mate. Any maid in this realm would be honored to have a man so fine as you."

Kier turned away. He knew now he'd never marry. If Cari was forbidden him, he'd have no one. He'd seek refuge in some remote corner of the Deg Tirith and put Alcor, and his agony, behind him. "When do the nuptials take place?" He cringed to hear the quaver in his voice.

"Midsummer's Day. The contract will be finalized tonight." Cari hesitated. "Will you come, Kier—to see me wedded?"

Kier's whole frame went rigid. How could she ask that of him? Surely she must know what it would do to him. "I'll be leaving Alcor within a fortnight," he said. "I don't expect to return." He saw Cari recoil as if he'd slapped her, and forced himself to look away, hating himself for causing her pain—and her, for making him want to.

Cari grasped his sleeve. "Kier, please try to understand. I did not want this."

He knew, but still he could not face her. He longed to crawl off to some private corner and nurse his wounds. But that was not to be. From beside the prince's empty chair, Duke Edmund urgently beckoned him. "I do understand," he said, gently lifting Cari's hand from his arm. The touch of her flesh seared his heart. "I... have to go. Your father wants me."

"Kier!" The tears in Cari's voice held him back. "You must know I will always love you."

Kier's eyes were brimming. He couldn't let her see. Swiftly, he turned to join the duke.

The prince and the rest of the council had left the hall. "They are in conference," the anxious Edmund told him, indicating the door to the family's private dining room. "Malcolm has broached the issue of your inheritance. He charges it a loss of his hereditary holdings, and Tor Connail champions his every allegation."

Kier tried to divide his attention between his uncle's hasty summary and the snatches of bilious debate he overheard within. "What shall I do? I'm not permitted to address Council."

"In formal session, no. But this is only an advisory sitting. Any decision rests with the prince alone. I requested an audience for you, and Prince

Rhynion has agreed to it. Yet the price of Tor Connail's acquiescence was high. You may speak only when a question is put to you. Any outburst and you will be removed from the chamber. That will effectively end your suit. Do you understand?" Kier nodded. "Come then. They're waiting."

The debate halted abruptly as Edmund ushered Kier into the chamber. Malcolm, seated at the prince's right, pointedly turned away. Beside him, the black-robed Penitarch Tor Connail's vulture-like eyes fixed on Kier with predatory intensity. Only the Earls Lochlainn and Ruark rose to greet him, the tall Lord Jaremy clapping Kier's arm encouragingly as he passed.

At the head of the table, the prince looked frail beneath his heavy robes of state. Kier dropped to one knee before him. Rhynion smiled. "Welcome, cousin," he said, his cheery voice still a boyish treble, though Kier calculated Rhynion must be nearly sixteen. "We have missed you at court. A pity your duties keep you so far from home."

Kier bowed. "I am pleased to serve wherever your Majesties have need of me."

Rhynion's brown eyes sparkled in the light of some two score candles. "I imagine you've seen some wondrous sights in all your travels. Alas, I am not permitted to leave Alcor. You must come to me soon and tell me of your adventures."

"Gladly, my Prince. Whenever you wish."

Rhynion smiled again and indicated a chair by the wall. "Bring that and sit beside me."

"Your Highness," Tor Connail said, rising, "it is an insult to the new Duke of Evorick and all others at this table for one not of the Council to usurp the privilege of those born to it."

Rhynion wilted.

"My Prince," said Duke Edmund, "I believe no one on this side of the table would object..."

"It's all right, uncle," Kier said quietly. "I'll stand."

"Very well," said Rhynion. "We have heard Duke Malcolm dispute the terms of his father's will. Yet I would have the matter restated for the benefit of Fitzmorwen. My lord Edmund, will you read the passage again?"

Edmund unfurled a parchment scroll. "This is the last testament of my late brother, Duke Morwen Devon of Evorick, given into my keeping some three years ago, to be presented on the occasion of his death. For the most part, it is straightforward enough. The only point of contention lies in the tenth paragraph, where he states: *I bequeath unto my illegitimate son, Kier*

Gareth-Alyn, called Fitzmorwen, the demesne of Cymworth, its treasures, fortifications... and so on, *to be his, and his heirs' for so long as his line continues.* The issue is whether or not..."

"There is no issue," Malcolm snapped. "Cymworth is mine by birthright. It cannot be granted to another—least of all to a halfblood bastard."

"*Evorick* is your birthright." Edmund's voice betrayed exasperation. "None here disputes that. Yet Cymworth belongs to the province of Glenneth, that wild mountainland that even now lies in the hands of our Branwyn enemy. The Tiernai conquered Cymworth forty years ago and since then, the Dukes of Evorick have held it in trust."

Tor Connail rose. "My Prince, may I speak?" The ruddy-faced penitarch allowed his dark eyes to travel slowly over the company. "You have heard me argue in Lord Malcolm's behalf. Yet now I see my facts were in error. Duke Edmund speaks aright."

Malcolm's head shot up, clearly caught off guard by his ally's change of tack.

"Indeed," said Connail, "the land of Cymworth was never truly a part of Evorick and, as such, was not Morwen's to leave to anyone. It belongs to the king—to Rhynion, now that he is regent—and he may grant it to whomever he chooses. I see but three choices." Tor Connail ticked them off on black-gloved fingers. "He may keep it himself, but there is little advantage to that; Cymworth brings forth no revenue. Yet, as it borders Branwyn lands, it has great strategic value. It could, of course, be returned to the Branwyns, but that is unthinkable. The third option seems the most logical: grant Cymworth to the lord best able to defend it against Branwyn incursion. Who is better positioned for that than Duke Malcolm, whose lands border it? Clearly, the Duke of Evorick must retain control of Cymworth, for only thus can we be sure it will not be recaptured."

"Your words have merit," Antony Ruark conceded. "Yet Morwen must ha' known the dangers, should Cymworth fall to enemy hands. Would he leave it to Fitzmorwen if he dinna think the lad could defend it? How can we, his friends, deny his dyin' request?"

"It was not his *dyin' request*," Connail mimicked sarcastically. "Did not Edmund say he received the petition three years ago? Why, we must ask, would Morwen grant Cymworth, a Dynian holy site, to his bastard? Fitzmorwen is a Legion officer and, as such, receives a generous income. What need has he of land? These past years he has demonstrated his preference to remain abroad, leaving those at home to fight Branwyn in his stead." Connail paused to let the innuendo sink in. "We've even found evidence that Fitzmorwen may not be Morwen's son at all."

Kier's knuckles whitened around the table's edge as he fought to bridle his temper. Tor Connail had a reputation as an expert orator, and a sly and subtle foe.

"What evidence?" Edmund growled. "There's never been any doubt Fitzmorwen is my brother's son. My Prince, Penitarch Connail only seeks to confuse the issue. I ask that Fitzmorwen be allowed to speak in his own behalf."

"No," cried Malcolm. "I would hear what Penitarch Tor has to say."

"Very well," said Rhynion. "But be brief, your reverence."

Tor Connail smiled thinly. "As you know, my brother Aran and I have long been committed to rooting out hotbeds of sinistral sorcery that plague our land and threaten the Divine Order."

"Murdering innocent peasants," Edmund rumbled.

"*Demon spawn*, my lord." The black-robed penitarch stalked to the far end of the table. "Some three weeks ago, my brother learned of a sinistral coven on the very border of his realm, in a Dynian village called Caerdewi—that same village where Fitzmorwen was born and reared. Several of those interrogated admitted that Fitzmorwen's dam, a spell-hand harlot named Allyn, used her sinistral arts to lure men to her bed— dozens of men. These confessions, *freely given*, indicate Duke Morwen was a blameless victim of sorcery and may well have been deceived into accepting that the son this Allyn bore was truly his own."

Kier scarcely felt his fingernails digging into his palms. Edmund clamped a restraining hand on his arm. "Curb your slanderous tongue, Connail. My brother was no one's victim. He openly acknowledged Fitzmorwen his son before the king and all the court. If you have proof of this absurd charge—besides the rantings of terrified peasants—produce it, and let us judge its merit."

"What more proof do you need? All know sinistral sorcery is condoned among the Dynian, who alone defy the crusade of my holy brethren to abolish it. This Allyn of Caerdewi was a branded spell-hand, a fashioner of charms and potions. It was holy Devoreth's rage at her licentiousness— of which Fitzmorwen is the sorry product—that drew pestilence to her village. Though my brethren ordered the witch destroyed, they were too late to stop the scourge."

Kier's throat constricted so tight he could barely swallow. He wanted to leap across the table and close his fingers about the smirking penitarch's throat.

"There is an ancient saying," Tor Connail went on. "*The poisoned vine bears blighted fruit.* Has not Fitzmorwen proved his own bent toward sinistral sorcery? He long studied in secret with that blasphemous Fithlon monk, Gwythion."

"That ended years ago," said Edmund. "Fitzmorwen is no more sinistral than you or I. You've seen him compete in tourneys. With which hand does he wield a blade?"

"A man may betray no outward sign, yet still possess sinistral talents," said Connail. "And be not deceived, Fitzmorwen's association with the Fithlon is not ended. Two nights ago, he was summoned to secret discourse with that same Gwythion to whom he has ever owed allegiance. For years, the two of them conspired to manipulate Duke Morwen into granting Fitzmorwen a land so coveted by our Branwyn enemy that..."

Kier's fragile rein on his temper snapped. "What of yourself, Connail?" he shouted. "Why not tell these good lords of your *own* Fithlon accomplice, and how, through you, he seeks to manipulate the High Council of Alcor?"

Penitarch Tor's expression hovered between fury and delight. "Remove him from the chamber," he cried. "He has broken his pledge."

"No!" With one arm, Edmund shoved Kier behind him, halting Rhynion's approaching guards. "I would hear Fitzmorwen's charge."

"But it was agreed—"

"My Prince." Edmund stiffly dropped to one knee. "This accusation strikes of something more serious than a mere protest over inheritance. I beg your indulgence."

Rhynion waved the guards away. "We will hear Fitzmorwen out."

Kier's finger trembled as he leveled it at Tor Connail. "Ask him," he said. "Ask him if the attainted heir of Anlawth, whose claim he upholds, is not one of those same Fithlon whose powers he pretends to abhor. You're not above using them for your own gain, are you, Connail?"

Tor Connail drew himself up, looking more scornful than ever. "A priest of Devoreth's holy Covenant relying on the profane powers of a Fithlon?" He gave a dismissive snort. "Who with any grain of sanity would believe such prattle? Fitzmorwen uses this pathetic falsehood to save his own hide. What evidence has he to support his slander?"

"Is it you who now cries slander? You, who would have these lords believe my mother somehow bewitched my father, based on 'confessions' you wrested from poor Dynian peasants under torture? My lords, I do have evidence, but I cannot yet reveal—"

"Aha, you see? Fitzmorwen uses this fabrication to malign me and my order because he *knows* what I say of him is true."

Rhynion slammed his palm on the tabletop. "Enough of this. Lord Edmund, you will investigate the matter of Anlawth and report to us your findings. For now, we discuss *Cymworth*."

"Then we would do well, my liege," Connail snarled, "to remind this bastard halfblood of the conditions of his presence here. Another outburst and he will be ousted from this chamber."

"Aye, Kier," said Edmund, laying a fatherly hand on his shoulder. "You'll defeat your suit if you cannot hold your tongue. Don't you see it's just what Connail is trying to goad you into?"

Kier nodded sullenly. The malignant penitarch had done an artful job of enraging him beyond caution. He dared not let it happen again. He might already have revealed too much.

"What I don't understand," said Jaremy Lochlainn, "is how, as you seem to imply, Duke Morwen's granting Cymworth to Fitzmorwen could possibly benefit our Branwyn enemy."

"That should be clear enough," Connail returned. "The Branwyns seek to use that land as a base from which to conquer all of Evorick."

"Perhaps," said Lochlainn, "but even if that is true, what has Fitzmorwen to do with it?"

"Aye, Connail," said Edmund. "Tell us *exactly* what you are getting at."

Penitarch Tor's dark eyes glistened. "The unavoidable truth, my lords: that Duke Morwen was manipulated by Dynian sorcery into granting this crucial holding to one whose true loyalties lie with our Branwyn foe."

Kier felt the blood drain from his face. How could he defend himself against so devastating a charge? He fingered the gold ring that displayed his family's crest. *Duál et Onóir*, it read, in the ancient Tiernai script. *Duty and Honor.* His innards roiled like molten pitch.

"Connail lies through his teeth!" said Edmund. "He spews slander and innuendo and calls it truth. Priest or no, he'd not recognize the truth if it came up and throttled him."

"Indeed, Lord Connail," said the prince, "I think you must be mistaken in this. Fitzmorwen has ever served the Tiernai loyally. His value abroad cannot be gainsaid."

"A clever deception, my Prince. All know that once a man is marked by the Dynian, he is theirs for life. Did Fitzmorwen not come to Cordon with a Branwyn spy? *Squire*, he calls him—an impudent knave and student of sorcery who, in the course of his whoring, has been tricked into divulging their true purpose. He and his master plan to seize Cymworth and hand it over to the infamous Dynian brigand with whom they conspired on their way here—the traitor, Gerit Mawr."

Rhynion's eyes hardened. "Is this true, Fitzmorwen? Did you have concert with this outlaw?"

Kier hesitated. Now that he finally had the chance to speak, there was nothing he could say in his own defense.

"Yes, or no?" Penitarch Tor demanded.

"We had no choice. We were taken captive. Gerit Mawr's forces control the road from the capital."

"Then why did *we* not encounter them? Why was this outlaw only interested in you? You see, my Prince, Fitzmorwen cannot deny his duplicity. He is a traitor, owned by the Dynian through secret and barbaric rites. My spies have found a tavern wench who once lay with Fitzmorwen. She will attest that his manhood does indeed bear the mark of the Dynian.

"And as for those who still defend him, I ask this: Why has this captain of the King's Legion never taken part in any action or reprisal against the Branwyns? He has declined to fight them on every occasion. Why should this be, unless his true loyalties lie with their cause?"

Tor Connail sat down, looking supremely pleased with himself. Beside him, the rotund Norris Hannon struggled to his feet. "I know not of the rest of you, but I've heard enough. Fitzmorwen deserves *nothing* of this council. I move that his claim be denied. He should be stripped of his commission and packed off to the heathen lands he's grown so fond of. We need no more traitors in Alcor."

"Aye," Malcolm echoed. "I'll not have my father's memory profaned by the likes of him. I am ashamed to call him brother."

"Well, Fitzmorwen?" said the prince. Beneath his boyish voice crept the pain of betrayal. "Should these accusations prove true, it could mean banishment—even your death. Yet the laws of Alcor are just. Is there aught you can say to refute Penitarch Connail's charge?"

Kier stood without moving, the anger that had seared his veins only moments before now chilled to icy humiliation. "My Prince," he began hoarsely, "how can I prove these accusations false other than simply by my word? I'm no orator like Penitarch Connail, but a soldier—and as such, I must rely on my deeds to speak for me."

He gazed slowly around the table. Of the six nobles seated there, only Duke Edmund would meet his eyes. "My lords, you all know me. I was schooled at court alongside your own sons. What have I ever done to cast doubt upon my loyalty to Alcor or her prince? True, I've not fought the Branwyns, for I've spent these past five years abroad. Alcor has enemies other than those at home. Yet I need not recount my assignments here. You know them, for they originated in Council. If you wanted me to fight Branwyns, why did you not summon me back to Alcor? I'd have complied as readily as I have answered all my orders.

"As to the matter of my servant, well," Kier chuckled grimly, "you've seen him. He is certainly Dynian. Yet you need only hear him speak to know he is of Castémaron, not Alcor. He saved my life there, and in recompense I accepted him into my service. He knows nothing of his race, for he was taken from them as a child and has no memory of his past. To call him a spy is ridiculous. Think on it, my lords: If you wished to infiltrate the Branwyn fortress, would you send a full-blood Tiernai, whose every move would be suspect? Of course not. Were the Branwyns such fools as to do likewise, they'd not remain unconquered."

Tor Connail stirred. "My good lords, Fitzmorwen only tries to cloud the issue. Of course he defends this spy. He is himself of Dynian blood."

"Ah, now we come to it. My Dynian blood. Penitarch Connail would have you believe that because my mother was Dynian, my whole being is somehow *possessed* by them." Kier gave a wry snort. "It would seem, my lords, that the Penitarch has little respect for the potency of Tiernai manhood. Add but one drop of Dynian seed and it is wholly overwhelmed."

Tor Connail glowered as the rest of the table took up the joke at his expense. "Aye, Kier, well put," said Antony Ruark. "Who's to say that all of mixed blood are not truly Tiernai? Surely the coloring's more potent, eh?"

"My lords," Kier went on, "all Alcor knows of the Connails' hatred for the Dynian. When their mother was killed in a Branwyn raid, thirty years ago, the reverend Tor and his brother Aran swore vengeance against the entire Dynian race. None here is unsympathetic to their loss. But how many innocent Dynian have paid for it with their lives?

"Aye, I was born among them, and came of age, as do all Dynian youths, at my twelfth nativity, in a ritual few Dynian discuss even amongst themselves. Yet such things do not long remain private when a Dynian youth is brought to live among the Tiernai. I have endured my share of scorn for it. Indeed, I cannot fathom why Penitarch Connail had to seek that information from a tavern wench. Surely he cannot imagine it was secret. I do indeed 'bear their mark,' as he so inelegantly put it. It is a mark of manhood and respect among the Dynian. Yet be assured, my lords, the penitarch is wrong in one thing: *they do not own me.* No one *owns* me, Connail—not the Dynian of my childhood, nor the Tiernai, among whom I also came of age, at sixteen, in a ceremony more elaborate and far less painful. By both races I am considered a man, and as a man, I claim responsibility for my own actions."

Kier wiped the beaded sweat from his brow. "The Penitarch builds his treason charge against me on what he calls the strategic importance of Cymworth. Yet have any of you been there? Connail? My lord brother?"

Malcolm squirmed in his high-backed chair. Beside him, Tor Connail's eyes reflected an avid wish that thoughts could strangle.

"I thought not. Well, I have. Years ago, I accompanied Sir Donal there on a scouting mission. We found Cymworth a wasted peninsula of rock— desolate. The ruined fortress of Carreg Cymworth is indefensible as it stands. The very notion that the Branwyns would seek to use such a site as a base from which to attack Evorick is madness. Some dozen leagues lie between Cymworth and the Branwyn fortress of Dorcalon—most of it rugged mountainland; another twenty-five between Cymworth and Castle Cordon. And without Cordon, Evorick is but open moorland. What attack could the Branwyns hope to launch from such a distance?—unless they only mean to conquer sheep. No, my lords, as a soldier I assure you, Cymworth lies strategically between nothing and nowhere. It is as worthless to the Branwyns as it is to the Tiernai."

"Penitarch?" the prince acknowledged, as Tor Connail raised a finger to speak. "What say you to this?"

"Only that I'd expect no other answer from one who promotes the cause of his own rebellious race. Of course he denies it. That of itself proves its veracity. Is it not strange, my lords, that a Legion officer should know so much about our enemy's intentions? Has Gerit Mawr advised you, Fitzmorwen, or have you conspired with Ross Branwyn himself?"

Kier smoldered. "I need none to advise me, Connail. What I say is no more than you'd hear at the Citadel, had you the wit to listen. If, as you claim, the Branwyns so desire Cymworth, why wait for me to give it to them? Is it defended? Does it house a garrison? You know well it does not—and *never has*. If the Branwyns wanted Cymworth, they could have it now. The truth is, the land is of so little value, neither race cares to expend the manpower to defend it."

Norris Hannon stood. "If Cymworth is as worthless as you say, why are you are so keen to have it?"

Kier shrugged. "What man would not want land of his own, however remote? Cymworth is no rich prize; my father would be first to admit that. Yet such as it is, he wished it to be mine, and for that alone, I desire it. As to its defense, I can at least promise that, should it be granted me, I'll see it is no *worse* defended than it has been till now."

Kier dropped to his knee before Rhynion. "My Prince, I know I am entitled to no inheritance unless it be by your decision. I am grateful you allowed me to speak. If, in your eyes, I am not worthy of this honor, so be it. I have served Alcor faithfully these past eight years and will continue to do so. I ask only that you judge me upon my own merits and not the prejudices of those who disdain my parentage—for in that, I had no say."

The firelit chamber felt like an oven. Rhynion's gaze was not unfriendly, yet it betrayed no hint of the thoughts behind it. The youth was learning his office well. It occurred to Kier that he had the power to place a thought in the young monarch's mind—one that would almost certainly sway Rhynion to his cause. It would be worth it; Gwythion said that his right to the Cábretaur depended on his ownership of Cymworth. Yet Tor Connail might discover such a move. Though the Covenanters possessed no sinistral talents, many were trained to detect them in use. He dared not take that chance. And he would not resort to subterfuge. Whatever the consequences, he must win or lose this battle on his own.

"We have heard your defense, Fitzmorwen," said Rhynion, "and indeed, your assessment of Cymworth's importance goes against all I have been told. I wish Sir Donal were here to advise me. As he is not, I must come to a decision alone. You may wait outside until we summon you."

Kier's stomach sank. He bowed stiffly. As he turned to leave, he saw his brother smirking at Tor Connail from behind his hand. Malcolm already felt assured of victory. Kier suddenly despaired of not using his Fithlon-enhanced talents while he had the chance. Perhaps this was the very reason he'd taken the training. He left the chamber on a wave of self-reproach.

He found JonMarc waiting for him. Even through his gloom, Kier noticed the Dynian's hair was more disheveled than usual, and flecks of straw dotted the shoulders of his worn leather tunic. Kier ushered him to a private corner.

"I've ruined it," he said. "I'm sure I've lost Cymworth. Tor Connail and my brother have Rhynion convinced it's a military target, and I made the blunder of my life by admitting I couldn't defend it." Kier cradled his forehead in his hands. "Gwythion will be furious."

"Have they made their decision?"

"Not yet."

"Then give it a rest. We may have another problem."

Kier warily raised one eye.

"Roderig's been back. I saw him limping around the stable not half an hour ago. He threw a bundle over the back of a horse and took off again as if the Death Hag's hounds were after him."

"You say he was limping?"

"Aye, and nursing a bloody lip. Someone popped him a good one. I only wish I knew—"

Kier cut him off. The prince had emerged from the arched doorway, followed by the councilors. Kier could read nothing in their faces as they took seats at the dais. Rhynion looked stately for his age, and very much in control. As he beckoned, Kier steeled himself for the worst.

"My lords. Captain Fitzmorwen. I have come to a decision." The stressed *I* made Kier wonder if perhaps Rhynion were attempting to establish his independence from the Council—a move he could only applaud. It seemed so, for Malcolm and the other lords did not appear to know the outcome either.

"The matter of Cymworth is complicated," said Rhynion. "Since none here *truly* knows what the Branwyns are plotting, the question comes down to a difference of opinion—that of Penitarch Connail against Captain Fitzmorwen's. Of the two, we would like to believe the captain. Fitzmorwen has experience in these matters and is highly esteemed by Sir Donal, whose judgment we respect. Yet in the years he has lived abroad, the situation at Cymworth may have changed." Rhynion took a sip of wine and offered Kier a subtle nod. Encouragement? Impossible to tell.

"There is an old adage: *Prudence is oft the wisest course.* In this instance, I believe it has merit. For that reason, I have decided to take Penitarch Connail's advice and cede Cymworth to the one best positioned to defend it. Henceforth, that land shall be part of Evorick and will fall under the protection of its lords."

Kier's defeated groan was overwhelmed by his brother's whoop of victory. Malcolm leaped up and embraced Tor Connail as if the Covenant penitarch were his father.

Rhynion held up a hand for silence. "In return, it is Our wish that, for his lifetime, and in accordance with his father's request, the fief in question be granted to Fitzmorwen. He shall swear fealty to his brother as liegelord, and agree to turn over to him, each year, one third of all revenues derived from that holding."

"But," Malcolm sputtered, "there is no revenue to be derived from Cymworth. It's a wasteland. Kier said so himself."

"When and if there shall be, one third will be your due."

"But that's not fair. Am I required to defend his lands for this? Why, it's not worth—" Malcolm caught Tor Connail's warning glare and halted.

The fealty vows were quickly exchanged, though not quickly enough for Malcolm. As soon as the ceremony ended, he slipped off to a corner with Tor Connail. When he returned, he appeared better pleased with himself.

The prince was in a merry mood, surrounded by those he trusted. Kier happily accepted his invitation to sit beside him and tell of his adventures in the far reaches of the Deg Tirith.

In the midst of one such tale, a young guardsman nervously approached the prince's chair. A hush fell around him. "Your Highness," he began, at Rhynion's nod. "Captain Daevlon, of your Highness' guard..."

"Yes?"

"He's been found dead, sire."

Rhynion stared, stricken.

Kier was instantly on his feet. "Where, and when?"

"Only a few moments ago. He lies near the foot of the stairs outside the west barracks. He looks to have been dead an hour or more."

Kier stood. "My Prince, with your permission..." He signaled JonMarc, who was watching from a corner nearby. "Come with me."

As the clamor of the great hall faded behind them, the stillness of the foggy courtyard felt eerie. Hazy globes of orange torchlight dotted the twilit walls. The few soldiers clustered around the body moved aside at Kier's approach. They eyed JonMarc with suspicion.

Captain Daevlon lay sprawled on his side in the shadow of the stair, his head twisted at a grotesque angle. Kier squatted on the wet flagstone to examine the corpse. "How many drinks did he have?"

One grizzled veteran moved forward, twisting a leather gauntlet in his hands. "None, so far as I know." He glanced about, to nods of confirmation. "The rest of us was just off duty, y'see—an' since we couldn't join the celebration, we thought to do some partyin' of our own. Cap'ain Daevlon came to check on us, but he didn't drink."

Kier spotted a curious track through the mud and gestured for JonMarc to investigate.

The veteran's head drooped. "I confess, we was a bit rowdy, Cap'ain. Why, didn' none of us e'en hear him fall."

"He didn't fall," Kier said, rolling the body onto its back. "His neck was snapped by pressure from behind. And there's blood on his hands and the back of his head. He put up a struggle before he died."

"But if there was a fight, why didn't we hear it?" asked another soldier.

"Because it didn't happen here," said JonMarc, reappearing around the corner. "This trail leads to the stable. Daevlon's body was dragged from there, probably to make it look like an accident."

"But, that don't make sense!" said the veteran. "Who'd want to kill Cap'ain Daevlon?"

Kier and JonMarc exchanged glances. There was one likely suspect, and he'd ridden away an hour since. The question now was *why*?

Chapter Twenty

"Preposterous!" Tor Connail hastily shut the door to the prince's bedchamber behind him and strode into the anteroom, where the rest of the lords stood assessing Kier's report. The fact that the Covenant penitarch reacted without hearing the whole tale convinced Kier he knew more about Captain Daevlon's death than he let on. "Of course it was an accident. Who at Cordon would have reason to wish the captain of the prince's guard dead?" A shrewd look. "—Unless it be your Dynian squire."

"JonMarc's doings are accounted for," said Kier. "And he had no more reason to wish Daevlon dead than I did. Yet there was another Dynian in the castle at the time—a white-haired fellow with a scarred cheek. I'm told his name is Roderig. He arrived yesternight, with the Connail party, and rode off again not an hour before Daevlon's body was found."

"A Dynian? With *my* party?" Connail scoffed. "You expect these lords to believe I would tolerate one of that accursed race among my following? I do not know this Roderig—if indeed he exists anywhere but in Fitzmorwen's imagination."

"Nor do I," echoed Malcolm. "How could a Dynian enter Cordon without my knowledge?"

Kier's lips hardened. He'd seen Malcolm talking to Roderig the night he and JonMarc arrived at Cordon. Yet it was pointless to argue. Connail and Malcolm would only deny their complicity and, if backed into a corner, they could make matters difficult for JonMarc. The Lady Yssolt's chambermaid, whose favors JonMarc had been enjoying at the time Daevlon was killed, would quickly change her story if she saw her employment in jeopardy. In any case, as Roderig was Dynian, he probably didn't belong to Malcolm or Connail, but took orders from Táranos directly. That left the question of why Táranos should want Rhynion's captain killed.

Jaremy Lochlainn intervened. "From Fitzmorwen's description, it seems clear Captain Daevlon was murdered. Perhaps it was some private quarrel. Is this Roderig being pursued?"

"I dispatched a patrol to track him." Kier noted his brother's panicked glance at Tor Connail. "With luck, we'll soon know more."

"Meanwhile," said Edmund, "what are we to tell the prince? He is already frail, and news of Daevlon's death shook him deeply. Is it wise to suggest murder before we ourselves are sure?"

Norris Hannon of Dandryth stroked the foremost of several layered chins and scowled. "I say no. The prince needs his rest. What point upsetting him further?"

"I think we are agreed," said Tor Connail. "So far as Prince Rhynion is concerned, Daevlon's death was an accident. Until we have proof to the contrary, I see no reason to tell him—"

"Tell me what?" Rhynion poked his tousled head out of the bedchamber.

Tor Connail started. "My Prince! I did not hear you stir. Did our talk waken you?"

Rhynion entered the anteroom, swathed in a robe of purple brocade that swished as he walked. "No, I just had much to think about. What were you not going to tell me, Connail?"

"Nothing urgent, my Prince. Only the matter of... of our return to the capital. I had thought to depart in three days, but after tonight's unpleasantness, it might be wise to leave Cordon tomorrow. Of course, I did not wish to broach the subject until I knew how well your Highness had rested."

"Very thoughtful." Rhynion took a seat and folded his hands between his knees. "And what is there in the capital that cannot wait a few days more?"

"Official business, Highness. Now that you are regent, our allies will be sending envoys to confer with you. My brother Aran and I would value the extra time to prepare you."

"But we just arrived. I do not wish to return so soon."

"My Prince, the chill and this accursed drizzle—not to mention the day's sad events—all conspire against your Highness' health."

Jaremy Lochlainn looked up from a conversation he'd been having with Malcolm and Ruark. "Perhaps we can offer an alternative," he said. "Malcolm has a thought that merits consideration. As you know, Ruark and I do not immediately return to the capital. We plan to take the western route and visit his fortress of Caerllyn, there, for a week or so, to take our ease, do some hunting, then continue on to Menythgar in time for the council session, a fortnight hence. Could not the prince travel with us? The western lands are rolling and green; the air far healthier than in the city. And Caerllyn is the mightiest fortress in Alcor, beside the Citadel itself. His Highness would certainly be safe there. Perhaps Edmund and his daughter might join us, and so make a merry company. How say you to that, my lords?"

Rhynion's young eyes brightened at the suggestion.

"No," said Connail. "It is out of the question. The western road lies too near Branwyn lands."

Rhynion's features drooped again. "How say you, my lord Edmund?"

"Much as it grieves me to counter your Highness' wishes, I fear Connail is right. That route is too dangerous."

"But the Branwyns have not been sighted in that vicinity for more than a year!" said Ruark. "An' if, as Fitzmorwen reported, the outlaw Gerit Mawr's camp lies near the road to the capital, the western route may be the safest." He drew Edmund aside. "An' think what it could mean to our cause to separate Rhynion from the Connails a while."

Kier overheard. "My lords, as senior Legion officer, I must concur with Duke Edmund and the penitarch. True, the Branwyns have been quiet of late, but this Roderig is still at large, and headed we know not where. Why invite trouble?" He darted a glance at Tor Connail. Did he detect a secret gleam in the penitarch's eye? Blazes, if only he had the courage to probe Connail's mind. Yet he dared not risk it. Tor Connail already suspected him of having sinistral powers, despite his obvious skill-handedness. Should the Covenant penitarch gain proof, the consequences could be dire. The Covenanters still commanded public fear. Even Kier's allies on the Council would hesitate to risk their reputations defending him.

"Well, I see no problem," said Malcolm. His break from Connail's leash seemed no more than an independent bid for Rhynion's favor. "His Highness clearly needs a diversion to make up for the unpleasantness this day. If such a journey will accomplish that, it seems well worth it. After all, he'd not go unprotected. With an entire legion to accompany him, as well as Ruark and Lochlainn's house guards, what Branwyn would dare threaten him?"

"There is *not* an entire legion," said Kier. "The Connails' private guard made up most of the prince's company on his journey here. Without them, His Highness' force will be greatly diminished—dangerously so, I deem it."

"Then I shall send half my guard to accompany him," said the penitarch, in an unexpected turnabout. "That is, if Rhynion is truly set upon this course."

Kier's belly cinched a warning. What did Tor Connail hope to gain by this? Rhynion's support? "And from whom will they take their orders?" he asked.

"Why, from the Legion captain, of course."

"The Legion captain is *dead*. Did Daevlon's passing mean so little to you, my lord, that you so swiftly thrust it from memory? His second is an unseasoned lieutenant to whom I would not entrust responsibility for the prince's safety on such a journey."

"Well, there it is," said Edmund. "We cannot send the prince westward without an experienced captain to lead his forces."

"But there is one," said Malcolm. "My brother is a captain of the Legion. Why could *he* not accompany the prince?"

The hammer fell on cue. Kier cursed himself for a fool for letting himself be blind-sided.

"But I have other plans..." he began, knowing his protest was futile.

"What plans could be more important than attending our prince in his need?" said Connail. Kier caught the edge of mockery in the penitarch's voice.

"Oh, yes!" said Rhynion. "With you in command, no Branwyn would dare attack us."

"But my Prince..." Kier gave it up. One look in Rhynion's eager eyes told him he was trapped.

"Then it's settled," said Lochlainn, rubbing his hands together against the chill. Kier felt sure that he, and the honest Ruark, had no notion of Tor Connail's duplicity. Like himself, they'd simply been played for dupes. "The weather is clearing. We may depart for Caerllyn tomorrow. Edmund, will you and Lady Cariwyn accompany us?"

Edmund frowned, then offered a grudging nod. Kier suspected his uncle liked the turn of events no more than he did.

"Excellent," said Lochlainn. "Then we must each to our charges. There's much to prepare before morning."

Tor Connail wrapped a fatherly arm around Rhynion's shoulders. "And you, my Prince, must get some rest. I'm sure there will be much excitement in store for you these coming days."

"So, the prince and company depart tomorrow?" JonMarc had gathered snatches of conversation as the lords hastened from Rhynion's chamber. He hadn't been allowed to enter, and so spent the time quietly sharpening his dirk, while four royal bodyguards glowered down at him.

"Aye," said Kier, "and we're to accompany them, as far as Caerllyn, at least." He turned toward the keep's main stair. JonMarc scrambled after him.

"Caerllyn? Where's that?"

"It's Ruark's fortress, in Galwyn, some twenty leagues southwest of here."

"But I thought we were going to Cymworth," JonMarc whispered.

"So did I. Connail and my brother had other plans." Kier grimly recounted what had happened. "Not three hours ago, they were condemning me for a traitor. Now, I'm the only one they'll trust with Rhynion's safety."

"So, you think it's a ruse?"

"Of course it is. And I'm a prize chump for not catching on sooner. Connail knows we meant to go to Cymworth. He probably arranged Daevlon's death just to delay us—so his Master could have more time to locate the Cábretaur." Kier exhaled bitterly. "Daevlon was a fine officer, JonMarc; one of the best. To think he died for this." Kier slammed his fist into his palm. "How many more will pay for the Cábretaur with their lives before this is ended?"

"But if you know it's a ruse, why go along with it?"

"How can I refuse? Rhynion is Alcor's prince, and I'm sworn to serve him. I'll send for a replacement to meet us at Caerllyn and we'll leave for Cymworth from there. At least it's not far off our route. The Cábretaur will just have to wait a few days more."

JonMarc recognized the smolder in Kier's amethyst eyes. It was pointless to protest. "So where are we going now?" he asked, as they descended a torch-lit stair beneath the keep.

"The armory. I'll need a mail shirt and some other gear. You'd do well to take one too—and maybe a better weapon than that dirk." Kier pondered a moment. "I know one that will suit you."

It took him some time to locate what he sought—in an old trunk, hidden beneath a pile of rusted chainmail that had lain untouched for a nine-year or more. Kier rooted through his boyhood treasures and at last drew out a parcel wrapped in skins. He laid it reverently on the floor. "My mother gave me this before she died. It belonged to my grandsire. I don't know much about him except that he was a Dynian warrior, killed in battle—I'm not even sure which one. She spoke of clinging to her mother's skirts as they searched the field for his body. They found him by the color of his sash, for his head had been struck off. By some miracle, the sword lay hidden beneath him. My mother treasured it all her life."

As Kier removed the last of the wrappings, JonMarc gasped. "By all the saints of Karithon, Kier—it's beautiful! May I handle it?" Kier moved aside to let him slide the gleaming broadsword from its scabbard. JonMarc hefted it cautiously with his left hand, then switched it to his right—the only acceptable way to handle a blade, he'd been taught. He bounced the weapon in his palm to feel the weight, admiring the way the filigreed gold on the hilt blazed torchlight in his calloused fingers. "Nice balance," he murmured, and carved a steel arc through the musty air. Then he grinned and drew himself up a little taller. "Mind if I play with it a while?"

"All you like," said Kier. "It's yours."

JonMarc's jaw dropped. He sought Kier's eyes for some hint of jest, but found none. "But—it's an heirloom. Why don't you wear it yourself?"

"I already have the sword my father gave me. And this is a Dynian blade. Can you imagine the suspicion it would rouse for a Legion captain to wear it? I have a measure of courage, but not a death wish."

"But... you'd actually *give* this to me?"

"Why not? I can't carry it with me, and if I leave it here, it's bound to be plundered eventually." He chuckled. "I've been told you look like a Dynian princeling. You may as well dress the part."

"A princeling, eh?" JonMarc grinned. "Who said that?"

"Doesn't matter. Come on, JonMarc. Any blade's better for being used. This one's lain idle long enough. Will you accept it?"

JonMarc whistled softly, unwilling to reveal how deeply the gesture had moved him. Few but Kier and Gwythion ever treated him as anything more than a slave and thief. "I will, but you know I can't return the favor—yet."

§

By morning, the sky had cleared and a thin rim of gold at the eastern horizon heralded a fair day. Kier viewed it from his saddle. He'd received no word from the patrol he'd sent after Roderig, though he expected none so soon. It would take daylight to track the villain properly. Gwythion, too, had been silent. Kier had lain awake last night while the rest of the castle slept, trying to contact his mentor—a nearly impossible feat, not knowing the Fithlon's exact whereabouts. He could only probe the blackness, hoping his mentor might, by chance or intuition, detect the summons and respond. But Gwythion had not answered.

The courtyard bustled as wagons were loaded and horses harnessed in preparation for the prince's departure. So far, none of the lords had appeared, save Edmund. The trusty duke was the Council's lone representative when Captain Alaric Daevlon was laid to rest, at dawn. Kier had attended the brief ceremony with the troops, and was formally placed in command. His men now assembled in the courtyard, as restless as he to depart. Much as Kier dreaded the prospect of trekking over muddy roads and swollen streams, he found the wait even more exasperating.

Devoreth's Orb rode high by the time he detected any stirrings from the keep. Edmund emerged again, somber as ever, followed by the other lords, who clustered in a great, doting lump around the prince. All but Malcolm and Tor Connail would accompany them on their journey.

Malcolm seemed to distance himself from the general excitement. His pallor, and the deep shadows beneath his eyes, indicated he, too, had not slept. Kier suspected the reason. All morning, rumors had circulated amongst the troops, and though hushed to silence whenever he approached, Kier could guess their nature. Last night, strange lights again shone from the new duke's apartments, and common sooth had it that Lord Malcolm colluded with demons.

It took yet another hour of petty problems and interminable farewells before the royal party was ready to depart. As Kier sat his mount before the gates, watching the procession pass, he sensed a presence at his elbow. Startled, he glanced down.

Malcolm stood there, staring intently after the prince, fingers flexing nervously at his sides.

Kier frowned. "So, brother, do you come to wish us safe journey?"

Malcolm's head shot up like a felon's. He glanced at Kier, then back to the castle, as though uncertain what to do. Abruptly, his rigid manner changed. Haunted eyes lifted to meet Kier's square on.

Kier's belly knotted. That gaze held a specter of the past—a plea from the brother who had once idolized him, before other influences turned that admiration to hate.

"Guard our princely cousin *well*," Malcolm whispered fervently.

Kier started to question. But as quickly as it appeared, the expression vanished. With a cowering glance over his shoulder, Malcolm turned and hastened back into the castle.

Chapter Twenty-one

A disheveled and saddle-weary centuriant stalked angrily from the captain's tent and nearly collided with a staggering intruder. His hand flew to his swordhilt before he recognized his new commander's Dynian servant. Muttering a curse, he elbowed the churl aside and strode off between the campfires.

JonMarc ducked into the tent. "What was that about?" he asked, his words slightly slurred. He lowered himself onto the edge of Kier's field cot with more than usual care.

Kier looked up from the report he'd been studying. "One would think," he said, flaunting the parchment, "that five trained legionaries would have no trouble capturing a lone Dynian fugitive."

"You mean, Ro—Roderig?" JonMarc belched. Kier caught a stale whiff of beer. "What happened? Didn' they find him?"

"Find him? They had him cornered in a cottage. He *escaped.*."

"Well, we knew he was—a slipp'ry bastard."

"Gods, JonMarc, he's no demon. To let him slip past them in the dark—with their prince's life at risk..." He loosed an irate snort.

"So, what're you gonna to do?"

"I've done all I can think of, for now. I've dispatched outriders; tripled the guard around the prince's tent. The whole camp's on alert. Blazes, I can feel the tension from here." Kier turned an exasperated eye on JonMarc. "And you're not helping matters! This camp's Dynian-mad already. Half the younger troops are so skittish they'd shoot at anything, out of panic. Yet you stagger around drunk, without a care in the world. If there were any women but Cari along, you'd likely be out whoring now—living down to their lowest expectations. It's a wonder you haven't got an arrow in your back already." Kier shook his head. "And here I'd hoped you'd set an example; maybe change a few opinions about the Dynian."

At the mention of Cari, JonMarc's head drooped noticeably. But he made no excuses for himself.

"Oh, get to bed," said Kier. "You're of no use to me like this."

"Yesss sir." With an exaggerated salute, JonMarc collapsed onto his bedroll. Seconds later, he was snoring.

What in Devoreth's name had gotten into him? Kier had hoped that by entrusting JonMarc with something as precious as the sword, his companion might grow into a role befitting it. Instead, JonMarc's behavior had worsened. This reeking specimen was a far cry from the JonMarc he'd witnessed this morning: the one who, when offered the unprecedented honor of riding escort to the Lady Cariwyn, had disappeared to the riverside, to return bathed and clean shaven, sporting a mailed jerkin over his cleanest shirt, and smelling like a Castémaron brothel. What had happened since then to change his mood?

Kier set the matter aside. He had more pressing concerns. His plans for finding the Cábretaur were careening out of control, and Malcolm's warning hung heavy on his mind.

JonMarc murmured in his sleep and rolled over to embrace his pillow. Kier watched with envy, wondering how it must feel to amble through life with few cares and no responsibilities. Now, more than ever, he longed to share in his companion's uniquely unbiased outlook. But that was not to be, with JonMarc rumbling in his sleep like a bear in hibernation. Kier settled down on his cot, listening to the camp noises recede around him. Eventually, he too drifted off, but his sleep was troubled and gave little rest.

His fears for the journey proved groundless. Whether by chance, or his own skill at command, there were no attempts on the prince's life. Even his concern that the Branwyns might spy the imposing silver and sable of the Connail houseguard and view it as provocation had not materialized. His scouts sighted no Branwyns. The lords took this for a healthy sign. To Kier, it only meant their luck had lasted longer than he dared hope. That made him even edgier.

On the afternoon of their fourth day, they crossed the upper waters of the river Averin and entered the province of Galwyn. Soon the company caught their first glimpse of Ruark's stately fortress of Caerllyn, its six hexagonal towers tinted rose-gold in the westering orblight. Built upon a rugged peninsula that thrust, like a flexed arm, into the crystalline waters of Loch Allain, the castle seemed to float, its gleaming walls mirrored in the lake's glassy surface.

Kier welcomed the sight. He'd pressed the company hard, setting out early each day and riding till dusk. There were protests, ostensibly on the prince's behalf, but Rhynion had held up well. The sunshine and brisk upland air agreed with him. Kier had never seen the youth more energetic. He suspected most of the grumbling was prompted by the chafing of noble buttocks.

Earl Ruark had sent messengers to herald their arrival, and onlookers already lined the streets of the walled town to cheer the prince and his entourage. Kier glanced over his shoulder. Behind Rhynion's litter, Cari and JonMarc rode side by side, as they had each day since JonMarc was asked to escort her. Kier envied him that task. Cari smiled as she pointed out the sights to her eager companion. Her raven hair, constrained by a silken veil, blew soft about her shoulders, her fair face haloed in a golden glow, as if Devoreth's Orb shone only for her. Kier's heart ached at the thought of losing her—though how could he lose what had never been his? He turned and spurred to the front of the line.

In the courtyard, the prince was greeted by the Lady Ruark and several of the earl's vassal lords, then ushered to the chambers prepared for him. Kier remained behind to oversee the quartering of his troops and stabling of their mounts. He might easily have delegated the task to another, but he preferred the company of horses to that of the flatterers and courtiers who swarmed around the prince.

It was dark when he finally dragged himself up the stairs to his own quarters. He found JonMarc sitting by the fireplace, polishing his new sword. Kier yawned. "Thank the gods that's over. I could sleep for a week." He pulled off his boots and collapsed across the horsehair mattress. "My relief should arrive tomorrow. Then you and I can finally leave for Cymworth." He glanced up. "Have you eaten? The soldiers' mess is almost done, but there's still food left. Why don't you go grab a bite? I'd rather sleep."

"I ate," said JonMarc. "I met a kitchen wench who..."

"Oh, no," Kier groaned, and rolled to face him. "Don't you ever stop? Caerllyn's not like Cordon, JonMarc. It's a border fortress. The only Dynian they see here are Branwyn raiding parties. If you don't stay clear of Tiernai women, you're going to end up in deeper trouble than even *you* can talk your way out of."

JonMarc's blue eyes flashed. "Blast it, Kier, I'm not a slave anymore, remember? What I do on my own time's my business." He took a breath to calm himself. "Anyway, it wasn't like that. She only directed me to the mess. I wasn't interested in..." His words trailed off.

Not interested? The admission astounded Kier even more than his companion's outburst. What could JonMarc find compelling enough to offset his preoccupation with sex? "I'm sorry," he said. "But you're still new to Alcor. I'm warning you as a friend: you're in mortal danger here. Don't do anything stupid."

JonMarc shot him the look of one whose judgment had been wrongly called to question. Then he got up and began to make ready for bed. As usual, he was asleep the moment his head touched the pillow. This time, Kier had no trouble matching him.

A pounding on the door woke him. Kier sat up with a start, battling the fuzziness in his brain. The rhythm of JonMarc's snoring continued, unbroken. Kier yanked his breeches on and stumbled to the door.

Earl Antony Ruark stood in the corridor, a candle fluttering in his brawny hand. He eyed Kier, standing barefoot and shirtless, and clicked his tongue. "I dinna think you'd to bed so early."

Kier yawned. "Why? What's the time?"

"Four hours past sundown. I came to tell you: we rise at dawn. The prince wishes to hunt."

"Hunt? But we only just got here! He needs to rest. There'll be plenty of time for hunting."

The earl shrugged. "'Tis what he's asked to do. I'll not be the one to refuse him. Earl Hannon made the suggestion, an' Rhynion seized on it. In truth, 'tis good to see the lad makin' up his own mind for a change. I've had my doubts..." Ruark's voice dropped. "You know what I mean. Rhynion's a good lad, an' in time he'll make a fine king, but they pamper him too much. Why, already he's twice the man he was when we left Cordon. Leave him with me another month an' I'll make a warrior of him his father Eduard would be proud of."

"I'm sure you would," said Kier. "But for now, he's still a boy, and until my relief arrives, I'm responsible for his safety. A hunt tomorrow leaves no time for scouting. I'll not have him venturing out unknowing of the dangers."

Ruark laid a patronizing hand on Kier's shoulder. "Kier, lad, dinna think just because this old warhorse has been away from home, he doesn'a know what goes on in his own lands. My responsibility is protectin' this valley—the shortest route between Branwyn and the capital. *No one* crosses my borders wi'out my knowledge. I've already dispatched scouts. If the enemy's about, I'll know of it ere morning. Does that ease your mind?"

It didn't. Kier let his disaffection show.

"Tell you what," the earl said. "We'll make it a short hunt; just enough to whet the lad's appetite for more. We'll ride to the forest by Galglenneth's Spire. That's but two leagues west of here. No Branwyn'd dare venture so near Caerllyn. How say you to that?"

Ruark was not to be gainsaid. Reluctantly, Kier gave in and the earl took his leave. Even as he turned for his bed, Kier's apprehensions closed in. They nagged at him well into the night.

§

At that same hour, a league to the east, a hooded figure crouched beside the bridge of the river Averin, waiting. Above the western hills, the red moon's new crescent hovered low, while the smaller white moon, now in its first quarter, floated amid the shredding clouds to cast its cold gleam on the rolling landscape.

The figure did not move, his gaunt form scarcely visible beside a stand of budding willows. On a hill nearby, his hobbled mount grazed the thick meadow grass, occasionally raising its shaggy head to sniff the breeze.

Suddenly, the beast gave a restless whinny. The hooded man cocked his head. Above the ceaseless melody of the river came the rolling rhythm of hoofbeats, approaching from the east. Soon the rider would be in view. The hooded man threw back his cloak and strung his bow.

Seconds throbbed by like labored heartbeats. At the foot of a long slope, the single torch that denoted the sleeping village of Averford vanished for an instant as the errand rider clattered past. The hooded man drew a slender shaft from his quiver and fixed it to the bowstring.

The hoofbeats slowed as the rider neared the bridge and noticed the saddled horse silhouetted against the russet moonlight. Warily, he glanced about. A soft breeze hissed among the grasses. He spurred his mount onward.

The bowman climbed the high bank and drew. The scar across his cheekbone pulsed with his quickening heartbeat.

The rider spotted him. His mouth opened and he reined in hard. With the whine of an angry hornet, the arrow split the air. The rider cried out as it pierced his tunic just below the collarbone. He swayed in the saddle, then toppled. His skittish mount snorted and reared in confusion.

The bowman bounded down the bank. He flapped his cloak, and the horse galloped off, reins dangling. Retrieving his lantern from behind a rock, he knelt beside his victim's head.

The rider still breathed. The bowman took quiet satisfaction in the man's livery—the white stag of the Citadel Guard. Swiftly he searched the rider's leather pouch until he found a small scroll. He broke the seal and held it open to the lamplight. He could make out little, but it was enough. He re-rolled the message and stuffed it back in the pouch.

Fear glistened in the errand rider's dark eyes as he stared at his attacker. A smile played across the hooded man's lips. He drew out a kerchief and gently dabbed his victim's brow. The rider struggled to speak. The hooded man regarded him with mocking pity. Then, drawing his knife, he calmly slit the young man's throat.

Moments later he was in the saddle, galloping southward over the moonlit hills, to Ruthland, and his Master's Connail allies.

Chapter Twenty-two

The royal hunting party breakfasted in the great hall at orbrise. There were thirty seated around the long trestle tables—a number Kier protested as insufficient for the prince's safety. Again, he was overruled. "After all," Antony Ruark chided, "ye canna stalk game with an army. My scouts report all quiet in the forest to the west. There's naught to protect him *from*."

Grudgingly, Kier yielded and settled down to the huge offering before him. He ate little. Casting his eyes around the horseshoe of tables, he noted a number of somber faces, and many a yawn carefully concealed behind a goblet of wine or a joint of cold fowl. Earl Hannon, whose rash suggestion had prompted this early morning jaunt, was absent entirely—taken to his bed with a chill, it was said. That only increased Kier's misgivings. Beside him, Duke Edmund stared grimly into his hands. Only Rhynion displayed excitement. For him, this was an all-too-rare opportunity to escape matters of state and simply enjoy himself.

Seated below, at one of the lesser tables, JonMarc appeared unusually pensive, his shaggy blond head propped upon his fist. After a time, his eyes stole up to the dais where Cari sat, two places to Kier's left. Kier was startled to see his cousin acknowledge that wistful gaze. Suspicions roiled in him. Cari and JonMarc? Impossible. Yet amid the bustle, those two pairs of eyes, the blue and the umber, seemed to share some unspoken message. Kier glanced from one to the other, feeling more alienated than ever.

"Shall we find boar, do you think?" Rhynion's excitement gleamed bright as the mid-morning orblight on the meadow grass.

Edmund offered a fatherly smile and drew his mount nearer. "Deer, most certainly, my liege. The winter has been kind to them and Ruark tells me great numbers roam the hills hereabouts. The hounds should have no trouble driving some in our direction."

Barely had he spoken when a hunting horn sounded shrill in the brisk air. Soon they heard shouts and the baying of hounds. Rhynion took up his bow with trembling fingers.

"There, my liege!" shouted Lochlainn, pointing. A yearling buck leaped into the clearing, panic flaming his eyes. Around him raced the hunting pack. Cut off, the buck swerved. Rhynion raised his bow and shot. The buck stumbled but continued to run, the prince's dart dangling from his belly.

"A fatal shot, Highness," said Ruark, reining up beside them.

"Aye, but not a clean one. I've not practiced since I fell ill."

"Never fear. The hounds will bring him down."

"Finish him, my lord Ruark," said the prince. "I would not see so fine a beast suffer."

Ruark raised his crossbow. A second later, the buck fell dead. The keeper of hounds called the milling pack off as the hunting party galloped up to inspect the first kill of the day.

"We shall feast well tonight, my liege," Jaremy Lochlainn exclaimed.

Rhynion looked down at the fallen buck with pity in his eyes, then turned away.

By mid-day, three deer hung gutted and bled, trussed upon carrying poles. The huntsmen and hounds were dispatched back to the castle, bearing the fruits of a successful enterprise. The remainder of the party stayed to enjoy a leisurely picnic before returning to Caerllyn. By the time they, too, set out, the shadows were beginning to lengthen.

"I just told Duke Edmund," Rhynion called gaily, as Kier galloped back to them along the trail, "I've a mind to take your Dynian to be my jester."

Kier bowed his head. "I'm pleased your Highness found him amusing."

"Amusing? Why, his tales of his boyhood in Castémaron were the funniest I've ever heard. He had us enthralled."

It was true. JonMarc had done a worthy job of entertaining the royal party while they ate. Even the stoic Edmund had chuckled at his exploits, and the look on Cari's face was nothing short of worshipful. Kier recalled the scene he'd witnessed at breakfast, and his curdling suspicion returned. Had anyone else noticed? How could they not? Even now, his cousin and JonMarc rode together, some distance behind the rest, laughing and jesting. It was unseemly for JonMarc to spend so much time with a betrothed woman. Kier determined to talk to him when they got back.

"What's wrong, Kier?" Edmund pulled up beside him, out of the prince's hearing. "Your thoughts have been elsewhere today. Did you not enjoy the hunt?"

Kier wrenched his attention back. "It wasn't undertaken for *my* enjoyment. But there is something, uncle. One of my scouts hasn't returned. He should've been back half an hour ago."

"What direction did you send him?"

"North, to check out the forest above Galglenneth's Spire."

Edmund scowled. "Not far from the way we're headed. Perhaps his horse went lame, or he became lost. The woods are thick up that way."

"That's what I keep telling myself. I rode out a while ago to look for him, but found no trace. The forest around the Spire is quiet as a tomb— *too* quiet."

"You think there's cause for concern?"

"There's always cause when the prince is among us. I sensed nothing specific, but I'm uneasy." Kier didn't trouble to hide his frustration. "You know I was against this from the start. But Ruark and Lochlainn—they're so ecstatic about getting the prince to themselves—like schoolboys with a new plaything. I honestly don't think they see the dangers."

Edmund clicked his tongue. "You cannot know the concerns we've all faced these past months, Kier, with the king at death's door, and Rhynion dominated by the Connails. This may be the opportunity we need to add our influence. And Ruark took precautions. His scouts combed the forest all night and found no sign the Branwyns even know we're here."

"Men see what they want to see," Kier said. "Or what they're *allowed* to." He smiled grimly. "You needn't humor me, uncle. I know what's being said: 'Fitzmorwen takes his duty too seriously. He sees Branwyns lurking behind every tree.' Doubtless there are charges less flattering that I've *not* been allowed to overhear." Kier sighed. "If this were any life but Rhynion's..."

Edmund laid a fatherly hand on his arm. "None fault you for taking your duty seriously. My brother would be proud. Why don't you ride with the prince while I scout ahead?" Without waiting for a reply, Edmund spurred up the trail and soon disappeared around a bend.

Kier slowed, allowing Rhynion to catch up. Lochlainn and Ruark rode beside him, with six mounted guards ahead and another eight behind. JonMarc and Cari brought up a distant rear.

"Shall we pass the Spire this time?" Rhynion asked. "I'd hoped to glimpse it when we came by this morning, but the mist was too thick. Is it truly so mysterious as they say?"

"It's very ancient," said Lochlainn, "and so far as I've heard, unique to Alcor. You've been abroad, Fitzmorwen. Are there like wonders elsewhere in the Deg Tirith?"

Kier fell into pace. "There is one, similar but not so tall, in the courtyard of the Fithlon cloister outside Castémaron. Legend says another stood in the central plaza of the ancient Nwtyrrans' capital, but it was destroyed when the lost realm fell."

"But what are they for?" asked Rhynion.

"No one knows," said Lochlainn. "I understand the Dynian hold this spire sacred, though they did not build it. It's said that within the ring of stones at its base, they perform manhood rites and child sacrifice. But that is only legend," he added, glancing sidelong at Kier.

"The Dynian have never performed human sacrifice," said Kier, ever astounded by the depth of Tiernai ignorance. "That tale was devised by Tiernai mothers to make their children behave. As for the other..." He pointed ahead. "You can see the tip of the Spire there, above the trees, Highness. Is it any wonder the Dynian chose such a site for conducting manhood rites? The Spire and stone circle surrounding it are held sacred to the god Devoreth."

"Devoreth? You mean the Dynian revere the same gods as we? Penitarch Tor told me they worship demons."

"He would," Kier muttered. "The Dynian worship Devoreth, as we do, but their bond is closer with Denia, the sacred Mother. The Dynian call themselves the Children of Denia." Kier met the prince's eager eyes. "With so many Dynian as your subjects, Highness, it might be useful for you to learn more about them than the Connails can teach."

"Indeed yes. You, cousin, must instruct me, for no Tiernai knows that race so well as you. Tell me of Galglenneth. Who was he and what had he to do with the Spire? Did he build it?"

Kier shook his head. "Only the Fithlon know who built it, and they do not say. It already stood when our ancient ancestors, the Edenists, arrived on Éclatan—and that was more than five hundred years before the coming of the Nwtyrrans. Galglenneth of the Wolf Staff was one of the five heroes of Dynian lore. He won renown by rescuing the sister of a Dynian chieftain from the dungeons of a powerful sorcerer. Their battle, mind to mind, lasted six days and nights, until the evil one's power was broken. The maid then chose Galglenneth to wed. It was he who summoned the first *Cyngor*,

which is like our High Council, and presented the Dynian Elders with
a unified law code. They elected him High King at the base of the spire
that now bears his name, and from his wife were sprung the Telynor High
Kings, whose line endured until the Tiernai conquered Alcor, fifty years
ago."

Kier looked up to find Lochlainn, and even the gruff Antony Ruark,
attending his tale. Tiernai lords never troubled to verse themselves in their
enemy's lore—an arrogance he found both aggravating and tactically naive.
Know your enemy, Sir Donal always stressed. If Kier had any say, young
Rhynion would not suffer similar blindness.

"Why do you say Galglenneth's line sprang from his *wife*?" Rhynion
asked.

"Among the Dynian, ancestry is counted through the female. While a
man may be unable to name his father, he will almost certainly know his
mother. So although a man may assume the role of king, his heir will not
be his own son, but his sister's, for only through her does the royal blood
run true. The coming of the Tiernai changed that, but it may interest you
to know that the conqueror, Melchor—your Highness' great-grandsire—
based his claim to Alcor on the right of his mother, who was of Telynor
blood."

"Then I am related to Galglenneth," Rhynion exclaimed.

"Indeed yes, though distantly. Melchor broke the line by passing the
kingship on, in Tiernai fashion, to his own son, Brendan."

"How if he followed the Dynian way? Who would now be king?"

"Well, the crown would have passed to his sister's son. That would
be—" Kier froze.

"Anlawth," Rhynion provided. "It would have gone to the attainted Earl
Táranos. This is fascinating, cousin."

Fascinating? Dread sluiced through Kier's veins. Was *that* what Táranos
wanted? The crown? And if so, did the Connails know?

"What happened to Galglenneth?" Rhynion pressed. "Did he die in
battle?"

Kier wrenched his mind back. "No. Legend says that after his wife's
passing, he found a way inside the Spire and climbed to the very top.
There, he broke his wolf staff, the symbol of his power, and raised it up to
Devoreth, who put forth his hand and bore him away."

"A strange ending," said Rhynion.

"And blasphemous," Lochlainn added, "or so Penitarch Connail would say." He and Ruark showed no sign the revelation about Táranos concerned them in the least.

"None of the Dynian heroes was ever said to have died," said Kier. "One way or another, they simply passed out of reckoning."

As he spoke, their trail narrowed between two tall sentinel stones and the company entered a broad meadow. Atop the long slope to their left gleamed a huge pillar of silver that looked to have been planted there by some ambitious god. From this distance, its metal surface appeared smooth and unblemished. Around its base clustered a ring of standing stones, like those flanking the path. Though nearly twice man-high, they were dwarfed by the towering monument in their midst.

"The Spire," Rhynion said in awe. "Why, it is a greater wonder than I e'er imagined! May we not ride up and view it more closely?"

Kier cast a swift glance about him. Ever since the revelation about Táranos, his warning senses had raged at him. Boding threat—or imminent danger? No point taking chances. "No," he said, disregarding royal protocol. "I'm uneasy here. We must leave—*now*." He pointed ahead. "Follow the right-hand trail. Hurry!"

Antony Ruark opened his mouth to protest. Suddenly, Duke Edmund appeared atop the ridge and galloped down toward them. "Fly, my liege," he cried. "The enemy is here!"

Kier seized the prince's reins and surged for cover. From somewhere in the trees ahead, an arrow sped. Edmund gave a sharp cry and grabbed his shoulder.

Eight of the prince's guard closed in to protect their lord. One fell with a grey-fletched shaft in his eye. Five others stormed the forest, and soon the meadow echoed with the clank of swordplay and the strident cries of men and horses.

"This way," Kier shouted, leading the prince toward a gap in the trees. A dark-clad form dropped from the branches and tried to pull Rhynion from his saddle. Kier hewed the man's arm off. More attackers sprang from the underbrush. The prince drew his sword to fend them off.

Kier reined his mount around, fighting like a berserker, his jerkin already spattered with enemy blood. Lochlainn and Ruark battled two pale-haired attackers who had closed from behind. They seized Jaremy Lochlainn and dragged him from his horse. Ruark thrust his blade between the shoulderblades of one, who went down with a cry. Lochlainn scrambled to his feet, striking furiously at the other. With a hoarse shout, the sturdy Ruark surged after the prince's opponents.

Fighting raged all around, but it had begun to abate. Kier reined in to avoid trampling a fallen guardsman and turned to check on Rhynion. The prince signaled he was unhurt. Through the dust and blood, it looked as if they might win their way clear.

Ruark grabbed Lochlainn's arm and pulled him onto the rump of his own mount.

"Follow me," cried Kier, and spurred off the trail.

A dozen men leaped from the cover of dense forest ahead and spread across his path, arrows trained on the royal party. Kier wheeled about, only to find more bowmen blocking the way behind. Trapped.

Kier took quick inventory of his own men. Only thirteen remained in their immediate party, including the prince. The rest were either captured or lay wounded on the path. Kier's belly wrenched. Where were JonMarc and Cari? They had been riding well behind the rest. Had they overheard the battle and fled to safety? He could only pray so.

From the shadow of the Spire, a small troop of Dynian horsemen galloped down the slope, halting some yards away. The two at the center urged their mounts forward. One, a youth in his early twenties, whose pale eyes burned like liquid fire, curled his lip and spat.

"Tiernai dogs." He used the common speech, though his voice bore a strong Dynian accent. "Lay down your weapons or your princeling dies. Your lives come cheaply here."

Kier felt Ruark stir beside him. "Not so cheap as yours," the earl growled, fingering his sword. "If ye want my weapon, piss whelp, come take it."

The young zealot flushed deeper than the orange of his wiry hair and beard. With a grunt, he nudged his mount in the flanks. His companion, older and swifter, seized his reins and yanked him up short. The horse reared. "Dai!" he barked, his voice a crisp baritone. "Keep your head."

Dai barely managed to keep his seat. His sword slipped from his grasp, embedding itself in the shaggy turf. Dai recovered it, seething.

"Ross Branwyn," snarled the outraged Ruark. "I mighta known ye'd be behind this. Devoreth take your traitorous hide."

The Branwyn leader acknowledged with the barest nod. Like his men, he was clad in weathered brown, with a jerkin and brow band of bronze-studded leather. A plaid cloak of green and black, caught at the shoulder with a silver brooch in the shape of a dragon, was his only emblem of authority. His hair, thinning at the temples, was tied back in a long braid the color of autumn grain. He paid Ruark no heed, but turned keen eyes on Kier. "Fitzmorwen, is it not?" His voice bore the melodic lilt of the Dynian.

Kier returned a slow nod.

"We competed as boys—archery, at Midsummer's Faire; you shot eight gold to my six." Ross's narrowed brows shadowed a twinkle of respect. "But I've improved since. Please accept my condolences on the death of your father. Duke Morwen was a brave man, an' less an enemy to Branwyn than most of your Tiernai lot." He shot a swift look at the steaming Ruark. "Dismount and lay down your weapons. Your prince will not be harmed so long as you obey my commands. You have my word." Ross touched two fingers to his heart in the Dynian gesture of oath-taking.

Kier loosed a tense exhale. Branwyn bowmen knelt to either side, arrows fixed on the prince. Grimly, Kier dismounted and tossed his sword on the grass, then helped Rhynion down. All but Ruark followed his lead.

"You canna mean you trust this Dynian whoreson!" the earl growled.

"No more than you, my lord," Kier replied, quite aware his words might be taken two ways. It was Ruark's stubbornness that had gotten them into this. "We're out-flanked and outnumbered. This seems the best bargain we can make for the prince's safety—unless you've a better plan."

Ruark snarled, but at last he, too, dismounted and clanged his sword down with the rest.

"Now," said Ross, "if you will follow—"

A disturbance at the meadow's edge cut him short. Amid the sharp neighs of horses came the clash of opposing swords. Kier's heart sank. JonMarc and Cari had not escaped. They'd lagged so far behind, they'd only now reached the gate of stones. Helpless, Kier could only await the outcome.

Soon, two of Ross's men led the struggling JonMarc into the meadow. Behind limped a third man, nursing a wounded thigh. Kier strained to see past them, but could not spot Cari.

Ross Branwyn frowned down at JonMarc. "Do Dynian now ride with Tiernai lords?"

JonMarc licked blood from the corner of his mouth and eyed the Branwyn chieftain as if Ross were a haunch of venison he considered carving. "My bond is with Kier Fitzmorwen and is one of blood. His foes are my foes." JonMarc gave a sly grin. "Would the Dynian captain have me prove my allegiance?"

A sudden jab of JonMarc's elbow, and the man on his left yelped in surprise and broke his hold. JonMarc stomped the foot of the other and shoved a solid elbow under his chin, then fell back into a fighter's crouch, his captor's dagger glinting in his hand.

Ross Branwyn chuckled and motioned to his men. A thicket of arrows trained on JonMarc. "What will you do now, firebrand?"

JonMarc drew himself up with a feral grin and pinched the dagger for throwing. "I'll take their captain with me."

"Well spoken," said Ross. "In that, at least, you do credit to our race." He waved the bowmen off. "I am Ross, War Chieftain of the Branwyns. This is Dai Caydyn, my lieutenant. But—where is the maid who rode with you? Was she not taken?"

JonMarc's head shot around. Clearly he'd thought Cari was behind him.

"She regained her horse and bolted south," grunted one of JonMarc's captors. "Madoc rode after her."

"Madoc?" Alarm showed in Ross's face. "He is one of yours, Dai. What will he do?"

Dai jerked a careless shrug, still smoldering from his earlier humiliation. "What matter? The wench is Tiernai. Let him do as he likes."

"By all the gods!" gasped Edmund, a red-stained hand clutching his wounded shoulder. "She is my daughter."

Panic seized Kier. Cari was a capable horsewoman; he'd seen to that himself. But did she have the skill to elude a Branwyn warrior, born to the saddle? He tensed, ready to lunge for his horse and gallop after her. The very thought of his beloved Cariwyn victimized by any man, especially one of Dai's brutish warriors, terrified him almost beyond caring.

Years of training yanked that passion to heel. Even if he managed to escape the Branwyn arrows, his flight would leave the prince at the mercy of his enemies. Kier's fingers closed around the crest-ring on his middle finger. *Duty and Honor.* The prince's safety was—*must* be—his first priority. Kier's principles raged at him. How could he abandon Cari? Crazed with frustration, he yanked off the ring and hurled it.

It struck Dai Caydyn's horse squarely between the eyes. With a grunt, the beast tossed its head and pranced, jostling the flank of Ross's mount which, in turn, lurched into the horse behind. Dai's fiery gaze was so intent on his captain he failed to see what had caused the mishap.

But JonMarc saw and understood. In the confusion, he ducked free of his captors and raced for his mount. Bowling aside the Branwyn who held her, he leaped into the saddle and kicked the mare's flanks. By the time the guard raised a cry, JonMarc was already galloping for the gate of stones. Several of Ross' bowmen knelt and took aim.

"Let him go," Ross ordered. "He is of no value to us; the woman's safety is."

Kier breathed relief and silently wished JonMarc godspeed. "If any harm comes to her, Branwyn," he seethed, "I'll not rest until I see you and your lieutenant flayed alive."

Ross Branwyn's face was granite. Sharply, he reined his mount around, barking orders over his shoulder in the Dynian tongue, then galloped back up the hill. Dai Caydyn followed.

With cold efficiency, Ross's remaining officers searched the prince and the Tiernai nobles for weapons, then ushered them, single file, to the menacing ring of stones. Kier was allowed to accompany them. The rest of Rhynion's entourage remained near the trail, under guard.

The afternoon sky had turned overcast and a brisk breeze rose from the north, whipping the prisoners' cloaks behind them as they labored up the grassy slope. By the time their captors pointed them to seats on a row of stone blocks near the altar, Rhynion was shivering. Kier removed his own cloak and draped it around the prince's shoulders, warning off a guard who moved to impede him. Rhynion raised bleak eyes to his. Kier tried to reflect back more encouragement than he felt. A quick glance showed where their horses stood tethered and their weapons were stowed—and how many Branwyns guarded them. Too many. For now, escape was impossible, but that could change.

Again, panic over Cari's fate stabbed him. Kier forced it down. JonMarc would rescue her. Right now, his only concern must be Rhynion.

From behind a giant monolith across the circle came the harsh strains of argument—Ross berating his lieutenant. The Tiernai lords paid little heed, but to Kier, who knew the Dynian tongue, the confrontation provided some insight. Dissent festered among the Branwyn ranks, and Dai was at its core.

Some minutes later, Ross Branwyn strode toward them, followed at a distance by a red-faced Dai Caydyn. "Who speaks for you?" Ross demanded. His gaze fell on the wounded Edmund, who struggled to his feet. Earls Ruark and Lochlainn were already standing.

Yet it was Rhynion who spoke. "*I* do," he said, sitting straight and regal, as if the rude stone bench were a gilded throne.

Ross Branwyn's face mirrored the others' surprise. A sober smile played upon his lips. "So, the Tiernai princeling has a tongue after all."

"Show some respect to your liegelord, Branwyn!" snapped Ruark.

"I grant respect to those who *earn* it. We Branwyns recognize but one ruler. Until my father, Glyn, returns from foreign lands, that office falls to me. We serve no scion of a usurper."

Rhynion bristled and tossed his head like a spirited colt. "Address your comments to *me*, Ross Branwyn. This land was by my ancestor truly claimed and truly won. *I* am your rightful prince. Why do you detain us here? Release us at once, or suffer the price of your treason."

From beside the prince's seat, Kier watched for Ross's reaction, ready to step in. The searchers had missed his hide-out dagger, and he would not hesitate to use it if the Branwyn chieftain threatened Rhynion in any way. He flexed his fingers, waiting.

Slowly, Ross Branwyn's expression softened. "I see I underestimated your Highness. You have spirit that belies your stature." He folded his muscled arms across his chest and his voice turned belligerent. "You ask why we hold you here. Can you truly pretend you do not know?"

The prince's brown eyes flashed. "I pretend nothing. These few years since Ceorl's Ford, there has been peace between our races. Why do you seek to destroy it?"

"*Peace*? When my people cannot tend their fields or go to their own beds in safety?"

"So, is this outrage retaliation for the Connail attack on that village— what was it, Caerdewi? That incident was regrettable. Yet the Connails assure me the village was a haven for traitors and sorcerers, and your actions do naught to persuade me otherwise. If you wish to start a war, Ross Branwyn, you have made a good start."

Ross went livid. "By the gods, how can we start what, for us, has never ended? For fifty years, you Tiernai have hunted the Dynian for *sport*. Aye, I do not doubt your Connail adders told you the sacking of Caerdewi was justified. Traitors and sorcerers, you say? Were that so, then women and babes and old men do threaten your kingdom, for that is who died at Caerdewi—most of them herded into their own homes to be burned alive. Have they kept you so ignorant of this, prince, or do you *choose* not to know what occurs in this realm you claim to rule?"

Rhynion started to reply. Ross Branwyn cut him off. "Aye, the sack of Caerdewi would be right enough cause for retaliation. But there is more. I can scarce believe Tiernai couriers are so slow bearing you word. 'Tis now three days since my sister Llydia was captured by Aran Connail and his accursed son, Aric, and she but bearing aid to the sick and homeless. Can your Highness still believe it is we of Branwyn who provoke war?"

Kier mouthed an oath as his earlier fears redoubled. Antony Ruark gave it voice. "The plague take those Connails," he hissed. "Are they tryin' to get us all killed?"

"Earl Aran was at his castle in Ruthland when we left for Caerllyn," whispered Lochlainn. "He cannot have known Rhynion was with us."

Kier drew closer. "Don't be so sure, my lords. You forget, his ally Táranos possesses Fithlon mind skills."

"So you've said," muttered Edmund. "But if he knew, why would Connail do something so rash? And the Branwyn is right—why did we not hear of the girl's capture? At worst, news should have reached Caerllyn last night. Had we known, I would *never* have allowed the prince to venture forth."

Ross overheard. "Aye, you may blame the Connails for your capture. In truth, when we spied Tor Connail's colors amongst your host, we'd hoped the Covenant viper traveled with you."

"Penitarch Tor is in the capital, attending matters of state," said Rhynion. "When he learns of this outrage, he'll dispatch the entire Legion against you. What do you mean to do with us, Branwyn?"

Ross rested one booted foot upon the altar stone. "You have knowingly trespassed on Branwyn soil. The penalty for that is death."

"Trespassed?" Ruark sputtered. "These lands belong to Galwyn. You know that full well."

"They are *Dynian* lands, my lord Ruark. All Alcor is Dynian land. You Tiernai have stolen the choicest holdings for yourselves, leaving us only the mountain forests, which you cannot tame. Yet here, we thrive. The mountains keep us strong. Now, in your arrogance, you dare cross our very borders to challenge us. Do you expect us to yield up more?"

"We came to hunt," said Rhynion, "no more than that. We meant no harm to you or yours. I give you my word."

"Your word?" Ross Branwyn scoffed. "What good is that? The Tiernai Council gave its word that all Glenneth province would belong to the Dynian. But the Council forgets its word when convenience strikes. How long have the Tiernai raided our villages; stolen our land? Yet when we retaliate, *we* are called aggressors."

"So, what will you do?" Edmund challenged. "Harm us, and you destroy your only hope for peace."

"*Peace*?" snarled Dai Caydyn. He had been standing to the side, leaning against one of the tall stones. Now he stormed forward. "We *spit* on peace. Kill them, Ross. Alcor will not be free till all Tiernai are driven from her shores or drench her soil with their craven blood."

"I warn you, Branwyn," said Edmund, pointedly ignoring Dai. "Raise a finger to harm us and it will mean the end of your race. The mountains will no longer protect you."

Dai thrust himself past Ross before his captain could counter. "What of that? We do not fear death. Better to be slain in battle than die the cowards' death you visit on us." Dai's trembling fingers gripped his sword. "Do it, Ross! *Kill* their leaders. Destroy the Council. Or, if you fear to act, grant me the task. Do you not see it is our one chance to drive them forever from our soil?"

Kier silently edged in front of Rhynion, his dagger marked for Dai Caydyn's heart.

Ross's eyes blazed. "Dai, *enough*!" he shouted, in Dynian. "I told you, this is not the time."

Dai spat again. "Coward. My blood is as good as yours. Were it not for purest chance I, not you, would rule our people."

Ross's face flushed. "Praise Denia you do not. You would bring death to us all." His glance darted to the clouded sky and he frowned. "Searchers will soon arrive from Caerllyn. Go. Ready the troops to depart."

"I don't take orders from—"

"You *do*, and you *will*." Ross thundered.

For a moment, uncertainty showed on Dai's face. Finally, he turned and stalked off toward the makeshift encampment.

Ross Branwyn's eyes followed. "Denia preserve us," he muttered. Abruptly, he realized Kier had understood their exchange. He straightened to face the prisoners. "Lords of the Tiernai," he said, returning to the common speech. "Though your actions merit death, on this occasion we grant you your lives. We have other need of you. In a week, your Council will decide whether to renew hostilities against the Dynian. Know you this: Though we of Branwyn do not seek war, we are well prepared for it. We have both the strength and the will to drive you from our shores.

"Know also that, if the decision be for peace, we will ne'er again be content with the pittance you toss us. These demands do we make of the

Tiernai Council: *First*, all raids and aggressions against the Dynian shall cease. The Tiernai will pledge, on pain of death, ne'er to set foot uninvited within Dynian borders—and those borders shall encompass the sacred Spire and its surrounding forests. *Second*, there shall be recompense in the amount of ten thousand silver arians to all Dynian made homeless or orphaned by the Connail raids. And *last*—though not least in importance—my sister Llydia will be returned to us, alive and unharmed. Let these demands stand as the price of your lives."

The Tiernai lords exchanged troubled looks. "Such demands are impossible to meet," said Lochlainn. "The Connail faction is too strong. You would destroy all we've striven to achieve."

"Aye," echoed Ruark. "Ask this, an' ye can be assured the vote will be for war."

"So be it," said Ross. "Then look to your lives when next we meet, for we shall at last drive you into the sea from whence you came. No more will we be slaves in our own land."

Duke Edmund raised a conciliatory hand. "Wait," he said. "Ruark and Lochlainn speak aright. None of us wants war, yet these demands, as a whole, will be impossible to get past the Connails. But if you will be patient, they may be broached separately and thus stand a better chance. This, at least, I vow: your sister will be returned. Her capture was unconscionable and shall be redressed."

Ross's face reflected bitter scorn. "Patient? Nay, we have *been* patient. 'Tis time to fight once more for what is ours. As for my sister, I need no vow from you to assure her safe return. For until her release, your prince remains our prisoner."

"You would not dare!" said Ruark.

"Would we not? If you are so keen to curb someone, why have you not leashed the Connails? Your prince will be well looked after; you have my pledge. As token of our good faith, we will allow one of you to accompany him. Choose who it will be."

Kier squatted beside Rhynion. "With your permission, Highness, I will attend you. The rest will be needed to persuade the Connails to release the Branwyn maid." Inside, Kier's spirits foundered. Another delay in reaching the Cábretaur.

"How say you, my Prince?" asked Edmund.

Rhynion nodded. "It seems we have little choice. Yet do not fear for me, my lords. It was dishonorable for the Connails to take a woman prisoner. I am willing to stand in her stead. Tell Earl Aran he has much to answer for when I return."

Ross signaled his men to move out. Two shaggy horses were provided for Kier and the prince. "Your indulgence, my lords," Ross told the others, "but you and your men must walk. We need your mounts to bear our wounded."

"But what of *our* wounded?" Ruark protested. "Duke Edmund needs care..."

"You will soon be met by searchers from Caerllyn. And mark you, do not try to follow, or you will be shot down. We shall meet you here at this same hour, three days hence, to exchange my sister Llydia for your prince. See that she is unharmed."

"Three days?" said Edmund. "That's not time enough to persuade the Connails to agree—"

"It will *have* to be, my lord of Hlanneth." Ross Branwyns voice was as unyielding as the standing stones. "*Be here*. And bring no troops. Should there be treachery, your prince will pay—with his life."

Chapter Twenty-three

A shrill cry sliced the forest air—a woman's terror, abruptly cut short. JonMarc reined the mare around, his breath heaving. Where was the path that would take him to her? The tangled undergrowth betrayed no sign. Sweat sliming his face, he abandoned his winded mount at the forest's edge and plunged headlong into the trees.

"Cari!" he shouted, elbowing his way through thorny scrub. A spate of dizziness seized him. The forest blurred, swirling in a lurid maelstrom of smoke and flame. Wildly, he staggered through branches that clutched at his arms and knees like beggars' fingers. "Cari, *where are you*?"

The words his reeling mind heard were different—strange syllables in a tongue he did not recognize. Yet somehow he knew the words were his own. An image wavered before him: a young girl with innocent blue eyes and hair the color of summer buttercups. Pleading hands reached out to him. Her lips suddenly parted in a shriek of agony as her face blackened, charred by the licking flames that devoured it. "*Jenna!*" JonMarc cried, plowing his way to her. A tree root caught his foot and he sprawled to his face in the leafy mould. The illusion vanished.

For some moments, JonMarc lay panting as the twi-lit foliage solidified around him. He felt spent as a drowned rat washed up on a rock. He dragged himself to his feet. The forest spun. He lurched to a gnarled treetrunk and clung to it with quaking fingers until his balance returned.

Some madness had overwhelmed his mind—he was sure of it now. It first assailed him in the tavern, the night he'd torched Modron, then several times thereafter, in fractured dreams. And once it began, he could not halt the fiery apparitions, the horror, the helplessness, each time more vivid than the last. But why did they torture him? What did they mean?

The dizziness was lessening, though JonMarc's legs still felt wobbly. Urgency stabbed him. Cari was somewhere ahead. The cries he'd heard couldn't all have been phantoms of his mind. Thrusting aside his lingering queasiness, JonMarc stumbled on.

At last he found a path that seemed to plunge straight into the forest's depths. Heartened, he hurried along it until the way was cut by a shallow stream. There in the muddy bank were the signs he'd been searching for: hoofprints—two sets. Some yards beyond, something pale caught his eye. Cari's head veil! JonMarc splashed across and snatched it from the branch that had snared it. Clutching it to his heart, he raced up the trail.

He found her at the edge of a clearing. She was leaning against a tree, so still he almost passed her by. "Cari!" he breathed, and reached out to take her in his arms.

With unexpected viciousness, she threw off his embrace and backed away, her brown eyes wild. Only then did JonMarc note the glint of steel in her fist, the torn bodice, the scratches on her face and neck. And, most obvious, the dark stain at the hip of her gown.

Fury consumed him. "Where is he?"

A flame kindled Cari's dark eyes. She nodded toward the bare ground behind him.

JonMarc spun. A body lay crumpled on its side, hardly visible in the waning light. He noted the man's size—shorter than himself, yet almost twice his girth. Bronze-colored hair hung, grimed and matted, halfway down the Branwyn warrior's back. A thick leather jerkin served him like armor. JonMarc scratched his head and stole a glance back at Cari, who was watching him with the eyes of a whipped animal. How had she managed it? How had a maid as slender and fragile as Kier's cousin brought down this hulk of a warrior all alone, with only a hunting knife? JonMarc rolled the man onto his back—and found his answer.

The deed hadn't required extraordinary skill or strength. Only cunning, and the fortitude to endure the brute's embrace until she could slip his weapon from the scabbard at his hip. His bruin weight against her had plunged the knife home. So the blood on her skirt must belong to him. JonMarc nodded sober admiration. There were women in his past life from whom he'd have expected no less—but they weren't gentlewomen like the Lady Cariwyn.

The warrior at his feet gave a low moan and tried to move. The stout blade had pierced his bowel—there was no mistaking the stench. Pooled blood darkened the forest duff around him.

JonMarc turned to Cari. "He won't last," he said, letting his satisfaction ring clear. "His own juices'll kill him by nightfall. Let's get out of here."

Cari shivered. "Finish it," she said. A cauldron of conflicting emotion seethed beneath her words. She held out the hunting knife as if it were caked with filth.

JonMarc took the weapon and knelt beside the body. The warrior's eyes widened, perhaps in the hope he'd found an ally. JonMarc left him no such delusion. With seasoned precision, he sliced through the jerkin's worn laces and ripped open the sweat-drenched shirt to bare the man's chest. Carefully, he positioned his knife just beside the breastbone.

The warrior made a gurgling noise and struggled, but he'd already lost too much blood. Whatever Cari's wish, the brute didn't deserve a quick death. Deliberately, JonMarc moved the knife point to miss the heart. Then, bracing his weight behind the blade, he plunged it deep.

Hot crimson erupted in a satisfying spurt that helped quell JonMarc's anger. For a moment the warrior lurched it his death throes, glassy eyes staring bewilderment. JonMarc kicked him onto his belly, to bleed out. He cleansed the knife in the weeds, then wrested its sheath from the Branwyn warrior's belt and slid it onto his own.

Cari had turned away at the last second. She now seemed impatient to leave. JonMarc could only imagine what she'd suffered, and this was no time to question. "Are you all right?" he asked.

Cari nodded but refused to take his hand. Pressing past him, she hastened down the trail.

JonMarc spared a last look around the clearing. The horses were gone and it was too dark to search for them. He turned and followed Cari.

The porridge dusk promised rain as JonMarc paused near the forest edge to get his bearings. "We won't get far tonight on foot," he said. "I left my mount somewhere nearby. With luck, she hasn't strayed." He knew Cari must be weary of struggling through the brush, but was loath to leave her alone while he searched. Instead, he scooped her up in his arms. She did not protest.

JonMarc found the mare complacently cropping grass, very close to where he'd left her. Gently, he lifted Cari onto the beast's back, then inventoried the contents of his saddlebag: a half-full wine skin and a quarter-round of bread he'd hoarded from their mid-day meal—enough for one meager supper, at best. He said nothing of this to Cari. She seemed content to let him make the decisions. He wrapped his fur-lined cloak about her and persuaded her to drink some wine and finish the bread.

Then, taking up the reins, he trudged off across the downs in what he
hoped was the direction of Caerllyn.

They had traveled less than an hour when the storm broke. It was an
hour of the most oppressive silence JonMarc had ever experienced. Cari
had said no word since they'd left the clearing, and JonMarc was hesitant
to intrude on her privacy. He wanted to wrap his arms around her; to kiss
away her lingering fears. Yet he'd felt her recoil at his touch, as if she blamed
him for what had happened. Blazes, he *was* to blame. He should never have
let her out of his sight when they were attacked. In all his experience with
women, JonMarc had never felt this way—unclean; almost ashamed of his
own manhood.

The rain fell harder. It pelted in his eyes and trickled down his collar.
His boots squelched with every labored step. "Cari," he said at last,
shielding his eyes from the downpour, "we'll never make it to Caerllyn
tonight. I don't even know what direction I'm going. I'll try to find us some
shelter." Cari seemed to nod at that, though she made no reply.

JonMarc quickly recognized the challenge he'd set for himself. What
little he could see of the countryside looked desolate, the few stands of
barren trees offering no protection. At last, as he was about to give up hope,
he spotted a coppice of shrubs in a cleft between two low hills, and made
for that. A path, of sorts, wended up the slope, leading to a rocky outcrop.
JonMarc left Cari with the horse and scrambled up to investigate. The rock
face looked solid, but at one point a narrow shelf jutted out. The space
beneath was too shallow to be called a cave, yet wide enough to provide
shelter from the rain. With a whoop, JonMarc leaped down to fetch Cari.

Moments later, she lay huddled at the back of the overhang while
JonMarc unburdened the mare. With his belt, he fashioned a makeshift
hobble to keep the beast from wandering. Then, trappings in tow, he
crawled beneath the ledge, grateful to be out of the downpour.

He felt Cari's eyes on him as he settled beside her. His guilt fashioned
her thoughts: she'd want him to keep his distance—not easy on so narrow
a ledge. JonMarc rolled onto his side, facing outward, and tugged the
saddle blanket over his shoulders. Its scent recalled generations of horses.
JonMarc was too exhausted to care. He shut his eyes and tried to ignore the
raindrops splashing his nose.

A swish of dead leaves behind him and Cari's gentle hand touched his
back. "JonMarc, you're shivering!" They were the first words she'd spoken

since the forest, and JonMarc was relieved to hear them. He vaguely wondered why she'd felt the need to wake him up to point out the obvious.

"I'm fine," he assured her.

Her hand again. This time it touched his shoulder and gently felt its way down his left arm. Cari clicked her tongue. "How could I have been so thoughtless? To leave you lying there in the rain, after you so bravely came to my rescue. Come, move in from the ledge and let me drape the cloak over you. The blanket should go underneath, to keep out the cold from the ground."

JonMarc appreciated her concern. But still, he feared to intrude. After all she'd been through, it was relief enough to know she did not hate him. "Cari, the cold doesn't bother me so much. I'm used to it. You wrap up warm and try to get some sleep. I can fend for myself."

Her response astounded him. "Am I so sullied, then, that you'll have naught to do with me?" Cari's voice broke with pent-up emotion. "You've spoken nary a word to me since we left the forest, JonMarc, and now you bid me keep to myself."

JonMarc rolled over to face her. "I... *no!* I never meant anything like that. I only thought you wanted… " It was too much to explain. Cari's eyes were brimming. Despite her bedraggled hair and dirty face, JonMarc thought her incredibly beautiful. He shrugged the saddle blanket off his shoulder and laid it on the ground between them. "Come on," he said, beckoning her onto it. "We can keep each other warm."

Cari hesitated, then finally settled herself against his side. JonMarc tugged the fur-lined cloak over them both. He'd given up trying to fathom her mood and simply accepted the improvement. Already, he could feel warmth returning to his limbs and knew it was not entirely due to the cloak. He drew Cari's arm across his waist and smiled into the darkness at the images his imagination painted for him on the canvas of his closed eyes.

They shattered abruptly as Cari pulled away. "JonMarc, your jerkin is soaked through."

"Well, *yes.* It's pouring rain out there."

"You needn't shout."

"*I wasn't shout...*" Frustrated, JonMarc forced his voice down. "I'm sorry. I just don't know what you expect me to do about it."

For a moment, Cari said nothing. Then: "You might let it dry."

JonMarc's thoughts raced. What was she suggesting? If this were any maid but Cari, he'd assume... Warily, he said, "Are you asking me to take it off?"

Cari's voice carried an edge of impatience. "I would not—object," she replied, carefully. "Perhaps 'twill be dry by morning."

Not a chance. Yet the message in her words conveyed trust—and perhaps more. These last several days, riding together, they'd shared many secrets. Did he dare imagine his feelings for her were returned?

Whoa, boy. JonMarc reined in his hormones. This was no peasant lass to be trifling with, but the daughter of a duke; his best friend's cousin. She was simply concerned for his comfort and had made a practical, straightforward suggestion. No need to read more into it than that.

JonMarc sat up as far as he could in the cramped shelter and fumbled with the laces. Before he could get them untied, Cari managed to negotiate the sopping leather up to his armpits. It left him in an awkward bind. "Your shirt is drenched too," she said, and yanked it from inside his breeches.

JonMarc's gluteals congealed. With a muffled shriek he jerked upright, slamming his head on the rocky overhang. Cari drew back, aghast. "JonMarc, I'm sorry. I didn't mean..."

JonMarc shook his head, momentarily unable to speak. He hauled the wet jerkin over his head, the laces still taut. "It's all right," he gasped, once he was free, and rubbed his scalp. He tugged the sopping shirt back down. No telling how a lady like Cari might react to the service stripes emblazoned on his back.

Cari laid her hand on his sleeve. "JonMarc, you're chilled to the marrow. A wet garment will not keep you warmer."

"I'm fine," he said, through chattering teeth. "Just—lend me a corner of the cloak."

Cari draped it over him half-heartedly, but did not settle back down. "Do the scars on your back embarrass you that much?"

JonMarc looked up with a start. Could she read his mind? "How do you know about those?"

A sly smirk. "I have my sources."

JonMarc didn't doubt that. In the close environs of a castle, word got around. And admittedly, these last few weeks he hadn't exactly been a monk.

Cari sighed. "Your scars do not trouble me, JonMarc. I've tended wounds before." She ran her fingers down his stubbled cheek. "You may as well take off the shirt. 'Twill be but one more maid to share your secret."

JonMarc gratefully peeled the drenched linen over his head and tossed it aside. When he lay back down, Cari cuddled into the crook of his arm, spreading the cloak over the two of them. "You'll soon be warmer," she said, rubbing his icy hands between her own. "Is that not better?"

JonMarc had to admit it was. He gave a low murmur of satisfaction and drew her nearer. Cari's damp hair spilled across his chest. On impulse, he leaned over to press his lips to her forehead, then closed his eyes to drink in her sweet scent.

"You're sure you don't think me a wanton for suggesting this?" she whispered. "I've ne'er lain beside a man."

JonMarc's lips quirked. "Then you can hardly be wanton, can you?"

Cari sighed. "Some will think otherwise—my betrothed's father, the Earl of Dandryth, for one. And the Connails. I fear the humiliation this may cause my father. Yet I am still a maid, JonMarc. The Branwyn did not dishonor me."

JonMarc kept his relief to himself. He'd suspected as much, but had feared to ask.

A shudder passed through Cari's slim body. "He told me what he meant to do, and gloated that none would hear my cries." She rested her head on JonMarc's chest, but did not weep.

To JonMarc, who was enjoying his role as protector, that came as something of a disappointment. Still, he reminded himself, this was the girl who'd tried to brain Kier with a chamber pot, their first night at Cordon. "You acted bravely," he said. "I'm proud of you."

"But I *killed* him. I wanted him dead."

"Now don't go taking all the credit yourself. I had something to do with that, you know." He thought he saw her smile—a healthy sign.

"You acted at my command. Do you not feel remorse?"

JonMarc shrugged. "For what? The bastard deserved to die."

"But do your gods not teach that taking life is sinful?"

"My gods, such as they are, believe in survival—for their followers, and thereby, for themselves."

Cari gave a soft snort. "You're teasing me, JonMarc."

"A little," he admitted. "But it's foolish to feel guilt over killing a man who would surely have killed you."

Cari seemed to ponder that. "Does it not trouble you that he was one of your own kind?"

"*My* kind? You mean Dynian?" He hadn't made the connection. Was that how Cari saw him? "I feel no kinship with the likes of him."

"No, thank the Lady you are not like him." Cari nuzzled her cheek against his bare shoulder, and for the first time JonMarc thought he felt warm tears. "He was cruel; hurtful. You've been with women, JonMarc. Why do they claim to take pleasure in a man's touch, when I found it only—degrading?"

JonMarc stroked her face with the back of his hand. What could he say that wouldn't sound hackneyed? "Cari, I know it's hard for you to believe right now, but one day you'll find that such things can be—"

"Will you teach me, JonMarc?"

JonMarc choked. He could scarcely believe his ears. Cari actually wanted him. Gods, if only she knew how he'd longed for this.

A nagging voice inside him resisted. It was not a voice he recognized.

"Cari, I don't think that's a good idea." What was he saying? It was a *wonderful* idea! It had dominated his every dream for the past week or more.

Cari turned away. "So you *do* think me tarnished by what happened. Or am I simply not so appealing to you as your chambermaids?"

"Cari, you're the most amazing woman I've ever met."

"Then why should the servants have you when I cannot?" There was anguish in her voice. "I do not care that you're Dynian, or even that you were once a slave. I love you, JonMarc."

JonMarc rejoiced to hear those words. Yet he was uncertain how to handle the beggar's stew of emotions battling within him. It would be so easy to give in. Blazes, he'd prayed for such an opportunity. Yet deep inside, he feared it wasn't real. He'd rescued Cari from deadly peril and, in the aftermath of fear, she had built a fantasy around him. To take advantage now might destroy everything. "You'll think more clearly in the morning," he said, goggling to hear his own words.

He sensed resignation in Cari's sigh. "Will you not even kiss me?"

"Cari, I'm afraid of..."

"What? My father's anger; or Kier's?"

Frustration welled inside him like storm surge. How could he explain what he himself didn't understand? Ghedrev's cods, why pick a moment like this to develop a conscience? "It's nothing like that."

Cari snuggled her head against his shoulder. "Do you love me, JonMarc?"

He drew her close and rubbed his jaw against her soft hair. "Yes," he whispered emphatically. Cari squeezed his hand. A short while later, he felt her breathing slow to a soft rhythm.

JonMarc heaved a long exhale. The moment was gone; it might never come again. He grimaced. His loins were bound up tighter than a catapult. Yet he dared not move, for fear of waking Cari. He adjusted his back on the scratchy horse blanket, shut his eyes and tried to make himself comfortable—to no avail. It would be a long night.

By the time morning crept beneath the rock shelter, the rain had ended, though the sky retained a flinty cast. Above the dark mantle of forest to the west, the fleeing clouds revealed a widening strip of blue. JonMarc rose early, feeling stiff and edgy. He saddled the mare, then climbed to the top of the outcrop to survey the countryside.

He could now roughly gauge their position. Several leagues north, the forested hills thrust eastward, into the plain. There, above the treetops, a fingertip of silver caught the rising orblight. The Spire. What had happened there after he rode off? Clearly, the Branwyn chieftain had sent no one to pursue them. But then, he and Cari were of scant importance. It was the prince and the nobles the enemy wanted. What had befallen them—and *Kier*? When he'd left, they were talking, not fighting. But between enemies, words could swiftly turn to blows.

JonMarc spied Cari laboring up to meet him and set his concerns aside for the moment. "There's a village in that valley," he said, pointing. "There, beyond the hedgerow. It can't be more than half a league off. We might've found more comfortable lodgings there."

Cari reached the top and took his arm. The brisk wind whipped her hair into long, sable streamers. "I was comfortable," she said, looking down at the clustered cottages, white and brown, with roofs of thatch. "Anyway, I doubt they'd have taken us in."

"Why not? Surely if you told them your father is..." JonMarc hesitated. "You mean, because I'm Dynian?"

"And I am Tiernai."

"It would scandalize them so much to see us together?"

Cari nodded and looked away.

"Are you scandalized too?"

Cari leaned against his shoulder. "You know how I feel."

JonMarc smiled, relieved that the morning had not changed her mind. The sleepless hours had allowed him to think things out, and now he was sure—as sure as he could ever hope to be—that what he wanted most in life was standing on the windy hilltop beside him. He put his arm about Cari's waist and held her close. "Cari," he began, "about last night..."

"You needn't explain, JonMarc. I understand."

"No, it's not what you think. I—" Blazes, man, spit it out. "Cari, I love you. I think I have since that first night at Cordon."

He hoped she would fall into his waiting arms. He was disappointed. The sadness never left her smile as she raised her eyes to his. "I know you do, JonMarc. But then, you've said that to a lot of women, haven't you?"

She was right. JonMarc found the admission disconcerting. After all, he'd never intended to deceive anyone. Whenever he'd professed his love, he'd meant it, just as he meant it now. Only now it didn't seem to mean quite the same thing. This feeling came from a different part of him—a place no woman had ever touched before. "Cari, I'm serious. I want you." Gently, he tilted her head back to search the fathomless depths of her eyes. Ghedrev's blood, a man could get sucked in there and never find the will to leave. A shiver darted through him.

Cari seemed to feel it, for she moved nearer and ran her delicate hands up the front of his jerkin. "Your garments are still damp, JonMarc," she murmured as their lips met.

To JonMarc, the minutes seemed to meld into an eternity that was not nearly long enough. Cari was first to break away. She drew back and tried to make some gesture of propriety by straightening her rumpled gown. JonMarc leaped in, ready for another go. Cari held him off.

"JonMarc, last night I'd have given anything to have you show your love for me. After what had happened, I needed to know you still found me desirable."

"I did!" JonMarc exclaimed. "I *do*." He moved to kiss her again.

Again she withdrew. "But you were wiser than I. I understand now what you meant when you said I would see things more clearly in the morning. Sadly, my love, you were right. We must leave this place. We dare not be seen together like this."

"But why?" he asked, still playful. "I'd spend my whole life up here with you."

"Do not say such things. I am promised to another—you know that. I should never have let this happen."

The laughter died on JonMarc's lips. "Cari, I was wrong last night. What happened was meant to happen. Surely you can feel that."

She smiled and laid her head on his chest. "You sound like a Fithlon."

"Maybe so. But this much I know: you'll never wed that Hannon brat. You'll marry *me*."

"JonMarc, that's impossible. Even if you were not Dynian, and my cousin's squire, we would never be permitted to wed. I represent an inheritance: a parcel of land and a dukedom—and the power that goes with them. I may not choose my husband according to my heart. I beg you, do not be like Kier and make this more difficult than it already is."

"You're the one like Kier," JonMarc countered. "You both wear duty like a badge of honor—as if it's noble to bend your lives to the will of others. Can't you see those *others* merely use you for their own purposes?" He seized her shoulders, forcing her to look into the ice blue intensity of his eyes. "Life is short, Cari. Don't waste it on what others tell you is your duty. Your first duty is to yourself; your own happiness. If you don't accept that, one day you'll look back and find naught in your life but might-have-beens."

Cari pulled away. "Please, JonMarc, say no more. Take me back to Caerllyn."

"All right. But remember what I've said." He scooped her into his arms and kissed her again, despite her protest. "One day you *will* be my bride."

They were soon cantering northward across the grassy downs of Galwyn. To their left, the deep fastness of the Berwyn forest blanketed the rising hills. JonMarc had set Cari behind him on the mare. With both riding, he hoped to reach Caerllyn before noon. That, at least, was the excuse he'd given her. For his part, he simply enjoyed the warmth of her body pressed against his own.

Just to the north, the mysterious Spire thrust its mighty head above the dark shoulders of forest, a silver-domed sentinel with black slits for eyes. JonMarc had meant to avoid the place, yet as they drew nearer, his earlier concerns intensified. What if Kier and the others lay wounded or dead on the grassy slope? How could he pass without finding out? He angled the mare toward the forest below the Spire.

Cari quickly recognized his intent and voiced her own concerns. "Do you think they're all right—Kier and the prince, and my father?"

JonMarc brought the horse to a halt near the twin sentinel stones where the Branwyns first attacked. "I don't know. I'm going to have a look around." He swung a leg over the mare's neck and dropped to the ground.

"I'll come with you."

"No. There may still be Branwyns about. Stay under cover of the trees and wait for me."

"But I want to know, too."

"You will, as soon as I return." Though hesitant to leave her alone, if there were bodies on the field—especially of those Cari loved—he did not want her to see. "Keep your ears sharp. I'll whistle when I approach. If you see or hear anything amiss, *ride*. Don't worry about me. Caerllyn lies that way: to the river, then east."

"But what if you meet trouble?"

JonMarc returned a cocky wink. "Trouble and I are old comrades."

He was relieved to find no one in the meadow, alive or dead. With eyes to the trodden turf, JonMarc carefully searched the battle site. In part, he sought the golden sword, which the Branwyns had seized when he was taken. He didn't expect to find it, but his belly wrenched at the thought of losing it. Instead, he discovered Kier's crest ring, trampled into the grass. He slipped it into his pouch, hoping against his deeper fears he'd find the chance to return it.

He followed a trodden path up the long slope to the curious ring of stones. The huge metal Spire, towering like a giant in their midst, utterly fascinated him. As he drew nearer, he began to make out threadlike lines in its surface, as though it were pieced together of many panels that fit each other with incredible precision. High above, a narrow platform with a low parapet encircled the spire like a crown, yet nowhere did he see any way to reach it.

So engrossed was he in his inspection, he failed to realize he was not alone until the snap of a twig sent him wheeling about—to confront a bramble of pikes. A half dozen Tiernai soldiers had crept from the shadow of the stones and now trapped him against the Spire.

They appeared as uneasy as he. Their slate-bearded leader stepped forward, a loaded crossbow resting on his arm. "Drop your weapons," he ordered.

JonMarc let the Branwyn knife fall. "I'm no enemy," he said, palms open. "Who are you?"

"*I'll* ask the questions," the captain barked. His men gripped their pikes with whitened fingers, as if fearing JonMarc might pounce on them. "You dare show your face here, Branwyn?"

JonMarc kept his eyes on the crossbow. "I'm no Branwyn. My name is JonMarc. I'm squire to Captain Fitzmorwen of the Royal Legion. We were with the prince and his hunting party yestereve when we were waylaid by enemies. I was searching for..."

"This is some trick." one of the pikemen interrupted. "No Dynian would be riding with the prince. He's a Branwyn spy. I say kill him. Let his death stand against our own losses."

"Aye," chorused the others. Their dress and manner seemed too rustic for legion troops. They must be from one of the neighboring villages.

"There'll be no killing unless I order it," said the leader, who looked more a soldier than the rest. "Who are you, Dynian? The *truth*."

"I've *told* you the truth."

The Tiernai officer handed his bow to another and picked up JonMarc's hunting knife. "You think I'm a fool? I know a Branwyn hilt when I see one." He seized JonMarc by the collar and slammed him against the Spire, pressing the huge blade to his throat.

JonMarc swallowed hard. "If you don't believe me, take me to the prince—or the Duke of Hlanneth. They'll vouch for me."

The man's grip tightened. "The duke lies wounded at Caerllyn; the prince and your so-called master, captured by the Branwyns. If you truly were squire to Captain Fitzmorwen—which I doubt—why did you desert him in his peril? Unless you had foreknowledge of the attack."

"I had no foreknowledge," JonMarc managed, as the man pressured the blade against his larynx. Cari could vindicate him. These men were Tiernai; they'd believe the Duke of Hlanneth's daughter. But could he afford the risk? Ruffians were ruffians, whatever their race.

The Tiernai captain suddenly spotted the frayed cord about JonMarc's neck. "What's this?" he demanded and yanked the dathana crystal from inside JonMarc's shirt.

"Just a trinket I picked up..."

"It's a charmstone," interrupted a heavyset pikeman, "used by the 'cursed *sinistrae* for spell-casting." He pointed to JonMarc's left hand. "What'll 'e wager that glove hides a serpent brand?"

The captain hastily let go of the pendant as if fearing it might sear his fingers. "Show me." he ordered.

JonMarc slowly removed his glove. He could have predicted the reaction.

"Sorcerer!" shrilled the pikeman, fumbling the sign against evil. "Kill him or we're all cursed!" His comrades took up the cry.

"*I'm no sorcerer,*" JonMarc shouted above the confusion. "If you'll let me explain..."

No one listened. "'Ware his eyes," someone cried. "He'll spell you with a look!"

They manhandled him around and slammed his face against the Spire. JonMarc braced for the stab of a half-dozen pikes in his back. He only prayed it would end quickly.

A small bump on the surface of the Spire caught his eye—a crystal, embedded in the metal wall, a mere hand's breadth from his nose. JonMarc's mind raced. The Citadel Square; Modron's ear crystal. It was worth a try. In the last instant, he let his charmstone touch the tiny gem.

Lightning stabbed his eyes, blinding white, accompanied by a screech so raucous it all but numbed JonMarc's senses. His terrified captors dropped their pikes and covered their ears.

The charmstone dazzled on JonMarc's chest as if a star had fallen in their midst. With a sound like a rake through dead leaves, the metal wall he leaned upon suddenly slid aside and JonMarc pitched forward into blackness.

As his head hit the cold floor, he imagined he heard a woman's scream. Then a male voice bellowed somewhere behind him: "What in blazes is going on here?"

Chapter Twenty-four

JonMarc opened his eyes to find Cari's brown eyes gazing down at him. He lay in tall meadow grass, his head cradled in Cari's lap, the warm rays of Devoreth's Orb beating against his face. He tried to push himself onto his elbows. A herd of hornbucks stampeded between his temples. With a groan, he dropped back. "What happened?" he murmured.

Cari gently brushed a wisp of hair from his brow. "Your comrade, *Trouble*, nearly got the best of you."

JonMarc recalled his flippant boast. "But—the pikemen. How did I escape?"

"Through no talent of your own, I'll wager." The young male voice sounded familiar.

JonMarc squinted. "Gaelin?"

"You've a keen memory, Dynian." Kier's former aide squatted on the grass beside him.

"What are you doing here? I thought you were in Menythgar."

"I arrived last night with Sir Donal and the relief force from the Citadel." Gaelin cocked his head toward the Spire. "Sorry about the mix-up. The local conscripts are a mite over-zealous in their hatred of Branwyns— though that's scarce to be wondered at, things as they are."

"Then what they said about Kier and the prince being captured...?"

"Unfortunately, true." JonMarc recognized wariness in the young centuriant's eyes. Despite Kier's endorsement, Gaelin didn't entirely trust him. "We're to exchange Ross Branwyn's sister for them in two days. Come, we're headed back to Caerllyn. Duke Edmund is near frantic for news of his daughter." Gaelin stood and offered a hand to Cari.

JonMarc struggled up on his own. The bright gold of mid-morning orblight glinted off the Spire. He shaded his eyes. "What happened up there?"

"According to your captors, some kind of door opened in the Spire and you fell in. If I hadn't witnessed the flash, and heard that infernal screech, I'd have guessed they'd been sipping from the wrong bottle. No one knew such an entry even existed, much less why it chanced to open just in time to save your Dynian hide." Gaelin's tone said he suspected chance had little to do with it.

JonMarc was inclined to agree. His charmstone touching the crystal in the wall had somehow triggered the door mechanism. "What was inside?"

"All we could make out was a spiral stair. The door slid shut the moment we dragged you clear and we could find no way to re-open it." Gaelin eyed him sidelong. "You're earning yourself quite a reputation for sorcery, Dynian."

A brisk west wind flapped the pennons on Caerllyn's gleaming towers as the small company rode through the gates. JonMarc scarcely had time to wash and change his clothes before a summons arrived from Duke Edmund.

As he neared the duke's guarded doors, he met Cari, exiting. He smiled, about to speak, but Cari shook her head. A warning. She hurried off down the corridor. JonMarc braced for a storm.

He found Duke Edmund seated in a curule chair beside the fire, his left arm bound a linen sling. The care lines in his face looked deeper than JonMarc remembered. Gathered around him in a small semi-circle sat the inseparable Ruark and Lochlainn, and the pasty-faced Earl Hannon of Dandryth, the latter apparently recovered from whatever malady had kept him from the hunt.

Edmund rose as JonMarc entered and embraced him with genuine gratitude, then motioned him to an empty chair. A servant set a round loaf and a wedge of cheese on the low table before him, next to a carafe of wine. "My daughter tells me you have not supped since yestereve," said Edmund. "Pray help yourself."

JonMarc did so, ravenously, much to the sober amusement of Ruark and Lochlainn, and the obvious irritation of the fidgety Earl Hannon.

Jaremy Lochlainn stood, rubbing his long hands together. "Well, I wish to hear the reports of Sir Donal's scouts before we confer with him this afternoon. How say you, Ruark? Hannon?"

Antony Ruark responded to a none-too-subtle nudge. Hannon remained seated. "I have questions for this fellow," he said, looking down his stubby nose at JonMarc, "regarding his association with the maid—if I may still *use* that term—contracted to be my son's bride."

Edmund's dark eyes flared. Beside him, Lochlainn gave an irate snort. "Hannon, you have all the subtlety of a rotting corpse."

Earl Hannon drew himself up. "Well, I could hardly ask *her*."

Lochlainn just shook his head and left the room, Ruark stalking along behind him.

"Well?" Hannon demanded, once the door shut. "What have you to say for yourself, knave?"

JonMarc purposely ignored the linen napkin on his tray and wiped his mouth on the back of his sleeve, only because it so plainly irritated Earl Hannon. "About what?" he said, chewing.

"Don't play the fool with me, Dynian. I've dealt with your deceitful race before."

JonMarc sat back, arms folded behind his head, and propped his boots on the tabletop.

"Confound your insolence. You *will* speak or I'll have you flogged."

"Calm yourself, Hannon," said Edmund. "There will be no floggings. JonMarc has done us both an immense service by returning my daughter safely. He has earned my gratitude and more. *I* will ask the questions."

"Then get on with it, man!" the earl huffed.

Edmund turned to JonMarc. "Sit up!" he snapped. "Remember where you are." JonMarc straightened. "Now, give us full account of what befell you and the lady Cariwyn after you left us at the Spire. Hold nothing back. I will know if you are lying."

"I've no cause to lie, your Grace. We did nothing wrong."

"Humph," grunted Hannon, "I find that hard to believe, knowing this one's reputation with the household sluts."

Edmund glared. "You forget yourself, Hannon. By impugning JonMarc, you also impugn my daughter."

"Women are a gullible lot, Edmund. The lady Cariwyn may easily have been beguiled. Or raped."

"I swear she was neither," JonMarc retorted. "Cari told me she still has her honor, and I laid no hand on her."

"I do not doubt it," Edmund said, trying to mollify the situation. "Now tell your tale."

JonMarc related as much of the truth as he deemed necessary, glossing over awkward details and elaborating on those of little consequence. When he finished, Duke Edmund seemed satisfied. Earl Hannon, predictably, was not.

"You say she disabled this Branwyn before he could ravish her? She, a maid—alone and unarmed?"

"Not unarmed. She had a hunting knife."

"Aye. *His* knife. How did she acquire it? I cannot believe he'd allow her a hand free, unless his own were occupied—elsewhere."

JonMarc silently cursed the loutish earl. "My lord, I was not there. I only know what I saw, and what the lady told me."

"Which is clearly more than you are telling us. Do you lie to protect her, or yourself?"

"I haven't lied."

Hannon gave an imperious snort. His stubby fingers toyed with some trinket hidden inside his broad belt. "Well, I believe the Lady Cariwyn was brutalized by the Branwyn villain, or at the very least, manhandled. Either way, she is no longer pure. I'll not bind my son to such a match."

Edmund stared at him. "What are you talking about, Hannon? The marriage contract is signed. You cannot break it now."

"I can, and I do. This incident abrogates our agreement. I pledged my son to a maid—unsullied. We will settle for nothing less."

"But she *is* a maid," said Edmund, reddening. "You've heard her swear it."

"I hear only that she spent the night alone with this Dynian knave. All know his reputation. Can you offer proof she was not compromised in *any* way? Of course you cannot. There will always be doubts. I'll not have my son's honor besmirched by such a match. However," Hannon added, an avaricious glint creeping into his eyes, "I may be willing to reconsider—for a price."

Edmund's graying brows narrowed. "What price?"

"If you were to raise her dowry to, say, five thousand gold koryns, I might forget your daughter is, shall we say, tarnished?"

Edmund swallowed back a cough. "*Five thousand*? Are you insane, man? How could I afford five thousand koryns? Is it not enough your son stands to inherit a dukedom?"

"Come, my friend," said Hannon, still fingering whatever he held in his belt. The gesture roused JonMarc's curiosity. "Let us not quibble. Your holdings in Glen Tierna alone net you that amount each year, and more. Is your daughter not worth the sacrifice? Besides," he added, with a touch of spite, "where else will you find a match for her without sending her over the sea? I know you cannot bear to part with her. You see, Edmund, you really have no choice."

Edmund jerked to his feet, eyes ablaze. "I'll show you choice. You think to extort money from me? I've had enough of your insults, Hannon. I'd not have my Cariwyn wed your pimple-faced oaf of a son if he were the last man on Alcor! The contract is dissolved. I don't want to see your flabby, over-fed face around me again. Now get out before I boot you out myself!"

Whatever Hannon's motives, he clearly hadn't expected this. He opened and shut his mouth several times, like a codfish, then scrambled for the door. JonMarc sprang ahead to open it for him. Hannon bowled him aside and beat an ignoble retreat into the hall.

JonMarc returned to his chair, smugly fingering the token he'd lifted from the earl's belt. He stole a glimpse at it before slipping it into his pouch: a small, blood-red crystal.

Duke Edmund did not notice. "Five thousand koryns," he fumed. "As if young Caulder's 'honor' couldn't be bought and sold for three sulls at any trollop's cot. To think I plighted my Cariwyn to that parasite." He sat down heavily and couched his forehead in his hands. "Hannon is right, though. The gods know where I shall find a suitable match for her now. I may well have to send her across the sea, to the Tiernai homeland—and in truth, I cannot bear the thought of that."

It occurred to JonMarc that, for the moment, the duke was addressing him almost as an equal. He seized his opportunity. "Your Grace, I beg you, let her marry me."

Edmund looked up, startled. "*You*? Devoreth's blood, I'm not *that* desperate. How dare you presume to ask this of me?"

JonMarc was taken aback by the duke's sudden animosity. "I love her," he replied simply.

"You think that reason enough for me to grant you her hand?"

JonMarc fidgeted with his wine cup. "Why not? She loves me, too."

Edmund's expression softened. "Aye, I think you are right. It was unwise of me to let you spend so much time together. I had other matters on my mind and did not realize what was happening. But she'll get over it," he added brusquely, "as will you. There can be no thought of marriage. The very suggestion is absurd. Did Cariwyn know you intended to approach me?"

JonMarc shifted uneasily. "She warned me not to."

"And rightly. After all, what are you? A Dynian lackey with no home, no income, no prospects—and a reputation, as Earl Hannon was pleased to point out, for knavery and lechery. Why, you don't even have a name."

"I can change all that," said JonMarc. "I swear, I'll do anything to have Cari."

Edmund shook his head. "I'm sorry, JonMarc. I would grant you much for bringing my Cariwyn safely back, for she is more precious to me than my life. Yet in this you ask too much. Indeed, I don't think you understand how far above yourself you aim. As my only child, Cariwyn will inherit all I possess, and the man she weds shall become Duke of Hlanneth after me. For that reason, the choice of her husband is not mine alone. The lords of the Council demand a say in who shall be permitted to join their ranks. Do you truly imagine they would ever accept *you*?"

"But surely, as her father, you could insist..."

"Why should I do that? Such a match could only bring shame and humiliation upon my daughter."

"But I don't want her for her inheritance. I love her! How can you ask me to lay that aside just so she can wed some pompous lordling with a title?"

"Nonetheless, I do ask it. I *demand* it. Forget her, JonMarc. She is not for you."

JonMarc glowered. He'd expected an uphill fight. He wasn't prepared for total dismissal. "I cannot forget her. I *will* not."

"Blazes, man, do you think you're the only one who's ever been in love? Your master, Fitzmorwen, has worshiped Cariwyn since they were both children, yet he knows he can never have her. Mayhap he is wiser than you, for he has accepted his disappointment and put it behind him. You must do the same. For my part, in consideration of what I owe you, I will do what I can to make your plight easier to bear."

JonMarc raised a suspicious eye. "How?"

"I will make sure you neither see nor speak with the lady Cariwyn again. As soon as this unpleasantness with the Branwyns is ended, I shall accompany her back to Hlanneth, and thence across the sea to Glen Tierna, where some lord of the Tiernai shall be found to wed her."

JonMarc's brow darkened. "You call that a favor?"

"I do, though it may not seem so now." Edmund's tone grew fatherly. "Come, JonMarc, one so worldly as yourself will love again soon enough. Perhaps one day, when men like the Connails and their cat's-paw, Earl

Hannon, are dead and their bigotries forgotten, a Dynian youth may aspire to wed into the ranks of Tiernai nobility. Sadly, that day may be years in coming."

"It will have to come sooner than that, my lord," JonMarc rejoined bitterly. "I cannot wait *years.*" He stood to go.

"Stay, JonMarc. Though your problem may be settled, to your liking or no, we have not yet touched upon the reason I called you here."

"I thought you just wanted an account of Cari's rescue," JonMarc grumbled, eager to escape and lick his wounds.

"In part. Yet there is a more pressing matter. In a few hours, we of the Council, and Legion Commander Donal, will meet to discuss the Branwyn crisis. I need information."

JonMarc's gelid eyes narrowed. "I spent only a few moments with the Branwyns. What can I tell that you don't already know?"

"News of Táranos, the attainted Earl of Anlawth. Before his capture, the prince charged me to investigate that matter. Kier mentioned that Anlawth is Fithlon trained. You know as much of this as he, do you not?"

"I suppose, though that's little enough. But why? Do you think Táranos was involved in the Branwyn attack?"

"I'd hoped you could tell me that. In all my years in Council, the name of Anlawth seldom arose—until a few months ago, when the Connails moved to restore him to favor. We of my late brother's party thought they only wished to add another voice to their bid for war, and so denied the suit." Edmund leaned forward, elbows on his knees. "But now it seems his influence runs deeper. That the Connails are in his sway is clear, though the notion of a Covenant Penitarch allying with a Fithlon is difficult to fathom. Still, their behavior has made their commitment to him obvious. They, in turn, dominate Malcolm Morwensen and Norris Hannon." Edmund stroked his chin. "What I cannot discern is Anlawth's purpose. Does he mean to bribe or threaten his way into favor? If so, he's in for a surprise. The High Council of Alcor is not so easily manipulated."

JonMarc frowned, wondering how much Kier meant to tell his uncle. Undoubtedly less than the duke deserved to know. Kier did not share secrets readily, even with those he trusted. Yet, what damage could it do now? Their plans lay in ruins. It could hardly hurt to have an ally on the Council. "It's more than that. According to Master Gwythion, who confronted him to learn his mind, it's not favor Táranos seeks, but power."

"You mean political power."

JonMarc shook his head. "The power to control minds; to force men to his will. Táranos seeks revenge against the races that named him outcast. To achieve it, he is willing to call upon a power strong enough to destroy all the Deg Tirith."

Edmund scoffed. "The attainted earl deceives himself. The Fithlon do not claim to possess such power. It does not exist." He frowned, suddenly uncertain. "Does it?"

"Master Gwythion believes it does." JonMarc swiftly recounted what he knew of the Cábretaur. When he'd finished, Edmund looked more dubious than ever.

"I know not what to believe. Gwythion is a learned scholar—though mysterious enough, as are all of his order. He won my late brother's friendship, much to the chagrin of Penitarch Tor, and for a while was tolerated at court. My nephew remains devoted to him, and Kier is as level-headed a man as I have ever known. Does *he* believe in this Cábretaur you speak of?"

"When first told of it, I think he was as skeptical as you, my lord. He may still be. Yet all we've been through has shown that Táranos, at least, believes the Cábretaur exists, and he is putting forth every effort to find it. His henchman, Roderig, followed us from Vilsolia to keep Kier from reaching the Cábretaur's resting place at Cymworth. We'd have left for there yestereve, had the Branwyns not attacked. Till now, I hadn't considered that Táranos might be involved."

"Indeed," muttered the duke, sounding even more troubled. "There is news you have not heard. On their way here, the relief troops from the capital discovered the body of a royal messenger. He had been murdered the night before, though no motive could be determined. They ascribed the deed to some roving Dynian brigand, for villagers reported seeing such a one in the vicinity." Edmund stood and began to pace. "I think I can put a name to that elusive Dynian: *Roderig*. And his motive: to prevent us from receiving word that Ross Branwyn's sister had been taken by the Connails. It seems Lord Táranos may have *wanted* the prince captured." Edmund pounded a fist on his palm. "But why? Simply to delay Kier's journey to Cymworth? The scheme seems too elaborate. Besides, how could he know Kier would choose to accompany the prince?"

JonMarc pressed a knuckle to his lip. This news added yet another dimension to the problem. "My lord, knowing Kier, do you honestly think he'd have left for Cymworth while the prince was in Branwyn hands?

Rhynion's capture might have fulfilled Táranos' purpose of itself. Nothing would please him more than to see Alcor ripped apart by war. What if he instigated the Branwyn girl's capture in order to provoke it?"

"If that's true," said Edmund, "then—what of the Connails? Only this noon we received word from Ruthland that they agree to the hostage exchange and will meet us at the appointed hour. Surely—*surely* it is within their own interests to see the prince freed." Doubt clouded Edmund's face. "What are we to do? The safety of the entire realm depends on the Connails' loyalty."

"Then I'd say the realm is in a lot of trouble." JonMarc's mind suddenly closed around a plan—one that, if successful, would place Edmund and the Council so irrevocably in his debt they'd have no choice but to grant him Cari. "My lord, I'm trained in Fithlon mind-touch." An exaggeration, but worth the risk. "Maybe I could use my skills to learn what the Connails intend."

"You mean, read their minds?" Edmund looked mildly scandalized. "Such information would certainly be of great value, but... Could you accomplish such a feat from here?"

JonMarc shook his head. "Too far. I'd have to get closer to their castle."

Edmund touched steepled fingers to his lip, clearly intrigued. "Then you would have to depart soon. We meet the Branwyns in but two days. And such a mission would require the approval of Sir Donal and the Council—at least, Ruark and Lochlainn. Yet, do you truly know what you propose, JonMarc? For one of Dynian race to venture near Ruthland would be extremely dangerous. Couldn't you remain here and read Earl Hannon's mind? He is their ally."

JonMarc rubbed his brow. Doing that would win him nothing—if he even had the skill to accomplish it. "I doubt Táranos or the Connails make Hannon intimate to their plans. I mean, if you plotted treason, would *you* trust him?"

"Treason," Edmund muttered. "I only pray it has not come to that."

The interview with Sir Donal proved difficult. JonMarc was amazed how much the Legion commander already knew about him—more than he could possibly have learned from Kier. The crafty officer must have spies all over the Deg Tirith. Even so, he grilled JonMarc for more than an hour about his life in Castémaron and his dealings with the Fithlon. By the time the session ended, JonMarc's brain felt like a haversack that had been hauled inside out and shaken clean.

Sir Donal leaned back in his sturdy chair and frowned into gnarled fists. "I see no harm in having someone practiced in the Fithlon arts spy out Ruthland for us."

A wonder he didn't add *expendable*. JonMarc found the gruff officer intimidating, and somewhat less than candid, yet he had to concede him grudging respect. In many ways, Sir Donal reminded him of Kier—an older, more self-assured Kier: stern, resolute, and bound by an unwavering sense of duty. A worn leather patch covered the officer's left eye, but the other seemed to conceal a universe of subtlety. And, as JonMarc had quickly learned, the Legion commander could cut through deception like a seasoned plotter.

Antony Ruark remained the least enthusiastic. "I know not how near Ruthland Castle the lad must go before his accursed Fithlon powers'll work, but wi' each step, his danger grows. What if he be taken? How do we explain it?"

"We don't," said Sir Donal. "The Connails will assume he was sent by the Branwyns. We must let them think that."

"You see, JonMarc," said Edmund, the first to address him directly since the interrogation ended, "whatever they may be planning, the Connails have as yet committed no crime. We dare not let them think we suspect their loyalty. Once you cross into Ruthland, you'll be on your own."

JonMarc understood. He hadn't expected the Council's help. The game of cover-your-arse was universal. "And if I return with the information you need?"

The three lords eyed one another skeptically. Ruark leaned over to whisper in Edmund's ear. The duke nodded. "We shall discuss your reward at a later date. Yet be assured, if your information proves reliable, you will not find us ungenerous."

It was the best he could hope for. JonMarc guessed what Ruark had whispered. They never expected him to return. But he would—and collect his reward.

Sir Donal was the last to speak to him before he set out. The Legion commander came alone to the stable where JonMarc stood, busily packing provisions into a well-worn saddlebag. "I didn't want you to go—unthanked," the gruff officer said. "'Tis a brave thing you offer, lad."

JonMarc shrugged and continued packing.

Sir Donal leaned against a stall post. "One thing puzzles me. Why are you so keen to risk your life? You cannot have developed such loyalty to Alcor and her prince so soon."

"I risk my life only when it profits me."

"You'd like to believe that of yourself. Tell me, then, how will this profit you?"

JonMarc fastened down the saddlebag and went to tug on the girth one last time. "The lords of the Council will be pleased to show their gratitude, once the prince is freed."

"You think so, eh? You don't know them as I do. But I don't think it's profit that sends you on so perilous a mission. I think you go out of fear— fear for your friend Fitzmorwen. And perhaps—fear of losing the love of someone even more dear?" Sir Donal eyed him shrewdly.

JonMarc avoided his gaze and began to saddle his spare mount. "What does it matter why I go, so long as you get your precious prince back?"

Sir Donal calmly stroked the horse's muzzle. "Why didn't you tell them the truth in there?"

"About what?"

"Let us be frank with one another, JonMarc. I know something of Fithlon ways. Though you're spell-handed and probably possess some measure of sinistral talent, you've no ability to read minds—not from any distance, at any rate. To do that would require the skills of at least a Second Tier adept. You've no such training. Did you fear the lords would not send you to Ruthland if they knew you actually meant to enter the castle? And you *do* mean to enter; you can acquire the information no other way. Such a mission is suicide, and may prove fatal to the Council as well, should you be captured and interrogated."

JonMarc scowled. What in blazes did the man want? "I'll manage."

"Not without my help. I carry in my head the plans of every fortress in Alcor. I can tell you the layout of Ruthland Castle; how to get in—and out."

JonMarc eyed the officer warily. "Why should you do that if you don't trust me?"

"It's not a matter of trust. I need that intelligence and I'm willing to take any risk to get it. You have abilities more valuable to me than Fithlon mind powers."

JonMarc guessed what Sir Donal meant: his skills as a thief and cracksman.

The Legion commander found a dry section of floor and smoothed it with his boot. "Bring the light," he ordered. He lowered himself with difficulty onto the cold ground and drew his dagger. "Now look, and remember. Some seven leagues southwest of here, the river Bron cuts diagonally across your path. That is the border of Ruthland. The road crosses it here, at Ceorl's Ford, half a league north of the castle. Do not go that way; it is too closely watched."

JonMarc knelt beside him. "Then how do I approach?"

"Travel overland till you reach the Southerwood, then skirt it to the west. Within three hours' ride, you'll reach the heathlands directly across the river from Ruthland Castle. Can you swim?" JonMarc nodded. "Good, for you must cross the river beneath the very walls of the castle. Ruthland is a new fortress, built only thirty years ago, as a defense against the Branwyns. It faces westward, toward the Berwyn forest. By approaching from the east, you're less likely to be detected. The land is rugged on that side, with many crannies in which to lie hidden. Wait out the daylight and make your crossing under cover of darkness."

JonMarc rubbed his neck. That would allow him to snatch some rest. By then he'd need it.

"The castle has two posterns, one to the south, beneath the chapel, another here to the north. Both are barred from within, so you cannot use them to enter, but they may provide a means of escape. The northern exit is hidden behind a tapestry in Earl Aran's bedchamber in the keep. Few know of it. Now tell me, how do you plan to enter the castle?"

JonMarc shrugged. "There are only three ways into any structure: over it, under it, or through the walls. I thought to use a grapple, and climb—or perhaps, take down a guard and pass through the gates disguised."

"Neither will work. Ruthland's walls are higher than most, and project outward. It would take many noisy tries before your grapple found a footing, and you would spend most of your climb dangling in mid-air. As for the other plan, the Connails are not a trusting lot. No man unvouched-for enters their inner ward. Though you might hope to conceal your Dynian hair beneath a helmet, how, pray, did you intend to hide your eyes?"

"No, there is another way, though not so pleasant." Sir Donal drew in the dirt with his knife. "As it reaches the castle, part of the river has been diverted through a sewage culvert that flows beneath the castle walls. Because the entrance is easy to spot, it is flanked by two guard towers. Yet at this time of year, the river runs high. The input will be totally submerged."

"Is it barred?"

"Of course. The Connails aren't fools. But after years at water's edge, iron rusts and stone housings deteriorate. You may be able to pry one of the bars loose enough to pass through. Once inside, you must feel your way. There are two accesses to the castle: one through the stable floor, the other beneath the kitchen. Neither is concealed, but they may be difficult to locate."

JonMarc wondered how the Legion commander had acquired such detailed information.

"From there, you're on your own. I don't know how you mean to accomplish this impossible task you've set for yourself—nor, I think, do you. It's not always wise to plan too far in advance. Yet there is a chance you may find an ally at Ruthland."

JonMarc looked up.

"Though the Council does not know it, I have long suspected the Connails and their dealings with the traitor-spawn of Anlawth. For years, I've maintained a spy within Ruthland castle. From him I learned much—until four months ago, when he suddenly went silent."

Sir Donal pursed his bearded lips. "At first I thought he had nothing to report, or could find no way of doing so discreetly. Passing intelligence from a stronghold like Ruthland requires patience and cunning. Yet after two months' silence, I dispatched another man, one of my best, disguised as a tradesman. He communicated only once, briefly, to say he was on to something important and would send word when he could." Sir Donal struggled to his feet. "That was a month ago, and still I've heard nothing."

JonMarc stood with a scowl. Sir Donal didn't paint a hopeful picture. Still, he was committed now. And the stakes were high. "Are you asking me to find him for you?"

"No. Your task will be difficult enough. I only tell you so that if you should encounter or hear word of him, you will know him for an ally. He passes as Aedan, the smith."

"And how will he know me?"

"We have a code. Ask if he has heard the black owl cry beneath the tower window. If you have the right man, he will understand."

"And if not, he'll think me a right fool." JonMarc swung into the saddle and started for the gate, leading the spare mount. He was eager to make full use of the darkness while it lasted. An alert sentry hastened to open the portcullis for him.

"JonMarc!" The gruff call from behind made him turn.

Sir Donal looked a forlorn figure, silhouetted against the flutter of torchlight. "Devoreth go with you, lad," he rumbled. "I think it unlikely we will meet again."

PART III: THE PROPHECY OF ANERYN

Chapter Twenty-five

The longer JonMarc stared at the stark gray keep of Ruthland castle, the worse his chances appeared. This was no gleaming showcase like Caerllyn, but a fortress, cold and austere. It dominated the landscape, its every grim detail reflecting the pride and arrogance of its Connail owner.

Yet it wasn't the stout walls and mighty towers that dampened his spirits. After all, what was a castle? Just a fortified dwelling. He'd been stealing his way in and out of those since he was a ragged urchin on Castémaron's squalid streets. No, something odd was going on at Ruthland. Yestereve, Duke Edmund told him the prisoner exchange would be a touchy affair at which no troops were allowed. Yet, from where he lay hidden on a scrubby slope east of the castle, JonMarc could see the road to the gates crawling with soldiers, packed tighter than maggots on a corpse, and more were arriving every hour. All afternoon he'd watched them straggle up from the south, small bands on horseback and larger companies on foot, most bearing the Connails' silver falcon. Their tents spread beyond the outwalls and onto the western plain. Why were the Connails mobilizing? One thing was certain—the sheer number of troops severely lessened his chances for success.

For a moment, JonMarc was tempted to concede the futility of his task and return to Caerllyn. None would blame him. But to give up his best chance to earn some status in this new land—maybe even win Cari? JonMarc set his jaw. He couldn't back out now. Curiosity spurred him as much as self interest. He had to learn what the Connails were up to. How much easier if he could simply remain where he lay, staring down at the castle's shadow-splashed walls, and read the minds of those within. But Sir Donal was right; he hadn't the skill for that. Bravado had gotten him into some tight spots before, but few so potentially disastrous as this.

Level shafts of orblight blazed crimson across the grassy slope. JonMarc prayed the guards on the walls couldn't see him, hidden beneath a tangle of gorse and maidenthorn. His belly rumbled. He'd eaten nothing since noon, on the road. Yet he'd left his provisions with the horses, now tethered in a hollow beyond the hillcrest. This task would go easier on an empty stomach.

At last, Devoreth's Orb sank behind the dark smudge of forest. A few early stars pricked the lazulite sky. Cautiously, JonMarc crept from hiding and started down the slope. As he neared the river's edge, a flock of yellowbills took to the air, flapping and squawking. JonMarc dropped. The sentries on the walls paid no heed. He swiftly crawled down to the bank.

The river had a musty smell, as if it carried down from the forest an entire winter's worth of debris. Though an easy stone's throw across, its smooth flow told JonMarc it ran deep—and cold. The far bank rose steeply against the castle wall. In only one spot did the dark waters wash directly against the stone. Above, just as Sir Donal described, loomed two square towers, their wooden hoardings extending a short way over the river. The culvert entrance must lie between them, hidden beneath the water. JonMarc made sure the few essentials he'd "borrowed" from the armory at Caerllyn were strapped securely to his waist. Then he sat behind the reeds on the soggy bank and pulled off his boots; their bulk would only hinder him. He tucked their tops over his belt to free his hands and slid into the icy stream.

He emerged beside the fortress wall, gasping from the cold. Waves gently lapped the stone. He found the culvert entrance a short way below the surface and measured the opening with hands and feet—easily big enough for a man to pass through, were it not for the bars. He counted six, spaced about a hand-span apart. They felt smooth, hardly corroded at all. JonMarc dove down to examine their housings. Firm enough. This must be a new grate, installed within the last few months, while the river was low. So much for trusting to luck.

JonMarc slid from his belt an iron pry bar and carefully began to chip away at the mortar. What he found was even more discouraging. The bars had not been placed individually. They were welded to a thick crosspiece on top, probably on the bottom too, and cemented into the wall's core. He could chip all night and not break the thing free. But that was out of the question. His body wouldn't take the cold much longer. He'd have to bend the bars apart. If he could make a space wide enough for his head, he knew he could squeeze the rest of his body through. That sounded simple.

JonMarc knew better. Working underwater, in total darkness, while trying to make no noise, the task was a challenge at best.

JonMarc braced his bare feet on the algae-slimed stones and tugged at the pry bar with all his strength. He felt it move. Yes, it was giving. Just a bit more... His right foot lost its grip and he capsized with a splash. The pry bar slipped from his hands. It gave a muted clang as it hit the grate, then sank like a rock to the river's bottom.

"What was that?" A sentry with a torch stepped onto the hoarding above and peered through the hole in its floor. JonMarc sank from sight. He emerged a few seconds later, out of range of the light, and prayed the speaker could not hear his chattering teeth.

"—only a mud-flapper," came a second voice. "Or a rat. There's enough of 'em down there."

The second grunted agreement and withdrew the light. JonMarc waited until their footsteps faded, then swam back to appraise his handiwork.

He'd widened the gap between the bars by only a few finger-widths, yet he could do no more without the pry bar. It might take hours to find that. He ducked down and measured the opening against the size of his head—a tight fit, but with time and patience he felt sure he could work his way through. Unfortunately, underwater he'd have neither. He felt the bars again. They'd been greased to keep them from rusting. That would help.

JonMarc stripped off his clothes and bound them into a tight bundle, then swam down for a last reconnaissance. The floor of the culvert felt even with the bottom of the opening, but the ceiling inside must be higher. How high, he couldn't tell, but Sir Donal hinted a man could stand upright in there. The presence of rats meant there was air. He pushed the bundle of clothes through the bars and strapped it with his belt, then came up for a breath he knew might be his last. Silently he slipped beneath the water.

He'd all but forgotten the cold; his body had ceased to feel it. Here below the surface lay another world, an aqueous void of darkness and muffled sound. JonMarc shut his eyes for concentration and thrust his right arm through the grate, feeling the rigid bars slide along the smooth muscles of his shoulder. He turned his head. Solid iron clamped his face; scraped past his ears. Through. JonMarc expelled half the air from his lungs and hollowed his chest. Steady... left shoulder. Blast, it was too tight! No, the first went through; this one wasn't that much more developed. Just— ease it around... There. JonMarc's lungs ached. Only his buttocks now, and his muscled thighs. He scooted up to where the space between the bars was wider.

An image flashed across his mind—as if he read the report himself: "...
*were found... remains... naked male... trapped between the bars of the sewage
culvert.*" Not an epitaph he fancied. With all his remaining strength, he gave
a final squeeze. He was through! But could he reach the surface in time?

It was only a foot above. JonMarc broke the waves, gasping and
coughing. He'd made it. The absurdity of that found its way into his brain
just as the stench found his olfactory nerve: he'd risked his life to enter a
damned sewer. He looked about. No light but a faint luminescence at the
culvert's far end. JonMarc straightened and found he could indeed stand
upright. The water reached just above his waist. Now all he had to do was
locate one of the trapdoors that led into the castle. He shoved the parcel of
clothes under his arm and began inching his way along, one hand blindly
groping the low ceiling.

Rats were everywhere, scurrying along the ledge, swimming beside
him. And—something else. Fish, he hoped. Now and again, a slimy form
would brush the gooseflesh of his thighs. The rats didn't trouble him; he'd
lived with their Vilsolian kin most of his life. Their squeals echoed from
the dripping walls, sometimes accompanied by a shallow trickle from
what JonMarc supposed must be privy shafts. He blinked, and swiped at a
cobweb that strung across his face.

The sludge at the bottom of the culvert deepened to his knees.
JonMarc's left hand made out an indented rectangle above—the trapdoor
to the stables. He gave a tentative push.

Rusted hinges protested as the hatch creaked open. JonMarc pulled
himself up. Cold air touched his nostrils. Even laden with stable scent,
it felt invigorating after the stench of the sewer. He peered into a dark,
cavernous room. At the far end, a flicker of torchlight marked the
entrance to the inner ward. It was enough for JonMarc to make out his
surroundings. The trapdoor lay at the end of a long row of stalls. Tack and
tools hung along the walls. But for the horses, the place looked deserted.
JonMarc tossed his bundle onto the wood floor. Shivering uncontrollably,
he scrambled out of the hole and quietly shut the hatch.

He heard voices outside—the low murmur and occasional laughter
of soldiers at evening mess. JonMarc tried to recall Sir Donal's rude map.
The common hall must lie two or three doors down. He was safe for the
moment, if he didn't freeze to death. He'd have given a year's pocket-
pickings for a blanket. He wrung out his clothes and was about to crawl

into them when a loud hail from outside sent him diving for the nearest stall. He crouched into a corner beside a skittish mare who whinnied in protest. JonMarc prayed the newcomers would continue on their way.

They didn't.

"Ho, Jeraint," called a genial voice. "Where're you off to? Come join me for a pint."

"Can't," said another. JonMarc heard the crunch of determined footfalls drawing nearer. "I have to meet with the outland captains. I'm to command them tomorrow."

"Aye, I heard. Quite a plume in your cap, eh? Must come of capturing that Branwyn wench." A disgruntled chuckle. "Some folk have all the luck."

"Talent, friend," said the one called Jeraint. He spoke with a self-assurance that bordered on arrogance. "Just a matter of knowing Lord Aric's mind and finding a way to get him what he wants, then letting him take the credit. He'll not forget who it was led him to her." The sound of a friendly clap on the back. "Come talk to me, Con, while I saddle up." The stable brightened with the light of a second torch. "Here, hold this."

"Why bother to ride?" Con asked. "The outland troops are just outside the gates."

Jeraint hoisted tack from a wall peg. "What respect would I earn from those bumpkins if I just walked out there like some common foot-wabbler? Nay, it's the subtleties make all the difference. You'd best learn that if you want to make more than centuriant."

"I suppose," said Con. "I just wish I could come with you tomorrow. D'you know what this is all about?"

"Only that the Branwyns have captured his Highness the prince—plague take their heathen hides—and we're to rescue him. Come, follow me with that torch."

JonMarc cowered to the back of the stall as the footsteps drew nearer. They seemed headed straight for him! He freed his dagger from the bundle and readied himself to spring. They wouldn't take him without a fight. The mare beside him grew more restive. JonMarc could barely keep her from trampling his toes. As the torch drew almost even with his hiding place, it halted. The door to the next stall creaked open.

"Here you go, Nemesis lad," said Jeraint. "Ready for some exercise?" JonMarc's mare whinnied and nervously stamped the floor. "Whoa, now, Tansy my girl, what's wrong? You want to go too, eh?" Jeraint reached across the dividing wall and stroked the beast's muzzle. His arm stretched right over JonMarc's head. "Don't worry, you'll get your chance tomorrow." He led his horse into the aisle.

JonMarc dropped back against the wall, panting. That was too close.

"D'you expect to see action?" Con sounded envious.

"I hope we do. Our men are up for it. I'm not so sure about the rest. The West Ruthlanders are all right, so long as they don't have to think overmuch. But the troop that arrived from Evorick this noon with their duke and Penitarch Tor—blazes, I wouldn't trust 'em to find their arses in the dark. Their captain's no better—a strutting little banty-cock who keeps all his brains in his breeches. He'd better know how to take orders, Con, or there'll be trouble."

"Is he the one called Halistan?" JonMarc's ears perked up at the name.

"Aye, you know him?"

"Only what I've heard. He'll be riding none too comfortably tomorrow. Seems he tangled with the Branwyn wench—bribed a guard to let him have a go at her. But she'd have none of it. Got him where it counts, she did. He's been walking tender ever since."

Jeraint guffawed. "Serves him right, bloody fool. She's a sinistral witch. Everybody knows it—though she's a looker, no mistake. And feisty. You should've seen when we captured her, Con—all claws and teeth. And she shoots like a warrior. Took down three of my best men before we got her from behind. Hand me that saddle blanket."

"So, where have you been all evening? I looked for you at mess."

"Closeted with the earl and his guests in the great hall. I'm to report back, once I meet with the outlanders. This might be the break I've waited for, Con. A chance to prove myself."

"Well, I'm glad for you." Con sounded skeptical. "But be careful when you report back. They hold private council in the great hall tonight. My sentries are ordered to stay clear of the keep till they're summoned. Don't go blundering in there unless you're sure the meeting's finished. It's not something you want to get involved in."

Jeraint chuckled. "Con, you worry too much. I've met them. There's naught to fear..." His voice dropped. "Except that Dynian—the scarred one. Gods, he makes my skin crawl. Those white eyes cut through you like brands. But he won't be there; he rode out an hour since."

"Aye, I know the one you mean. No one wants aught to do with him." Con lowered his voice so that JonMarc had to strain to hear him. "But he's not Dynian. Believe it or not, he's as Tiernai as you or I. They say he's *demon-spawn*—born without color. Outcast. I don't know what the earl sees in him, but he's a trusted confidant. I wouldn't be heard speaking ill of him."

Roderig—*Tiernai*? The revelation floored JonMarc. Táranos evidently used him to keep an eye in both camps; more than an eye, judging from Roderig's inflammatory speech at the *Jackal and Hounds*. It explained a lot.

The conversation faded as Jeraint and Con led the saddled horse into the courtyard. JonMarc seized the opportunity to struggle into his wet clothes, then stealthily crept down the corridor. By the time he peered into the torch-dotted night, the two had disappeared.

He shivered in the chill air. He had to find his way into the great hall. From what Con said, the Connails' council might last well into the night. And guards were barred from the keep. A stroke of luck, that. He'd wondered how he might get close enough to overhear what the Connails plotted. Now Earl Aran's own order neatly solved that. For the first time since his arrival, JonMarc began to feel optimistic. But first he had to find a cloak, and something to cover his hair. He'd not get far looking like this.

There were few soldiers in the courtyard. Most went about their duties, unlike the outland troops whose revelrous voices echoed from beyond the gates. Keeping low, JonMarc skirted the torchlight and silently crept along the shadowed wall. The next building would be the forge; a good place to start. With luck, he might encounter Sir Donal's spy, the missing *Aedan, the smith.*

It turned out to be a low, fieldstone structure with a wide doorway and a single, shuttered window. JonMarc peeked in through a crack. No one inside—just the glow from a banked fire in the central hearth. The promise of warmth beckoned him. Noiselessly he slipped inside.

The place looked well ordered. There was no sign of the smith. On a shelf near the back, JonMarc spotted a row of helmets awaiting repair. He chose one that looked newly patched. It had no liner, but he needed disguise, not protection. A further search showed him a woolen cloak hung on a peg behind the door. It was shabby, with conspicuous burn holes, but at least it was warm. He found no weapons but a broken spear. His hunting knife would have to serve. Skirting the firelight, JonMarc again slunk outside.

The keep of Ruthland castle was a fortress of itself. It dominated the north end of the compound, its five stark towers thrusting crenelated heads a third again as high as the surrounding curtain wall. In front, two lesser drum towers flanked the gates. JonMarc watched from a distance as a half-dozen guards, temporarily banished from the keep, clustered outside, muttering. Occasionally one would raise a wary eye to the lighted window slits above.

Cautiously, JonMarc followed the base of the outer wall to the pair of towers he'd seen from across the river. One of them must house a stair to the wall-walk above. All afternoon he'd watched sentries appear and disappear at this point. The door to the right-hand tower stood ajar. JonMarc sidled over to it and ducked inside.

Utter blackness. He groped his way up the winding stair, his gut taut as a bowstring. He reached the top and glanced out. Denia's white moon floated high in the star-pricked canopy. Low voices murmured somewhere to his right, but he couldn't make out words. He crouched below the level of the inner parapet and cautiously peered around the corner.

Four sentries took their ease against the wall—or so it first appeared. Looking closer, JonMarc realized they were watching something. One pointed. The horses? What if they'd broken free and wandered within view? But no, the sentries' eyes were trained skyward, not at the ground. One of them fearfully circled thumb and forefinger in the protective sign of Devoreth's Eye. What could they be looking at? JonMarc crept out to search the eastern sky.

Footsteps approached from the left and he ducked back, praying he hadn't been spotted. The swish of a cloak, a blurred shadow, and the sentry hastened past to join his comrades on the wall. They welcomed him with muted excitement. JonMarc strained to hear. He made out only a few, tense syllables, but they were enough to confirm his suspicions.

"*Torch star. Omen. Peril.*"

The *Death Seer* had appeared.

Chapter Twenty-six

The *Death Seer's* arrival heightened JonMarc's urgency. Conjunction with the Life Star, and the Cábretaur's re-discovery, could only be days away, and he and Kier were further than ever from reaching Cymworth and the ominous power crystal.

The guards at the wall began to disperse. Hunched nearly double, JonMarc scurried along the narrow walkway to the keep's rear towers. He saw no sentries; they must be among those still at the wall. JonMarc entered a short, arched tunnel where the wall-walk passed through the first tower. To his left, another staircase twisted like a segmented worm, up to what must be a guard chamber. He followed it downward.

An ensconced torch threw flickering polygons of light across the circular walls, but beyond the second spiral, the glow disappeared. Surely this must be the rear entrance to the keep. JonMarc halted on the landing and tried a wooden door. Locked. He knelt to examine the mechanism, then reached into the pouch of oddments he always carried and selected one of several re-worked nails. After a moment's careful manipulation, he eased the bolt open and gave the door a gentle tug.

Voices carried up from below. JonMarc peered inside, but could discern only a dim fire-flicker against the far wall. Very carefully, he braced the door up with his fingers to ease pressure on the hinges. Inch by cautious inch, he opened it enough to maneuver himself inside.

He found himself on a narrow balcony that encircled the great hall on three sides. Tapestries hanging from the stout railing concealed him from below. He crawled past a staircase that led down to the hall and crept on stealthily a few more yards. Peeking around the edge of a dusty hanging, he viewed a long table before a hearth in the keep's northern wall. The evening meal had been cleared; little remained but a pewter flagon and a few bowls of sweetmeats scattered amongst the crumbs. At the table's far end stood a bronze candelabrum bearing three stout candles. Their tallow light fluttered across the faces of the four men seated there.

Three JonMarc recognized instantly. Aric Connail faced the fire. The stark shadows that played across the young lord's face made his broken nose seem some hideous deformity. Across from him sat Kier's brother, the new Duke Malcolm, with the black-robed penitarch, Tor Connail, perched at his side like one of the Death Hag's harbinger crows. The man at the table's head was a stranger—older than the rest, and sharp featured, with graying hair to his shoulders. Black slits of eyes mirrored the firelight. He must be Aric's father, the earl Aran Connail, master of Ruthland. Even from a distance, the resemblance between father and son was striking.

There remained one vacant chair, undoubtedly where Roderig had been seated. Its very emptiness gave the illusion of some unseen presence watching over the proceedings. JonMarc thought of Táranos. The impression might not be far from wrong.

Below, Earl Aran stood, wine cup in hand, and cleared his throat. "My friends," he said, "we know what is required of us tomorrow. Before we retire, I offer a toast."

Retire? JonMarc's jaw fell. They couldn't retire! Not after all he'd gone through to get here.

"I drink to our success," said Earl Aran. "To the final annihilation of the Branwyns, and to the one soon to be our king—may his reign be memorable."

All rose except Malcolm. Why, JonMarc wondered, would the young duke remain seated in a toast to Rhynion? Did he hold some grudge against the prince?

The others drained their cups and sat again.

"The day we have awaited at last approaches. Tomorrow, ere dawn, our armies will depart. My son Aric will hold the castle until our triumphant return."

Malcolm cocked his head, frowning. "But this I do not understand. How can we keep so large a force hidden from the Branwyns until the time to attack?"

"We need not keep it hidden." Earl Aran folded his gloved hands on the table, looking slyly satisfied with himself. "The Branwyns believe Roderig is their spy within Ruthland. Even now, he supplies them false report of our numbers. By the time Ross Branwyn learns his mistake, it will be too late. We'll have the bastard by his heathen cods."

"But Duke Edmund's message warned against bringing troops. Once

Ross Branwyn learns the truth, he may be so enraged he will refuse to bring forth the prince."

Earl Aran chuckled. "He will certainly be enraged; I am counting on that. But he'll not withhold the prince. Ross may bluff and bluster, but above all he wants his sister returned. That will never happen if he withholds Rhynion. In the end, he will bring the lad forth as a gesture of good faith. That will be all we need."

His brother, the Covenant Penitarch, thoughtfully stroked his pointed beard. "In truth, it seems a pity to relinquish the girl. She could be a powerful weapon in our hands."

"Relinquish her?" Earl Aran laughed. "Rest assured, brother, I've no intention of giving her up. As long as Llydia Branwyn is our prisoner, her brother Ross is in my power. His affection for her is his weakness. He'll do nothing that might jeopardize her safety."

"But if we keep her, our intentions will appear dishonorable from the outset," said Penitarch Tor. "An army one may explain as simple precaution. But this? 'Twould serve us better if the Branwyns appeared the first to break faith."

"And so they shall. We will bear with us a litter, curtained and guarded, and even our own men will believe it conceals the she-witch of Branwyn. Yet inside will be a wench of my own household, veiled and disguised in the Branwyn girl's clothes. When the prince is publicly betrayed and the battle joined, we will bear her to safety. All the while, Llydia Branwyn will remain here, secured in the tower."

The Penitarch appeared uncertain. "I fear you underestimate Ross Branwyn. He will capture the litter and discover your deception."

"What matter? The wench is expendable. And when the Branwyn discovers she is not his sister and he has been doubly deceived—why, brother, that will be sweet revenge for us."

"But, if he should take her before the Council..?"

"It will be too late. Ross Branwyn will be hard pressed just to save himself. Even if he should make his accusation known, who among the Tiernai will believe him? They'll take him prisoner, or cut him down where he stands. In any case, nothing can be proved against us. You forget, brother: by then we shall have an ally on the throne." His eyes turned to Malcolm.

A queasy knot tightened in JonMarc's belly.

Malcolm seemed ill at ease with the attention. His be-ringed fingers fidgeted with the contents of a shallow nut bowl. The incessant rattling plainly infuriated Aric. "My brother Fitzmorwen is Prince Rhynion's protector. If you mean to kill him, I want no part of it."

Across the table, Aric's narrowed eyes betrayed utter contempt for the young duke. His father addressed the issue. "Fitzmorwen's death is inevitable. Tor has already planted seeds of doubt in the councilors' minds. After the battle, all will believe your brother turned his coat and sided with his Branwyn countrymen. The Council will declare him traitor and demand his execution." Earl Aran gave a careless shrug. "Like as not, he won't even survive the battle."

Aric stirred at that. "I would not have it so. I do not wish Fitzmorwen slain out of hand."

His father turned to him, startled. "*You* say this, my son? After what Fitzmorwen did to you?"

Loathing kindled Aric's brown eyes. "Bring him to me, Father. I know what to do with Fitzmorwen. And I promise you, Malcolm, your brother will not die against his will. When his hour comes, he'll have begged for it, long and piteously. Death will take Fitzmorwen by inches, I swear it."

Malcolm shuddered, but returned a grudging nod. "So long as I am not blamed. I'll not bear the curse of a brother's murder."

JonMarc let slip a muffled oath, and instantly regretted it. Below, the larger of two mastiffs that lay dozing at Aran Connail's feet pricked up its ears and sniffed. It emitted a predatory growl. JonMarc froze. The beast's scarlet eyes fixed on his position. These were the biggest hounds he'd ever seen. For an awful moment JonMarc waited for the creature to lunge, knowing that if it mounted the stair, it would cut him off before he could reach the door.

Earl Aran kicked the hound in the ribs. It settled, but trained watchful eyes on the balcony.

"What's wrong, Malcolm?" Penitarch Tor laid a talon-like hand on the young duke's shoulder. "Do you now have second thoughts about your commitment to our cause? You were eager enough when we spoke of this at Cordon."

Tor's eyes evidently held some kind of warning, for Malcolm shifted and looked away. "I do have—misgivings. The *torch star* seen tonight: I fear it forebodes our defeat."

"Nonsense!" snapped Earl Aran. "If the star bodes ill, it is for our Branwyn foes, and their defeat is our victory. Lay aside fear, Malcolm.

Tomorrow night, you will rule Alcor."

"Aye," Malcolm muttered, "but with Rhynion's blood on my hands."

"*Your* hands? Nay, that deed belongs to another—one who has no qualms about killing. Whatever the outcome, you, Malcolm, will remain blameless."

Malcolm toyed with a walnut between thumb and forefinger, bouncing it on the table again and again until JonMarc thought Aric might strike him. "Is there no other way? There was no talk of killing when we first made our plans."

Earl Aran's face darkened. "How then did you expect to gain the throne? Did you expect Rhynion to simply relinquish it for the asking? If so, you're a greater fool than..."

Penitarch Tor clamped a cautioning hand on his elder brother's arm. "Malcolm," he said, his tone fatherly, "great ends cannot be achieved without sacrifice. We have committed to serve one who shall soon be Master of our world. To those who are loyal, he offers great rewards." Tor's voice turned ominous. "But greater still will be the punishment for those who break faith. I warn you, he will not tolerate this wavering."

"I do not waver!" Malcolm nervously dabbed a napkin to his brow. "I simply don't understand. *Why* must the prince be murdered? Rhynion is sickly and might die at any time. Could we not postpone this until...?"

"*No!*" said Earl Aran. "Rhynion must be killed and the Branwyns made to look responsible. Only thus will the Tiernai be inflamed enough to rise against them."

"Think on this, Malcolm," said Tor. "We do Alcor a great service. The Branwyns grow more powerful each day, and no one lifts a hand to stop them. Rhynion is influenced by arrant cowards who would sell this land out at any price, just to gain a few years of peace. Their timidity will allow the Branwyns time to build a force mighty enough to destroy all the Tiernai on Alcor. You *know* that is their plan. The fact that they captured the prince proves they've already grown dangerously strong. Would you see us all their slaves?"

"But with a staunch monarch like you on the throne," said Earl Aran, "we shall wage a campaign to wipe out the entire Dynian race—to the last man, woman, and child—and so rid ourselves forever of their menace."

Malcolm twisted a lock of long, raven hair between his fingers. "How can we justify such deeds to the Council? However noble our ends, it is treason to plot the death of a prince."

"Treason? Nay, not when we *win*. Once you are king, all we have done to secure your crown will be judged loyal service. Those who oppose you are the traitors—to their own race." Tor Connail seized Malcolm's shoulders. "Think, Malcolm—to be *king*. To live in the Citadel and be served by those arrogant lords who now scarcely guess your abilities."

"And with my daughter Tríona as your consort," said Earl Aran, "you will found a mighty dynasty that will last centuries."

Malcolm seemed to like what he was hearing. "Still, the old king lives," he reminded them. "I'll not inherit the kingship, but a regency only. Should we be found out, King Brendan might yet name another to succeed him."

"Nay, he cannot. After Rhynion, you, as Duke Morwen's son, are rightful heir to the throne. Only a unanimous vote of Council can alter that. And Brendan is a witless dotard, senile and bedrid. His hour nears— I have our Master's word on that. Do not fear, my future son. Our plan cannot fail. By tomorrow night, you shall rule Alcor, in fact if not in name."

Malcolm nodded decisively and rose from the table. "Your counsel is sound. When this unpleasantness is over, you'll find me generous in my gratitude. I will retire now, for dawn must find us already on the road. I bid you goodnight, my true friends."

The others stood as Malcolm pressed their extended hands in turn. Then, with a quick about-face, he exited through the great double doors. JonMarc heard them shut with a loud thump.

High time for him to leave as well. Once he reported all he'd heard to Sir Donal, the Connails and Malcolm would surely face the headsman's block. That intelligence would win him a respectable place in the kingdom—and Cari for his bride.

Below, Aric leaned heavily on his elbow and refilled his wine cup; drained it; filled it again. He slumped back in his seat with a petulant snort. "I don't know how much longer I can abide that squeamish milksop," he growled, wiping his mouth on the back of a scarlet glove. "I swear I'd have expected better of old Morwen's loins. For all that I despise his guts, the bastard Fitzmorwen is at least a man. Watching *him* die will be well worth the effort."

His father Aran smiled sourly and took a seat beside him. "Were it up to me, tomorrow would see a Connail on the throne. Yet our Master has other plans." He shrugged. "For now, we must humor him, for we've much to gain. Yet soon we will have our way—if your sister Tríona does her duty by her new husband and quickly bears a sturdy son to succeed him. That son will be reared a Connail, and with his birth, Malcolm will have outlived his usefulness."

"Aye, if we can but wait so long," muttered Aric. "I fear our new ruler may be harder to put up with than the one we dispose of."

The candles on the long table fluttered, moved by some undetectable eddy of air. A yellow flash lit the room, followed by a low, ominous rumble that seemed to boil up through the hall like the deepening roll of a monstrous kettledrum. Penitarch Tor cupped his hands protectively around an object that seemed to pulse through his fingers with its own sanguine glow, like a living heart. He placed it at the center of the table. JonMarc could not take his eyes off it. It looked much like the token he'd lifted from the Earl of Dandryth.

A burst of wind howled through the window above him. The candles on the table danced wildly and went out, plunging the hall into blackness broken only by the hearth embers and the lurid gleam of the jewel. Startled, JonMarc dropped to his belly. The room filled with a sense of presence so potent the very air felt charged. *Táranos!*

JonMarc peered from behind the tapestries. The three Connails sat ringed around the jewel, hands joined. The gem's crimson light seemed to bathe their faces in fresh blood. JonMarc conceded grudging respect. The renegade Fithlon certainly knew how to make an entrance.

Penitarch Tor bowed his head. "We welcome you, Master," he said aloud. "What would you have of your faithful servants?"

From somewhere in the living air there came an answer. JonMarc could sense it, like the shimmering warmth around a desert rock, though it remained beyond his hearing.

"We have, my lord," Tor Connail intoned. Clearly, the Connails hadn't the skill to answer the renegade Fithlon mind-to-mind. "All is arranged according to your instructions."

JonMarc's pulse raced. Gods, how he would love to eavesdrop on the other half of that conversation; to see in his mind the visage of this adept even Master Gwythion confessed to fear. He knew he should leave—now, while the Connails sat totally absorbed. Even the hounds, monsters though they were, lay cowering beneath the table. Time to escape and warn the others of the Connails' treachery. But Táranos, *here*. JonMarc couldn't resist. He had to experience it, just for a moment. Then he would leave. He might even learn the renegade Fithlon's whereabouts so he and Kier could shape their plans accordingly. JonMarc knew he had the skill to tap in on the conversation; he'd done so with Gwythion. As long as he didn't open his mind fully, the charmstone's power would shield him from detection.

"Aye, lord, we have beheld it," said Tor. "Does it, as we guess, portend our victory?"

JonMarc knelt behind the tapestry and wrapped his fingers around the charmstone at his throat, straining to seek out the level of contact. He felt a dull ache behind his eyes—nothing he couldn't handle. In fact, whether due to the strength of Táranos's thought-sending, or perhaps an increase in his own skill, JonMarc found it easier than he'd expected.

"—*no time to lose.*" The cold, disembodied voice grew in his mind. "*I need the Amulet here—quickly. Send it with Roderig, or bring it yourselves, I care not which, but I must have it within the week.*" The voice of Táranos of Anlawth, inside his brain. JonMarc's limbs trembled with excitement. The image that took shape in his mind was not at all what he'd expected. It was a noble face, like that of a great sage, only more rash and haughty; a face that could inspire followers, and as easily cut them down.

"It shall be as you say, lord," said Tor Connail. "But how shall we recognize this token when we find it, if you yourself do not know its appearance?"

Táranos sounded testy. "*The predictions refer to something that resembles a hand. I am sure Fitzmorwen has it somewhere on his person. Send me every charm and ornament he either wears or carries. And I charge you, see that he is taken alive, and is neither searched nor despoiled by your minions. Is that understood?*"

"It is," Penitarch Tor replied, nodding acknowledgment to Aric's prompting. "And how long must he be *kept* alive?"

"*Until I find what I seek. There is a chance Fitzmorwen may yet be of service to me. Keep him safe. Many tomorrow will crave his blood. Once I acquire the Cábretaur, then you may do with him as you like.*"

JonMarc's knuckles whitened. A death sentence.

"How soon shall we see our rewards?" asked Earl Aran. "You ask much, and we shall deliver faithfully, as always. Yet our risk is great. We require more than promises."

"*You shall have your rewards,*" said Táranos, in a tone that made JonMarc shudder. "*The kingdom for the three of you, and wealth beyond imagining. Yet the prize is not yet won. When all is achieved, then shall you reap return for your service. Until then...*" Táranos hesitated. "*Where is Earl Hannon?*"

"Why, at Caerllyn, as you instructed," replied Tor, seemingly taken aback by the query.

"*No, I sense his beacon crystal.*" The face in JonMarc's mind suddenly stared right at him, as though trying to pierce his thoughts and come up with an image as clear as the one he himself beheld. The charmstone tingled in his fist. "*Who is there with you?*"

"None but ourselves, lord," Tor Connail assured him.

"*There is another; a stranger—there in the castle.*"

"Impossible!" snarled Earl Aran.

"*Find him.*"

JonMarc tried to empty his mind, to stifle every modicum of thought before Táranos could fix on him. He could not. He felt as if a great vise had clamped down on him. Something crimson gleamed from the pouch at his belt—Earl Hannon's crystal. Panic seized JonMarc. He fumbled for the perilous gem and hurled it over the balcony. Too late. An opposing will, like a huge, repressive hand, pinned him down. Searing waves of pain flooded his brain like molten lead. JonMarc fought to stifle a cry. The agony sent him writhing on his back. It grew and grew until it could not possibly get worse—and yet it did. It was as if all the pain ever spawned in the universe had suddenly erupted inside his head. JonMarc screamed, his skull a huge ball of flaming gasses, expanding with a pressure beyond enduring. In seconds it would burst and splatter the entire hall in pulpy shreds of brain matter.

He heard voices but could not make them out. Searing heat shimmered before his eyes and a silent roaring filled his ears. The charmstone burned his palm like a blazing coal. Woodenly, JonMarc thrust it into his shirt. Did he imagine it, or was the agony at last beginning to abate?

"Careful," came a distorted voice. "I think the Dynian's about to be sick."

Sick? He was well beyond sick. Yet his stomach was empty. There was nothing to... A convulsion wrenched JonMarc's belly and tried to force it up through his tonsils. He gagged and moaned. His mouth felt like parched leather.

"—an unexpected prize." JonMarc's eyes focused on Aric's misshapen face. "I could not have wished for better! If Fitzmorwen's end must be postponed, I can at least enjoy watching this one die."

"But how long has he been here?" demanded Penitarch Tor. "What did he overhear?"

"Aye, and how did he get in?" said Earl Aran. "An entire army guards the gates."

Aric waved a hand before his nose. "Through the sewer, by the stink of him. This Dynian is a conjurer, father—the one Tuán and I encountered in Menythgar the night Modron vanished." JonMarc felt Aric's boot press down on his wrist as, with a jeweled dagger, the Tiernai lordling sliced the glove from his outstretched left hand. "You see? He conceals a serpent brand."

"Profligate," snarled Penitarch Tor. "For that alone, he should be flayed alive."

"Fear not, uncle, I'll see to him," said Aric. "Your Covenant brethren will be well satisfied with his punishment."

"Very well," said Tor. "I do not doubt the villain overheard all we said. I leave the manner of his torture to you, Aric. Be sure you learn all he has to tell before you finish him."

With a gloating grin, Aric ordered two newly-summoned guards to haul the prisoner to his feet. JonMarc's knees were flaccid. The guards draped his limp arms around their shoulders and half-dragged, half-carried him down the stair to the great hall.

The two mastiffs sprang at him, yellow fangs bared, their eyes narrowed slits of fury. JonMarc groaned and struggled. Yet one glance at Aric told him the attack was for show. The Connail heir had other plans for his prize—slower, more painful.

They dragged him down a narrow stair to a deep chamber beneath the gate towers. There, in fetid darkness, JonMarc watched with growing horror as torchlight revealed a trapdoor in the floor. A stocky gaoler hastened to open it. The other guards placed hands over their noses as the stone slab grated aside. The stench of decay pouring out of it grew overwhelming. JonMarc choked and gasped, his dulled senses jarred back to reality. The charnel scent. It evoked memories of the Death Quarries—worse than the most hideous nightmare. JonMarc trembled. Death lurked in that pit, and they meant to put him there. He struggled with returning strength.

Aric laughed. "What's wrong, Dynian? Don't you like your accommodations? They were especially devised for spies and traitors like you." The guards dragged JonMarc to the edge of the pit. The reek that rose from it enveloped him like a smothering blanket. Those around him coughed and gagged and turned their faces away. JonMarc tried not to breathe. Sick and terrified, he looked into blackness, seeing nothing but tiny pinpricks reflecting the torchlight.

"You see," said Aric, "bastard halfblood though he is, your master was at least sired of noble blood, and so must be better housed. But you—" Aric's thin lips twisted in the same taunting sneer JonMarc learned to despise at the Citadel. "You, Dynian, are dung—less than the filth heap you were spawned upon—and so deserve no better."

The gaoler slid a ladder into the pit. It all but vanished. A guard clapped chains to JonMarc's wrists and ankles. "I've no doubt the others down there will find you a refreshing diversion," said Aric. The gaoler, a filthy creature with a bent back and arms like tree limbs, cackled heartily. He alone seemed oblivious to the stench. JonMarc did not understand their joke, but his hopes kindled. If there were other prisoners, they might band together to escape.

"I'll return for you at dawn, Dynian," said Aric. "Be ready to talk, for I have many questions, not the least of which concerns the fate of my henchman, Modron. You will tell me your part in his disappearance, and more. You will purge yourself of information as an ox purges himself in the field. And when you're finished, we shall await your master, to let him witness the last of your interrogation." Aric's lips peeled back in a feral grin. "Perhaps he'll wish to bargain for your freedom—costly on his part, but not impossible. To Fitzmorwen, it will seem like mercy. But you and I know better. I may be persuaded to free you: blind and gelded, with neither hands nor tongue with which to ply your accursed skills. And ever after, I shall take delight, knowing that somewhere you still live and remember by whose hand you were—disfigured."

With the last word, Aric reached up to touch his broken nose and all semblance of humor left him. He ordered JonMarc onto the ladder.

JonMarc's limbs had recovered some of their strength, but the heavy leg irons hampered his movements. He descended slowly into the loathsome pit. Impatient, Aric gave the ladder a kick. JonMarc lost his grip and fell to his back on the muck-slimed floor. A dozen rats scurried for the corners. He recovered quickly and grabbed for the ladder. If he could haul that down too...

The stocky gaoler anticipated his move and levered it. The bottom rung smashed beneath JonMarc's jaw. He dropped back with a curse, spitting blood. A roar of laughter echoed from above, and the gaoler spat into the cell. "Good try, lad," he said, "but ye'll 'ave to do better'n that. I've minded this 'cursed 'ole nigh on ten year. No one escapes."

Aric drew the gaoler aside, managing not to get too close. "Do not underestimate him," he hissed. "That Dynian is a sinistral sorcerer. He may try to talk, or bargain, or even *conjure* his way out. If he succeeds, you will pay—with your life."

At the mention of the sinistrae, the gaoler lost his cockiness. His thick fingers circled in the all-too-familiar sign of Devoreth's Eye. "Superstitious bastard," JonMarc growled.

Then the heavy slab ground back into place. He was trapped in the stifling blackness of a tomb.

Chapter Twenty-seven

JonMarc staggered to the pit's dank wall and leaned heavily upon it. The noxious air was almost unbreathable, yet he knew from grim experience that his senses would numb to it, in time. His head still throbbed and he felt sick and chilled. No good. He had to pull himself together; find a way out of this loathsome prison before Aric returned. If he failed, there would be no second chance—or if there were, he'd be in no condition to take it. JonMarc snorted impatiently. No sense pondering that. He'd made a mess of things already.

He heard a rustling in the darkness and his hopes sparked. "Is someone there?"

Pressure on the toe of his boot told him it was only a rat. There must be scores of them down here, chittering and scrabbling in the straw. If he could discover where they were coming in from, perhaps he could widen that opening enough to make use of it. It was a desperate hope, but hadn't many options. JonMarc began to work his way around the damp walls, groping like a blind man, alert for any crack or loosened stone. The two-foot span of chain between his wrists jangled brazenly against the rock like lepers' bells.

Halfway across the second wall, he caught a whiff of freer air. At first he was loath to believe it. Excitement surged. A few inches above his head, a narrow shaft angled upward, to open somewhere outside—probably into the dry, inner moat below the drum towers. On tiptoe, JonMarc pressed his face to the opening, greedily drinking in stale remnants of what, farther up the shaft, would be chill, midnight air. It refreshed his lungs as a cool sip of water would have refreshed his parched throat. To JonMarc's tortured mind, that tiny niche became a refuge—his only thread of contact with the outside. Just to know it existed was a balm to his heart. Come morning, it might even yield a shred of sunlight to this gruesome hole. But he couldn't wait. He had to be gone by then, and the air shaft, though comforting, provided no escape.

As he drew back from the blessed opening, a spate of dizziness seized him. The room pitched like a foundering ship, and he suddenly felt feverish; soaked with sweat. He dug his fingernails into the wall. *Steady now. Keep going. Concentrate on the coldness of the stone, the grit of mortar. No cracks yet; no openings.* JonMarc searched the corner and staggered along the adjacent wall, fumbling high and low in the darkness. Rats milled, squealing about his ankles. He plowed through a thick mass of them at the base of the wall, then lurched into something larger. He heard a jangle of chains. An overwhelming stench of death dragged him back to his senses.

He needed light. Why hadn't he thought of it before? He might manage it, if he could find something in this gods-forsaken hole dry enough to burn. His clothes were still damp, and the straw underfoot felt downright mucky. JonMarc backtracked around the pit, groping in corners until he gathered a scant handful of dry straw. Squatting on his heels, he set to work.

The guards had taken his dirk, but they'd overlooked the pouch of tools hidden inside his belt. JonMarc fumbled until he found a worn flint and the battered scrap of knife blade he used as a striker. Their familiarity gave him comfort, like old friends in an alien place. His dwindling store of tinder, tightly sealed in a little tin box, thankfully remained dry. The task required all of it. JonMarc nursed the tiny spark between trembling palms until a wisp of flame took hold. It traced an eerie pattern on the ceiling. He looked about.

The upper walls were lined with stone blocks, rough, but cunningly fitted together. No cracks showed. He lowered the light. The rats formed a seething mass along the base of the opposite wall. Tiny pinpricks of red stared back at him through the gloom. JonMarc's queasiness grew. A ragged mound loomed in their midst. Before it lay an object: round, and oddly shadowed. JonMarc moved the light nearer.

A skull stared at him through the flame, teeth parted in a skewed grimace. Remnants of rotting flesh still clung to the bony lips. The hollow eyes, alive with crawling things, regarded him with sardonic disdain.

JonMarc's stomach lurched. The blaze in his hand flared, and suddenly he beheld Modron, shrieking through the ravenous flames that consumed him. Then the vision changed to another face—one JonMarc knew but could not name: a tender cheek, flushed crimson; terror-filled blue eyes that melted to ooze as blackened skin crinkled from the bone.

With a strangled shriek, JonMarc careened backward. The room whirled. His head hit the wall with a crack and he sank to the floor, broken and shaking. The tiny flame died in a hiss of noxious fume, and fiery nightmares closed in.

The black walls of a ruined tower drifted above roiling sea mists, stark; desolate. Crumbling battlements, like rotted teeth, grinned a ghostly silhouette against a moon-shimmered sky.

On the plain below, two armies writhed in combat, the distant clamor borne upon the wind: the hue and cry of men in battle, the shrill screams of horses, the endless clash of steel upon steel.

A figure stepped onto the tower wall and gazed down on the turmoil, a smile of scorn twisting his wizened face. His robes, long and silvery, like the hair that blew wild about him, made him appear some mighty wizard of an ancient age. JonMarc knew better. His mind and thoughts were filled with that face of hate.

The robed figure raised his hands aloft. Between them he held a gleaming casket. His laughter froze the air like an icy blast of winter. In a mighty voice, he issued a command, and the shadow figures on the plain below dropped their weapons and groveled in the trodden mud.

Yet one man stood apart, refusing to kneel, and with pride and horror JonMarc recognized Kier. He looked a forlorn figure before the decaying walls, defiance gleaming in his eyes. Yet somehow JonMarc knew his friend hadn't the strength for this confrontation. It would destroy him.

The robed figure turned his scalding glare on the young upstart who dared challenge him. Kier reeled and staggered as slowly, inexorably, Táranos willed him to his knees.

JonMarc's anger flared. He knew that pain. None better. He tried to reach Kier, but some impediment held him back. He fought and raged at it, and finally won free.

Too late. Kier lay on his face, dead, on the muddy field of carnage.

"No!" JonMarc's hoarse cry wrenched itself from the deepest dungeon of his soul. His eyes opened to blackness in which the vivid images of his dream were slow to fade.

Gradually, awareness of his present plight returned, a nightmare of itself. His head pounded. How long had he been out? He groaned and stretched his legs—to indignant squeals, as his movement disturbed a cluster of enterprising rodents doing reconnaissance on his left boot. JonMarc scattered them with a kick and struggled to his feet.

His head felt like he'd been hit with a post. He staggered to the air shaft and took a deep draught. There were noises outside: men and horses; the clink of harness. JonMarc recalled hearing them even in his dream. He strained to see, but could only catch the occasional glow of a passing torch. The Connail troops were moving out for their deadly rendezvous with the Branwyns.

Anxiety tore at him. He had to get out of here! He fumbled about him for anything dry enough to ignite another fire, but there was little to be had. He settled for a webby tangle of rats' nest, gathered from the cell's far corner. Using the blade scrap, he sliced off his drying shirt sleeve and rolled the linen tightly for a torch.

It took many tries before a spark would catch. Painstakingly, JonMarc nurtured the infant flame to life. This time he knew what to expect. Even so, he could not repress a shudder as his torch spilled its mottled gleam on the grisly scene.

Two figures sat a few feet apart, propped against the wall. The one JonMarc had stumbled over was only a moldering heap of rag and bone, leaning at a precarious angle. Rats had eaten away most of the flesh. The fallen skull stared up vacantly from the putrid straw. JonMarc suspected the remains had lain there several months.

The second corpse appeared in better shape, though little remained of the face and gut cavity. Judging from the matted remnants of black hair, the man had been Tiernai. His limbs were chained, so he must have been alive when thrown in the pit. Whether he died before the rats began their gruesome work on his flesh, or after, was hard to say, but he'd certainly been tortured; the rotted flesh of his back was sliced to blackened shreds. He looked to have been a brawny man. A blacksmith?

JonMarc squatted beside him, muttering Sir Donal's coded words: "Have you heard the black owl cry...?" The hollow eyes stared up at him with mournful disregard. "No, I suppose not."

He turned away, leaving the rats to their meal. No wonder there were so many. They must be breeding down here. The implication hit him like a sledge. He'd failed to find their passage to the outside because they needed none. With food so plentiful, an entire host of rodents could happily live out their lives here.

JonMarc recalled Aric's parting gibe. The rats must be the *others* the Connail heir had spoken of, and JonMarc represented not so much a diversion for them as another course. He'd never truly believed Aric meant to free him, in any condition. His captor might haul him out now and again, torture him until his mind and limbs were jelly, but in the end, like Sir Donal's luckless spies, he'd simply end up as so much rat dung.

Despair assailed him. He couldn't die like this. Not when he'd barely begun to live. Maddened, JonMarc raged about the chamber, shouting and flailing his chain at the walls until at last, exhausted, he collapsed in a corner.

Something sharp grazed his knuckles. "Blast it," he bellowed, flinging aside an inquisitive rodent, "I'm not dead yet."

There was a scraping sound above and the stone slab moved. JonMarc panicked. Aric? But it wasn't yet dawn. Perhaps the Connail lordling had grown impatient to begin the torture.

Quickly, JonMarc concealed his torch, careful to leave the fibers smoldering. A brighter light from above replaced it. JonMarc blinked and shaded his eyes.

"Hoy, Dynian, what're you up to?" the gaoler barked. "Move where I can see you."

With a jangle of chains, JonMarc stood and skirted the torch glow, measuring the distance with his eyes. The opening lay only a yard beyond his reach.

The gaoler seemed aptly wary of him. "What was that racket? Been brewin' up some o' yer spoil-hand deviltry? Well I'll 'ave none o' yer tricks, you hear?"

JonMarc glared into the torchlight. "What're you afraid I'll do, weevil brain? Turn myself into a rat and climb out the air shaft?"

The gaoler blenched. "Just don't ye be tryin' nothin' *unnatural*. Lord Aric'll be here soon." Fumbling the protective gesture, he heaved the stone slab back into place.

JonMarc responded in the dark with a gesture of his own. If only he had the skills that superstitious dolt attributed to him. If only he weren't so confounded *helpless*. JonMarc paced the putrid straw. He'd always believed that for every impediment Fortunea placed in one's path, she also offered a solution. One only needed the ingenuity to see it. What powers did he have to draw on? A beginner's ability to touch minds, and his own native cunning. That didn't amount to much.

JonMarc halted. Blinked. Looked back at the opening. Or did it? There was a power he hadn't considered: suggestion. Aric had his gaoler convinced their prisoner could work sorcery. Maybe he could use that. *A rat through the air shaft*. Blazes, Táranos's attack must have addled his thinking. There was only a fool's hope it could work. Still, a fool's hope was better than none.

Methodically, JonMarc set to work. He breathed the smoldering torch back to life, then slipped a nail from his pouch and began disposing of his chains. There was some risk, for if the ruse failed—as seemed likely—Aric would demand to know how he'd come to be free and deprive him of the one advantage he had: the precious pouch of tools. No point worrying about that. If the ruse failed, he'd be in little condition to use it again.

The chains slipped off with a rattle and clank. JonMarc placed them, and the ragged remains of his shirt, in the center of the floor, directly below the opening. He searched about him for a weapon, something he could wield noiselessly. A leg bone? Now that the eerie madness had passed, JonMarc felt no qualms about using what circumstance provided. Sir Donal's spy would not miss the limb. With his meager blade, JonMarc pried apart the last tenacious remnants of sinew and swung the grisly club over his head. It would serve. He doused the torch.

A pale rectangle of moonlight shone on the soggy floor beneath the air shaft. JonMarc sniffed the scant breeze. It would be dawn soon. Denia's moon rode low in the west, its silver light perfectly framed by the walls of the air channel. JonMarc mumbled a silent prayer to the Lady, hoping she, a stranger, might heed the entreaty of an insignificant and none-too-reverent pickpurse. Fat chance. He'd have to rely, as always, on his own luck and ingenuity.

JonMarc squatted against the wall and grasped the charmstone in his left fist. The crystal felt cold and strangely fragile, as though it had been shattered from within, like his own mind, by the power of Táranos's attack. Rats milled about his ankles. JonMarc ignored them and willed himself to concentrate. Gwythion said the charmstone would amplify his thoughts, assuming it wasn't too damaged to function. He banished that concern and turned his mind to locating the gaoler.

It was, in effect, like groping through impenetrable darkness to find the thoughts of an unfamiliar mind. JonMarc sensed no one in the chamber above. He tried to recall the layout of the keep and set his mind exploring.

The task proved easier than he'd dared hope. Perhaps Táranos's assault had actually enhanced his perceptive powers. He touched the minds of two guards outside the gatehouse. They were cold and hungry, eagerly awaiting their relief. But where would the gaoler be? JonMarc let his mind range farther. He found the courtyard all but deserted. Most of the castle's defenders must have ridden north with the earl. Pain intensified behind his eyes.

What would take a man so far from his post when he knew his master might require him at any moment? It must be something pressing, to risk Aric's ire. JonMarc's mouth quirked. The privy? It was as good a guess as any. It must lie somewhere above the sewage culvert. He calculated the location and willed his mind there with surprising ease.

He found the gaoler, straining and fidgeting, well aware of the need for haste. His bowels would not cooperate. JonMarc chuckled, and resolved to give him something more urgent to worry about. As he reasoned it, if he could picture the scenario he wished to convey, he might be able to project that image into the gaoler's mind. Here in the lonely hour before dawn, with his fears already roused, the superstitious dolt might be willing to believe almost anything of his mysterious prisoner—provided JonMarc could hold the contact long enough. His temples throbbed unmercifully, and the charmstone's power felt erratic.

JonMarc imagined himself standing in the middle of the chamber, arms held high above his head. He had his image chant a string of nonsensical syllables—actually the ribald chorus of a Syrmian drinking song—and perform an intricate gesture he hoped would read as a magical incantation. The image spun three times, then blurred. Chains and clothing sank to the floor as the projection shrank, fattened, sprouted black fur and whiskers and a long, whip-like tail. The rat wrinkled its nose and cautiously climbed the rough stone wall toward the air shaft. It paused a moment to sniff the breeze, then, with a joyous squeal, scurried up the angled path to freedom.

A corner of JonMarc's mind checked on the gaoler. The man had gobbled the bait like a hungry mullet. Already he was hurtling toward the stair, tugging his breeches as he ran. JonMarc severed the contact. The experience left him lightheaded. Steadying himself, he picked up his club and made his way to the corner farthest from the opening.

Seconds crept by like hours, and still no sound from above. JonMarc's hopes began to dim. Maybe he deceived himself; his powers weren't up to the task.

Heavy footsteps pounded above. JonMarc's heart caught. Stone rasped stone as the trapdoor slid open and orange light stabbed the chamber. "You, Branwyn! Come stand where I can see you." The gaoler's obstinate voice carried no trace of panic. Had he recognized the ruse? JonMarc grudgingly conceded he might have underestimated the man.

"Branwyn, d'ya hear me? Come stand in the light, you miserable maggot."

JonMarc bit his lip. His fingers trembled around the greasy club. The torch dropped lower, and at last the gaoler spotted the shirt and manacles lying on the floor. A long silence followed in which JonMarc could almost see the alternatives flashing across the gaoler's mind.

"Ye canna trick me so easily, Branwyn. I know yer still down there."

Doubt, and fear—unmistakable now. What would the man do? Too tense and head-weary to attempt another mind touch, JonMarc could only wonder.

A bale of straw dropped into the pit and scattered, followed by the torch. JonMarc caught his breath. He hadn't anticipated this. The straw began to flame. Ghedrev's blood, he could roast down here like a capon in an oven. In a moment, the fire would start the damp straw smoldering. The smoke would suffocate him. JonMarc plastered himself against the wall and tried to avoid looking at the flames. Fire seemed to trigger his attacks of madness. He dared not risk that.

He heard the clomp of impatient footsteps. At last the gaoler leaned into the hole for a better look. Dancing flames curled the straw; the fume grew thick. JonMarc held his breath as more of the gaoler's shaggy head appeared. With all his strength, he swung the grisly club.

It smashed into the gaoler's skull with the force of a battle ram. The man yelped and struggled to withdraw. JonMarc clubbed him again, and yet again. The leg bone snapped. One end, still held with dried sinew, whipped around and caught the gaoler between the eyes with a squishy thump. He groaned and went limp.

JonMarc discarded the club and leaped up to grab the gaoler's dangling arm. The body, like a beached whale, completely blocked the opening. JonMarc's eyes streamed. His boot soles began to smolder. At last he managed to shift the gaoler's weight and dragged him into the pit.

The body fell with a muffled thud, largely smothering the flames. JonMarc quickly relieved him of a coin pouch and a well worn dirk. The gaoler still breathed. JonMarc used his great ale belly as a platform to boost himself up to the opening. Fingers straining against the rim, he clawed his way out of the pit, then heaved the stone lid back into place.

The chamber was silent, and hazy with smoke and the first light of dawn. JonMarc crept up the stairs. Two bored sentries still stood before the keep. One blew warm breath on his fingers. The stench of burning had not yet alerted them; its scent melded with the smoke of dozens of hearth fires throughout the castle. JonMarc waited until the pair turned away, then hastened back to the great hall.

He'd made no plans beyond his escape from the oubliette, yet he knew what he must do: find the Branwyn leader's sister—what had they called her, Llydia?—and take her to the Spire with him. It was the only way to prevent a massacre. Aran Connail said she was held in a tower—one of the five keep towers, JonMarc presumed. He need only determine which one.

The great hall lay dark and deserted. JonMarc shivered as he mounted the stair and crept past the spot where he'd suffered such pain and humiliation last night. What an ass he'd been to think he could conceal his mind from Táranos. Once again, bravado had nearly cost him his life.

He found the door to the outside locked again. JonMarc reached into his pouch and made quick work of it. He climbed the stair to the level of the wall-walk and peered around a corner.

A blushing rim of satin lined the clouds above the eastern hills. A chill breeze ruffled his hair. It bore the tantalizing aroma of bacon broiling in the kitchens below. JonMarc filled his lungs with it. It was all the breakfast he was likely to get. He sighted along the wall in either direction. No movement. The tower where Llydia Branwyn was held must be guarded. That ruled out the one beside him. JonMarc crept to the next, right behind the keep. Still no guard. He passed through the archway and continued on.

Torchlight flickered ahead. JonMarc breathed relief. This was the last tower he could reach without re-entering the keep. As he neared the tunneled entrance, he saw a shadow move within and dodged into the corner between the arch and the outer parapet. He heard shuffling; a yawn. JonMarc nibbled his lip. How best to lure the guard out without raising an alarm?

Even as he pondered, he heard the man inside sniff loudly; and again. The sound moved closer. Blazes, the guard smelled him. Backed to the wall, JonMarc watched the shadow on the floor lengthen. As the guard reached the arch, JonMarc spun.

The guard barely had time to register astonishment before JonMarc shoved his dirk in the man's side. With a retching sound, the guard bent double. JonMarc quickly relieved him of his sword, purse, and a stout ring of keys, then pitched him over the wall. The body hit the ground below with a muted thud. JonMarc gave him no further thought. He leaped up the turret stair to the uppermost chamber and knelt before the keyhole.

All was dark inside. "Llydia!" he whispered. "Llydia Branwyn, are you in there?" Silence. She must be asleep. "Answer me, girl. I've come to get you out." Nothing. Could she be drugged? He felt an almost irresistible urge to enter the chamber.

Something rustled just inside the door and a large blue eye appeared at the keyhole. It blinked, startled, when it met his. "Who are you?" came a muffled voice.

"A friend. Wait a moment; I'll get you out."

JonMarc fumbled with the stolen keys. One fit. He pushed the door open.

Llydia Branwyn peered from behind it, then warily stepped out, clutching a length of cord between her fists. She scrutinized him up and down as he stood revealed in the torchlight. JonMarc had the feeling those suspicious eyes missed nothing. Neither did his. Llydia was clad only in a woolen shift. Her red-gold hair, wild to the waist, framed a round, freckled face and a pair of huge, uniquely expressive blue eyes. They regarded him dubiously.

"I've never seen *you* before. Are you sent by my brother?"

"We'll talk later," said JonMarc, feeling the pressure of time. "Get dressed."

He stepped outside to scout for additional guards. When he returned, he found Llydia clad in a man's breeches and tunic, several sizes too large. "They took my gown and left me only these," she said, tying her hair back with the length of cord he'd seen her holding earlier.

"Planned to garrote your guard, did you?" JonMarc chuckled, recognizing a kindred spirit.

Llydia eyed him up and down where he stood, filthy and shirtless, then shrugged. "I tried to lure him in, but his iron cap turned my thoughts."

Uneasiness pricked JonMarc's backbone. The Branwyn girl possessed sinistral talents. He'd sensed their tug himself, when he'd stood outside her door.

"How do you mean to escape?" Llydia asked.

"There's a secret exit hidden behind a tapestry in Earl Aran's bedchamber." According to Sir Donal, that chamber lay in the northeast corner of the keep, just off the great hall. With the earl gone, it was likely empty. He and Llydia could be well on their way before Aric Connail even realized they were gone.

Llydia pushed past him. "Then let's find it."

The hall was still deserted. JonMarc took the lead down the main staircase, then circled behind it. There were two doors in the east wall, spaced well apart. The earl's bedchamber was most likely the one on the left. JonMarc squatted before the keyhole and tried every key on the guard's ring. None fit. He drew out his lock-pick.

Llydia watched over his shoulder. "I hear voices," she whispered, glancing about.

JonMarc did too—male voices, in animated conversation. They were too muted to determine their direction. "I'll check the main doors," said Llydia.

JonMarc was having trouble with the lock. This mechanism was more complicated than the last. "Be quick," he said, tossing her the gaoler's dirk. Then, frowning, he sat on his heels and searched his pouch for another tool.

Llydia barely made it across the vaulted hall when the voices grew louder. She spun back. JonMarc shot her a panicked look and leaped to his feet just as the right-hand door burst wide.

Aric Connail strode out, laughing with a comrade behind him.

He instantly spotted JonMarc and the laughter died on his lips. "*You!*" he cried, and drew his sword.

Chapter Twenty-eight

Aric's stunned gaze darted from JonMarc to the lock-pick protruding from the keyhole, then back again. "How did you escape my dungeon, Dynian?"

Nervously fingering the sword he'd taken from Llydia's guard, JonMarc summoned up a sneer of defiance he hoped would mask the hammer-pounding of his heart. "Sinistral sorcery. Did you not believe your own warning, Connail?"

Trepidation flickered in Aric's dark eyes, but only for an instant. Then a humorless smile oozed across his face. "Did you hear that, Con?" he said to his companion. "The Branwyn whoreson simply *conjured* himself here." He tossed a flippant hand. "Perhaps we shall see him conjure his way out again." His gaze tracked over JonMarc's pathetic exterior, narrowing on the charmstone, still dangling from the ragged cord about his neck. "But I think not."

With the speed of an adder's tongue, he whipped his slender blade across JonMarc's bare chest, leaving a seam of red. The precious pendant flew across the floor.

JonMarc's confidence crumbled. He'd heard Aric ranked among the finest swordsmen on Alcor—on a level with Kier and Sir Donal. By comparison, he felt a lumbering oaf. He fumbled with his sword, frantically striving to recall the lessons taught him in secret by his swordmaster-owner, back in Castémaron. That was eight years ago. It seemed eons. He recalled his master's tenet: *No worthy swordsman wields a blade with his spoil-hand. It is an insult to swordsmanship and the blade itself.* JonMarc shifted the weapon to his so-called *skill*-hand, though it had never proven so for him.

Aric eagerly took up his stance. With subtle grace, he tapped JonMarc's weapon with his blade tip. JonMarc circled his point to disengage. The guardsman's sword was stouter; less manageable than Aric's. The Connail lord chuckled and performed the maneuver again, and yet again. Each repeat further unsettled JonMarc. His arm grew heavy and he gripped the weapon as if it were a serpent that might set fangs to him.

Aric's blade darted for his shoulder. JonMarc jerked to parry, but felt a slash of fire as Aric's point instead opened the skin across his belly. That blood melded with the rivulets oozing from his chest. Shaken, JonMarc jerked the sword across to protect his ribs. The Connail's blade sliced his arm from wrist to elbow. JonMarc lurched backward. Before he could collect himself, Aric's lightning swing drove the weapon from his grasp.

Aric's triumphant smirk was as shallow as cheap veneer. "So, Dynian, it seems your sorcery has merely hastened your appointment with my torturer." He pressured his weapon point against JonMarc's throat, forcing him back to the wall. "You'll find him a true master of his craft as he dismembers you piece by piece, allowing you to savor every moment of your laborious dissection. Where shall I have him begin?" He pricked the skin above JonMarc's heart. "Here? Or perhaps—" He lowered the point to JonMarc's groin. "—Here?"

Cold stone pressed the small of JonMarc's back as Aric's point gnawed deeper into his cods. "What's wrong, Dynian? Squeamish already? Why, the amusement's barely begun. Con," he called to his aide, "summon the—"

"*Ayee-aah!*" The rending war shriek shivered the hall as if the Death Hag's ravenous soul-eaters swooped from the rafters. Llydia Branwyn! JonMarc had forgotten her. She flitted among the shadows near the main doors, brandishing the dirk.

Aric shot a glance over his shoulder. It was all JonMarc needed. He rammed his boot into the lordling's shin and scrambled free.

Aric spat an oath and hurtled after him. "Take the she-wolf alive!" he shouted to Con.

Only when JonMarc had skidded to the far side of the long dining table did he stop to catch his breath. Aric rested one slim hip on the table's edge, watching him, his marred face twisted in a mocking counterfeit of a smile. "Is that the best you can do, sorcerer? It seems your magic has deserted you. Surrender now, and save us both this futile chase. In exchange, I'm prepared to offer you a relatively easy death."

JonMarc returned a bitter laugh. "The way you offered me my life, at the Citadel? I know the worth of your promises, Connail. I'm afraid you'll just have to come get me."

Aric's face hardened. "All right, Dynian. But you *will* die—and painfully. That promise you may be *sure* I will keep." In a fluid motion, he swung his long legs over the table, landing lightly as a malkin on the other side. JonMarc retreated along its length, hurling bowls, goblets, whatever he could lay hands on. Aric deflected them with his sword. Their contents littered the floor.

As he backed around the table's far end, JonMarc stumbled against a chair. Grinning, Aric lunged, scoring the flesh on JonMarc's shoulder. JonMarc stumbled clear. He snatched up a pewter wine carafe and hurled the liquid in Aric's face.

Aric's countenance darkened beyond the deep murrey of the wine. With a roar, he charged.

JonMarc smashed a crockery dish on the table's edge for a weapon. Then, seizing the nearest object at hand—the bronze candelabrum—he turned and ran.

At the center of the hall, he spun back. Aric advanced, swinging. With a mighty clang, JonMarc snared the blade between the stout branches of the candelabrum. The impact sent numbness crawling up his left arm. He stabbed the bowl shard at Aric's trapped sword hand and felt it graze flesh.

A savage kick hurled him backward, freeing Aric's blade. JonMarc's foot lit on a dog bone and he slammed to his rump on the slate floor. Aric leaped after him. JonMarc rolled, fending off the Connail's strokes with the candelabrum. A furious swing, and Aric sliced it in half. Its top flew against the wall. JonMarc chucked the base at Aric's chest and scuttled aside, crablike, until he could regain his feet. He grabbed a high-backed chair and shoved it between them.

Aric halted, hands on hips, looking only minimally fatigued. "So, Dynian, you flee as nimbly as a frightened hare on a summer's morn. You are indeed a credit to your cowardly race."

JonMarc's body streamed like a melting snowbank. The salty sweat burned the cuts on his chest and arms, melding with rivulets of red. He could barely take in enough air to satisfy his lungs. "Throw away your sword, Connail," he panted, "and fight me man to man. Then we'll see who's the coward."

"Fight you? Does a falcon creep through the mud to catch a serpent? Learn your place, Dynian. Your race is for killing, not fighting, and there will be a mighty slaughter of them today, you may be sure—starting with you. Con!"

"My lord?" The centuriant's harried response came from the shadows beneath the balcony where Llydia still managed to evade him. He'd drawn his sword, but seemed uncertain about using it against a woman.

"Summon the Guard," said Aric. "We'll have this one alive."

"But lord Aric, the wench..."

"Forget the Branwyn bitch. She cannot escape the castle. Do as I say."

"Aye, lord." Con exited through the main doors.

"What's wrong, Connail?" JonMarc scorned. "Afraid you can't take me alone? Did I wound your pride so much when I wounded your arm?"

Aric aimed him a look—half haughty, half puzzled. JonMarc indicated the Connail lord's sleeve, where the linen soaked up blood like a thirsty rag. Aric blanched. "You'll pay for this a thousandfold."

This time JonMarc did not doubt his word. Victory was all but impossible. Flight, equally so. It appeared faithless Fortunea had at last turned on him, weaving him a web from which there was no escape. Yet while he lived, he could not give up hope. If he could find some way to enrage Aric past caring, perhaps the Connail lord would blunder. That might offer him a chance, albeit a slim one. It was that, or surrender. At any second, Con would return with soldiers.

"You claim to be a swordsman, Connail? What kind of swordsman must cry for aid just to capture a single, unarmed man? Where's all your skill? In your bragging tongue?"

Aric's thin lips twitched. His fingers whitened around his sword hilt. "I'll see the tongue cut out of you."

"That won't make my words less true. You're a coward, Connail. All Alcor knows it. You won't fight me because you fear I'll win. How would it feel to be bested by a Dynian?"

"Silence, worm!"

JonMarc could sense Aric's restraint slipping. The lordling's crimson face resembled a kettle about to spew. It suddenly occurred to him that he might have inadvertently hit upon the very trigger he needed. It was a guess, but he felt sure he must be right. "Who was it broke your nose, Connail? A pretty trophy of your skill. Was it the halfblood, Fitzmorwen?" JonMarc saw confirmation in Aric's smoldering eyes and grinned wolfishly. "Aye, I see now why you hate him so. To bear the proof of his victory the rest of your days? To face it every time you look in a glass? Is that the canker that festers in you, Connail?"

Aric's sword hand trembled.

"Tell me. Was it a fair fight, or did you again reserve all the odds for yourself?"

With a shriek, Aric's self-control broke. He attacked like a berserker, slashing wildly at the chair JonMarc held between them until splintered fragments littered the floor like kindling. The force drove JonMarc backward, his arms near to buckling beneath Aric's demented blows.

Behind him, the huge doors groaned open. It could only be Con, returning with the guards. JonMarc's stomach sank. He'd be seized, tortured, executed. All he'd tried to achieve would be for naught. He'd never see Cari again, or Kier. And the Connails' treachery would wipe out a race JonMarc was startled to realize he actually cared about.

Aric's assault halted in mid-stroke. JonMarc looked to the Connail's face, expecting a leer of triumph. Instead, he saw confusion—even alarm. But why...? JonMarc spared a swift glance over his shoulder. He saw no soldiers—only the Branwyn girl, bolting the doors behind her.

"Llydia!" he cried. "Find me my sword! It's somewhere beneath the stair."

The girl hastened to obey. Aric sped off to stop her. With a shout, JonMarc leaped, tackling the Connail lord's ankles. They both crashed to the ground.

Llydia found the sword and slid it to him across the floor. But even as JonMarc reached for it, Aric rolled, smashing his boot heel down on JonMarc's outstretched hand.

Pain lanced through JonMarc's right palm. Fighting down nausea, he grabbed the hilt without feeling it and followed Aric to his feet.

Aric's eyes glittered satisfaction at crushing his enemy's sword hand. JonMarc fumbled the weapon to his left and hooked his throbbing fingers through the iron key ring at his belt. He barely managed to duck Aric's flailing stroke, then lunged in behind it. His blade pierced Aric's leather tunic just below the ribcage. The tip came out bloody.

Eyes burning, Aric groped for his side, then stared in disbelief at the blood on his fingers. His face contorted. "*Guards,*" he bellowed. "Guards, to *me!*"

His words echoed against the chill walls and died there. No one came. Slowly, realization crept in on Aric. His summons had miscarried. He was alone.

His narrowed gaze turned on JonMarc with a death promise so real JonMarc girded himself for the end. The fingers of his mangled hand tightened around the iron ring of keys.

Aric swung with all his strength. There was an ear-shattering clang as JonMarc's blade forced Aric's aside. JonMarc drove in with his right fist, his damaged knuckles reinforced with stout iron.

The blow caught the bridge of Aric's nose, stunning the Connail lord instantly. His sword dangled from his fingers like a broken twig, then clattered to the floor. JonMarc flung aside his own. Bracing his enemy by the collar, he pounded him again. All control left him. Rage and loathing remained. Their momentum gave him strength. Mindless, he pummeled Aric, blow after blow, feeling his enemy's face reduce to spongy pulp beneath his fist.

He was oblivious to the pain that screamed through his injured hand, to everything around him, until Llydia's cry broke his distraction. "Soldiers in the corridor. We must flee."

JonMarc heard shouts; the stomp of booted feet. Someone rattled the door, calling Aric's name. JonMarc released the lordling's collar and Aric collapsed at his feet, a bloody rag.

JonMarc swayed, about to drop as well. Llydia shoved his sagging six-foot frame against the wall. "We've no time for that!" A loud boom reverberated through the hall. "The bar won't hold them long. Hurry!"

"I can't," JonMarc gasped. "I need a moment..."

"We don't *have* a moment." Llydia's eyes tracked over him dubiously, as though assessing the soundness of a swaying tower. "I'll help you to the earl's chamber."

"But—the door's still locked. I had no chance to..."

Llydia scowled. Swiftly, she knelt and searched Aric's tunic. Another boom shook the hall. Llydia snapped a chain of keys from Aric's neck. "Come," she said, grabbing JonMarc's arm.

JonMarc glanced one last time at the bloody porridge that had been Aric's face. The gorge rose in him and he stumbled to follow. "Wait! My charmstone..."

"I have it." Llydia pressed the crystal into his palm. Miraculously, his pain seemed to lessen. Llydia helped him to the door. One of Aric's keys fit the lock. They scrambled through just as voices sounded from the balcony overhead and footsteps thundered down the stairs.

Another boom, and the hall doors burst open. The confusion of shouts and barked orders muted as JonMarc bolted the chamber door behind them.

He found the tapestry and the secret exit behind it, exactly as Sir Donal had described. Blindly, they plunged into a lightless passageway between the walls. Llydia took the lead, feeling her way down a steep stair that descended almost to the level of the sewage culvert, then veered left. A door stood at the end. Together they fumbled to withdraw the bolts, and pushed.

Orblight blinded them. The postern opened into a narrow trench, concealed by a line of hollies that grew close about the castle's foot. Below, the river carved its rushy course around the castle's eastward side, its surface shot with flecks of gold and grey morning.

The keep wall rose behind them. JonMarc could already hear the commotion inside as soldiers scoured the castle for the escapees. "Connail's men must not know about the postern," he chuckled painfully. "They're racing to beat us to the front gates."

"We must cross the river before they think to look this way," said Llydia. "We've no weapons to engage them."

"But you have the dirk..."

Llydia shook her head. "I lost it."

"*Lost* it?"

"Aye," she said. "In the centuriant's ribs—when he fell down the stair."

They covered the leagues to Galglenneth's Spire as swiftly as their horses would allow. If soldiers pursued them from Ruthland, they did not stay to learn of it.

Devoreth's hazy Orb lengthened their shadows to gaunt stick-figures when, from a hillcrest, they spied the last stragglers of the Connail army. Llydia reined westward, and soon they came to another track, narrower and less trodden, that paralleled the road from the cover of forest.

They had followed it less than three leagues when JonMarc finally caught sight of the Spire, jutting above the treetops like a huge silver spike. His pulse quickened. All around them, Branwyn foot-soldiers slipped through the forest on their way to the prisoner exchange. They seemed far too few to stand against the Connail host.

The trail brought them to the upper end of the meadow, just behind the ring of stones. To their right, the Spire's long shadow clove the circle like a sword of doom. The Branwyn and Tiernai deputations stood near the flat altar stone. Though he could not make out their words, JonMarc sensed the rancor boiling between them. The reason for it was clear. The Connail army covered the hillslope—a tide of color and glinting steel.

Duke Edmund, at the head of his party, looked furious, while Malcolm, flanked by the brothers Tor and Aran, fidgeted nervously and glanced about as though wishing the whole affair were over. Behind them, outside the circle, JonMarc made out the grim figure of Sir Donal, mounted beside Gaelin at the head of some two dozen of the prince's guard.

In stark contrast, the Branwyn force of some hundred men, with Dai Caydyn at their head, seemed small and threadbare. The most regal figure among them was the young prince. Close beside him, hovering like an anxious mastiff, stood Kier. Even with half the circle between them, JonMarc recognized the furnace smoldering beneath his companion's dark brows.

He saw no sign of Roderig, yet the creature must strike soon—before the Connails were compelled to bring forth their hostage.

JonMarc dug heels into his horse's flanks and charged straight for the altar stone, ignoring the gasps as the company suddenly became aware of him. "Kier," he cried, reining in amid the Branwyn troops. "Look to the prince! The Connails plan treachery."

Kier heard. He instantly thrust Rhynion behind one of the tall standing-stones, using his own body to shield the boy from the Connails' direction. JonMarc leaped down to join him.

He barely heard the quiet *zzzip*, and did not grasp its significance until he saw Kier stiffen. Slowly his friend began to sag against the stone, cradling Rhynion to his chest. A moment later, JonMarc reached them. It was a moment too late.

Rhynion leaned upon his cousin like a weary child, brown eyes registering only surprise. But the firm hand that supported the young monarch's back trickled crimson. As JonMarc looked closer, he saw that Kier's palm was pierced by a crossbow bolt. And that bolt, despite the impediment, had found its mark.

Shouting rose all around them, punctuated by the clang of swordplay. Gaelin galloped up with a handful of royal guardsmen to form a protective wall around Kier and the prince. Branwyn men-at-arms impeded his effort, and for a while the fighting was intense. Gaelin downed two of Dai's men and forced his way forward, dismounting to use his horse as a shield.

"Come with me, Highness. We can escape—" JonMarc seized his arm, forcing him to look at what had happened. Gaelin went white. "Who...?" he gasped.

"*Roderig*. He's somewhere behind Branwyn lines." JonMarc traced back along the missile's probable path. He pointed. "There, inside the Spire! Táranos must know about the door."

Fighting broke out near at hand as a fragment of the Connail force tried to reach the prince. For a moment, the Branwyns and Gaelin's men inadvertently joined forces to hold them off.

JonMarc yanked out the fatal bolt and tried to pull Kier's hand away. His friend resisted. "Kier, the Connails are after *you*. We've got to get out of here!"

Kier shook his head, stubbornly clinging to Rhynion's limp body. JonMarc felt for a pulse at the boy's neck—a waste of time; he knew death when he saw it. "Kier, there's nothing more you can do for him. The Connails seek your blood."

Kier cradled the boy closer, like a mother refusing to acknowledge the death of her only child. "They can have it."

"Captain, you did all you could," cried Gaelin. "Come back to Caerllyn. You'll be safe there."

"Kier, the prince is *dead*," said JonMarc, hoping the shock of his words would jar Kier to action. "You can't help him by staying. Your duty's not ended. There's still the Cábretaur—"

"Curse the Cábretaur!" Kier returned. "I've failed my prince."

JonMarc chewed his lip. Kier's stubbornness would keep him from abandoning Rhynion's body, though it cost him his life. He cast about, desperate. The Connails were winning ground; they'd soon reach the ring of stones. There was no choice. He balled his fist and swung.

The blow caught Kier below the temple. His head hit the tall stone beside him and he slumped into JonMarc's arms like a sack of meal. Gaelin caught the prince.

The scene had turned to madness. Battle raged all around. JonMarc spotted Llydia, fighting on horseback beside her brother's men. He shouted to her and she made her way to him. JonMarc hoisted Kier over her saddlebow. "Take him to safety," he cried, slapping the horse's rump.

His action took Gaelin by surprise. "But I thought you'd return to—"

JonMarc grasped the young officer's shoulder. "Listen well," he said, doing his best to make himself understood above the din. He swiftly recounted what he'd overheard at Ruthland.

"Tell Sir Donal I heard Malcolm and the Connails plotting Rhynion's murder." He grabbed the reins of Gaelin's mount and leaped into the saddle. Standing with Rhynion's body in his arms, Gaelin could only nod.

Another bolt zipped past, mere inches from JonMarc's chest. It took down a man a few yards beyond. JonMarc spotted movement atop the Spire. "That was meant for *me*. Guard the Spire. Don't let Roderig escape." Without waiting for a reply, he turned and spurred after Kier.

Chapter Twenty-nine

Kier opened his eyes with a start, to the sound of rain beating a sonorous tattoo against the roof slats. Shreds of pallid light creeping in from the chimney hole told him dreary day still lingered outside. What day? How long had he been asleep?

He recognized the knotted ceiling staves of the rude cabin where he and Rhynion had been imprisoned. He thought he remembered leaving there for the prisoner exchange, but perhaps that had been part of his dream...? A leaden ingot formed deep in Kier's belly. Panicked, he groped beside him on the pallet. *Empty.* He bolted upright.

His head pounded and his left palm felt as if it had been gored by a lance. He tried to flex his fingers, but found the hand tightly bandaged. The crushing truth descended on him. The incident at the Spire had been no nightmare. Rhynion was *dead*.

Tears welled in Kier's eyes—tears of frustration; of pain; of unbearable loss. These past three days, he and Rhynion had grown so close, forging a bond few ever shared with their sovereign. Over many a challenging game of *King's Board,* they'd discussed history, politics and strategy. Kier had listened to Rhynion's thoughts and fears; related his own experiences abroad—insights gleaned from five years of service. He'd enlightened the prince in the ways of his Dynian subjects, hoping such instruction might influence the way the young monarch ruled. And he'd been delighted to find Rhynion an apt pupil, keen of mind, compassionate, and eager to learn. Now, all that lay in ruin.

Had he heard aright? Roderig had shot the fatal bolt? Kier prayed he might one day lock his fingers around that traitorous creature's throat. Yet most of his rancor he reserved for himself. He'd known Rhynion was in peril; had accepted full responsibility for the prince's safety. Yet despite all his efforts, he'd utterly failed to shield the boy from their enemy's treachery.

The rain hammered on, a tedious drum roll, the day as desolate as his mood. Kier got up and peered through a chink in the log wall. A guard stood outside. So, he was still a prisoner. Kier clumsily poured some wine to warm himself until he could get the fire stoked. He found his boots and leather jerkin laid out for him, as well as a clean woolen shirt to replace the bloodstained one he wore. Kier examined the stains. At least some of the blood was his own. The bolt must have passed right through Rhynion's frail body and nicked him below the ribcage. That wound had gone unnoticed by whoever had tended his hand. Kier fumbled at his belt for the Amulet, then breathed relief. The silver charm remained safely hidden. Yet his wrist dagger and scabbard were gone. Kier felt naked without them.

The cabin door suddenly burst open. Kier spun, and his heart leaped. But no, he recognized his error the moment his eyes adjusted to the light. A girl had entered, though clad as she was in breeches and jerkin, she reminded him so much of... Kier shoved the wrenching thought aside.

His visitor squinted into the gloom. "Oh!" she said, when she saw him staring back at her. "You're awake. JonMarc asked me to look in on you." She pulled off her rain-soaked hood and shook out a wealth of reddish curls. Kier watched with reluctant curiosity.

"Does the shirt fit? It belongs to my brother."

So, she must be Ross's sister—the kidnapped Llydia Branwyn. The resemblance was canny enough. "I haven't tried it on yet," Kier replied.

Llydia folded her arms, making it clear she expected him to do so now. Kier was very conscious of her gaze as he slipped off his bloodstained shirt and reached for the other.

"Ah, I see you truly are Dynian!"

Kier reddened to the ears. How could she know he bore the Dynian mark? He glanced down to where his breeches had sagged low about his hip bones. Blazes, they weren't *that* low. What was she staring at? "Only part," he managed.

Llydia recognized his discomfiture. "Your chest," she hastened. "You are fair. I'm told Tiernai men are—darker..." She trailed off awkwardly. "I have to go."

"No, wait!" Kier tugged the shirt on over his head. "You spoke of JonMarc. Where is he?"

"Closeted with my brother and the War Council. They've questioned him since early this morning—and he with barely two hours sleep since we fought our way out of Ruthland."

Ruthland? So JonMarc had rescued Llydia Branwyn from the Connails. And, as the girl was privy to his lack of sleep, Kier presumed he also shared her bed.

"I cannot stay," said Llydia. "There are wounded to be tended." She drew the hood back over her head.

"But I have questions..."

"They will wait." Llydia glanced at him over her shoulder, her eyes not unfriendly. "I'll return in a while with your supper. Then you may ask all the questions you like."

It was more than a while. Alone with his thoughts, Kier fretted and chafed and paced the earthen floor. Questions tore at him like harpies. What had become of Cari? Through all the turmoil of the prince's capture, she had seldom left his thoughts. Yet he'd had no word of her since JonMarc rode to her rescue. His companion had evidently returned unharmed. That raised his hopes that she was safe. Yet, had she been compromised by the Branwyn warrior, or... JonMarc?

Kier recalled his cousin's wistful expression when she gazed upon JonMarc. She'd never looked at *him* that way. What could the Dynian be to her? Some romantic fantasy; the reflection of a distant, brazen world she could never know. It was hardly her fault JonMarc encouraged her attentions; he did that with every woman he met. The very idea of counting Cari among his companion's random conquests left Kier livid.

And why did the Branwyns still guard him? With Rhynion in his charge, he'd actually welcomed Ross's protection from frothing fanatics like Dai Caydyn. Kier had kept the boy with him always and would not sleep until Rhynion lay sheltered at his side. Now, the guard's presence only reminded him how completely he'd failed.

Outside, the sky faded toward dusk and the rain turned to snow. Restless and bored beyond measure, Kier sat with a blanket around him and watched the lacy crystals drift down from the chimney hole to melt in a muddy puddle. Llydia had forgotten him. Kier began to contemplate escape—and blast the consequences—when at last there came a staccato tapping at the door. At least this time the girl had thought to knock. "Come!" he said.

The door swung wide, but it was JonMarc who entered, shaking snow from his hunched shoulders. He sniffed and wiped his nose on his sleeve, then squatted before the fire to warm his hands. He glanced back over his shoulder. "How do you feel?"

Kier merely snorted, his relief at seeing his friend overborne by maddening impatience. "Why am I still kept prisoner?"

JonMarc seemed to select his words carefully. "The Tiernai have put a price on your head."

He need say no more. Kier understood. The Council wanted him back to pay for his failure—as if there could be any greater punishment than bearing the terrible guilt of Rhynion's death. "Does Ross Branwyn keep me *from* them, or *for* them?"

JonMarc looked uneasy. "The Branwyn demands of the Council all fell through when the prince was killed."

"So I'm their only bargaining tool."

JonMarc nodded grimly. "But if Gaelin got through to Duke Edmund with my message, it's only a matter of time before they arrange to have you freed. Ross is still willing to negotiate."

Kier turned away. The irony was infuriating. That he, who had been raised among the Dynian, should remain their prisoner, while JonMarc, an outsider who didn't even speak their language, was free to wander as he chose. He'd even taken to wearing a leather brow band, such as the Branwyns wore. "So you're now a confidant of Ross Branwyn's, are you?"

"He only questioned me about Ruthland and my escape with Llydia. Did she tell you of that?"

"She mentioned it. I'll give you this, JonMarc: you're a great rescuer of women. Are they all expected to show their gratitude in the same way?"

JonMarc's fair brows narrowed. "What's that supposed to mean?"

"You know bloody well. What happened to Cari?"

"She's safe at Caerllyn. I took her there myself." JonMarc's expression reflected a subtle change when he spoke of Cari.

Kier saw in it what he expected to see. "How long were you out there alone with her?"

JonMarc's eyes flashed. "I told you, she's unharmed. Blazes, I should think you'd be grateful I got her back safely."

Kier was grateful. Immensely so. He had no chance to voice it.

"Here," JonMarc said, tossing Kier's crest-ring and sheathed dagger onto the bed. "I didn't want Llydia to find the weapon when she tended your hand. You might need it."

Kier picked up the crest-ring. He'd thought it lost for good. He ran his finger over the gold letters: *Duál et Onóir*. Duty and Honor. Guilt lanced him and he handed it back. "Keep it," he said. "Sell it, if you want. It's meaningless now." He turned away before JonMarc could see the moisture again welling in his eyes. "Gods, I wish I'd never returned to this festering land. At least Rhynion would be alive."

"Kier, quit blaming yourself. Táranos's scheme was well planned. I overheard the plot at Ruthland and I *still* couldn't prevent it. What more could you possibly have done?"

"I don't know." Kier drove an impatient fist into his thigh. "Something. *Anything.*" He tried to imagine some way he could have used his sinistral powers to pinpoint the threat and protect Rhynion. In truth, the atmosphere around the Spire had been so charged with hostility his senses had been unable to differentiate one peril from another.

"Look, no one expects you to be infallible—except *you*. Why don't you climb down off that sacred mountain of yours and join the rest of us mere mortals?"

Kier reddened.

"Oh, what's the use?" said JonMarc, before he could reply. "There's no point trying to reason with you; you're as stubborn as your cousin." Kier scarcely had time to wonder what he meant by that. JonMarc tossed the crest ring back to him and opened the door to leave, only to come face to face with Llydia, entering. "You talk to him," he said, stalking out. "He won't listen to me."

Kier felt a cold blast as Llydia shut the door behind her. Now that she'd finally come, he preferred to be alone; or maybe he didn't. Blazes, he didn't know what he wanted.

"What's the matter?" Llydia asked.

Kier rested elbows on his knees and studied the ground. "I'm sick of talking about it."

Llydia did not probe further, which rather surprised him. Even Cari, whom he prized above all women, could be a great wheedler of information when she wanted to be. "Here's your supper," Llydia said, laying the contents of a fair sized basket on the stool beside him. "The broth is good; I made it myself. And there's cheese and bread—"

"I'm not hungry."

Llydia did not chide him or cajole. She simply stood there, silent, until finally Kier raised his eyes to see what she was up to. Then her face went smug. "I knew I could get you to look at me. Now come and eat, before anger burns a hole in your belly. When you finish, I have news."

"What news?" Kier asked, trying not to reveal how sheepish he felt. "Eat!"

Kier gave in. He discovered he was hungrier than he'd thought, having had nothing since yestermorn. Llydia watched him with knowing blue eyes that seemed to hold a million secrets just below the surface. Kier found her rather pretty, in a buxom sort of way; far different from the willowy Cariwyn—but then, he'd never known JonMarc to discriminate. Kier felt sudden envy for the ease with which his companion related to women. He put it aside; such things could never be, for him.

"So, what's your news?" he asked, when he'd reached the slowing down point.

"My brother summons you to the sitting of Cyngor tonight."

"*Cyngor?*" The High Council of the Dynian seldom welcomed outsiders. They hadn't even invited Rhynion. Suddenly wary, he said, "You're sure you're not mistaking me for JonMarc?"

Llydia's eyes tracked boldly over his torso and her lips twitched as she repressed a smile. "I don't think so."

She was teasing him. It irked Kier that she couldn't be serious. Yet a part of him felt oddly flattered. "Why does he want *me*? These past few days, he's treated me like excess baggage."

Llydia shrugged. "My brother keeps his own counsel. Shall I tell him you do not wish to come?"

"No!" The invitation represented his first chance to get some real news. Kier wasn't about to pass that up. "When do we go?"

"As soon as you're ready."

Ready? Devoreth's blood, she had no idea how ready he was.

Llydia led him through the slushy streets to the rear of the settlement. High cliffs ringed Dorcalon on three sides, their sheer faces looming wet and black as slabbed obsidian. As they neared one rock wall, Kier discovered it was not the solid barrier it appeared. At the western corner, a nearly invisible cleft provided a passageway that must lead right into the mountain. A pair of sentries stood before it. "These two will guide you to the sacred hall," said Llydia.

"But, aren't you coming?"

"I will follow shortly." Llydia hurried off before he could question further.

The sentries motioned Kier between them. They looked surprisingly young for guard duty—scarcely into their teens. It made Kier wonder what casualties the Branwyns had sustained at the Spire, to have to rely on children to stand watch.

One of the "children" jabbed a quarterstaff in his ribs. "Move, Tiernai dog," he snarled.

Kier checked his temper. The pair had probably never seen a halfblood before. In their eyes, he was the enemy. It frustrated him that his few fair features, so instantly apparent to the Tiernai, became equally invisible to the race of his youth.

They led him through a narrow passage between the steep cliff walls. After several minutes' climb, the path snaked to the right at the brink of a wide chasm and continued on, hugging the edge of the drop. With but a single bobbing torch to light the way, Kier found the narrowness of the slippery trail, and the gusting wind, disconcerting. He could not judge the chasm's depth, though at rare moments when the wind paused, he heard the rush of churning water far below. At one point, he spied what appeared to be the start of a path, plunging downward. A postern? That would satisfy his conviction that a fortress as well designed as Dorcalon must have an escape route.

The youths left him, without a word, at the torch-flanked entrance to a cave. From there, another guard, equally taciturn, escorted him into a virtual catacomb of chill, musty tunnels that delved into the very heart of this, the Dynian sacred mountain.

The Caverns of Dorcalon. Kier had heard of them as a boy, spoken of with reverence and dread. It was said that anyone unfortunate enough to become entangled in the endless maze was doomed to grope in darkness until the Death Hag snatched away his soul. The deepest of the passages were known only to the Holy Elders—those who possessed the *sight*.

To Kier's relief, he was not taken nearly so far, only to a small chamber off the main tunnel. JonMarc was already there, having obviously been invited as well. He sat with his back to the wall, arms encircling his knees. His uneasiness in these eerie surroundings shone in his eyes.

Kier settled opposite him and, for a time, neither spoke. Then, as if haunted by the awkward silence, they both blurted their words at once. Kier began again, at his friend's nod.

"JonMarc, what I said before—I didn't..."

JonMarc dismissed it with a wave. He glanced anxiously about the chamber. "What do you know of this—this *Cyngor* we've been summoned to?" His words echoed off the rocky walls.

"It's the ruling council of the Dynian."

"But I thought Ross Branwyn ruled the Dynian."

"In a practical sense, he does. Yet the duties of War Chieftain have only existed since the Tiernai invasion. Before that, Alcor was ruled by Cyngor, and its chosen representative, the High King. But the last High King was murdered by the Tiernai; you've heard the tale. Since then, the War Chieftain has taken his place. As I understand it, Cyngor now meets only at times of major upheaval, like the death of..." Guilt again wrenched Kier and he trailed off.

They heard the rustle and patter of footsteps approaching down the corridor. JonMarc crept to the doorway just as a litter passed, bearing a cowled figure. "Who was that?" he asked the rugged youth guarding them. The fellow didn't understand his words. JonMarc rephrased the query in the best Dynian he could manage. It came out: "*Who him am carry?*" Kier chuckled, wondering how JonMarc would fare tonight, for it was said Cyngor conducted business in no language but its own.

JonMarc carried the guard's answer back with him. "What's *Émam Nácian Dynian?*"

Kier's brows arched in surprise. "Literally, the Birth Mother of the Dynian. The matriarch."

"So women are allowed at Cyngor?"

"More than allowed. Women are the power of the Dynian—or were, until the Tiernai came. I'm not sure how it stands now..."

Their guard poked his head around the corner and gestured for JonMarc to follow him. Kier, too, scrambled to his feet. "Sit, Tiernai," the fellow said. "You are not yet summoned."

Kier fumed. He was fuming still, a half-hour later, when a commotion in the tunnel roused him. A breathless Ross Branwyn poked his head into the chamber. "Fitzmorwen, come with me," he barked. Kier followed at a run.

The sentries at the entrance to the sacred hall leapt to attention as their leader thrust his way in. But their quarterstaves crossed with a clack in front of Kier. Ross cuffed one aside. "Cannot you see he's with me?" He ushered Kier into the chamber.

Kier barely repressed a gasp. The cavern's walls and ceiling, lit by some five score candles, were encrusted with thousands upon thousands of luminous magien crystals: shimmering clusters of purple, brown, pink and gold, that clung to the rock face like flowing pillows of many-faceted ladymoss. Their very power seemed to steal his breath away. His sinistral senses felt keener, more alert than ever before. Only with effort did he shift his attention from the dazzling display above to the dour company seated on the ground before him.

A few faces he recognized. JonMarc sat beside Llydia, opposite a semi-circle of robed figures. Right now, his eyes, like all the rest, were turned toward the newcomers.

"Ross Branwyn," said an elderly man, robed in gray. He was seated near the center of the semi-circle in what Kier judged a place of prominence. "Why do you come late to Cyngor?"

"Why do you start without me, Terryd Rhys?" Ross countered, bristling. Like Rhys, he used the Dynian tongue. "My spies have just returned from the eastern borders. Does it mean naught to you that the Tiernai now send their entire force against us?"

Small hairs prickled Kier's neck. The murmured undercurrent that rippled through the gathering told him he was not alone.

"That is not news," Terryd Rhys replied bitterly. "When do the Tiernai *not* attack? Yet these doings are the charge of the War Council, not Cyngor." He looked at Kier as though noticing him for the first time, and his voice grew stern. "Why do you bring one of *their* kind among us? No man but those proved so in the sacred rite of *Ym Torrath* may come before Cyngor."

"I *am* so proved," Kier broke in, wondering how JonMarc had escaped that proscription. He guessed the answer. Since JonMarc *looked* Dynian, no one had even bothered to ask whether he'd actually come of age among them.

"I bring him because I wish him to join us," said Ross. "Fitzmorwen has vital knowledge of the Tiernai legions. If this is not of interest to Cyngor, then Cyngor's interest is misplaced."

Kier scarcely heard Rhys's angry rebuttal. "You know I can't betray my allegiance," he said Ross Branwyn's ear. "I still serve the king."

"Be not so sure," Ross growled through the corner of his mouth. Then louder, in response to Rhys's challenge: "Word has reached us this night. The Tiernai king, Brendan, is dead."

Kier felt the blood drain from his face.

"Malcolm Morwensen now rules Alcor, though it is our enemies, the Connails, who hold true power. All who oppose them are imprisoned: Edmund of Hlanneth, and our old adversary, Sir Donal. Aran Connail

now commands the Legion, and the force he leads against us is the greatest
we have faced in fifty years." He half-turned toward Kier. "Who will you
support now, Fitzmorwen—the Tiernai, who seek your blood? Or us?"

"Enough of this!"

Kier's eyes leaped. The voice was crinkled and thin, yet strong
enough to carry with ease through the rocky chamber. It belonged to the
Émam Nácia. She sat in a low chair at the center of the half-circle, beside
Terryd Rhys who, despite his years, appeared young by comparison. The
matriarch's shrunken form was robed in white, and a deep cowl shaded her
eyes. "Ross Branwyn, you have entered the sanctum—the holy womb of the
Goddess Denia. You will perform the ritual cleansing, as demanded of all
males who enter Her sacred body. Then you will *sit*."

Ross glowered. "Ritual. Is that all that matters here? What good is ritual
when our people face annihilation? Will Blessed Denia arm our men, or
protect our walls with thunderbolts?"

"You dare to blaspheme...?" exclaimed Terryd Rhys.

The Émam Nácia raised a wrinkled hand and Rhys went still. "You ask
an eternal question, Ross Branwyn. We Dynian are the Children of the
Goddess, called to her service generations ago. Without Her ritual we are
already extinct—no better than the Tiernai, who leave matters of faith to
their priests, and feel it not in their daily lives. Would you have us become
what we fight against?"

Ross grudgingly conceded. Together, he and Kier knelt before a low
altar and performed the required obeisance: a trickle of blood from their
left wrists, mixed with a chalky cave secretion referred to as *Denia's Milk*,
then applied in a line down the middle of their foreheads. As Kier took his
seat on the floor beside JonMarc, he noted that all the men in the chamber,
including his friend, wore a similar mark, though the women did not.

"As for you, Fitzmorwen," said Terryd Rhys, "you are come to this
sacred hall at the bidding of a member of Cyngor. Are you prepared to
show proof you have indeed been tested and bear the mark of Dynian
manhood?"

"I am," said Kier.

"But Fitzmorwen is our enemy!" cried a robed figure at the far end of
the semi-circle. Kier recognized the ever-contentious Dai Caydyn. "To
let him remain is an insult to the wisdom and valor of all of us elected to
Cyngor."

Another member stirred at that, a hardy veteran of middle years, with a creased and war-ravaged face. "How do you include yourself in that tally, Dai? *You* were not elected. You but sit in the place of your uncle, who lies wounded. Save your pious rantings for those who may be impressed by them." His keen grey eyes scanned the company. Ally, or foe? Kier wondered. So far as he knew, the man had no cause to be either.

"I know Fitzmorwen only by reputation," the veteran said, "yet I stood witness the day he came of age. That, I recall clearly, for he impressed me with his courage and resolve. He endured the sacred cutting without any outcry—which is more than can be said of others I've witnessed." He aimed a telling glance at Dai. "His ordeal binds him to us in a way no loyalty oath ever could. I say, let him remain. A man cannot prove himself trustworthy unless he is first trusted."

The vote was taken—an informal affair of nodded heads, with only Dai Caydyn's dissension. When it ended, Kier held himself a little straighter.

"It has been charged," said Terryd Rhys, "that because Cyngor does not concern itself with matters of war, its interest is misplaced. That is untrue. Ross Branwyn warns of impending peril, and of course this is of gravest concern. Yet there are other powers at work, beyond armies and politics. These are the matters Cyngor must address." The gray-haired Rhys cast his eyes over the gathering. "Our prophets tell us that endings are also beginnings, and that such an ending is at hand for the Dynian. They speak of sacred portents that, one by one, now come to pass. The Wanderer of the heavens, called in ages past the *Death Seer*, is again come amongst us, heralding change for the Children of Denia. Soon, it will conjoin with the sacred *Life Star*, and when that happens, legend tells us, a world will end. So spoke the prophetess Morganwy, in ages past:

> *And at that time, a great Power shall re-awaken,*
> *and to the Children of the Mother will return a Hero:*
> *Born of the line of Kings;*
> *Bred of the Dynian, yet sundered from them.*
> *And he shall bear the Sword of his Fathers."*

Terryd Rhys lifted a fur coverlet before him and slipped his palms beneath the treasure it concealed. He held it up. "Behold, the Sword of the Telynors, ancient treasure of the High Kings. For two generations it was lost to us, but now, in fulfillment of prophecy, it has returned."

There were murmurs of astonishment as members of Cyngor craned their necks to see. Yet no eyes grew wider than JonMarc's. "That's my sword!" he blurted in the common speech.

Silence followed, and glares. "You will not profane the Hallows with the use of a heathen tongue," declared Terryd Rhys.

Kier hastened to JonMarc's defense. "I apologize for my friend. Yet surely Cyngor must have realized that JonMarc was not raised on Alcor and speaks no Dynian."

Rhys looked startled. Apparently Ross Branwyn had not provided that information. Nor had Llydia. The latter surprised Kier, for if JonMarc now shared her bed, she must also know he did not meet the most basic requirement for male attendance at Cyngor.

"If the stranger is not of Alcor, how did he acquire the sword?" asked Rhys.

"I gave it to him. And I cannot believe it is truly the weapon you seek. This sword has been in my family for generations. It belonged to my grandsire."

"And who was he?"

"I—don't know. A warrior of the Dynian, killed in battle; that much I was told. My granddam retrieved the sword from the battlefield, and my mother passed it to me."

The Émam Nácia raised her head. Her cowl had fallen back, revealing thin hair the color of winter snows, trussed back in a silver band, and sightless, milky-white orbs that bespoke deep wisdom despite their fixed stare. She leaned over and whispered to Rhys. He nodded. "What is your name?" he asked.

Kier's brow furrowed. "Kier Fitzmorwen."

"That is what the Tiernai call you. I ask your *true* name."

"Kier Gareth-Alyn," Kier amended, wondering what they were getting at.

"The female form being *Allyn*—your mother. And by tradition, the other name keeps alive the memory of one who is gone. Your grandsire?"

"I—believe so," said Kier. That brought more whispers between the two senior members.

"Kier Gareth-Alyn," said the Émam Nácia, "kneel before me."

Kier did. The hand that reached out to him had a dry surface like crumpled parchment. Kier shut his eyes and let the aged matriarch touch his face. He opened them like a shot when he realized her true intention was to touch his mind. The Émam Nácia possessed Fithlon skills!

Kier's stomach writhed. Her powers of mind were potent—far stronger than his own. He could block them no more easily than Gwythion's. He did not try, though it ripped him apart to have his innermost secrets laid naked to a woman.

The Mother of the Dynian sought within his memory, unmindful of his torment. When finished, she seemed well pleased. "It is true," she said. "The sword's authenticity can no longer be in doubt. It is indeed the Sword of the Telynors, passed down from one High King to the next, for generations beyond count. The last to bear it into battle was my own son, Gareth Branwyn—your grandsire. From the day of his death until now, the sword has been lost to us. But now it is returned, and the prophecy fulfilled."

Kier nearly choked. Gareth Branwyn, the Tiernai's most relentless foe, his grandsire? If Duke Morwen ever knew that, he'd wisely kept it to himself. Word of such a connection would have ruined Kier's career, and might even have cost him his life.

"Part of the prophecy may be fulfilled," said Ross, "yet it also speaks of a hero's return. Fitzmorwen is no hero to the Dynian. Why, he does not even look Dynian."

"Nor did any of the Dynian heroes," Terryd Rhys reminded him. "Our legends tell that each of the five was dark-featured."

Ross frowned. "Nonetheless, there can be no doubt the hero foretold is my father, Glyn: Gareth Branwyn's true son. How the sword arrived before him, I do not know, but I shall await *his* return before I count the prophecy fulfilled."

"Your father will not return," Kier said quietly. "He is dead."

Ross Branwyn stared hard at him. "What lie is this? All know Glyn Branwyn travels the far lands of the Deg Tirith, gathering arms and allies for our cause."

"It's no lie. How long is it since you've had word from your father? Four years ago, the Connails captured him and secretly paid Syrmian slavers to deliver him to the calstone quarries on Vilsolia. The *Death Quarries*, they are called. There, he was killed while trying to escape."

Ross paled. "How do you know this when we ourselves have heard naught?"

"Sir Donal wished it kept secret lest it inflame passions and start the war anew. Yet it can do no harm to tell you now. Sir Donal has ever distrusted the Connails. He learned of their deed and ordered me to Vilsolia to discover the truth. By the time I arrived, Glyn Branwyn was already dead. Yet not so long that I, who had seen him in life, could not identify his remains."

Ross Branwyn was having trouble maintaining his control. "Inflame passions? Aye, it surely would have! Yet Glyn Branwyn was my father. It was my *right* to know." He paused to rein in his temper. "Have you proof of this?"

Kier shook his head. "None but my own eyes."

JonMarc was fairly aching to speak. For nearly an hour he'd sat, barely comprehending, until two realizations came to him: If he ceased to concentrate on words and let his mind relax, he could pick up the gist of what was being said. He had no idea why this worked, it just did. And if he needed a more precise translation, he could tap Llydia's mind and read her perceptions of what was happening. If she recognized the intrusion, she seemed not to mind.

Yet neither scheme would allow him to formulate his own contributions into words acceptable to Cyngor. Even a translator would not help, for, as Llydia's understanding told him, simply to utter his non-Dynian syllables to such a person would be considered sacrilege. JonMarc tried to communicate his desperation to Kier, but ever since his friend had knelt before the Émam Nácia, his mind had shut tighter than a colloch shell. Llydia was his only hope.

At first, the girl seemed startled as he placed his thought in her mind. She eyed him questioningly, then nodded. "Reverend Mother," she said, "the stranger, JonMarc, knows something of this matter. He would have me voice his thoughts—as you use my eyes to see with."

The Émam Nácia cocked her head, intrigued. "Then let those thoughts be known."

Llydia began to recount the message she heard in her mind, haltingly at first, then with greater surety. "He says—he was imprisoned in the Death Quarries at the time Kier spoke of. When another of Dynian race arrived, he sought JonMarc out as an ally, to plan escape. JonMarc says he agreed to the scheme, but later learned the guards had set a trap. He tried to warn his companion but—too late. They loosed their hounds upon..." Llydia froze. "No, JonMarc, *please!*. I don't want to see it through your memory. Glyn Branwyn was my father, too."

JonMarc reached for her, aghast. He'd been so intent on making himself heard, he hadn't considered how Llydia might react to his tale.

"You say that is how he died?" her brother demanded, switching to the common speech. "They set attack dogs on him?" JonMarc gave a sharp nod. Ross Branwyn regarded him with scorn. "And why did you, his *ally*, not share that fate?"

JonMarc shot him a seething glance, then responded aloud. "If you think I betrayed him, you're wrong. Your father betrayed himself. He was reckless; bent on escape—or martyrdom. I'd already survived two years in that accursed filth hole. I had no wish to die for nothing."

Few but Ross heard his answer above the din that arose over the exchange. Terryd Rhys shouted for quiet. He'd have expelled them both, had the Émam Nácia not stayed him.

"This news changes nothing," declared Ross, again in Dynian. "If my father, its true heir, is dead, then the sword should come to me. I, at least, have proved my valor by leading the Dynian in battle. With the sword of the High Kings before us, think what havoc we may wreak against the Tiernai. Clearly it has returned for that very purpose."

His declaration met with enthusiastic support from much of the gathering. Once again, the Émam Nácia intervened. Her frail body rocked with passion as she drew herself up and pointed a bony finger. "Ross Branwyn, again you show that your ardor for battle is greater than your knowledge of what you defend. Were we Tiernai, then indeed the sword would be yours. But among the Dynian, your inheritance derives from your mother, as you know well, and will go to your sister's son, not your own. It is Llydia that bears the Branwyn line. As for Kier Gareth-Alyn, he received the sword from his mother, and she from hers. It belongs to him."

"But Fitzmorwen is a bastard," protested Dai Caydyn. "And so was his mother—a witch and outcast, stoned to death for summoning pestilence upon her village. If right to the sword be determined so, it should come to *me*, for I am descended of Gareth Branwyn's true wife, and also bear the blood of Telynor High Kings. And my valor is no less than Ross's."

"And your knowledge is no greater," said the Émam Nácia, "for like him, you speak in our enemy's terms. Alas for the Dynian, when their own sons forget the foundations that make them a people. 'Tis the Tiernai who require a vow of marriage to prove the heirs of a man's property are also the heirs of his body. When descent is measured through the mother, what need to prove fatherhood? As for your Telynor blood, Dai Caydyn, it earns you nothing. All the true heirs of the Telynor line are dead. From a distance, all claims are equal. The sword has come to Kier Gareth-Alyn, and by him, and him alone, is the prophecy fulfilled."

Kier slowly shook his head. He was sick to death of being prophecy's pawn. "But I gave the sword to JonMarc."

The Émam Nácia looked pensive. "It is true," she admitted at last. "If the sword was a freely-given gift, it must belong to the outlander. And he does possess *talents* to a measure I've not felt for many years—not since the days of Jaimie Telynor, before his tragedy took him from us." The Émam Nácia went silent.

"Yet that one can tell us nothing of himself," Ross protested. "A former slave, with no family, no name. He doesn't even speak our tongue. Do the Dynian seek heroes from such as this?"

"Then how do we unravel this riddle?" asked Terryd Rhys. "The candles burn low, and still we are no closer to an answer."

"Why hurry?" said Ross. "I say we hold them both as bargaining tools."

"You cannot bargain with the Connails," argued the veteran who'd earlier defended Kier.

"Why not? So long as we hold something they want, we may at least buy ourselves time."

"Or bring them down on us that much quicker."

"But we cannot stay here," Kier protested. "We've a mission to perform for the Fithlon."

"What mission?" asked Terryd Rhys.

Kier scanned the faces of the Cyngor members. Roderig might not be Táranos's only agent among the Dynian. "I cannot speak of it here, yet it, too, deals with a matter of prophecy. Master Gwythion is no stranger to you. Ask him. He should arrive here any day now. He'll tell you the *Death Seer* portends doom for more than just the Dynian." Kier glanced at the Émam Nácia, hoping she might take his side, but the aged matriarch had dozed off. "The *Death Seer's* conjunction with the *Life Star* will soon occur. JonMarc and I must leave."

"Impossible," said Rhys. "With the enemy marching against our gates, none may leave Dorcalon, least of all the two of you; certainly not before Cyngor determines which of you is the foretold hero. That cannot be tonight, for the Émam Nácia is wearied."

"Aye," said Dai Caydyn, "these two should remain under guard—especially Fitzmorwen, who makes no secret of his loyalty to the Tiernai. Like enough, he is their spy."

His words struck a desperate chord. The Cyngor members agreed that Kier alone would be held in confinement until a decision could be reached. The timing of that would depend on the Émam Nácia. The frail matriarch had to be carried from the hall, asleep in her chair. Dai slipped out behind her.

"Of all the cursed luck," Kier sputtered. He and JonMarc had managed a few moments privacy by walking some paces ahead of the guards. "*Days*, they said. We haven't got days! Why doesn't Gwythion show up and explain it to them? They'd listen to him."

They reached the hut where Kier was to be held. No guard had yet been posted. Kier lit a taper from JonMarc's torch and clapped his friend on the shoulder. "I'll see you in the morning," he said, and ducked inside. The door shut with a thud.

Kier's senses instantly warned him something was amiss. He spun, reaching for the sword no longer at his hip. A face leered at him through the candlelight. Then a bludgeon struck the side of his head and he crumpled.

Chapter Thirty

"*Kier!*" JonMarc's sharp whisper startled the elderly guard snoring in his seat beside the hut's entrance. The man jerked upright, fumbling for his sword. JonMarc calmed him with an upraised hand and rapped on the door. "Kier, are you all right?"

Silence. High above, the star-spattered sky wheeled toward morning, perhaps three hours off. JonMarc knocked again, and again received no answer. He threw the bolt and let himself in.

The light from his lantern swept the room. "Ghedrev's cods," he groaned when he saw Kier's prone form sprawled across the floor. He knelt; pressed fingers to his friend's neck. The only pulse he felt was his own, and it was racing. He rolled Kier over and laid an ear to his chest, then breathed relief.

Clotted blood smeared the side of Kier's face and matted his black hair. More darkened the mud beneath his head. JonMarc glared at the sentry, who had followed him in. "He's been like this for hours! Didn't you think to check on him?" The man did not understand. JonMarc pointed to a pewter basin. "Fill that." The flustered guardsman hesitated, uncertain. "*Now.*"

Eyes bulging, the guard snatched up the basin and hurried out.

JonMarc rolled up a blanket to cushion Kier's head and ran his hands over the rest of him. No broken bones. Yet another discovery renewed his urgency. He shook Kier's shoulder.

Kier groaned. A moment later his eyes fluttered open. "JonMarc?" He tried to rise, but instantly rejected the idea. The room whirled like a waterspout. "How did I...?" Kier suddenly recalled the intruder. He touched his scalp. "Blazes, he must've hit me with an oak bough."

The guard returned and set a brimming basin on the floor. JonMarc waved him off. He soaked a rag and pressed it to Kier's temple. "Did you see who it was?"

Kier winced. He was having trouble keeping his attention focused. "Aye," he said, taking over pressure on the rag. "Dai Caydyn. I've suspected that he—" Kier's hand flew to his belt, where he kept the Amulet hidden.

"It's gone," said JonMarc.

Kier dragged himself upright. "Then we've got to get after him. If Dai serves Táranos..." The room began to sway again and he dropped back. "What made you think to come check on me?"

"Gwythion's arrived in Menythgar. When he couldn't touch your mind, he contacted me."

Kier shut his eyes. He recalled sensing Gwythion's summons through murky dreams, but he'd been powerless to answer. He held the cloth to his brow, feeling humiliated.

"Stay still; you've lost a fair bit of blood. I'll go check the gates to see when Dai left."

The door slammed shut behind him. Kier pulled himself up onto the edge of the bed.

The Amulet was gone; the Cábretaur's key, entrusted to his care. Again, he'd failed. And if Dai Caydyn succeeded in getting it to Táranos, that failure could mean the ruin of all he knew.

Kier cradled his head in his hands, feeling devastated; alone. Loneliness was no stranger; it had been his companion most of his life. Yet never was there loneliness like this. This was a desolation of the soul, an emptiness that left no hope, no dignity, only bitter self-recrimination that did not fill the void, but only left it more empty.

Kier fingered the gold-hilted dagger at his wrist. It had been a gift from his father at his coming-of-age, and meant much, bestowed by the man Kier admired above all others. Duke Morwen had seen great things in his son's future. How wrong he'd been. Alcor's Iron Duke, the chronicles would say, had sired two sons. One was to become a king. The other...?

Kier stared at the muddy floor. He'd let his father down, as he had Sir Donal, who'd always had faith in him. And Rhynion, who trusted him with his young life. And his mother. And now Gwythion. He'd failed them all. And the world had no use for failures. One less would be a blessing. Kier drew the blade from its sheath. He'd always loved this deadly toy for its shininess and secret dependability. It had ever been a friend to him when he'd had no others. It could be a friend now...

The hut door burst open. Kier jumped and the dagger fell. For an instant it flashed back the gleam of JonMarc's lantern. Kier hastily retrieved it and slipped it into his sleeve.

"Dai hasn't been seen." JonMarc's voice caught as he reasoned what Kier had been up to. "Maybe... he hasn't left yet. Maybe..."

"He's gone," said Kier. "He probably used the rear exit."

"How do you know there's a rear exit?"

"I spied the path last night, on the way to the caverns. It headed west—the direction Dai must take if he's to deliver the Amulet to his Master. Táranos is either at his fortress in Anlawth, or at Cymworth—or somewhere between. Whichever it is, it lies west of here."

"Dai might as easily deliver it to the Connails. They're a lot closer. You can see their watch fires from the gates."

Kier shook his head. "Dai Caydyn and the Connails may serve the same Master, but I sincerely doubt they're allies. Like as not, they don't even know about each other. Roderig's acted as Táranos's agent in both camps. Even if Dai was told to bring the Amulet to him, it still has to get to their Master—and that route lies westward."

JonMarc rubbed his chill hands together. "Then we'd best get going. Gwythion said he'd meet us at Cymworth in three days. We've that long to find the Cábretaur. You feeling any better?"

"Aye," Kier lied. He struggled to his feet, waving off JonMarc's assistance, and steadied himself against the wall. "What about the guard?"

"Asleep." JonMarc offered a telling wink and handed Kier the man's sword.

They made their way around the edge of the fortress, keeping to the shadow of the defense wall. Despite the hour, the tension in the air was palpable. In the aftermath of battle, with besiegers within sight, even those who slept did so fitfully. In some nearby hut, an infant squalled. Dogs growled their watchfulness as sentries hurried by with the clank of arms.

A brisk breeze had beaten back the clouds, and the waxing sphere of Denia's moon rode low in the west, a precious pearl on a gem-spangled cushion. Yet more worthy of wonder was the newcomer to the skies—the Death Seer, directly overhead, its wraithlike mantle trailing behind it like a shroud of the undead. Kier measured its distance from the Life Star. When the two converged, the fate of the world would be decided. *Three days.*

The entrance to the passage through the mountain was still guarded. "We'll have to disable them somehow, before they can cry an alarm," said Kier. "I'll creep up on the one to the left. You circle 'round and surprise the other." Shaky as he was, the task seemed daunting.

"Wait," JonMarc whispered. "Maybe I can lure them off." He gripped his charmstone.

Kier stared at him. "What makes you think...?" He swallowed the rest. A hooded figure was nearing the portal. As they watched, the newcomer traded words with the sentries. Then he beckoned and the pair followed him away, leaving their post deserted.

"Dai?" JonMarc ventured.

"Not unless he's shrunk." The inexplicable turn of fortune left Kier suspicious. He did not trust coincidence. Still, they'd be fools to throw away the opportunity. At his nod, they hastened for the opening.

Again, fortune seemed to be on their side. They made it to the gate, and through the narrow passage, without encountering anyone. Kier quickly located the path he'd seen earlier and, with caution, they eased their way down the rocky slope.

At one point, Kier hit a muddy patch and skidded some way on his feet before coming to a halt on a sandy platform. JonMarc had stopped there already. So had the path.

JonMarc uncovered his lantern and dangled it over the edge. The sound of churning water echoed, near at hand. "It's a dead end."

"It can't be. Why would they make a path that goes nowhere?"

"Well, it looks like a sheer drop to me. We'll have to go back up and find another route."

Kier glanced impatiently over the chasm rim. They hadn't time for this.

"Do not move, either of you!" The clear voice came from the blackness of the trail above.

Kier pressed himself to the cliff face, cursing. "Cover the light," he whispered.

Too late. An arrow hissed and the lantern flew from JonMarc's hand to clatter over the ledge.

"You have no permission to leave Dorcalon," their pursuer cried.

"I didn't know I needed it," JonMarc shouted back. "Who is that? Llydia?" As their eyes grew accustomed to the moonlit dark, they made out her slight form above them. "Look, we had no choice. We have a task—"

"I know. You told me of your quest, JonMarc, and though my brother does not believe in it, I do. Why else would I draw the sentries away?"

So that was it. "Then why hinder us now?" Kier demanded, his exasperation growing.

"Because you cannot find the way on your own. The secrets of the path are known only to the members of the two councils. You must take me with you."

Kier shot a glance at JonMarc. He was obviously the reason the girl followed. "Look, this is no springtide outing. You could be hurt..."

Another arrow zipped past. Kier jumped as it hit a stone near his foot and sent it skittering over the edge. "I can handle danger as well as either of you. And I'm not the one stranded on a cliff. Take me along, or remain there till my brother discovers you're missing and sends men to fetch you back."

Kier frowned. The last thing they needed was Ross Branwyn's sister tagging along. Yet they had no time to puzzle out the route on their own. Grudgingly, he jerked a nod. "Come, then."

Llydia wasted no time. She slid onto the platform, a bundle on her back, bow and quiver slung over her shoulder. She was still dressed as a boy, her long hair tucked up under a huntsman's cap.

"So how do we get down?" JonMarc asked.

Moonlight caught Llydia's smile. "There are foot and hand-holds cut into the rock." She dropped her bundle to the next level. They could dimly see it below, perhaps thrice man-height. Llydia slipped over the edge and made her way down as easily as a spider on a wall. "You'd best take off your boots and toss them down first," she called up to them. "And be sure to start with your left foot."

JonMarc followed easily enough. Kier took longer. His head still pounded and his balance was unsteady. He breathed profound relief when his bare feet touched the landing.

Llydia led them on a tortuous route along the edge of the ravine. They climbed up again, then down, squeezed through cracks and slithered beneath overhangs no higher than Kier's knees while water churned, invisible and menacing, over the rocks below.

The light grew as they made their way westward. Once or twice they found signs that someone traveled the path ahead of them. At one infrequent stop, Llydia pressed them about Táranos and the stolen Amulet.

"I wonder how long Dai has served such a master," she said. "'Tis true he was ever jealous of his standing among the Dynian, for he holds himself heir to the Telynor High Kings. Of late, he's spoken out loudly against the Tiernai incursions. Yet never was he wont to evil."

"He may not be now," said JonMarc. "If Táranos promised him victory for his people and the death of their enemies, as he did the Connails,

Dai may believe what he does in service to his Master will truly help the Dynian. He probably sees himself a hero."

Llydia gazed wistfully at the dawn-streaked hills. "Poor soul," she murmured, "to be so wickedly deceived."

By the second hour of daylight, the sheer walls of the ravine at last began to widen. The river, now a rushing torrent swollen with spring runoff, churned and boiled its way through a notch between the hills, tumbling beyond with a muffled roar to yet unseen depths. The cliff path ended in a rough stair of strewn boulders leading down to the water's edge.

Kier halted them at the brink and pointed. "I think we've found our thief."

Llydia laid a hand on his arm. "Let me go down first."

Dai was not having an easy time. He sat on a rock, muttering impatiently to himself, and did not notice Llydia until she stood a short way above him. His whole countenance brightened.

"Llydia! Thank the Lady. Come help me, girl. I think I've broke my leg."

Llydia carefully picked her way down the rude stair. The icy ground made the footing treacherous. Twice she slipped, sending stones tumbling before her.

"'Twas just such a misstep defeated me," Dai told her as a particularly large rock dislodged and clattered almost to the riverbank. "I've managed to splint the leg, but I cannot find a crutch. Help me down beyond yon hillock. A horse waits there—left by one who knows my mission."

"What mission is that?" Llydia asked.

"A way to defeat the Tiernai and save our people," said Dai, in a near whisper. "At last I've come by the means to buy us that power. Look you at this." Dai reached inside his jerkin and handed her the silver Amulet. The encrusted gems dazzled in the morning orblight.

Llydia turned it over in her hands. "This is not yours to bargain with, Dai."

His eager smile faded. "Of course it is. It's a relic, and so belongs to whoever claims it."

"Then I claim it," said Kier, climbing down the rocky stair with JonMarc behind. "And did so long before you laid hands on it, Caydyn."

Dai flashed Llydia a look of betrayal and tried to grab the Amulet back. She kept it from him. "Why did you bring them?" he cried. "Traitors! Scavengers! Go back to your Tiernai overlords."

Kier held out his hand. Llydia returned the Amulet to him.

"No!" Dai screamed, turning on her with venom. "So you're in league with them. Traitoress. You deny victory to your own people!"

"Dai, Táranos deceives you," said Kier. "He only uses you for his own purposes."

Dai spat. "What do you know? You, an avowed puppet of the Tiernai."

JonMarc crouched beside Dai's pack. "Kier, look," he said, lifting the golden sword.

"So, you sought to rob your people of that, too," Kier said.

Dai glared at him. "Why not? I am the prophesied hero. Only I can lead the Dynian to victory. *He* has promised it. Llydia, why do you take their side against me?"

"Dai," she said, kneeling beside him, "you're a brave man and a fine warrior. Why run off on this futile errand when you could be leading men against the Connails?"

"Futile? He has promised weapons to make us invincible; power such as we've never known. He only wishes to help us, and I've no cause to doubt him." Dai aimed Kier a spiteful glare. "After all, he managed the death of the Tiernai prince, despite this one's efforts to prevent it."

It was all JonMarc could do to hold Kier back. "It was the Connails who plotted that," he said. "I heard them. And they're the ones who profit by it. Your Master will give you nothing, Dai, for he has nothing to give—just words and false promises. When he's done with you—when you can't bring him what he wants—he'll toss you aside like yesterday's slops."

Doubt crept into Dai's pale eyes, to be quickly replaced by contempt. He braced himself against a boulder and brandished the stick Llydia had fashioned into a crutch. "You think I don't know what you're after, outlander? You, who pass yourself off as a Dynian hero. You wish to deliver it to him yourself. Well, it won't work. The Dynian will never follow you!"

"Come on, JonMarc," said Kier. "There's no point arguing. He's as far gone as my brother." He started back for the trail.

"But we cannot just leave him here, alone and injured," Llydia insisted.

"Why not? If he can't fend for himself till your brother's men arrive— and they must be well after us by now—then he's no warrior. Stay with him yourself, if you're so concerned."

"I need no one to coddle me," said Dai, struggling to stand. "Go with your new friends, Llydia. See where it leads you."

Llydia hesitated.

"Go on, wench! You think I crave your company? You've already ruined me."

"Dai, I—"

"*Go!*" he thundered, swinging the crutch at her.

Llydia turned and fled after the others.

When Kier glanced back, he saw that Dai had followed them a short way, hobbling like a pitiful beggar on his crutch. He perched upon the rocks, staring out over the thunderous falls, a fey gleam in his eyes. "You may bear it to him, Fitzmorwen," he cried, his words echoing off the chasm walls. "Yet you'll find your reward more bitter than you bargain for."

Kier ignored him and started down the rocky path beside the falls.

Only Llydia saw what happened next. Her scream brought the others running back.

JonMarc leaned over the ledge and shook his head. "I'll go down and see to him."

It was some time before he returned, sweaty and panting. "He only fell part of the way, before the rocks caught him and broke his back. He died quickly," he added, for Llydia's benefit. "I let the river take him. But I thought you might want these." JonMarc laid a ring and other small, personal items on the ground before Llydia. "And I found this," he murmured, handing Kier a blood-red crystal. "The token of his Master's service."

Kier nodded darkly. "Throw it in the river. If we take it, Táranos will use it to track us."

They easily found the mount Dai said would be waiting for him. There were, in fact, two horses—one saddled for riding, the other burdened with supplies. The latter greatly pleased JonMarc, who had rued the haste which forced them to escape Dorcalon without provender. To Kier, the unexpected good fortune of finding two horses when there should only have been one struck him as suspicious. Dai's final words weighed heavily on his mind.

They rode single file, with Llydia seated behind JonMarc on the saddled bay. It was well past dusk when they found a craggy hollow and made camp. At Kier's insistence, they set a watch, though they were all bone weary from the long trek through rugged terrain. Yet they did not know what agent of Táranos had delivered the horses for Dai's use, or where he might be now.

JonMarc claimed first watch and, for a time, Llydia sat with him, which further confirmed Kier's assumption about their relationship. He left them to it and drifted off to a much needed sleep.

Llydia sidled up to the fire and drew her cloak about her. "I saw Dai go over the cliff," she admitted quietly. "I lied when I said he slipped; it was what I wanted to believe."

JonMarc poked at the fire with a jointed stick. A billow of sparks flew up and vanished into the brisk, night air. "I know," he said. "I've seen the same with other servants of Táranos."

"But why do they take their own lives?"

"Because they fear their Master's wrath." JonMarc shut his eyes. "I experienced that wrath myself, at Ruthland. They're wise to fear it. It nearly killed me."

"Yet you fought to live. You are braver than Dai and those others."

JonMarc responded with a grim laugh. "I'm not brave, Llyd. Far from it."

"I don't believe that. I've seen the scars on your back, JonMarc. Only a brave man could endure such torture without flinching."

"Who told you I didn't flinch? Blazes, girl, don't go making me into some kind of hero. Truth is, I screamed like hell."

Llydia sought humor in his eyes, but found none.

"The only point to torture is to break a man down. The sooner you give them what they want, the sooner they get bored and quit. I've seen brave men flogged to death because they wouldn't cry out. What good did it do them? A corpse rots the same whether it belonged to a brave man or a coward."

"You are certainly no coward, JonMarc."

He shrugged. "I've been called one—by your father, in fact, when I wouldn't throw my life away, back in the Death Quarries."

"Then my father was wrong."

"Maybe. But I've done things I'm not proud of." JonMarc forced himself to smile, though sadly. "I kept myself alive. At the time, that's all that mattered."

Llydia sat with her knees drawn up to her chin. She rested her round, freckled face on her fists and stared at him with those probing blue eyes that reflected a depth of insight unusual in one so young. "Do you fear death, JonMarc?"

"Aye," he admitted frankly. "Oh, not of itself; we all have to die sometime. It's *not living* that scares me. I've been cheated out of half my life already. I don't want to lose the rest."

"What about Kier?"

JonMarc looked at his companion, lying curled in a blanket meant for Dai, and shook his head, recalling the scene he'd interrupted back at Dorcalon. "Sometimes I think he looks forward to it. What terrifies Kier is failing to live up to what he sees as his duty. Right now he blames himself for Prince Rhynion's death, and the guilt is eating him alive."

"You are concerned for him, then."

JonMarc avoided her eyes. "He's like a soldier who's foreseen his own end, yet marches to it anyway, unquestioning." JonMarc hesitated. An image flashed across his mind, and suddenly, with a chill that froze the blood, he realized he, too, had foreseen Kier's destruction. When had the vision come? At Ruthland? JonMarc fingered the serpent scar on his left hand. What if it was a true foreseeing and not just a product of his fire-madness?

Kier murmured something in restless dream and rolled over. JonMarc banished the image, fearing his companion might be picking up remnants of his own thoughts.

"You fear his vision of death is a true one," said Llydia. "You do not then believe Kier is the Dynian hero prophesied?"

The question took JonMarc aback. Llydia's probes were as sure as her arrows. "He may well be. He, or your brother. They're both fine warriors."

"What of you?"

JonMarc tried to laugh the notion off. "I told you, I'm no hero."

"You rescued me from Ruthland, when you might simply have escaped with your own life."

"That's different. I planned to use your rescue to buy myself status with the Tiernai."

"Yet you did not try to do so."

"I never had the chance." Llydia's lips crinkled in a knowing smile. Blast the girl. "Look, I don't *want* to be a hero—to the Dynian or anyone else. It's too much responsibility. I only want to live my life as I please for a change."

"Yet you follow Kier to an outcome that may spell doom for all of us."

"I follow Kier because I still owe him my life and I don't like being indebted." The smirk remained in Llydia's eyes. "But I only do it because I *choose* to; not in fulfillment of some moth-eaten prophecy. Kier's the one whose life is charted, not me. I'm my own man."

Llydia's gaze grew thoughtful. "Have it your way, JonMarc. Yet I will tell you this: Dai and my brother were mistaken. None of the five Dynian heroes was named so for his prowess in battle. Each won renown for the service he did the Dynian people. Your actions are your own, and they speak louder than any prophecy. Whether the title of hero be yours will be determined by what you *do*; it does not work the other way 'round."

They set out again at dawn, for many leagues lay between them and Cymworth. Thusfar, they had detected no sign of pursuit, yet deep inside, Kier had a feeling their coming was known. True, Dai had no chance to contact his Master after they found him on the trail. Yet one coincidence continued to plague Kier. According to Gwythion, they must reach Cymworth by tomorrow. On foot, such speed would be impossible. Were the horses and Dai's death all part of Aneryn's prophecy? And since Táranos knew of that prophecy, might they not be riding into a trap?

Of course, it was possible Táranos was still in Anlawth, waiting for Dai to deliver the Amulet. No Fithlon had the power to will himself from place to place. If Táranos miscalculated the hour of Conjunction—and without the unique instruments Gwythion had invented for himself, that was quite possible—he could not reach Cymworth in time, even if he left Anlawth today.

Kier knew such conjecture was futile; they could only go on. So far, he'd sensed no danger. But such musings helped take his mind off a more immediate predicament. Upon waking, he'd been told it was his turn to bear Llydia behind him on his horse. Kier balked. He'd never wanted the girl along. She obviously followed just to be near JonMarc, and so was his friend's responsibility. Kier was awkwardly conscious of her arms wrapped around his middle—and the rest of her, pressed against his back. He couldn't relax. That made the journey even more taxing.

Gradually, as the day wore on, the mountains gave way to hills, and the hills to rolling downs, shaggy with coarse grass. A salty tang in the air spoke of the sea.

They made camp before sundown in a sheltered hollow between two wind-sculpted dunes, close to fresh water, yet within echo of the breaking surf. Tomorrow, they need only journey north a few leagues to reach their destination. Camping here was Llydia's idea, though Kier heartily seconded it. To approach Cymworth at dusk would be foolhardy, not knowing what, or who, they might encounter. Now they would have all day to locate the Cábretaur—and, hopefully, turn it over to Gwythion the moment he arrived. The Fithlon Master could deal with it from there.

While Kier and Llydia set up camp, JonMarc stood off to himself, gazing across the low hills, his left hand shading his eyes from the angled rays of Devoreth's Orb. "What ruin is that?" he asked, pointing toward the heights a little south of the way they'd come. The charred remnants of an old keep tower stood on the edge of a scrubby cliff, its blackened windows, like hollow eyes, staring sadly across the flats to the sea.

Kier rose from the fireside where he'd been spitting two hares Llydia had shot earlier. He wiped his hands in a clump of sedgegrass and followed his friend's finger. "That's Castle Correth."

"What happened to it?"

"I don't know. It was like that the last time I came through here, years ago. The walls are still intact, though the interior's gone. Must have been quite a fire."

JonMarc didn't take his eyes off the ruined castle. "I'm going to have a look." Without waiting for a response, he trudged off across the dunes.

"Don't be long," Kier called after him. "The meal will be ready..." JonMarc waved over his shoulder and kept going. Kier frowned. It wasn't like JonMarc to go exploring when there was even a hint of food to be had.

Llydia, on her way to fetch water, overheard the exchange. As she watched JonMarc amble off, her face showed quiet satisfaction.

They ate in strained silence. JonMarc had not returned and Kier was growing impatient, not so much out of concern for his friend—there were few better able to defend themselves than JonMarc. He simply felt uncomfortable alone with Llydia. After the meal, he wandered off to busy himself with the horses, rubbing them down with a dry bristlecone, and picking caked mud from their hooves. He was at ease with horses. At least when *they* lowered their eyes to look at him, he knew what they wanted: a feeding or a brushing. There were no subtle signals to be deciphered or, better still, ignored.

When he'd seen to their needs and could think of nothing more to do, Kier wandered to the edge of a low bluff and gazed out over the vast gray plain of the sea. Devoreth's Orb was setting in a fiery blaze of reds, golds and purples, that shot sparks across the rippling surface. A brisk breeze ruffled his hair. Kier took a deep breath and savored it.

Some distance north, atop the rising chalk cliffs, stood another ruin—the skeletal remains of Carreg Cymworth, the ancient fortress of the Nwtyrran refugees, where tomorrow he would face his fate. Kier tried to banish that thought, yet it continued to weigh on him like a dragging anchor. The tower appeared oddly distinct, as though penned by an expert hand in starkest black and the sullen blood-red of orbset. The *last* orbset? When Conjunction occurred, a world would end—so Dynian legend said. The last Nwtyrrans might have beheld just such an orbset while gazing back toward their ruined land. Perhaps they could not wrap their minds around such a cataclysm any more than he. That tiny band of fugitives, all that survived the holocaust that devastated their civilization, had made landfall near here—perhaps on this very spot. They had brought with them a treasure and a curse; had hidden it well from a world not yet ready to receive it. Now, nine hundred years later, he himself was destined to recover it—or die trying.

Was his world any more ready? Would it ever be? Kier doubted it. True, thanks to the Fithlon—to men like Gwythion—they were capable of more. There were better laws, faster travel. But history was the story of people, and fundamentally, people did not change. Ambitious men like Táranos, and Malcolm, and the Connails—those who put their own desires above the needs of their fellow beings—would always be found. They were no different from the selfish few who brought Nwtyrra to her doom. Advanced though the Nwtyrrans were, they'd proven incapable of controlling the wondrous power they had found—a power that might have built a paradise. Instead, it had destroyed their civilization, just as it might now destroy his own.

Kier sensed someone approaching behind him. His right hand flew to his sword and he spun, half-expecting to encounter Táranos. Yet it was only Llydia.

"'Tis indeed a glorious orbset," the girl said, smiling.

"Aye." Kier turned to leave. She'd likely prefer to be alone with her thoughts, as he did.

"Kier, why will you not talk to me?"

Kier halted and looked back over his shoulder. "About what?"

"I don't know. Anything. You've answered me in naught but grunts and monotones since we set out this morning."

It was true. Kier studied the ground, feeling awkward. "I'm sorry. I guess... I've had other things on my mind." Again he sought escape.

"Kier!" Llydia's voice, urgent at first, abruptly softened. "Please stay."

She sighed. "Will you not even look at me?"

He did. She wore a simple gown of dark green wool that clung well to her ample curves. It was the first time Kier bothered to appreciate that she had curves. "Very nice," he said. "JonMarc will be pleased."

"I do not wear it for JonMarc."

Kier's stomach cinched. He couldn't deal with this. Not now. He always felt a simpleton with women, helpless to unravel their mysterious messages. "I.... need to go check on the horses."

"The horses are fine; there's nothing more for you to do there." Again, Llydia's tone softened. "Will you not stay a while?"

He didn't want to stay. Everything in his being told him to retreat while he had the chance. Yet he could think of no good excuse to leave. He didn't want to hurt the girl's feelings. Blazes, why didn't JonMarc return and rescue him, like he always did? "Llydia, I don't know what you want of me."

"Friendship. Nothing more. I'm not a leper, Kier."

"No, but you're JonMarc's..." Unable to come up with the right word, he reddened. Llydia stared at him with wonder. "I mean, you and JonMarc are..." Oh, bloody blazes.

"He and I are what?" Suddenly Llydia laughed. It had a musical sound. "Is that what this is about? You think JonMarc and I are lovers?"

"Well, aren't you?" Kier began to doubt himself.

Llydia smiled indulgently and shook her head. "No. It's true, JonMarc and I have grown close since he rescued me from the Connails. We confide in one another, almost like sister and brother." She chided him roguishly. "I would not bed my brother, Kier."

Fine. She'd succeeded in making him feel a fool. "Then, if not for JonMarc's sake, why did you insist on coming along?"

"The Émam Nácia bade me follow."

"The Émam Nácia...?" The revelation floored him. "Why?"

"Because she recognized the importance of your quest, and its need for secrecy. Also, she knew the question of Morganwy's prophecy of a Dynian hero would not be settled by debate, but by deeds. My brother and his followers would never have let you go. There is too much suspicion and rivalry amongst them. It could only be done by stealth. So the Reverend Mother feigned sleep to end Cyngor, then sent me to aid your escape."

"Did she send Dai as well?" Kier bitterly fingered the tender spot on his scalp.

Llydia shook her head. "She did not know Dai's mind—or, if she did, she said naught of it to me. Dai played his part unwittingly, to his own destruction. You must forgive him for doing what he thought best for his people."

That was something Kier was disinclined to do. "So, why were you sent? To observe how JonMarc and I behave, and report back to the Reverend Mother which of us is the hero foretold?"

Llydia ignored the sarcasm in his voice. "If that does not become apparent of itself, the prophecy is likely false. I am only sent to help you, if I can."

Kier scowled. Gwythion never mentioned Llydia on this quest. "What help can you be?"

Llydia's chin flew up. Defiance glinted in her eyes. "You mean besides supplying your supper? I do not know yet. I am trained of the Émam Nácia and possess the healing powers of blessed Denia. I can see things you do not."

"What kind of things?" Kier asked, suspicious now. Llydia Branwyn must possess sinistral talents, though, like him, she bore no serpent brand. That part wasn't surprising. It was the Covenant priests who insisted on branding spell-handers, and here on Alcor, most Covenanters were Tiernai. No member of their order would ever be welcomed at Dorcalon.

Llydia tried to search his eyes, long and deeply. "I see that of the many demons that possess you, there is one whose power for harm is greater than the rest. You are eaten away with jealousy for your friend JonMarc— because he dares to love one whom *you* love but cannot claim, and knows he is loved in return."

Kier's discomfort grew. He didn't need to be reminded of Cari. "I'm not jealous!" he insisted, realizing his vehemence only confirmed her statement. "Did JonMarc tell you this?"

"He did not have to. The symptoms are plain."

Kier turned and walked a short way down the beach. "Did he tell you that he can't have her either? That she's betrothed to another?"

"He said that arrangement is dissolved."

Kier's head shot up and a spark of hope leaped in his heart. It died just as swiftly. "That changes nothing. JonMarc has no more chance of winning her than I do. He may as well just leave her alone."

"Why? Because she is *your* goddess, and if you cannot possess her, no one can? Isn't that a bit selfish of you, Kier?"

"It's not that. I'm not the one who makes those decisions. To the

Tiernai, JonMarc is a nobody. He's no more worthy of her than I am."

"You underestimate him—and yourself, too, if you think you are unworthy. Circumstances change." Llydia gazed southward, toward the ruined tower JonMarc had gone to explore. "For JonMarc, the change may come sooner than either of you expects."

Kier tried to puzzle her meaning. "What change? What's going on?"

Llydia shook her head. "I cannot say. Yet perhaps JonMarc has gone in search of his past."

"His past? You mean—he's from Castle Correth?"

"We cannot know until he returns. Yet I suspect..." Her voice trailed off.

Kier's hand leaped to his hip. "Is he in danger? I'll go after him."

"No. If there is danger, it is not from any force that can be slain with a sword. Whatever truth JonMarc encounters, he must deal with himself— alone."

She would say no more, though Kier pressed her mightily. At last, dejected, he sat down on the sand and cradled his pounding head in his hand. "Happy JonMarc," he sighed, "to have the chance to find himself at last."

Llydia knelt a little behind him. "And what of Kier?"

He looked up, startled. "What do you mean? I know my parentage; who I am. *What* I am," he added with disgust.

Llydia reached out to touch his shoulder—hesitated—pulled her hand back. He might not understand; might recoil or, worse, try to escape. She couldn't risk that now that she finally had him talking. She sensed his fears, his frustrations, aching to come out yet trammeled behind the stout walls he'd built to protect himself. The Émam Nácia had warned her he was self-destructive. Her talk with JonMarc had borne that out. If she could only get him to let go, there was a chance she might save him. Llydia was honest enough to admit her motives were not entirely unselfish.

The last, pink afterglow faded beyond the water, and faint stars began to appear. Night birds swooped low over the rolling breakers, crying and scolding one another. The tide was going out. Llydia decided to take the chance. She laid her hand gently between Kier's shoulderblades and began to soothe the taut muscles there. As she'd feared, Kier went rigid and jerked away. "Relax," she said softly. "This will ease your headache."

"How... did you know my head ached?" Kier asked, feeling self-conscious with her so near.

"I'm a healer," she replied simply. "Close your eyes and let the pain flow from you."

Kier tried, and was amazed when her suggestion worked. Llydia knelt behind him, her fingers kneading the hard shoulder flesh beneath his collar. Once he got used to it, Kier felt his breathing slow and deepen as his body began to sink into the rhythm of her touch.

Llydia's hands moved to his neck, circling, soothing, then down across his shoulders. Like a sculptor, molding his flesh to fit her fancy, her palms caressed his back, his shoulderblades. Kier felt a shudder pass through him and found it not an unpleasant sensation.

"There," said Llydia. "Is that not better?" Kier chewed his lip and nodded.

She hadn't quite finished. Gently, she moved her left hand down the side of his head, stroking the thick hair away from his ear. Kier cocked his head to expose his neck. It was the first time he'd opened himself to her, and Llydia counted it a victory. She let her hand linger there, sliding it inside his collar to run her fingers along the line of his bare shoulder.

Kier heaved a tremulous gasp. "Llydia, I... I'm..." The words jammed up in his throat.

Llydia laid her head on his shoulder. Her hair, soft and sweet-smelling, piled in a cushiony mound against his cheek. He nuzzled it, then abruptly turned away.

"Llydia, I have to confront Táranos tomorrow. I know it. Yet... I haven't the strength to defeat him." The words ripped out of him. Kier wasn't even sure why he'd voiced them. She didn't have to know the doubts that were killing him inside.

"You have the skills you need, Kier. It is your fear that keeps you from recognizing them."

"Fear? I'm not afraid to die."

"No, you only fear to fail." Llydia sighed and rubbed his shoulder. "Kier, a man can only fail if he gives up trying."

The rumble in Kier's throat told what he thought of that platitude. He'd sought reassurance he knew she could not provide. Yet, for a moment he'd hoped... Angry words spilled out in spite of him. "What if a man *does* try—again and again, with all his heart—yet his every choice leads deeper into darkness?" It was less a question than a self-accusation.

Llydia touched his forearm. He did not recoil, but neither did he respond. "Kier, you cannot see all ends. Do not let your guilt over Rhynion's death make you doubt yourself. You bear no blame for that."

"Don't I? I knew Rhynion was threatened, yet I failed to save him." He looked away. "But it's more than that." How could he expect her to understand? He'd harbored the guilty secret most of his life. "Dai told the Cyngor my mother died because she summoned disease upon our village. It's not true." Blazes, he didn't want to talk about this. It was as if some alien will suddenly usurped his own. "My mother died because of *me*."

There. The wall was breached. Kier stole a glance at Llydia, expecting her to recoil in horror, but she betrayed no reaction at all. Her silence urged him on.

"She was like you—a healer, respected by her village—until she dared give birth to a half-Tiernai bastard and refused to stake him out to die." Kier snorted bitterly. "You can imagine how things changed then. She was spat on in the streets, shunned and humiliated. She pretended not to care, but even as a child I felt her torment. When she came home one evening, bloody and trembling, I swore to myself that every man who'd touched her would pay."

A sullen breeze rattled sand against the swaying salt-grass. Kier fingered a broken colloch shell, then hurled it away. "That night I made a blood offering to Denia. I entreated her to raise a plague that would smite down all who had shamed my mother." Kier shut his eyes. "Three days later, a pestilence struck. A third of the village died. When the Tiernai Covenant priest came seeking the cause, the villagers were quick to cast blame. At his urging, they dragged my mother from her bed, where she too lay stricken, and stoned her to death as a sinistral sorceress."

Llydia sat on the sand beside him. "Kier, surely you cannot believe the wish of an anguished child caused that plague."

Kier stared into the salt-mist. "Maybe not," he admitted. "But even then I knew I had sinistral talents. I tried to use them to protect her, but it wasn't enough. She was hauled off and murdered because *I failed*. Gods, why didn't they take *me*? I'm the one they wanted to be rid of."

"You cannot continue blaming yourself, Kier. The past exists only in your mind—and there, you have the power to change it. Nothing is ever as it appears." Llydia paused a moment, thoughtful. "Perhaps the Goddess had a reason for sparing your life."

Kier lanced her with his gaze. "What reason?"

"Perhaps... she intended that you one day become the savior of your people."

It sounded like a callous jest. "My *people*? Blazes, Llydia, who are my *people*? I'm a mongrel; a beggar's cloak, pieced together from warring scraps: Dynian and Tiernai, noble and peasant, skill-hand and sinistral. I have no people." Kier threw his hands up in frustration. "Even if I did, how could I save them? I hadn't power enough to save my own mother—or my prince."

Llydia shook her head. "I speak not of sinistral talents. Don't you see, Kier? You carry within you the seeds of all the embattled peoples of Alcor. That is not your weakness but the source of your strength. Use it. Make peace with them, for no army can prevail that is in conflict with itself. United, you will find the strength you need to challenge Táranos."

Kier pondered that a moment. Then his eyes drooped and he shook his head. "I don't know how. That war's raged inside me all my life—like demons, ripping apart my soul. I've tried to battle the darkness, but it's too powerful."

Llydia laid her hand on his. "Kier, you only battle *yourself*. Darkness cannot be fought; it is *nothing*. It has no power but what you give it. To banish darkness you need only open yourself to light—to the knowledge that you are worthy and whole. There is nothing to fear, for in light, the *Infinite* works *with* you." Llydia's moist eyes reflected the starlight as she moved nearer. "Make peace with yourself, Kier. I am a priestess of Denia. I can help."

Kier's breath caught in his throat. He knew what she offered, yet he could scarcely believe she'd want him for *that*. Mocking laughter filled his mind: the laughter of a tavern wench whose name he'd long since forgotten—a raven-haired vixen who'd enticed him to her stable cot, and there discovered the mark of his Dynian past. She'd scorned him for it, taunting him to a failure made all the more humiliating because she'd laughed of it with her friends. "I'm... not any good with women," he stammered. It was a less searing echo of the tavern girl's words—words which, because she was vastly more experienced in such matters, he'd always accepted as true.

Llydia dismissed the myth with a toss of her head. "That is just another demon, Kier. It has no power. Let it go." Then gently, as before: "I can help you."

She knelt before him, her full body very near his own. Kier could see her breasts move, hear her rapid breath as she gently reached up to stroke his hair. An uncontrollable tremor seized his jaw. It was echoed lower down, where his physical response to her nearness was swift and overwhelming. Kier reddened, wondering if Llydia sensed it, yet too caught up now to retreat. He reached for her, feeling the passion of her lips against his throat. He swallowed hard, shut his eyes and drew her against him, losing himself in the depths of her kiss.

The shirt fell from his shoulders. Llydia's hands caressed his bare skin while he fumbled with the tangle of laces at her bodice. He tore it away and ran his stubbled cheek along the smoothness of her shoulder to seek out the warm, swelling mounds that overflowed his fingers. His mouth attacked them like a starving man, tasting her clean, salt-sweet flesh.

Llydia's fingers sought the front of his breeches and freed them with an urgency now equaled by his own. Her skirt slipped away and she pulled him down to her, his breeches scarcely below his knees. She wrapped her legs around him and they were magically together, clinging and thrashing in a primal rhythm that seemed to make them one with the universe.

"Release your demons, Kier," Llydia whispered in his ear as he bore down on her. "I am a priestess of Denia. In Her womb they will be purified."

He found he could not answer. When the final moment came, he gave a groan of sweet agony and swayed above her, near collapse.

At that same instant, far away upon the unfeeling wind, it seemed to Llydia that she heard a cry wrenched from another tortured soul, and for a moment her heart went out to it. Yet it lay beyond her healing powers— and Kier still needed her.

"That was wondrous, Kier," she murmured, as he settled on top of her. "How could you ever doubt yourself?" Too exhausted to speak, Kier acknowledged with a breathless nod, still fighting his way back from the little death. Llydia drew him down onto her skirt, spread out on the salt grass beneath them. Kier buried his face against her neck and slept.

Llydia held him close, savoring the musky odor of his maleness, lulled by the soft rasp of his relaxed breathing beside her ear. He had willingly laid open his defenses to her, and now their souls were forever entwined.

Kier murmured something in his sleep and softly began to snore. Llydia smiled—a little smugly. She had made her choice.

Chapter Thirty-one

Kier woke to the shrill cry of sea birds squabbling over a moldering scrap of fish. Devoreth's Orb had not yet risen above the eastern foothills, but the sky was growing brighter. He realized he was cold. Sometime during the night. Llydia had drawn some random scraps of clothing over them, but his movements had long since scattered them.

Kier gazed at the girl lying naked beside him, her red-gold hair spread across the sand, and tried to untangle the unaccustomed emotions that welled up inside him. Too confusing. He got up, shook out his small-clothes and breeches, and tugged them on.

He'd just slipped his shirt over his head when Llydia awoke. She smiled up at him, then stood and began sorting out her garments. For a moment Kier felt oddly embarrassed. Darkness had at least overcome the problem of decorum. Yet it did not trouble him so much that he turned away. When Llydia bent to pick up her shift, Kier's breath caught. This was sensual overload such as he'd never experienced, and his eyes feasted on the appealing vision like a famished beggar at a banquet. He recalled his cousin Cari's slender form: all graceful lines and cylinders, classically elegant, like an alabaster statue. Llydia's figure was mostly curves and spheres. It amazed Kier how two women could be so different, yet both be beautiful. Of course, he'd never seen Cari like *this*. The very thought seemed sacrilegious. Llydia had hit it on the head last night when she'd called Cari his goddess. That's exactly what his cousin represented to him: a divine being, to be worshiped, but never possessed. It must be what he'd found so infuriating about JonMarc's earthy attentions toward her.

The thought of JonMarc hit Kier with an abrupt pang of guilt. He'd given no thought to his friend since last evening. What had been JonMarc's reaction when he returned to find the camp empty? Surely, he must have come looking for them. Kier reddened at the thought of the royal razzing he could expect when he and Llydia got back. Then he chuckled. Let JonMarc tease him. Knowing his friend, the gibes would mask a fair measure of respect.

But JonMarc had not returned. His blanket and scant belongings remained stowed at the edge of the camp where he'd left them yesterday. Worried, Kier belted on his sword to go after him.

"No, Kier, wait." Llydia laid a hand on his arm. "Look."

There across the grassy dunes, a tall, bedraggled figure was laboring toward them. "Devoreth's blood," Kier gasped, when he got a better glimpse. JonMarc seemed to have aged ten years in as many hours. His face was drawn and smudged with soot, his clothing blackened and disheveled. He trudged toward the encampment with eyes fixed on the ground.

Kier hastened toward him. "JonMarc, what happened?"

JonMarc slowed and raised his eyes, red and swollen. He focused blankly on Kier and Llydia as though not really seeing them. "They're dead," he murmured thickly.

Kier aimed Llydia a quizzical look, then turned back to JonMarc. "Who?"

JonMarc's lips tried to formulate words, but no sound came. He looked imploringly at each of them, as if expecting them to understand. Llydia's sharp inhale hinted that she did. Kier remained in the dark.

"I couldn't save them. I *tried*."

"Save *who*?" Sudden panic seized Kier. "Not... Cari?"

Llydia shook her head, signaling him to let JonMarc continue.

"We were off playing in the forest. The tower bell rang an alarm. I made Jenna hide, then went back to look. They were everywhere! Running and shouting—their serpent ships all drawn up on the beach. I didn't know what to do." Tears filled JonMarc's pale eyes.

Kier tugged Llydia aside. He indicated JonMarc, then measured his hand to waist level. A child? She nodded. Kier's lips formed a silent "O."

JonMarc sank to his knees in the sand. Sooty fingers raked his hairline. He shook his head, as if desperate to rid it of the memory. "I watched them drag her from the hall. They threw her down and took turns hurting her. She screamed. Cried—and screamed. I threw rocks to make them stop, but then they grabbed me." JonMarc covered his ears and shut his eyes tight. "Maman," he whimpered.

Kier could hardly bear to see his friend so ripped apart. He wanted to shake him back to the present, but Llydia held him back. "Not yet," she whispered. "He must tell it all. He has hidden the memory deep inside. He needs to set it free."

JonMarc wiped grimy hands across his eyes. "They wouldn't let me get to her. They left her bloody on the ground—so still, all naked and alone. The torches! Flames and fire, everywhere—roaring like thunder—falling on us." Suddenly JonMarc's eyes widened, seeing something the others did not. "Jenna!" he cried, "Jenna, *no*! Go back. Run and hide. *Jenna!*" The name escaped him in a tangled shriek. JonMarc hugged a small bundle to his breast. At first Kier took it for a lump of rag and wondered why his friend clutched it so tightly. Now JonMarc buried his face in it, his slim body rocking back and forth, lost in a memory the others could not share.

"What happened to her?" Llydia asked softly.

JonMarc looked up, his face streaked with tears. "They threw her in the fire. She screamed to me; tried to climb free—her hair, her face, all wild with flames. I couldn't get to her. They carried me away to their ship." JonMarc shook the bundle in his arms. "Jenna, I told you to hide. Why do you never listen?" His eyes suddenly fixed Kier and he jabbed an accusing finger. "Where were *you*? I couldn't save them myself. I tried!" Then louder, hurling his fist at the sky: "Papa, where *were* you? Why didn't you come when Maman called? Why didn't you *come*?"

Llydia knelt beside him. "May I see?" JonMarc let her pry the ragged bundle from his arm. She studied it a moment, then handed it to Kier.

"It's... a doll," he said. "Whose?"

JonMarc's head bowed over his chest. "It was Jenna's. I found it on the ground."

Llydia reached up and gently stroked the hair from his sooty brow. "What is your name?"

"What?" he stammered, confused. "It's JonMarc..." He stared a moment, then understood. His lips quivered with sluggish syllables trying to escape. "Mm..." He hesitated, struggling. "My... kal?" A look of triumph came over his grimy face. "Mykhal," he said at last. "Mykhal...Telynor."

Kier touched Llydia's arm. "You asked in Dynian, and he understood. How did you know?"

"I only suspected. The Émam Nácia had me bring him here—to see what might happen."

"But how could she guess that JonMarc...?"

"When he communicated through me at Cyngor, she sensed the power of his mind. Many of the Telynor clan possessed sinistral sight. The last was Jaimie Telynor—a Dynian High Elder who died of grief some eighteen years ago. Word reached him at Dorcalon that his entire family had been slaughtered by Syrmian raiders. He returned to Castle Correth to find it a smoldering ruin, the reports true. The charred remains of his wife and daughter he found. The body of the son was never discovered—" She raised her eyes to JonMarc, who was making a valiant effort to battle his way back to the present. "Until now."

"So—JonMarc is descended of the Telynor High Kings; at least on his father's side."

"Of both sides. His mother bore the Telynor line. She was gifted herself, and had trained with the Émam Nácia, as I do now. JonMarc bears her blood, but cannot carry on her line. Had his sister lived, the Telynors might continue, but now... JonMarc—Mykhal—is last of that clan."

"Then the sword belongs to him by right as well as chance." Kier spoke with awe. "He's the hero of your prophecy."

"No. That is not determined by heritage, but by deeds. The task ahead..."

Kier nodded. Since dawn he'd felt the weight of that charge closing in. While Llydia's ministering had at least made the burden bearable, fears still plagued him. He pulled the wineskin from their packs and pressed JonMarc to drink. "He can't ride to Cymworth like this. He hasn't eaten or slept. Stay with him, Llyd. I'll go on ahead and see what I can find."

It was JonMarc who answered. A pained but familiar twinkle found its way into his blue eyes as he wearily hauled himself to his feet. "I'm all right," he said, looking embarrassed. "Let's get out of here."

Kier regarded him curiously. How much of a transformation had he undergone? There was nothing apparent beyond the utter exhaustion JonMarc was already taking pains to hide. Kier suspected the change went deeper. "I'm not even sure what to call you now," he said.

JonMarc cocked his head. "Same as always. Mykhal Telynor's a stranger to both of us."

JonMarc appeared to have suffered no ill effects from his experience. He quickly made a connection between his recent revelations and the waking dreams his fire-madness evoked.

"It must've started when Gwythion first touched my mind," he said. They were riding northward toward the wind-whipped ruins of Carreg Cymworth. Devoreth's Orb brooded low and sullen above the eastern horizon, a florid ball, casting the landscape in a wash of ruddy gold. "I'd never experienced visions like that before. And it's grown worse since Ruthland, when Táranos..." JonMarc's voice faltered. They might soon encounter the renegade Fithlon again.

By the time they reached Cymworth, the lingering haze had melted the shadows into one vast monochrome. Kier sent JonMarc and Llydia to scout the grounds while he dismounted and explored the fortress. Carreg Cymworth was ancient even by Dynian standards. The years, and relentless sea wind, had not been kind to it. The crumbling walls still stood, proud yet impotent, like a maimed and battle-weary veteran who had lost the strength to bear arms. They enclosed the entire tip of the peninsula, their bleached stones looking like mere extensions of the sea-washed cliffs. Behind the ruined curtain wall, a stout tower stood grim and forbidding, its wooden roof long since collapsed. Yet some of the fortress could still be made tenable, and it was with a seasoned soldier's eye that Kier assessed the possibilities. Cymworth was, after all, his own demesne. A more desolate property he could not imagine.

JonMarc and Llydia reined in as Kier exited the fallen gates. "We've found no sign that Táranos has been here," he said, "but not much shows in this chalky ground. Did you discover anything?"

Kier shook his head.

JonMarc swung his leg over his horse's neck and dropped to his feet, then helped Llydia dismount. "So where do we look for the Cábretaur?"

"You've got the book," said Kier. "I figured you'd have those verses memorized by now."

In fact, JonMarc did. During the endless days at sea, when his enthusiasm for the venture was at its zenith, he'd spent many an hour curled in a corner with his nose in the Fithlon's sacred text. But that was a fortnight ago. Since then, events had moved so swiftly he'd scarcely thought of the writings. He thumbed through the damaged pages until he found the place he'd marked with a scrap of cordage. He recited the first verse aloud.

> "A Chamber wrought by salty-fingered Time
> Where seeks the Jackal for a kingly Cache,
> Entombed deep, in weighty Walls of Stone:
> The Sovereign's Secret lies beneath the Ash.

Sounds like a cave."

"There are hundreds along these cliffs." Kier rubbed his brow. "We'd best start looking. If we're *supposed* to find the Cábretaur, I expect we will."

They spent the rest of the day scrambling among the chalk cliffs, searching for Aneryn's tomb. They scouted dozens of caves, some wide and shallow, others little more than deep fissures in the cliff—and all of them empty, but for the droppings of bats and other small creatures. When at last Devoreth's Orb cast its bleared brilliance through the arrow loops of Carreg Cymworth, Kier sat down on a rock and stared at the breaking waves below. "This could take months!" he groaned. "We should've come here days ago." He swiped a lock of sweaty hair from his eyes. He felt tired and footsore, and his legs ached from climbing.

JonMarc clambered up, breathless, from the other direction and rubbed his neck. He pulled out the book, as he had a dozen times already, and studied the verse again. He scratched his head. "We must be missing something. I wish I could figure out what Aneryn meant by the *Jackal*. I've seen no animals at all today—only their leavings. Then there's that bit about the secret lying *beneath the ash*. I haven't come across any sign of fire either. Have you?"

Kier shook his head and glanced apprehensively at the westering orb. If Gwythion was right, Conjunction would occur tonight. That left little time.

Llydia scrambled up beside them. She, too, was powdered with chalk dust. She wore her red hair tied back in a fat braid. Kier brightened when he saw her and took her hand.

"I hate to tell you this," she said, "but there are dozens more caves over on the windward side."

The news came as no surprise. Kier struggled to his feet. "Then I guess we'd better go have a look at them."

They found the peninsula's western face combed with even more crevasses than the other—and they were harder to reach. Kier sent Llydia back to the horses for a rope and, with it, they continued their search for several hours more until at last, as if by mutual agreement, they all sat down at once, too worn out to try further.

Devoreth's Orb was sinking fast beyond a blood-red sea. From the south, a storm approached, trailing black clouds gilded intermittently with flashes of white. Something else welled before it—a great, brownish plume of dust.

Kier wiped his face on his sleeve and tried to reconcile himself to failure. He could hardly believe it had come like this—not the sudden, terrible defeat he'd been dreading, but a long, worn-out surrender. He scarcely felt it when JonMarc nudged his arm.

"Kier, look." JonMarc pointed along the cliffs. "The shape of that rock; doesn't it look like—I mean, couldn't you be convinced it was some animal climbing the cliff? A jackal, maybe?"

Kier followed his finger, almost afraid to hope. Yet, in this light, the effect was uncanny. "Is there a cave above it?"

JonMarc leaned out for a better view. "I think there may be."

They wasted no time getting to it. The spot lay farther down the coast than it appeared—perhaps half a mile from the ruined fortress—and could scarcely be recognized from near at hand. In fact, seeing the changes in the feature as they approached, Kier suspected that the only place, and perhaps the only conditions, from which one could view the silhouette were those from which JonMarc first glimpsed it. He secured the rope to a gnarled tree trunk and Llydia tended it while he, and then JonMarc, carefully eased themselves down the wind-chiseled cliff.

A cave yawned into the sunset like a huge, bloody maw. As they ducked inside, they found it deeper than any they'd explored so far. As soon as they turned the first bend, they lost the meager orblight. JonMarc lit the stump of their last candle. In the darkness, they began to lose all sense of time. The echoes of their footfalls might have been the first sounds these walls had witnessed in centuries.

They hadn't ventured far before they found the passage blocked by debris fallen from the roof. Searching for a way around, they came instead upon a small chamber, hollowed into the solid rock by the same natural forces that had formed the rest of the cave. Awe and apprehension tugged Kier's belly as he followed JonMarc inside.

In the center of the chamber lay a sepulcher of stone—a massive thing, perfectly rectangular, and so black its surface seemed to absorb the light of their candle rather than reflect it back. They examined it inch by chilly inch, but found no mark or inscription. On the floor beside it, Kier's toe caught the remains of an ornate brazier, now green and pitted with age, that had evidently once stood atop the coffin. The ashes of ceremonial incense lay strewn about the stone lid. "*The Sovereign's secret lies beneath the Ash*," murmured JonMarc. Together they heaved on the lid.

"Nothing?" Llydia exclaimed.

They had climbed back up and now huddled together beside a wizened tree that looked to be as ancient as the rest of the ruins they'd explored. It was still barren of leaf, but at least it would provide some shelter from the approaching storm.

"Nothing," Kier repeated with disgust. "No bones, no grave goods. Whoever got there ahead of us did a thorough job."

"But why wouldn't there be bones?" asked Llydia. "Surely no one would steal those."

"The tomb was completely empty. We didn't even find dust."

"Then maybe it wasn't a tomb," said JonMarc. He'd been prodding among the grassy boulders as though searching for something.

"What do you mean?" said Kier. "What else could it have been? It fulfilled all the prophecy's requirements, except the Cábretaur was gone."

"Assuming it was ever there."

Kier cocked his head, intrigued. "Are you saying we searched the wrong place?"

"I'm not saying anything, except that there are two possible explanations: either someone got to the Cábretaur before us, as it would appear—or it was never there to begin with, in which case, we *were* searching the wrong spot."

"But everything fit: the cave, the jackal, the ash. If it wasn't there, where would it be?"

"I don't know. But for someone of Aneryn's cunning, it just seemed a bit too easy."

Kier snorted. He'd hardly call what they'd been through easy.

JonMarc leaned against the ancient tree trunk. The first drops of rain were beginning to fall. From the look of the sky, they'd be well drenched before it ended. "Aneryn must've guessed that, over the years, people were bound to search for the Cábretaur. Else, why bother to hide it—if the only ones to seek it would be those he intended to have find it?"

Kier gave an impatient nod. "So?"

"Well, if I had something to hide, I wouldn't just put it out of reach. I'd provide a decoy—something obvious enough to let people think they'd found it, and disappointing enough to make them quit the search."

Kier rubbed the back of his neck. "So you think this tomb was just a diversion?"

"Maybe."

A glimmer of hope crept into Kier's heart. "Is that the opinion of a professional thief?"

JonMarc's grin broadened.

"All right, you're the expert. Where do we search?"

JonMarc glanced about. "Well—it could be another cave altogether, but for now, let's assume this one's right. We never did reach the back."

"It was sealed off by debris. I checked."

"But it would come out pretty close to here. And the cave turns, so the back part must lie just beneath us." JonMarc wandered among the boulders, probing the ground with a knotted stick. When he looked back, he was smiling. "I knew this place looked familiar! My sister and I used to race our ponies across that plain."

His words caught for a second. He went on tentatively, as if following a thread he feared might break. "We came to this spot once, looking for buried treasure. There's a deep pit nearby. Jenna got caught and I had to fetch her out. I remember thinking the place looked interesting, but I never had a chance to return. Here," he said, after another minute's search. "I've found it! Bet it leads down to the back of that cave."

The opening was so well hidden under grass and scrub, Kier could easily believe an unwary child might fall in. It amazed him JonMarc had enough of his old memory to locate the place, after so many years. The opening was no wider than a badger hole. "Can you fit?" he asked, then chided himself, remembering who he was talking to. "Wait a minute, I'll get the rope."

JonMarc squeezed through. His shaggy head disappeared last. Kier heard soft cursing, then a thump. "It's all right," came his muffled voice. "Lots of blasted tree roots. Hand me that candle, will you?"

Kier used his sword to widen the hole for himself and Llydia. He secured the rope to the tree trunk and dropped it down. Llydia slipped through with little effort. His own broad shoulders proved a tighter fit.

"The storm's getting worse," he panted as his feet touched down. He brushed muddy hair out of his eyes. An arm-sized tree root poked at him. He ducked, only to collide with one the width of his thigh. Kier rubbed his scalp, muttering.

Llydia and JonMarc stood just ahead. As Kier's eyes adjusted to the gloom, he began to make out the dimensions of the cavern. It seemed larger and brighter than the part they'd entered earlier. Here, the chalk walls had been scraped smooth. He stepped up behind the others, and caught his breath. There, in a crypt against the wall, stood a tomb, undisturbed, and magnificent in its solemnity.

"You were right!" he whispered to JonMarc.

His friend nodded, clearly awestricken by his own discovery.

Before them lay the dead king—an image in luminous white calstone, life-sized, and so exquisitely detailed they had to stare hard to be sure the figure did not breathe. A feeling of reverence came over Kier, and for a time he could only stand and gape, like a child intruding on a forbidden shrine. "He looks asleep," said Llydia in a hushed voice.

Kier stepped closer to examine the stony features, stern, yet with a gentleness that bespoke deep wisdom. "He must've been a great man. It's odd, I almost feel as if I knew him."

A shaft of light split the blackness behind them, followed by a deep, booming rumble that shook the ground. The candle fluttered in JonMarc's hand. Kier shifted uneasily. "We'd better get on with this. The flame won't last much longer. We've got to open the tomb."

The suggestion seemed blasphemous, yet the verses left little doubt the Cábretaur lay hidden inside the sepulcher. With all their strength, Kier and JonMarc heaved on the lid. It didn't budge.

"Devoreth's blood," Kier gasped, "I don't see how *anyone* could get in there. The thing's massive! Wait— It must be locked. Don't the verses speak of...?"

JonMarc riffled through the pages and read the second verse.

> *"The Power which sleeps in Death's profound Embrace,*
> *Enclosed in Bonds beyond men's Strength to free,*
> *Shall by a Finger's Touch be once discharged.*
> *The Hands of Aneryn are both Lock and Key."*

Kier nodded. "So, a finger's touch will open it." He drew out the Amulet. It looked tiny beside the huge figure of the king. "This must be the finger Aneryn spoke of." He examined the sleeping monarch's left hand, which lay near the front of the coffin lid. Like the Amulet, it was shaped as a fist, the forefinger outstretched. A cabochon ring gleamed upon that stony finger—the only part of the sculpture not of calstone. The oval seal of black onyx bore upon it, in silver, the eight-pointed Nwtyrran star. "If the hands are both lock and key, then this should be the lock." He fiddled with the cabochon and found that when he pressed on the star, the entire sigil could be moved to one side. There was an opening beneath it. Kier slipped the metal forefinger into it. It fit perfectly. They heard a metallic click and Kier cocked his head. "I think it's open. JonMarc, help me lift the lid."

This time the sculpted calstone stirred. Slowly, they raised the lid enough for Llydia to peer inside. "Make it quick," JonMarc gasped. "This thing's bloody heavy."

Llydia lowered the candle inside and waved a hand in front of her nose.

They could all glimpse what lay within. The Nwtyrran king's body appeared undisturbed, though the remains bore scant resemblance to the majestic figure carved above. He was robed in gleaming white cloth, still miraculously intact. The body was another matter. Centuries of sleep had reduced the corpse to a dried husk, the bones to brown relics that betrayed little hint of their former stature. The hollow eyes stared as if woeful at having their rest disturbed.

But what caught their attention instantly was the wooden casket once clutched in the king's withered grasp. It was stained with age, and heavy. Its weight had crushed the pelvic bones that cradled it and left it resting on the coffin floor.

"Can you reach it?" asked Kier, growing desperate.

Llydia lugged the box out and set it on the ground. Kier and JonMarc lowered the stone lid. It settled into place with a boom that rattled the chamber. A more menacing rumble echoed from outside. Kier felt a chill and cast an anxious glance over his shoulder.

"Lucky there were three of us," said JonMarc. "No one could've done this alone." The implication of that suddenly struck him. He looked at Kier, then Llydia, but both were too preoccupied to notice.

Kier was trying to remove his amulet from the effigy's grip. It would not release. At last, he braced his legs and yanked with all his might. The effort hurled him backwards. The silver hand glinted in his fist—but only part. The outstretched finger had broken off and remained within the lock. Kier stared dismally at the remnant.

"I'm afraid it's in there to stay," said Llydia. As she touched the signet, it snapped back into place and would not open again. "I guess Aneryn intended for the tomb to be opened only once."

"It says as much in the verse," said JonMarc. "And *we three* were the ones destined to open it. I'm getting a better feel for how Aneryn's mind worked. His prophecies are full of twists and double meanings. He must've known exactly who would fulfill them. Remember that bit about the Jackal? That wasn't just the image on the rock outside. It's *me*. The Syrmian pirates named me Jaha'an Maurek—*the white jackal*. As a child I hunted for treasure here—a *Kingly Cache*. Somehow Aneryn knew that." JonMarc searched from face to face but found only skepticism. He grasped a dangling tree root. "What do you wanna bet this tree's an *ash*?"

Kier nibbled his lip. "I'll admit it makes sense. I've just never heard of foresight that could determine specifics—like what you were named as a boy. It's hard to believe someone with Táranos's powers couldn't have done the same as we did, if he possessed the Amulet. To say it had to be us is like arguing that everything that happens was *meant* to happen." He shrugged. "It may be true, but there's no proving it." He knelt beside the wooden casket and motioned for the others to join him. "What do you make of this?"

JonMarc set the argument aside. "It seems awfully heavy for its size. Must be whatever's inside. We'd better make sure it's the Cábretaur before we trouble to carry it out of here."

Kier agreed. "But how do we get into it?" He'd already tried the lid, with no luck. And the Amulet was now useless. He tipped the casket on its side. "There's no obvious lock; only these three panels. What do your verses say about this?"

JonMarc managed to recite this passage from memory.

> "*And Whom hath Fate ordained men's Doom to free?*
> *The Lost, whose Strength is found in Unity;*
> *The Heir to Wisdom, Power's Steward to be;*
> *And Denia's Touch, to seal the Trinity.*

"It's the last one," he added, as if expecting Kier to request more specification.

Kier ran his finger over the metal panels. Two were shallow indentations; the first, an irregular shape he could not recognize; the third, an oval the size of his thumbnail. The middle panel was inlaid with the Nwtyrran star, a tiny white crystal embedded in its center.

JonMarc drew the charmstone from around his neck. "If my guess is right, each of those panels represents one of us, and the middle one has to be mine. I've seen its like before. Hold your ears." Gingerly, he touched the crystals together.

But this time there was no deafening squeal; no flash of light. In fact, nothing happened at all. JonMarc examined the charmstone, then the box. His face showed puzzlement. "It must require something from each of you before it'll work."

Llydia drew a small pendant from inside her bodice—oval-shaped, and bearing the sigil of the Life Tree. "*Denia's Touch*," she said, "the emblem of the healer." She pressed it to the indentation in the third panel. It fit perfectly.

All eyes turned to Kier. He scratched his head and pointed to the remaining panel. "I don't have anything that looks like that."

"What about the silver charms you wear?" Llydia suggested.

"But that indentation's not a stag or a dragon." He lifted the chain over his head.

"May I see?" Kier handed her the charms. Llydia toyed with the small figures a moment, then gave them back. "Perhaps the key lies in *unity*."

Kier glanced at her, then at the charms, then at the box. Slowly, he took up the small, right-facing silhouette of the Tiernai stag and placed it in the indentation, turning it until it snapped into place; then the Dynian dragon, overlaid upon it. At first, the charm would not fit. In a flash of insight, Kier turned it to face left. The space was filled. Kier shook his head, not quite believing. "Try your crystal now, JonMarc."

Again, they heard no squeal. As if the charmstone had at last found its intended function, there was only a small, metallic snap, and the lock released. The three gathered close in the darkness. Kier raised the casket lid.

Inside lay another box, this one of some dark metal, black as a midnight pit. Its surface was nicked and marred with age and much handling. Kier lugged it out. "Here's the weight," he said. The box was unadorned, save for some writing around the edge and a simple figure encircled on the lid—the Life Tree's double trident, inset with crystals placed to represent the stars in that constellation. The one at the center, in the position of the Life Star, was larger than the rest, and bright amber.

"I thought it would be grander than this." JonMarc echoed Kier's sentiment. This plain box hardly seemed a fitting casket for the gem they'd gone to such pains to find. "What are the words around the rim?" The letters were engraved in an ancient, flowing style, like the script of Nwtyrra transcribed in his book, yet the words were Dynian. Kier translated them aloud:

> "*May proud Nwtyrra's Doom smite all who dare*
> *To seek Her lost Power without Compassion;*
> *To subdue it without true Purpose;*
> *To wield it without Restraint.*"

He drew a tense breath. "So, this is really it—the last remnant of Nwtyrra's lost power. *The Miril Cábretaur.*"

"We'd better make sure," said JonMarc, "knowing Aneryn's fondness for decoys."

They heard a muted rumble outside. The candle shimmered with the dank breeze that smelled of mould and decay. Kier shivered and nervously glanced back toward the opening. "How could you tell? No one knows what miril looks like. And Gwythion warned us not to handle it."

"I'm not going to handle it. I just want to look."

Kier gave in, as much to satisfy his own curiosity as JonMarc's. He held the box while his friend worked the lid. The metal latch came easily undone and JonMarc peered inside.

At first, all they could see was a hint of green that made Kier wonder if perhaps this really was just another decoy. But as JonMarc raised the lid farther, Kier began to make out the dimensions of a crystal. It was huge, the size of his fist, and glowed at its core with a green light that gradually began to pulse and grow, like a living thing. The light spilled over the edges of the box, touching the walls, his hands, everything around it, with a sickly luminescence reminiscent of corpse light. JonMarc shuddered but could not turn away.

"Shut it!" Kier shouted beside him. JonMarc continued to stare until Llydia slammed the lid down. The sound jolted JonMarc from his trance.

"Gwythion said the Gem's too powerful to handle without its protective casket." Kier tucked the box under his arm. "The sooner we're rid of the accursed thing, the better."

"*That is easily arranged.*"

The soft voice oozed from the darkness behind them. The three spun. The candle's sputtering light fell upon shimmering robes, a gaunt and bearded face, and deep violet eyes that JonMarc recognized at once.

"*Táranos!*" he growled.

Chapter Thirty-two

A peal of thunder convulsed the chill air. The buried chamber trembled and clods fell from the roof. Kier scarcely noticed. He stared at the gray-robed figure before them.

Even in the feeble light, Táranos's flesh looked pale and translucent, like that of a sightless slug that had crawled from beneath a rock. His silver hair and beard were liberally peppered with black, as were the slender strands that sprouted like limp weeds from either side of his upper lip. Yet it was his eyes that held Kier's attention—eyes so deep and piercing they looked more like hearth coals, glowing crimson at the edges. The heat of them was almost painful.

Táranos gave a satisfied smile, though his bloodless lips betrayed no trace of humor. "You truants certainly burned no boot leather getting here. I was beginning to despair of your arrival."

The sarcasm was not lost on Kier. They'd have been here a week since, had Táranos not set impediments in their path. "A pity we caused you such inconvenience."

"Not at all. It allowed me time to locate this chamber, and the tomb of Aneryn. As soon as I was certain I could not open the sepulcher without you, I did what I could to facilitate your journey—even providing you with horses."

"Which were meant for Dai," said Llydia.

Táranos's hollow smile transformed into a sneer of utter contempt. "Ah, poor, pathetic Dai Caydyn. He wanted to be a *hero.*" Táranos spat the word. "Well, I've made him a martyr. He'll have to be content with that."

Llydia bristled. "*You* killed him."

"Alas no, my dear. You did that yourselves. It was Dai's despair that led him to take his own life—though I confess, I did naught to discourage it. I had no further use for him."

"Aye," said Kier, "that's the fate of all who put trust in you, once they outlive their usefulness, isn't it, Táranos? JonMarc tried to warn him. He might've saved his breath."

Táranos's eyes smoldered. "Trust is for fools. None put trust in me except to further their own ambitions." He chuckled. "And I've given them exactly what they wanted. To the Tiernai I promised Dynian to kill—to the Dynian, Tiernai." Táranos nodded toward the opening above. His violet eyes glittered with malicious glee. "Even now they gather to annihilate one another."

Above the steady drumming of the rain, Kier could feel the vibrations of horses and wains rumbling and clanking on the soggy plain above. But who? Kier recalled the dust plume they'd seen rising above the southern hills. Táranos must have summoned the Connail forces to him; nothing else would make them abandon their siege of Dorcalon. And if the Tiernai retreated, the Branwyn army was sure to follow.

"In but a few hours, all will be dead," Táranos said. "Alcor shall founder in her own blood, and I shall savor my victory—and my *revenge*."

Kier recoiled, sickened. He gripped the metal casket. Táranos had already spotted it. A ravenous glint lit the renegade Fithlon's eyes. "You will, of course, relinquish that to me."

Kier met his fiery gaze straight on, though it took every ounce of will. "The Cábretaur is mine by right of inheritance. You have no claim to it." A pointless argument, yet it might at least buy them time. Gwythion had promised to meet them here tonight. This would be a perfect moment for him to appear.

Táranos laughed. "Claim? *I* am Aneryn's true heir, descended in direct line from his only son. My family possessed these lands long before your Tiernai sires e'er set foot on Alcor. And though *both* races have conspired to deny me my birthright, no ruling—least of all that of a witless council and a dead prince—can change that."

Aneryn's *heir*? Doubt wormed into Kier's heart. Gwythion never mentioned *that*.

"All here is mine," Táranos went on, "including your precious Amulet— your *Hand of Lidialis*. Perhaps you neglected to note, Fitzmorwen, that Aneryn's prophecy applies as easily to me as to you: *Born of Love and Hatred; skilled of the Stag and the Serpent*. Did you imagine you were the only halfblood *Abominari* on Alcor?"

Táranos gave a cursory wave. "But I no longer need your trinket. The

Cábretaur is the prize. It belongs to whoever owns the power to wield it, and I alone possess that."

Kier and JonMarc exchanged anxious glances.

"Still, I can afford to be magnanimous. You three have discharged your duties admirably in retrieving the Gem. As reward, I shall allow you to depart with your lives. Give me the Cábretaur, and you may go your ways, unharmed. Be assured, I will not make the offer again."

Kier considered the renegade Fithlon's words. To abandon the Cábretaur was unthinkable, whatever resistance might cost him. "Let the girl go," he said. "She has no part in this."

"No!" Llydia moved up beside him, clasping her bow. "I stand with you."

"As I say, I will let you all go—as soon as I possess the Cábretaur."

Kier nudged Llydia behind him and drew his sword. "Then you'll have to kill me for it."

Again, Táranos laughed. The malignant sound curdled Kier's loins. "Do you imagine that is a challenge? I can kill you with a thought."

Kier's sword suddenly blazed with searing heat. With a yelp, he flung it down. Pain stabbed his brow, as though someone plunged hot pokers into his eyes. He tried to hold off the spell, but it bored into his mind like an auger of fire. He felt JonMarc wrench the casket from his numbing fingers. "No, JonMarc. He'll kill you. The Cábretaur is… my responsibility…" Kier's mouth felt full of cotton wadding.

Abruptly, the pain veered off. Gasping, Kier staggered into Llydia's arms.

JonMarc held the casket before him like a weapon. Táranos appeared amused. "Fool. Do you think your puny powers can counter mine? The mere taste you had at Ruthland sent you crawling on your belly. Do you now plead for more?"

JonMarc's lips peeled back in a savage grin. "My powers may be no match for yours, Táranos, but I've got the Cábretaur. Let's see you come and take it."

"And what do you expect to do with it? You've no idea how to wield it."

"Nor have you," said JonMarc. Despite Táranos's bluster, JonMarc detected uncertainty. The renegade Fithlon didn't know the Cábretaur's powers any more than he did. If the Nwtyrran gemstone could make Táranos invincible, might it not do the same for him?

Táranos regarded him down the length of his blade-like nose.

"Impudent spell-hand," he said, and lifted one wizened finger. JonMarc braced himself and raised the casket higher.

A flash like heaven-fire filled the chamber. Kier gasped as the gold-hilted dagger he'd hurled at Táranos exploded in mid-flight, spattering to the ground in sizzling drops of molten metal.

"I've no time for this childs' play!" Táranos thundered, focusing his mind on Kier and Llydia.

Llydia gave a little scream and her bow dropped from her ready hands as she slumped in a heap beneath his eyes of fire. Kier cried out when he saw her fall, but could do nothing to aid her. He braved the pain with all the fortitude he could muster, ready to die rather than let Táranos see him grovel. Yet he hadn't strength to withstand so ruthless an attack. In the end, the agony proved too much. He crumpled, a last, strangled cry of defiance on his lips.

"And now, my valiant fool," said Táranos, turning vengeful eyes on JonMarc. "You expect Gwythion to save you?" His voice brimmed with scorn. "He has no power left. I destroyed your Fithlon Master, just as I'll now destroy you."

Harsh cries echoed from the plain above. The pounding of hoofbeats dropped more clods from the unstable roof. "Do you hear?" Táranos said, with delight. "It has begun! The ancient Nwtyrrans had a phrase for it: *Har Maggithon*; the final battle. A pity you'll not live to see it."

JonMarc fumbled with the casket as Táranos's mind assault hit. He could feel a kind of power ripple through his hands, even with the casket closed, but he had no idea how to focus it—and no time to learn. His fingers suddenly felt huge and spongy, and would not obey his will. Searing waves battered him like a fiery wind. He raised the heavy box to shield his mind. For a while, it worked. His thoughts remained clear, while his body was enveloped in a seething cauldron of pain, made all the more exquisite because of the part of him that remained detached. His blood turned to molten liquid, boiling him from within. JonMarc felt the flesh drop from his bones like overcooked meat while he looked on, too horrified to scream. The casket glowed in his hands, a huge green fireball. Then JonMarc's arms cooked away and the box crashed to the ground, shattering into a million tiny motes of mocking laughter.

His exposed brain was a shriveled ember, charred and blackened. Somewhere at its core, a tiny voice whispered: "Give in. If Táranos thinks he's won, he'll stop." Slowly the message filtered to his reflexes. JonMarc's will shut down. He sank to the ground, a crumpled doll.

He awoke in darkness, to the smell of dirt. Damp, musty, it dusted his face and sprinkled inside his collar. He tried to rise and shifted a great weight of it off his side.

What had happened? Táranos was gone and had taken the Cábretaur with him. JonMarc sensed no power nearby, except... His left hand clutched the dathana crystal at his chest. JonMarc flexed his arms, ecstatic to find them still intact. Táranos must have used some power of illusion to make him think they'd burned away. He tried to move his legs, but could not feel them. What if...? JonMarc levered himself onto one elbow and tried again. This time, dirt shifted. He felt a prickling sensation as his buried limbs stirred.

Much of the cavern roof had collapsed: Táranos's attempt to bury them alive. Panic seized him. Where were Kier and Llydia? JonMarc called out, but received no answer. He struggled against the mountain that held him pinned. His head hit a tree root. A whole tangle hung above him, probably what had saved him from being fully interred. He grasped the largest and slowly worked his legs free. Crawling on his belly, he began to grope for his friends.

A shaft of white light illuminated the chamber, growing ever brighter: Denia's moon, rising above the escape hole. JonMarc dragged himself toward it. He found Kier and Llydia lying side by side. The cave-in had spared them. From the warmth of their limbs he knew they still lived, yet he couldn't rouse them. Recovery from such a mind assault might take hours, and Kier had faced it unprotected. It was a credit to his strength of will that he'd managed to survive at all. JonMarc had no such delusions about his own escape. It wasn't the Cábretaur that had saved him. He'd certainly failed to control that. No, his charmstone once again deserved the credit for protecting his life.

JonMarc knew what he now had to do: keep Táranos from using his new-found power to destroy Alcor. It seemed an impossible task. Yet he was the only one left to attempt it. Kier, should he awaken, hadn't the strength to challenge Táranos again with any hope of survival.

That thought unwittingly recalled his dream: Kier facing Táranos alone—and falling. What if it had been an accurate foreseeing? He now knew he had Telynor blood, and Llydia said the spell-handed of that line possessed true foresight. JonMarc's mind recoiled, remembering a passage from the Fithlon sacred book: *An event foreseen cannot be altered; it must and will occur as witnessed.* Blazes, what good was foresight if he couldn't prevent what he'd seen? There must be some way to change the outcome.

From somewhere deep inside him, the answer came. The charmstone. JonMarc grasped the small white crystal with the fiery heart. It fitted his palm perfectly, matched his own warmth so precisely that when he held it, it seemed to meld with his hand. It had saved his life three times—too valuable a token to simply relinquish. He might as well cut off his arm. Besides, there was no need. When he'd saved Kier from Táranos by seizing the Cábretaur, the last of his blood-debt had been discharged. He owed Kier nothing now. He could leave with a clear conscience. Kier was a capable soldier; he might yet survive. Best think about saving his own skin. JonMarc slipped the charmstone back inside his shirt.

"Wear it until ... you find someone you would offer your life for ... as I would for you." Ma'ardhi's words, that rainy night behind the Dragon Sword. It seemed a lifetime ago. Back then, Kier was just a brassy he'd meant to take advantage of—a tool to get him out of Castémaron. So much had changed. Had they truly grown so close?

The light of Denia's moon cast his kneeling shadow across Kier's face. Something in JonMarc stirred—a feeling of companionship, of brother-love such as he'd never known. He trusted Kier with a treasure he'd never before entrusted to anyone: his life.

JonMarc fingered the charmstone. The gift of life, thrice given, was as much as he had any right to expect—certainly more than he deserved. He lifted the braided silk cord over his head and strung it around Kier's neck, hiding the small crystal well inside his friend's shirt. Then he clambered to his feet.

His legs tingled with returning life. They must have been buried for hours. JonMarc looked toward the back of the cave but saw nothing but debris. The dead king's rest would remain forever undisturbed. A shaft of moonlight touched Llydia's face and she murmured in her sleep, soon to awaken. JonMarc wanted to be well away by then—no farewells, no arguments or explanations. His footprints in the soft ground would tell them he lived.

The rope was gone. Táranos must have removed it. JonMarc leaped up with all the strength his flaccid legs could muster. Bracing his elbows at the edges of the hole, he dragged himself out. He found the rope, still tied to the tree, and tossed it down for the others to use.

The sky had cleared since their arrival. The look of the field had changed dramatically. Two armies now camped on the open plain, their sprawling numbers, like great seething anthills, illuminated by a thousand campfires and the light of two full moons. Between lay a deserted swath of no-man's-land. JonMarc stood at its western end. Along either edge ran a ragged line of watchfires behind which sentries marched and restless soldiers edged their weapons. Tension pervaded the air, as thick and heavy as the smoke from the fires.

JonMarc crawled atop a low hillock for a better view. He could make out no colors to tell which force was which, but he made a fair guess. The Tiernai would have been first to arrive. They'd be the ones camped before the crumbling walls of Carreg Cymworth, where Táranos awaited Conjunction to proclaim his mastery. The Dynian had followed, and now penned their enemy against the peninsula's tip. JonMarc frowned. To reach the fortress, he must pass right through the Tiernai lines. Earls Ruark and Lochlainn would likely grant him safe passage, but how would he reach them?

A bray of horns far out on the field seized his attention. A party of Dynian bowmen had crept in low and taken its toll on an outlying Tiernai encampment. Now, with the Tiernai alarm sounded, a sortie of Dynian horsemen galloped up to cover their comrades' retreat. Such skirmishes must have been going on since the armies arrived. JonMarc recalled hearing one right above them, hours before. Were there casualties? He slipped behind the mound for a quick reconnaissance.

The ground was well-trampled, and blood had certainly been spilt. On the leeward side, hidden in shadow, two bodies lay side by side—one Tiernai, the other Dynian—staring blindly into the moonlight. The Tiernai had died from a sword thrust through the belly. The Dynian's throat was pierced by a crossbow bolt. The weapons that had done the damage lay beside them. JonMarc relieved the Dynian soldier of his dagger and bloodstained cloak. From the Tiernai, he borrowed a leather helmet and a short corselet that fitted snug across his chest. He also took the crossbow and quiver. He'd never used such a weapon, but it would help him pass for Tiernai. He gently closed the soldiers' sightless eyes and left them to their rest.

The field was bright for midnight, almost like murky day. Denia's full white moon now floated directly overhead, a gleaming alabaster beacon.

The larger red moon of her consort Devoreth, drifted amid the scudding clouds, its pitted face, like a worn copper skillet, casting a russet glow upon the landscape. But more brilliant still was the grim wanderer that traversed the skies between them—the Death Seer—the shimmering yellow jewel of the Life Star embedded in its tip. In a matter of hours, maybe less, Conjunction would be complete.

JonMarc made no attempt to conceal himself as he staggered across the wold, hoping the Tiernai sentries would take him for a wounded scout returning belatedly to his unit. He only prayed they would not shoot before hearing his tale.

He'd barely gone thirty paces when a shout up ahead told him he'd been spotted. He ambled on—no choice, now that they had him in their sights. With luck, the helmet would hide his blond hair. The blue eyes he must remember keep averted.

No one intercepted him; they only watched, and waited. Not until he neared a watchfire did someone shout a challenge. JonMarc grasped his belly with his weaponless hand. Two soldiers wearing the emblem of Dandryth ran out to help him. They clasped his biceps and did not let go.

"Name's Alun," JonMarc said, in answer to their questions, his pronunciation a flawless mimicry of Tiernai speech. "Me an' my comrades met a party of Branwyns at dusk, back by that hill. I was gut punched; knocked cold. Came 'round a bit ago an' found I'd been left for dead."

The excitement over, most of the curious began to move off. "Who d'ye serve?" asked the sentry who'd first spotted him.

"The Earl of Galwyn. I have to find my unit. Can you tell me where they're camped?"

The dark-eyed sentry still looked suspicious. He cocked his head eastward, along the front lines. "Who's yer captain?"

Blast. JonMarc couldn't recall the names of any of Ruark's officers. He dared not risk a blunder. "Captain M—" Suddenly he gagged and doubled over, clapping a hand to his mouth.

"Devoreth's cods," the sentry exclaimed, backing away. "He ain't spillin' his guts here! Get him behind them rocks." JonMarc's captors led him off, then turned away. One made a crude jest. For a while, they heard only retching sounds, punctuated by an occasional groan of supplication. By the time they realized the noises had ceased, JonMarc was gone.

He cautiously picked his way through the midst of the Tiernai army, keeping his distance from the campfires. With dawn still hours off, many foot-weary soldiers were trying to catch some sleep. Few paid him any heed. He came upon the banners of Galwyn and Derwenth flapping in a stiff breeze at the eastern end of the field, near the front lines. Clearly the Connails intended their shakier allies to bear the brunt of the casualties. Now he need only find Ruark's tent and contrive a way to speak with him; convince the doughty earl of the Connails' treason.

A figure stepped out from between two wagons to bar his path. Moonlight glanced off the intruder's blade. "Halt, soldier! Place your weapons on the ground."

JonMarc's belly cinched. All about him, weary troops stood clustered beside campfires. He couldn't run without drawing attention. Slowly he set down his crossbow and sword.

His captor picked up the bow. Without taking his eyes off JonMarc, he methodically set a bolt, then turned the weapon on him. "Who are you?" he demanded. JonMarc started to answer. The newcomer gestured impatiently. "Yes, yes, you call yourself Alun; I heard all that. You'll pardon my asking, *Alun*, how you managed to take part in a skirmish with the Branwyns at dusk when no Galwyn troops arrived on the field till after nightfall?"

JonMarc's mind raced. Why had his captor followed him all this way without crying an alarm? He could tell little about the man except that he was Tiernai and probably held some kind of rank. If he'd questioned JonMarc's story from the first, why hadn't he voiced his suspicions in front of the others?

His captor eyed him attentively. "So, you've nothing to say for yourself? Perhaps the blow to—your belly, was it?—addled your memory. *Look* at me when I talk to you, soldier."

JonMarc hesitated, then met the officer's eyes.

The man chuckled. "No, you certainly are *not* of Galwyn. Tell me your true name, Dynian."

JonMarc was thankful the officer kept his voice low. Until he could determine what lord the man served, he dared not reveal too much. "I am Mykhal Telynor," he replied. "I scout for Earl Antony Ruark. A week ago he sent me to spy out the Branwyn defenses at Dorcalon. For obvious reason, I've been unable to report till now."

The officer smiled disbelief. JonMarc had the uneasy feeling the man knew more than he let on. "Telynor? That's a royal name among the Dynian. How do you come to serve the Tiernai?"

"My loyalty is to Lord Antony alone," JonMarc answered, "my mission of utmost secrecy. Would you expect him to send a *Tiernai* spy into Dorcalon?" The last was one of Kier's favorite arguments. JonMarc threw it in, hoping its sheer logic would strike a responsive chord. His captor seemed no fool. "Do not doubt he pays me well for what I do," he added. Every race understood greed.

The officer licked his lips, considering. JonMarc decided to press his luck. "Take me to the earl. He'll confirm what I've said. Surely you've nothing to lose by that."

"Haven't I?"

A disturbance nearby cut him short. A lone rider came galloping heedlessly through the encampment. Startled soldiers cursed and shouted as they sprang out of the way. One man, not so lucky, was trampled where he lay and let out a howl that brought his comrades running. The rider blundered on without apology. He nearly careened into JonMarc and his captor.

The officer managed to keep the crossbow trained on JonMarc even as they leaped off the path. "Addle brain!" he bellowed. "Why don't you watch where you're going?"

The rider pulled up short. "I'm on official business," he snapped. "Where do I find Ruark?"

"You mean the *Earl of Galwyn*?" the officer growled, furious.

"Well, who d'ya think I mean, fool?" The rider hesitated. "Denys, is that you?"

"Aye," the seething reply. No love lost there. "The earl has retired for the night."

"Then wake him. Aran Connail will meet with his captains within the hour." The rider suddenly spotted JonMarc. "What've you got here? Some trouble you Galwyn boys can't handle?" He edged the horse nearer until it nudged JonMarc nearly off his feet.

"Everything's under control, Jeraint," said Denys. "You needn't concern yourself."

Jeraint ignored him. "What is he? A deserter?" He puzzled hard at JonMarc, who had already matched the name to the voice he'd overheard in the stables at Ruthland. So this was the Connails' self-esteeming captain. JonMarc was not impressed.

Jeraint's brown eyes narrowed. "Take off that helmet, soldier."

JonMarc cringed inwardly, but obeyed. For some reason, Denys, too, appeared uneasy.

"By the gods, he's *Dynian!*" shouted Jeraint, loud enough for the whole camp to overhear.

"He claims to be the earl's spy," said Denys.

"More likely Ross Branwyn's." Jeraint touched his sword to JonMarc's chest. "Have you interrogated him?"

"I was about to seek the truth from Lord Antony," Denys replied, trying to keep things down. Murmuring soldiers were already starting to cluster around them.

Jeraint smiled slyly. "So, the Earl of Galwyn has one of the enemy in his employ. Aran Connail will be very interested to hear *that*. What's your name, churl?"

"Mykhal Telynor," JonMarc replied. "Shall I spell it for the captain?"

Jeraint backhanded him.

"Blast it, Jeraint," said Denys, "we haven't determined whether he works for Lord Antony or not. But it would make sense. You'd hardly expect the earl to send a Tiernai spy into Dorcalon."

JonMarc raised an eye at hearing his own argument parroted back. Had Denys bought his tale?

Jeraint rubbed his goateed chin. "You know the Connails seek a particular Branwyn spy—the one who mutilated Aric Connail in a vicious and unprovoked attack. This one may know of him. Be sure to find that out. If so, report it to me immediately."

A greenish glint shone in Jeraint's eye. Denys clearly detected it. "Why to you, and not Earl Aran himself?"

Jeraint drew himself up proudly. "I am Earl Connail's right hand in this matter. The spy they seek is squire to the traitor Fitzmorwen. He goes by the name John Mark. There's a sizeable reward for his capture—Fitzmorwen's as well—so be watchful."

"I will," said Denys, "though I doubt either would be fool enough to show his face here."

"Pray that they do." Jeraint grinned. "We'll both be the richer for it." He reined his mount around and cantered off between the campfires.

Denys glowered after him. "Pompous ass," he muttered. He looked up to find perhaps a score of soldiers loitering within earshot. "All right," he said, "the excitement's over. Go back to your posts. And keep your eyes sharp. You heard the captain; there may be Branwyn spies about."

The men dispersed. Denys picked up JonMarc's sword. "Let's get you to the earl. He'll be interested to hear what you have to say for yourself—*John Mark.*" JonMarc's head shot up. "Did you think I didn't recognize you? I was with those who rode from Cordon with the earl and Prince Rhynion, Devoreth rest his soul. I knew you the moment you set foot in camp."

"Then why didn't you turn me in for the reward?"

Denys shrugged. "I still may." He jerked his head after Jeraint. "But not to him. I'd never see a sull of that money. Besides, there's not a few of us believe Aric Connail got what he deserved. For myself, the only thing I hate worse than a Dynian is a damned Connail."

The audience with Ruark and Lochlainn went badly from the start. To their minds—and they made their feelings abundantly clear—JonMarc was an opportunist who maneuvered his way through political crises with the finesse of a courtesan in a roomful of suitors. That he dared show up here, on the eve of battle, bearing tales of conspiracies and magical gemstones, only confirmed their conviction.

"We heard Duke Edmund speak his treason aloud," said Lochlainn. "He proclaimed within hearing of Aran Connail that he would not rest until he saw Malcolm and his cohorts brought down. Now, like it or not, Malcolm is our king. To speak against him is to speak treason."

"But Malcolm and the Connails plotted Rhynion's murder! I heard them at Ruthland."

"But you bring no *proof,*" said Ruark. "Who'll accept the word of a Dynian fugitive with a price on his head? Your very presence is an embarrassment. How d'ya think 'twill sit with the Connails that you claim to be in my employ?"

"Not well," said JonMarc, fuming. "I'd hoped, when I came, to find allies whose loyalty to Alcor went deeper than the safety of their own hides. I see I was wrong. But as you've said, my lord, you are implicated now. If you won't help me for Alcor's sake, maybe you'll do it to keep your own neck from the axe."

Ruark went livid.

"No one can doubt *our* loyalty," said the ever-sensible Lochlainn. "Least of all a Dynian lackey so recently come from the Branwyn camp. One may be loyal to Alcor and still question *you.*" His keen brown eyes probed JonMarc's. "Yet my heart tells me you speak truth. What aid do you require of us?"

"I need to reach the ruined fortress."

"Impossible," said Ruark. "The whole Connail army lies between."

"Well, I've made it this far. The fortress tower is where Táranos will proclaim his mastery."

"So you keep saying. Yet we've seen nothing of the attainted earl. So far as we know, he's still at his castle in Anlawth and has naught to do with any of this."

"He's *here*. I've met him. Why do you think the Connails brought the army all this way? Táranos came to seize the gemstone that will give him the power to dominate Alcor. Is that what you'd have your men fight and die for?"

Lochlainn thoughtfully rubbed his chin. "If this gemstone you speak of will give Earl Táranos such power, what makes you think you have any hope of stopping him?"

JonMarc frowned. "I may have none," he admitted. "But Kier lies wounded in a cave, Duke Edmund and Sir Donal are imprisoned, you two won't help me and Master Gwythion is not here. Blazes, *someone's* got to try and stop him."

Lochlainn leaned to Ruark and for a time they spoke too low for JonMarc to hear. Finally they reached a decision. "We hold no allegiance to Táranos," said Lochlainn. "Take what action you will against him. To that end, we will help you. You may pass through our lines disguised as one of Ruark's bodyguard—Devoreth help us if you're discovered. But Malcolm is our king, and the Connails, his chosen servants. Without *proof* of their treason, we dare not move against them. If we join Edmund on the headsman's block, Alcor will indeed be at the Connails' mercy."

"What if I find you proof?" said JonMarc. "Would you pull your men from the battle?"

Ruark scowled. "Aye, I would stay my men. 'Tis the Connails seek this battle. I've no wish to sacrifice my people to secure a tyrant's crown. But the proof must be beyond question. An' the Branwyns must agree to the truce. I'll not hamstring or dishonor my men."

JonMarc nodded. It was a tall order, one he had little likelihood of filling in the scant time left. "If I fail, is there any way you can save Duke Edmund?"

Lochlainn soberly shook his head. "The Connails are not a forgiving lot. Sir Donal and Kier's young centuriant are to be tried with him, all charged with treason."

So Gaelin had gotten through to Sir Donal with his message about the

Connails' guilt, and now the youth would die for it. "What will become of the Lady Cariwyn if her father is executed?"

"The duke's lands will be forfeit to the crown, which is to say, they'll be granted to the Connails. Lady Cariwyn will be disinherited, left penniless, though she'll not starve. As she is niece to my wife, I shall, of course, take her in. But her future is not hopeful. No young man of any standing would agree to wed a traitor's scion."

JonMarc's hopes brightened. Was this the answer to his dilemma? Cari could be his. He need only stay alive and forget about saving Alcor from Táranos's wrath—a futile task anyway. He and Cari could escape and live out their lives on some foreign shore.

Of course, Kier would die. Duke Edmund, too. And Gaelin, and Sir Donal, not to mention a host of Dynian and Tiernai soldiers. The cloud that darkened JonMarc's hopes set his temper boiling. What kind of choice was that? He could almost hear Fortunea's laughter, mocking him.

The ruse worked well at first. Denys returned JonMarc's sword and, disguised in a helmet and tunic of Galwyn, he marched in a small company behind Antony Ruark. JonMarc hunched his shoulders and tried to remain inconspicuous. The rest of the men ignored him.

They had nearly passed through Connail lines when they heard hoofbeats ahead. JonMarc slunk down and waited for the horse to come into view. It was familiar. So was the rider.

"I'm relieved to see you finally on your way, my lords," said Jeraint as he trotted up. "Earl Aran was growing—concerned." He spied Denys near the rear and turned to ride beside him. "Have you brought him?" he whispered, perusing the small detachment. "Ah, I see you have. Excellent! And he's well guarded. Wise of you to disguise him so." Jeraint winked. "We wouldn't want him taken for an intruder and killed out of hand."

"No, there'd be no profit in that, would there?" said Denys.

"Did he tell you anything of value?" The wink again. JonMarc was growing tired of being discussed as if he were the newest addition to the local brothel.

"Nothing we didn't already know."

"A pity. But no matter. Aran Connail wants to interrogate him anyway."

"But it's a waste of the earl's time!"

"My master will take that risk. Bind the Dynian's hands. He comes with me."

Ruark and his lieutenant exchanged troubled glances. Yet they could do nothing. JonMarc had sworn not to incriminate Ruark, though that would hardly matter once Aran Connail recognized him. JonMarc suspected Ruark must feel his future very tenuous right now. He was more concerned about his own.

Denys looped a rope several times around JonMarc's wrists, then tied a stout knot. The job appeared formidable enough. He drew the hem of JonMarc's tunic over the exposed sword hilt, hoping Jeraint wouldn't notice that the scabbard was not empty.

"Remove his helmet," said Jeraint. "I want him to be *seen*." He cinched the other end of the rope around his own waist, then set spurs to his horse's flanks. The beast leaped forward, nearly jerking JonMarc off his feet. That seemed to amuse Jeraint. "Come, Dynian. Earl Aran has a few surprises for you." JonMarc's belly churned.

Jeraint trotted him through the camp, taking a circuitous route to keep JonMarc stumbling and off balance. He deliberately dragged his prisoner through as many campfires as he could find, unconcerned with the disruption it caused. Rousted soldiers showed their displeasure by pelting JonMarc with whatever came to hand. By the time Jeraint neared the ruined fortress, JonMarc was breathless and bleeding—and well-singed.

Some yards from the walls, they came upon an outer defense ditch which now served the armies as a communal latrine. With a yip of glee, Jeraint raced for it, dragging JonMarc along on legs that were about to give out from sheer fatigue.

The wind whipped up from the south in a roar that sounded for all the world like massed voices. Men suddenly ran and shouted near at hand. JonMarc struggled to make out their words. What he heard resurrected his dying hopes. The Branwyns were attacking!

Jeraint pulled up in confusion. JonMarc swayed, his legs begging to collapse. He girded himself. Planting feet in the clumped turf, he yanked on the rope with all his remaining strength.

The action caught Jeraint by surprise. The horse lurched and sent the officer sailing backward to land on his rump in the mud. JonMarc raced past, tearing the knotted rope from his wrists. It formed a huge loop which he draped over the neck of Jeraint's mount. Then he slapped the beast hard. It took off at a gallop down the center of the ditch, Jeraint yelling and flailing behind.

JonMarc swayed, exhausted, and sank to his knees. He knew he should run to save himself, but he could scarcely move. His arms felt as if they'd been ripped from their sockets. He raised his eyes to the bright heavens and caught his breath. The Death Seer glared overhead, a blazing harbinger of doom. Behind it, the Life Star could barely be seen.

JonMarc struggled to his feet, forcing his spent legs to obey, and followed the shadow of the ditch back toward the fortress tower. He had only one thought: to stop Táranos before the madman could summon the power of the Cábretaur. He had no idea how he might do it.

Battle sounds echoed from the south, but here, behind Tiernai lines, the situation remained quiet. Most of the troops had surged forward in disorder at the first alarm. JonMarc saw figures clustered at the fortress gates, but the light was too dim to identify them.

Even as he watched, a robed form stepped onto the battlements. Moonlight shone pale in his silvery hair. JonMarc's heart caught. At the base of the tower, another figure stood in challenge. JonMarc didn't need to see his face. He knew it was Kier. He scrambled up the bank.

An unexpected noise stopped him—the sound of a steel bolt being drawn. JonMarc spun.

He found himself confronting hueless eyes, hueless hair, a blanched and waxen face with a scar like a deep, muddied river carving the left cheek.

Roderig smiled, a death's-head grin, and leveled his crossbow at JonMarc's heart.

Chapter Thirty-three

The Tiernai sentry would not be appeased. Kier had to commend the man for his diligence, while at the same time cursing the fate that led him to cross such an attentive soldier's path.

He'd managed to flank most of the Tiernai forces by following the sea cliff around the peninsula's westward edge. The bright moonlight had been no friend to him. Even so, he'd nearly succeeded in avoiding the outlying Tiernai pickets. Nearly.

"I'm sorry, captain," the sentry said, in response to Kier's obvious impatience. His manner was polite, yet brusque. "I was ordered to watch for an officer of your description. If my commander accepts your account, you'll be free to go."

The tale Kier had concocted to explain himself would not hold up under scrutiny. He glanced about, seeking some escape before the Legion officer, whoever it might be, arrived to call his bluff. What might JonMarc do in such straits? The answer that came to mind went entirely against Kier's nature—or would have, a few short weeks ago. His outlook seemed somewhat different now. Either he had changed, or he simply faced more desperate circumstances. Either way, he found himself contemplating an unpardonable breach of etiquette: the assault of a fellow legionary.

Kier let his restless gaze wander back toward the cliffs. He drew a sharp breath and pointed. "Blazes, they're flanking us!" Alarmed, the sentry's eyes followed. Kier crumpled him with a neck chop the moment his head turned, and slunk off like a shadow into the night.

A massive Tiernai host sprawled across the plain, campfires blazing like beacons in the blustery dark. JonMarc was out there somewhere, trailing Táranos. Kier was sure of it. He rubbed his aching temples, wishing his friend had waited. He hated the thought of JonMarc wandering alone amongst the Tiernai. Llydia was gone as well. Kier had sent her back to her brother's camp—the safest place, with a battle in the offing. She'd protested, but her presence would make his task impossible. Deep in his heart, Kier feared he'd never see her again. That knowledge pained him far more than his throbbing head.

He forced both matters aside. He had to stop Táranos, even if it cost him his life. To fail again meant the death of all he cared about. Yet try as he might, he could think of no way. His defeat in Aneryn's cave proved he hadn't the strength to face his enemy mind to mind. And now that Táranos had the Cábretaur, the renegade Fithlon was all but invincible. The only one with any chance of stopping him was Gwythion. But the Fithlon Master had not arrived. Kier clung to hope that he would, at the last moment—like an avenging god in a mummers' play. In all their years' acquaintance, he'd never known Gwythion to betray a trust. Yet time was running out.

Kier picked his way along the cliff's edge, while breakers churned and thundered against the rocks below. He felt as if poised at the entrance to some long, lightless tunnel, fearful to enter, yet knowing his only path to daylight led through the darkness. Two days ago he'd have welcomed death with honor. Yet against all reason, he'd suddenly found something to live for—Llydia, who saw through his stout defenses as if they were glass; who seemed to love him *for* his fractured parts, not simply in spite of them. Kier never imagined such a miracle could happen. That Fortunea should send her to him now, when he faced almost certain annihilation, only emphasized why the harlot goddess was dubbed *heartless*.

The path began to narrow. Ahead, Carreg Cymworth's jagged walls glowed pale and ghostly in the cloud-shredded moonlight. Watchfires burned before the gates. Táranos was in there; Kier could feel his enemy's presence lurking at the edge of his senses like a brooding storm.

There were no sentries posted this far behind the lines—none to mark his passing but a handful of weary troops huddled around campfires, and they didn't even glance his way. Kier reached the dry moat that protected the fortress. Using its high bank as cover, he could follow it all the way to the ruined gates without being seen. Kier scrambled down. Thorn scrub and debris choked the bottom. He cautiously made his way along the edge, keeping low.

As he neared the watchfires, a muted roar surged up from the south. Kier cocked his ear. A shiver lanced through him. He recognized the sound of battle. Shouting erupted near the gates as horsemen leaped upon their mounts and spurred for the front. Kier ducked beneath the newly-repaired drawbridge as an errand rider reined in above.

"I bear news for the king!" the man shouted, breathless. "The Branwyns have attacked!"

Kier blew a bitter breath. Ross Branwyn was proving himself a brilliant tactician. His pre-dawn assault had clearly caught the Tiernai off guard. It also dashed Kier's desperate hope that, by stopping Táranos, he might end this needless conflict before it started.

The rider's news raised a frenzy at the gates. The roar of battle already rolled in from the front like an ferocious tide, charging the night air with tension. Above the clangor of armies in collision came a more chilling sound: the blood-freezing war shriek of the Dynian. Kier had witnessed the terror that cry evoked in daylight. Here in the dark hour before dawn, its effect upon the rousted Tiernai could be devastating.

That sentiment was being voiced above by a furious Antony Ruark. Kier peered over the lip of the moat as the doughty earl strode up to the gates, snorting like an incensed bull. Lochlainn, Hannon, and Aran Connail hastened in his wake. What in blazes were they doing back here when they should be at the front, leading their troops?

"Where is the king?" Ruark demanded. "There's a battle out there that wants his attention!"

"Calm yourself, Ruark," said Aran Connail. "There's naught to fear. Our victory is assured."

"Don't waste my time with false promises, Connail. The only way to assure victory is to *fight*. Let me go to my men. While you talk, they're being butchered!"

Aran Connail drew himself up haughtily. "Our ruler commands you to remain."

"Does he, now? We'll see about that." Ruark elbowed Connail aside and stalked up to confront Malcolm, now exiting the gates, Penitarch Tor, beside him. Kier was amazed at how haggard his brother looked. Beneath his royal robes, Malcolm's shoulders sagged as if he bore a heavy weight of care.

"I don't understand, my lord," Malcolm said, addressing Ruark's protest. "What prevents you joining your troops?"

Ruark's eyes nearly bulged from their sockets. "Your Majesty ordered us to stay. What else could keep me here when the Branwyns make mincemeat of my men?"

Malcolm's brow furrowed. "I gave no such command."

Penitarch Tor touched his shoulder. "'Tis Lord Táranos's wish, Majesty."

Malcolm's brown eyes flashed. "Táranos is not your king. How dare the Earl of Anlawth presume to command my captains?"

"Silence, fool," hissed Tor Connail.

But Malcolm had clearly reached a breaking point. "I'll *not* be silent! I am your king, not your boot rag. It's time you remembered that."

The black-robed penitarch's fingers tightened around his staff of office. "Miserable worm, you are whatever we *tell* you to be. Do not forget who placed you on the throne."

"Forget?" Malcolm replied, heedless of who might overhear. "How can I? You Connails and Táranos conspired it, though I said I wanted no killing. Now I see you only meant to use me to feed your own ambitions. I'll no longer take orders from you, Connail! The throne is mine by right of blood, and I'll be no man's puppet."

Through the press of legs, Kier caught the defiant gleam in Malcolm's dark eyes. It reminded him of the duke, their father.

Antony Ruark gripped his sword hilt. "So Edmund spoke aright. You Connails *did* plot Rhynion's murder."

Tor Connail's smile reflected supreme confidence in his own invulnerability. "You cannot prove that. You've naught but the word of this spineless creature you call king, and he'll soon regret his lies." His eyes darted to the tower above, and Kier knew his meaning. Táranos would not forgive his brother's rash tongue. "Do not think to summon the Guard," the penitarch added, as Ruark opened his mouth to do just that. "These men obey *me*. Raise a hand and, like Edmund, you will pay the price of treason."

Ruark glanced about. He had little support. Norris Hannon of Dandryth stood wringing his hands, a quivering mass of near-hysteria. Only Jaremy Lochlainn held staunch at his right.

"Join us, Ruark," urged Aran Connail, from behind. "Lord Táranos possesses powers you can scarcely dream of. And you cannot hope to challenge us—just the two of you, alone."

"*Three*," Kier shouted, mounting the bank. Ruark's face lit with surprise when he saw him. He lent Kier a hand up and clapped him fondly on the shoulder.

Tor Connail's eyes blazed. "Guards! It's the traitor, Fitzmorwen. *Kill him!*"

"No!" Malcolm thrust himself between Kier and the sentries. "I forbid it. Put up your swords." He pointed south, toward the mounting fray. "Don't you see? The enemy is out there!"

"No, Majesty," the penitarch seethed, whisking out his blade, "the enemy is *here*." Before anyone could react, Tor Connail plunged a foot of steel through the young monarch's belly.

Malcolm gasped and stared down at Connail's blade as though he could not fathom what he saw. The astonished guards stood paralyzed, not knowing what to do, who to follow.

With a bellow of rage, Kier drew and lunged. Tor Connail barely tugged his weapon free of Malcolm's sagging body when Kier drove his sword straight through the penitarch's heart.

Connail gave a strangled scream and slowly slid backward off the blade, disbelief chiseled on his ruddy features. He tumbled from the drawbridge and lay twitching his death throes in the muddy ditch below.

Kier left Ruark and Lochlainn to deal with the confusion at the gates. He lifted Malcolm in his arms and bore him off the bridge. Gently, he laid his half-brother in the coarse grass and knelt beside him, wiping blood from his lips. Malcolm clawed Kier's forearm as a spasm of pain laced through him. Then his slender body relaxed and his breathing seemed to ease. Kier bundled the velvet cloak beneath his head.

Malcolm gazed at him, brown eyes clear and completely lucid. "I'm glad... you still live," he whispered hoarsely. "There is... so much you need to know."

Kier shook his head. "Rest now. I know someone who can help you. She's a healer..."

"Don't... trouble yourself." Malcolm seemed to smile, though blood oozed from the corner of his mouth. "It's better this way. It is easier to die than it is to kill. Rhynion's face haunts me always. But—" Malcolm coughed, spattering Kier's sleeve. "Believe me, Kier, I never wished your death. It was Táranos..."

Kier dabbed his brother's chin. "I'll end his power if I can."

Eyes glistening, Malcolm clutched his arm. "You cannot. He is merciless. He turns your greatest desires against you." Malcolm's eyes squeezed shut. Kier felt a shudder pass through his brother's body and grasped his hand, trying to will life back into him. The fingers felt icy.

Malcolm opened his eyes once more as the pain in his belly seemed to ease. "I'm sorry Kier, for the things I said at Cordon. I never told you..." A pained sigh. "All my life, I only wanted... to be like you." Malcolm's head drooped and his last, ragged breath hissed away.

Kier's jaw trembled. He closed his brother's eyes and stared at his ashen face. Like *him*? All these years he'd thought Malcolm despised him. Yet now...

He quickly wiped the moisture from his eyes as Antony Ruark strode up with two of Malcolm's guards. The earl removed his helmet in the presence of death. "Poor Malcolm," he murmured. "He had no chance to be much of a king."

"He tried," Kier said bitterly. "In the end."

A crackle of profane laughter echoed from above. "So, the carrion eaters feast on one another. That is fitting." Táranos stood on the wall above the gates, his shining robes fluttering in the blustery moonlight.

Kier turned flashing eyes. "*You* are responsible for this."

The renegade Fithlon nodded graciously. "I like to think that, in my small way, I had a hand in the havoc you see around you."

"You're mad," Kier growled, under his breath.

"No, Fitzmorwen, I am *king*—of Alcor and, very soon, of all Éclatan. Look to the sky. Conjunction is nearly complete. Look—and behold my triumph!"

Kier refused to follow his finger. "I see only murder and betrayal. Is that what you set out to achieve?"

"*Yes*. For what the Dynian and Tiernai did to me. Disinherited. Outcast. I swore one day I'd take revenge. Now, at last, comes the day of reckoning." Táranos held aloft the metal casket. Few but Kier knew its significance, though it was clearly a token of some dread power.

"Táranos!" Aran Connail's ragged cry intruded on the scene. He stood beyond the drawbridge, under guard, and had been clamoring for attention since Táranos first appeared. Thusfar, the renegade Fithlon had refused to acknowledge him. "My brother is dead, Táranos. You promised us victory, yet you allowed this. I demand retaliation!"

Táranos sneered. "Blundering fool. You and your Covenanter brother botched every task I set you to. Incompetence merits no reward."

"But we were your true allies. We did all you asked." Aran Connail mopped sweat from his craggy face. "How will you recompense me for my brother's murder?"

Perverse humor tugged at Táranos's lips. "You want recompense? Very well, here is the reward your service merits." Táranos flicked his finger.

Like the kick of a giant mule, Aran Connail was lifted off his feet and hurled backward, onto the guard's poised halberd. The weapon plunged into his back and out again through his chest, its razor point dripping heart and lung tissue. The guard cried out in terror and leaped aside. For a moment, Aran Connail stood there, lips spewing blood in a soundless accusation. Then he collapsed in a heap.

The sounds of battle grew nearer. An errand rider galloped up in a billow of dust and scanned faces still in shock from the horror they'd witnessed. "Where is the king?" he cried.

"Here," said Táranos.

The rider glanced at the battlements, confused. "The Branwyns have broken through our defenses," he shouted, to no one in particular. "They come this way."

"What casualties?" demanded Ruark.

The rider dismounted, more at ease with someone he recognized. "Impossible to say, my lord. It's madness up there. No one commands."

Kier laid a firm hand on Ruark's shoulder. "Go to your men, Lord Antony."

Ruark gave a curt nod. "Aye, an' past time for it, too." Through the corner of his eye, he looked to see if Táranos meant to stop him, or worse, mete out the same punishment he'd inflicted on Aran Connail. But Táranos was in a jubilant mood.

"Yes, brave Lord Antony, go and die with your men. I've no more need of you here. Your comrade Lochlainn, and Captain Fitzmorwen, will suffice to witness my ascendancy."

Ruark snarled something inaudible and leaped onto the errand rider's horse. He spurred away before the new "king" could change his mind.

The rider's report had unnerved Norris Hannon. He wrung his pudgy hands and glanced furtively over his shoulder as though at any moment Ross Branwyn would lead a pack of shrieking heathens down on them. "We must flee, my liege!" he cried. "Take refuge behind the walls before it's too late!"

"Let them come," said Táranos, regarding the portly earl with a condescending sneer that made Kier's flesh crawl. "Poor Hannon. Do the nasty Branwyns frighten you?" Táranos's eyes glittered, savoring the game. "But I am your king now. Do you not trust me to protect you?"

Hannon's glance darted from the dead face of Aran Connail, gaping in betrayal, to Malcolm's body, lying nearer at hand. He nervously licked his lips. "Of... of course I do."

"*Liar.*" Táranos narrowed his brows. Instantly, Norris Hannon's hands flew to his own throat and began to squeeze, tighter and tighter, while he made little gurgling sounds and tried to tear them away. Táranos focused his thoughts and Hannon's bloated face purpled. Slowly, he sank to the ground, gasping for the air his own fingers denied him. A final wrench, and he fell on his side, unmoving.

Kier looked on, helpless. Táranos alone seemed unconcerned. "And you, Lochlainn. Will you now honor me as your liegelord?"

The tall lord Jaremy drew himself up proudly, despite the terror he must feel. "I see no king," he said. "Only an executioner."

For an instant Táranos seemed taken aback. Then his features hardened. "Very well," he said. "Remember that sight."

Lochlainn gave a sharp gasp as a glance from Táranos forced him to his knees. He covered his face with his hands. Kier knelt beside him and grasped his arm. "My lord?"

Lochlainn slowly withdrew his hands from his eyes. "Devoreth preserve us, Kier," he whispered. "I am blinded."

Kier stood, trembling with rage. Unmindful of the wild cries, the clatter of a half-dozen skirmishes now nearer at hand, his only thought was of Táranos, and how his power might be broken. He could think of no way.

"What will you do to *me*, Táranos?" he shouted in futile challenge. "I'll not kneel to you either."

He felt the heat of Táranos's eyes, as he had in the cave, and his belly knotted.

"Do you pretend you do not fear me, Fitzmorwen?"

"I fear you. I'd be a fool if I did not."

"True," said Táranos. "And you admit it. You are wiser than the rest. Do you not wonder why I let you live, back at Aneryn's tomb? It was no oversight. I've had my eye on you, Fitzmorwen. We are of a kind, you and I—both halfblood Abominari, both rejected by the society that fostered us. We must find our strength and our succor within ourselves. Yet perhaps we can be of use to one another."

"What use?" Kier asked warily.

Táranos's robes fluttered in the brisk sea wind. "I will soon rule this world." A statement of simple fact; no uncertainty there. "I suddenly find myself in need of reliable captains."

Kier's eyes smoldered. "I'm not surprised."

"The rewards will be great. Oh, not for scum such as these." Táranos gave a careless wave toward the bodies below. "You and I know what manner of men the Connails were. They deserved their fates. But for one like yourself—valiant, bright, able to follow orders, yet with formidable strength of will—you are one I could rely on; one with more at heart than his own ambition. In return, I will grant you all you've ever dreamed of: success, riches, even the Lady Cariwyn for your bride."

"I'm flattered," said Kier, sounding otherwise. "But it seems to me you already have a captain. What of your murdering viper, Roderig? Do you abandon him as well?"

"Roderig is a useful tool—and supremely loyal, since I delivered him from those who would have burned him alive simply because he was born without color. His hatreds run deep. He relishes slaughter, and soon I shall send him forth to glut himself on it. Yet he cannot savor the irony as you and I can. Dynian and Tiernai, the races that rejected us, destroying one another for our pleasure. Is it not the perfect revenge?"

Kier turned away, sickened. "I desire no revenge. How can you imagine I would ever serve you, Táranos? I despise all you stand for."

Táranos glanced at the sky and clicked his tongue. "A pity. I see Gwythion has poisoned your mind. Then hear the *truth*, Fitzmorwen. Your Fithlon Master is using you. Why else would he desert you now, when you most need him? He has coveted the Cábretaur for years; deceived you into risking your life to attain it for him. But now that it is mine, he fears to show himself, for he knows he is no match for my power. Your Master Gwythion has deserted you, just as he forsook my own master, years ago. He cares only for himself and cannot comprehend the torment this world wreaks upon such as us. But *I* understand what you've endured: the scorn, the humiliation, for I have known it as well. Tiernai and Dynian, Fithlon and Covenanter, skill-hand and sinistral: they all revile us. We will never fit their narrow world. Yet with the Cábretaur's power, we will create a new order, purged of all who despise us. Join me, Fitzmorwen, and never again know rejection. I can make you great."

The unexpected overture shook Kier to his core. After all he'd seen of Táranos's treachery, why would the renegade Fithlon court him to be his champion? Only to have someone with whom to share his warped notion of revenge? It defied all reason. Still... what if Táranos's allegations about Gwythion were true? At times, Kier had indeed suspected his mentor of using him. And where was he? He should have been at hand when they found the Cábretaur. Had Gwythion abandoned him? His mentor knew he hadn't the strength to face Táranos alone; had reassured him it was not his task to do so. Yet now...

Kier shut his eyes to banish doubt. "I've seen what happens to those who follow you, Táranos. I'd sooner stumble on my own than succeed with your malignant power behind me."

He expected a furious backlash, but Táranos only laughed. The eerie sound of it carried over the field, seeping into Kier's bones and turning his blood to icy brine. "Did you think this a request? You *will* serve me, Fitzmorwen, willing or no. You will witness my ascendancy and bear my will to all the Deg Tirith. Roderig has neither the skill nor finesse for that. Still, I prefer you do so willingly. To compel you would leave you, shall we say, less effective. Perhaps you require greater inducement: a demonstration of what the Cábretaur can do? Very well. *See*."

Before Kier could even brace himself, the force of Táranos's mind hit him like a giant fist, compressing his chest and stealing his breath. A storm erupted inside his brain. The skirmishes around him became a blur as choking corpse dust swirled through his nose and mouth, entering his eyes and stopping his ears. Kier groaned and swayed, adrift on a billowing sea of blackness.

Abruptly, the mist cleared and Kier again found himself on the battle plain. But it had changed. The chalky turf lay strewn with bodies, rotting in a bleared, mid-day heat. Kier wandered, sickened, among endless heaps of decaying carcasses and severed limbs. The stench of all the dead ever left unburied filled his nostrils. Carrion eaters flapped and shrieked among the ragged piles, feeding on moldering flesh of Dynian and Tiernai dead. Nothing else moved.

Then, across the battle plain rose a fierce wind, and Kier was lifted upon it. The scene below broadened. He floated above the rolling hills of Alcor, no longer green. Slag and ash covered the landscape, as if a rain of fire had blasted the land. Smoke rose high in the fetid air as armed brigands battled through the countryside, torching all they encountered. The Berwyn forest was a sea of blackened stumps and wasted villages. Children screamed over their parents' mangled corpses, only to be skewered themselves and tossed upon the ever-growing pyres.

Horror stricken, Kier drifted over Dorcalon, now a smoldering ruin, and saw the white walls of once-proud Caerllyn leveled to dust. Far in the distance, he saw Castle Cordon, now an island of smoking rubble amid a charred and pillaged landscape. The mighty river Averin pooled stagnant, its flow choked with corpses, Dynian and Tiernai, indistinguishable in death.

The phantom wind carried Kier higher still. He gazed out over the wide sea to the rest of the Deg Tirith. Plumes of grey smoke rose from Castémaron and Glen Tierna. Fires burned the ancient forests of Tarim and across the grassy plains of Chalcedon. Everywhere, Kier could hear enslaved peoples shrieking and groaning their agony. But from Alcor there was only silence.

Táranos's laughter clove the scene like a knacker's blade. The cloud pictures vanished and Kier again found himself before the ruined fortress. Táranos still stood on the battlement above him, now holding aloft the casket that housed the Cábretaur. Amid the havoc of a nearby skirmish, a soldier cried aloud: "Look! The Wanderer; it turns to flame!"

Still reeling from his vision, Kier raised his eyes heavenward and caught his breath. The Death Seer was wreathed in a dazzling orange brilliance that lit the night sky as if a blast of fire had erupted behind it.

Táranos cackled his exuberance. "The hour of Conjunction is come. This is the age of my ascendancy!" His voice carried far onto the battlefield. With trembling hands, he withdrew the Cábretaur from its metal casket. The gem glowed pestilential green as he brandished it on high. "Behold, *I am your God.* Kneel and worship me!"

The fighting before the gates ground to a bloody halt as Tiernai and Dynian soldiers discovered their limbs would no longer obey them. Weapons dropped and an eerie quiet fell as the combatants sank to their knees, compelled there by the staggering power of Táranos's will.

Kier fought with all his strength to remain standing, yet beneath the weight of Táranos's command, his legs would not support him. He dropped to his knees like a severed string-puppet.

Táranos could barely contain his glee. "The world as you have known it is ended. From this hour, all will revere me. And my reign shall be as mighty as Nwtyrra's of old, for the dread power they possessed is now *mine.*"

Kier's mind spun. Táranos wielded the Cábretaur unshielded. Was there any force in all Éclatan mighty enough to stop him? What if his only choice was to join with the renegade?—use what influence he had to temper Táranos's revenge? The scenes of destruction he'd witnessed could not have been foresight, for Gwythion said Táranos did not possess that talent. They must merely be projections of what Táranos intended. If so, there was still a chance Kier might change them. But—could Gwythion's word be trusted?

Far across the plain, the battle clamor stilled echoed, but those who knelt before the ruins of Carreg Cymworth could only stare like mindless thralls.

"Warriors of the Tiernai and Dynian," Táranos cried, eyes aflame, "your will is mine to command. Go forth and destroy your enemies. Let none survive: women, children, infants in their cradles—slaughter them all, and by their blood let this land be cleansed. You now fight at my command; kill at my command; *die* by my command! And the slaughter shall not cease until every one of your foes is vanquished. This you will do to avenge me, your ruler and your *God*."

Kier's belly writhed. How could he take part in such madness? Táranos would never heed his puny words of protest. Yet how else could he stop the carnage? Kill the Fithlon renegade? He'd tried, back at Aneryn's tomb. Táranos sensed his intent before he could act. Kier sought through his military training. *Exploit your enemy's weaknesses.* But Táranos *had* no weaknesses. He'd made himself invulnerable. Alcor would founder in her own blood to satisfy the madman's festering hatred.

Hatred... a mask for fear. Duke Morwen's words. Kier seized on them. What did Táranos fear? Defeat? With the Cábretaur at his command, he was invincible. Rejection, then? But Táranos had the power to compel men to his will. He could no longer *be* rejected.

A pale light glimmered in Kier's mind. Not rejection of itself, but... the notion that such rejection was warranted? That indeed, he was *not* worthy? The revelation slapped Kier like a splash from an icy spring. He knew that fear; it was his own, enlarged and distorted, like a shadow play on a giant screen. Táranos sought to destroy all who had rejected him. Yet men only attacked what they feared. If Táranos could still imagine himself threatened, when by all logic he was unassailable, that belief must come from within. Kier's pulse raced. It was a chink—if only a minute one—in Táranos's armor. But could he use it? Blazes, he hadn't even strength to move his limbs!

"*You have strength. Only your fears keep you from recognizing it.*" Llydia's voice. He could hear the words almost as if she spoke them to his face. "*No army can prevail that is in conflict with itself. Make peace with—*" Who? All those he'd ever deemed the source of his rejection? And in doing so, cast out the festering fear that he was unworthy. The revelation stunned Kier. In seeking Táranos's weakness, he had discovered the source of his own.

An oppressive weight lifted from Kier's soul, and behind it a power stirred; not sinistral talent or his Fithlon skills, but a deeper, more fundamental strength of will. He tried to move his limbs and found that he could overcome Táranos's control. He sought about him for some means to drive the Cábretaur from Táranos's grasp. Nearby, one of Malcolm's fallen standards lay trodden in the mud. Kier cautiously dragged himself toward it. Táranos did not see. Still absorbed in his tirade of retribution, the Fithlon renegade laughed wildly and gestured to the sky.

"Soon my triumph shall be complete. When the Nwtyrrans return—as they soon shall, for the summons has been sent—they will find themselves subject to my will!"

Nwtyrrans return? Summons? A chill shook Kier. He thrust the distraction aside. Seizing the standard pole, he hoisted himself to his feet and, with his every ounce of remaining strength, he hurled the makeshift spear.

His movement caught Táranos by surprise. Only by sheer luck did the Fithlon renegade dodge in time. The lance missed the Cábretaur by a hair's-breadth.

With an outraged snarl, Táranos turned on Kier, his violet eyes blazing like flames from the pit as shock and fury overwhelmed him. "You *dare* defy me? You haven't the power."

Dismayed, Kier threw back his head and laughed. He could not have said why. Hopelessness? The numbing fatalism that comes when the depth of despair shuts out fear? Gods, he must be as mad as Táranos. "Haven't I?" he cried. "Look again, Táranos. I reject you and all you stand for. You're a weakling and a coward. I'll play no part in your hate."

Táranos's face contorted. With a roar, he hurled the Cábretaur's empty casket. The leaden box caught Kier square in the chest, staggering him, yet he managed to hold his ground.

"Aye, strike at me, Táranos," he cried, his hoarse voice maniacal to his own ears. "Strike at Alcor. But when all those you hate are dead, who then will you blame for your cowardice?"

A searing claw seized Kier's mind. Terror flooded him; anguish, outrage—*but they were not his own.* Their force beat against him from without, like a violent hailstorm. Táranos howled his humiliation. A whirlwind of fire surrounded Kier as the full force of the Fithlon's rage assailed him. Pain imploded his mind and his knees buckled.

Through the conflagration—as if on the ragged fringes of dream—
Kier thought he saw the figures around him rouse and struggle to their
feet. But that was impossible. How could they move? Unless... Kier hardly
dared hope. Had he done it? Had his challenge broken Táranos's will? Then
perhaps he did not sacrifice his life in vain. Kier felt his consciousness
shrivel like crackling tinder. With a last, strangled cry of defiance, he let his
mind embrace death.

§

The scene was just like his dream. Beneath the tower walls, Kier lay
still, struck down by the force of Táranos's wrath. Swaying on his knees,
JonMarc blinked hard, trying to decide whether the spectacle he beheld
was real or just the backwash of some tortured nightmare. It seemed hours
that he'd knelt there, spewing his guts, powerless to rise.

Roderig's scarred face grinned at him like the cracked head of a
toppled statue. The henchman's torso sprawled on its belly, drenched in
its own spurted blood. In the last, desperate second, JonMarc had hurled
himself sideways, then slashed across in a wild backhand, decapitating the
malignant henchman in one stroke.

A tingle of life returned to JonMarc's limbs as the paralyzing weight
that had held him prone miraculously lifted. Unmindful of the burning
hole in his left shoulder where Roderig's bolt had passed through, he
grabbed up the sword, dragged himself to his feet and staggered toward the
tower. He dropped to raw knees beside Kier's body and yanked his friend's
face out of the mud.

All around, soldiers of both races, looking as dazed as he, groped for
their weapons and struggled to stand. Off to the south, the sounds of the
main battle drew nearer. A few tentative altercations renewed nearby as
soldiers faced their adversaries, knowing they too should be fighting, but
not quite remembering why.

Táranos stood upon the battlements, his hair and robes flying wild. His
face was a mask of bewilderment as he beheld the conflict renewing around
him.

"To your *knees*," he cried. "I *command* it!"

Another errand rider made his way through the confusion. "An army
approaches from the east," he shouted. "They bear the standard of Gerit
Mawr."

The wild yells and scraping of steel intensified as more soldiers again found their limbs and joined the fray. Táranos raised the Cábretaur high. *"Cease fighting. You obey my will."*

The combatants regarded him no more than if he were a screeching night-hawk.

JonMarc gripped his sword and gazed about. He could not comprehend what was happening any better than Táranos. Beside him, the lead casket that had housed the Cábretaur lay edgewise in the mud. Even as Táranos bellowed his command a third time, one of the crystals set in the lid suddenly came to life—a tiny golden star, glowing steadily brighter.

Memory stirred. As at the Spire, and Aneryn's tomb, JonMarc knew what to do. He groped inside his shirt for the charmstone. Gone! Blazes, what had...? No, wait, he'd given it to Kier. JonMarc thrust his hand inside Kier's jerkin and yanked the dathana crystal from his friend's throat. He touched its point to the glowing crystal.

There was a blinding flash, as if the Life Star herself had plummeted from the sky to cast her fiery brilliance among them. Soldiers cried out in terror and covered their eyes.

Then, as swiftly as it appeared, the grueling light faded. Only a green shaft remained, connecting the Cábretaur in Táranos's hands with the smaller yellow crystal on the casket lid.

Táranos stood frozen, staring at the wonder in his grasp. The gangrenous light shone up to illuminate his cadaverous features. The Cábretaur grew brighter. Like a living thing, it swelled to a massive sphere in his hands. Then the shaft of light diminished and only the Cábretaur remained, glowing its lurid hue.

Táranos cackled in triumph as those on the field at last appeared to heed his will. "You see?" he cried, as the crystal grew, "I alone possess the talent to wield the Cábretaur unshielded. I am Nwtyrra's heir!" The green light continued to spread, enveloping his hands, his arms. "The power is *mine.*" His voice sounded strangely garbled. "To your knees and worship me!"

The ground rumbled, as if Éclatan herself recoiled, and the fortress walls tremored. Still the Cábretaur grew. Táranos's shout of triumph became a shriek of agony. To JonMarc, shielding his eyes from the glare, it seemed the renegade Fithlon's arms began to wither in that ghastly light. The hands that held the Gem aloft shrank to bony claws.

Táranos's screams filled the air as the green light consumed him. He ran along the battlements, a wraith of fire, while the ground convulsed beneath him and blocks of stone crumbled from the walls. At last he stopped, high above the raging waves, his emaciated body like a charred sapling wreathed in flame.

There was a deafening roar, and a mighty rift opened before the walls. Wailing men teetered on the brink, then toppled, as the ancient fortress and the rocky cliff beneath it collapsed. Debris rained down. JonMarc covered his head with his arms.

Táranos gave a last shriek as the fortress walls disintegrated beneath him. Like a soaring star, he plunged into the waves, a shrunken cadaver of dazzling white within a spew of green fire.

From the sea there rose a huge mushroom plume of steam that whirled and fizzled with the fury of a hundred gales. Then, slowly, its passion receded. Clammy mist spread a moiling blanket over the land, glowing corpse-pale in the first dim shafts of dawn.

And there was silence.

Chapter Thirty-four

In the frozen fortress yard, an army chafed for battle. The smoke-filled air echoed with the clank and clatter of cavalry; of wagons and foot soldiers massing in confusion while, beyond the walls, horns brayed a raucous challenge. Kier knew these men marched to futile death. Against this enemy there could be no victory. The conflict was contrived to suit one man's perverse ambition. Yet no one would listen. He'd looked into their glazed eyes, leering with battle lust; seized their faceless captains by the shoulders and shaken them to get his warning across. No one listened. No one cared.

Close beside him, someone was edging a sword blade. The infernal rasp of steel on stone grated on Kier's nerves. He reached out to stop it...

The movement jolted him awake.

He lay in semi-dark. A lantern fluttered in an iron stand nearby. Its feeble light shone upon JonMarc, splayed out in a chair beside Kier's cot, his shaggy blond head thrown back in blissful slumber. His snores abraded the chill air. Kier chuckled.

Outside, a brisk wind blew. The patched tent walls rippled and snapped with every gust, sending pinpricks of daylight bouncing across the woolen blankets. A fresh sea smell was prominent, though beneath it lurked another: the battlefield stench of rotting flesh. They must be near Cymworth. Anxiety clutched Kier. Táranos! How had the battle ended? JonMarc would know. Kier nudged the Dynian with his knee.

JonMarc snorted and sputtered. Kier prodded him harder and JonMarc's blue eyes flew open. "I wasn't aslee..." His guilty expression transformed to a grin of relief. "Welcome back."

"Thanks," Kier said, a bit muddled. "How long have I been out?"

JonMarc's hair and clothes were rumpled, the worry lines on his face slow to smooth. His left arm was bound in a sling. "Three days."

Kier could scarcely believe it. "You haven't been here all that time..?"

"Well, me, and Llydia. We feared you might be halfway to Devoreth's Realm. She's been in day and night, working her magic on you. Just left a while ago, to catch some sleep."

Kier's expression drooped.

"Don't worry, she'll be back. Oh, and Gwythion's been by to check on you, too."

"Gwythion!" So the Fithlon Master made it after all. "Was he able to defeat Táranos?"

JonMarc shook his head. "No, the Cábretaur did that. Táranos thought he had mastery enough to use it unshielded. But it proved too powerful, even for him. Gwythion says he suffered Nwtyrra's fate: burned and consumed by the sea, just as Aneryn predicted."

Kier passed a hand over his eyes. The vision of ruin Táranos had shown him would remain a phantom. He breathed profound relief. Yet the death scent was real. "Who won the battle?"

"Stalemate. The Branwyn attack evened the numbers—which is saying a lot—but in the end, more Tiernai were scattered than killed. Then Gerit Mawr arrived, with his forces and Gwythion at his side. He sent word that he'd set his might against whichever side refused to halt the fighting. It proved enough threat for both sides to take notice. They called a truce, and that's the last thing they've managed to agree on. They've been conferring ever since, trying to work out what comes next."

JonMarc propped his feet on the edge of Kier's cot. "I sat in on the negotiations a while, but it's all noise and bluster. Neither side trusts the other. They can't even agree on where to retreat to. So here we sit, in the midst of the carnage, trying to bury our dead before pestilence sets in." He dropped his voice. "I think it's all part of Gwythion's plan: to make them so sick of the battle stench they'll consider twice before taking up arms again."

"Very astute."

JonMarc jumped at the voice. Gwythion stood in the doorway, daylight dazzling behind his wind-fluttered robes. "Since you know my mind so well, JonMarc, why don't you go sit in my place a while, so I can talk to Kier."

JonMarc scrambled to his feet. "Guess that means I'm dismissed," he said, offering Kier a telling wink. "I'll drop by in a bit, to rescue you." Kier waved after him as he ducked out beneath the tent flap.

Gwythion assumed his vacant seat. "So," the Fithlon said, looking Kier up and down, his bearded lips pursed in solemn appraisal. "You managed to survive. I confess, I don't see how. The power Táranos leveled at you would have felled a warhorse." Gwythion's gruff expression softened; indeed, he almost smiled. "You did well, Kier. Very well. I am immensely proud of you."

"But we needed you. Why did you take so long to get here? You might have saved Malcolm—or, at least, Jaremy Lochlainn's sight."

"I am sorry, Kier. I came as quickly as I could. I was delayed—by matters I will speak of shortly. But even had I been here, I could not have vanquished Táranos. Only the Cábretaur had the power to do that." Gwythion sat back and rubbed his wizened hands together. "As for the rest, you'll be pleased to know Earl Jaremy's sight is returning. I was at least able to reduce the damage. In a few weeks, he should be nearly healed. Your brother Malcolm is another matter. His fate was ordained the moment he chose to ally with Táranos. It is to Malcolm's credit that he found the strength to break from that allegiance before he died. Now he will rest at peace."

Kier recalled his brother's final words. "He said... he'd always wanted to be like me. Blazes, Gwythion, I never guessed. I thought he despised me."

Gwythion nodded soberly. "Malcolm craved a place in your father's affections the duke reserved only for you."

"If only I'd known, I could've helped him. He didn't need to go to Táranos."

"But you did *not* know," Gwythion said sternly. "Malcolm made his choice. Do not blame yourself, Kier. You're not infallible."

"So I've been told," Kier murmured wryly.

"Ah, well—" Gwythion drew himself up and resumed his brusque tone. "You may be wondering why I have taken time from a supremely important council, just to visit you."

"The thought had occurred to me." Kier eased back against the stacked pillows, savoring his release from the burdens of the past weeks. He could scarcely remember the last time he'd felt free of responsibilities.

Gwythion steepled his knobby hands, forefingers pressed to his lip. "These last few days have been difficult," he said. "It is not only the inevitable problems that arise after a battle; those are being dealt with. It's the daunting—some might say impossible—task of forging together a deeply divided land that has seen three of its rulers die within a week. Yesterday, the leaders of the three armies, and their advisors, sat in conference for sixteen hours. And still they reached no agreement. The major point at issue is: who will now rule Alcor?"

"Duke Edmund is next in line for the throne." Sudden dread struck Kier. "He's not...?"

"Dead? No, he is as well as can be expected for a man who was wounded, then forced to spend much of the week in the dungeons of Caerllyn. A deputation was sent the morning after the battle, to free him. Yet Branwyn has made it clear they will not consent to be ruled by him or any other Tiernai. They support only Ross Branwyn—who, of course, the Tiernai will never accept. Making matters worse, Edmund sent word that he is too ill to make the journey and, in any case, that he does not want the crown. He cites what many Tiernai already fear: that without a strong heir, the problems with Branwyn will only be postponed, should he take the throne."

Kier rubbed his temples to ease the nagging ache behind his eyes—the aftermath of Táranos's mind assault. He suspected Gwythion must have felt something similar in recent days. "Whose side does Gerit Mawr take? Surely if his forces could halt the battle..."

Gwythion snapped his fingers. "Ah, now you've hit on it. Gerit Mawr is in a position to dictate terms—all the more because of what occurred in the capital. I told you I was delayed. When my ship docked at Menythgar, I found the Citadel under siege and the rest of the city taken—by Gerit Mawr. The conflict did not last. The Connails, thinking themselves invincible, had all but emptied the city of troops. Gerit had enough supporters among the populace to make the overthrow almost bloodless. He now holds the capital and will not relinquish it unless his terms are met. Of course, the Tiernai demand the city's return before they will agree to anything. There is even talk of leading an army to take it back. And the Branwyns claim it for themselves."

"Will they not accept Gerit Mawr as king? He at least represents both races."

"Aye, he would be a good candidate. Yet there is no hope of that. To the Tiernai, he is Dynian, and so, an impossible choice. To the Dynian, he is a renegade and turncoat, with no trace of Branwyn blood. I fear Gerit Mawr's greatest strength lies in his wisdom—of which he has no shortage—and the army at his back. He knows that if a solution is not found, the races will go to war again, and Táranos will have his revenge, though he be not here to see it."

"What about JonMarc?" said Kier. "Did you know he's heir to the

Telynor High Kings?"

"Not heir," Gwythion corrected. "According to Dynian law, the kingship would have passed, not to him, but to his sister's offspring. In any case, the claim cannot be proven, nor would it carry any weight with the Tiernai if it could. They'll not relinquish Alcor to a Dynian, be he descended of royalty or not."

Kier's thoughts whirled. He did not envy Gwythion the task of finding a way around the impasse. He counted himself fortunate to be well out of the fray. There were substantial advantages to being a pawn.

Gwythion fingered his newly-trimmed beard, which seemed to have grown whiter since Kier last saw him. "There is one candidate who might win approval from both sides, though not without persuasion. Gerit Mawr and I came up with the name some days ago, but could not put it forward until now. In truth, it is the candidate Gerit wanted all along."

Kier looked up to find his mentor watching him keenly. He knew that look—and distrusted it. His stomach began to curdle. "Who?" he asked warily.

The Fithlon Master looked straight into his eyes.

Kier squirmed. "No, Gwythion. Don't jest with me."

"It is no jest. You are the only candidate who stands any chance of being accepted by all sides."

Kier felt as if his face were on fire. He only wanted to escape. "But I *can't* be king. I'm illegitimate."

"Only in Tiernai reckoning. That is one concession they would have to make. The fact that you are Duke Morwen's eldest son counts for much. And to appease the Dynian, you are also descended of Gareth Branwyn."

Kier stiffened. "You knew about that?"

"Since you first came to Cordon, though your father forbade me to speak of it. He feared for your life, should word leak out."

"But I hold no loyalty to the Branwyns. Ross knows that."

"And that is a concession *they* must make. You've already earned favor from Terryd Rhys, the head of Cyngor, and he has the confidence of the Émam Nácia. Her word will prevail over all the Dynian of Alcor—not just the Branwyns. In addition, you ritually came of age among both races. That is something few can boast."

Kier felt stunned. The prospect of ruling Alcor had never entered his wildest fantasies. The fact that anyone would even consider him boggled his mind. "But I know nothing about kingship. I'm not even a noble."

"You know how to lead men and instill confidence. Ruark and Lochlainn were impressed by the way you dealt with Táranos. And you've earned the respect of Legion Commander Donal. In that sense, you are better experienced than most who are *born* to rule."

"But I'm a soldier, not a peacemaker. Surely there must be someone better qualified. To tell the truth, I'd made up my mind that, if I survived, I'd ask Sir Donal for a permanent assignment abroad. I don't *want* to stay in Alcor. I've always felt ripped apart here."

Gwythion searched his eyes. "Then perhaps it's time to seek unity, Kier—for yourself *and* the kingdom. Alcor *needs* you."

Kier felt cornered. With Llydia's help, he'd managed to forge an alliance among the rival factions within himself, but it was, at best, an uneasy truce. He had no idea how to extend that to an entire country. And with the matter of the Cábretaur finally ended, he was sick and tired of having his life dictated by others.

Gwythion read his thoughts. "Consider this, Kier. What better way to control your destiny than to rule the kingdom?"

It sounded like a rebuttal JonMarc would use. Try as he might, Kier could find no way around the impasse. "I still can't believe they'll accept a halfblood as king," he muttered.

"I did say it would take persuasion. For all our sakes, I hope *you* have been the hardest to convince." With that, Gwythion rose to return to the council.

Kier watched his mentor leave, grateful for some time alone with his thoughts. He had no conviction anything would come of the matter, nor did he want it to. The task of forging a nation from two races that had spent the last fifty years clawing at each other's throats would be monumental; not a responsibility he wanted hoisted upon his already weary shoulders.

Yet late that afternoon, as he sat with JonMarc and Llydia, comparing tales of the past several weeks, a deputation from the council arrived to offer him the crown.

"There is one stipulation we had not foreseen," said Gwythion, casting his eye on Llydia. "The Branwyns demand assurance that your heirs will bear the Branwyn line. Ross insists that, if you wish Branwyn support, you must wed his sister."

Kier brightened as the prospect of kingship suddenly took on a whole new dimension. He turned to Llydia, seated on a stool beside his cot. "And what does the Lady of the Branwyns say to that?"

Llydia smiled. "What do you think?" she chided, grasping his ready hand. "That is a choice I made days ago!"

Chapter Thirty-five

"Gwythion, do you think we can persuade the Branwyns to divide
Glenneth into three provinces to warrant their three new Council seats,
or will they demand Cymworth as well? And what about Gerit Mawr? If
I grant him Ruthland, the Connails' followers are sure to..." Kier gave a
drawn-out sigh. "Gwythion, are you listening?"

A fortnight had passed since the battle of Cymworth. Kier now
occupied the royal apartments at the Citadel. He sat beside a huge table,
feeling more weary than regal, the stained riding clothes he'd worn during
the long progress to Menythgar, now hidden beneath a robe of dark blue
wool. Before him lay a map of Alcor, weighted with candlesticks at the
edges. He'd been poring over it for nearly an hour, with the acuity of a
military strategist. Yet his heart wasn't in it.

The journey from Cymworth had been tedious, but not nearly so
tiresome as the endless greetings and ceremony that confronted him
in Menythgar—ceremony he'd once been able to escape by retreating,
unnoticed, to the stables. No more. Though he would not officially be
proclaimed king until his coronation, a week hence, the responsibilities had
already descended on him. Kier felt uncomfortable with the protocol; with
being addressed as *Sire*, and *Majesty* by those who, until a few weeks ago,
he'd considered his betters. Gwythion assured him he would grow used to
the attention—perhaps even come to enjoy it. Kier doubted that.

The hour candle sputtered toward midnight. Kier grew impatient.
"Well, Gwythion? What do you think?"

The Fithlon was leaning over the casket that had housed the Cábretaur,
thoroughly engrossed in a tattered volume. He looked up with a start. "I'm
sorry, my liege, what did you ask?"

Kier cradled his brow. "Gods, not you, too. Not when we're alone. If
I'm *Your Majesty'ed* or *My Liege'd* once more tonight, I'm going to smash

something."

The Fithlon nodded passively, accepting the rebuke. "You were asking—?"

"Do you think—"

The rapid clatter of footsteps in the hall interrupted him. The chamber door flew open and JonMarc burst in, breathless. He grinned when he spotted Kier. "I've done it!" he cried, his exuberance wilting only a little when he caught Gwythion's frown. "*Your Majesty*," he amended, with an awkward bow. Kier rolled his eyes.

JonMarc's excitement instantly resumed. "Duke Edmund's accepted me. I don't know if it's because I'm descended of kings, or that I'm now advisor to one, but he's finally given his consent. Cari's to be mine!"

Something clutched inside Kier—the last, stubborn remnant of an outgrown dream. JonMarc noticed and sobered. "You—you're not angry, are you?"

Kier shut his eyes, banishing the feeling for good. "Of course not," he said, embracing his friend like the brother he'd become. "She deserves better, you know, but I'd be hard put to find it. Congratulations, JonMarc."

JonMarc nudged Gwythion with a surfeit of familiarity that made Kier wince. "Aren't you going to congratulate me as well?"

Gwythion murmured his good wishes without breaking his concentration.

"What's the matter with him?"

"He's sulking," said Kier. "He doesn't think the prophecies turned out as they should have."

Gwythion straightened indignantly. "If you will bother to read, you'll see that there are indeed discrepancies between Aneryn's predictions and the happenings at Cymworth. I am at a loss to understand them."

"Maybe Aneryn's predictions were wrong," said JonMarc, refusing to have his exuberance quashed by what seemed a minor technicality.

"Impossible. Aneryn's foresight could not have shown him events that would not occur."

"Well, I'm not convinced *any* of the prophecies were really fulfilled," said Kier. "True, some things happened that were spoken of, but we might simply have caused them to come about because we knew they were supposed to." He rolled up the map and laid it aside. The chore of apportioning lands could wait. "I don't expect I'll ever truly understand prophecy. But what does it matter now? Táranos and the Cábretaur are destroyed. Who's to know or care whether it happened as Aneryn foresaw it?"

"*I* know," said Gwythion, "and I care. If the Cábretaur was destroyed, I want proof; if merely lost, I must know what became of it. According to Aneryn, it should have come under my protection."

Kier hid a frown, recalling Táranos's allegation about Gwythion. He didn't truly believe it, but his mentor's intensity tweaked a smattering of doubt. Besides, it was too late at night to become embroiled in pointless argument. Now that his own work was stymied, he only wanted to go to bed and leave the difficult problems till the morrow.

"I can't help you there," he said. "But if it will make you feel any better, I'll give you the casket that held the Cábretaur. Then you can ponder the matter all you like—on your own time. I'm exhausted." It was as close as Kier dared come to dismissing his mentor.

Gwythion did not take the hint. His eyes lit with sudden interest and he stared at Kier as if seeing him anew. "What did you say?"

"I said, I'm exhausted."

"No, before that."

"Look, can't this wait till morning?"

"No, it cannot."

Kier reddened. "I said take the casket. It's *yours*. Just get the blasted thing out of here. I want..." Kier's brow furrowed. "Now what?"

Gwythion was thumbing furiously through his worn copy of the *Book of Ygair*. He tapped a passage with his finger. "Beloved Son and Adept of the Faithful, he shall receive his Legacy *at the Hand of the King*."

"I don't understand," said Kier. "I gave you an empty box. The Cábretaur's gone. JonMarc saw it burn up."

Gwythion shook his head. "Miril is not so easily destroyed."

"I know what I saw," said JonMarc. "Unless you think the Cábretaur could have survived all that fire, to wash up on a beach somewhere."

"Perhaps. Yet that would not fulfill the prophecy either."

Kier exhaled exasperation. "How can you be so certain the Cábretaur was meant to come to you? Táranos was an adept of the Faithful, whether the Fithlon acknowledged him or not. He told us he was directly descended from Aneryn's only son. Maybe Aneryn intended *him* to acquire the Cábretaur just so he could be destroyed with it."

Kier felt the air crackle, as it always did when Gwythion's ire was kindled. "Táranos was no descendent of Aneryn's."

"You can't know that for sure."

"I can indeed." Gwythion scowled into his clasped hands as though battling with some dark secret. At last he looked up. "You ask how I know the Cábretaur was to come to me? I'll tell you, Kier. It's time you knew the truth."

Gwythion displayed the cabochon on his left forefinger.

Abruptly, Kier recognized it. "Aneryn's ring! The same as the one on his tomb effigy." His mentor had worn that ring as long as he'd known him, but somehow, in the excitement of finding Aneryn's resting place, he'd failed to make the connection. "How did it come to you?"

Gwythion smiled sadly. "For the best of reasons: it was my birthright. I am Aneryn's son."

Kier cocked his head. "You mean, he was your ancestor."

"Dyveth Aneryn was my *father.*"

Kier stared at his mentor's face. "That's impossible. Aneryn died nine hundred years ago. How could you be his son?"

Gwythion chuckled softly, as though he hadn't expected to be believed. "The Nwtyrrans enjoyed longer life spans than the peoples of this world. The miril crystals they found when they arrived here extended them even further."

"Aye, you've said that. But—surely not nine hundred years."

"No one knows. Nwtyrra was too quickly destroyed. I was born here on Alcor, just before my father's death. I never knew him. Yet by some accident, the deadly residue of Nwtyrra's destruction, which cut short the lives of its few survivors, only served to lengthen my own. I cannot explain it more than to say that my body ages more slowly than others."

Kier frowned. If he didn't know Gwythion so well, he'd have found the assertion utterly preposterous. "Did Táranos know this?"

Gwythion laughed bitterly. "No one knows, save the two of you. I do not choose to share a truth that would instantly mark me a madman."

"But how could the Fithlon not suspect?" said JonMarc. "Surely when you failed to grow old and die like the rest, someone must have noticed."

"I have been cautions," said Gwythion, "living many lives under a variety of names and guises, careful never to remain in one place too long—even dropping out of the Fithlon and re-entering anew. But Alcor is my home, and the Dynian, the race that sheltered me when my own folk were destroyed. Here, I have spent most of my years, helping them in whatever ways I could. They have known me as Keron and Killian, Aurelin and Galglenneth—and many other names."

"All the heroes of their legends," said Kier, awed.

"Not all. Cyngor has still to determine the identity of the last. I suspect, when the verdict is reached, the two of you will share that title."

Kier regarded his mentor with new insight. If what he said was true, Gwythion's huge collection of artifacts suddenly made sense. Kier even recalled seeing an ancient harp among his possessions; the original *Kreuth of Killian*?

"But you do age," said JonMarc. "I mean, I can see a change since I first met you."

"Thank you very much!" Gwythion's lips compressed in feigned indignation. "But you are right, JonMarc. It is happening more swiftly since my conflict with Táranos and our sojourn in the Death Realm. The living cannot cross that portal without paying a heavy price. Táranos felt it more than I, for he actually dwelt there for a time. Though he looked an old man, he was even younger than your father, Kier.

"But my time, too, is passing, and I do not lament it. A long life takes its toll on the emotions. I will welcome the peace, when it comes. Yet in my remaining years, I was to be custodian of the Cábretaur—to unlock its secrets and train one to receive it after me. This, my father made clear to me when I crossed into the Forbidden Realm. We have seen that, in the wrong hands, the Cábretaur can be a great danger. If it survived Táranos's demise and did not come to me, it must be accounted for."

"Who do you fear might retrieve it?" asked JonMarc.

"Many might be tempted to use miril's power to further their own designs. Though the Covenant Priesthood claim to abhor such power, they would rejoice to find a weapon they could use against their foes. They hold to the exclusionist doctrines of the original Eden colonists, the founders of the Deg Tirith, and have ever been deadly rivals of the Nwtyrrans and their Fithlon disciples. Remember, JonMarc, it is not the weapon alone that destroys, but the hatred that wields it. And the Covenanters are not the only ones susceptible to such intolerance. It exists all around us."

Kier suddenly recalled something Táranos declared from the battlements—something he'd barely attended at the time, being so preoccupied with his efforts to bring the renegade down. "Táranos said the Nwtyrrans would one day return; that some kind of summons had been sent. But how, and to whom? I thought all the Nwtyrrans were destroyed."

Gwythion looked troubled, as though Kier's news confirmed some deep suspicion. "Not all. Only those who colonized Éclatan. Do you recall the Dynian prophecy that when Conjunction occurred, a world would end? That world was the Nwtyrrans' original home. You saw it perish yourselves, when the Orb that gave them life—that which the Nwtyrrans who came here dubbed the *Life Star*—consumed itself. That end was long anticipated. It is why, thousands of years before, they dispatched scouts to visit other worlds and send back reports of what they found. Those who came here to Éclatan discovered miril, which they thought to use to power their civilization—with disastrous result.

"Aneryn communicated word of that catastrophe from one of the towers his predecessors erected when they first visited Alcor—the place the Dynian call the Spire of Galglenneth. Táranos must have found the mechanism and used it to again attempt contact. If any Nwtyrrans come in answer, I see little hope they will have learned from their ancestors' mistakes. Táranos likely counted on that, expecting their lust for miril's power to give him a potent bargaining tool. That makes it even more imperative we discover what became of the Cábretaur."

"But if, as you fear, it wasn't destroyed with Táranos, where might it be?" Kier asked.

"It could be anywhere—in the sea; on a beach. But my father said it would come to me, and his foresight was reliable. To witness an event before it happens means it *must* happen as foreseen. The only variable is interpretation."

JonMarc murmured the verse Gwythion had marked. *"He shall receive his Legacy at the Hand of the King."* He tipped the metal casket on end. "So Kier is king, and this is what you received from him—an empty box which formerly housed a gem said to be—too powerful to use without its protective casket..."

"Then the casket..." Kier began, following his logic trail.

His mentor interrupted him. "Tell me exactly what you saw, JonMarc, just before Táranos was destroyed."

JonMarc chewed his lip. "I saw the Cábretaur glow green in Táranos's hand. He held it up before the armies and shouted for silence, but no one listened."

"Where was the casket at that time? Did he still hold it?"

"No, it was on the ground beside Kier. A spear of light from the Cábretaur touched it."

"What part of it?"

JonMarc's brow creased. "I don't know. Probably one of the crystals on the lid. I think it glowed yellow."

"This one, then. The Life Star. Did it glow of its own?"

"At first, yes." JonMarc nervously tapped the tabletop. "I took a chance and touched it with the charmstone."

"What happened then?"

"I don't—wait. *That's* when the shaft of light appeared."

"Going from Táranos's crystal to the box?"

"It could have gone either way. It happened so fast. Then it stopped, and the Cábretaur began to glow by itself—until it consumed Táranos."

"Yet you say the commands Táranos gave once he'd thrown the casket away were not obeyed." Gwythion traced his finger over the figure of the Life Tree inlaid on the casket lid and he smiled, suddenly comprehending.

"*The Miril Cábretaur will shine again for Aneryn—in the Second Conjunction of the Life Tree.*" His finger came to rest where the second branch of the trident crossed the stem, the spot where the yellow crystal was set.

"Then—Aneryn wasn't just talking about a time," said Kier. "He meant a place, as well. This is the *real* Cábretaur. We've been looking at it all along!"

"Then the gem that destroyed Táranos was just another decoy!" JonMarc grinned. "I suspected it at first, but Aneryn made the thing look so convincing. If Táranos had just been content to use the Cábretaur within its protective casket, as Aneryn warned..."

"Then we would likely all be dead," said Gwythion. "Táranos's own arrogance destroyed him. By risking your life to provoke him, Kier, you goaded him into throwing away the very power he'd spent his life pursuing. Your instincts served you well."

"I thought I'd failed," Kier marveled. "But then the soldiers around me started moving, and I wondered how that could be."

"So the green gem had no power of its own," said JonMarc. "Only what it took from the real Cábretaur on the casket lid. And that was activated by my charmstone. But—" JonMarc frowned. "Wasn't the Amulet—the *Hand of Lidialis*—supposed to be the Crystal's Key?"

Gwythion smiled. "Perhaps the true reading of that verse should be: 'He who bears the Amulet *also* bears the Crystal's Key.' I suspect that is what enabled Kier to survive Táranos's attack. Am I wrong, Kier, or do you not carry them both?"

Kier had wondered at that himself when he'd first discovered the charmstone hanging around his neck. JonMarc had insisted it was a gift. Now, Kier fished it from inside his shirt. "You'd best take it, JonMarc. I'm grateful for the loan, but you'll need it more than I, if you're still determined to work with Gwythion. You two will have your hands full, trying to determine what the powers of the Cábretaur really are."

The excitement in JonMarc's blue eyes indicated he felt more than ready for the challenge. "I suppose it's just as well everyone thinks the Cábretaur's destroyed," he said.

Gwythion hushed him. "It must remain so. Our world is not yet ready to accept the responsibility such power demands. Until it is, *no one* else must know the Cábretaur exists."

Epilogue

It was the grandest affair Alcor had witnessed in decades—the marriage of her new monarch to the heiress of Branwyn.

Crowds began packing the Citadel Square at first light, for, over Commander Donal's objections, Kier had ordained that no one be turned away. While Táranos had seen his own mixed blood as an excuse to tear the kingdom apart, Kier was determined his should be an instrument of healing.

He knew he took a huge risk. Many disapproved the marriage and his kingship. Resentments ran high, and probably would for years to come. Already, there were reports of uprisings in the former Connail province of Ruthland. Yet most of his new subjects seemed more curious than hostile, willing to put aside their differences and see how matters fared. Kier hoped that by inviting them all to witness the long-overdue joining of Alcor's two ruling houses, he might instill in them the enthusiasm needed to make the union work.

A crisp breeze snapped the many-colored pennons above the Citadel Square, and garlands of spring blossoms bedecked the walls. Kier prayed it would soon be over. He felt restless, clad in a tunic of white brocade, with a floor-length cloak of gold flowing from his shoulders—looking more a king than he ever would have credited. He'd even begun to feel like one, the weight of responsibilities settling on him as heavy as the jeweled crown itself.

Yet his eyes sparked like amethysts when he caught sight of Llydia, gliding down the aisle in her bridal finery. Behind her walked his cousin, the Lady Cariwyn Telynor, whose quiet marriage to JonMarc had taken place two days earlier. Kier had stood beside his friend as groomsman, just as JonMarc now stood beaming beside him.

The platform was draped with Alcor's new crest: two hands clasped

palm to palm, beneath the gold-embroidered words: *In Unity, Strength.*
Kier had come up with the design himself and desperately hoped that in
this, its first public viewing, it would stand up to his subjects' scrutiny.

The aged justiciar stepped forward and cleared his throat. Kier tried to
keep his attention on the ceremony, but it proved difficult. His mind still
reeled from this sudden turn of fortune.

"Do you, Kier Gareth-Alyn Fitzmorwen, of the Royal House of Devon,
take this, the hand of Llydia Alais Branwyn, to you as your mate and
consort for as long as..."

Kier's head shot up. The hand of *Llydia alais...?*

Beside him, JonMarc gave no sign that he noticed. Kier sought
Gwythion, seated below, as a waiting stillness descended upon the square.
The Fithlon met his eyes with a slow nod. He, too, had noted the reference.

JonMarc subtly nudged him. Kier overheard nervous grumbling from
the Branwyn faction to his left. Llydia quizzed him with her eyes.

The Tiernai justiciar spoke quietly: "You are to answer, my Liege."

"The hand of Lidi-alis. Yes! Yes, I *do.*"

A sigh of relief passed like a soft breeze through the gathered host. The
justiciar droned on, now addressing Llydia, while Kier shook his head in
silent wonder. *Heir to the Hand of Lidialis.* So Aneryn's prophecy referred
not only to the Amulet, but to this union.

Llydia spoke her answer with reassuring gentleness. Her fingers sought
his hand and squeezed it. Kier looked into her knowing blue eyes. On
sudden impulse, he drew her to him. Their lips met and parted.

The aged justiciar hesitated, then continued to finalize their vows in
his ritual monotone, while a murmured undercurrent passed through the
crowd.

Kier chuckled to himself. What matter that their embrace was
premature? He and Llydia belonged to each other now. And everything had
worked out better than he ever could have imagined on that dark street in
Castémaron, a lifetime ago.

And holding Llydia felt good. Gods, how good it felt. Kier closed his
mind to all but her eager embrace.

Note from the Author: Good reviews and feedback are gold to authors. If you enjoyed your experience reading this book, please "like" *The Talent Sinistral* page on Facebook and consider rating and reviewing the book with Amazon.com, Barnes & Noble, or any other review site. Thank you!

For more background information about L.F. Patten and upcoming books in the *Sinistral* series, visit us at www.dathana.com.